ALWAYS

anthony

ALWAYS anthony

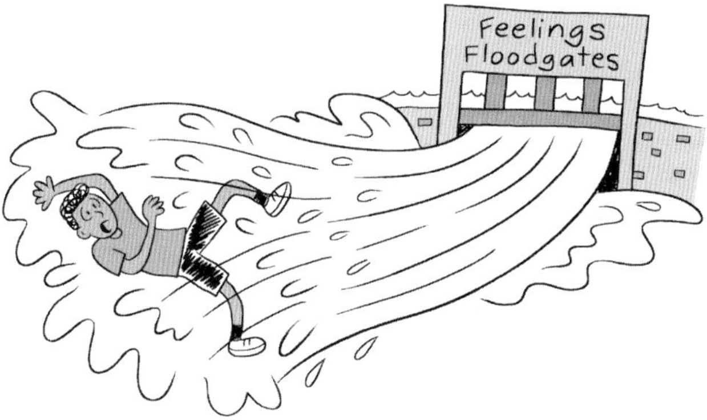
Feelings
Floodgates

TERRI LIBENSON

BALZER + BRAY
An Imprint of HarperCollins*Publishers*

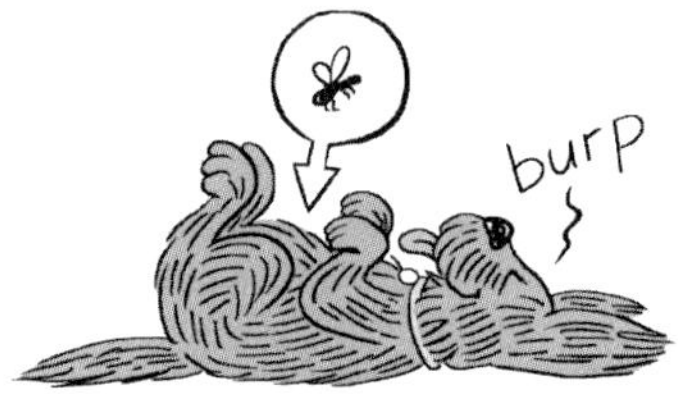
burp

Balzer + Bray is an imprint of HarperCollins Publishers.

Always Anthony

www.harpercollinschildrens.com

Library of Congress Control Number: 2023943328
ISBN 978-0-06-332093-2 (hardcover)
ISBN 978-0-06-332092-5 (pbk.)
ISBN 978-0-06-339582-4 (special edition)
ISBN 978-0-06-339584-8 (special edition)

Typography by Terri Libenson and Laura Mock
24 25 26 27 28 PC/TC 10 9 8 7 6 5 4 3 2 1
First Edition

To unlikely friendships, my favorite kind

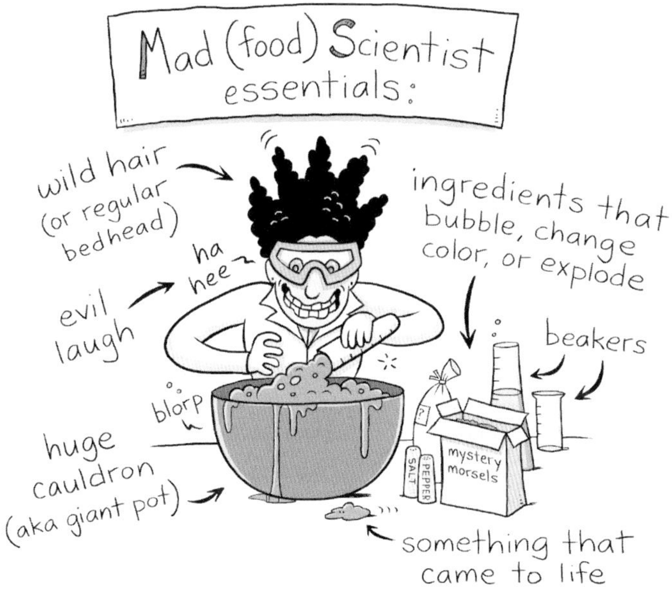
Mad (food) Scientist essentials:
wild hair (or regular bedhead)
ha hee
evil laugh
blorp
huge cauldron (aka giant pot)
ingredients that bubble, change color, or explode
beakers
SALT
PEPPER
mystery morsels
something that came to life

PROLOGUE
ANTHONY

I've never been what you'd call an open book.

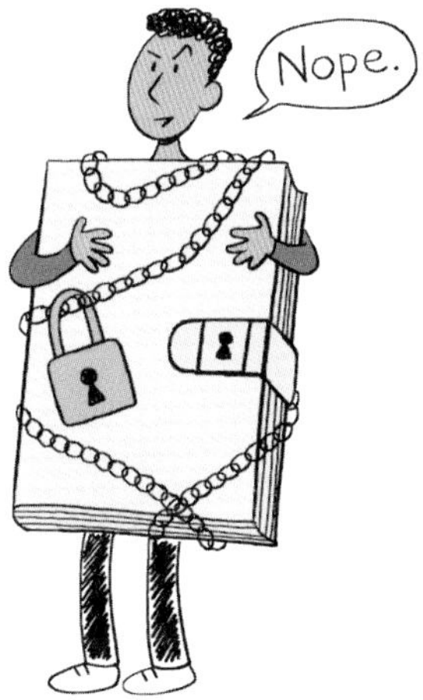
Nope.

Not to say I don't have feelings or anything. I do. I just hide 'em well. My best friend, Tyler, once made a chart documenting all my moods.

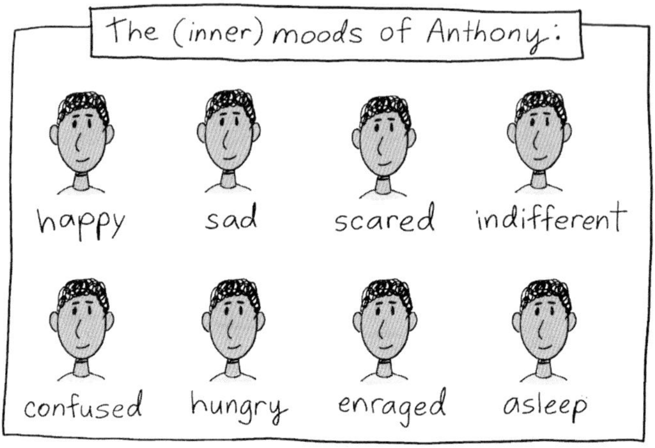
The (inner) moods of Anthony:
happy
sad
scared
indifferent
confused
hungry
enraged
asleep

When I saw it, I laughed.

But I didn't actually think it was funny. It kinda made me feel like a robot or something. Which sounds cool in theory but not in practice.

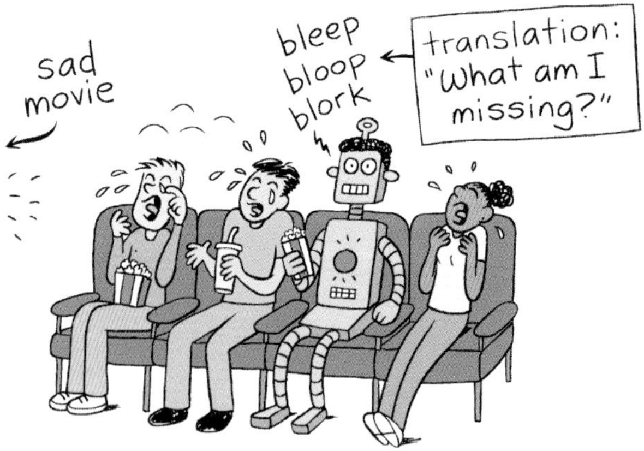
sad movie
bleep bloop blork
translation: "What am I missing?"

It also had me wondering if that's how other people see me, not just Tyler. But eventually I shrugged it off. I mean, it was a joke. I was making too big a deal of it, right?

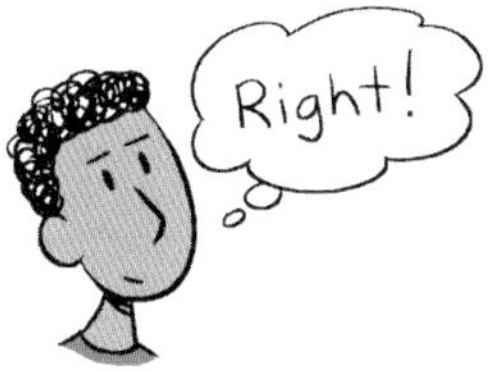
Right!

But if that's true . . .

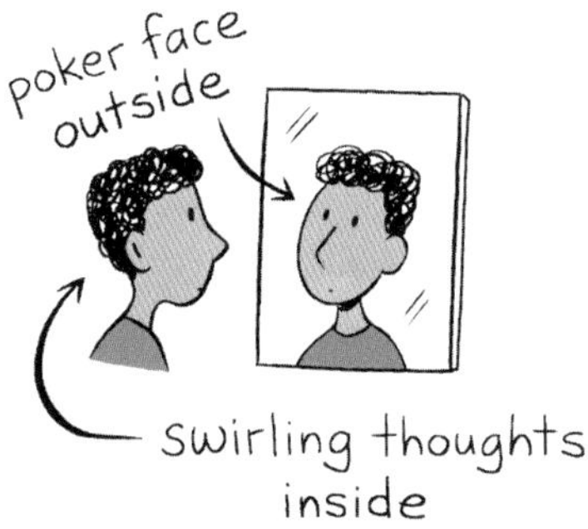
poker face outside
swirling thoughts inside

. . . why do I still think about it?

ANTHONY

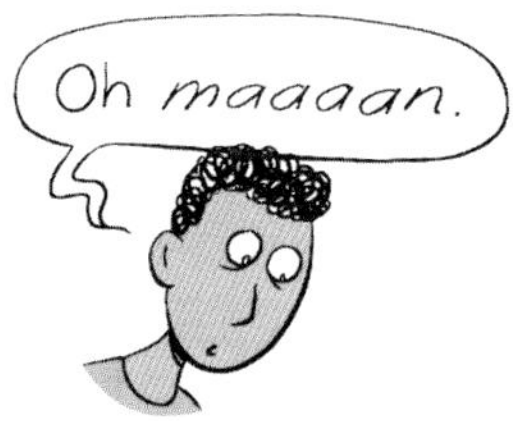
Oh *maaaan*.

I'm staring down at my Language Arts paper. And not liking what I see.

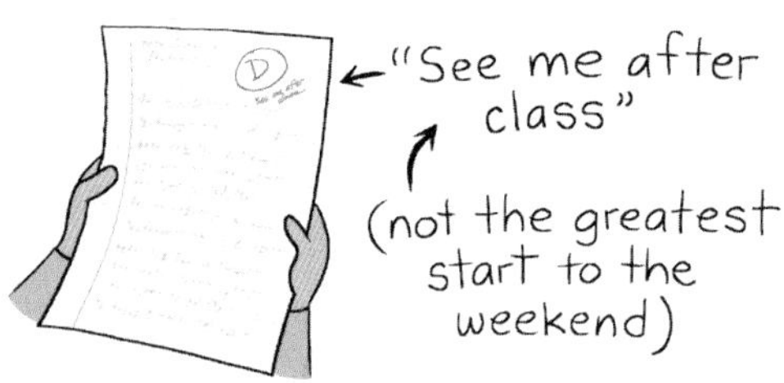
"See me after class"
(not the greatest start to the weekend)

I don't know what went wrong. I thought I had this in the bag. The topic was cool, too:

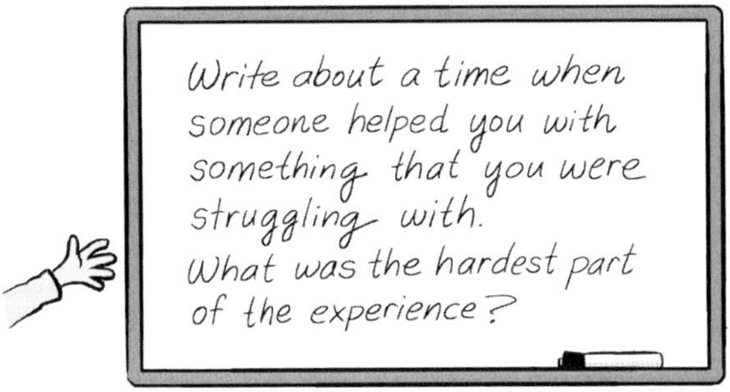
Write about a time when someone helped you with something that you were struggling with.
What was the hardest part of the experience?

So I wrote about last year when Tyler's older brother, Zach, helped me with my layups.

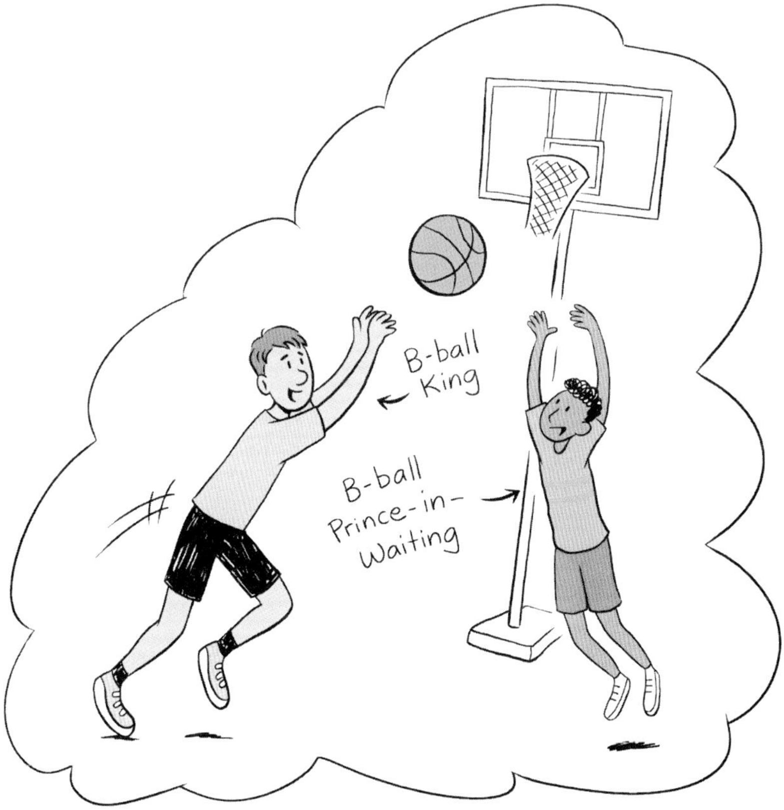
B-ball King
B-ball Prince-in-Waiting

The bell rings. I get up and walk over to Mrs. Winn's desk while everyone else files out. I'm jealous. It's Friday and I wanna get home asap. Malik waves to me from the door and tilts his head. That's his signal for "See you tomorrow?". We practice at the Y most Saturday afternoons.

Mrs. Winn doesn't look stern. In fact, she smiles at me. She's my nicest teacher. I wish I were better at her class.

Anthony. Your paper.

I nod. I should be more concerned, but I really just wanna get out of there.

The reason you got a D: Any guesses?

I shake my head.

Well, the subject you chose was fine.

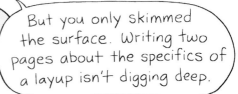

But you only skimmed the surface. Writing two pages about the specifics of a layup isn't digging deep.

I don't say anything. I mean, I wrote every detailed step on the precisions of that shot. What more does she want?

And, unfortunately, you had a lot of grammatical errors. Almost like you didn't check your work.

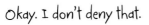

Okay. I don't deny that.

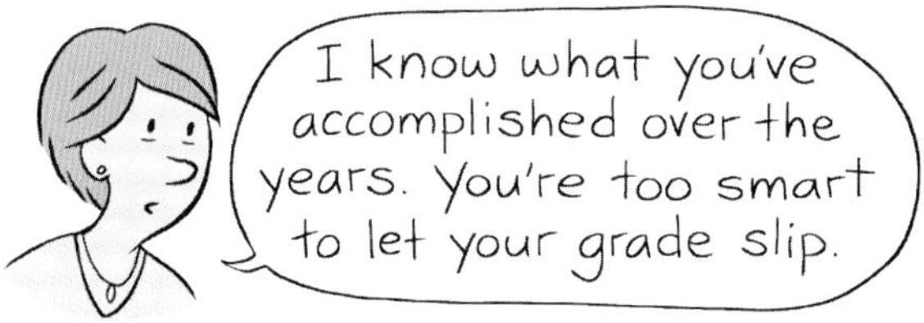

I know what you've accomplished over the years. You're too smart to let your grade slip.

If you rewrite your paper over the weekend, I'll give you extra credit, which will boost your overall grade. What do you say?

I think about it.

for a nanosecond → POOF

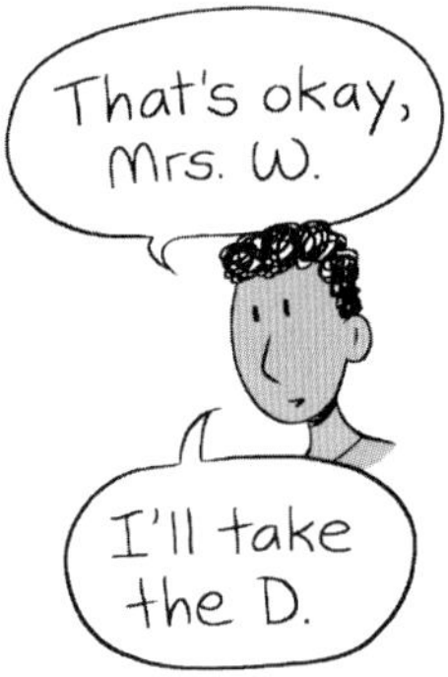
That's okay, Mrs. W.
I'll take the D.

She looks surprised.

Truth is, I have a lot going on this weekend. I have a big game next week, and I wanna get in as much practice as possible. I also have science and math tests on Monday and Tuesday, and I'd rather focus on those.

Yeah, I've had my issues and worked through them. But now I've gotta be choosy. English isn't that big a deal to me. I'm not great at it, but I **am** at STEM. I follow my strengths.

Mrs. W shakes her head as I head out. I try not to feel too guilty.

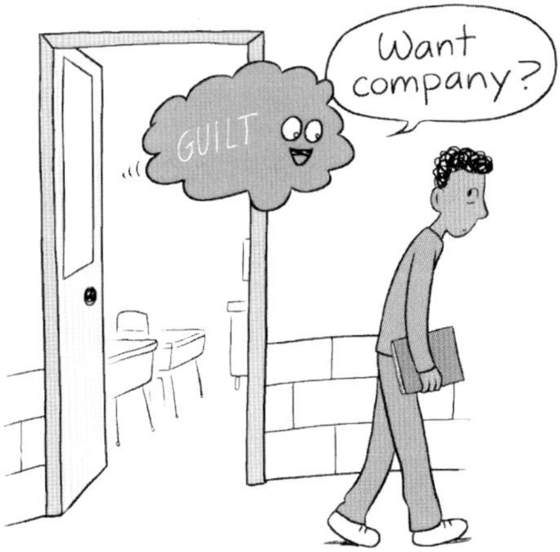
GUILT
Want company?

Tyler joins me in the hall as we walk to our buses. We always meet up after eighth period.

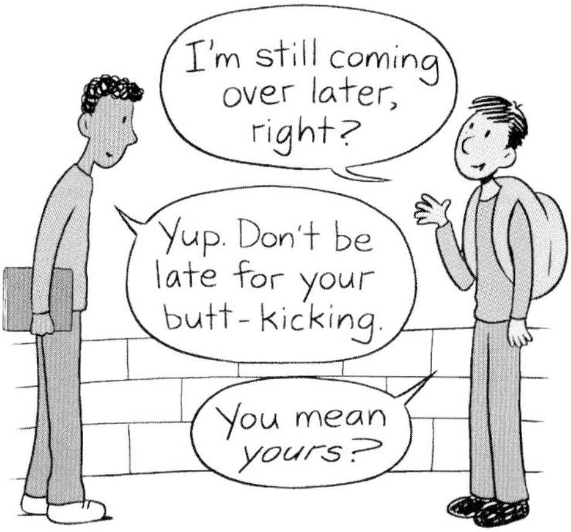
I'm still coming over later, right?
Yup. Don't be late for your butt-kicking.
You mean yours?

Tyler's sleeping over tonight. We're gonna have a Super Smash Bros. marathon.

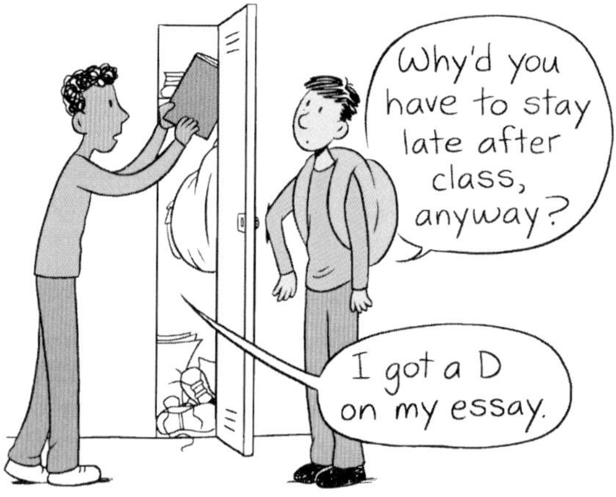
Why'd you have to stay late after class, anyway?
I got a D on my essay.

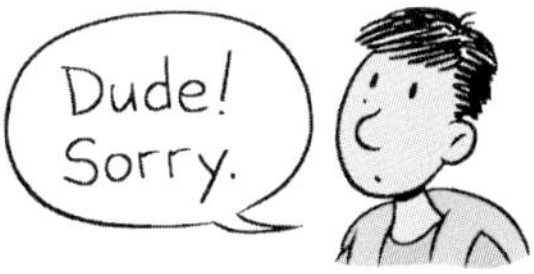
Dude! Sorry.

I shrug.

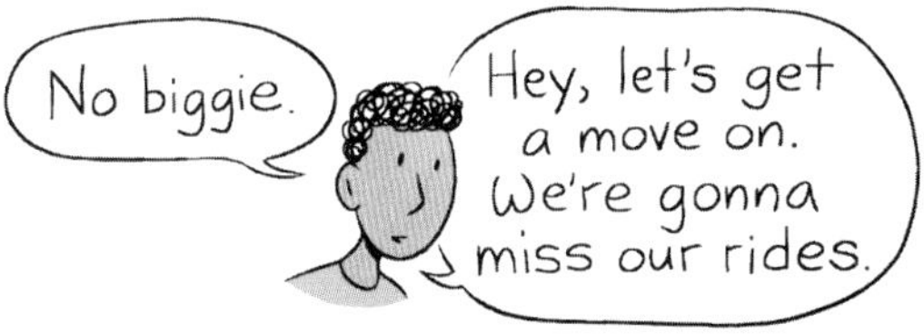
No biggie.
Hey, let's get a move on. We're gonna miss our rides.

We rush out the door and just make it. It was good of Ty to wait. Then again, he's my best friend and I'd do the same for him.

When the bus drops me off, I meander up my block, checking my phone for the time and trying to keep from spitting on the grass. It's a bad habit that started when I was little. Lately I've been bringing a water bottle from home to sip on instead of spitting, but today I forgot.

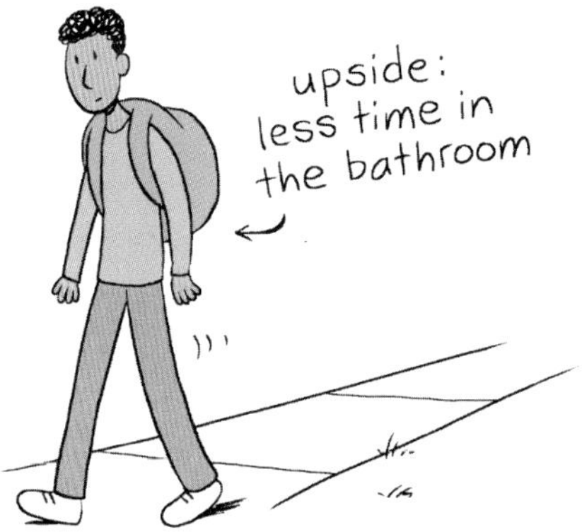
upside: less time in the bathroom

My mom usually takes a break from (virtual) meetings at two thirty and then hops back on at three. I slow my pace. I'm trying to time it so that I miss her and she won't grill me about my Language Arts paper. I swear she checks my online grades every hour.

I get home at exactly 3:03. Yes!

Nooooo!

I can hear my twin sisters, Lulu and Jada, arguing in the kitchen. Probably over the last potato chip or something. That stirs up Phineas, our five-year-old chocolate labradoodle. He's woofing in the background. It's like a three-part horror-harmony. My mom has tuned everyone out.

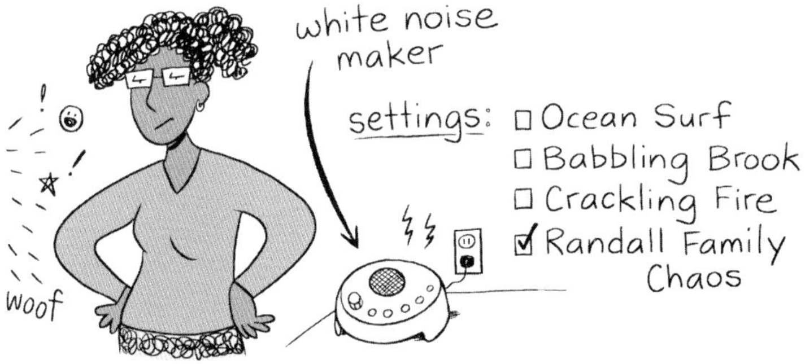
white noise maker
settings:
Ocean Surf
Babbling Brook
Crackling Fire
Randall Family Chaos
woof

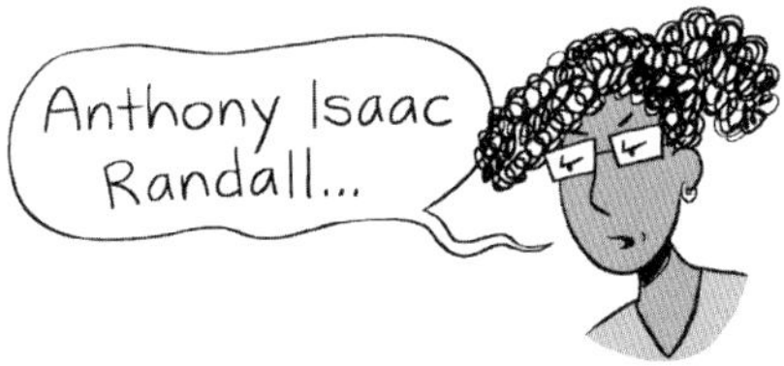
Anthony Isaac Randall...

Uh-oh. I've been middle-named. She definitely knows about my grade.

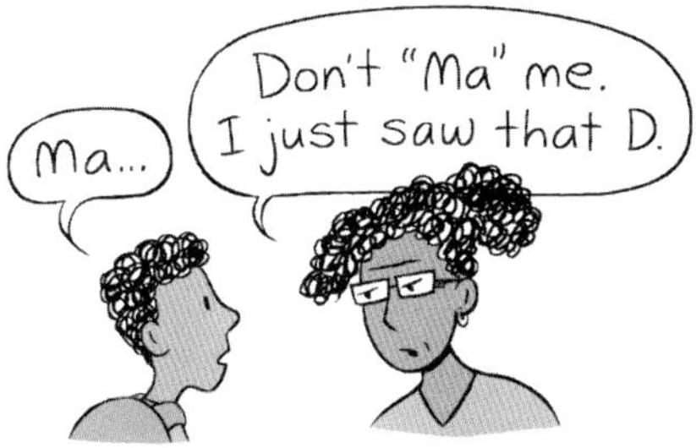
Ma...
Don't "Ma" me. I just saw that D.

Whoa, that was fast.

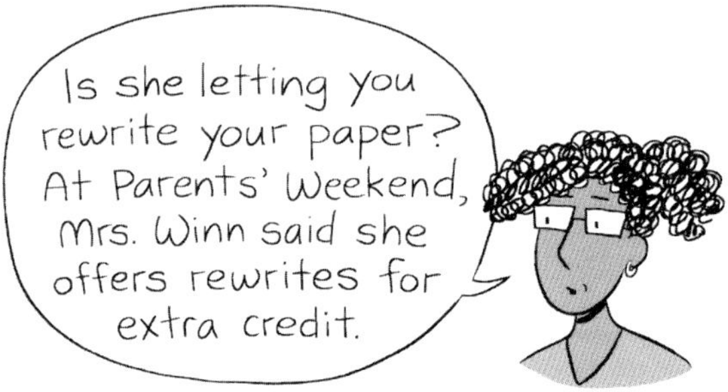
Is she letting you rewrite your paper? At Parents' Weekend, Mrs. Winn said she offers rewrites for extra credit.

The woman has a memory like a computer chip.

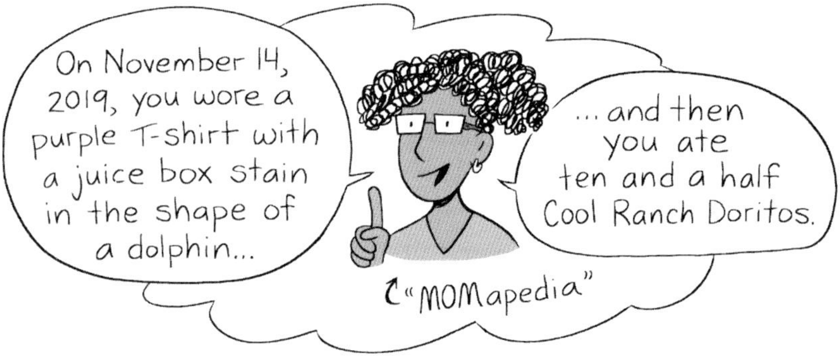
On November 14, 2019, you wore a purple T-shirt with a juice box stain in the shape of a dolphin...
...and then you ate ten and a half Cool Ranch Doritos.
"MOMapedia"

Oh man, I can't lie. She'll see right through it.

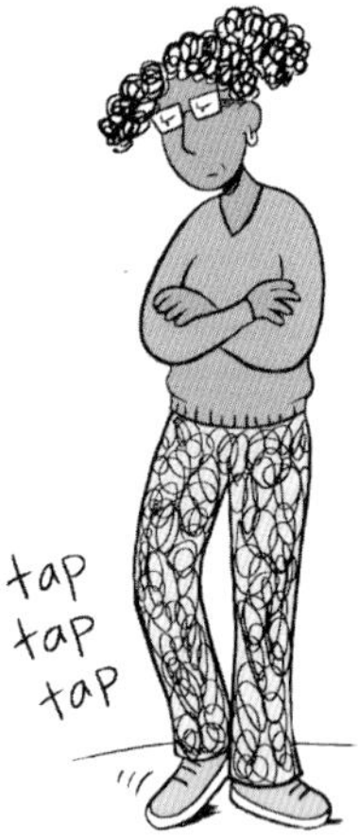
tap
tap
tap

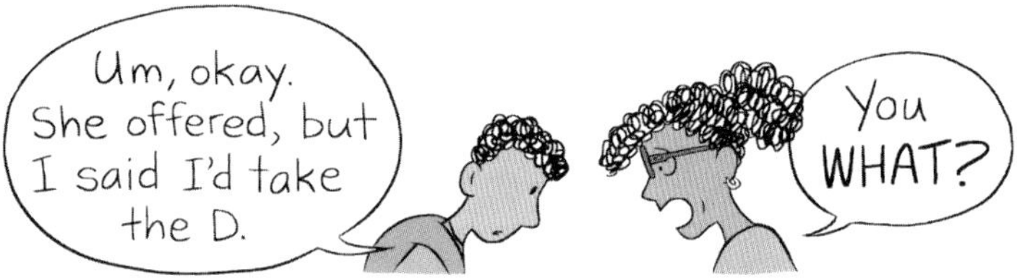
Um, okay. She offered, but I said I'd take the D.
You WHAT?

That sets the dog off again.

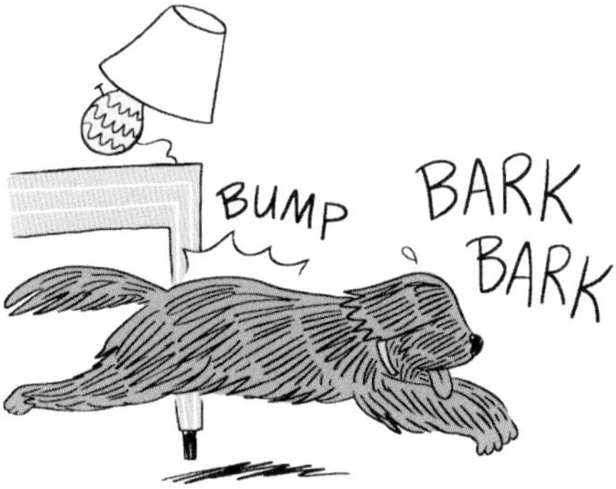
BUMP
BARK BARK

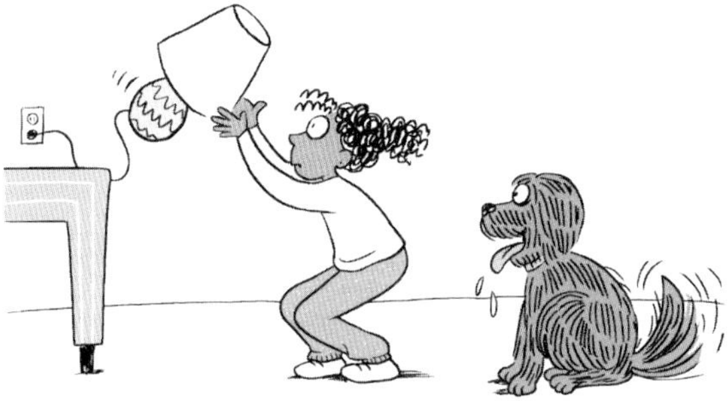

I groan.

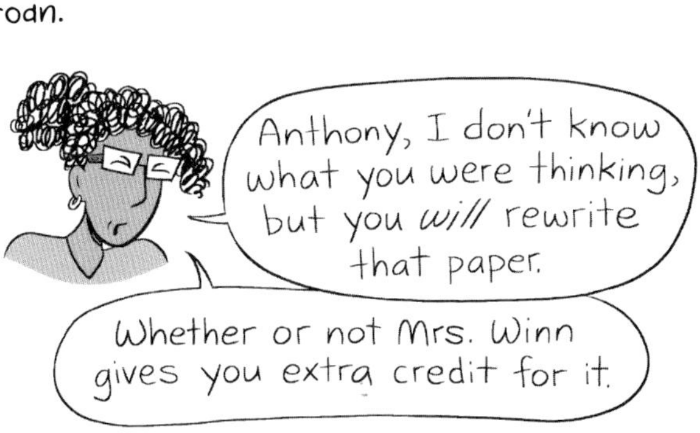
Anthony, I don't know what you were thinking, but you *will* rewrite that paper.
Whether or not Mrs. Winn gives you extra credit for it.

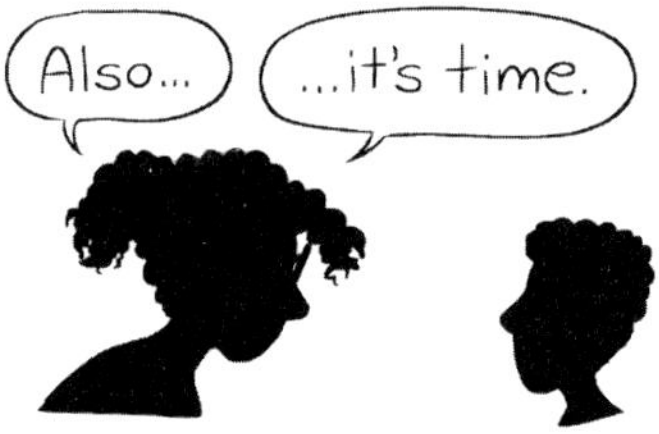
Also...
...it's time.

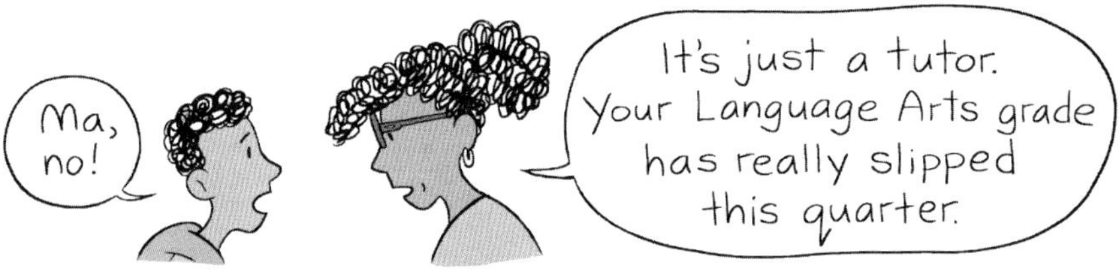
Ma, no!
It's just a tutor. Your Language Arts grade has really slipped this quarter.

Of course, that's when Things 1 and 2 walk over and get all in my business.

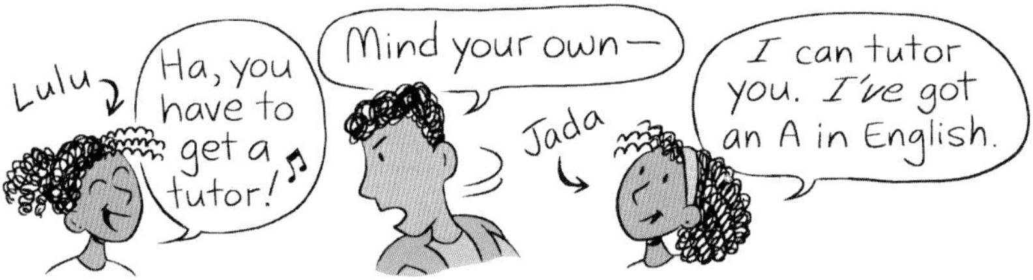
Lulu
Ha, you have to get a tutor! ♫
Mind your own—
Jada
I can tutor you. *I've* got an A in English.

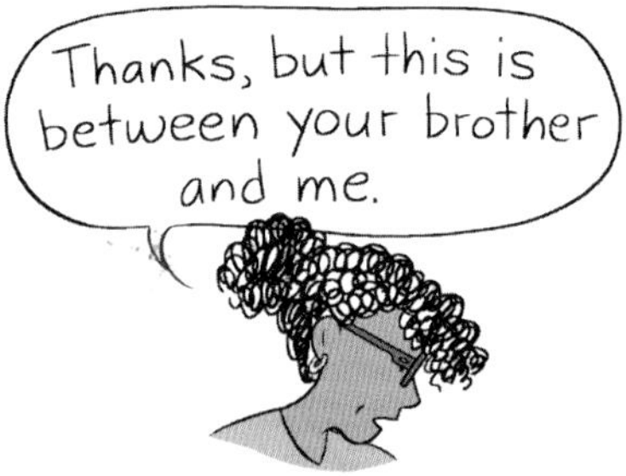
Thanks, but this is between your brother and me.

She kisses Jada on the top of her ten-year-old head. I roll my eyes when Mom's not looking.

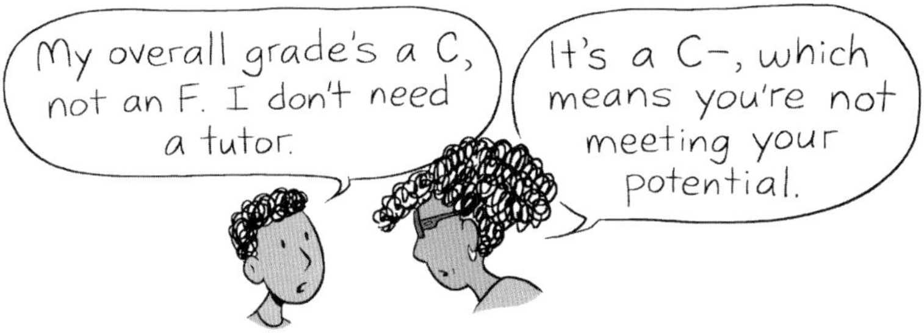
My overall grade's a C, not an F. I don't need a tutor.
It's a C–, which means you're not meeting your potential.

My parents always insist that we "meet our potential." I don't even know what that means anymore. Maybe my potential in Language Arts is a C-. I'm good at math and science and stuff. Maybe my "potential" is higher in those classes. Besides, I've gone through tutors and programs before. I'm so done.

Problem is: my mom is a work-at-home software developer, and my dad is a pediatric psychiatrist. They set the bar, well . . .

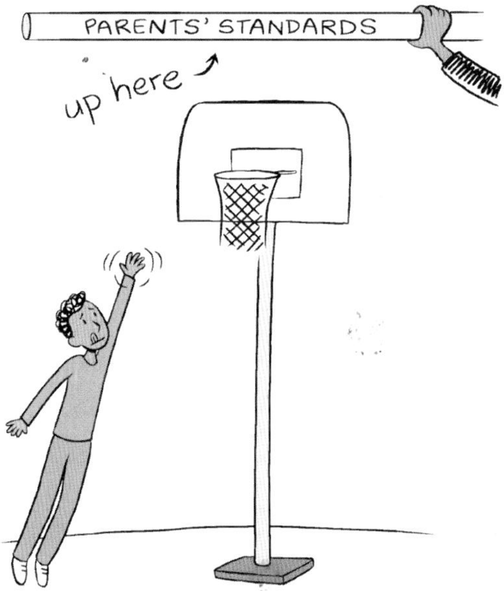
PARENTS' STANDARDS
up here

And they want the best for me. So, really, there's not a lot I can get away with. Even in Language Arts.

Look, I know it's more work, but you can do it.

You've already come so far, babe. Besides, we had an agreement.

It's true. If any of my grades start slipping, I'm s'posed to tell my parents right away. My Language Arts grade started a down-hill slide when we began writing longer essays, and I never said a word.

Mrs. Winn is notorious for not entering graded papers right away; I guess she finally did, and Hawkeye Mom saw everything come through at once.

So I don't get a say in this?

Nope. We'll talk more later. I've gotta get back to my meeting. Peach pie in the fridge.

To say my mom is no-nonsense is like saying Phineas hates baths. It's just a total given.

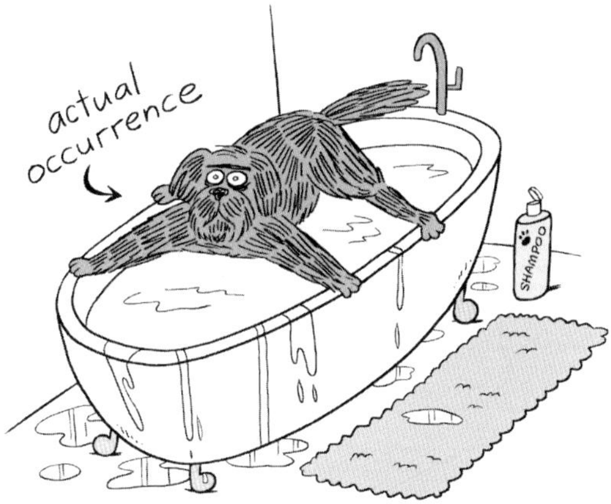
actual occurrence
SHAMPOO

I can't help it. I open the fridge and grab a giant helping of pie. I may be mad at my mom, but that won't stop me from eating her superior dessert. I race up the stairs, two at a time, while Lulu shouts:

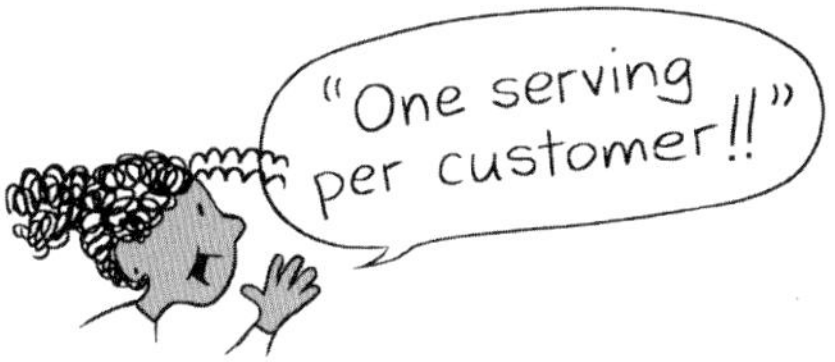
"One serving per customer!!"

I go in my room and close—and lock—the door. No chances taken with the nosy twosome.

I flop on my bed, practically inhaling the pie. Still, I'm sooo mad at my mom. **And** my pop, even though he probably doesn't know anything about this. But once he finds out, he'll take Mom's side because they're a "team."

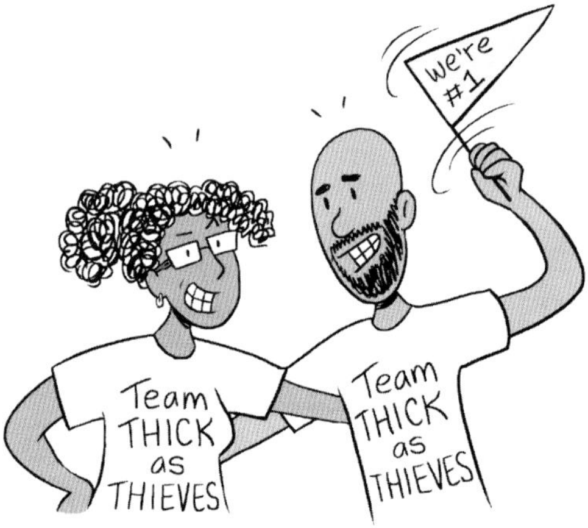
we're #1
Team THICK as THIEVES
Team THICK as THIEVES

At least my sleepover is still on. I start to text Tyler to let him know when to come over.

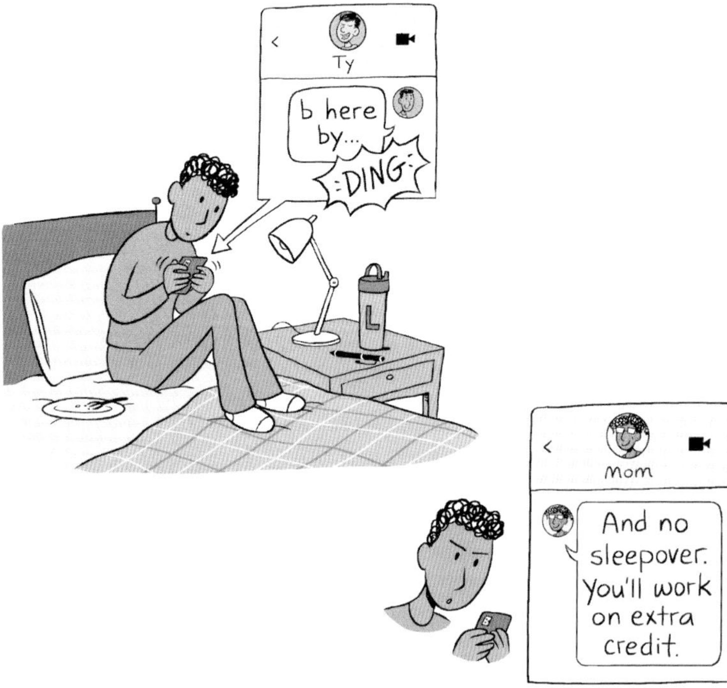
Ty
b here by...
DING
Mom
And no sleepover. You'll work on extra credit.

I slam my phone into the cushy mattress. This is totally UNFAIR.

But what can I do?

I sigh and give Tyler the update. He's (clearly) not happy.

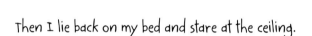

Then I lie back on my bed and stare at the ceiling.

dusty light →   (not much else up here)

It's gonna be a looooong weekend.

Leah

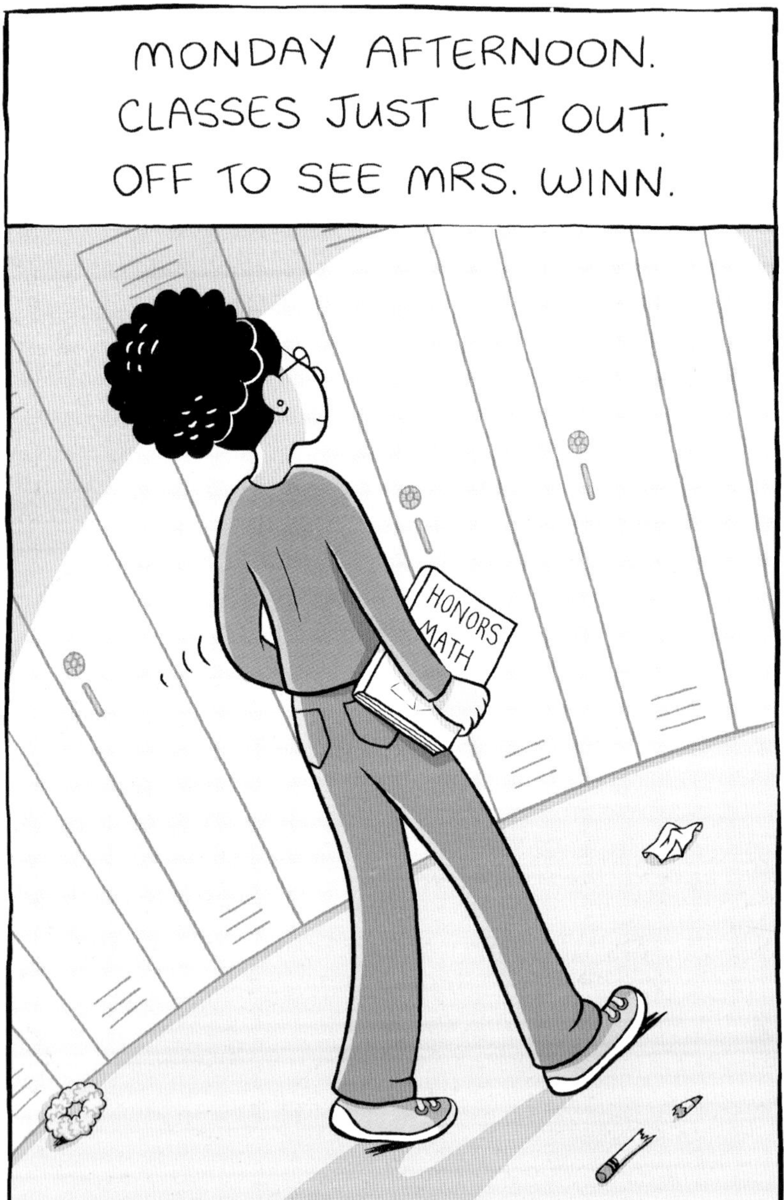
MONDAY AFTERNOON.
CLASSES JUST LET OUT.
OFF TO SEE MRS. WINN.
HONORS MATH

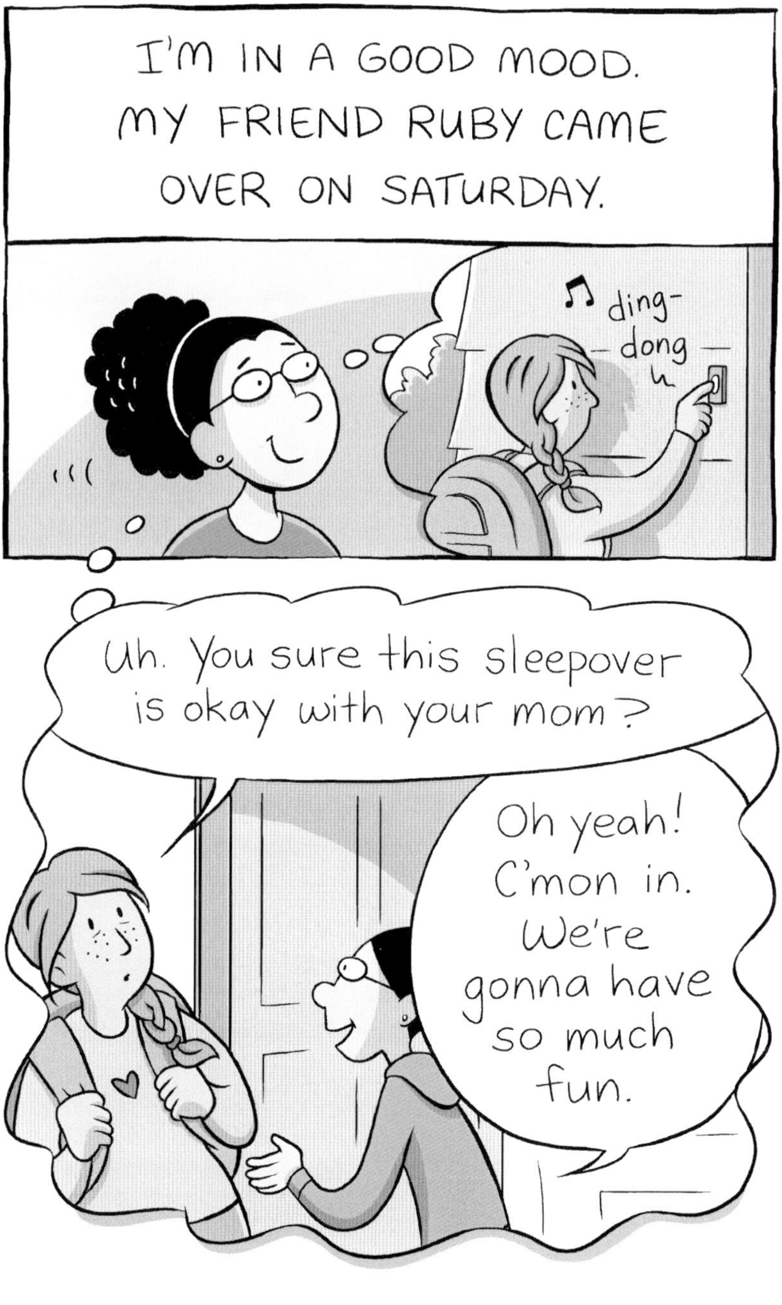
I'M IN A GOOD MOOD. MY FRIEND RUBY CAME OVER ON SATURDAY.
ding-dong
Uh. You sure this sleepover is okay with your mom?
Oh yeah! C'mon in. We're gonna have so much fun.

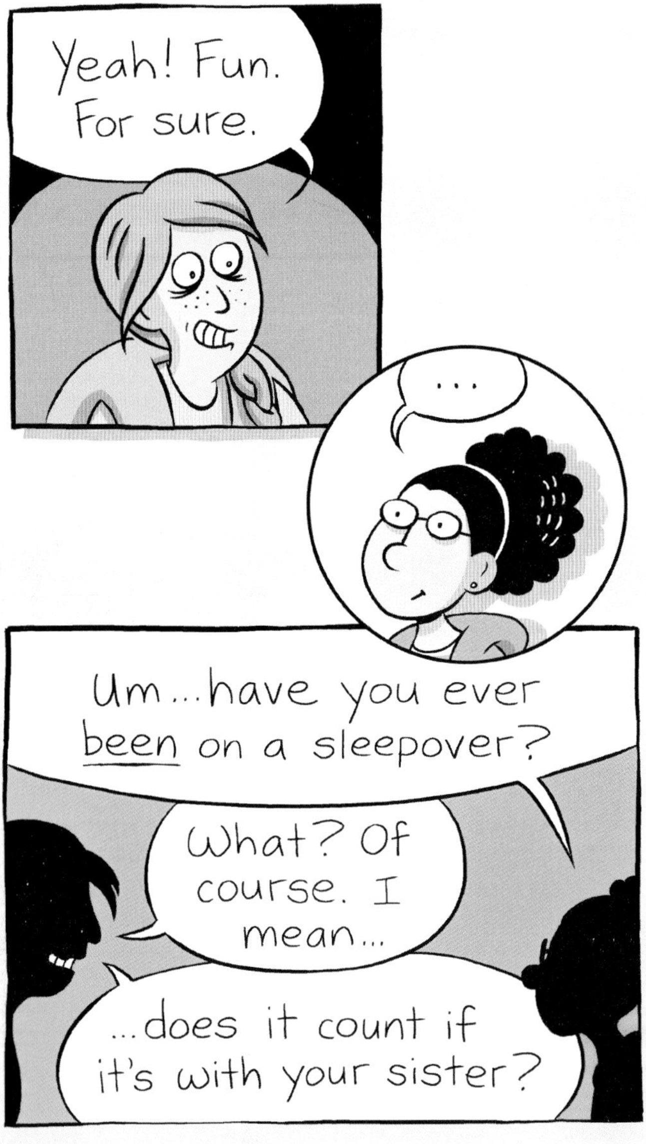
Yeah! Fun. For sure.
...
Um...have you ever been on a sleepover?
What? Of course. I mean...
...does it count if it's with your sister?

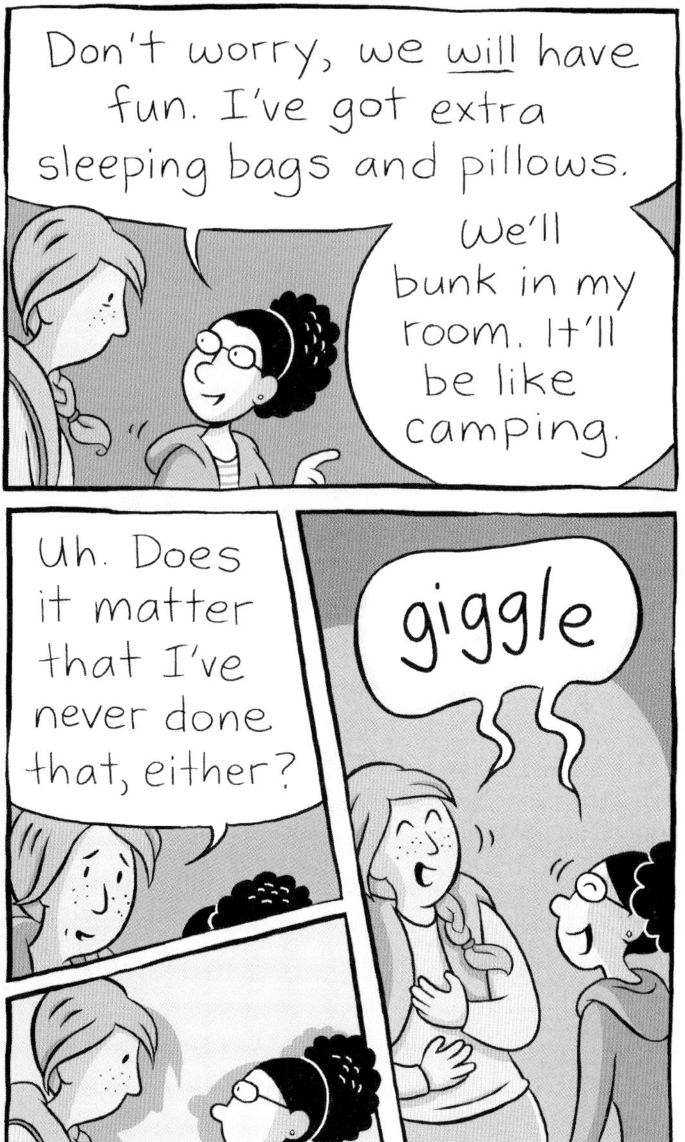
Don't worry, we will have fun. I've got extra sleeping bags and pillows.
We'll bunk in my room. It'll be like camping.
Uh. Does it matter that I've never done that, either?
giggle

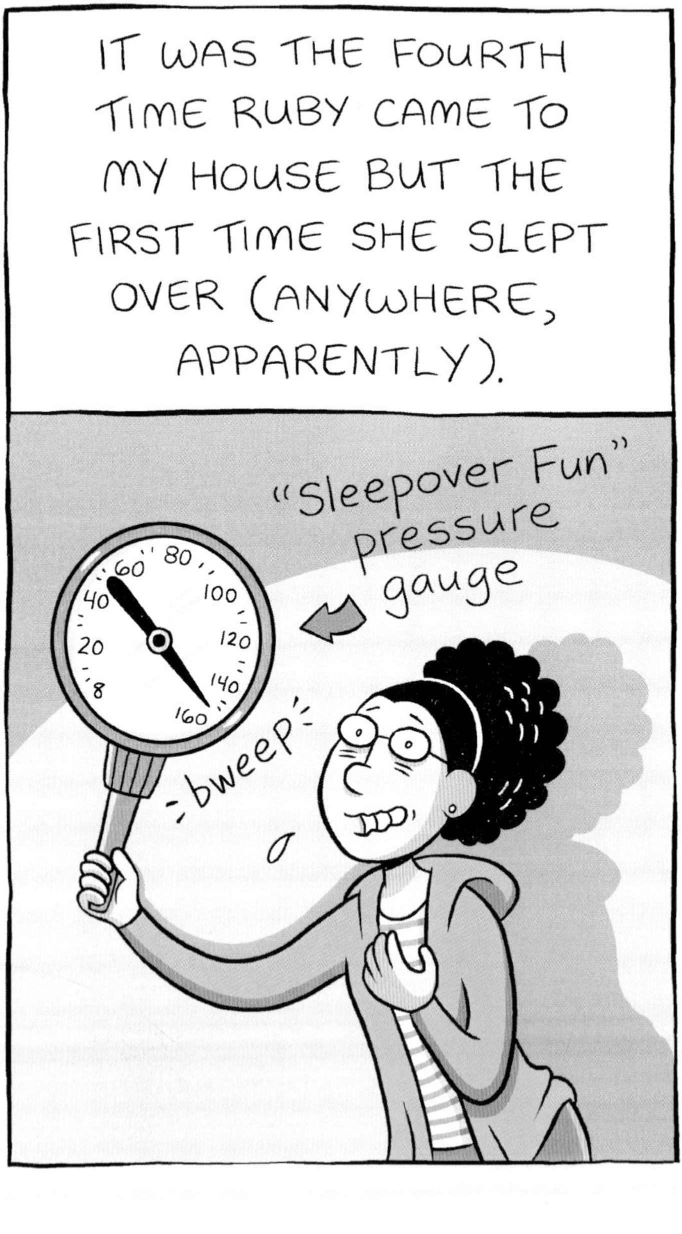
IT WAS THE FOURTH TIME RUBY CAME TO MY HOUSE BUT THE FIRST TIME SHE SLEPT OVER (ANYWHERE, APPARENTLY).
"Sleepover Fun" pressure gauge
bweep

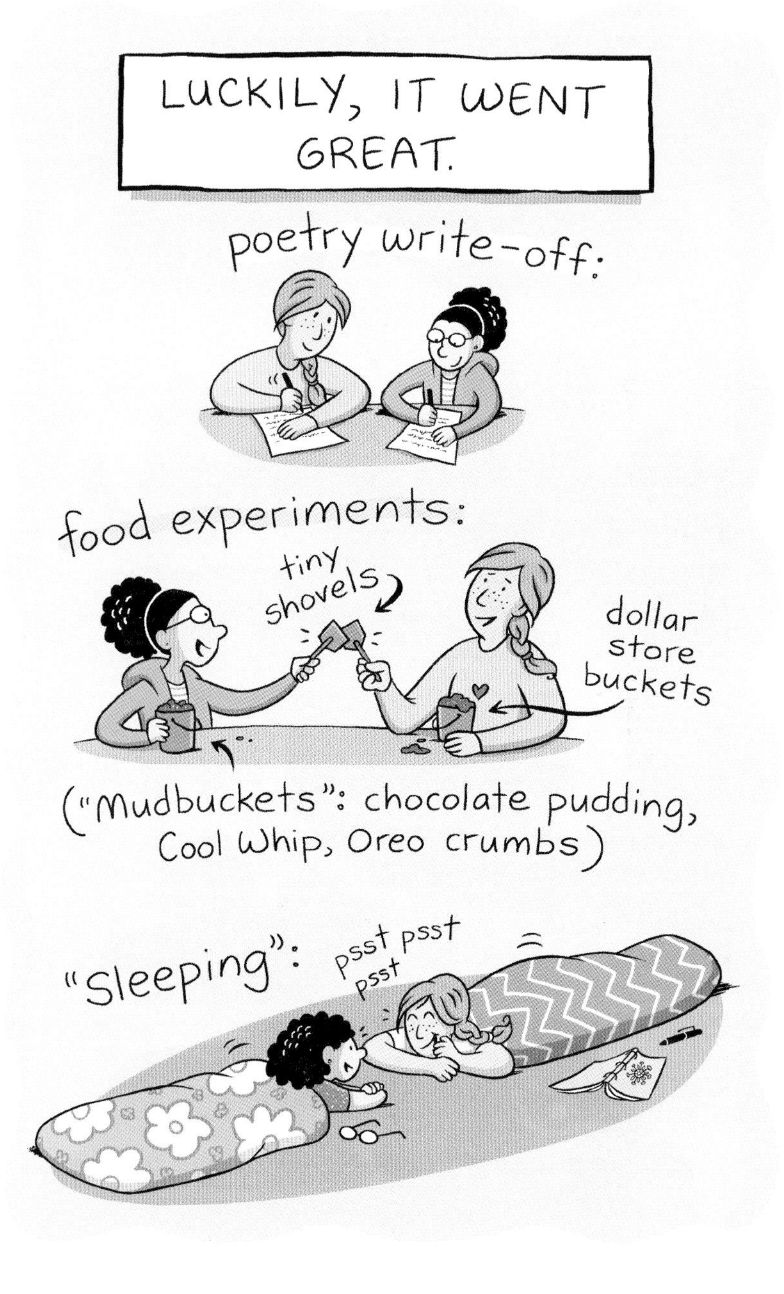
LUCKILY, IT WENT GREAT.
poetry write-off:
food experiments:
tiny shovels
dollar store buckets
("Mudbuckets": chocolate pudding, Cool Whip, Oreo crumbs)
"Sleeping":
psst psst psst

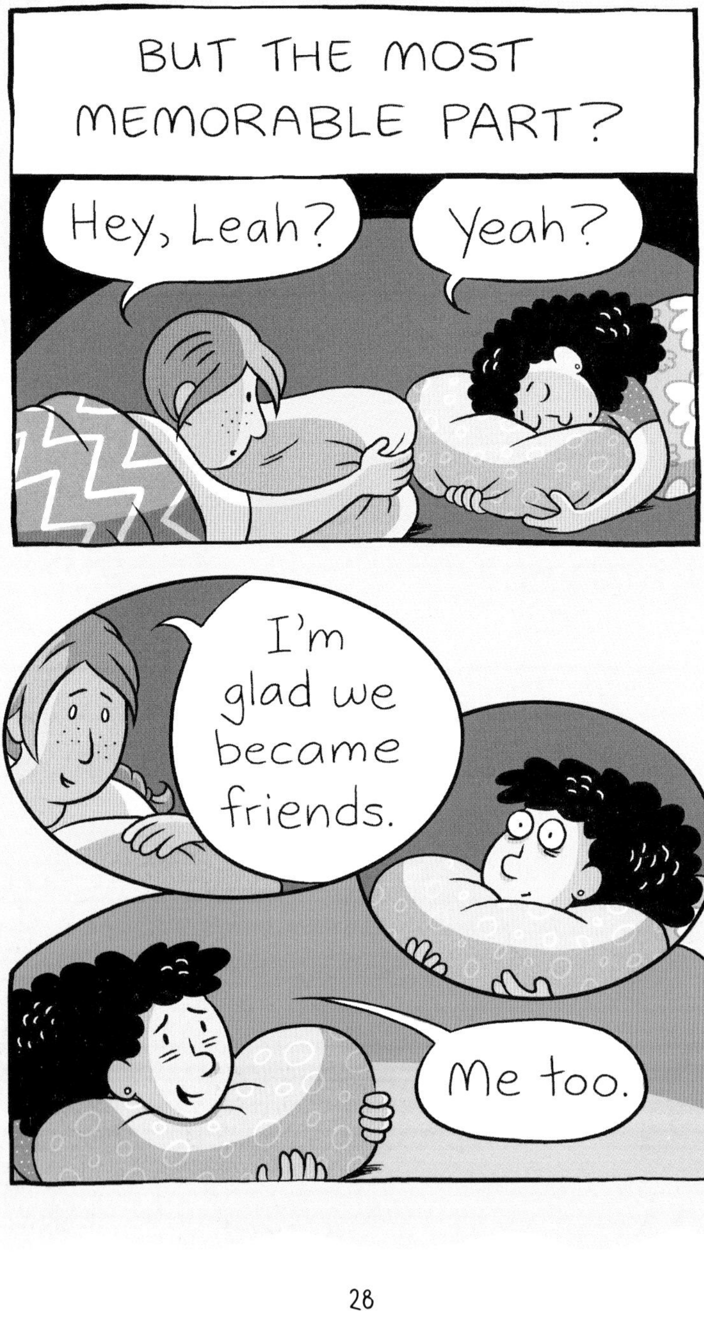
BUT THE MOST MEMORABLE PART?
Hey, Leah?
Yeah?
I'm glad we became friends.
Me too.

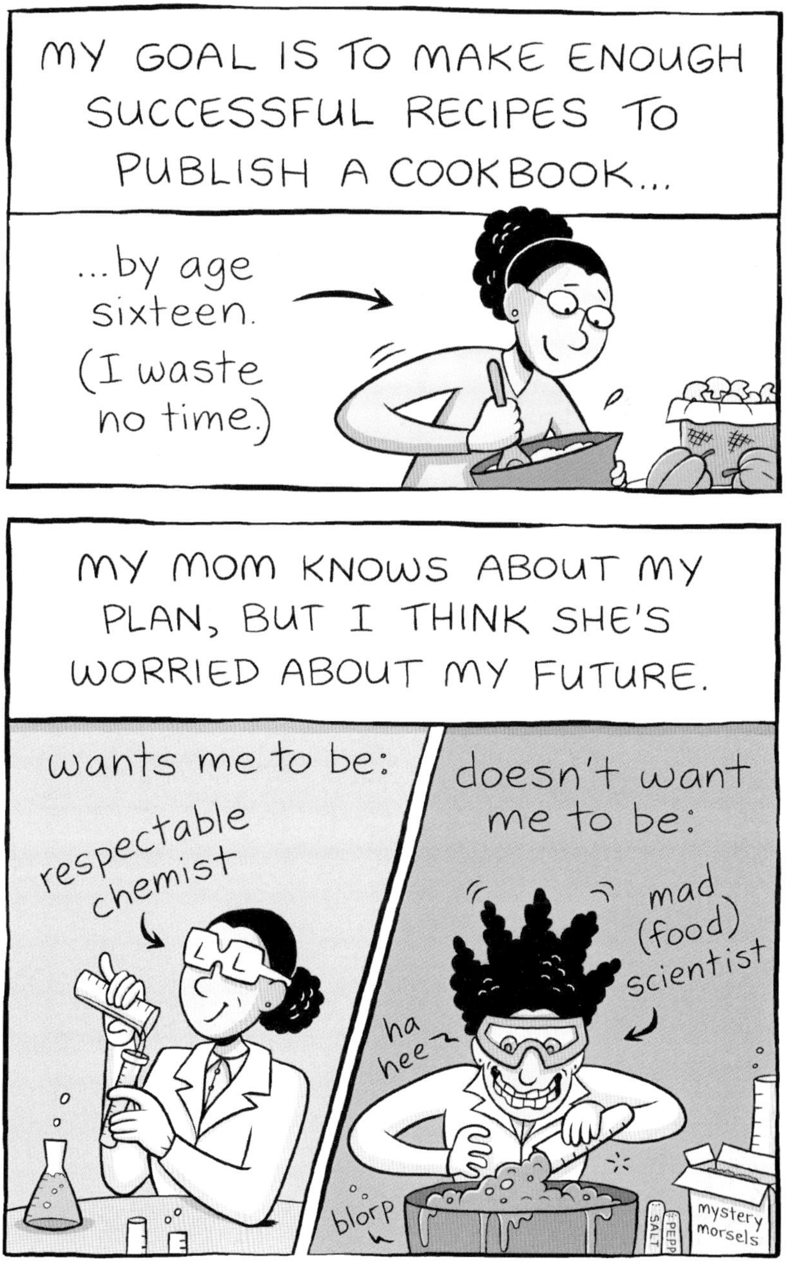
MY GOAL IS TO MAKE ENOUGH SUCCESSFUL RECIPES TO PUBLISH A COOKBOOK...
...by age sixteen. (I waste no time.)
MY MOM KNOWS ABOUT MY PLAN, BUT I THINK SHE'S WORRIED ABOUT MY FUTURE.
wants me to be:
respectable chemist
doesn't want me to be:
mad (food) scientist
ha hee
blorp
SALT
PEPP
mystery morsels

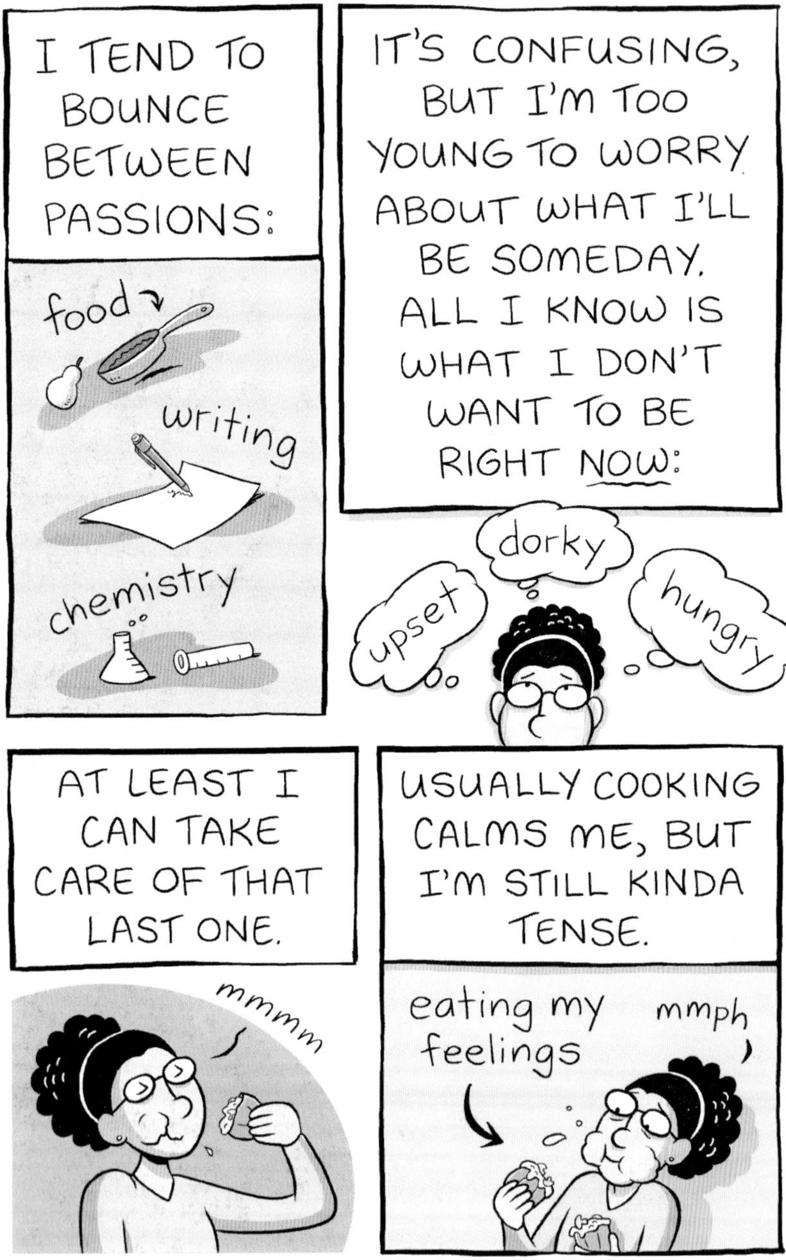
I TEND TO BOUNCE BETWEEN PASSIONS:
food
writing
chemistry
IT'S CONFUSING, BUT I'M TOO YOUNG TO WORRY ABOUT WHAT I'LL BE SOMEDAY. ALL I KNOW IS WHAT I DON'T WANT TO BE RIGHT NOW:
upset
dorky
hungry
AT LEAST I CAN TAKE CARE OF THAT LAST ONE.
mmmm
USUALLY COOKING CALMS ME, BUT I'M STILL KINDA TENSE.
eating my feelings
mmph

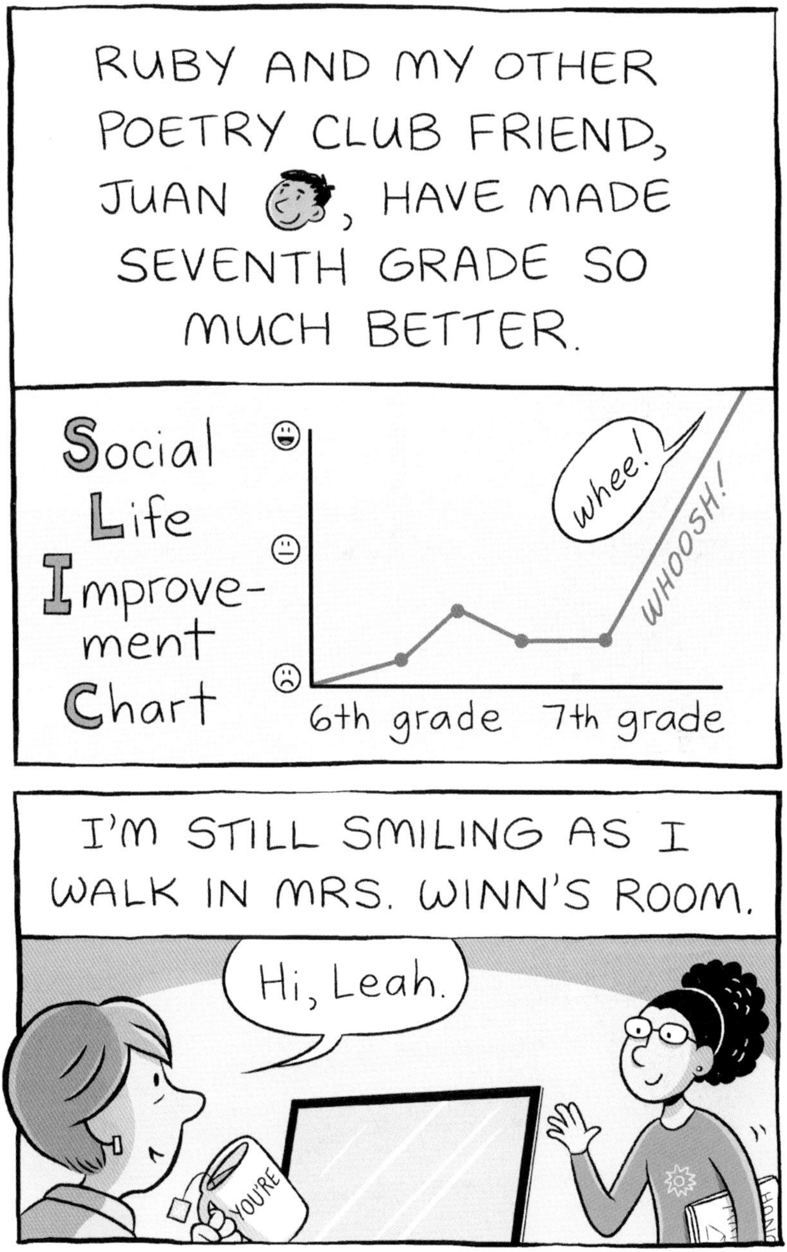
RUBY AND MY OTHER POETRY CLUB FRIEND, JUAN, HAVE MADE SEVENTH GRADE SO MUCH BETTER.
Social Life Improvement Chart
whee!
WHOOSH!
6th grade
7th grade
I'M STILL SMILING AS I WALK IN MRS. WINN'S ROOM.
Hi, Leah.
YOU'RE

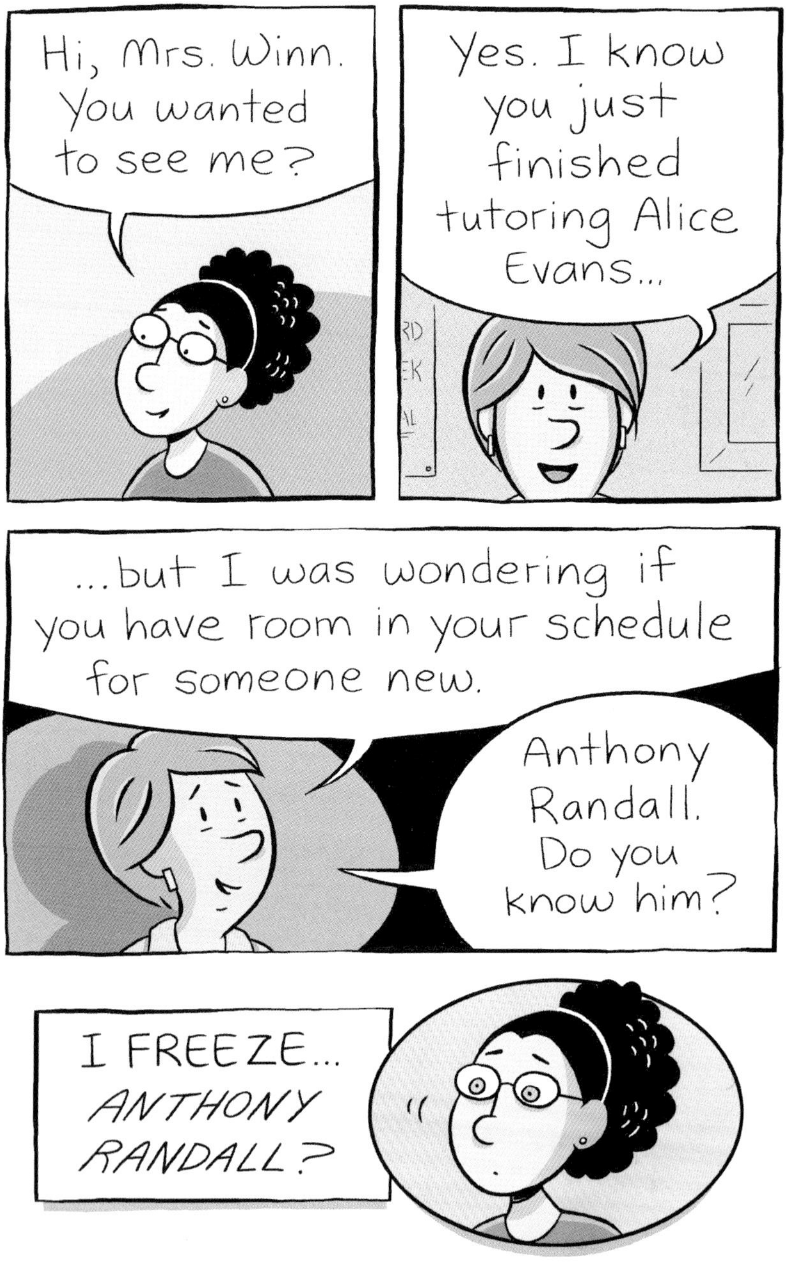
Hi, Mrs. Winn. You wanted to see me?
Yes. I know you just finished tutoring Alice Evans...
...but I was wondering if you have room in your schedule for someone new.
Anthony Randall. Do you know him?
I FREEZE... *ANTHONY RANDALL?*

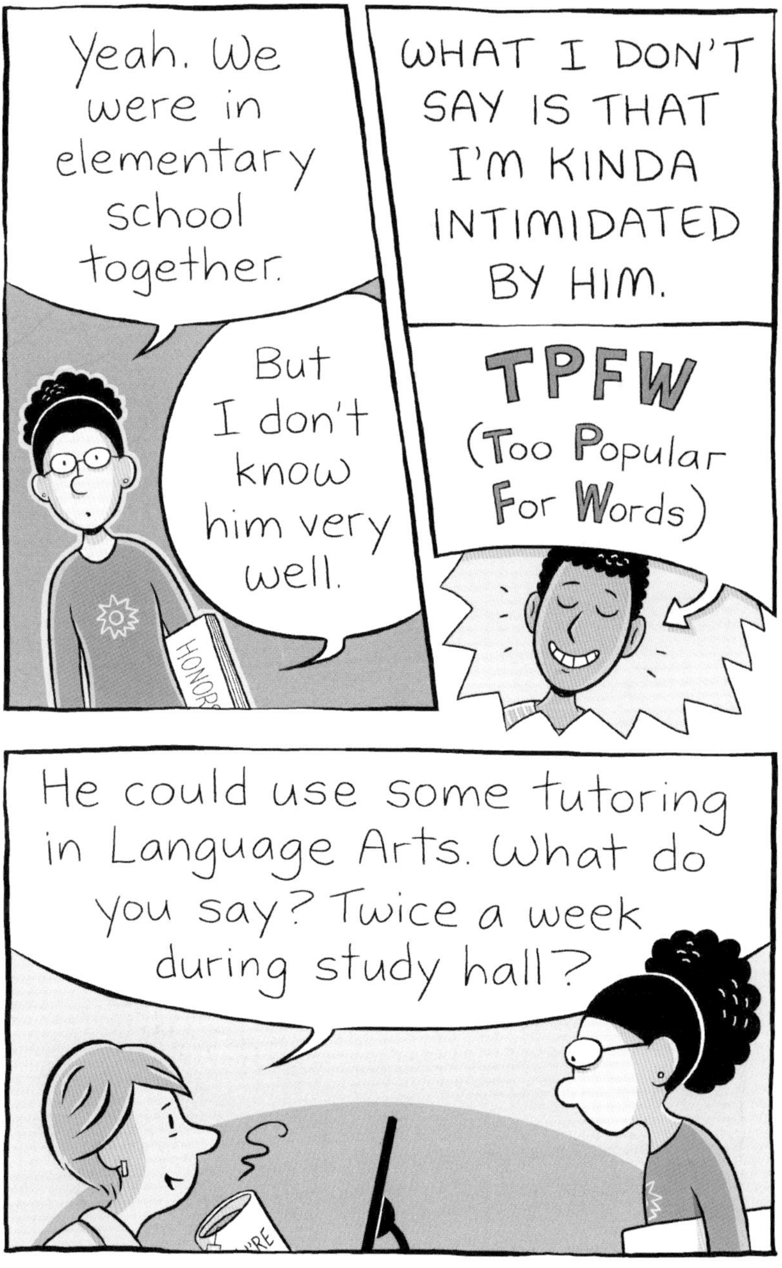
Yeah. We were in elementary school together.
But I don't know him very well.
WHAT I DON'T SAY IS THAT I'M KINDA INTIMIDATED BY HIM.
TPFW
(Too Popular For Words)
HONORS
He could use some tutoring in Language Arts. What do you say? Twice a week during study hall?

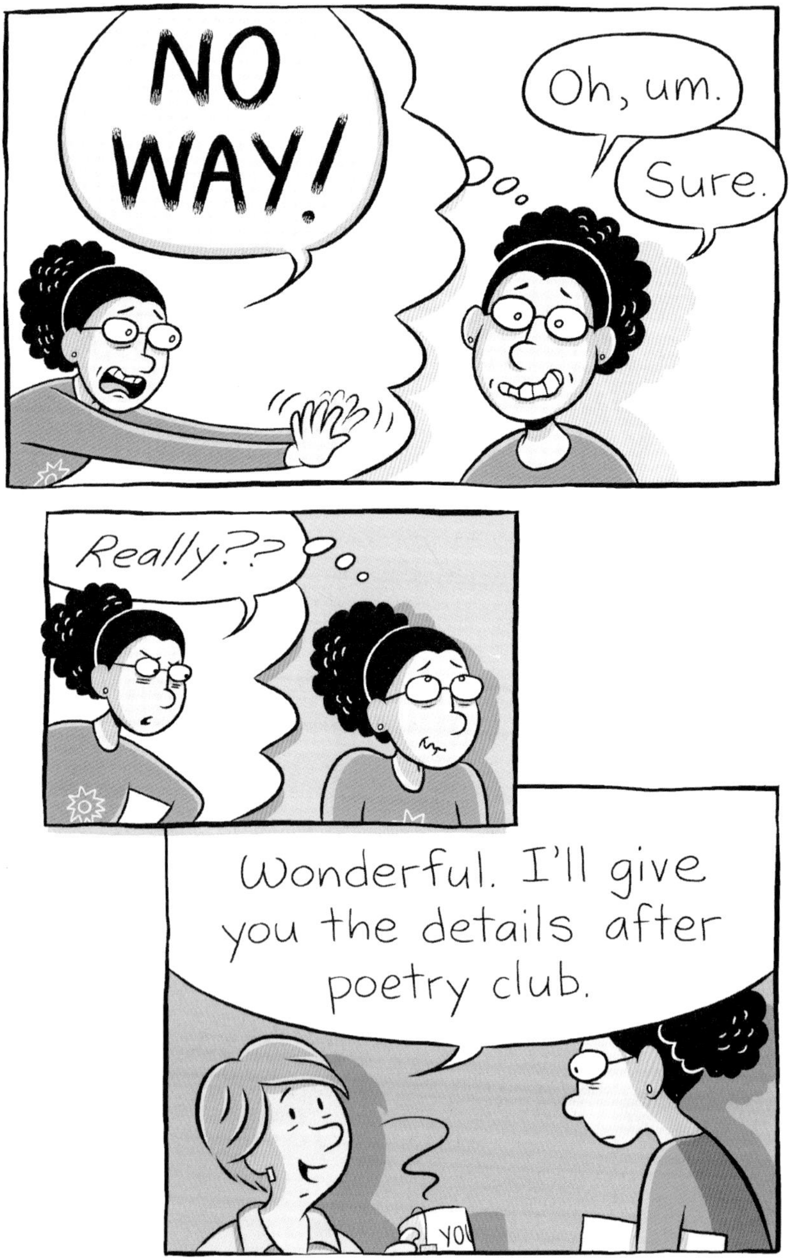
NO WAY!
Oh, um.
Sure.
Really??
Wonderful. I'll give you the details after poetry club.

IT'S HARD TO SAY NO TO MRS. WINN. AND I *DID* SIGN UP TO BE A TUTOR — IT'S NOT LIKE I CAN BE PICKY.

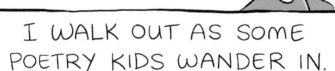

Sounds good.

Just gonna go to my locker. Be right back.

I WALK OUT AS SOME POETRY KIDS WANDER IN.

Hi, Leah. You going to poetry club?

Uh, yeah.

You okay?

Oh. Uh...

HONORS MATH

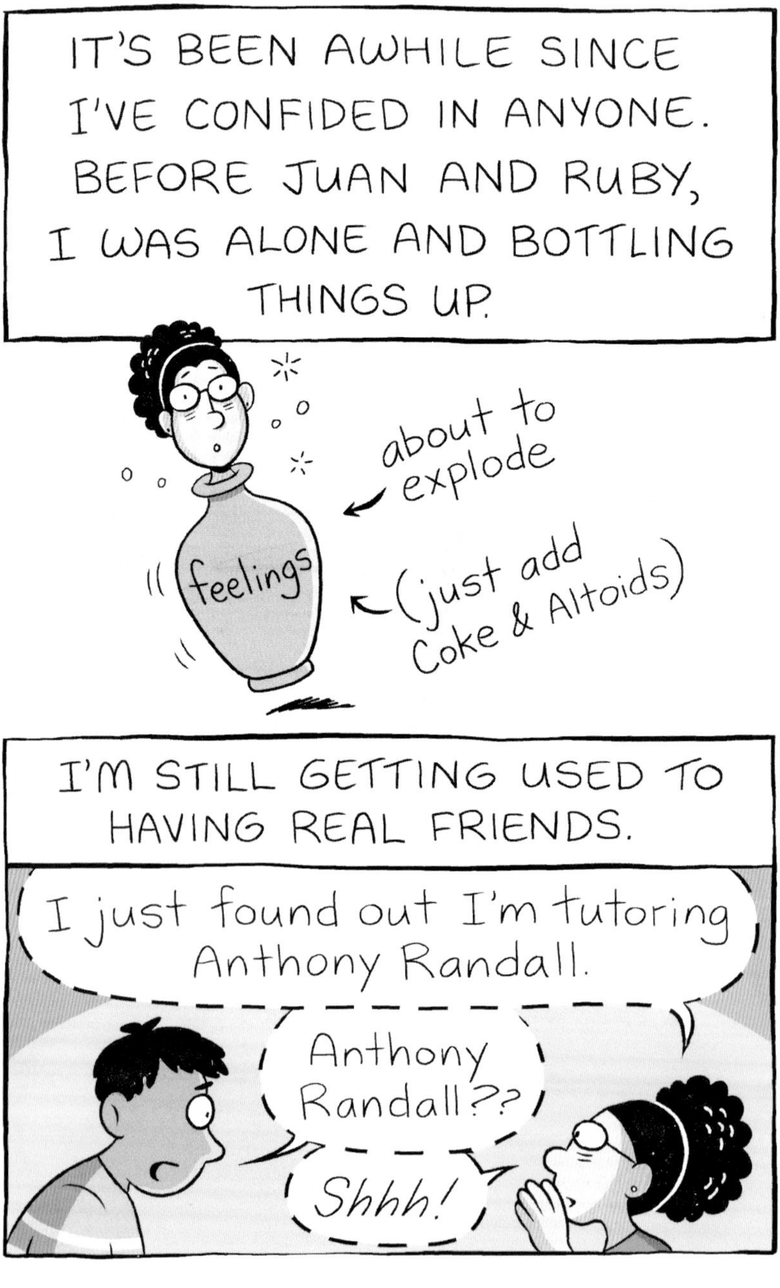
IT'S BEEN AWHILE SINCE I'VE CONFIDED IN ANYONE. BEFORE JUAN AND RUBY, I WAS ALONE AND BOTTLING THINGS UP.
about to explode
feelings
(just add Coke & Altoids)
I'M STILL GETTING USED TO HAVING REAL FRIENDS.
I just found out I'm tutoring Anthony Randall.
Anthony Randall??
Shhh!

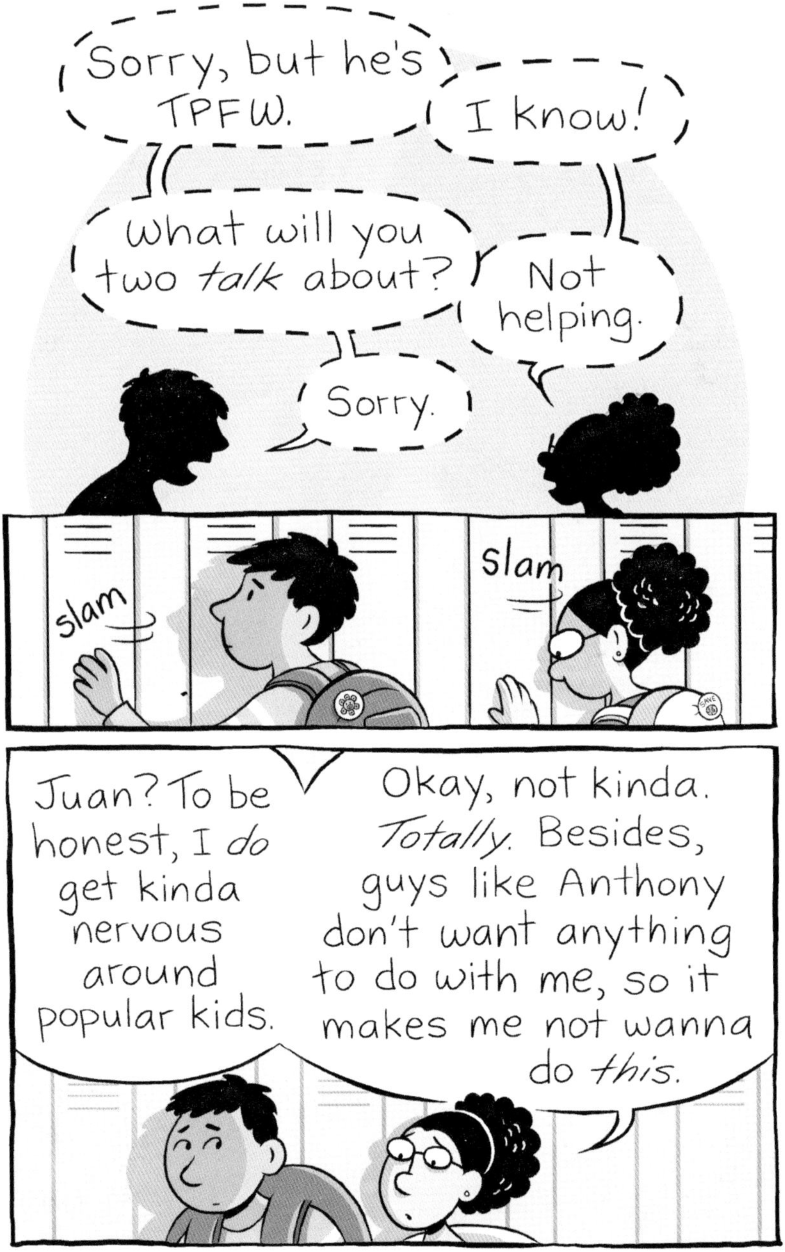
Sorry, but he's TPFW.
What will you two *talk* about?
I know!
Not helping.
Sorry.
slam
slam
Juan? To be honest, I *do* get kinda nervous around popular kids.
Okay, not kinda. *Totally.* Besides, guys like Anthony don't want anything to do with me, so it makes me not wanna do *this.*

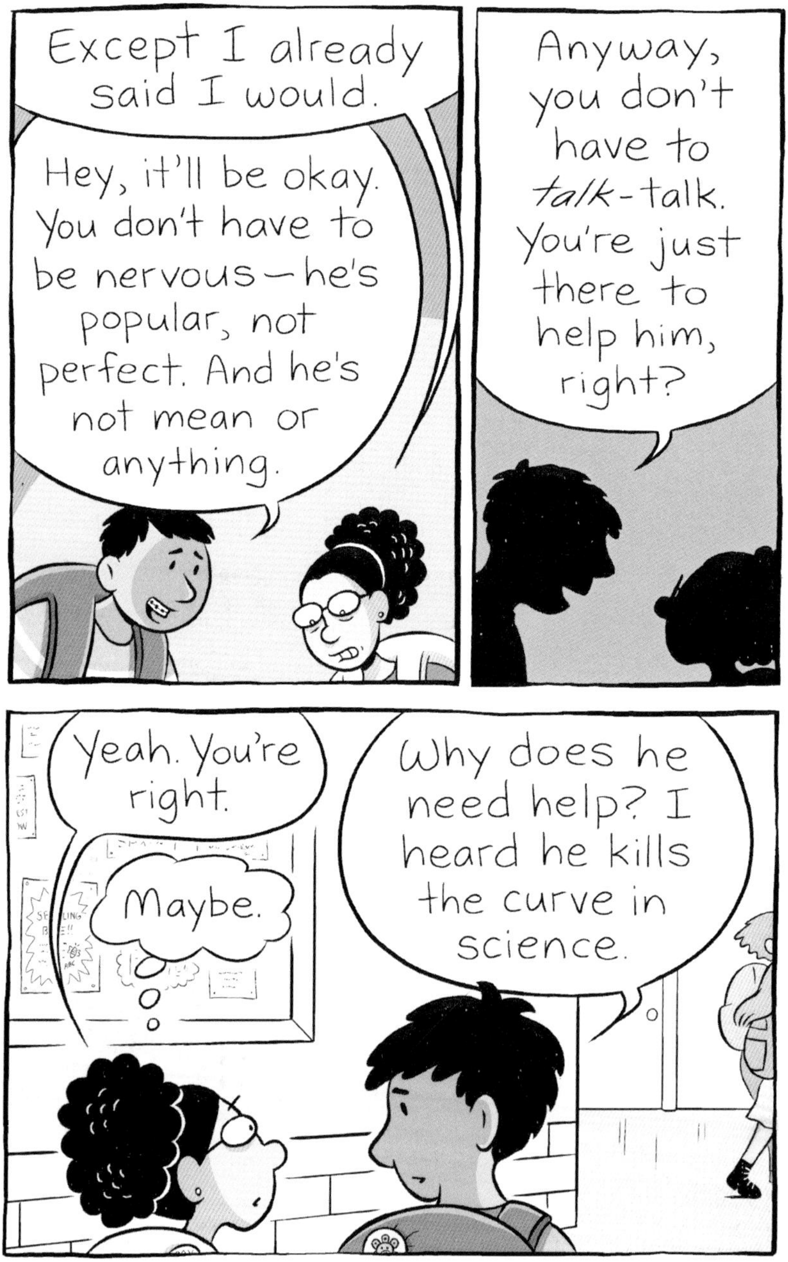
Except I already said I would.
Hey, it'll be okay. You don't have to be nervous—he's popular, not perfect. And he's not mean or anything.
Anyway, you don't have to *talk*-talk. You're just there to help him, right?
Yeah. You're right.
Maybe.
Why does he need help? I heard he kills the curve in science.
SPELLING BEE!!

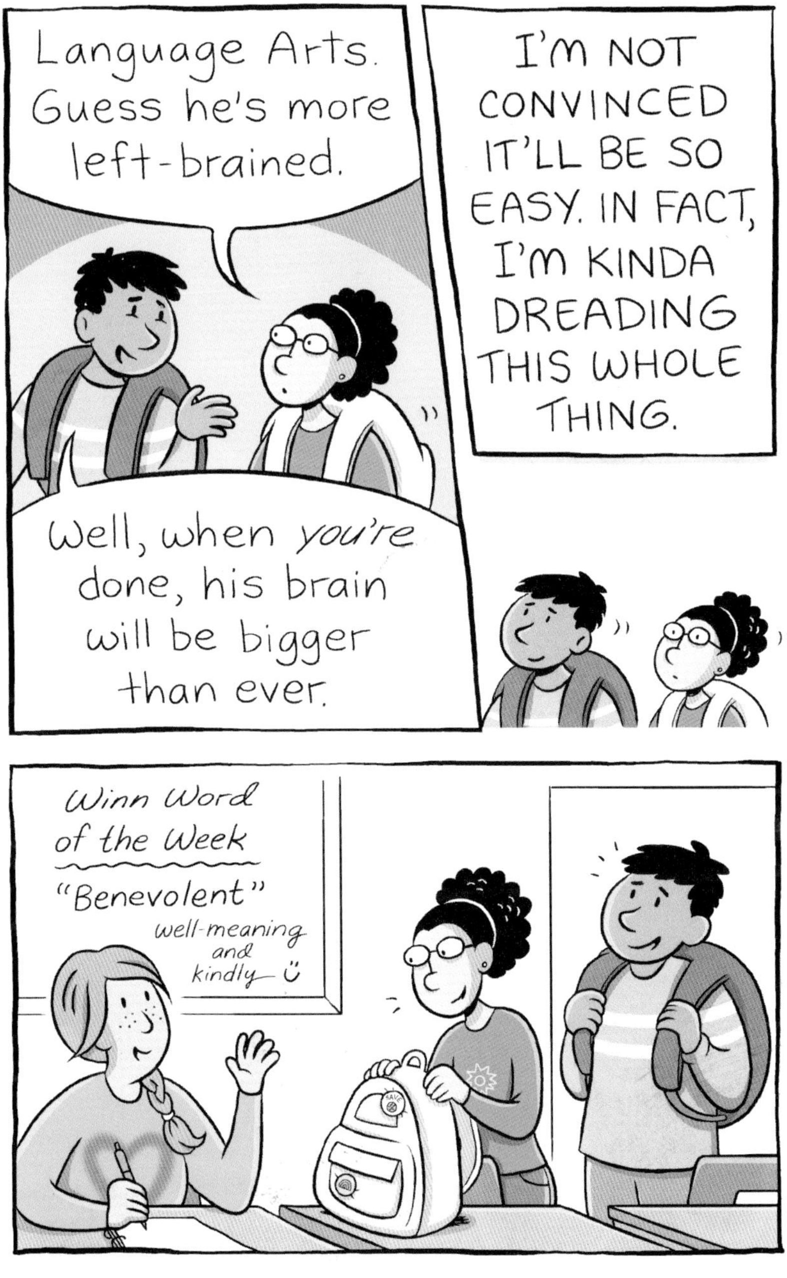
Language Arts. Guess he's more left-brained.
I'M NOT CONVINCED IT'LL BE SO EASY. IN FACT, I'M KINDA DREADING THIS WHOLE THING.
Well, when *you're* done, his brain will be bigger than ever.
Winn Word of the Week
"Benevolent"
well-meaning and kindly

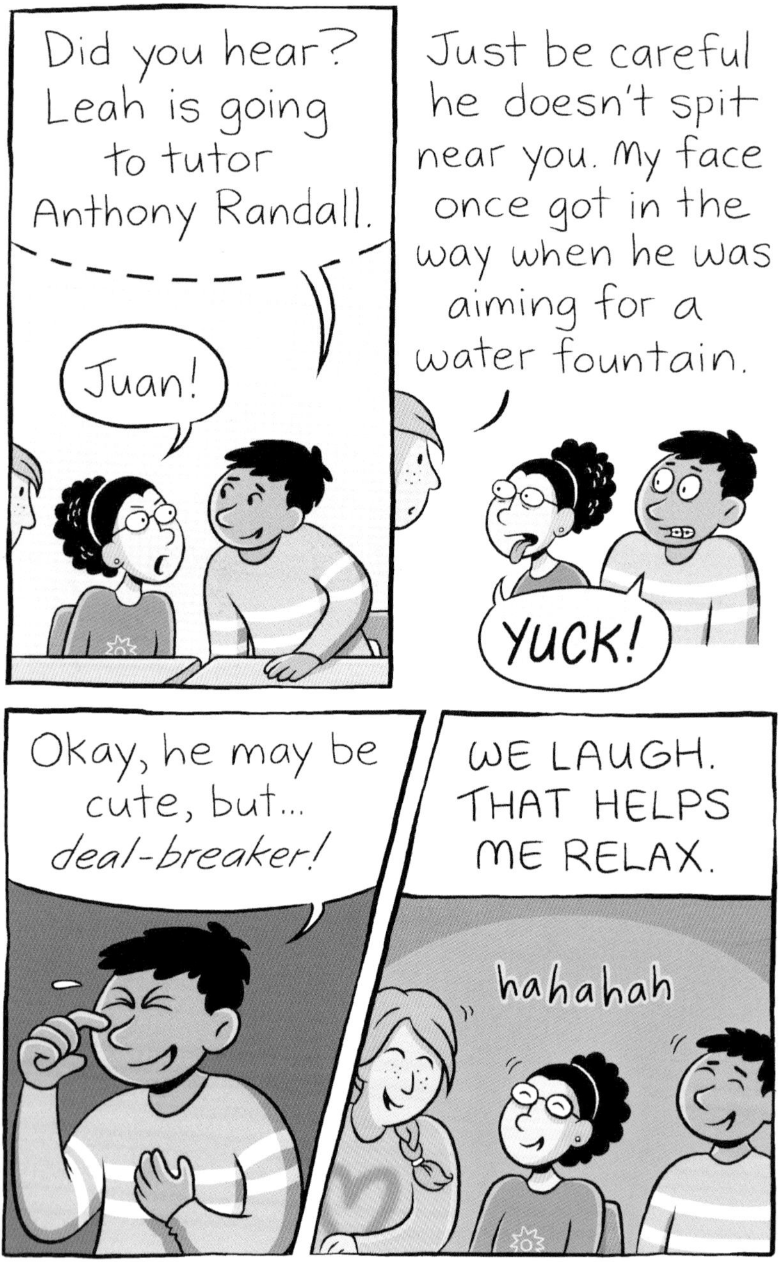
Did you hear? Leah is going to tutor Anthony Randall.
Juan!
Just be careful he doesn't spit near you. My face once got in the way when he was aiming for a water fountain.
YUCK!
Okay, he may be cute, but... *deal-breaker!*
WE LAUGH. THAT HELPS ME RELAX.
hahahah

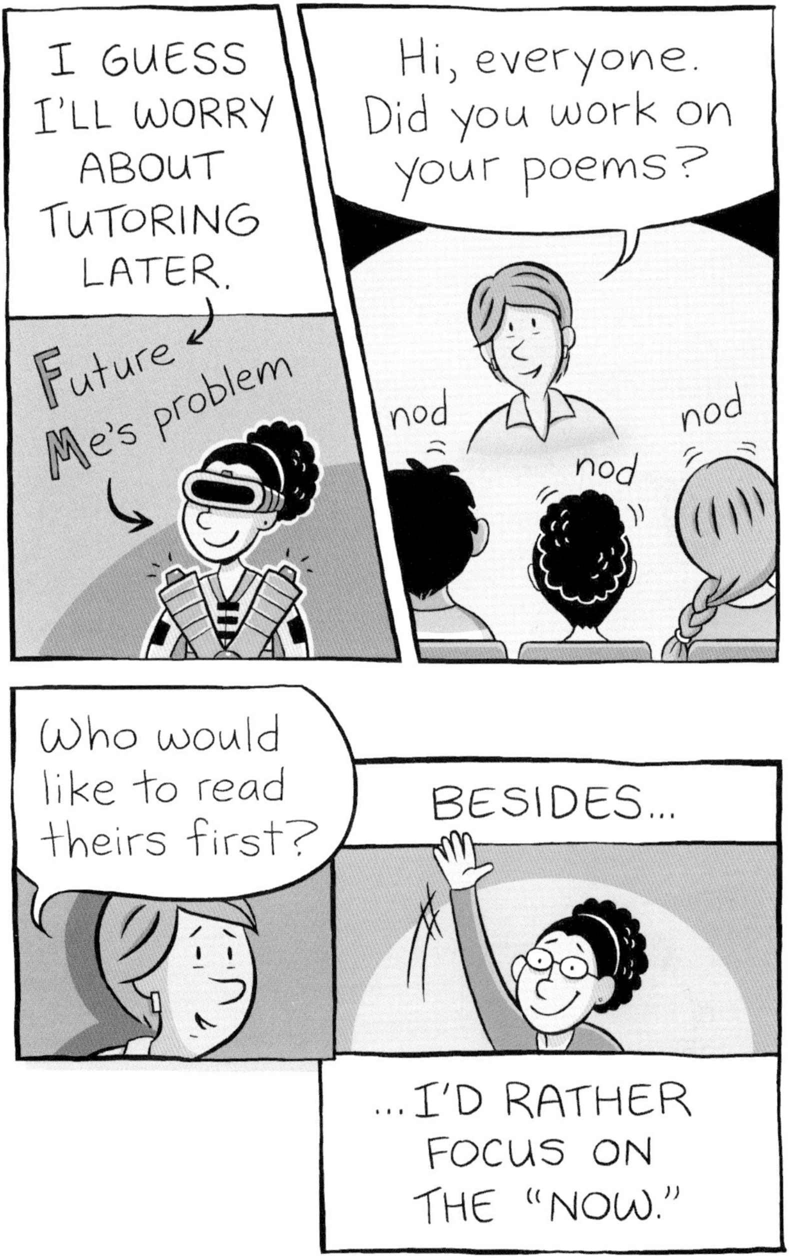
I GUESS I'LL WORRY ABOUT TUTORING LATER.
Future Me's problem
Hi, everyone. Did you work on your poems?
nod
nod
nod
Who would like to read theirs first?
BESIDES...
...I'D RATHER FOCUS ON THE "NOW."

ANTHONY

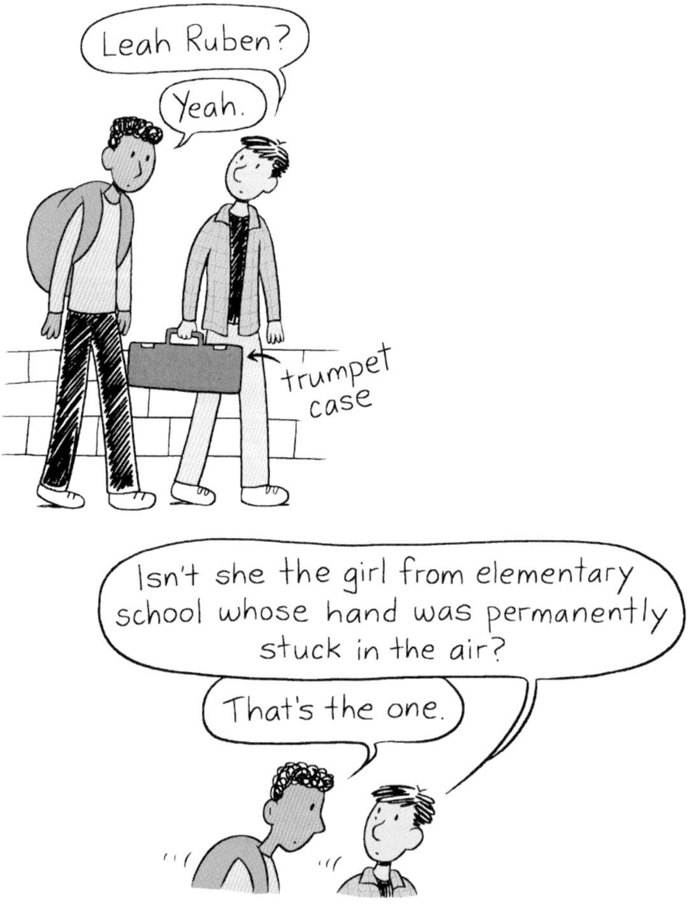
Leah Ruben?
Yeah.
trumpet case
Isn't she the girl from elementary school whose hand was permanently stuck in the air?
That's the one.

Mrs. Winn arranged this. It's kinda strange to me. I didn't think students tutored other students. My parents have hired tutors before, but they were always adults and either teachers or "experts."

We reach the library.

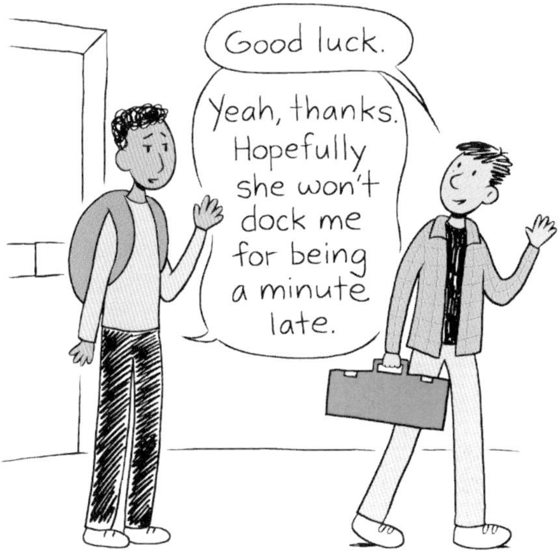
Good luck.
Yeah, thanks. Hopefully she won't dock me for being a minute late.

Tyler snorts and heads to Band.

I'm a little grumpy. I missed both the sleepover and b-ball at the Y because of that D. My parents made me work on extra credit, yeah, but they also made me watch YouTube videos to help with my grammar and hovered over me until I finished the rest of my homework and studying. Anyway, the whole weekend was a bust and a total waste of time. There was so much I could've gotten done (besides schoolwork).

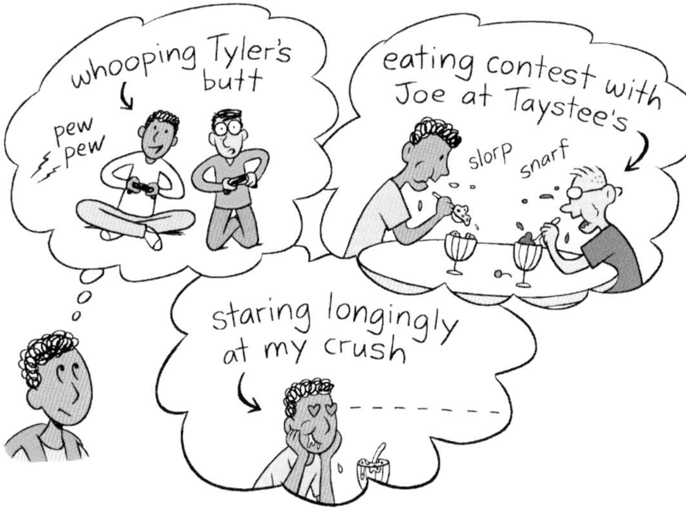
whooping Tyler's butt
pew pew
eating contest with Joe at Taystee's
slorp
snarf
staring longingly at my crush

I tried to rewrite my essay but couldn't. I don't know what Mrs. Winn meant by "digging deeper." I should've asked, but let's face it: in the moment, I didn't really care. Luckily, her class isn't until the end of the day, so there's still time to fix it.

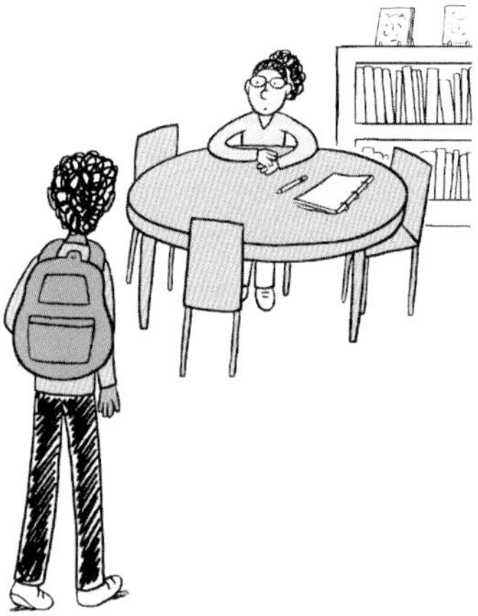

I don't run into Leah often, so seeing her now is kind of a jolt. Takes me back to elementary school.

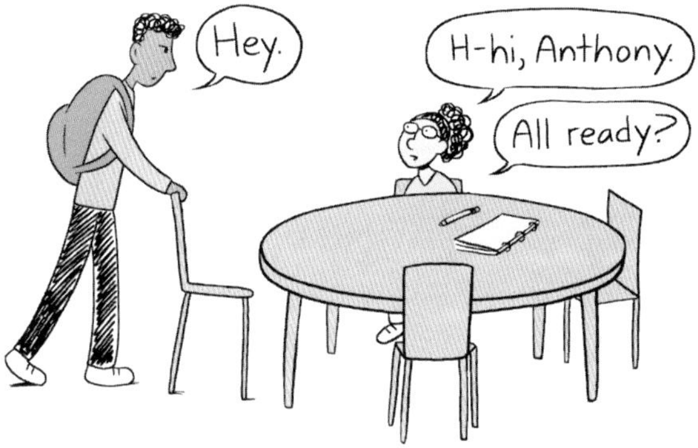
Hey.
H-hi, Anthony.
All ready?

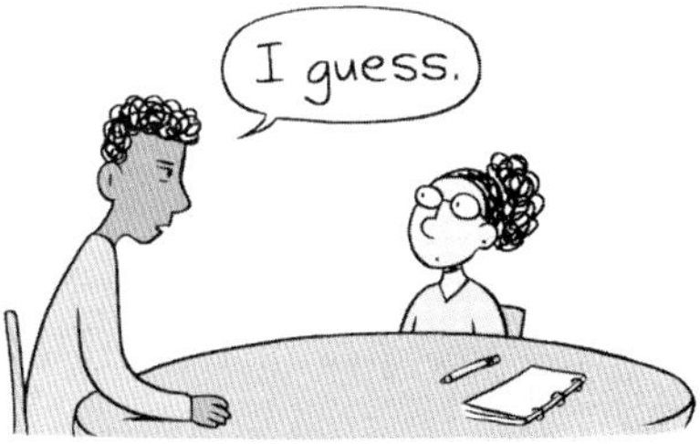
I guess.

Okay, that was sorta rude. It's not her fault I'm peeved at my parents.

But I've gotta admit, Leah's not my favorite person. In grade school, she was a total brownnose. She wouldn't talk much to other students, but she sure didn't mind answering the teachers' questions . . . like **all** the questions. It was really annoying.

I try to get past my negative thoughts. Gotta move forward. Anyway, she **is** smart.

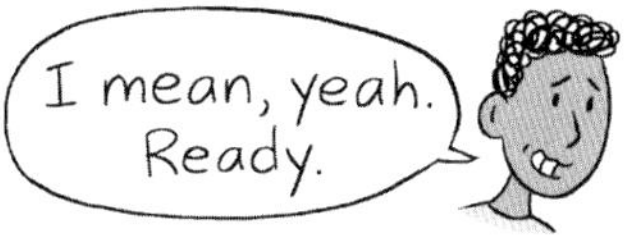
I mean, yeah. Ready.

She doesn't look convinced.

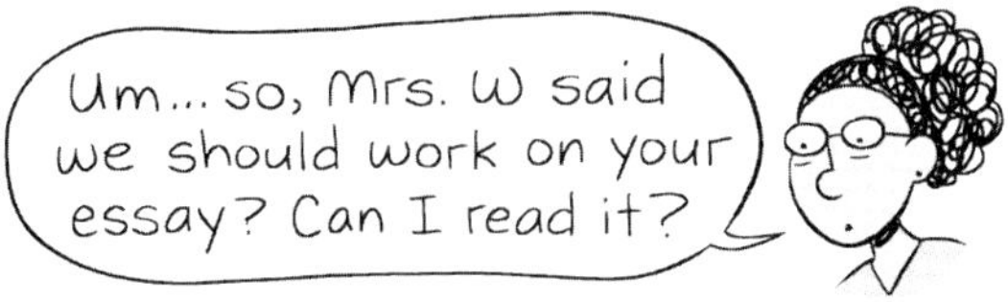
Um... so, Mrs. W said we should work on your essay? Can I read it?

She looks down when she talks. I don't remember her being this shy. It's hard to be around shy people 'cause I feel like I'm doing all the work, talking for two. Great, this'll be fun.

I dig my essay out of my backpack.

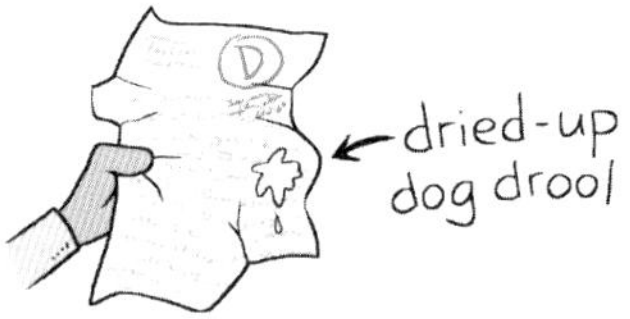
D
dried-up dog drool

I joke:

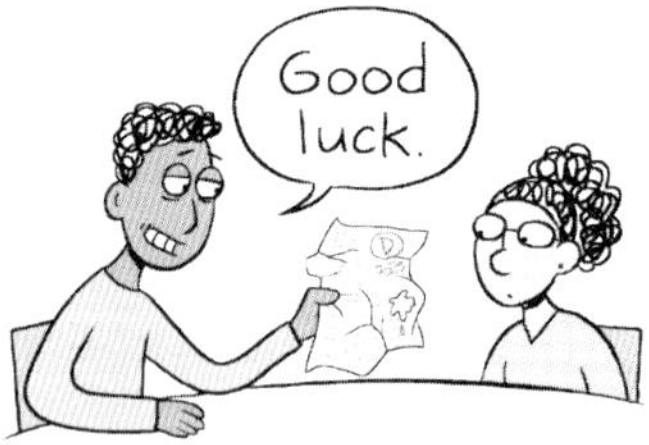
Good luck.
D

She turns bright red but takes the paper.

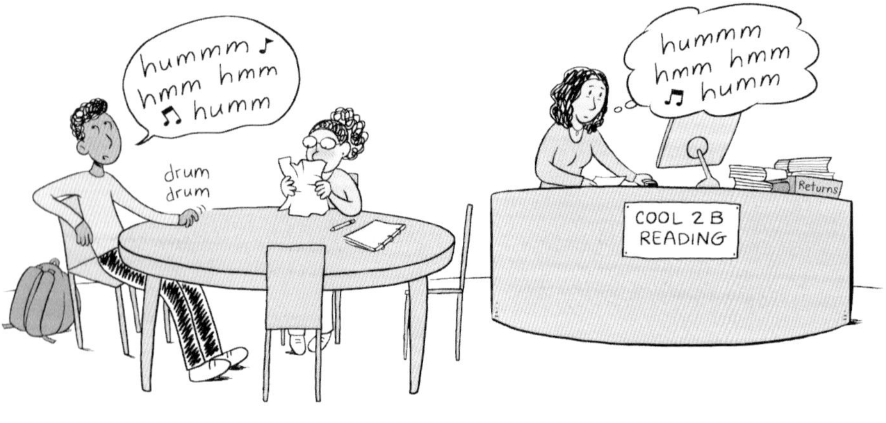
hummm hmm hmm humm
drum drum
hummm hmm hmm humm
Returns
COOL 2 B READING

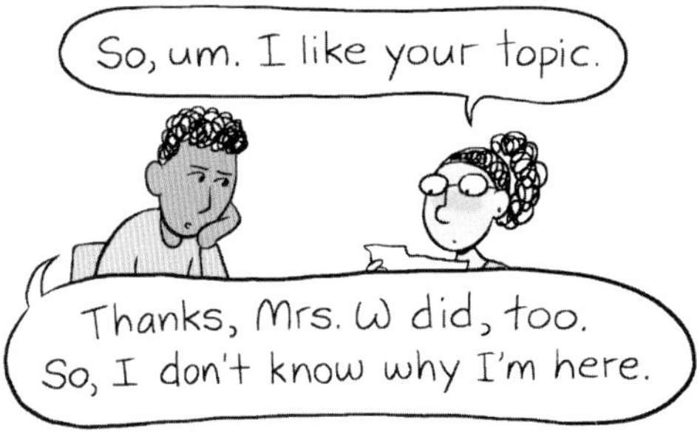
So, um. I like your topic.
Thanks, Mrs. W did, too. So, I don't know why I'm here.

She turns even redder. Is that possible?

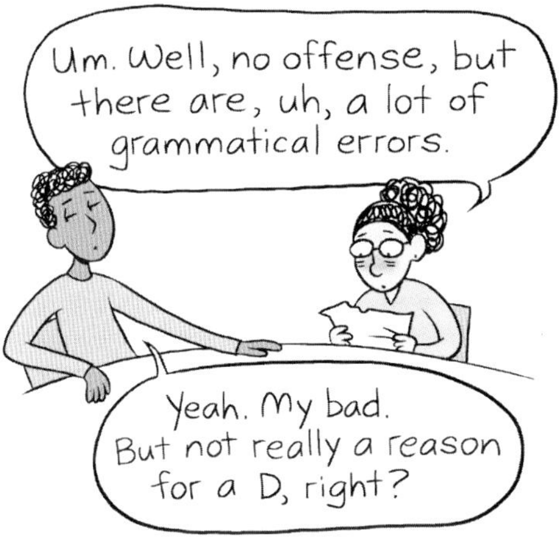
Um. Well, no offense, but there are, uh, a lot of grammatical errors.
Yeah. My bad. But not really a reason for a D, right?

Leah looks like she wants to run away. I guess I'm putting her on the spot.

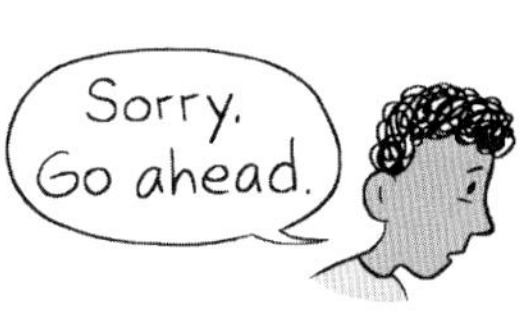
Sorry. Go ahead.

Now it seems like she's trying to figure out how to say something without insulting me.

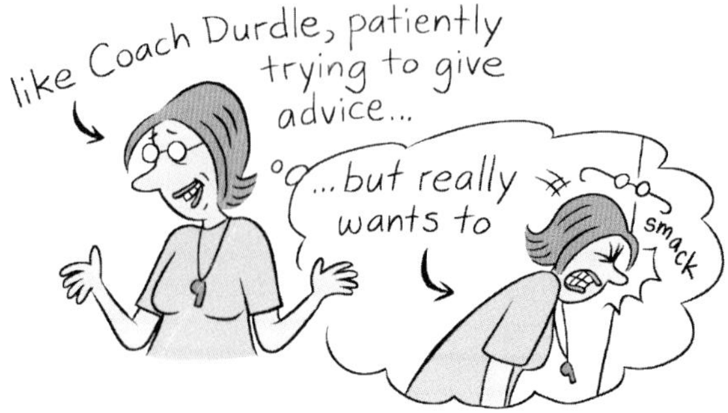
like Coach Durdle, patiently trying to give advice...
...but really wants to
smack

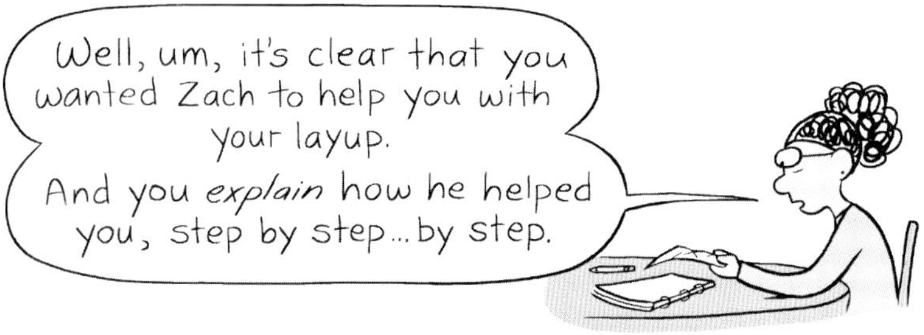
Well, um, it's clear that you wanted Zach to help you with your layup.
And you *explain* how he helped you, step by step... by step.

Seventeen steps, to be exact. And Mrs. W thought I didn't put any effort into this.

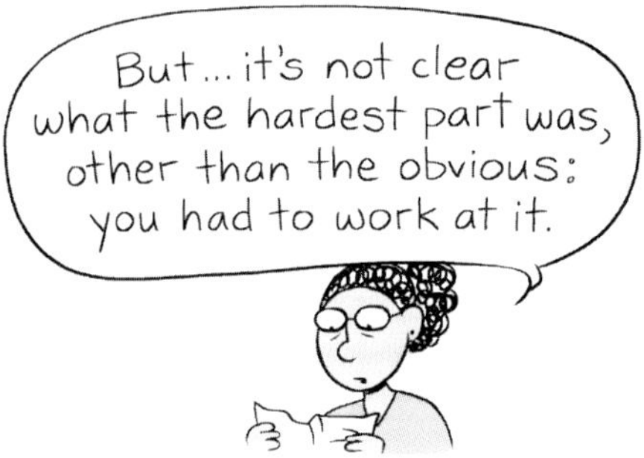
But... it's not clear what the hardest part was, other than the obvious: you had to work at it.

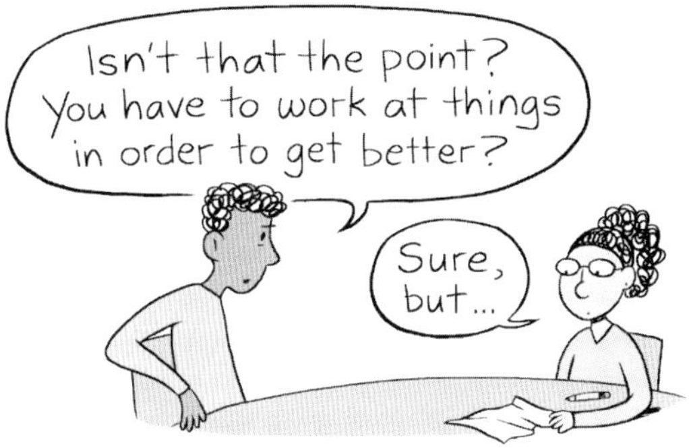
Isn't that the point? You have to work at things in order to get better?
Sure, but...

She scratches her head and sighs, with that same searching look on her face. I knew it: this was a mistake. She has no clue what she's doing.

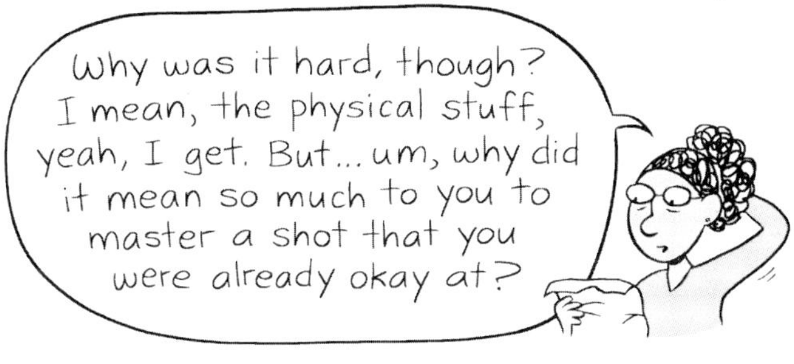
Why was it hard, though? I mean, the physical stuff, yeah, I get. But... um, why did it mean so much to you to master a shot that you were already okay at?

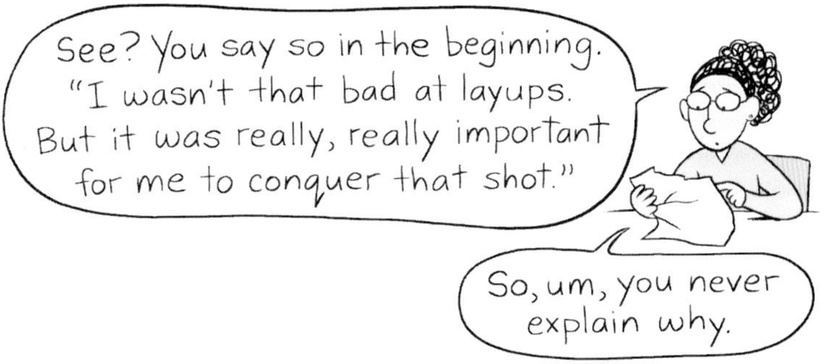
See? You say so in the beginning. "I wasn't that bad at layups. But it was really, really important for me to conquer that shot."
So, um, you never explain why.

Oh.

I mean...
...I don't know.
I guess I just wanted to
be better. To be...the best?

She finally looks at me.

Um. The best?
Yeah. Isn't
that reason
enough?

She bites her lip, thinking.

Um, you
sure that's it?

Why does she keep at this? So annoying.

Yeah. I'm sure.
Okay. Um, well,
let's just work on
grammar then....

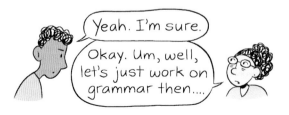

We go over my paper, sentence by sentence. It's boring, but I start to relax and so does she. Things are still tense, though. I guess that's my fault. I don't wanna be here and she knows it.

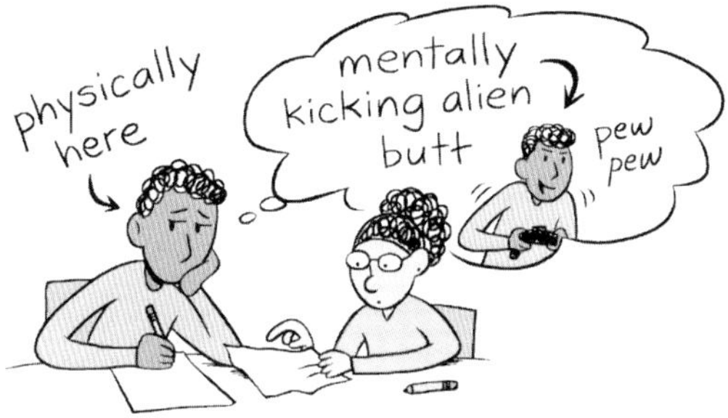
physically here
mentally kicking alien butt
pew pew

When the bell rings, I quickly hop up and grab my stuff.

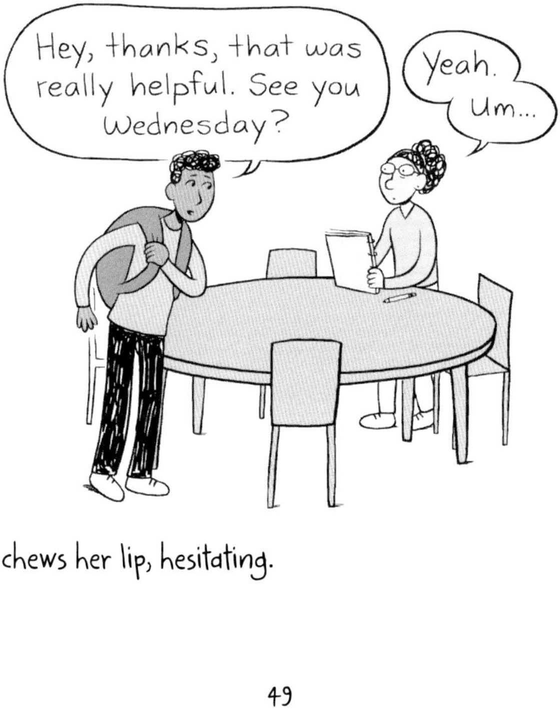
Hey, thanks, that was really helpful. See you Wednesday?
Yeah.
Um...

She chews her lip, hesitating.

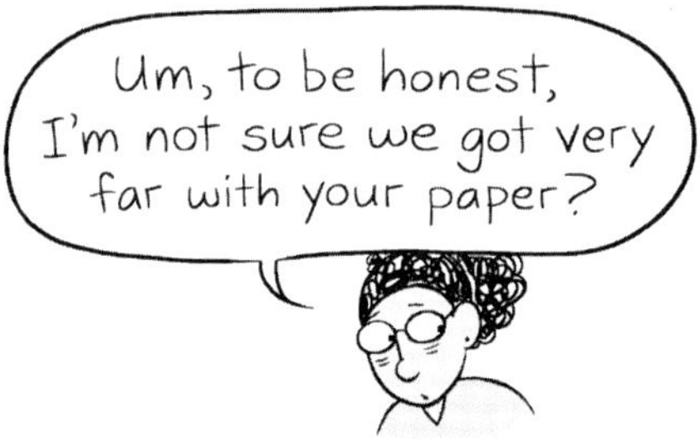
Um, to be honest, I'm not sure we got very far with your paper?

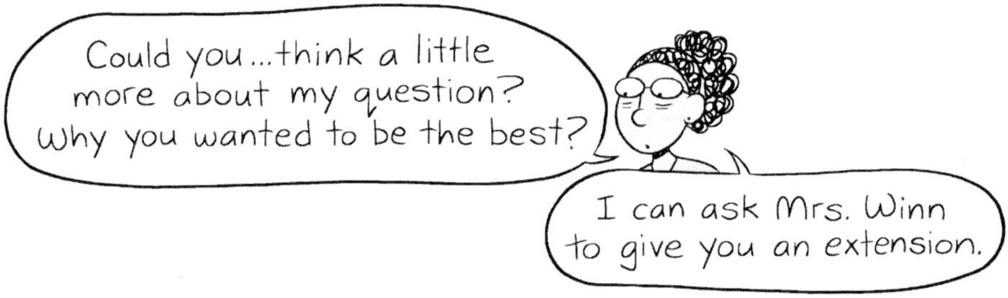
Could you...think a little more about my question? Why you wanted to be the best?
I can ask Mrs. Winn to give you an extension.

She waits.

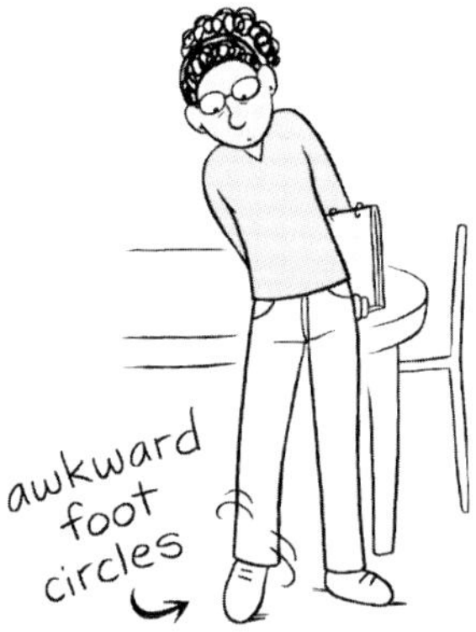
awkward foot circles

I groan inwardly. But I don't want to be a jerk.

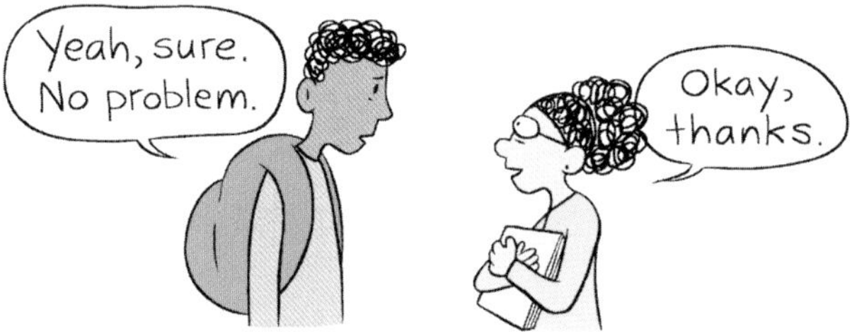
Yeah, sure. No problem.
Okay, thanks.

We head out.

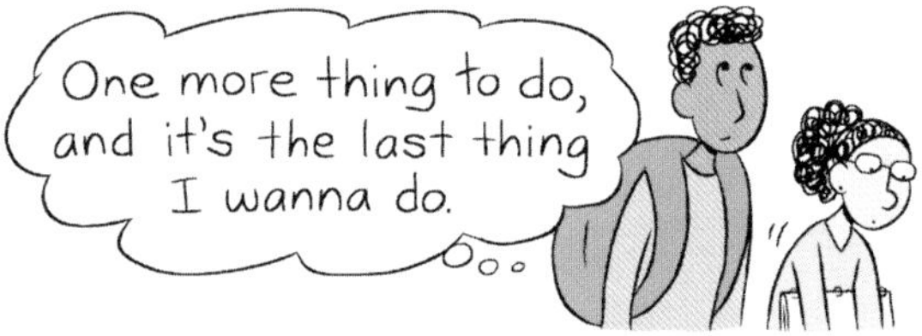
One more thing to do, and it's the last thing I wanna do.

But I guess I'll try. Not just to get a better grade . . .

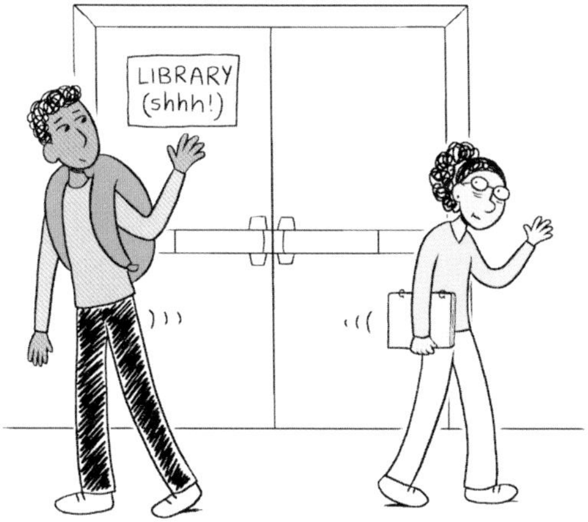
LIBRARY (shhh!)

. . . but to get one step closer to "no more tutoring."

Leah

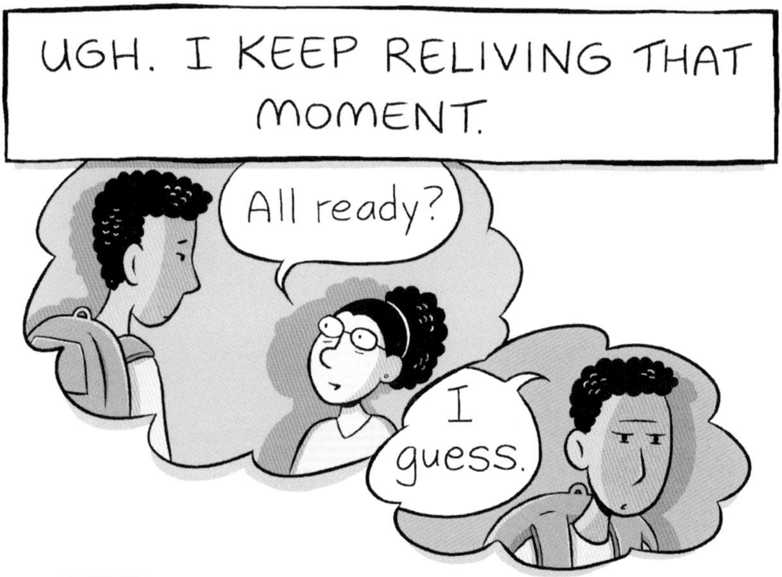
UGH. I KEEP RELIVING THAT MOMENT.
All ready?
I guess.

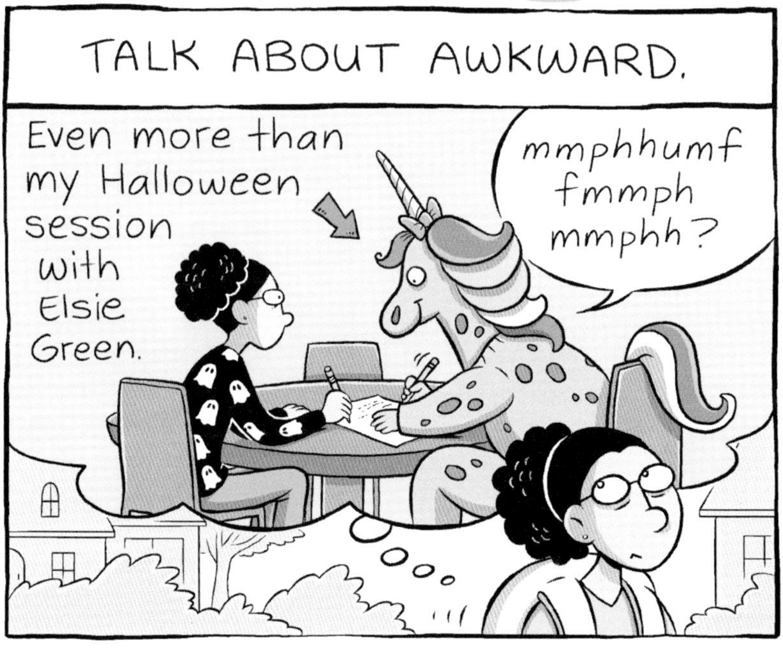
TALK ABOUT AWKWARD.
Even more than my Halloween session with Elsie Green.
mmphhumf fmmph mmphh?

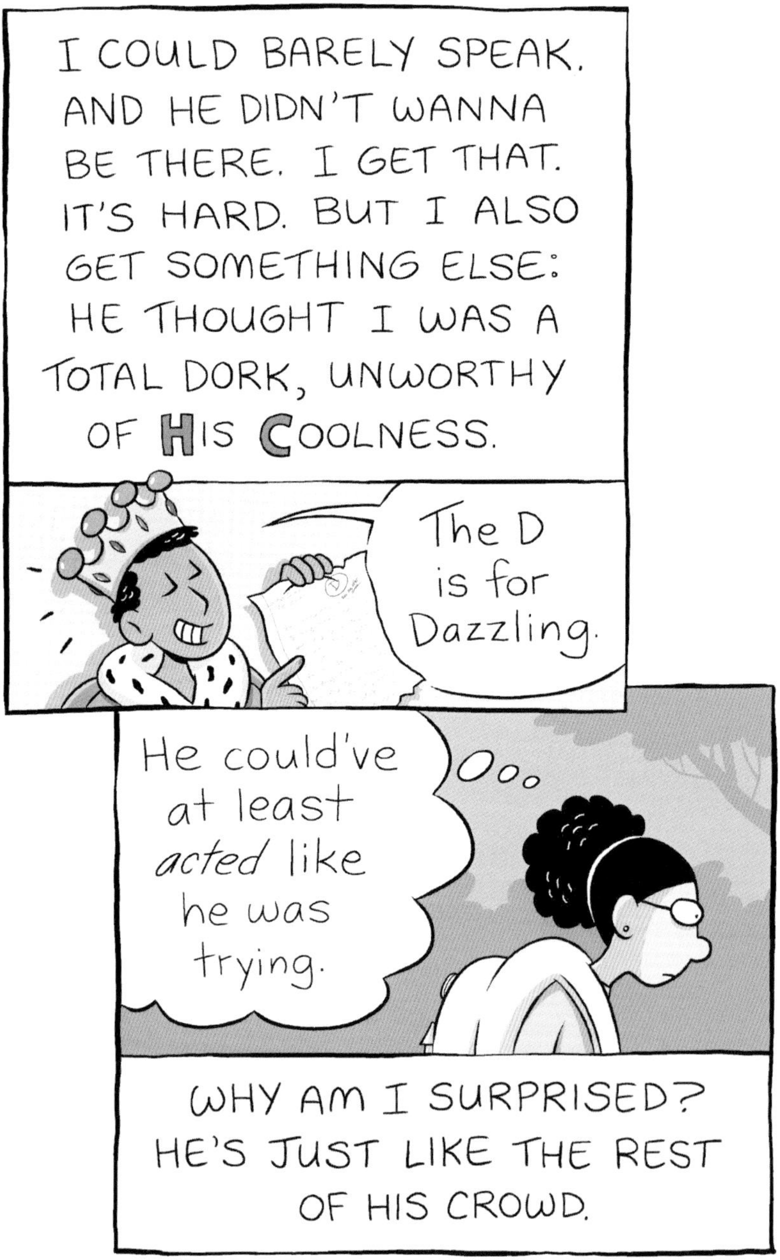
I COULD BARELY SPEAK. AND HE DIDN'T WANNA BE THERE. I GET THAT. IT'S HARD. BUT I ALSO GET SOMETHING ELSE: HE THOUGHT I WAS A TOTAL DORK, UNWORTHY OF HIS COOLNESS.
The D is for Dazzling.
He could've at least *acted* like he was trying.
WHY AM I SURPRISED? HE'S JUST LIKE THE REST OF HIS CROWD.

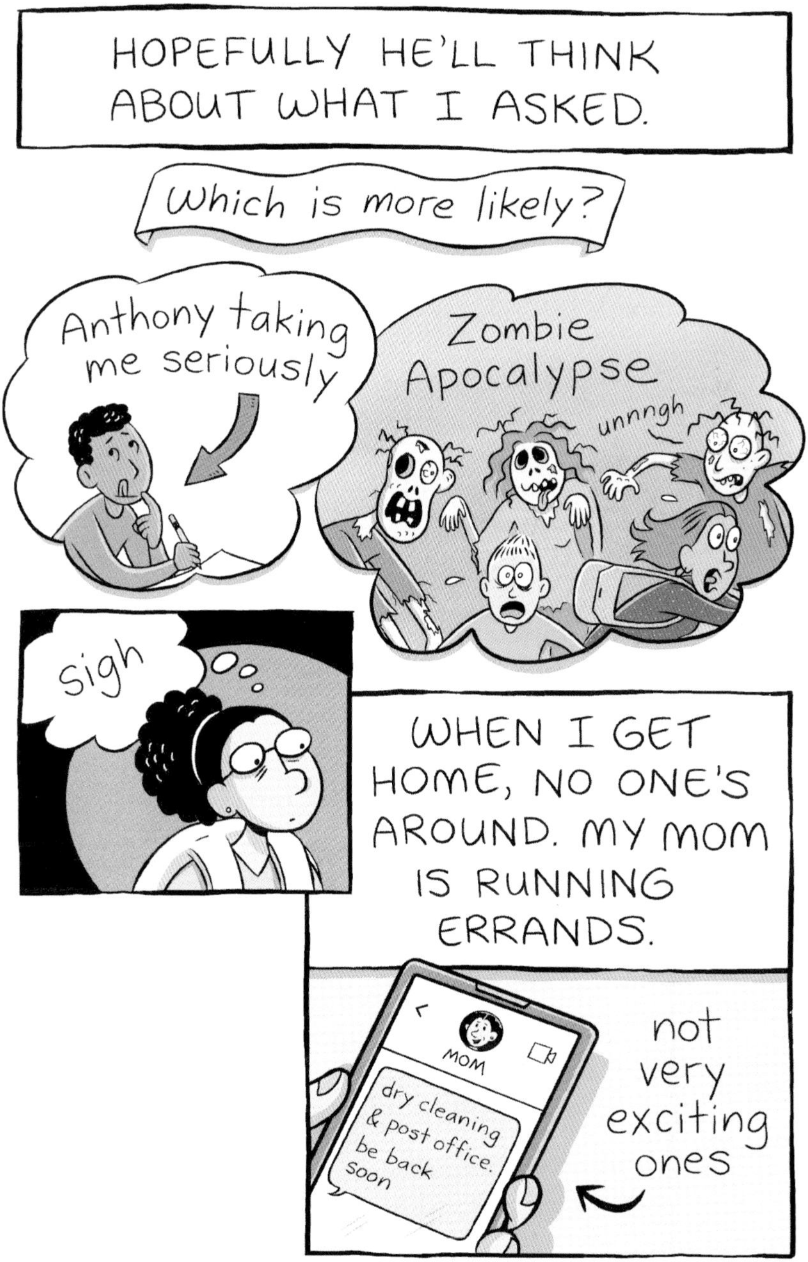
HOPEFULLY HE'LL THINK ABOUT WHAT I ASKED.
Which is more likely?
Anthony taking me seriously
Zombie Apocalypse
unnngh
sigh
WHEN I GET HOME, NO ONE'S AROUND. MY MOM IS RUNNING ERRANDS.
MOM
dry cleaning & post office. be back soon
not very exciting ones

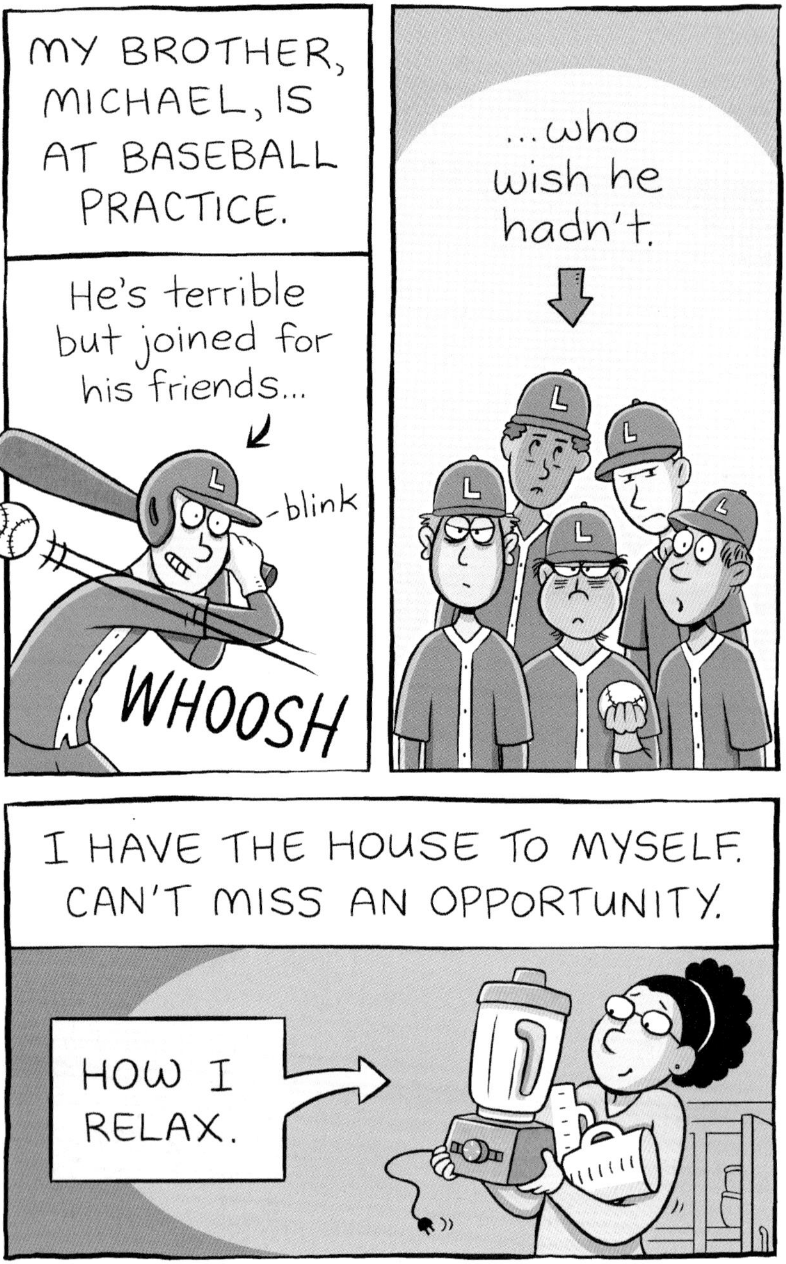
MY BROTHER, MICHAEL, IS AT BASEBALL PRACTICE.
He's terrible but joined for his friends...
-blink
WHOOSH
...who wish he hadn't.
I HAVE THE HOUSE TO MYSELF. CAN'T MISS AN OPPORTUNITY.
HOW I RELAX.

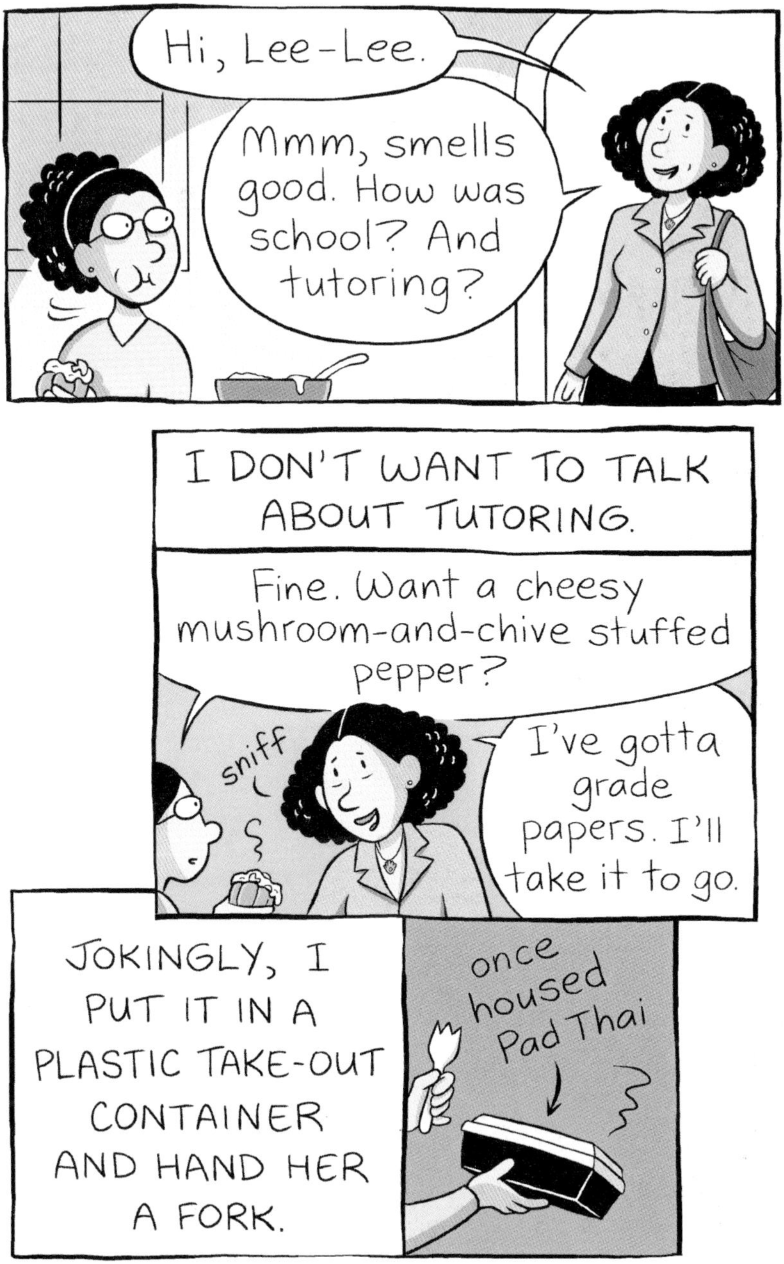
Hi, Lee-Lee.
Mmm, smells good. How was school? And tutoring?
I DON'T WANT TO TALK ABOUT TUTORING.
Fine. Want a cheesy mushroom-and-chive stuffed pepper?
sniff
I've gotta grade papers. I'll take it to go.
JOKINGLY, I PUT IT IN A PLASTIC TAKE-OUT CONTAINER AND HAND HER A FORK.
once housed Pad Thai

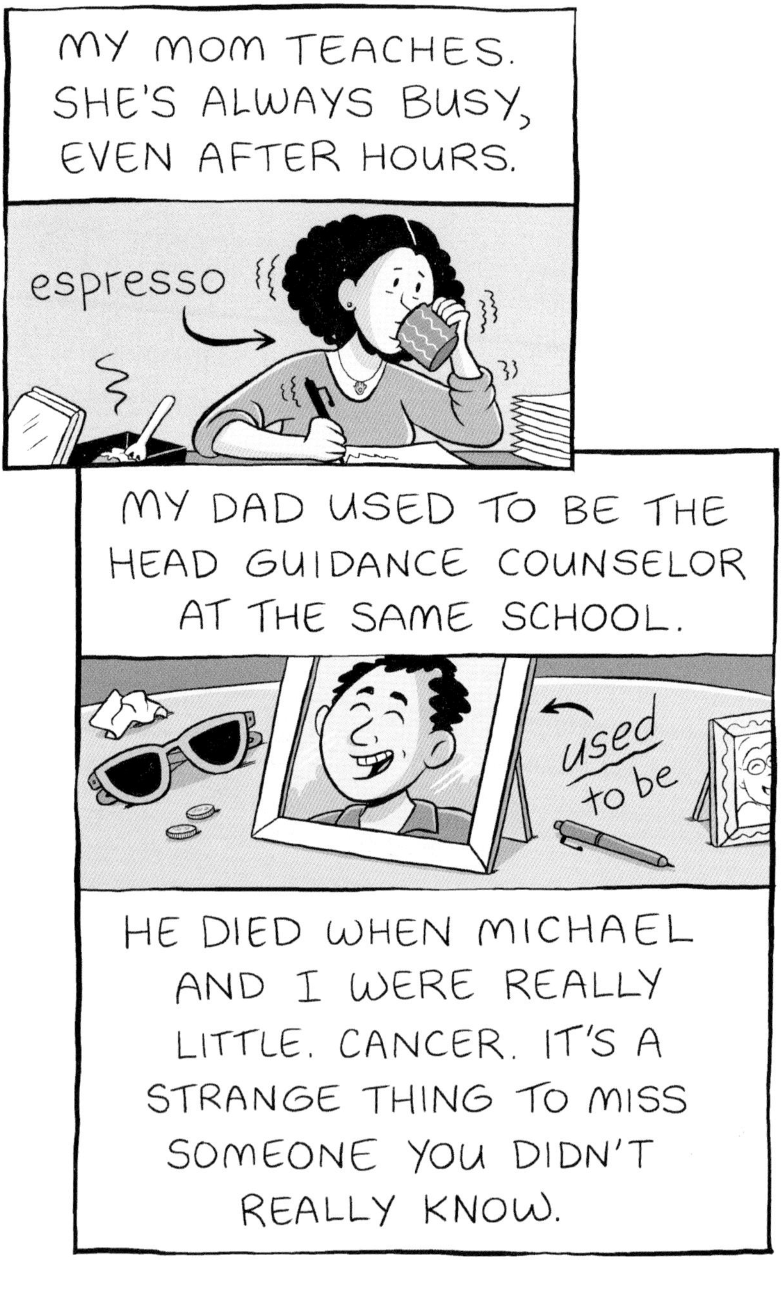
MY MOM TEACHES. SHE'S ALWAYS BUSY, EVEN AFTER HOURS.
espresso
MY DAD USED TO BE THE HEAD GUIDANCE COUNSELOR AT THE SAME SCHOOL.
used
to be
HE DIED WHEN MICHAEL AND I WERE REALLY LITTLE. CANCER. IT'S A STRANGE THING TO MISS SOMEONE YOU DIDN'T REALLY KNOW.

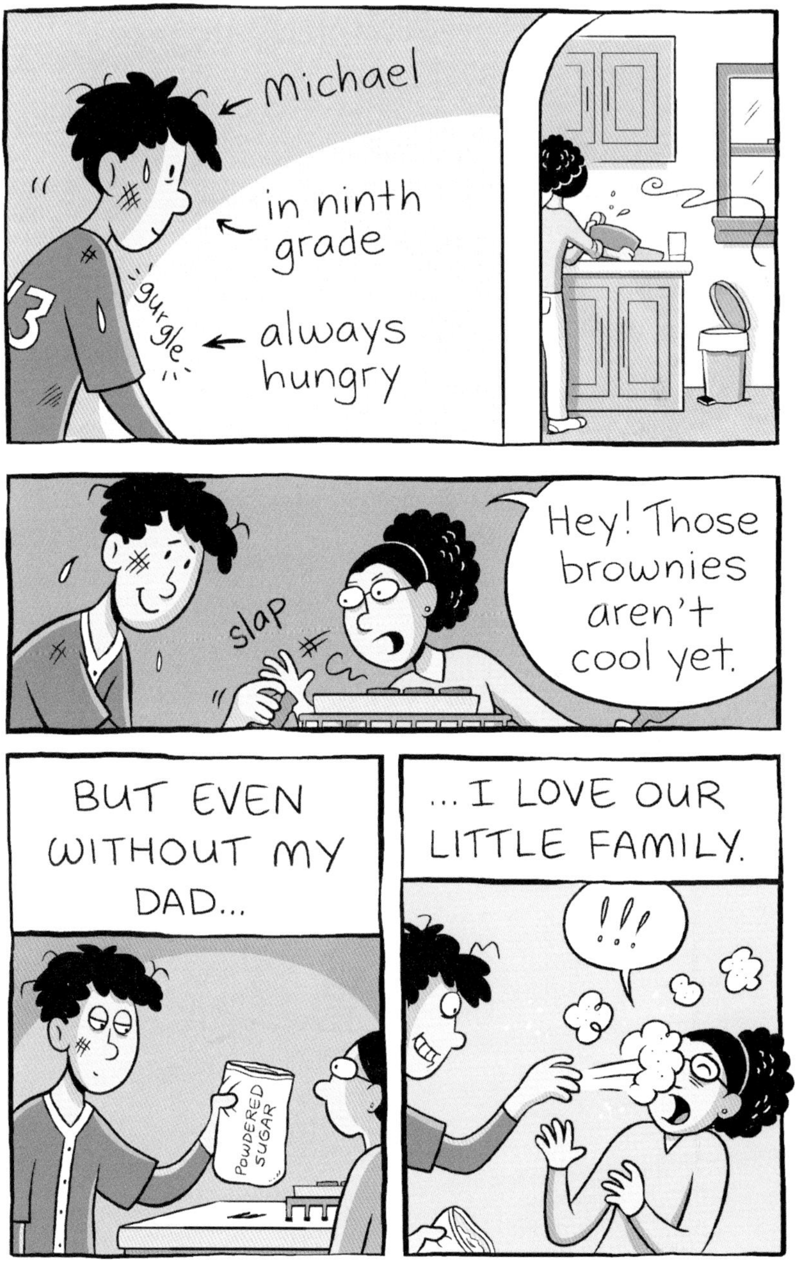
Michael
in ninth grade
gurgle
always hungry
slap
Hey! Those brownies aren't cool yet.
BUT EVEN WITHOUT MY DAD...
POWDERED SUGAR
...I LOVE OUR LITTLE FAMILY.
!!!

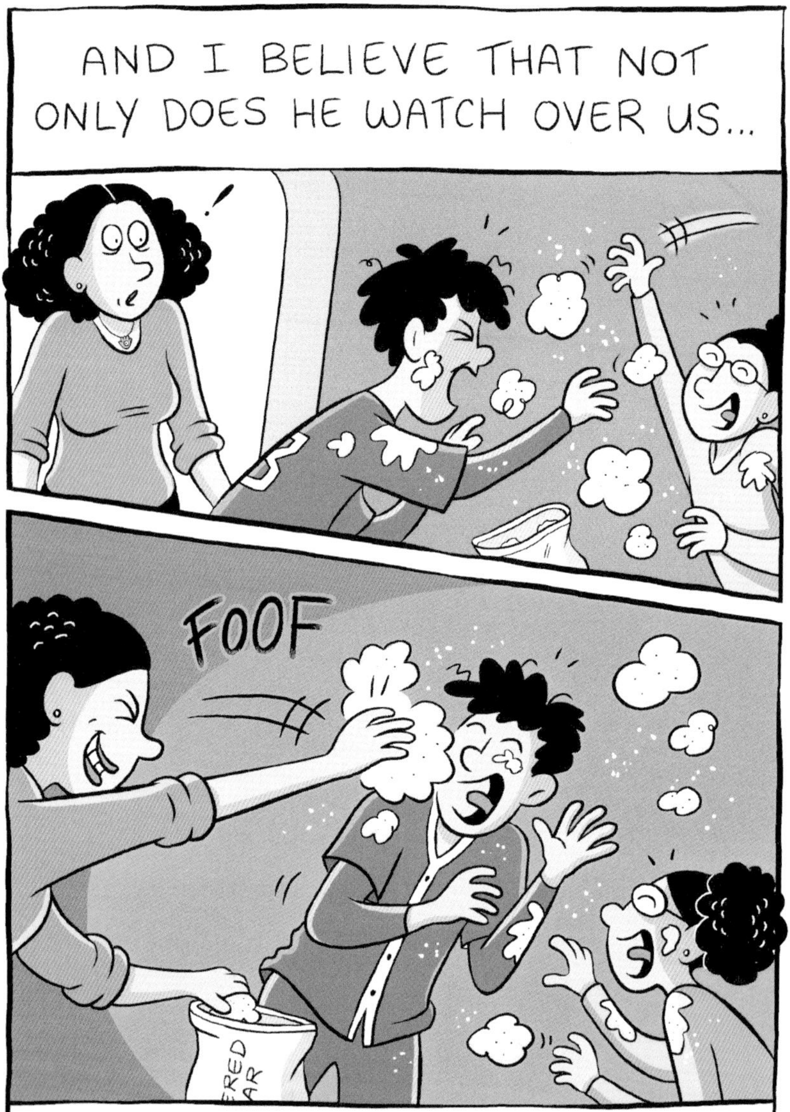
AND I BELIEVE THAT NOT ONLY DOES HE WATCH OVER US...
FOOF
...HE SOMEHOW KEEPS US LAUGHING.

ANTHONY

Tuesday night. I'm in my room. Just finished a math take-home quiz.

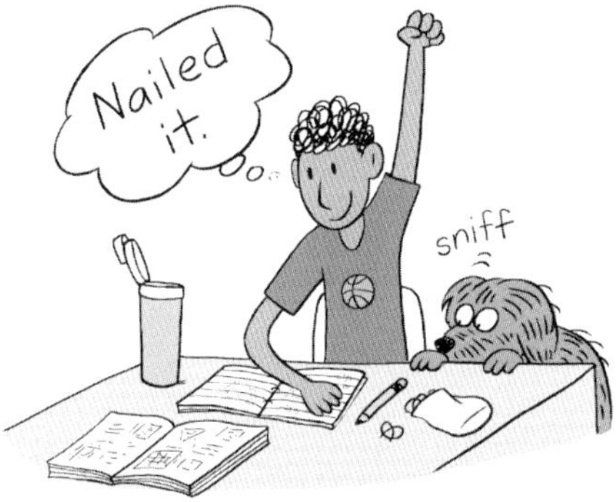
Nailed it.
sniff

I wish Language Arts came as easy. It would make the **rest** of my life easier.

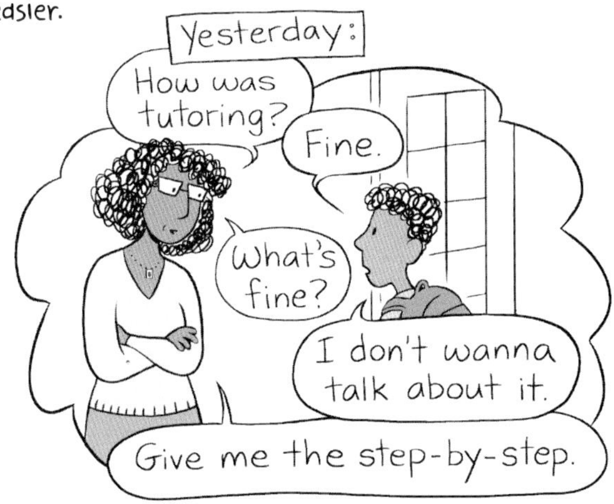
Yesterday:
How was tutoring?
Fine.
What's fine?
I don't wanna talk about it.
Give me the step-by-step.

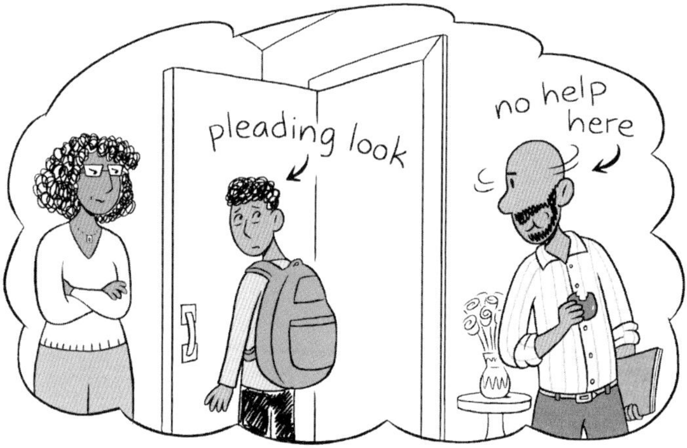
pleading look
no help here

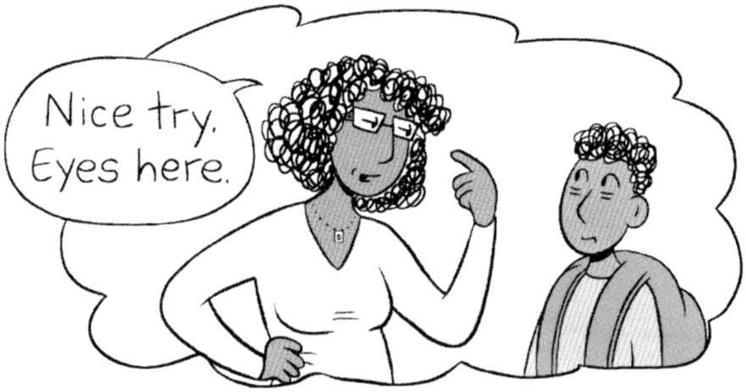
Nice try. Eyes here.

But it's no use. I'm just not good at writing. Or pouring my feelings onto paper. I can put all my heart and soul into a game. If only English was like basketball.

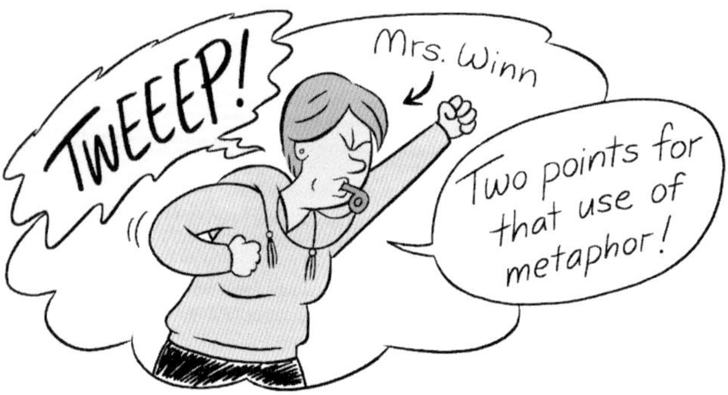
TWEEEP!
Mrs. Winn
Two points for that use of metaphor!

Seriously, I'm even passionate about layups. That's why I asked Zach to help.

Wait.

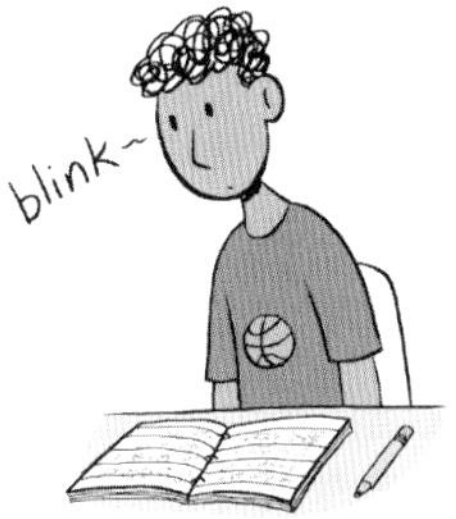
blink~

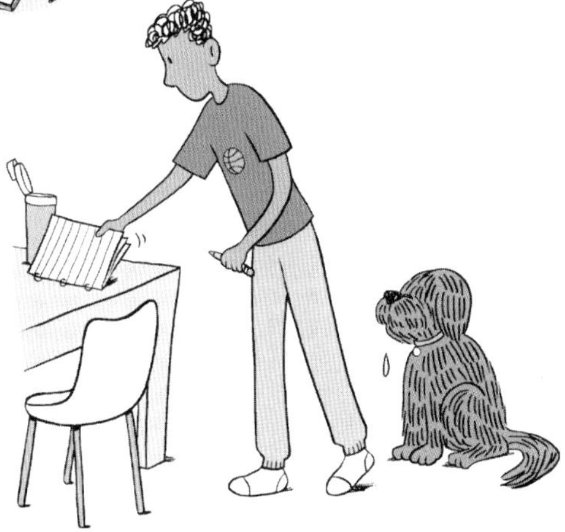

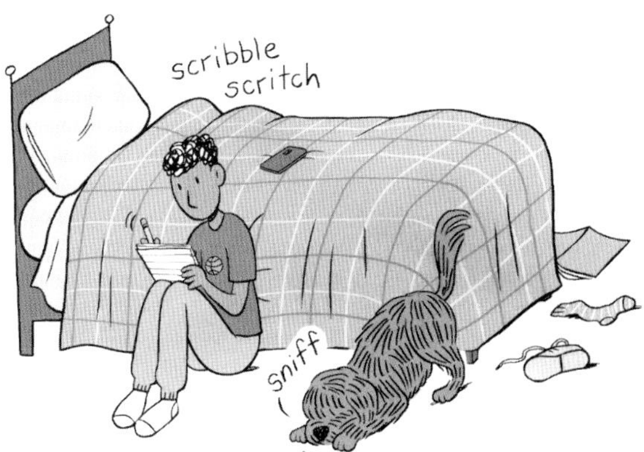
scribble
scritch
sniff

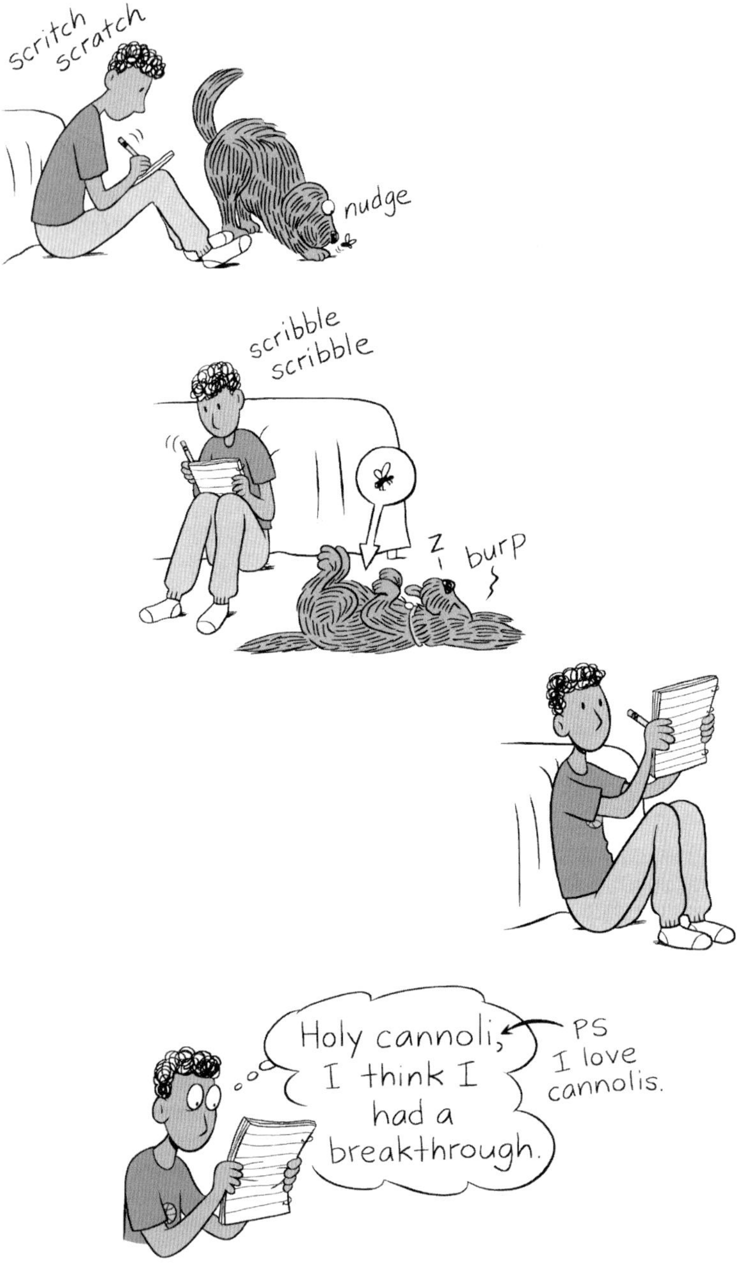
scritch scratch
nudge
scribble scribble
z
burp
Holy cannoli, I think I had a breakthrough.
PS I love cannolis.

I guess I have something to show Leah tomorrow.

But... do I *want* to show it to her?

This is, like, personal. Well, kinda. I mean, it'll help my paper, I think. But it's . . .

... a little embarrassing.

Still, no one's gonna see it except for Leah and Mrs. Winn. Not a big deal, right?

A
embarrass-
ment
decent
grade
tip
winner
A

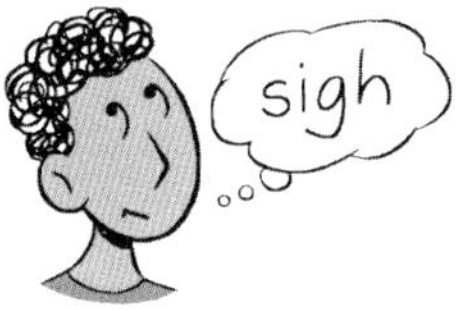
sigh

I quickly shove the paper in my Language Arts binder and stuff it in my backpack before I change my mind.

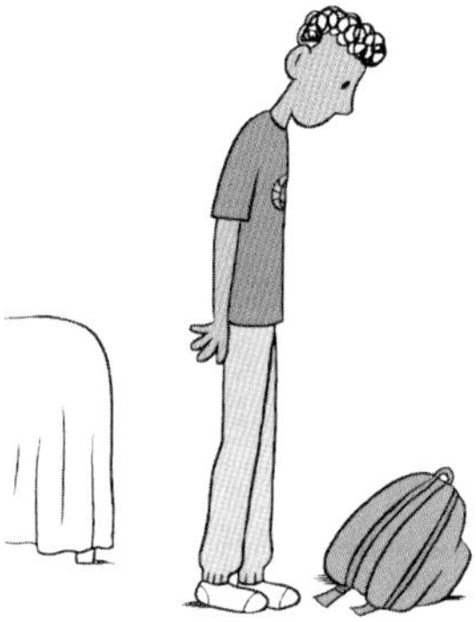

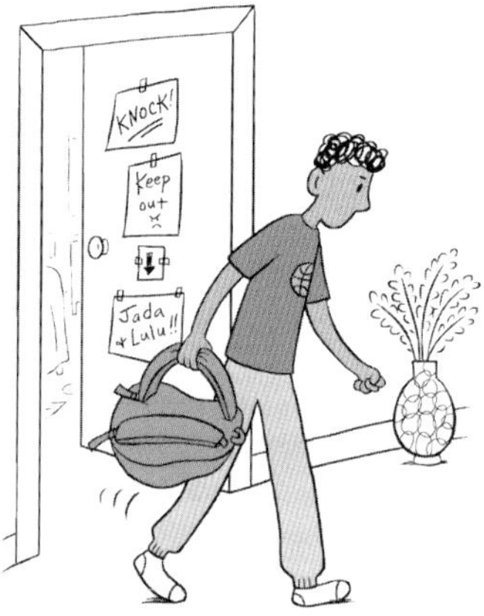
KNOCK!
Keep out
Jada & Lulu!!

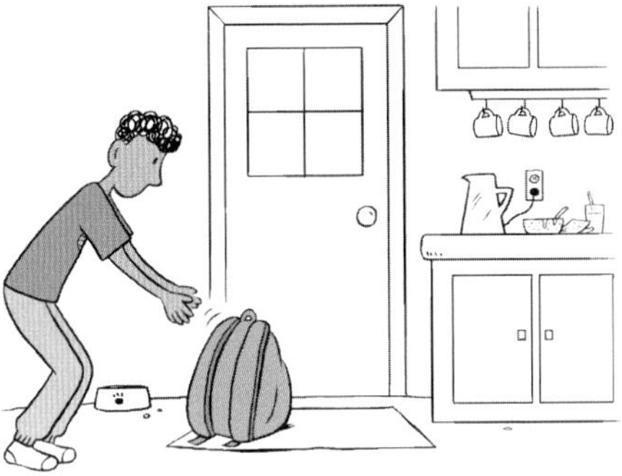

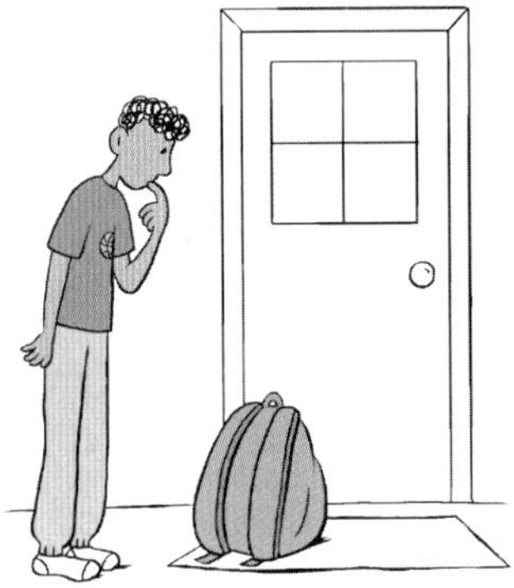

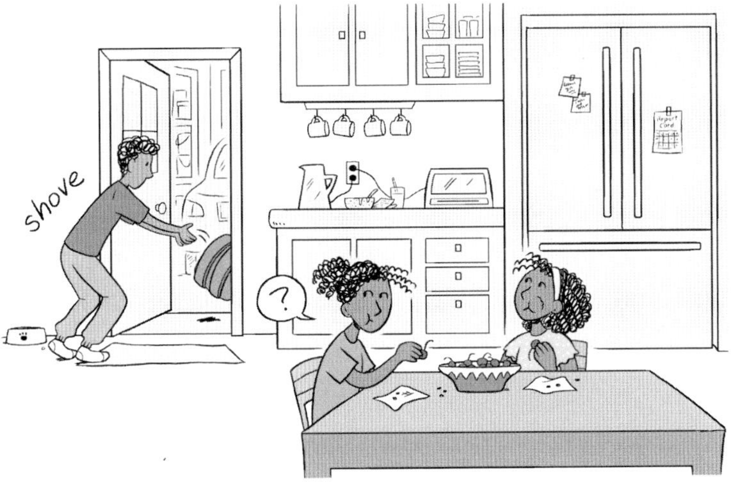
shove
?
Report card

I head back upstairs.

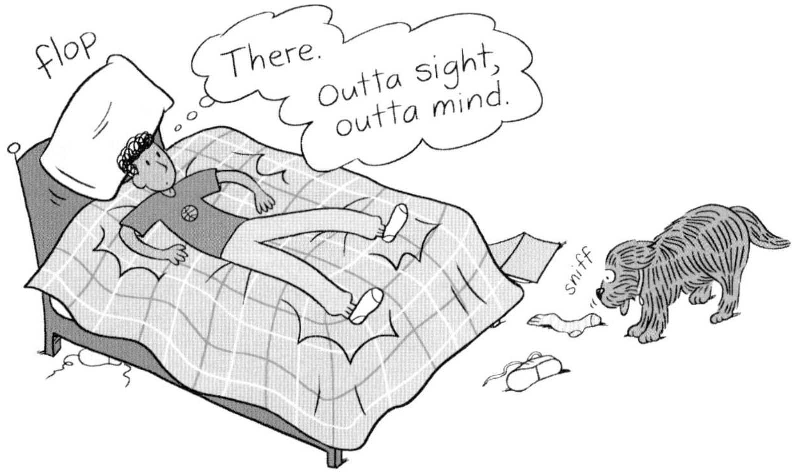
flop
There.
Outta sight,
outta mind.
sniff

Now I just have to get tomorrow over with.

Leah

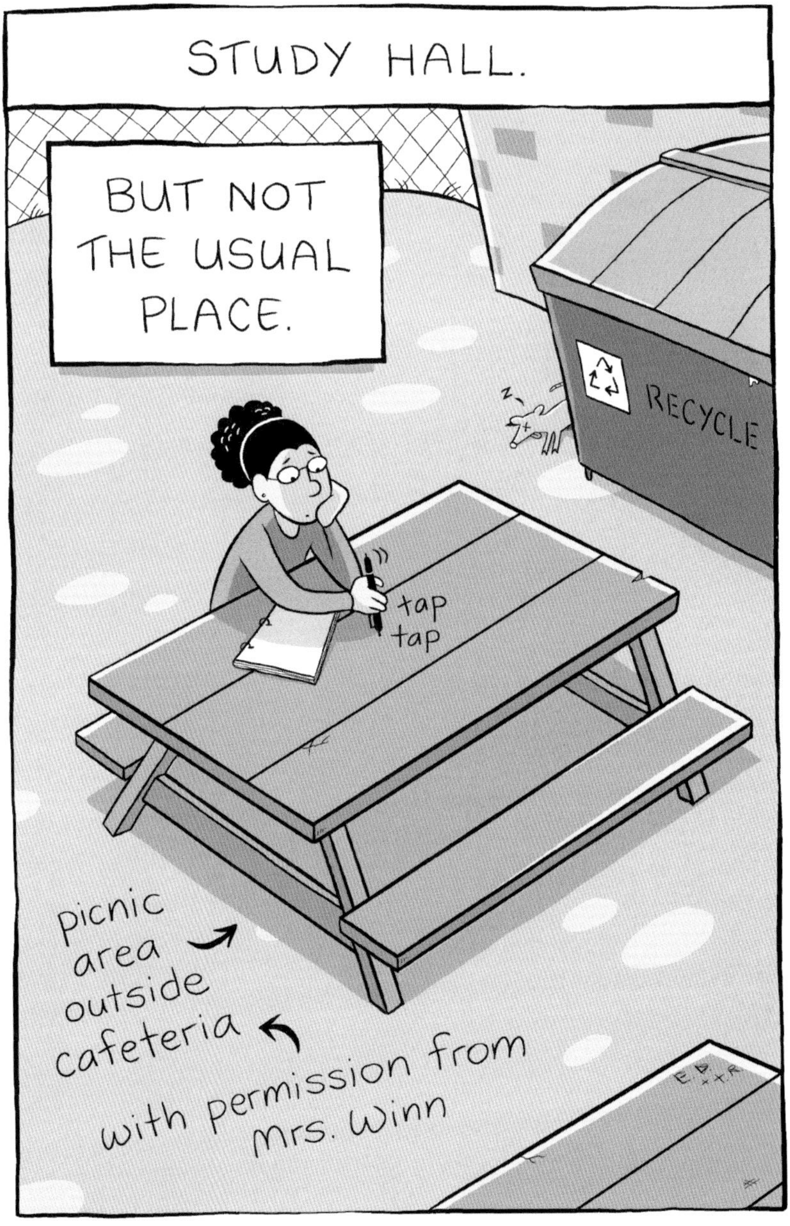
STUDY HALL.
BUT NOT THE USUAL PLACE.
RECYCLE
tap tap
picnic area outside cafeteria
with permission from Mrs. Winn

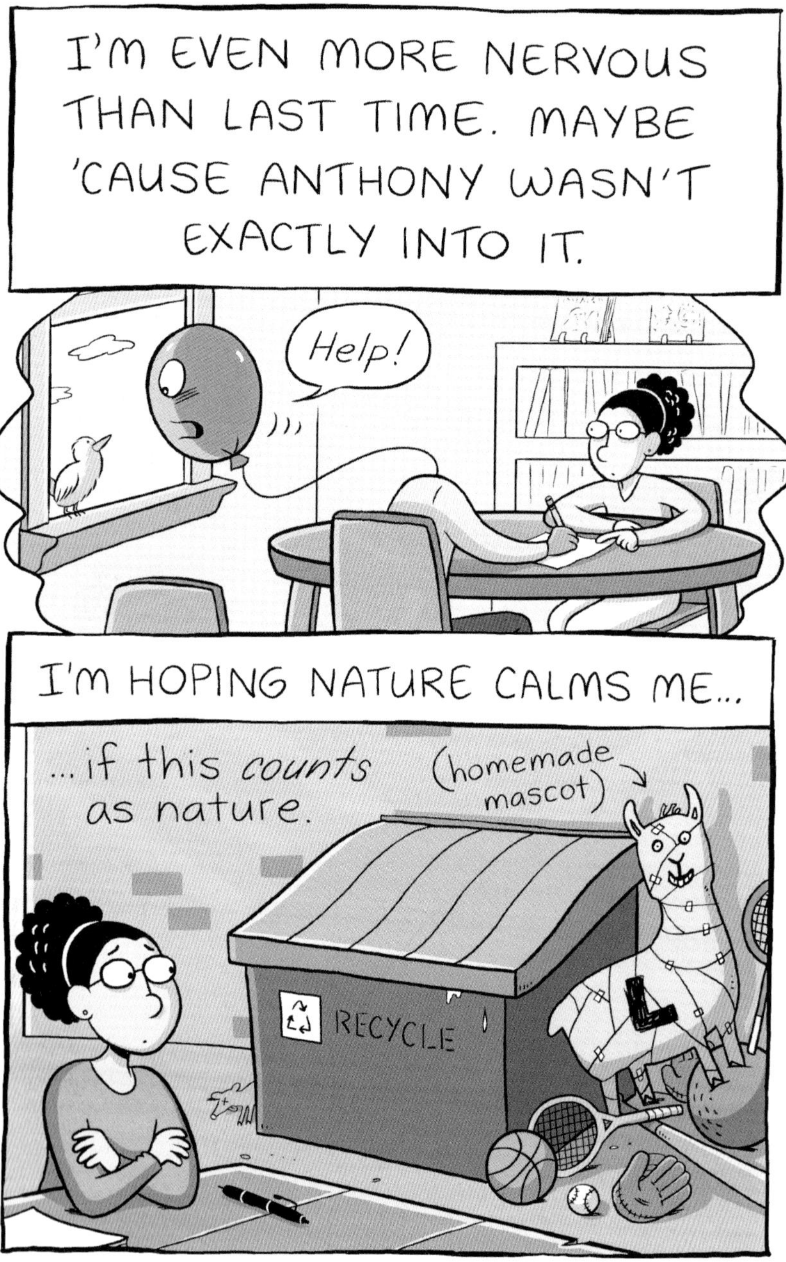
I'M EVEN MORE NERVOUS THAN LAST TIME. MAYBE 'CAUSE ANTHONY WASN'T EXACTLY INTO IT.
Help!
I'M HOPING NATURE CALMS ME...
...if this counts as nature.
(homemade mascot)
RECYCLE

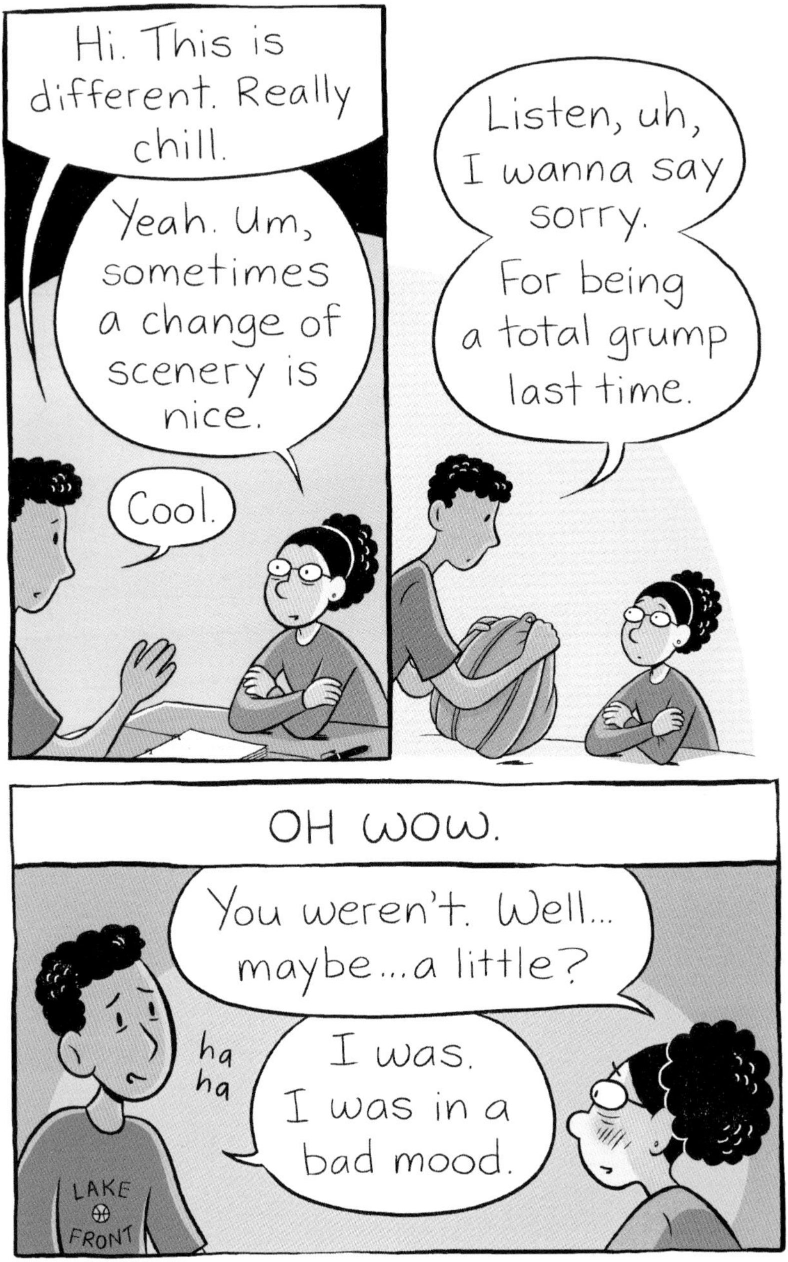
Hi. This is different. Really chill.
Yeah. Um, sometimes a change of scenery is nice.
Cool.
Listen, uh, I wanna say sorry.
For being a total grump last time.
OH WOW.
You weren't. Well... maybe...a little?
ha ha
I was. I was in a bad mood.
LAKE FRONT

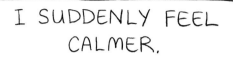
I SUDDENLY FEEL CALMER.

It's okay. Um, were you able to think about my question?

Yeah, kinda by accident. I was thinking of something else, and I had... I guess... an epiphany?

Winn Word!

HE LAUGHS. I DEFINITELY FEEL MORE AT EASE.

I sorta spilled out everything at once. Maybe...

...maybe we can work it into the paper?

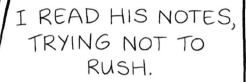

I READ HIS NOTES, TRYING NOT TO RUSH.

fidgety

drum drum

WAIT, HAVE THE TABLES TURNED? IS *HE* THE NERVOUS ONE NOW?

I FINISH READING.

So... it meant a lot for you to conquer that shot because...

...you really look up to Zach, who's like a mentor, a big brother... *and* a "layup god."

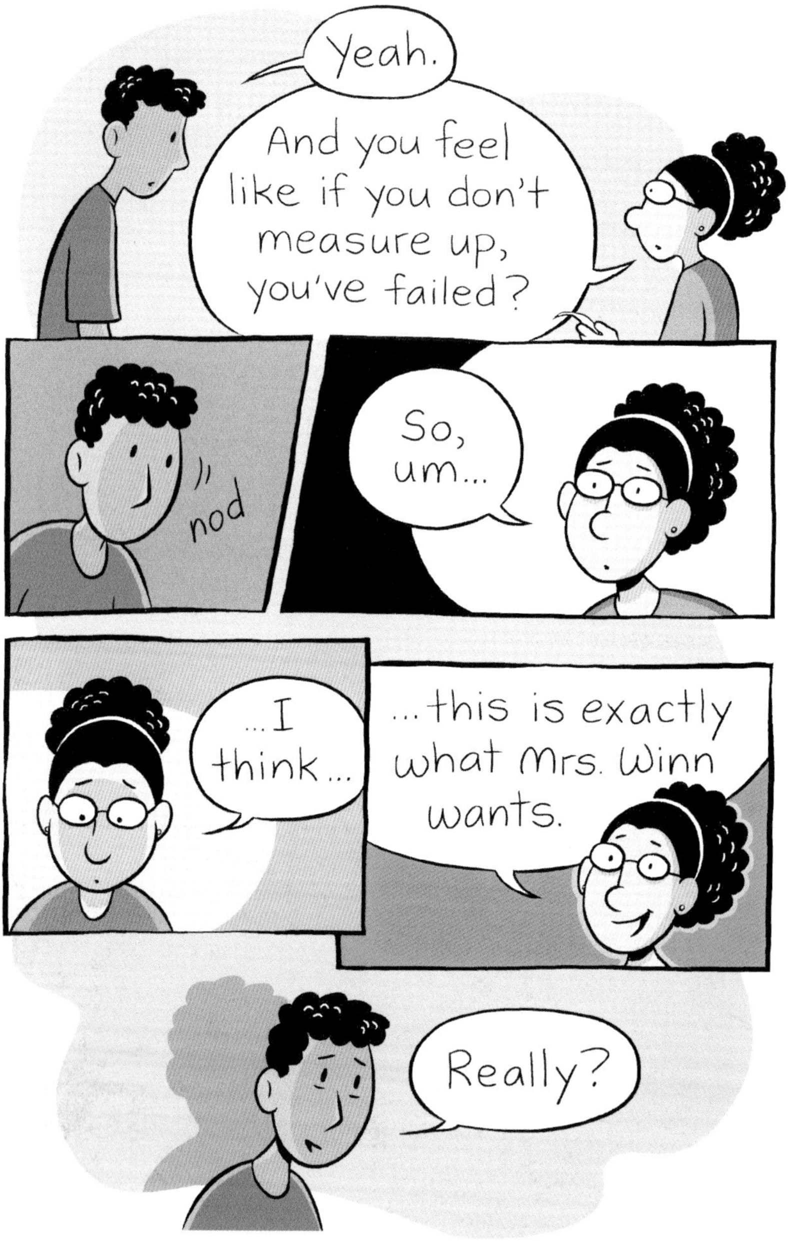
Yeah.
And you feel like if you don't measure up, you've failed?
nod
So, um...
...I think...
...this is exactly what Mrs. Winn wants.
Really?

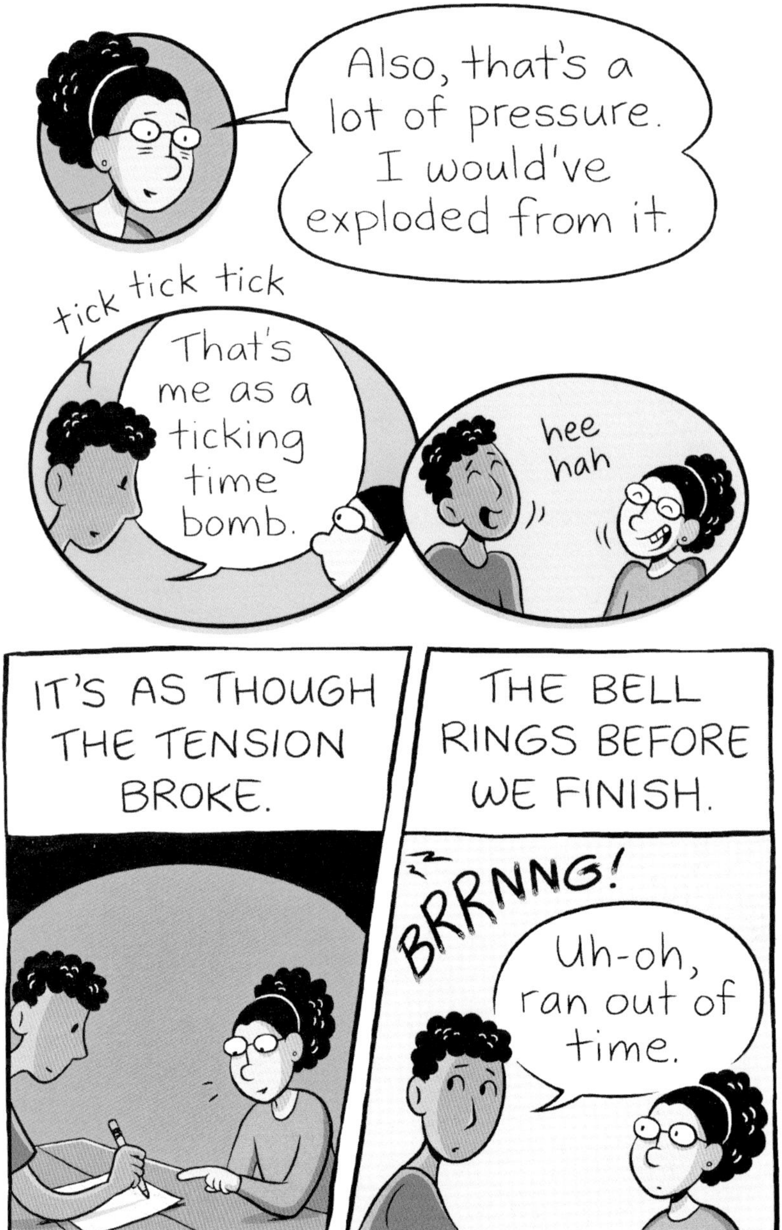
Also, that's a lot of pressure. I would've exploded from it.
tick tick tick
That's me as a ticking time bomb.
hee hah
IT'S AS THOUGH THE TENSION BROKE.
THE BELL RINGS BEFORE WE FINISH.
BRRNNG!
Uh-oh, ran out of time.

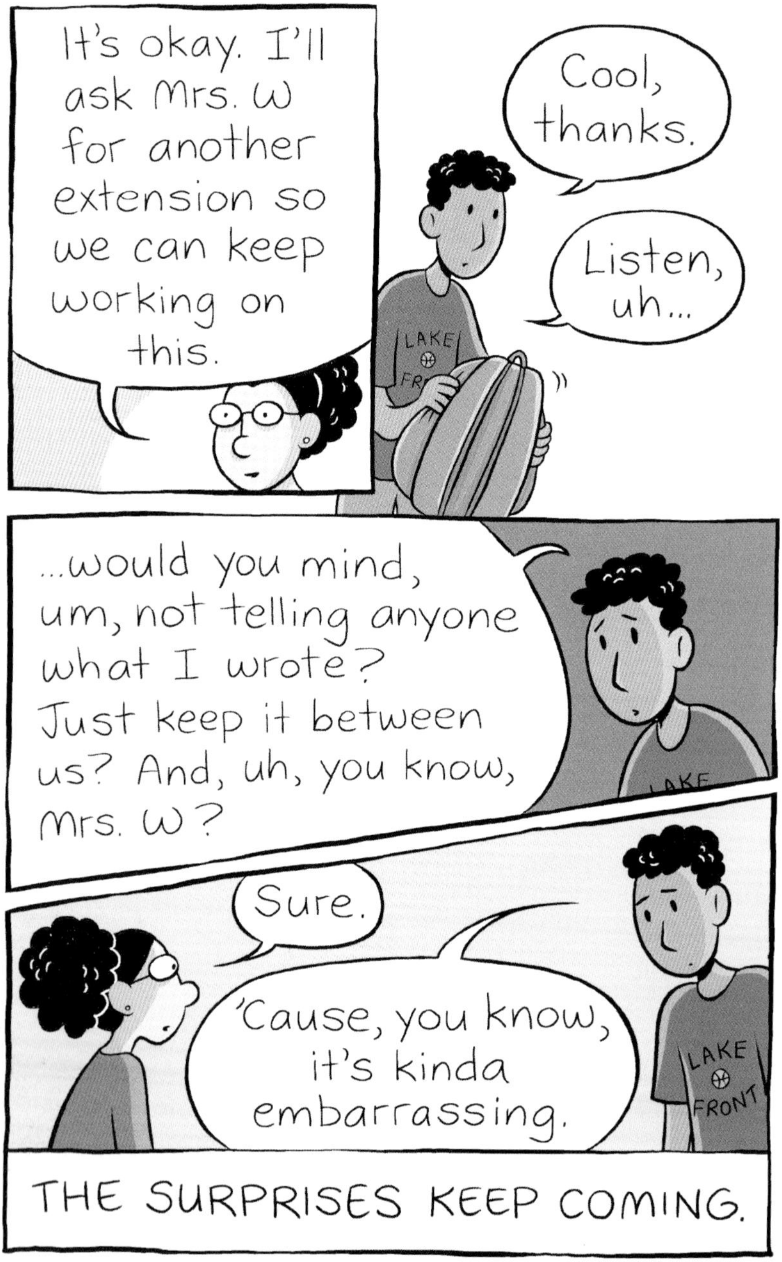
It's okay. I'll ask Mrs. W for another extension so we can keep working on this.
Cool, thanks.
Listen, uh...
LAKE FRONT
...would you mind, um, not telling anyone what I wrote? Just keep it between us? And, uh, you know, Mrs. W?
Sure.
'Cause, you know, it's kinda embarrassing.
LAKE FRONT
THE SURPRISES KEEP COMING.

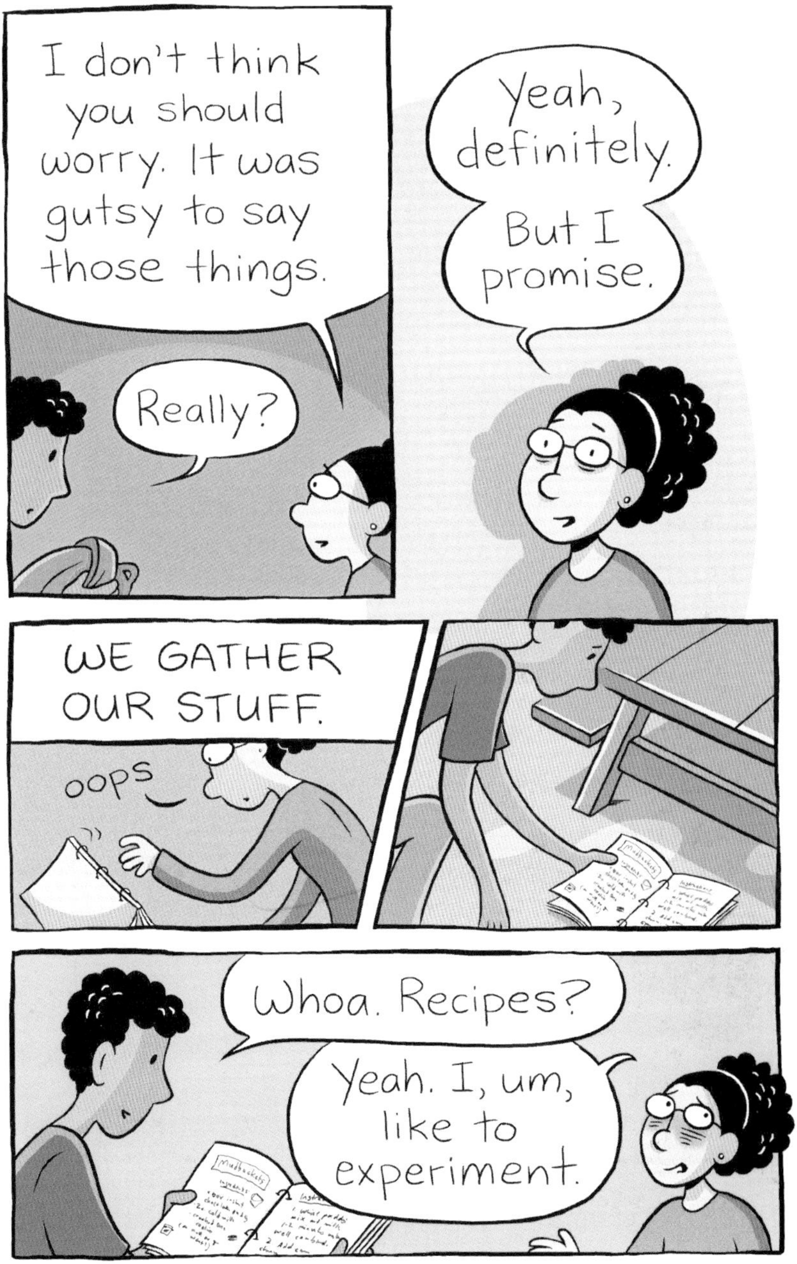
I don't think you should worry. It was gutsy to say those things.
Really?
Yeah, definitely.
But I promise.
WE GATHER OUR STUFF.
oops
Whoa. Recipes?
Yeah. I, um, like to experiment.

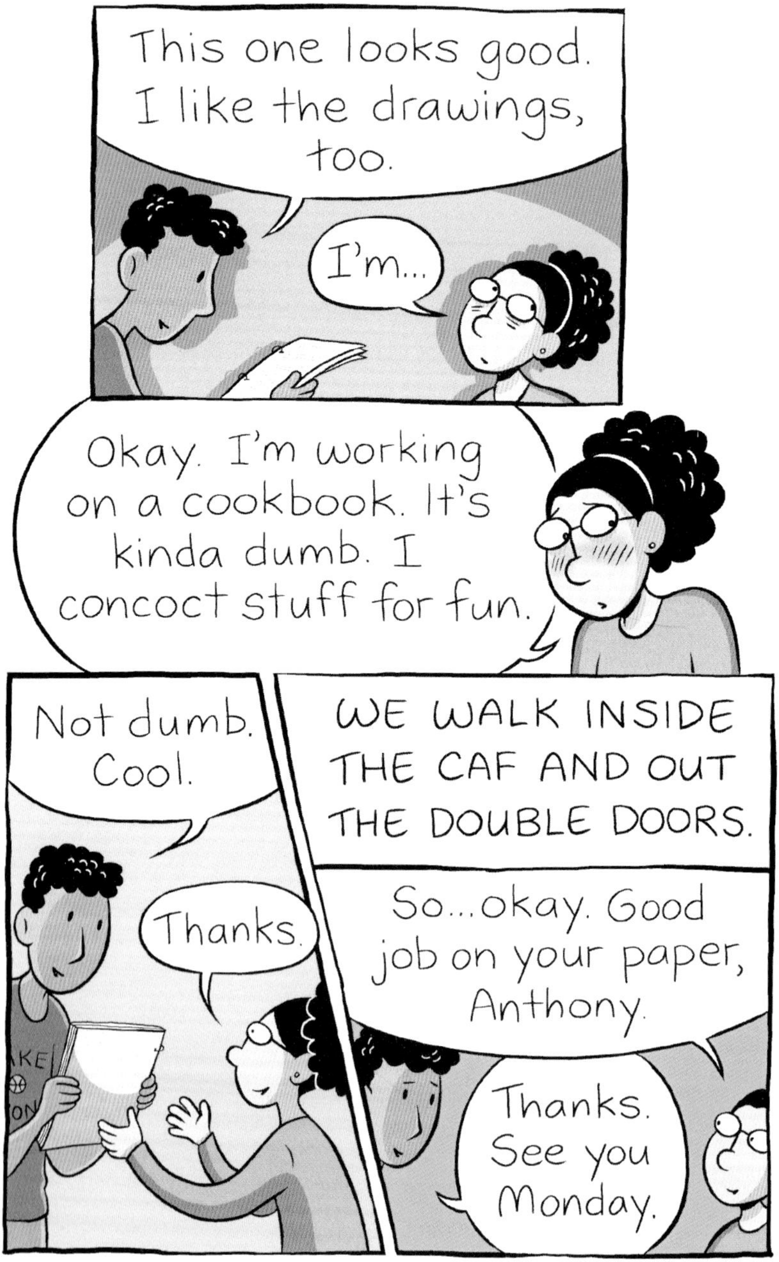
This one looks good. I like the drawings, too.
I'm...
Okay. I'm working on a cookbook. It's kinda dumb. I concoct stuff for fun.
Not dumb. Cool.
Thanks.
WE WALK INSIDE THE CAF AND OUT THE DOUBLE DOORS.
So...okay. Good job on your paper, Anthony.
Thanks. See you Monday.

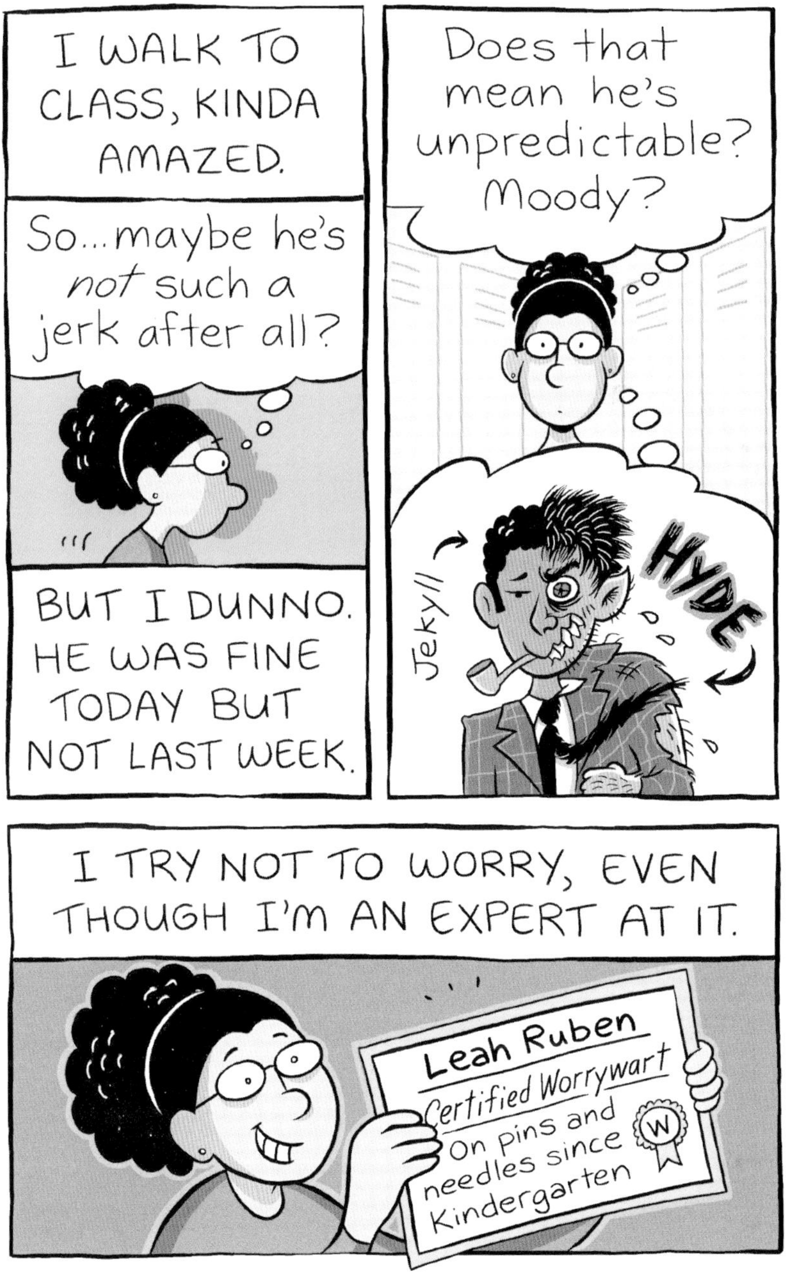
I WALK TO CLASS, KINDA AMAZED.
So...maybe he's *not* such a jerk after all?
BUT I DUNNO. HE WAS FINE TODAY BUT NOT LAST WEEK.
Does that mean he's unpredictable? Moody?
Jekyll
HYDE
I TRY NOT TO WORRY, EVEN THOUGH I'M AN EXPERT AT IT.
Leah Ruben
Certified Worrywart
On pins and needles since Kindergarten
W

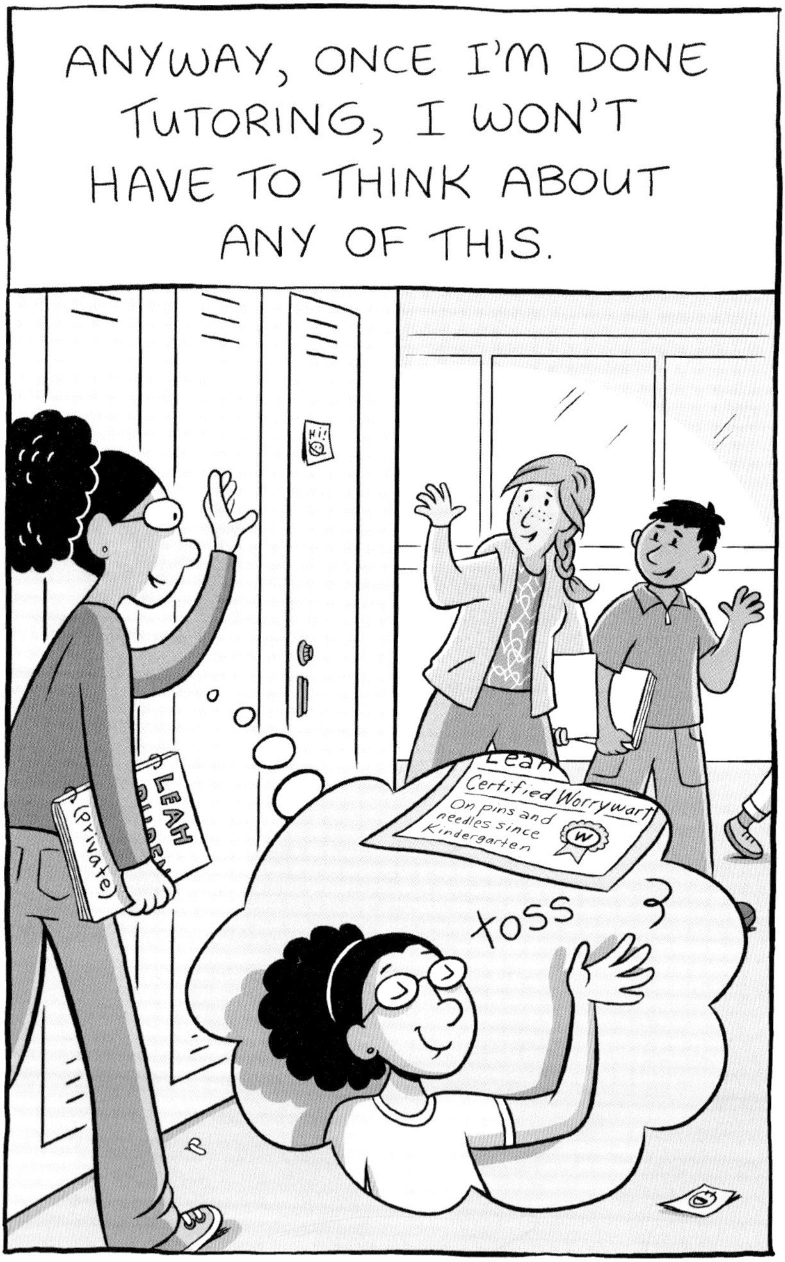
ANYWAY, ONCE I'M DONE TUTORING, I WON'T HAVE TO THINK ABOUT ANY OF THIS.
HI!
LEAH
(private)
Leah
Certified Worrywart
On pins and needles since Kindergarten
W
TOSS

ANTHONY

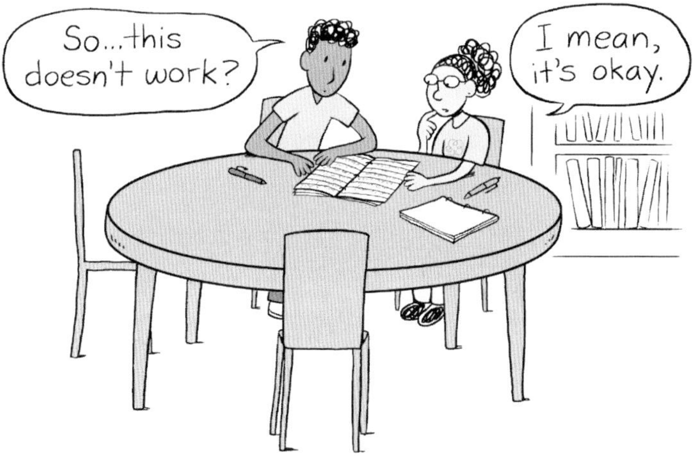
So...this doesn't work?
I mean, it's okay.

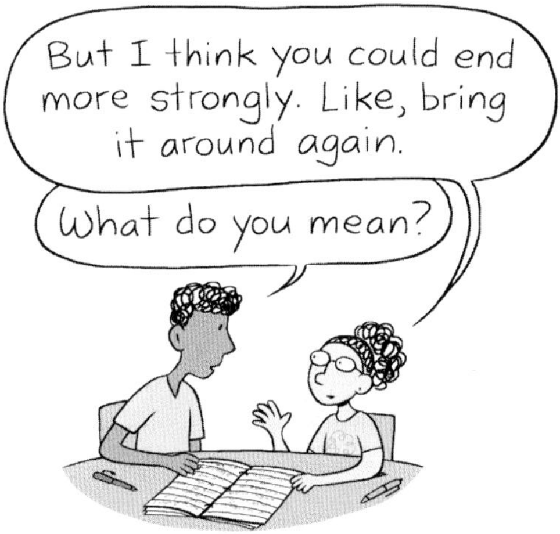
But I think you could end more strongly. Like, bring it around again.
What do you mean?

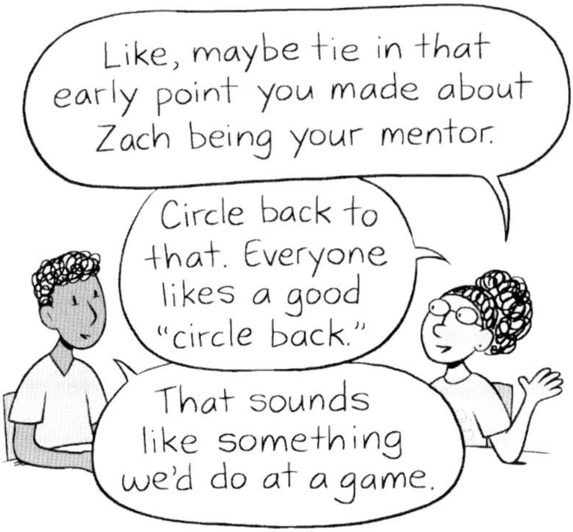
Like, maybe tie in that early point you made about Zach being your mentor.
Circle back to that. Everyone likes a good "circle back."
That sounds like something we'd do at a game.

We're back in the library, finishing my essay. Leah talked Mrs. Winn into another week's extension. I guess she still has a way with teachers. It's kinda like a superpower.

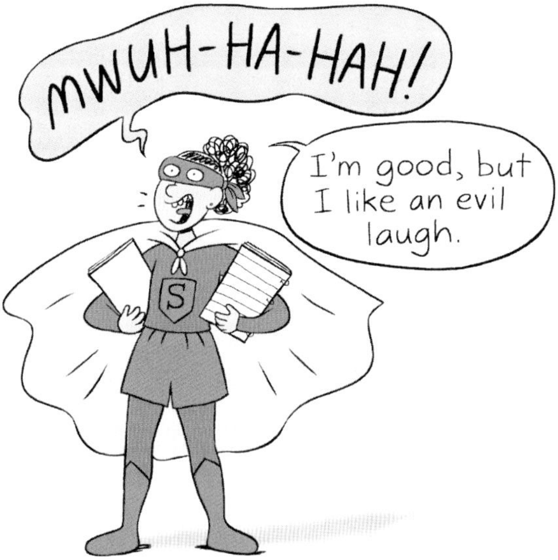
MWUH-HA-HAH!
I'm good, but I like an evil laugh.

We still have about ten minutes. I'm rewriting my ending when some girls walk into the library.

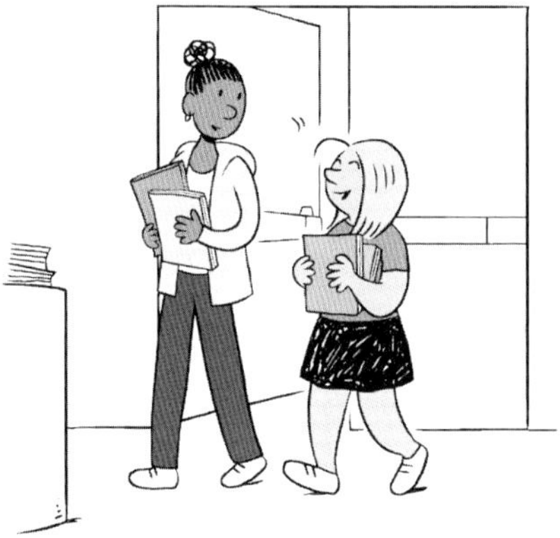

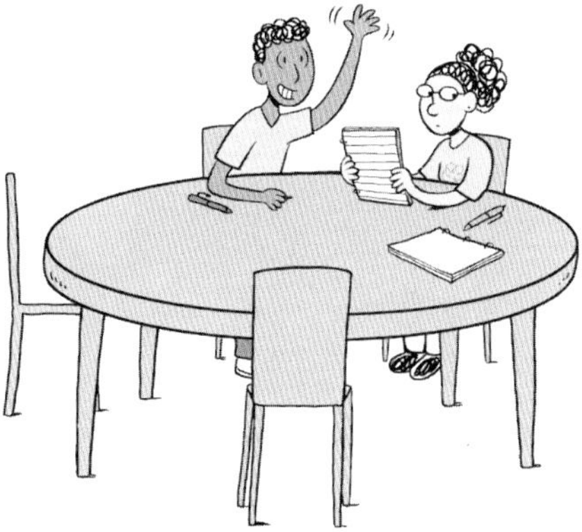

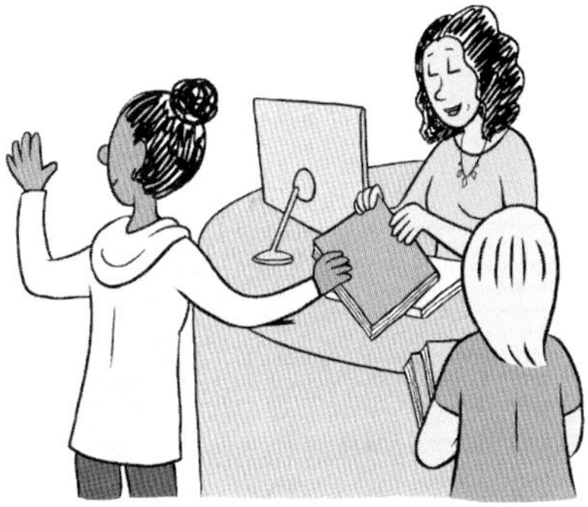

I catch Leah staring.

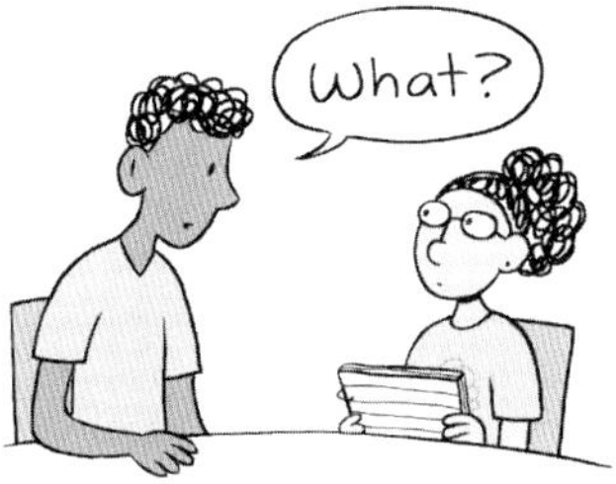
What?

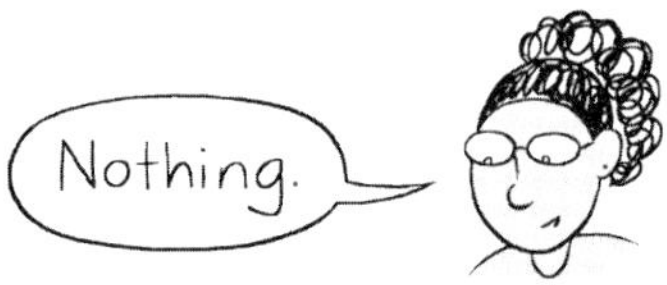
Nothing.

I go back to finishing my paper and Leah goes back to writing.

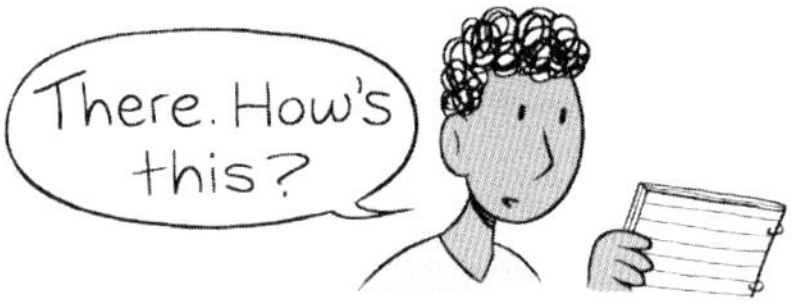
There. How's this?

She reads my work slowly and carefully.
Then she smiles widely.

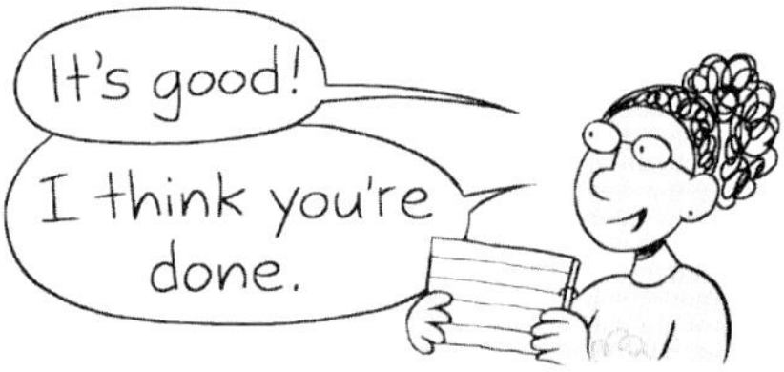
It's good!
I think you're done.

Not only did Leah help me rewrite my paper, but she's also helping defeat my nemesis:

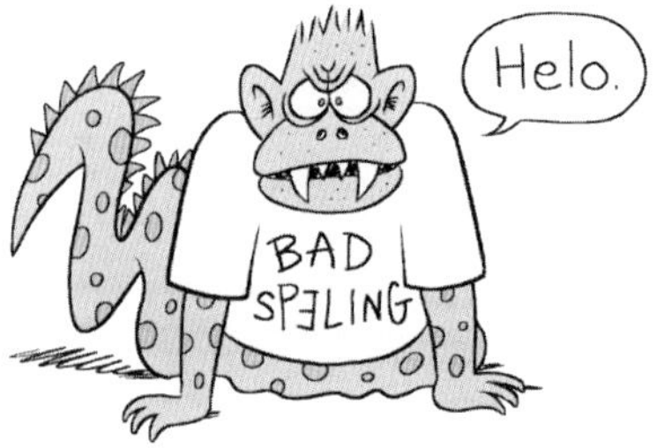
Helo.
BAD SPΞLING

I've definitely got a ways to go, but she promised to keep tutoring me for a while. Not that I have a choice.

Yeah, no. You're in this until that overall grade is up. WAY up.

Helicopter Mom: the one nemesis I'll never defeat.

Hey, what's that you're writing, anyway? Homework?

Oh. No, um... poetry. It's a hobby.

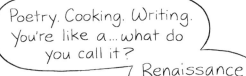

Poetry. Cooking. Writing. You're like a... what do you call it?

Renaissance Woman.

I don't know about that. But I do love all those things. I wish I could combine 'em.

Well, why not?

She throws me a strange look. But before we can say anything else, the bell rings. We gather our stuff and head for the door. Jaime and Maya are checking out some books.

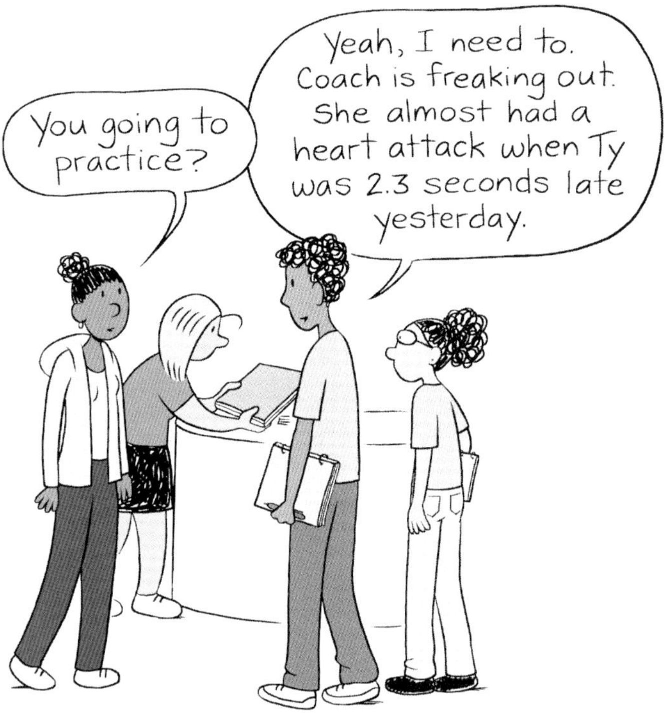
You going to practice?
Yeah, I need to. Coach is freaking out. She almost had a heart attack when Ty was 2.3 seconds late yesterday.

Jaime cracks up. I love making her laugh.

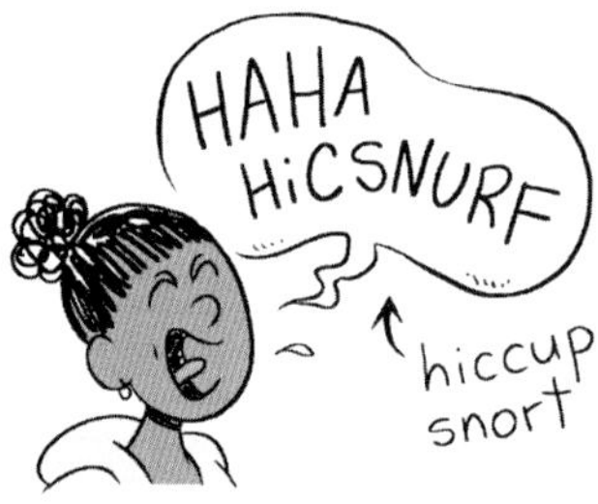
HAHA HiCSNURF
hiccup snort

Jaime has volleyball practice at the same time that I have basketball practice. We share the gym. We usually walk to Taystee's for a shake or to Ramone's for a pizza slice afterward. Maya and Tyler like to come along, but sometimes it's just us.

As we head to our next classes, I notice Leah glancing curiously at me.

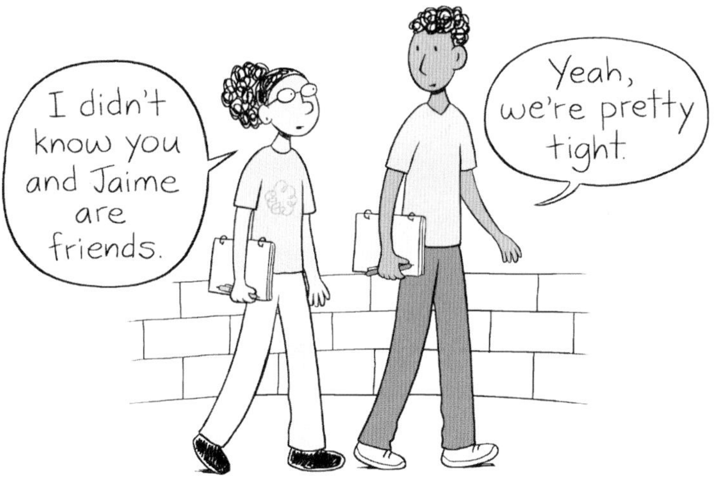
I didn't know you and Jaime are friends.
Yeah, we're pretty tight.

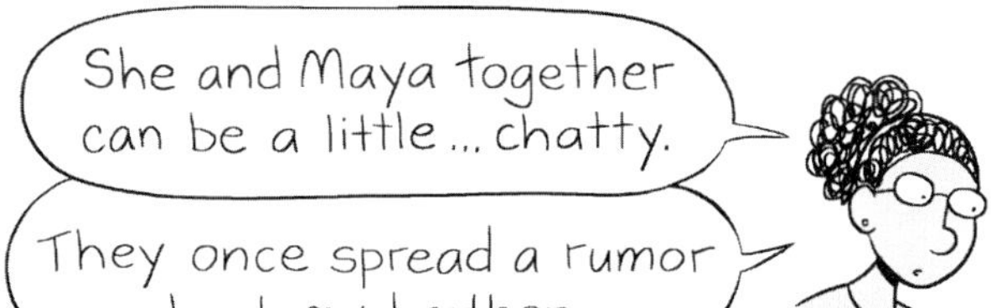
She and Maya together can be a little ... chatty.
They once spread a rumor about my brother.

I stop.

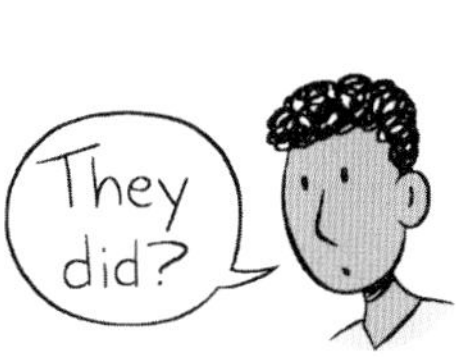
They did?

Yeah, last year. Um, that he and Anita Garcia were an item, even though he hates her guts.

Oh wow. Yeah, they can be like that.

That's the one thing I don't like about Jaime: around her friends, she can turn into . . . not a **mean** girl, but she can be hurtful. Not on purpose, but still. Same with Maya.

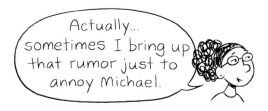

Actually... sometimes I bring up that rumor just to annoy Michael.

I laugh.

See you next week.

Good luck at the game.

DONUT

BULLY

We wave and head in different directions: me to Language Arts and her to math.

When I get to Mrs. Winn's class, I walk to her desk and hand her my essay. Gotta admit, I'm still a little nervous about it.

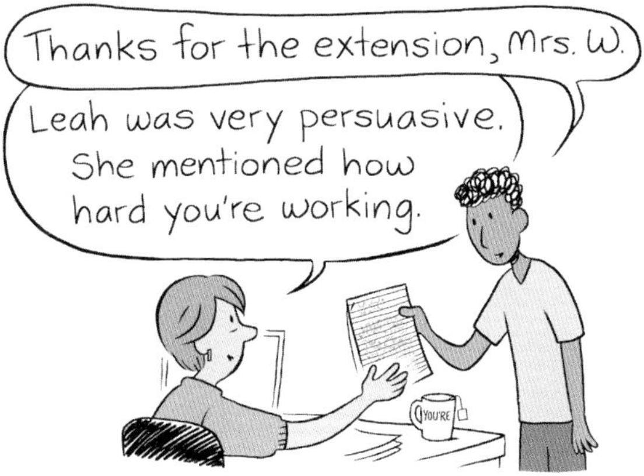
Thanks for the extension, Mrs. W.
Leah was very persuasive. She mentioned how hard you're working.
YOU'RE

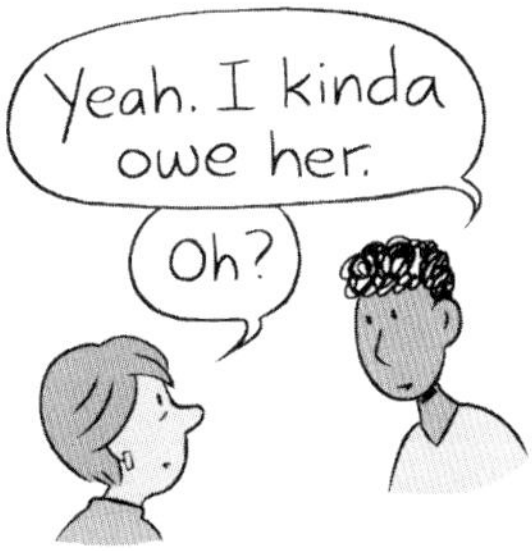
Yeah. I kinda owe her.
Oh?

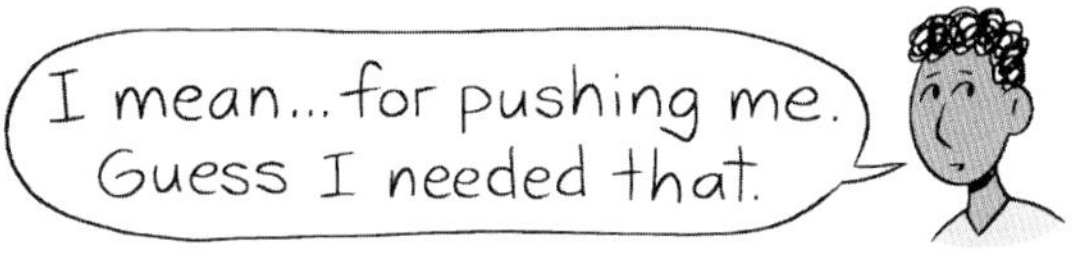
I mean... for pushing me. Guess I needed that.

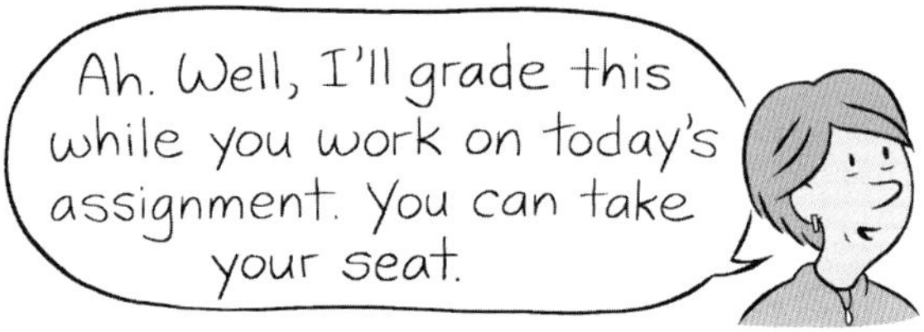
Ah. Well, I'll grade this while you work on today's assignment. You can take your seat.

Mrs. W starts the class. She assigns some reading and a follow-up worksheet. I'm kinda on edge, wondering how I did on my rewritten essay. I can't believe it's been two weeks since I didn't even care.

I try to be more careful on this in-class assignment. I read the short story twice and I check over my worksheet twice (although the bell rings before I can finish reviewing my last answer). We turn in our assignments.

Mrs. W calls me over.

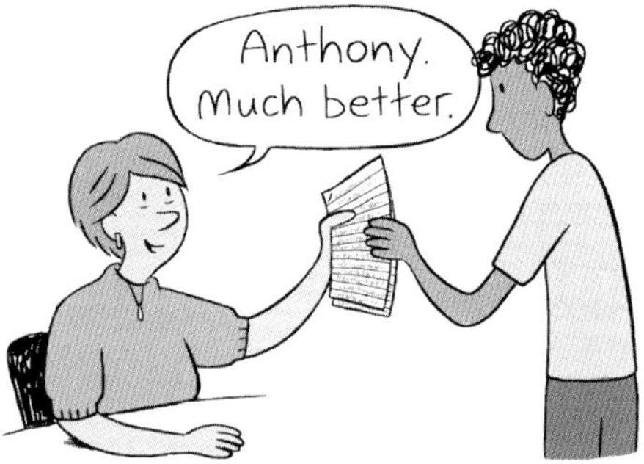
Anthony. Much better.

I look.

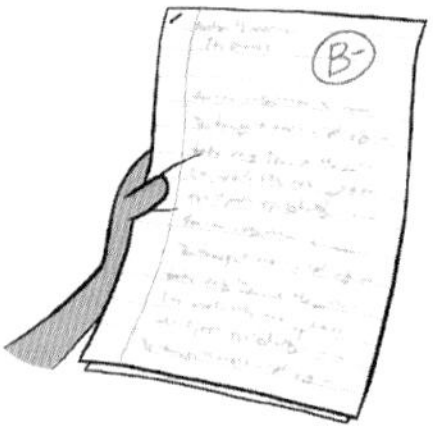
B-

There's still room for improvement. It's a little choppy, and I think it could use another paragraph about how you improved your layup and what its consequences meant to *you*... not to Zach.

But still...a big improvement. It's the small steps.

Thanks, Mrs. W.

I head out. Part of me is happy for the B-. That's huge. But another part is disappointed that I didn't do better after all that work. And writing about something that's . . . well, private. Still, I guess Mrs. W is right: it's the small steps. If anyone should know about that, it's me.

Tyler meets me in the hall, and we walk to practice together. He's in a good mood, chatting about art class and his new assignment: linocuts or something. We head to the locker room to get changed. Then we go to the gym. It's a little early, so Ty and I practice our baseline passes.

That's when the girls show up for volleyball.

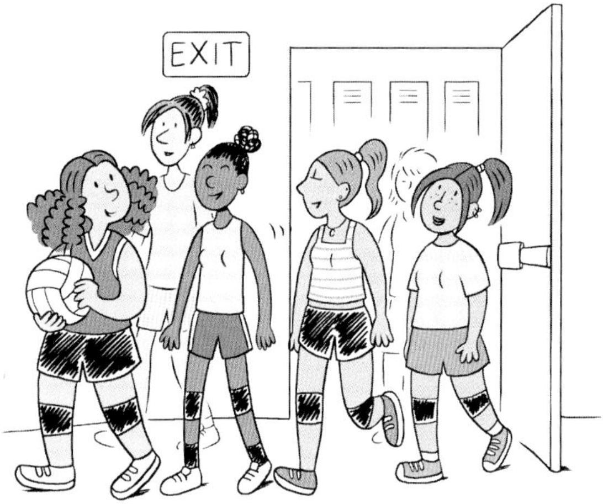
EXIT

And I see her.

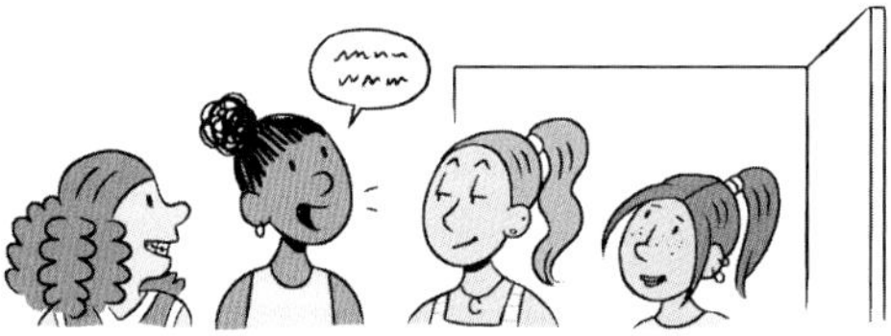

The girl who makes me light up like a thousand-watt bulb.

although no one would know it from the outside

Nikki Lourde.

Leah

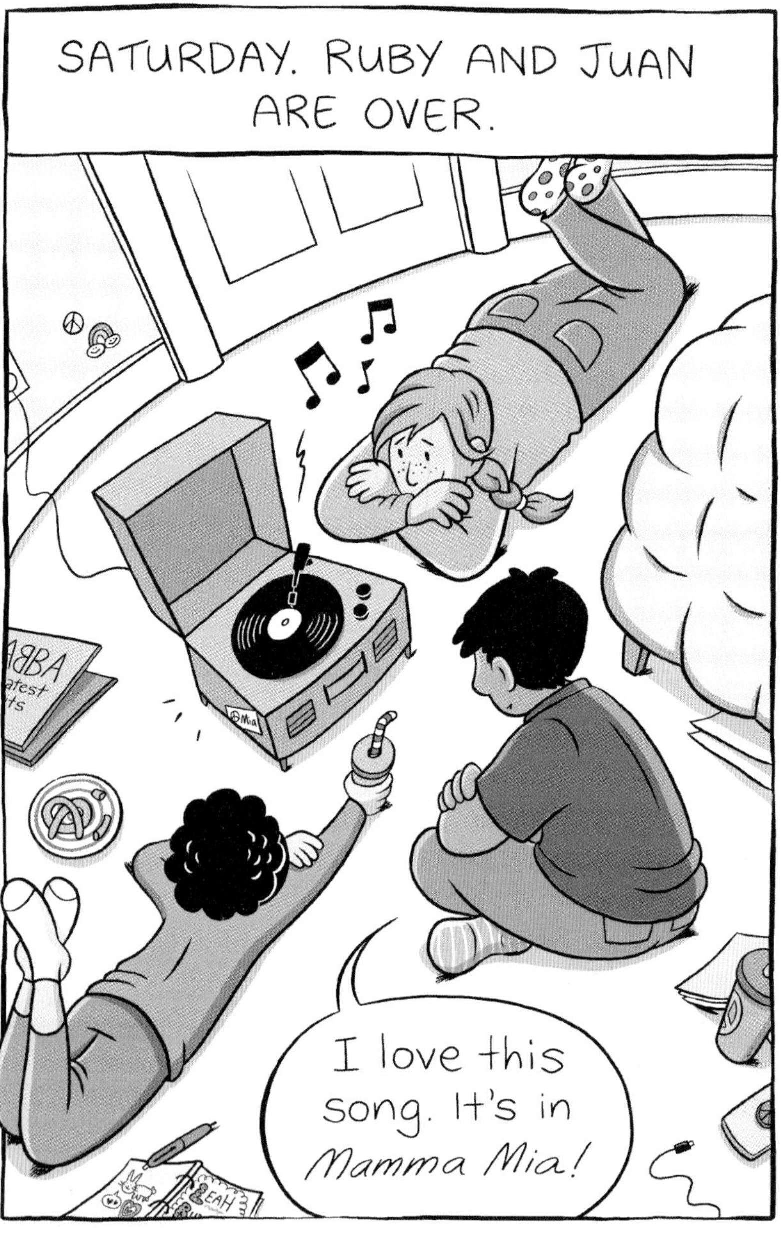
SATURDAY. RUBY AND JUAN ARE OVER.
ABBA Greatest Hits
Mia
I love this song. It's in *Mamma Mia!*

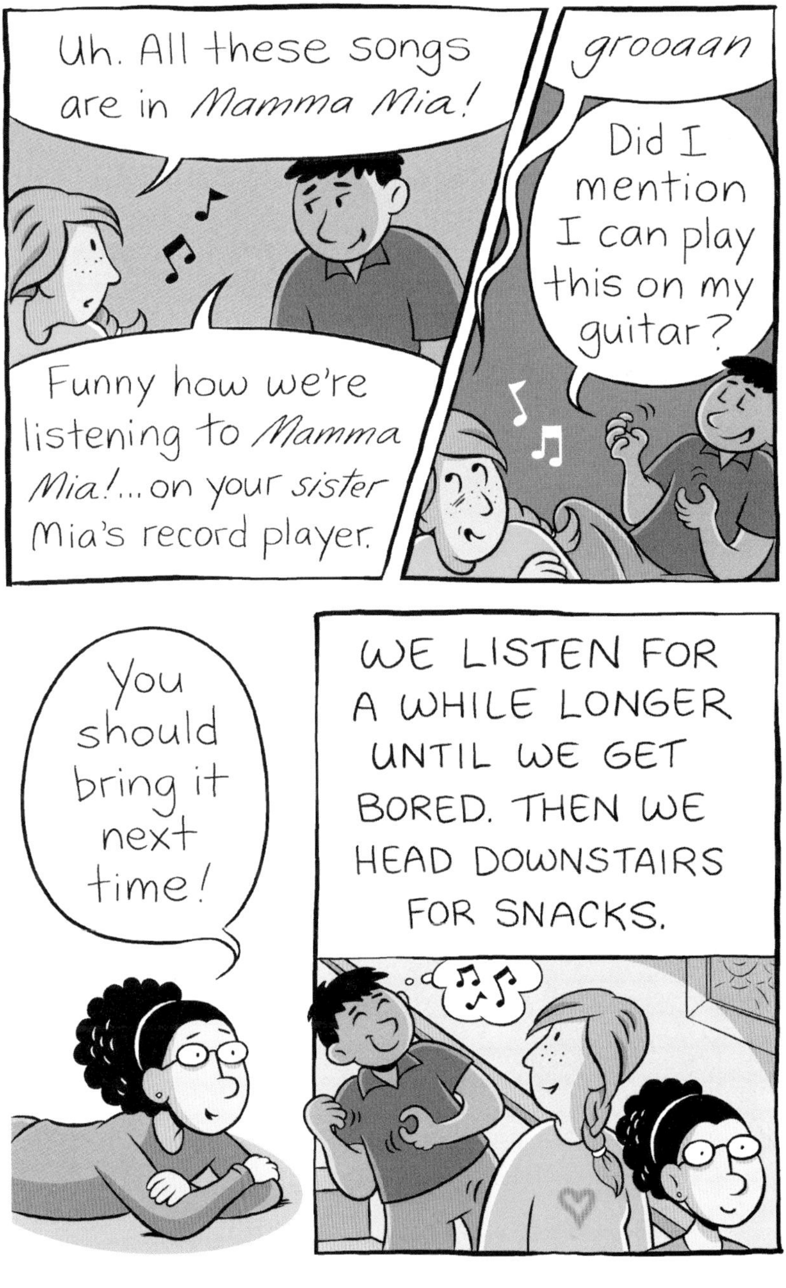

Uh. All these songs are in *Mamma Mia!*
Funny how we're listening to *Mamma Mia!*... on your *sister* Mia's record player.
grooaan
Did I mention I can play this on my guitar?
You should bring it next time!
WE LISTEN FOR A WHILE LONGER UNTIL WE GET BORED. THEN WE HEAD DOWNSTAIRS FOR SNACKS.

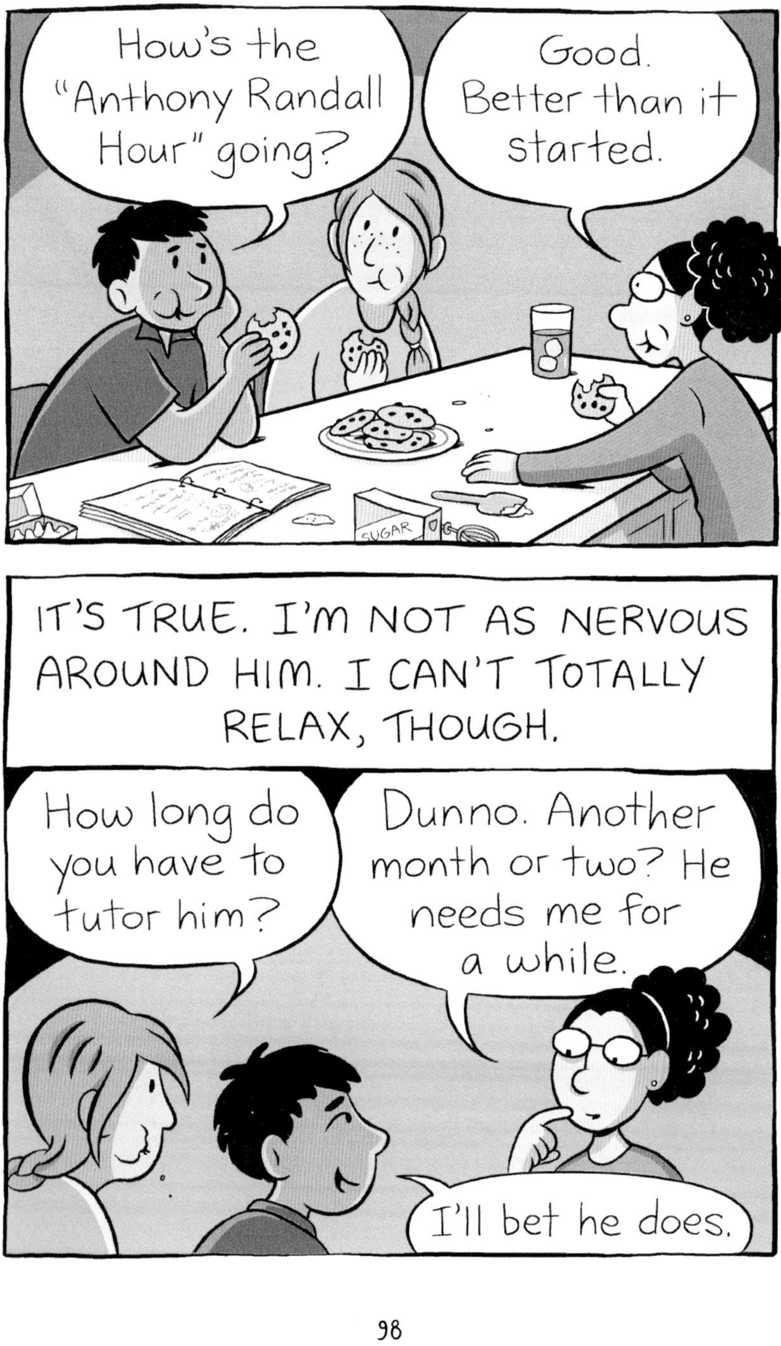
How's the "Anthony Randall Hour" going?
Good. Better than it started.
IT'S TRUE. I'M NOT AS NERVOUS AROUND HIM. I CAN'T TOTALLY RELAX, THOUGH.
How long do you have to tutor him?
Dunno. Another month or two? He needs me for a while.
I'll bet he does.

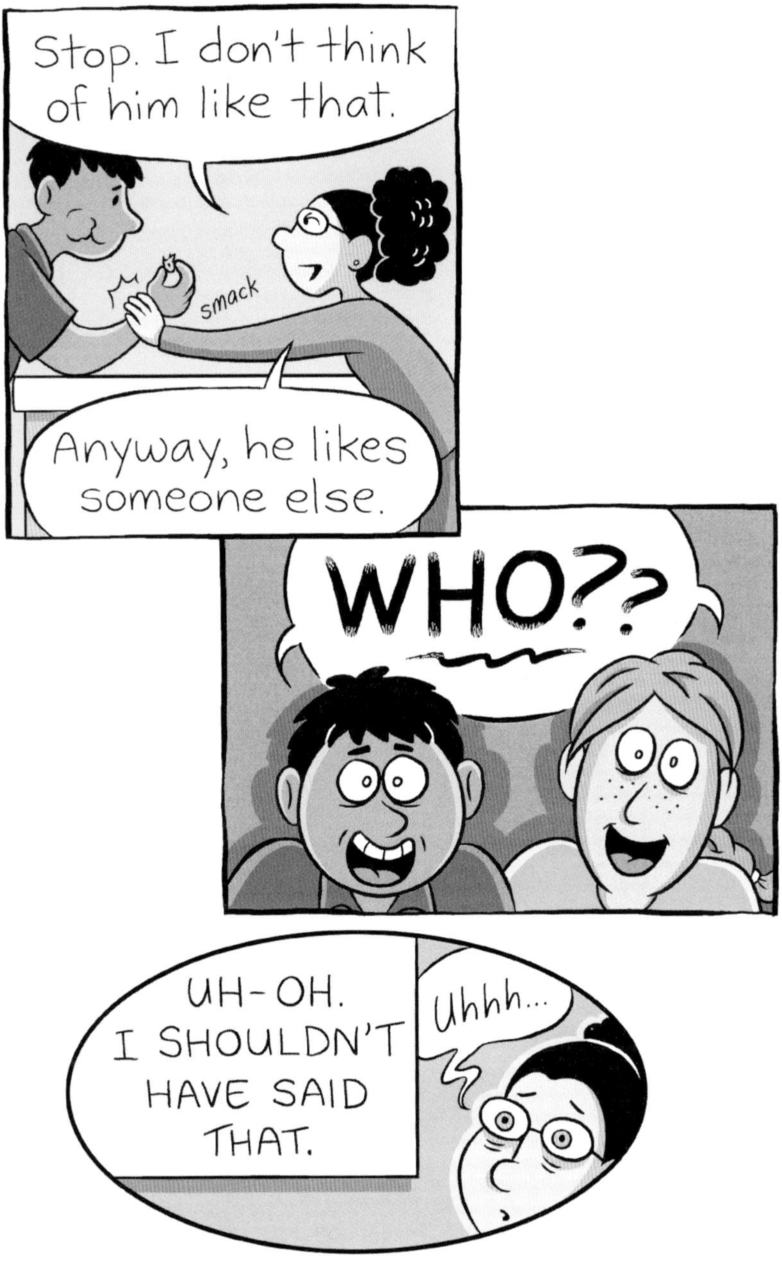
Stop. I don't think of him like that.
smack
Anyway, he likes someone else.
WHO??
UH-OH. I SHOULDN'T HAVE SAID THAT.
Uhhh...

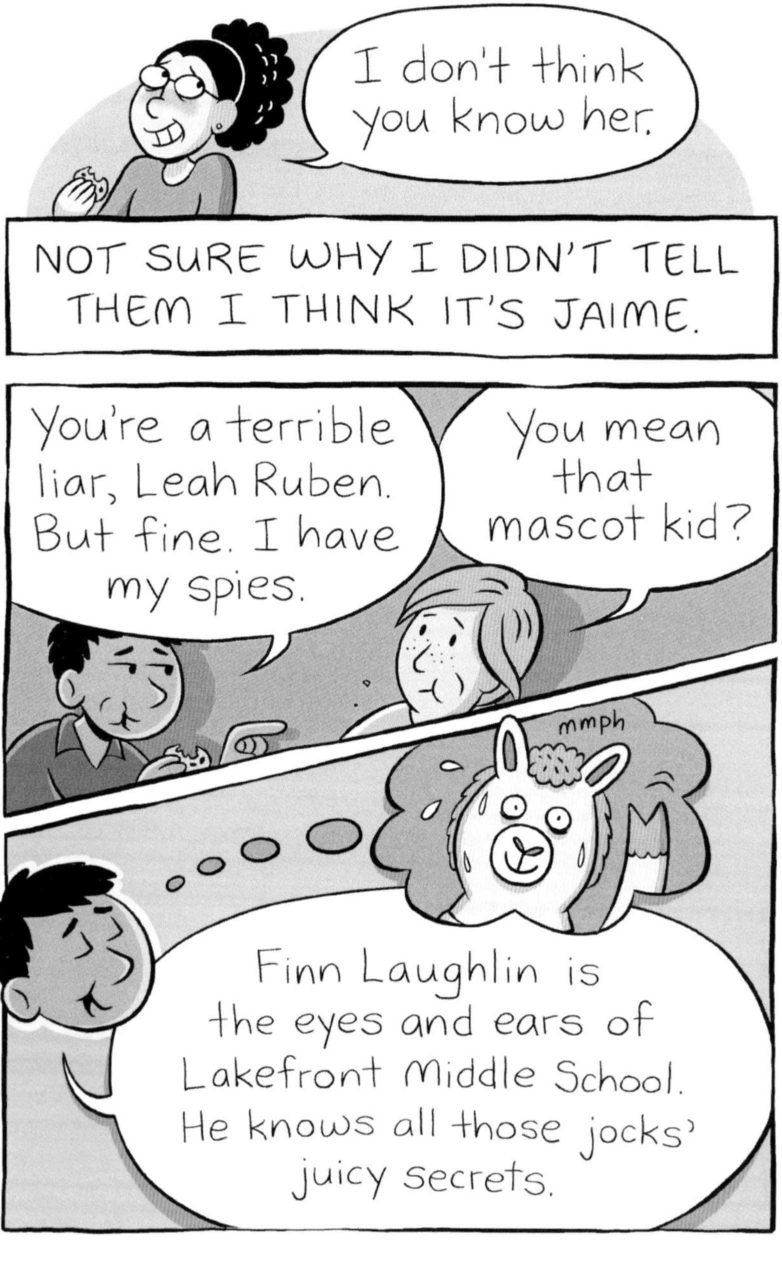
I don't think you know her.
NOT SURE WHY I DIDN'T TELL THEM I THINK IT'S JAIME.
You're a terrible liar, Leah Ruben. But fine. I have my spies.
You mean that mascot kid?
mmph
Finn Laughlin is the eyes and ears of Lakefront Middle School. He knows all those jocks' juicy secrets.

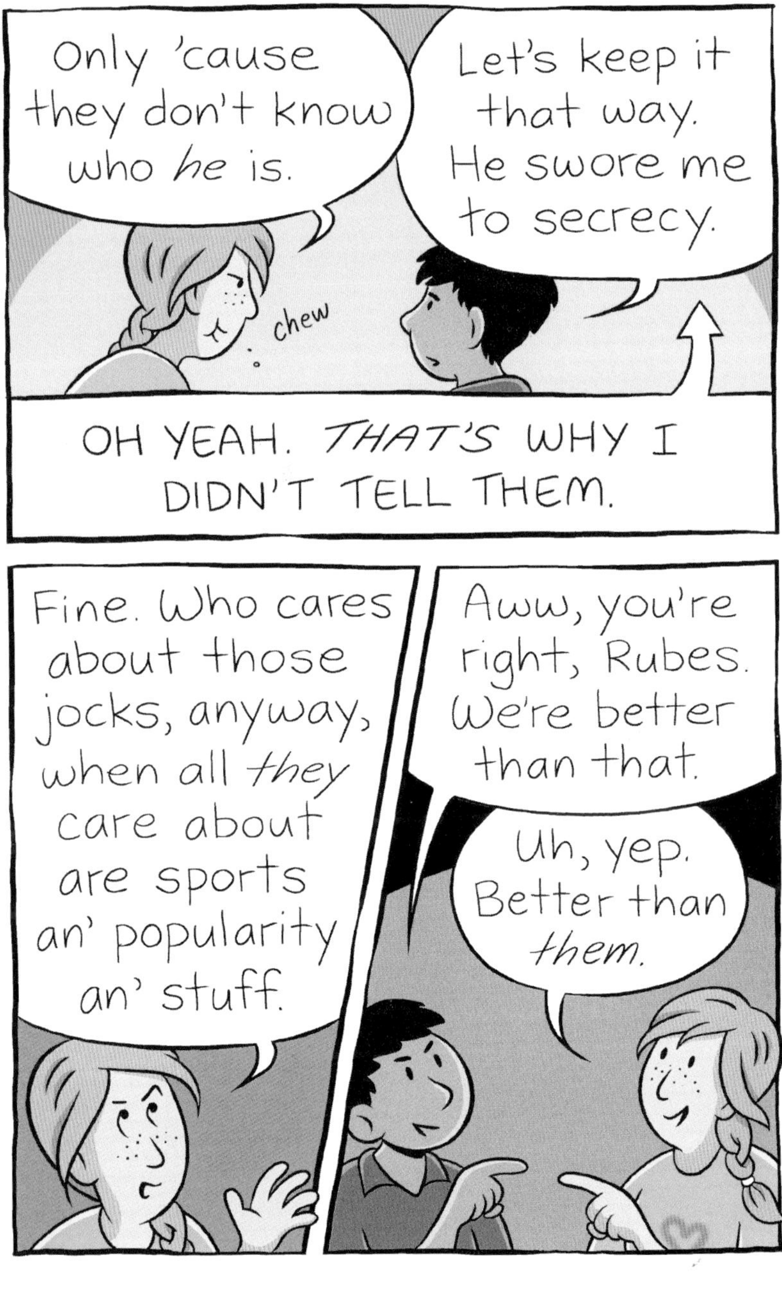
Only 'cause they don't know who *he* is.
Let's keep it that way. He swore me to secrecy.
chew
OH YEAH. *THAT'S* WHY I DIDN'T TELL THEM.
Fine. Who cares about those jocks, anyway, when all *they* care about are sports an' popularity an' stuff.
Aww, you're right, Rubes. We're better than that.
Uh, yep. Better than *them*.

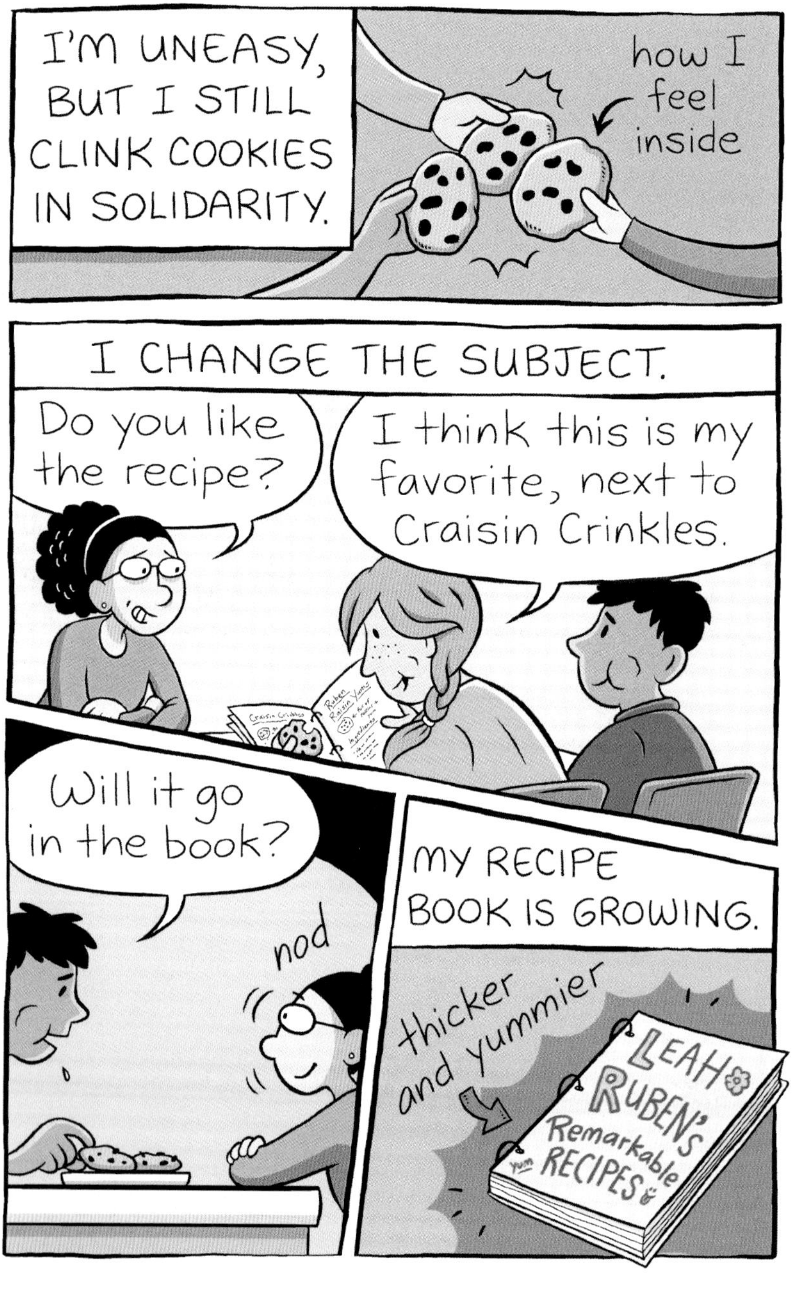
I'M UNEASY, BUT I STILL CLINK COOKIES IN SOLIDARITY.
how I feel inside
I CHANGE THE SUBJECT.
Do you like the recipe?
I think this is my favorite, next to Craisin Crinkles.
Will it go in the book?
nod
MY RECIPE BOOK IS GROWING.
thicker and yummier
LEAH RUBEN'S Remarkable RECIPES
yum

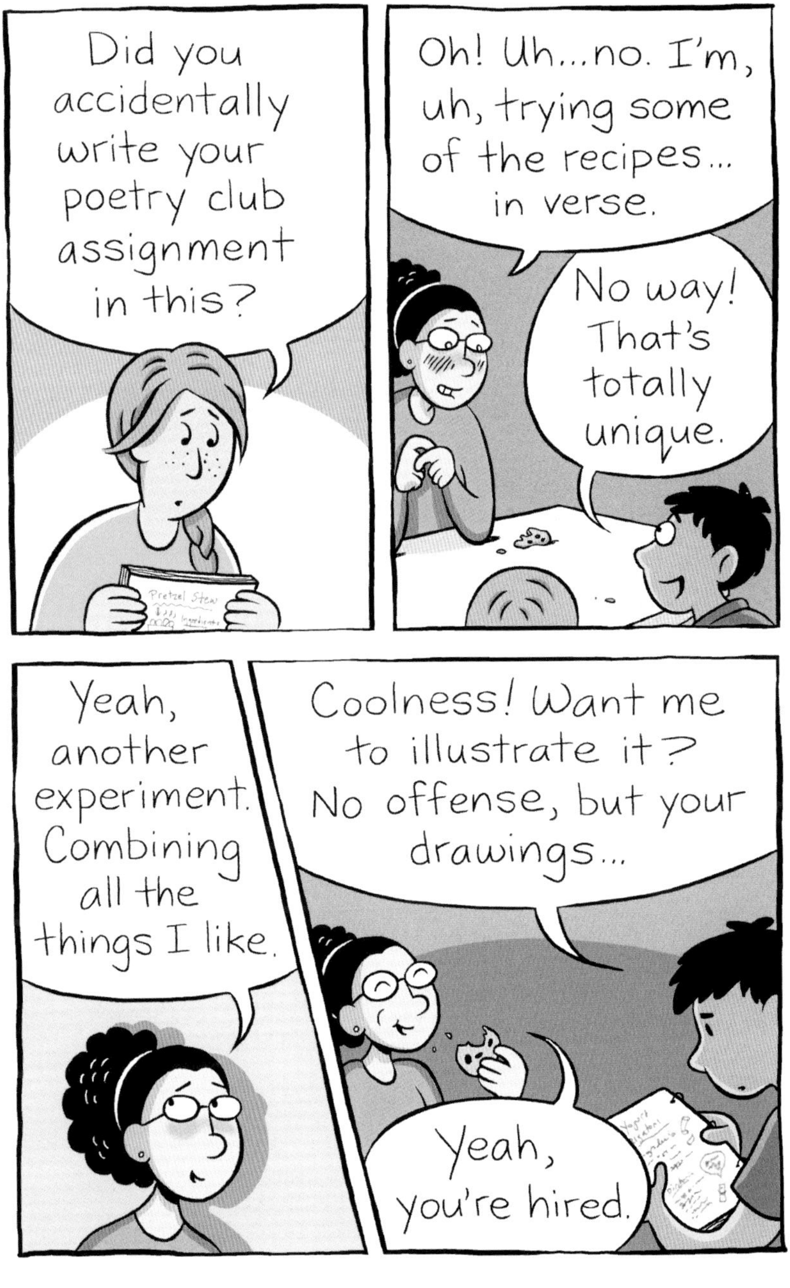

Did you accidentally write your poetry club assignment in this?
Pretzel Stew
Oh! Uh...no. I'm, uh, trying some of the recipes... in verse.
No way! That's totally unique.
Yeah, another experiment. Combining all the things I like.
Coolness! Want me to illustrate it? No offense, but your drawings...
Yeah, you're hired.

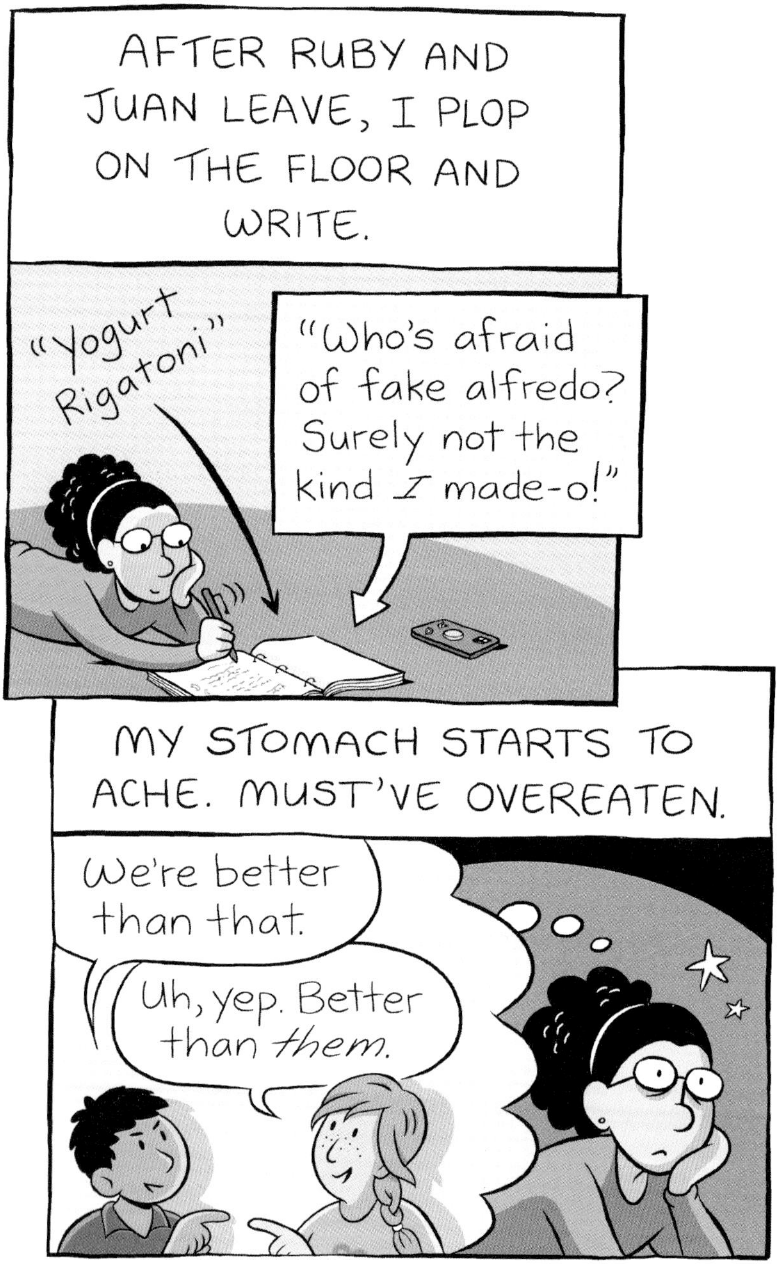
AFTER RUBY AND JUAN LEAVE, I PLOP ON THE FLOOR AND WRITE.
"Yogurt Rigatoni"
"Who's afraid of fake alfredo? Surely not the kind *I* made-o!"
MY STOMACH STARTS TO ACHE. MUST'VE OVEREATEN.
We're better than that.
Uh, yep. Better than *them*.

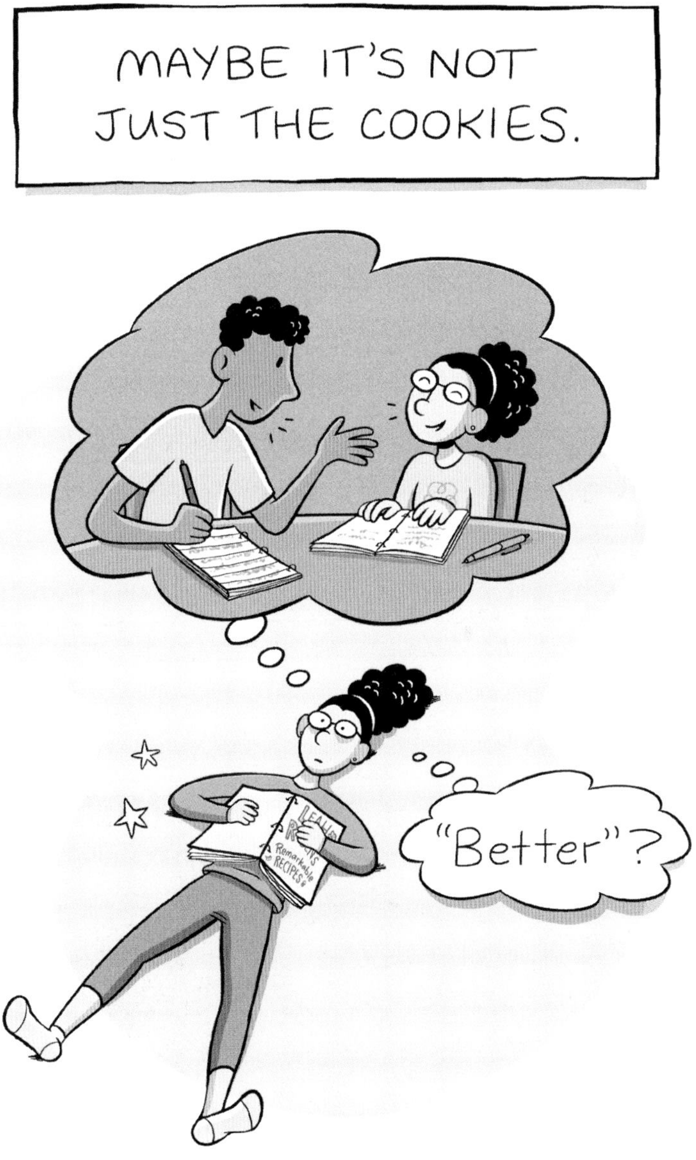
MAYBE IT'S NOT JUST THE COOKIES.
"Better"?

ANTHONY

Monday. Leah and I decided another change of scenery is in order.

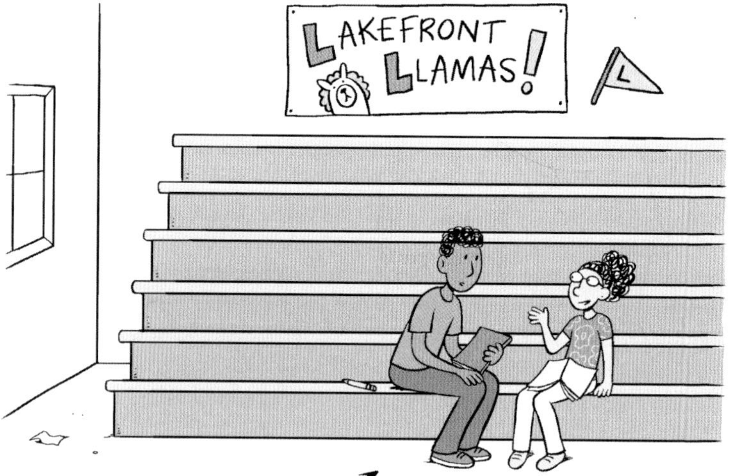
LAKEFRONT
LLAMAS!
L

trying out all the quiet places in the building

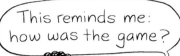

This reminds me:
how was the game?

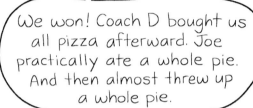

We won! Coach D bought us all pizza afterward. Joe practically ate a whole pie. And then almost threw up a whole pie.

Joe...Lungo? He's on the team?

Nah, but Coach lets him hang out...like an unofficial player.

Or pet.

We take bites of the chocolate power bars I snuck in, checking first to make sure no one's watching. Coach Durdle sits in her office behind a window, but she's glued to her computer monitor.

watching
kitten
videos

mew

You should come to a game.

Did I really say that? But I meant it.

I... can't.

Why not?

Um...well, I'm Jewish and we keep Shabbat. It starts Friday at sunset and goes till Saturday, sundown.

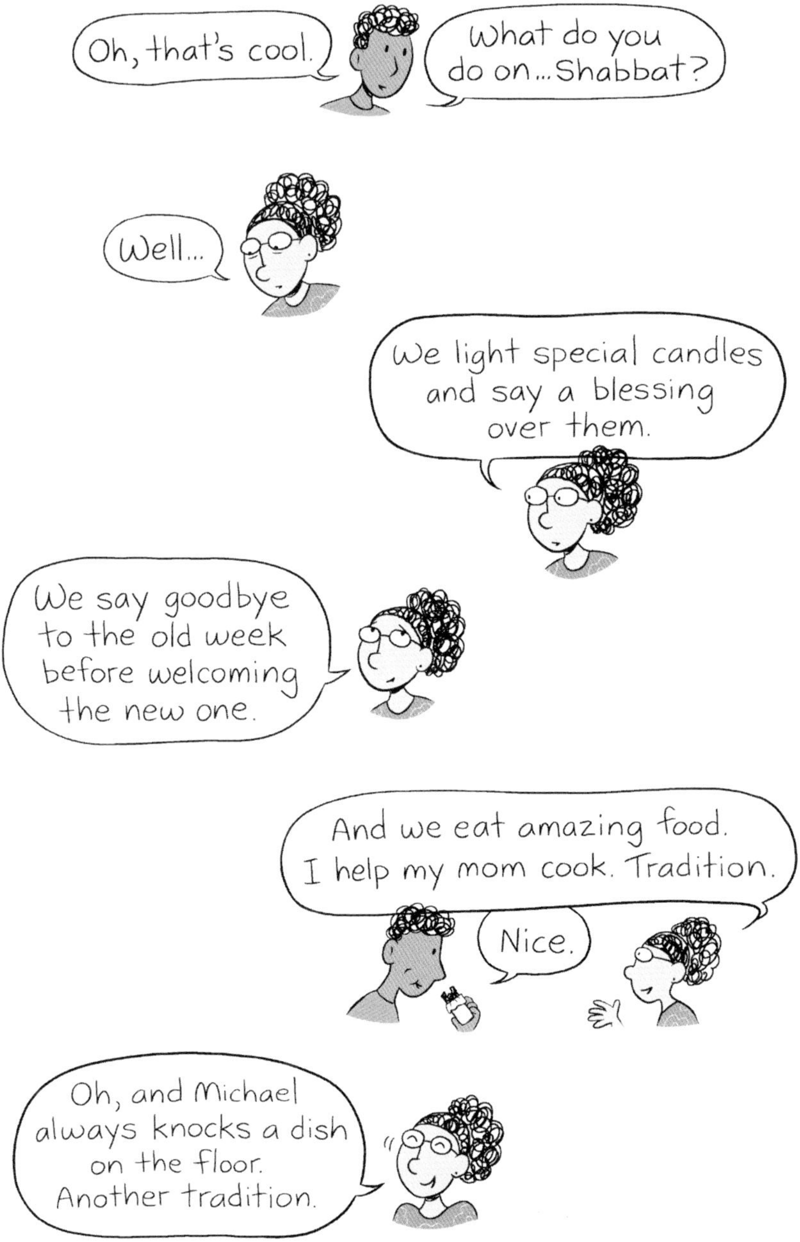

Oh, that's cool.
What do you do on... Shabbat?
Well...
We light special candles and say a blessing over them.
We say goodbye to the old week before welcoming the new one.
And we eat amazing food. I help my mom cook. Tradition.
Nice.
Oh, and Michael always knocks a dish on the floor. Another tradition.

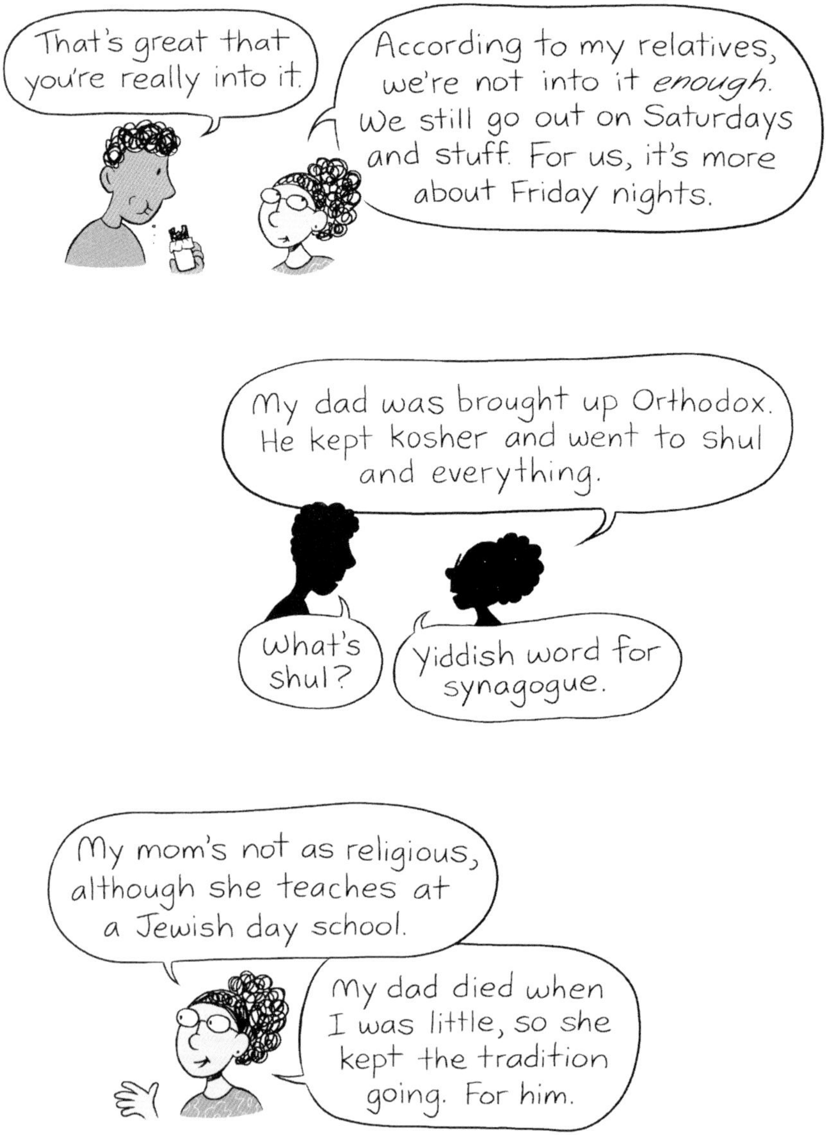
That's great that you're really into it.
According to my relatives, we're not into it *enough*. We still go out on Saturdays and stuff. For us, it's more about Friday nights.
My dad was brought up Orthodox. He kept kosher and went to shul and everything.
What's shul?
Yiddish word for synagogue.
My mom's not as religious, although she teaches at a Jewish day school.
My dad died when I was little, so she kept the tradition going. For him.

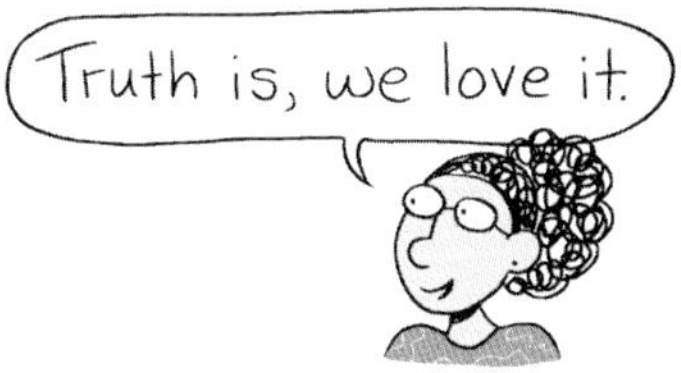
Truth is, we love it.

I knew Leah was Jewish, but I never knew her dad had died. Whoa.

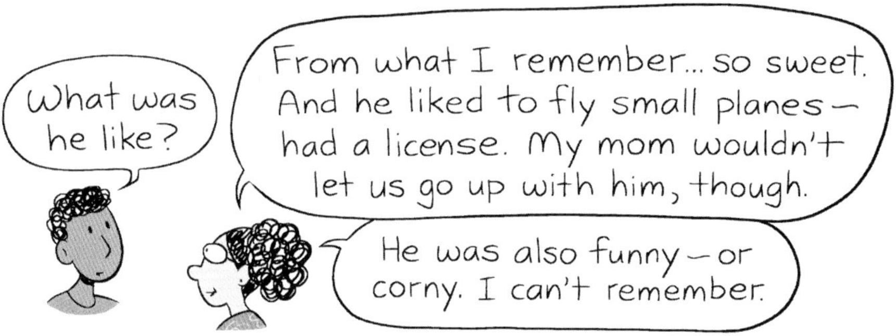
What was he like?
From what I remember... so sweet. And he liked to fly small planes—had a license. My mom wouldn't let us go up with him, though.
He was also funny—or corny. I can't remember.

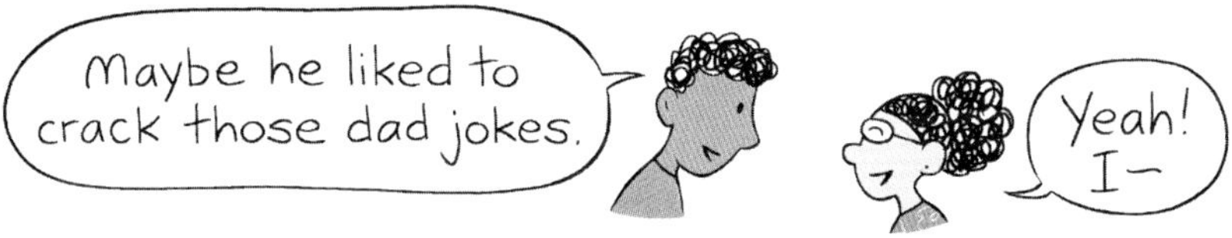
Maybe he liked to crack those dad jokes.
Yeah! I—

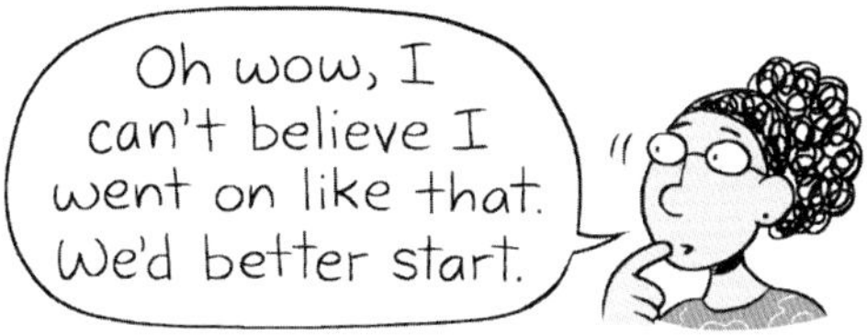
Oh wow, I can't believe I went on like that. We'd better start.

Truth is, I'd rather hear more. I like listening to people's stories. I guess I'm like my pop that way. He listens to them all day long for his job. But, like his patients, he always tries to get me to talk about my feelings. For some reason, that makes me not want to.

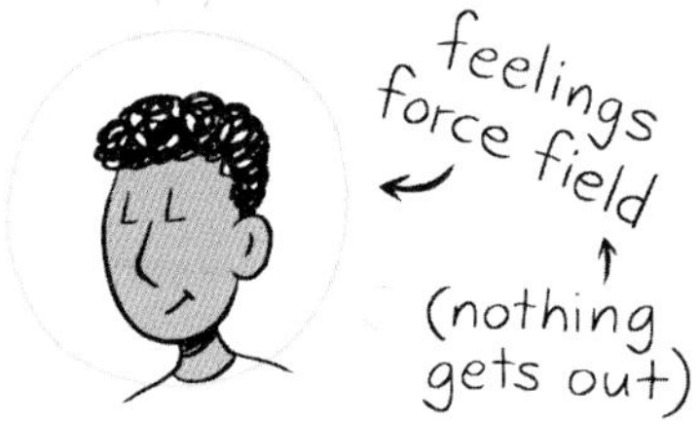
feelings force field
(nothing gets out)

We get started.

In class, we did a worksheet on Author's Purpose and Point of View. We were also assigned a related essay for homework over the weekend. I brought mine with me.

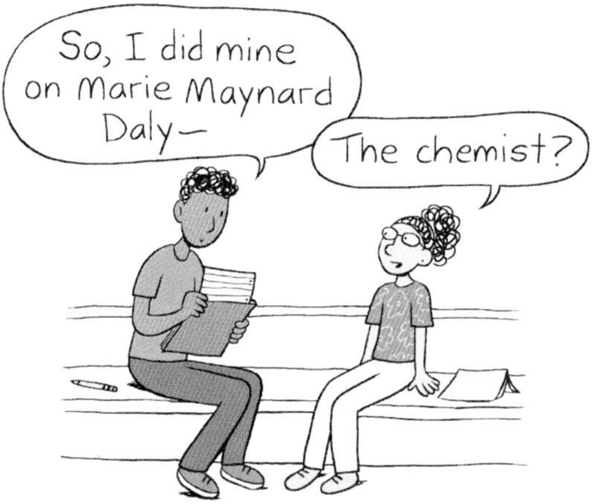
So, I did mine on Marie Maynard Daly—
The chemist?

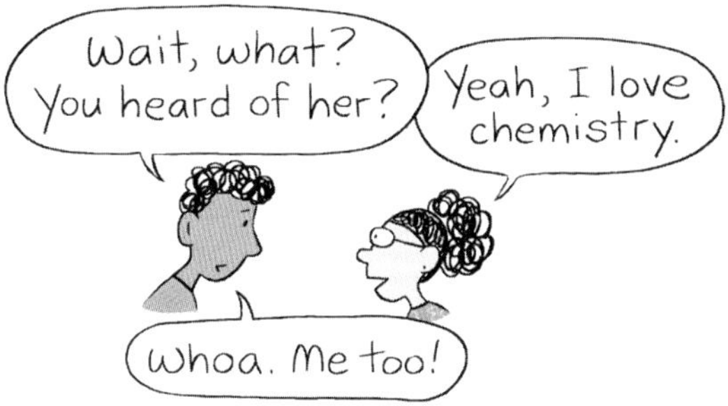
Wait, what? You heard of her?
Yeah, I love chemistry.
Whoa. Me too!

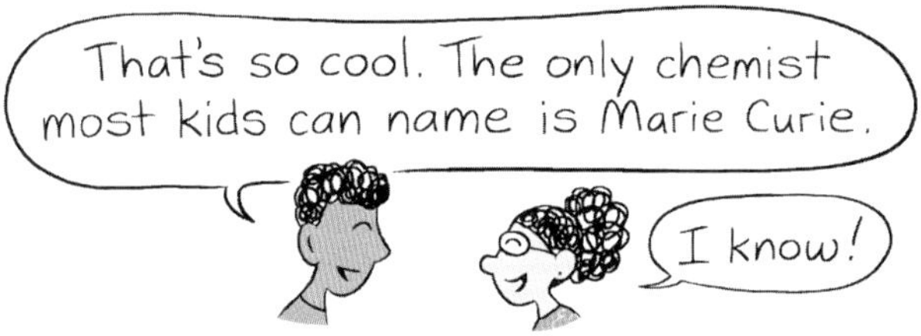
That's so cool. The only chemist most kids can name is Marie Curie.
I know!

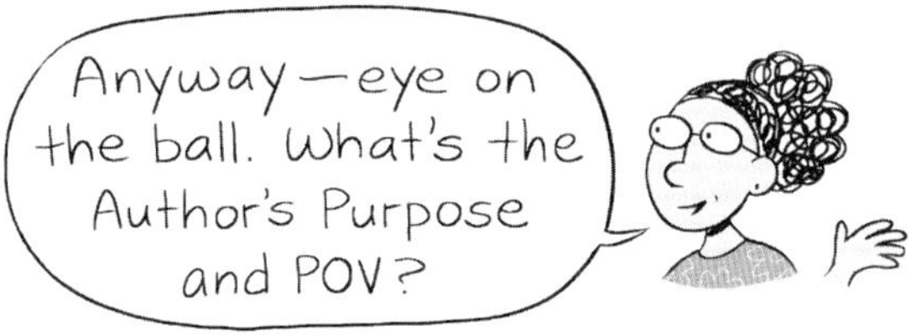
Anyway—eye on the ball. What's the Author's Purpose and POV?

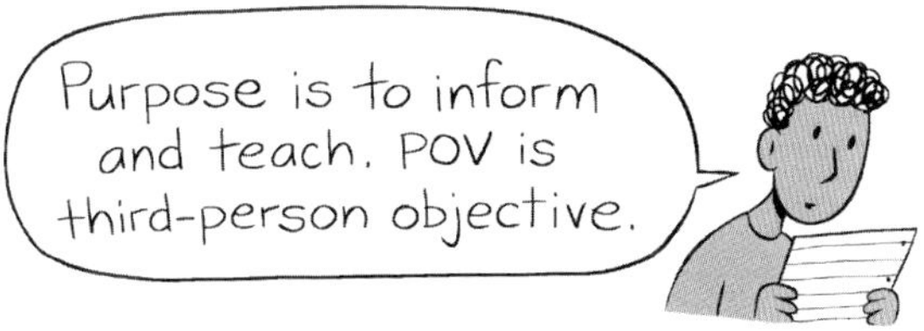
Purpose is to inform and teach. POV is third-person objective.

She reads my work. Afterward, she helps me with some grammar and punctuation stuff.

The bell rings and we head out.

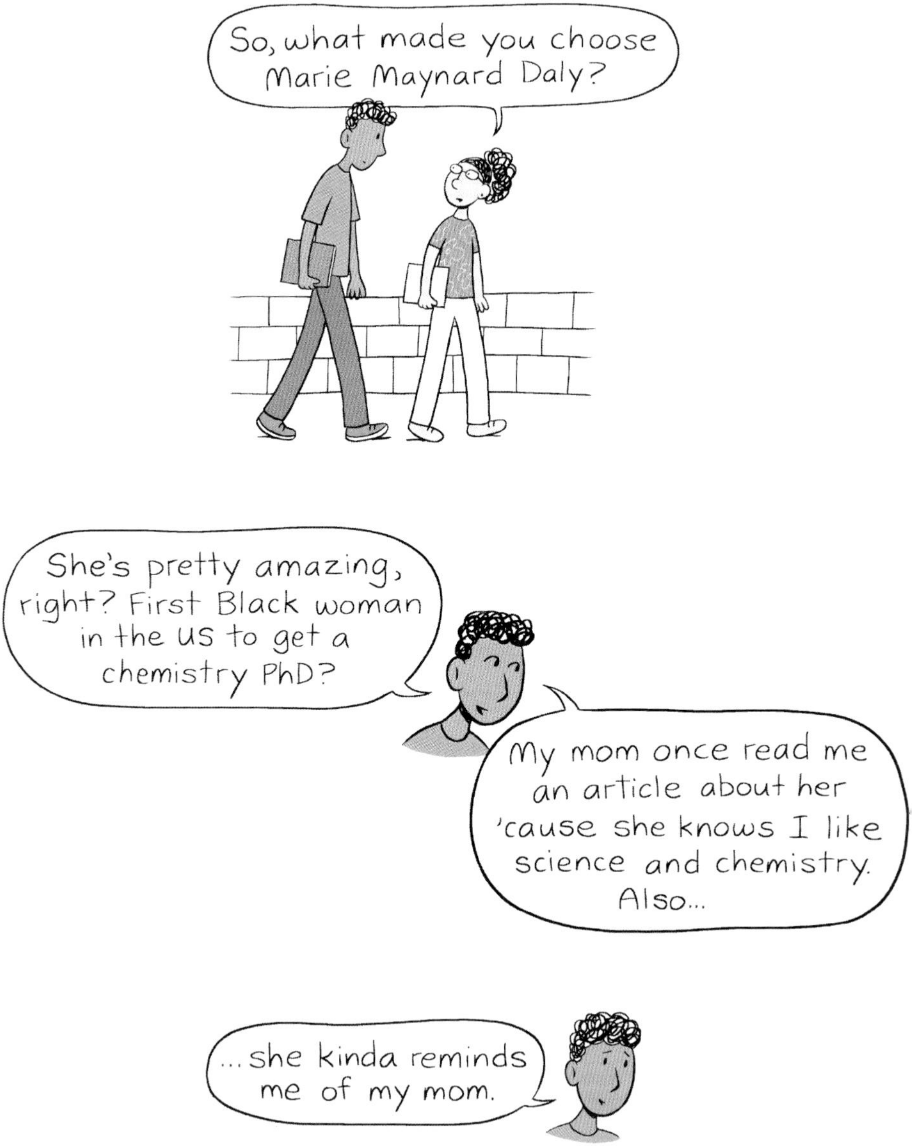
So, what made you choose Marie Maynard Daly?
She's pretty amazing, right? First Black woman in the US to get a chemistry PhD?
My mom once read me an article about her 'cause she knows I like science and chemistry. Also...
...she kinda reminds me of my mom.

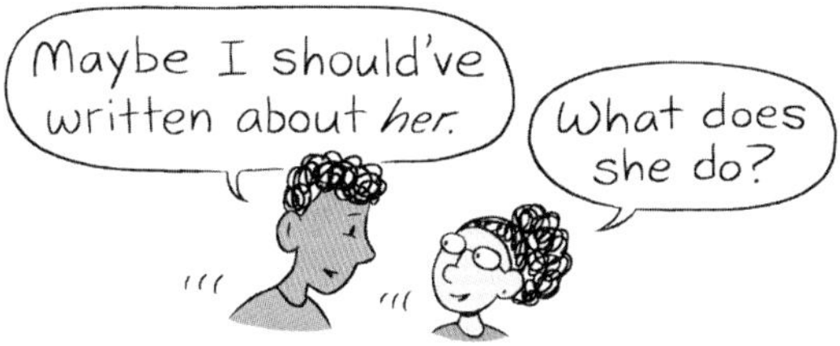
Maybe I should've written about *her.*
What does she do?

I tell her, but I just give her the basics. How I have supersmart parents, know-it-all twin sisters, and a lovable (but drooly) dog.

What I don't say is:

How my mom is the first person of color to head her department (just wish she wasn't the boss of **me** all the time). How my pop is always interested in people and how he—embarrassingly—grills every friend I bring home, like they're his patients on the couch. Or how my cute-but-irritating sisters totally annoy me, but—as hard as it is—I still wanna be a good big brother.

It feels kinda weird and embarrassing to mention all that. I guess I'm not a big sharer.

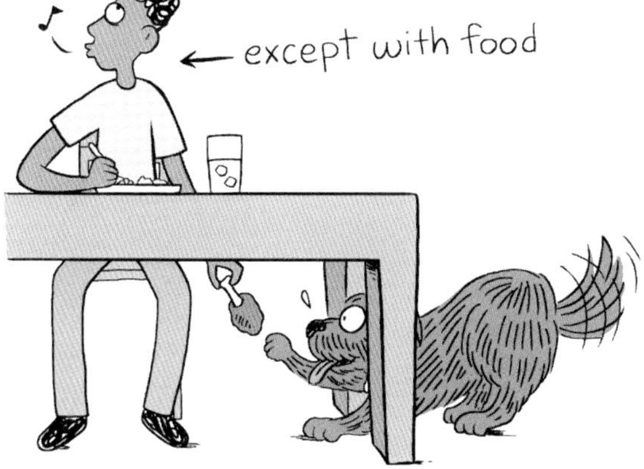
except with food

Other than my family, only two people really know me: Ty and Jaime. And I don't always keep it real around **them**. Especially when I'm feeling down or frustrated. I don't like to bum anyone out. With my b-ball friends, we just talk hoops. And with Joe . . . well, he just likes to clown around. Makes a joke of everything. So, I do it, too.

I'm known for being "cool and laid-back." And I guess . . . it's what I've come to expect of myself.

me as a cool... well, you know ↳

So what's Michael like?

She starts to tell me about her own "annoying" brother. How he's great at soccer but gave it up for baseball. How he's smart but struggles in school. And how he loves to crack jokes (ughh!)—which he may have inherited from their dad. I can tell she loves him a lot—you can hear it in her voice.

And then, all of a sudden, she stops talking.

SLAM

GASP

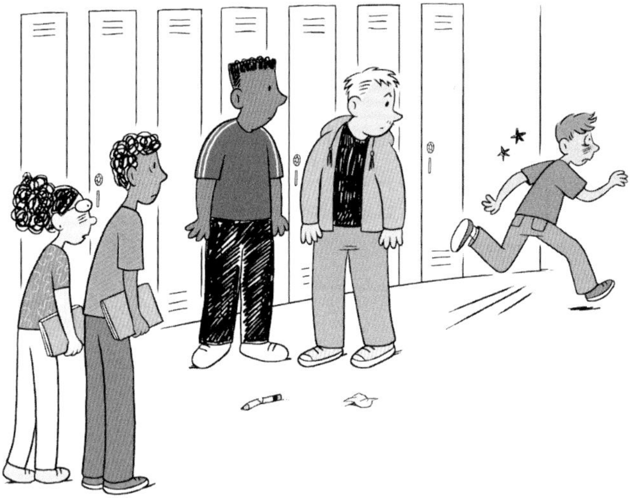

I can't move.

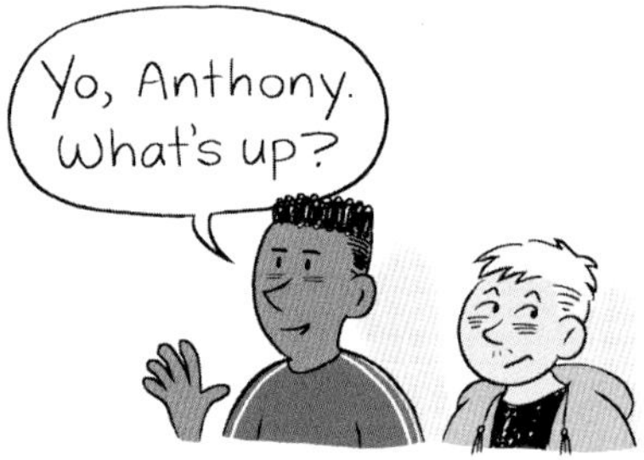
Yo, Anthony. What's up?

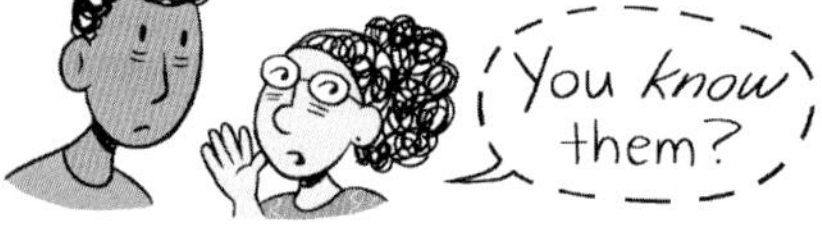
You *know* them?

Unfortunately, I do.

Leah

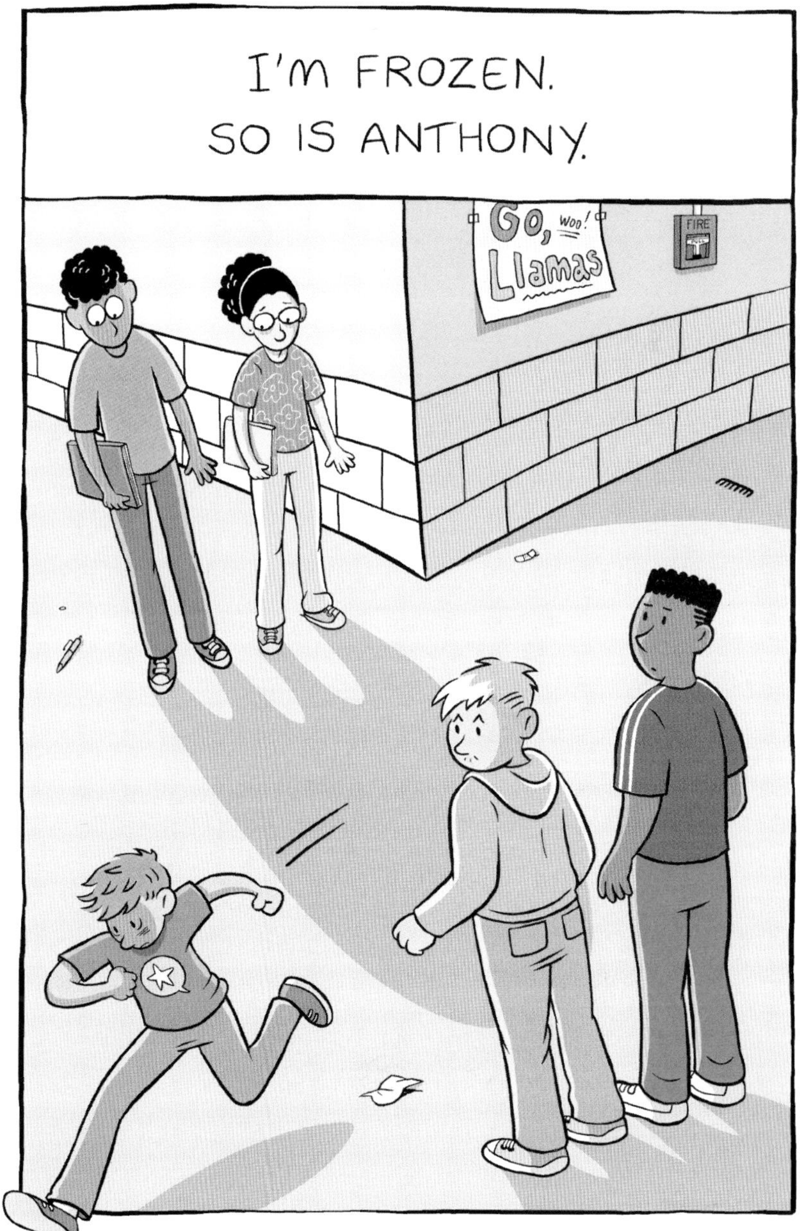
I'M FROZEN.
SO IS ANTHONY.
Go, WOO!
Llamas
FIRE

Yo, Anthony. What's up?

You *know* them?

They're my teammates.

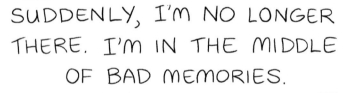

SUDDENLY, I'M NO LONGER THERE. I'M IN THE MIDDLE OF BAD MEMORIES.

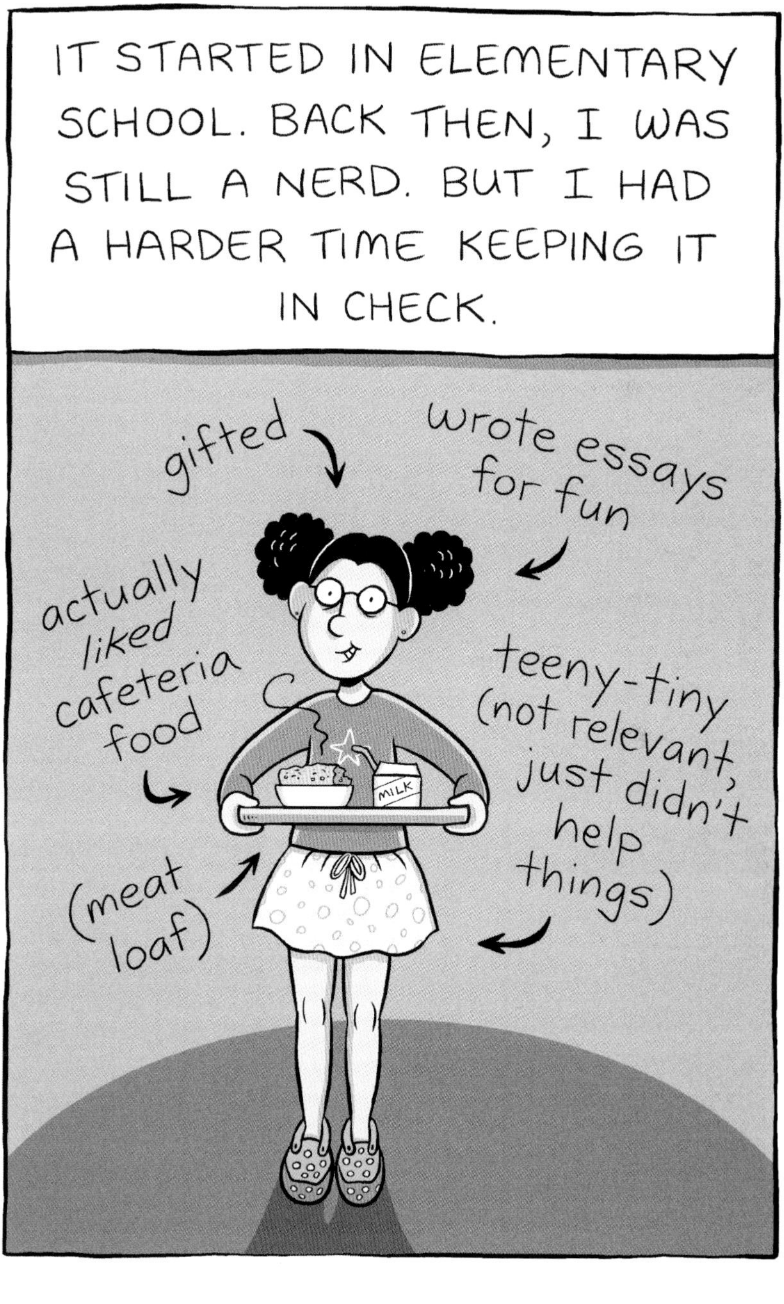

IT STARTED IN ELEMENTARY SCHOOL. BACK THEN, I WAS STILL A NERD. BUT I HAD A HARDER TIME KEEPING IT IN CHECK.
gifted
wrote essays for fun
actually liked cafeteria food
(meat loaf)
teeny-tiny (not relevant, just didn't help things)
MILK

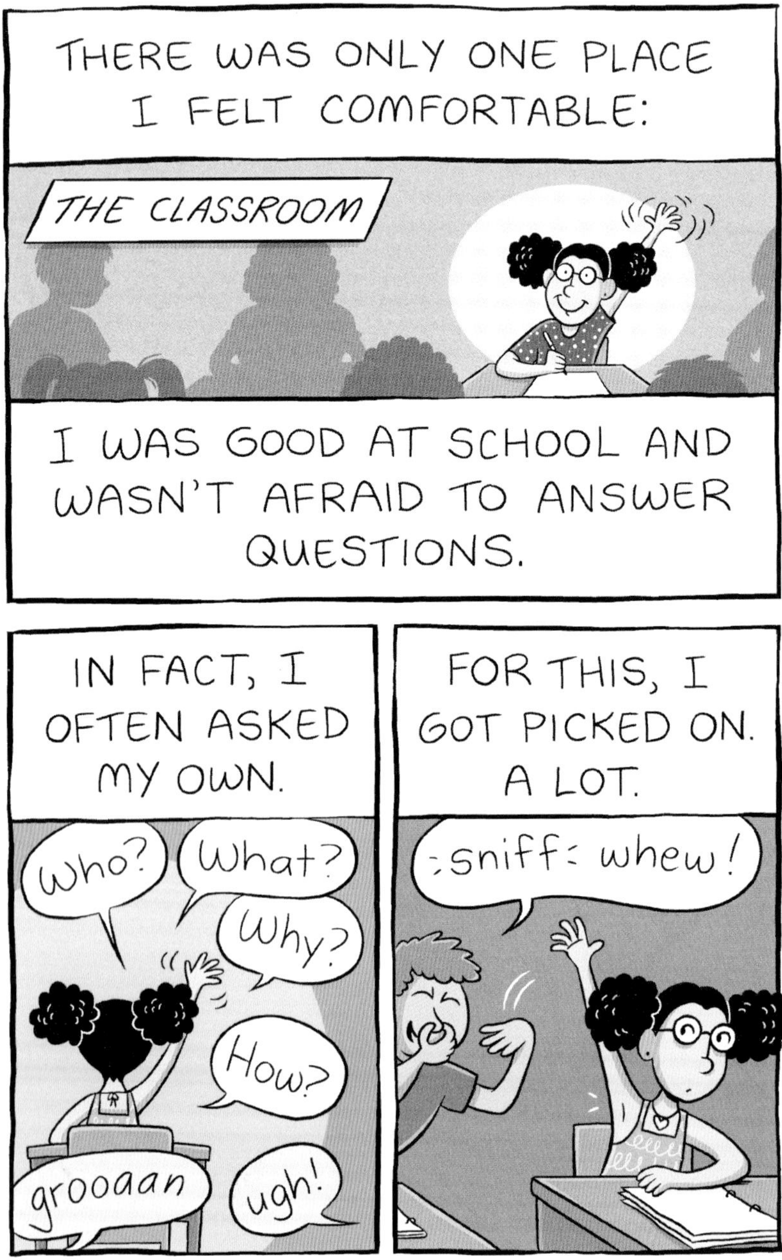
THERE WAS ONLY ONE PLACE I FELT COMFORTABLE:
THE CLASSROOM
I WAS GOOD AT SCHOOL AND WASN'T AFRAID TO ANSWER QUESTIONS.
IN FACT, I OFTEN ASKED MY OWN.
Who?
What?
Why?
How?
grooaan
ugh!
FOR THIS, I GOT PICKED ON. A LOT.
:sniff: whew!

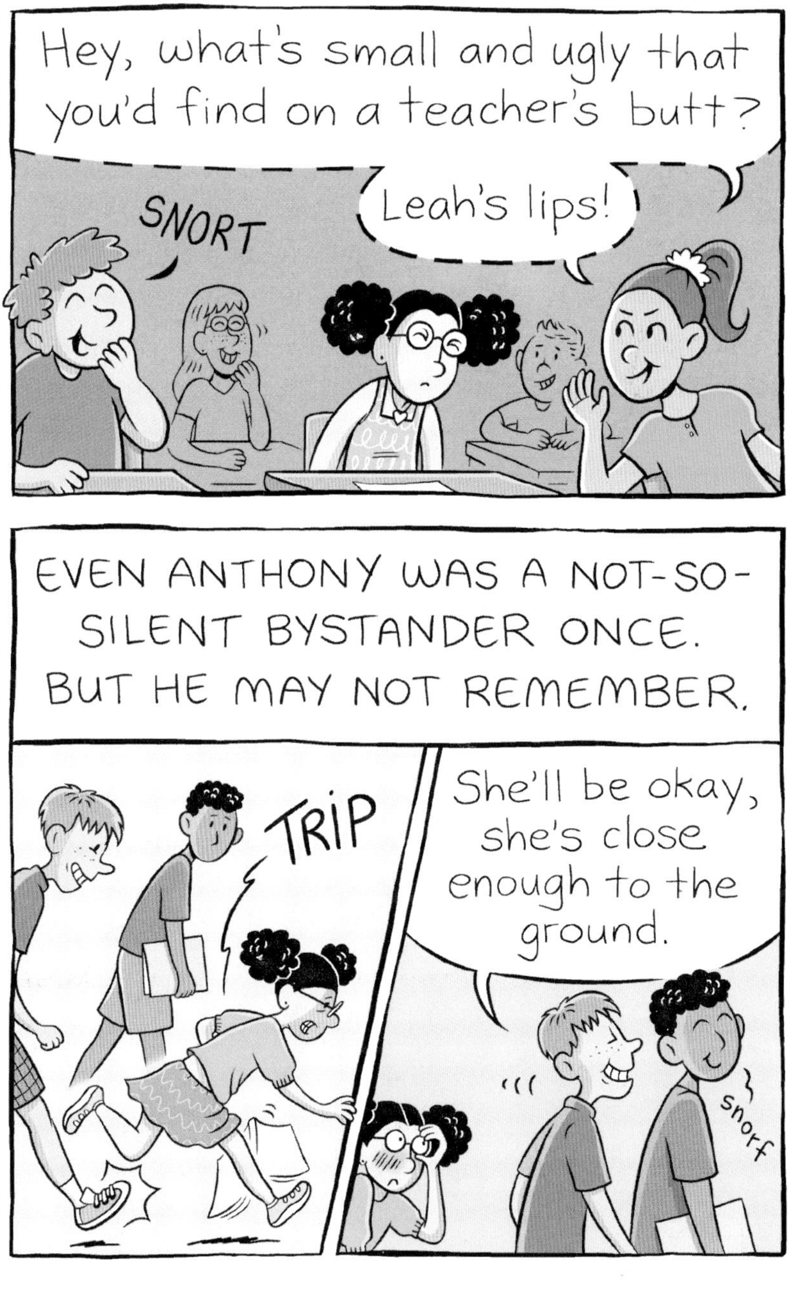
Hey, what's small and ugly that you'd find on a teacher's butt?
SNORT
Leah's lips!
EVEN ANTHONY WAS A NOT-SO-SILENT BYSTANDER ONCE. BUT HE MAY NOT REMEMBER.
TRIP
She'll be okay, she's close enough to the ground.
snorf

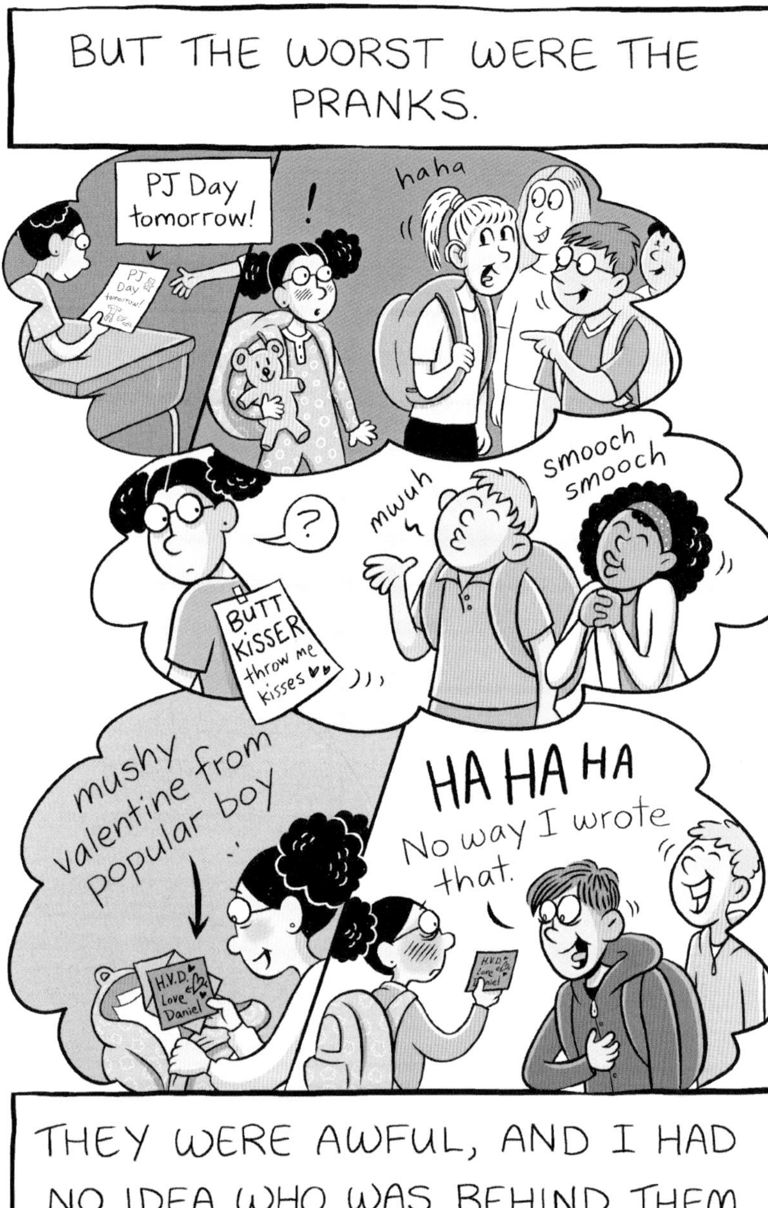
BUT THE WORST WERE THE PRANKS.
PJ Day tomorrow!
!
haha
?
BUTT KISSER throw me kisses
mwuh
smooch smooch
mushy valentine from popular boy
H.V.D. Love Daniel
HA HA HA
No way I wrote that.
THEY WERE AWFUL, AND I HAD NO IDEA WHO WAS BEHIND THEM.

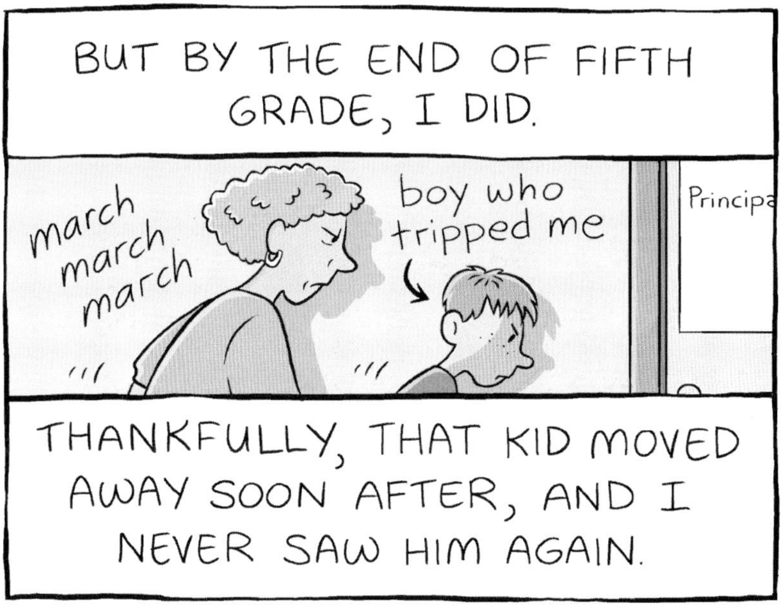
BUT BY THE END OF FIFTH GRADE, I DID.
march march march
boy who tripped me
Principa
THANKFULLY, THAT KID MOVED AWAY SOON AFTER, AND I NEVER SAW HIM AGAIN.

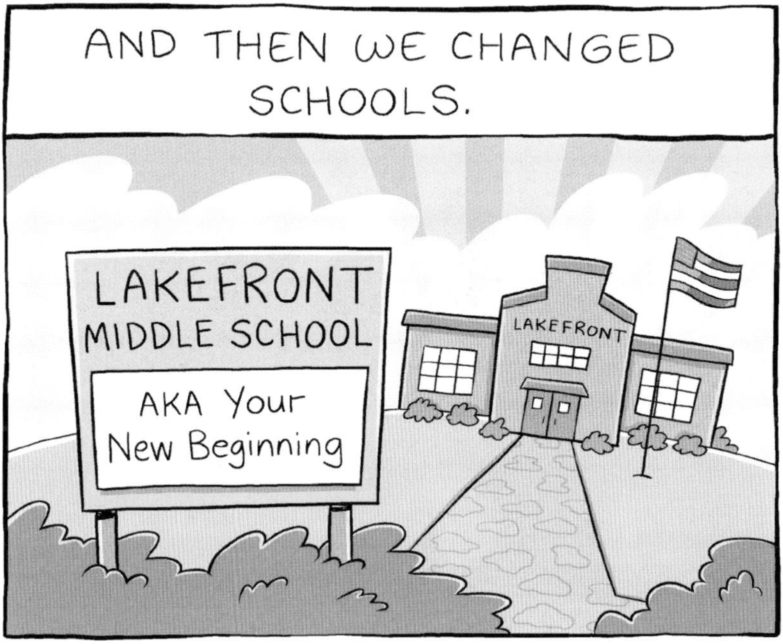
AND THEN WE CHANGED SCHOOLS.
LAKEFRONT MIDDLE SCHOOL
AKA Your New Beginning
LAKEFRONT

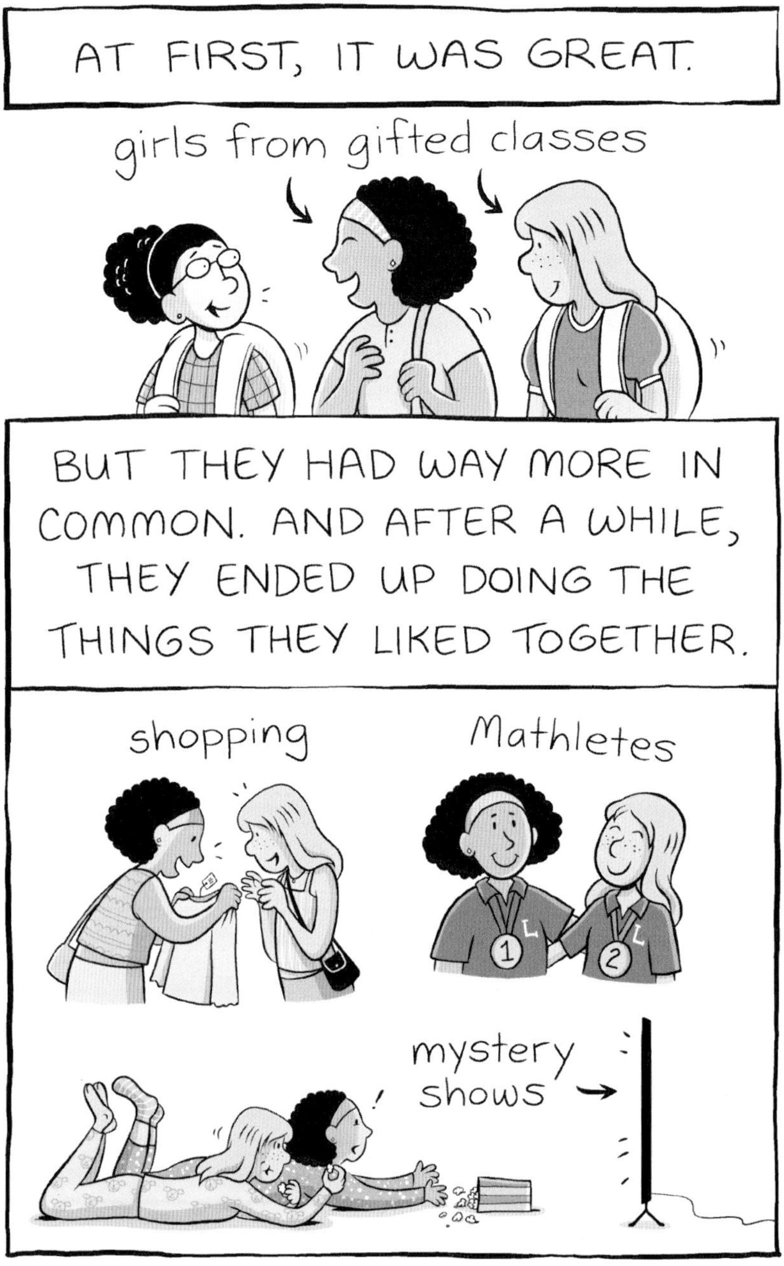
AT FIRST, IT WAS GREAT.
girls from gifted classes
BUT THEY HAD WAY MORE IN COMMON. AND AFTER A WHILE, THEY ENDED UP DOING THE THINGS THEY LIKED TOGETHER.
shopping
Mathletes
1
2
mystery shows

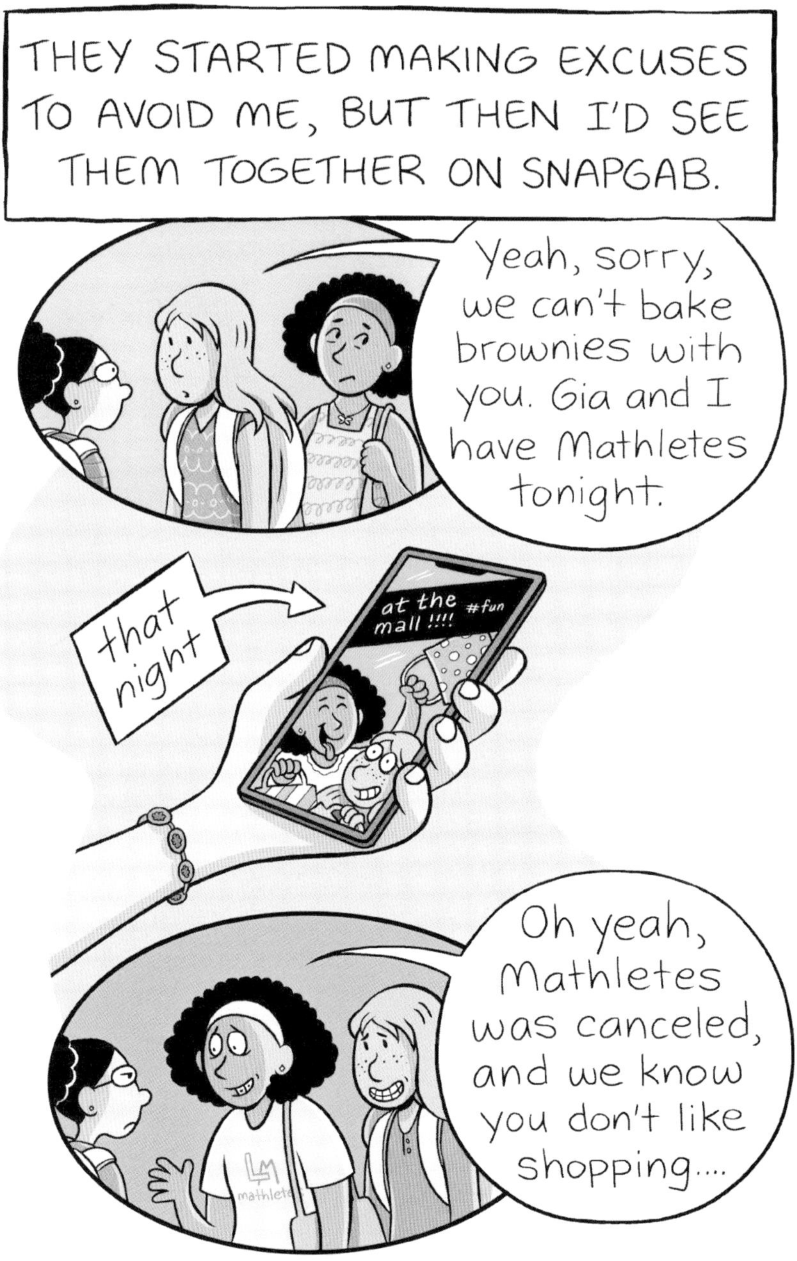
THEY STARTED MAKING EXCUSES TO AVOID ME, BUT THEN I'D SEE THEM TOGETHER ON SNAPGAB.
Yeah, sorry, we can't bake brownies with you. Gia and I have Mathletes tonight.
that night
at the mall !!!! #fun
Oh yeah, Mathletes was canceled, and we know you don't like shopping....
mathletes

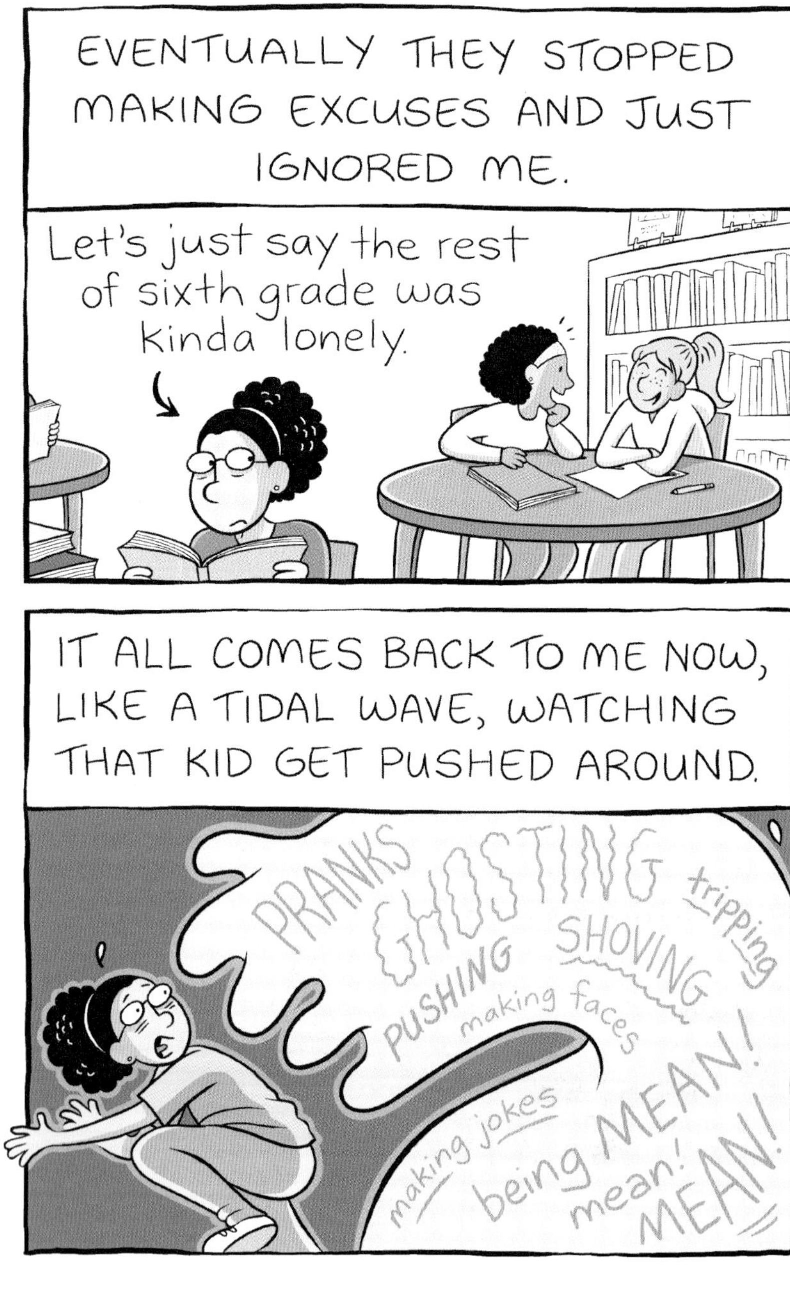
EVENTUALLY THEY STOPPED MAKING EXCUSES AND JUST IGNORED ME.
Let's just say the rest of sixth grade was kinda lonely.
IT ALL COMES BACK TO ME NOW, LIKE A TIDAL WAVE, WATCHING THAT KID GET PUSHED AROUND.
PRANKS
GHOSTING
tripping
SHOVING
PUSHING
making faces
making jokes
being MEAN!
mean!
MEAN!

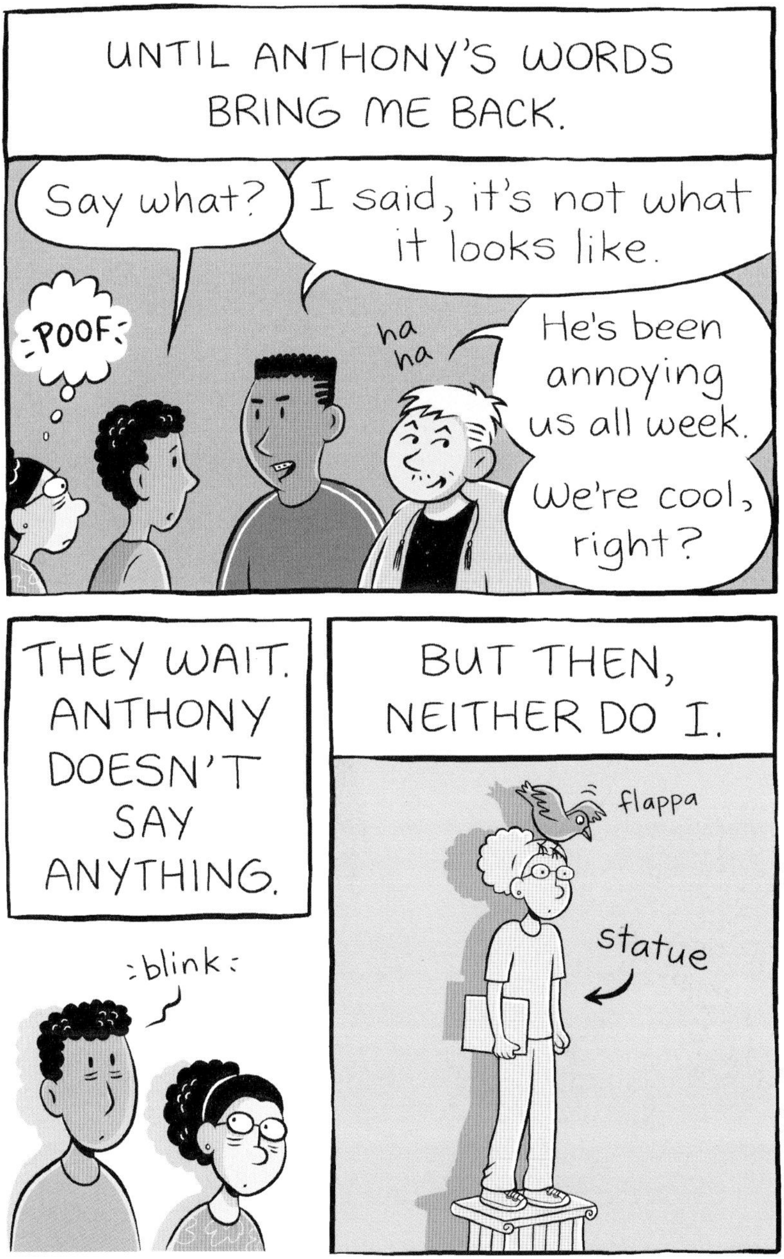
UNTIL ANTHONY'S WORDS BRING ME BACK.
Say what?
I said, it's not what it looks like.
POOF
ha ha
He's been annoying us all week.
We're cool, right?
THEY WAIT. ANTHONY DOESN'T SAY ANYTHING.
blink
BUT THEN, NEITHER DO I.
flappa
statue

ANTHONY

Ohhhh man. What do I do?

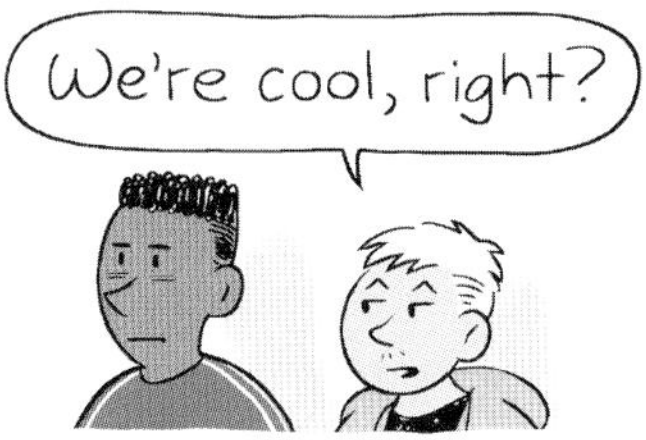
We're cool, right?

I hate to say it, but I'm not all that surprised by these dudes. They're always looking to pump themselves up by making others feel like, well . . .

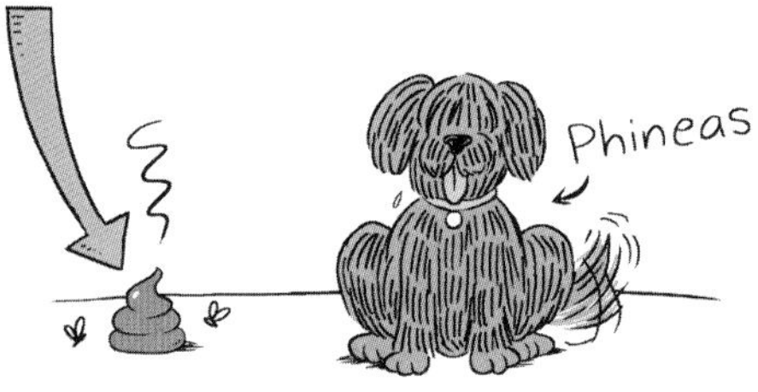
Phineas

I'm familiar with their technique. Before I knew better, I acted like that, too. But I wised up. Partly 'cause I knew it was wrong and partly 'cause my parents caught on.

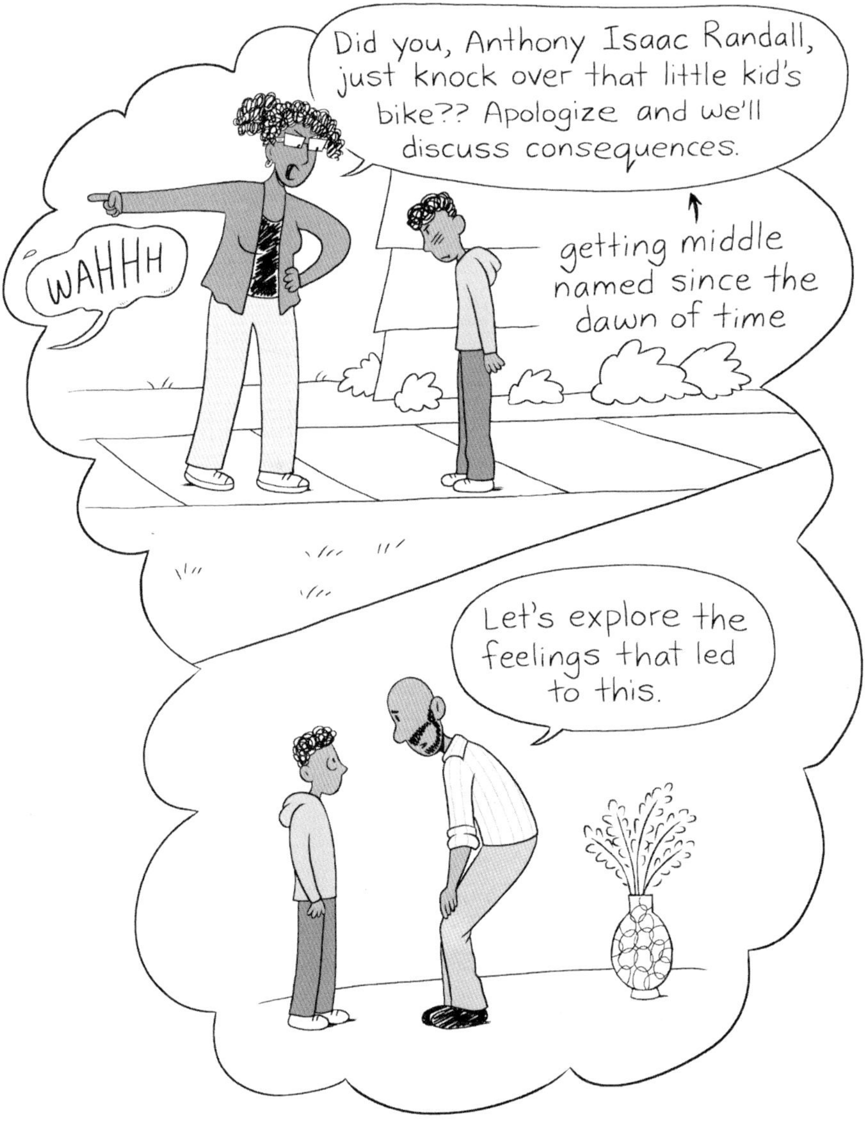
Did you, Anthony Isaac Randall, just knock over that little kid's bike?? Apologize and we'll discuss consequences.
WAHHH
getting middle named since the dawn of time
Let's explore the feelings that led to this.

PS My pop's reaction got more results.

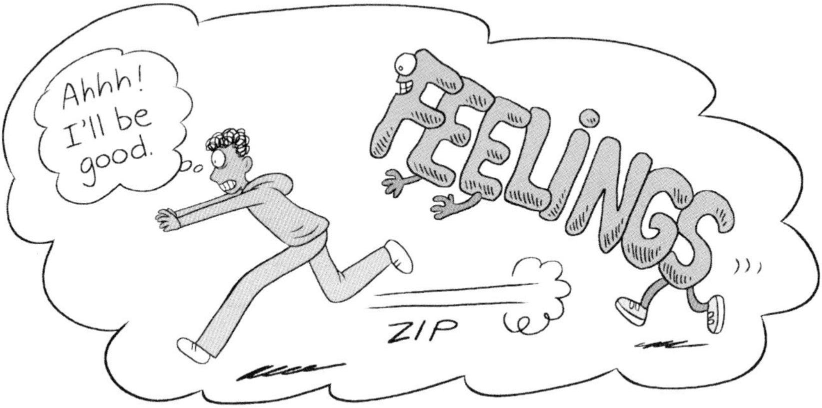
Ahhh! I'll be good.
FEELINGS
ZIP

Anyway, Lucas and Eddie can be total jerks during practice (especially together). They don't do outright physical stuff, but they'll rip on teammates when they make dumb mistakes or force you to pass the ball to them when you know it'll be intercepted. Stuff like that.

But I've never seen them throw someone against a locker. Especially someone smaller.

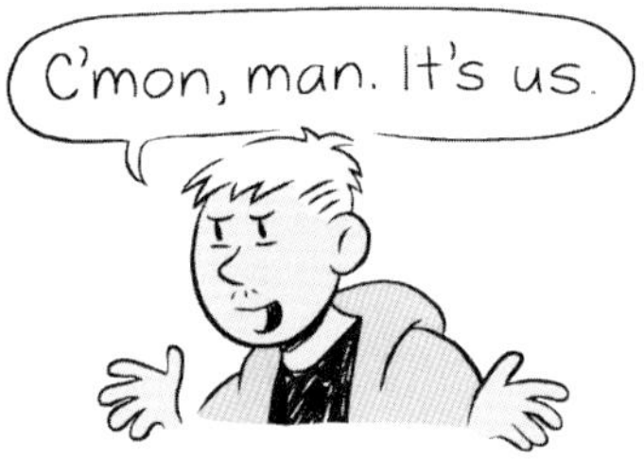
C'mon, man. It's us.

What can I do? They're eighth graders. Even if they're jerks, they're a big deal on the team. If I say anything, they'll make my life miserable. **And** I'll be known as a snitch. Fate worse than death.

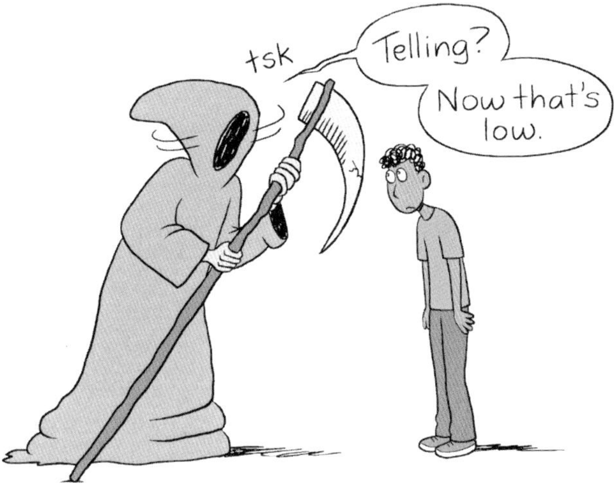
tsk
Telling?
Now that's low.

I glance at Leah, who looks like she just saw Death herself. It also looks like she's leaving the decision up to me.

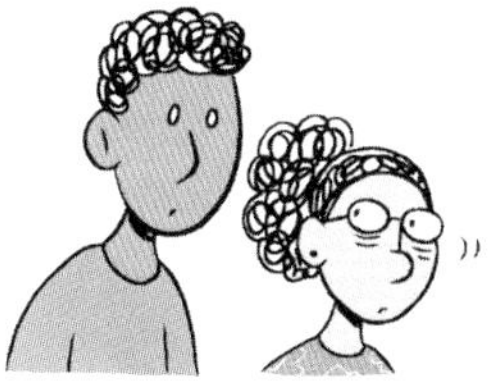

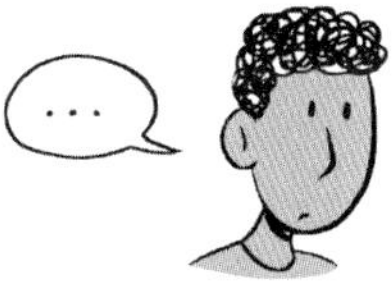
...

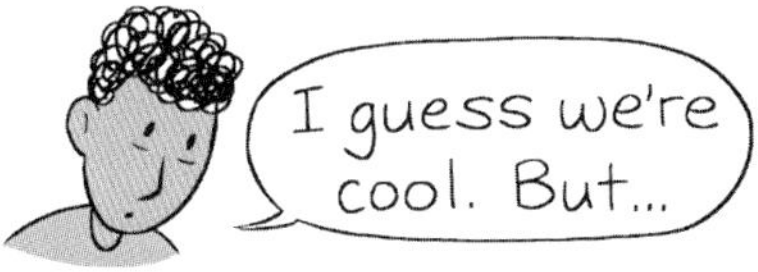
I guess we're cool. But...

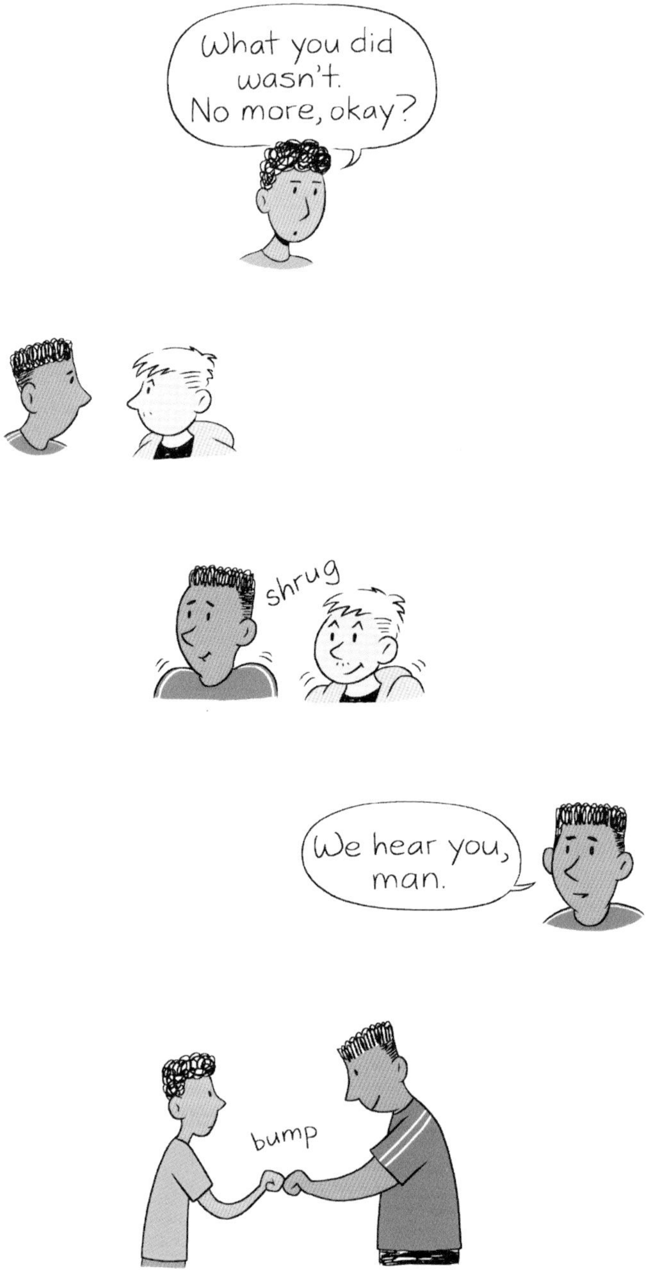
What you did wasn't. No more, okay?
shrug
We hear you, man.
bump

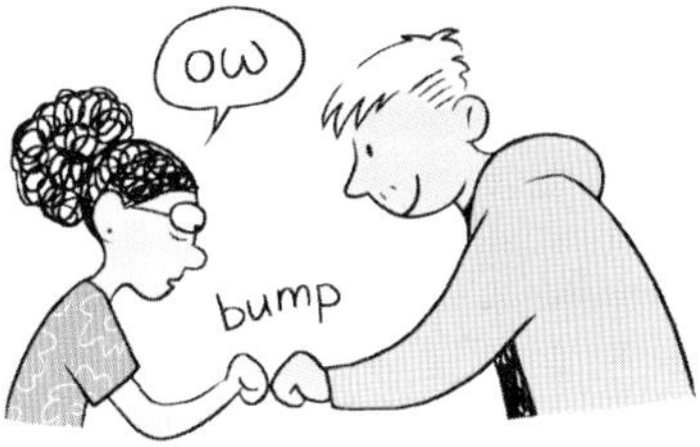
OW
bump

Then, just as the late bell rings, they take off down the hall, joking and play-punching each other.

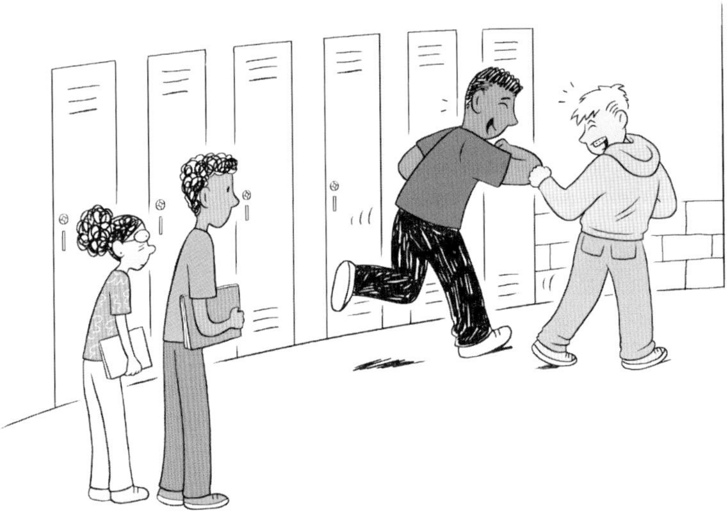

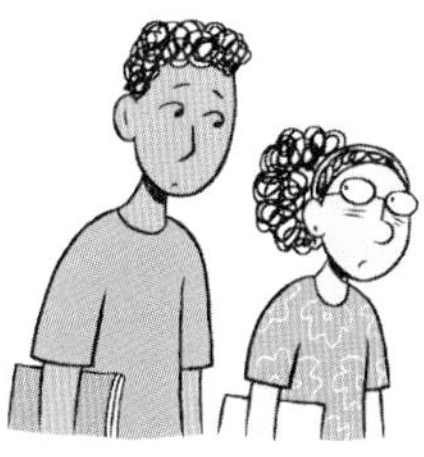

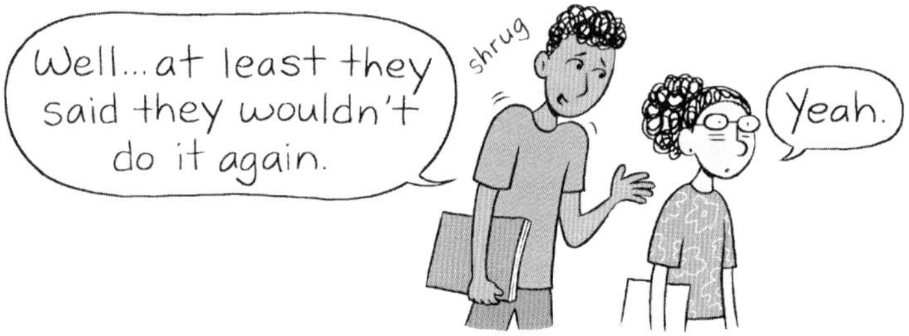
Well...at least they said they wouldn't do it again.
shrug
Yeah.

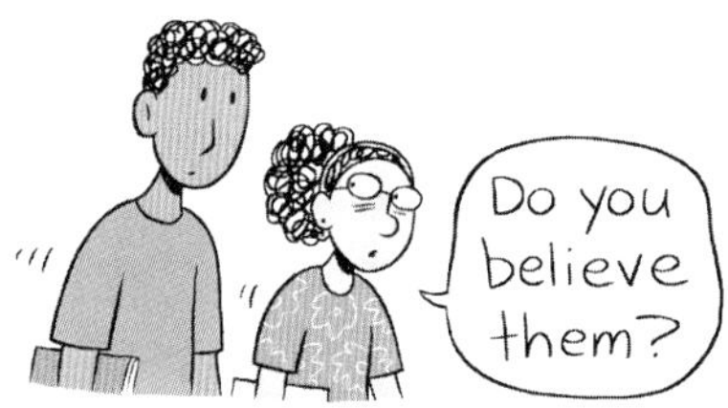
Do you believe them?

I don't know how to answer, so I don't.

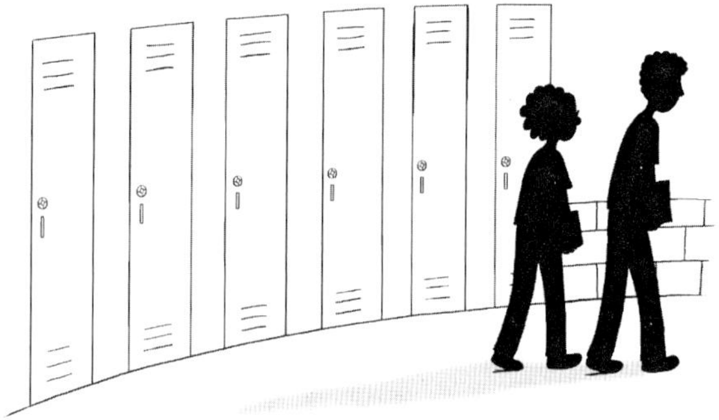

Which might be an answer in itself.

Leah

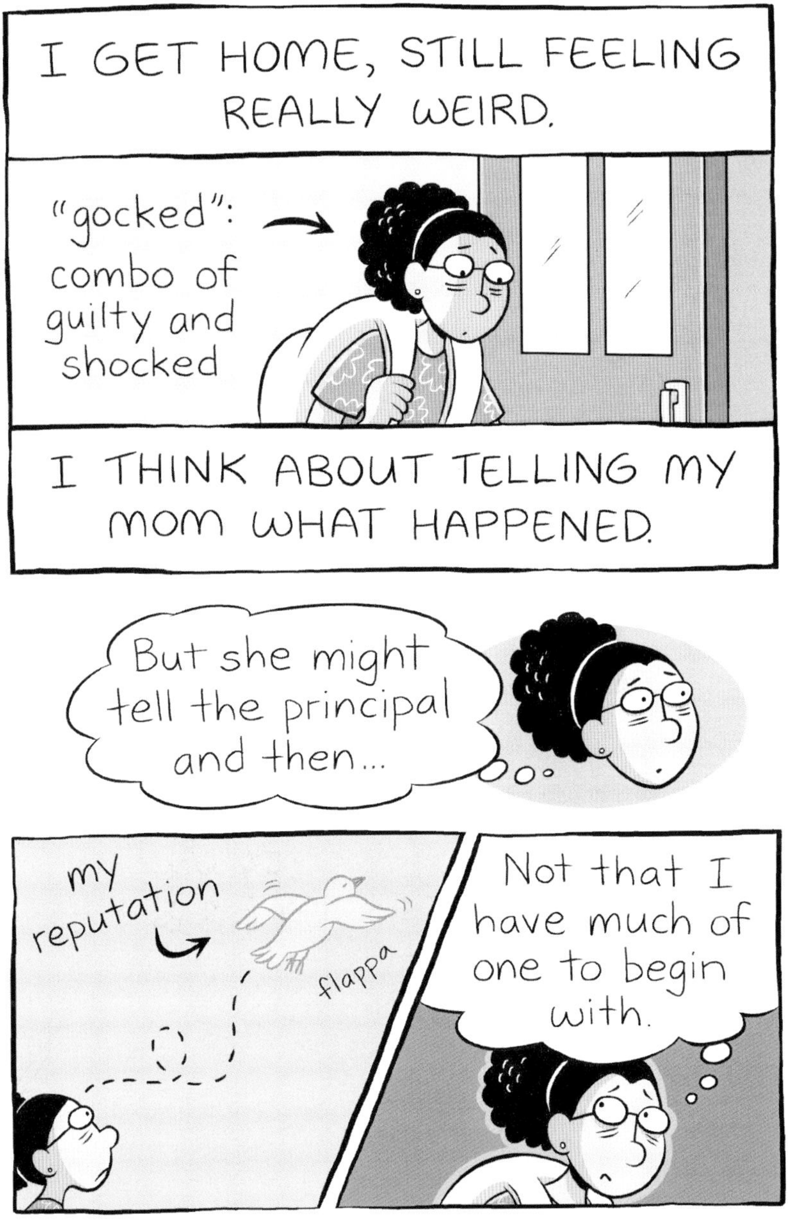

I GET HOME, STILL FEELING REALLY WEIRD.
"gocked": combo of guilty and shocked
I THINK ABOUT TELLING MY MOM WHAT HAPPENED.
But she might tell the principal and then...
my reputation
flappa
Not that I have much of one to begin with.

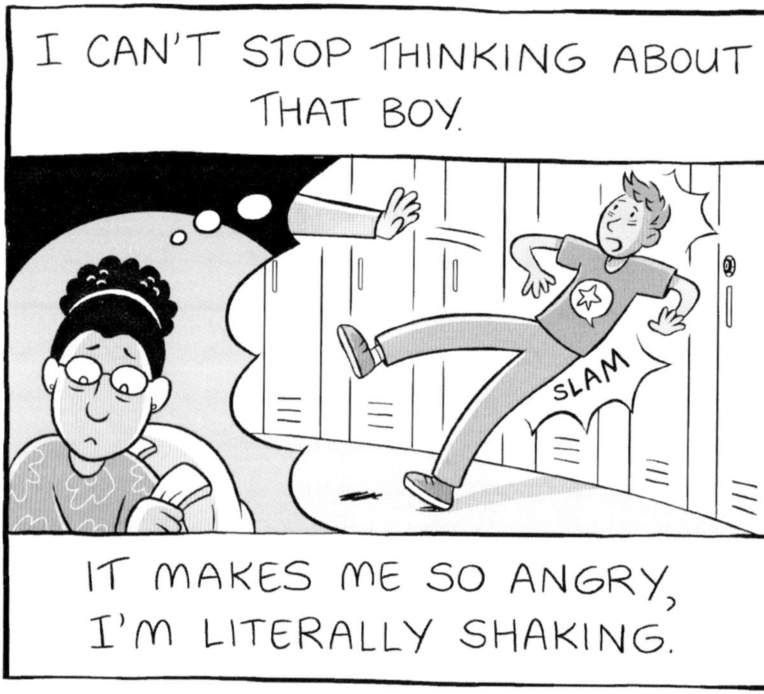
I CAN'T STOP THINKING ABOUT THAT BOY.
SLAM
IT MAKES ME SO ANGRY, I'M LITERALLY SHAKING.

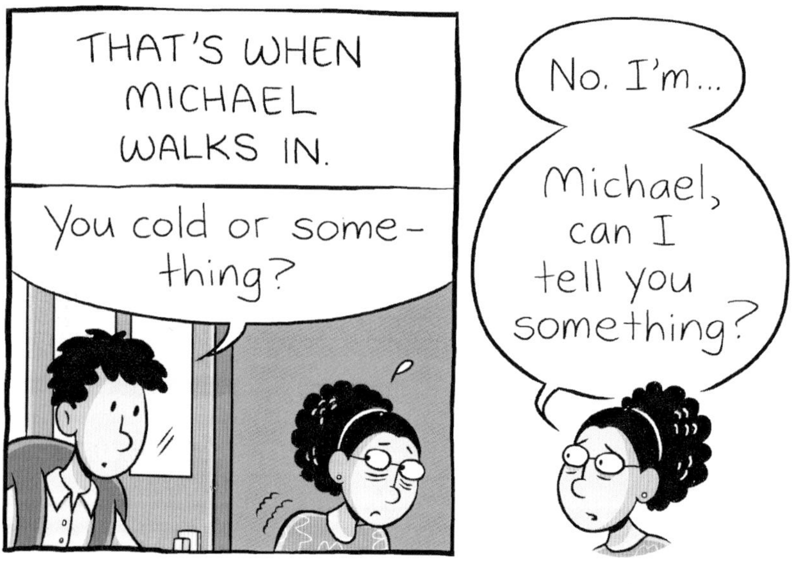
THAT'S WHEN MICHAEL WALKS IN.
You cold or some-thing?
No. I'm...
Michael, can I tell you something?

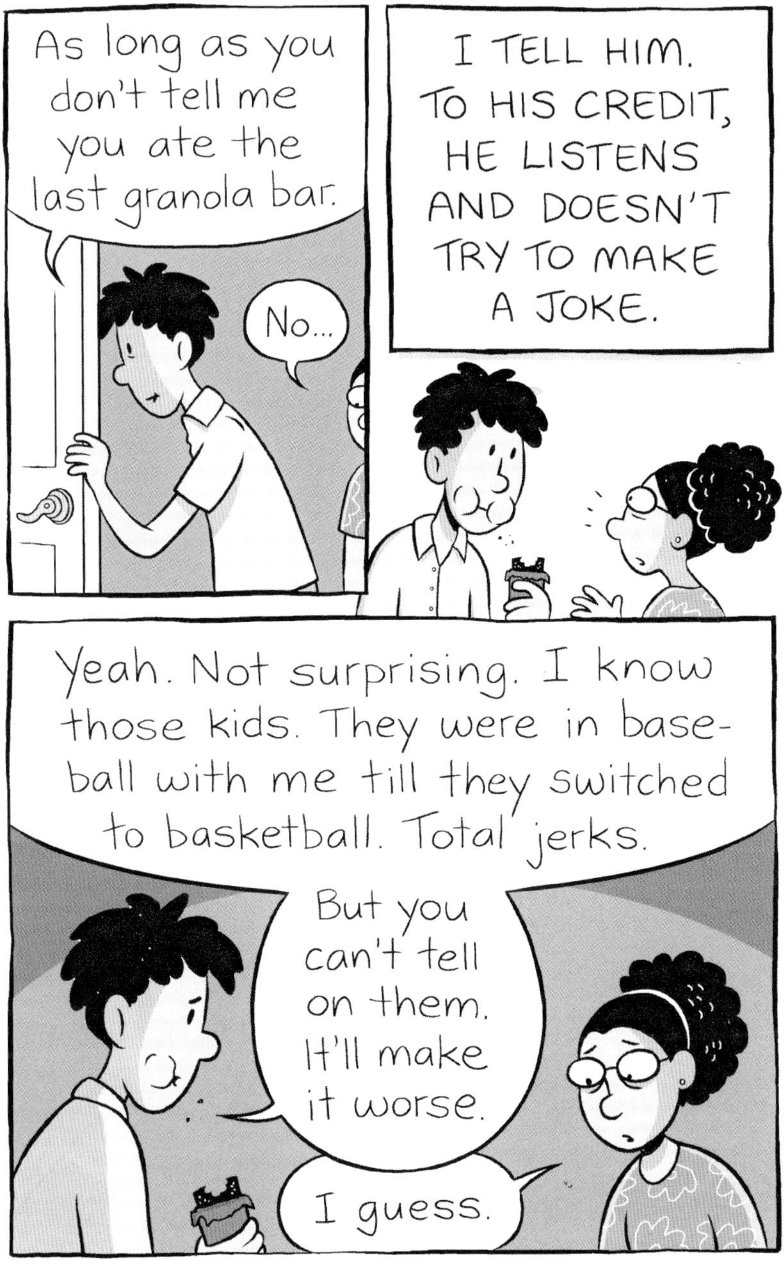
As long as you don't tell me you ate the last granola bar.
No...
I TELL HIM. TO HIS CREDIT, HE LISTENS AND DOESN'T TRY TO MAKE A JOKE.
Yeah. Not surprising. I know those kids. They were in baseball with me till they switched to basketball. Total jerks.
But you can't tell on them. It'll make it worse.
I guess.

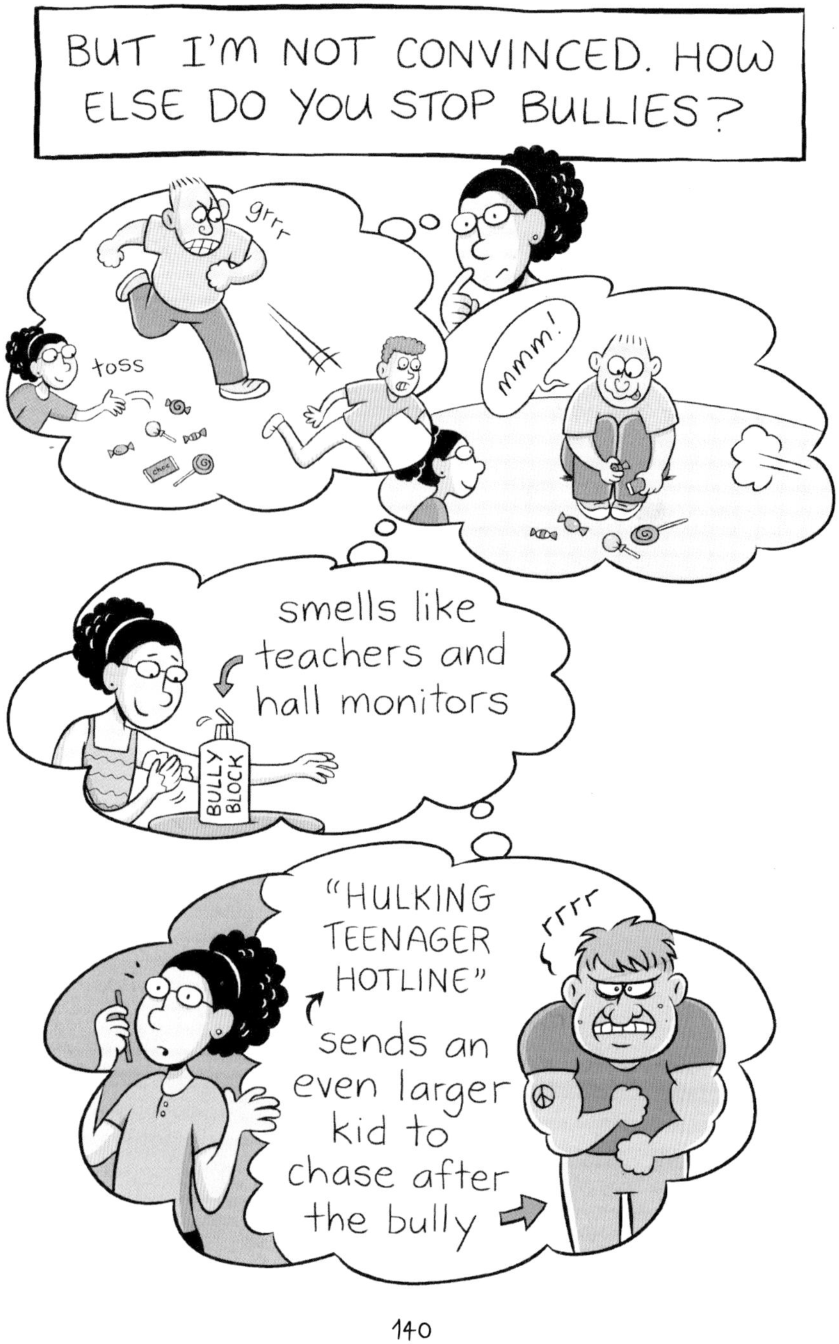
BUT I'M NOT CONVINCED. HOW ELSE DO YOU STOP BULLIES?
grrr
toss
choc
mmm!
smells like teachers and hall monitors
BULLY BLOCK
"HULKING TEENAGER HOTLINE"
sends an even larger kid to chase after the bully
rrrr

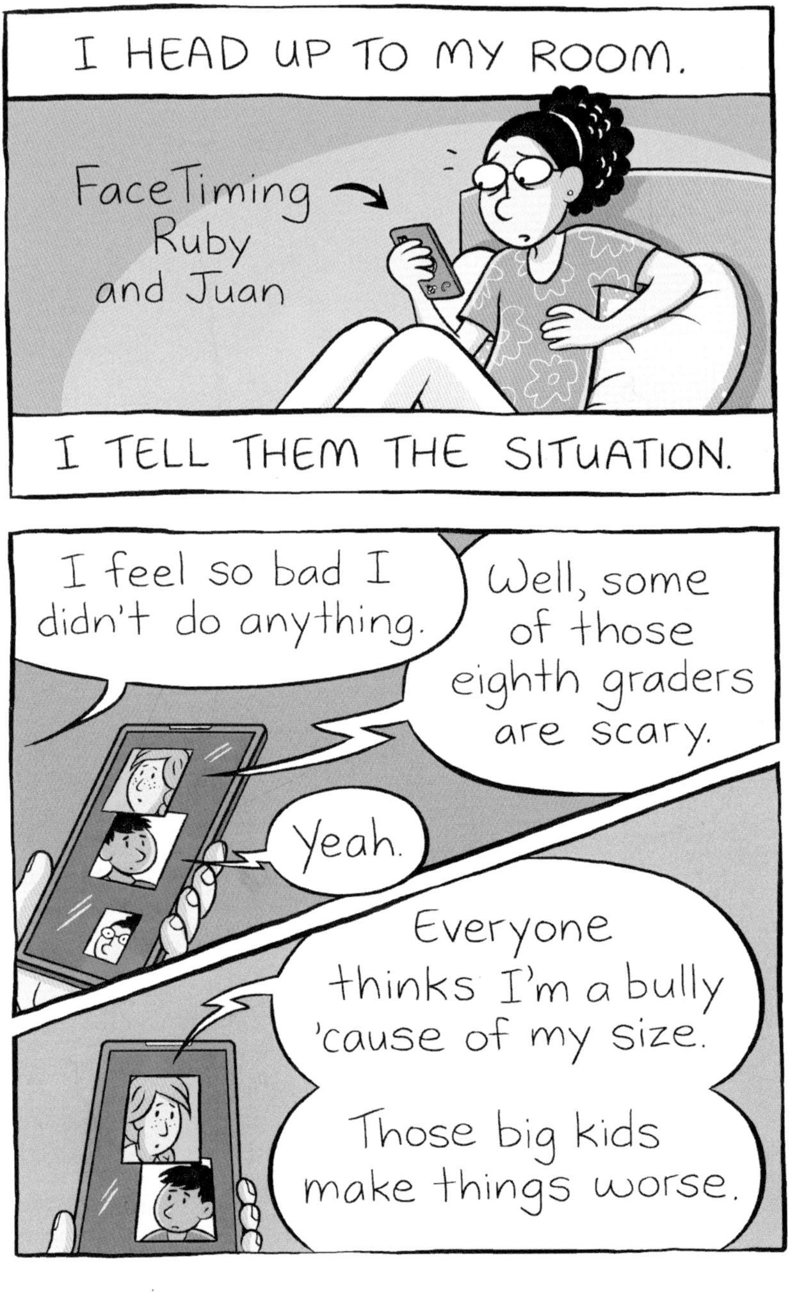
I HEAD UP TO MY ROOM.
FaceTiming Ruby and Juan
I TELL THEM THE SITUATION.
I feel so bad I didn't do anything.
Well, some of those eighth graders are scary.
Yeah.
Everyone thinks I'm a bully 'cause of my size.
Those big kids make things worse.

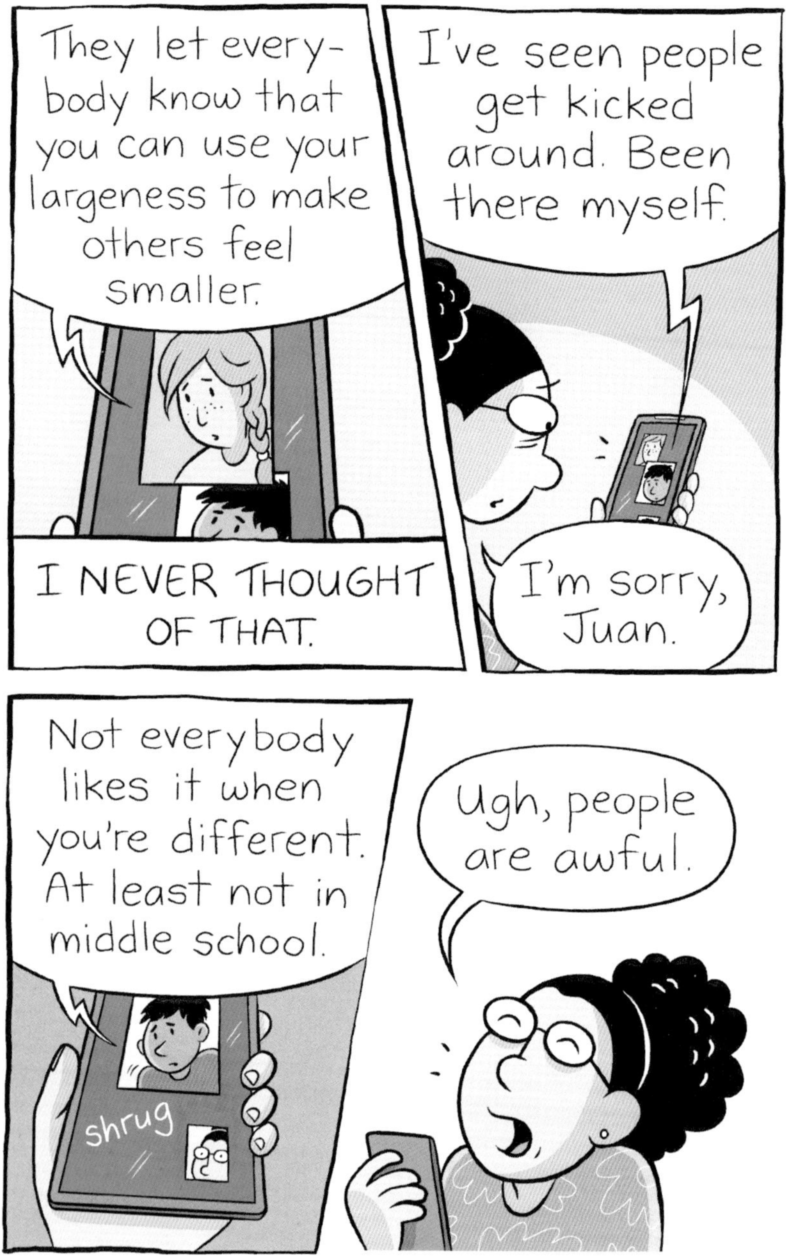
They let everybody know that you can use your largeness to make others feel smaller.
I NEVER THOUGHT OF THAT.
I've seen people get kicked around. Been there myself.
I'm sorry, Juan.
Not everybody likes it when you're different. At least not in middle school.
shrug
Ugh, people are awful.

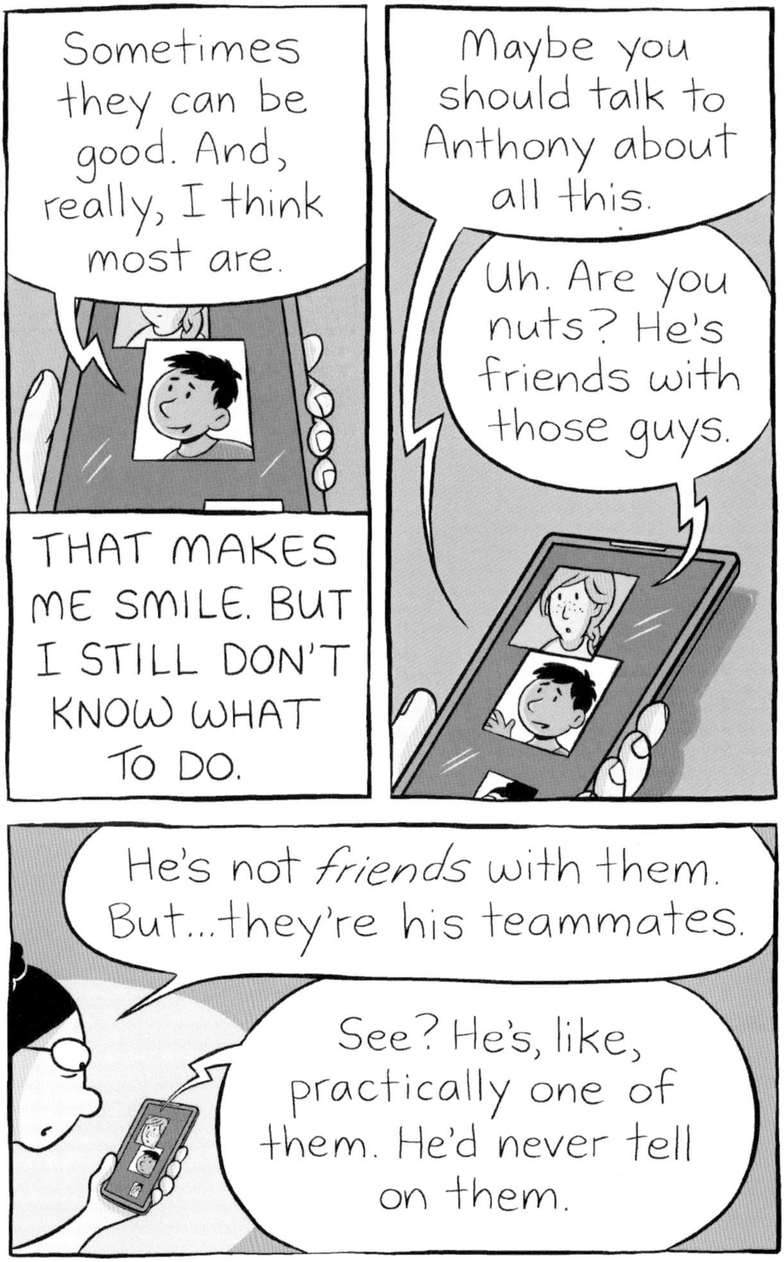
Sometimes they can be good. And, really, I think most are.
THAT MAKES ME SMILE. BUT I STILL DON'T KNOW WHAT TO DO.
Maybe you should talk to Anthony about all this.
Uh. Are you nuts? He's friends with those guys.
He's not *friends* with them. But...they're his teammates.
See? He's, like, practically one of them. He'd never tell on them.

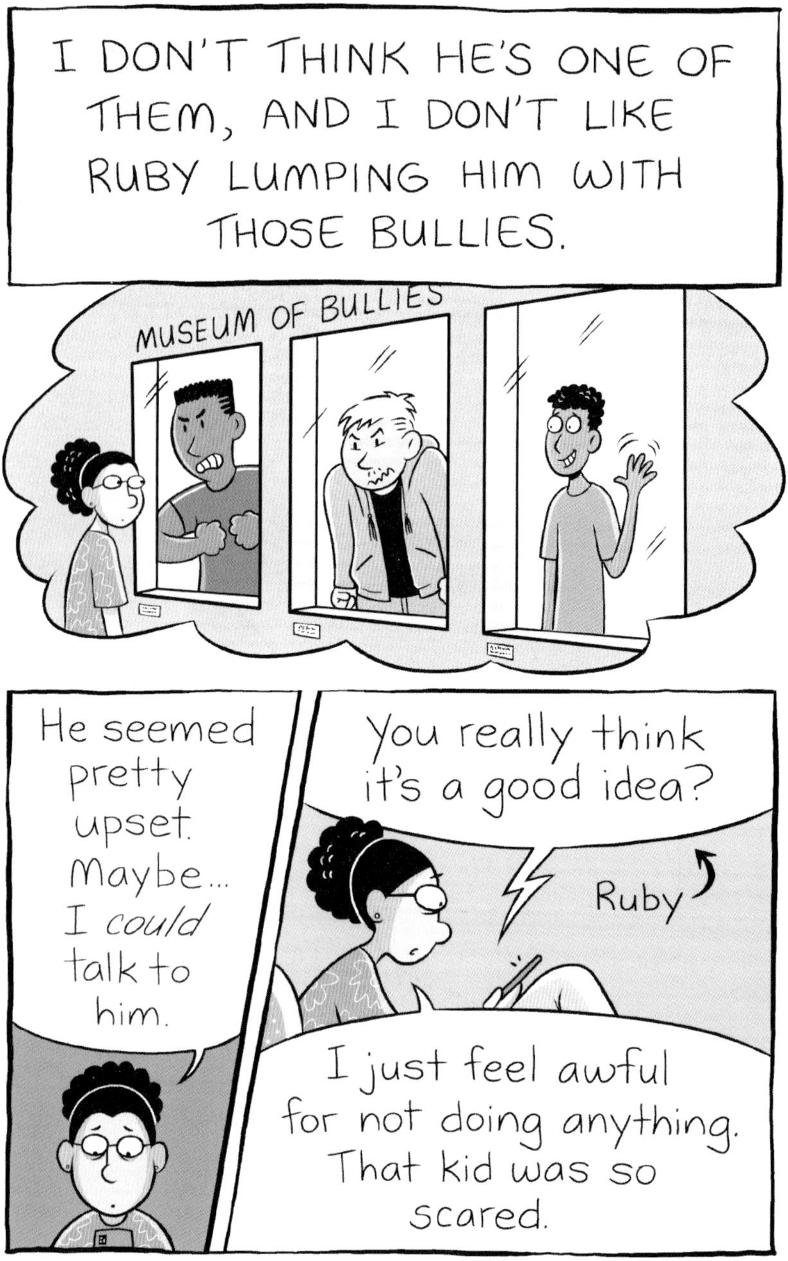
I DON'T THINK HE'S ONE OF THEM, AND I DON'T LIKE RUBY LUMPING HIM WITH THOSE BULLIES.
MUSEUM OF BULLIES
He seemed pretty upset. Maybe... I *could* talk to him.
You really think it's a good idea?
Ruby
I just feel awful for not doing anything. That kid was so scared.

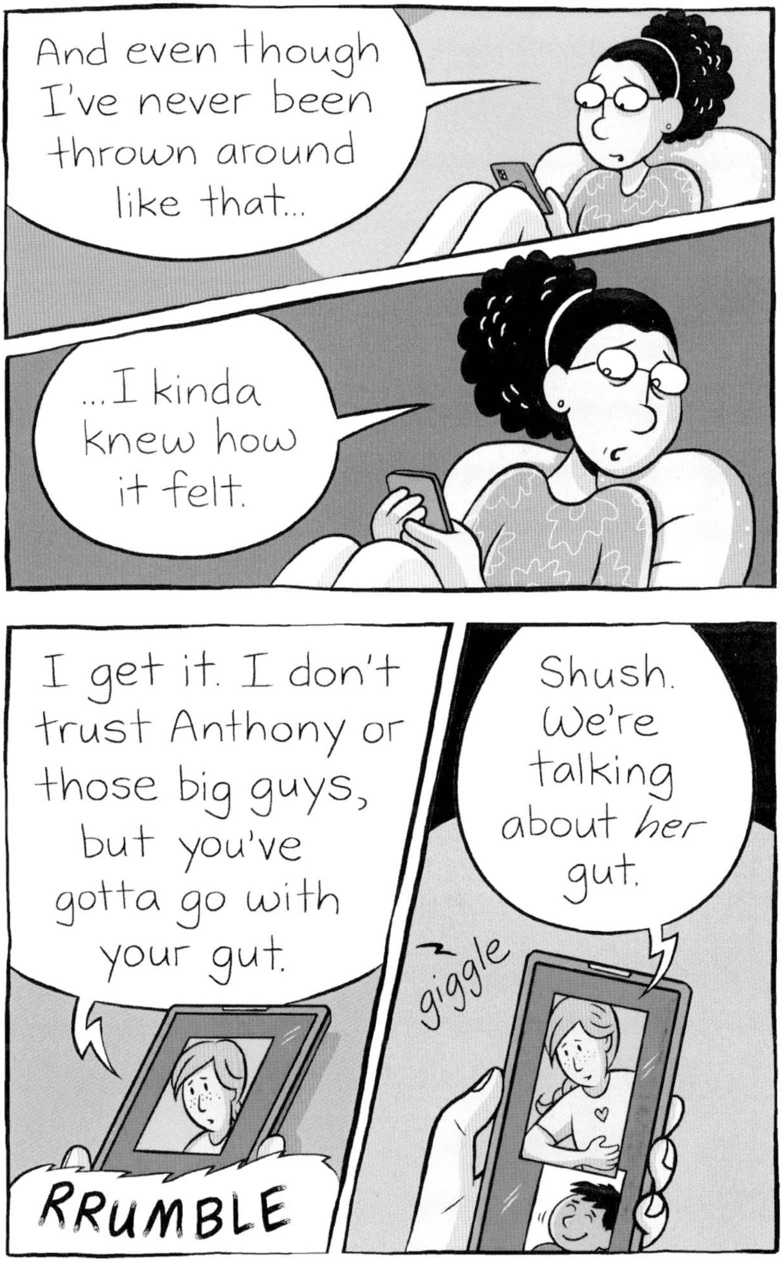
And even though I've never been thrown around like that...
...I kinda knew how it felt.
I get it. I don't trust Anthony or those big guys, but you've gotta go with your gut.
RRUMBLE
Shush. We're talking about *her* gut.
giggle

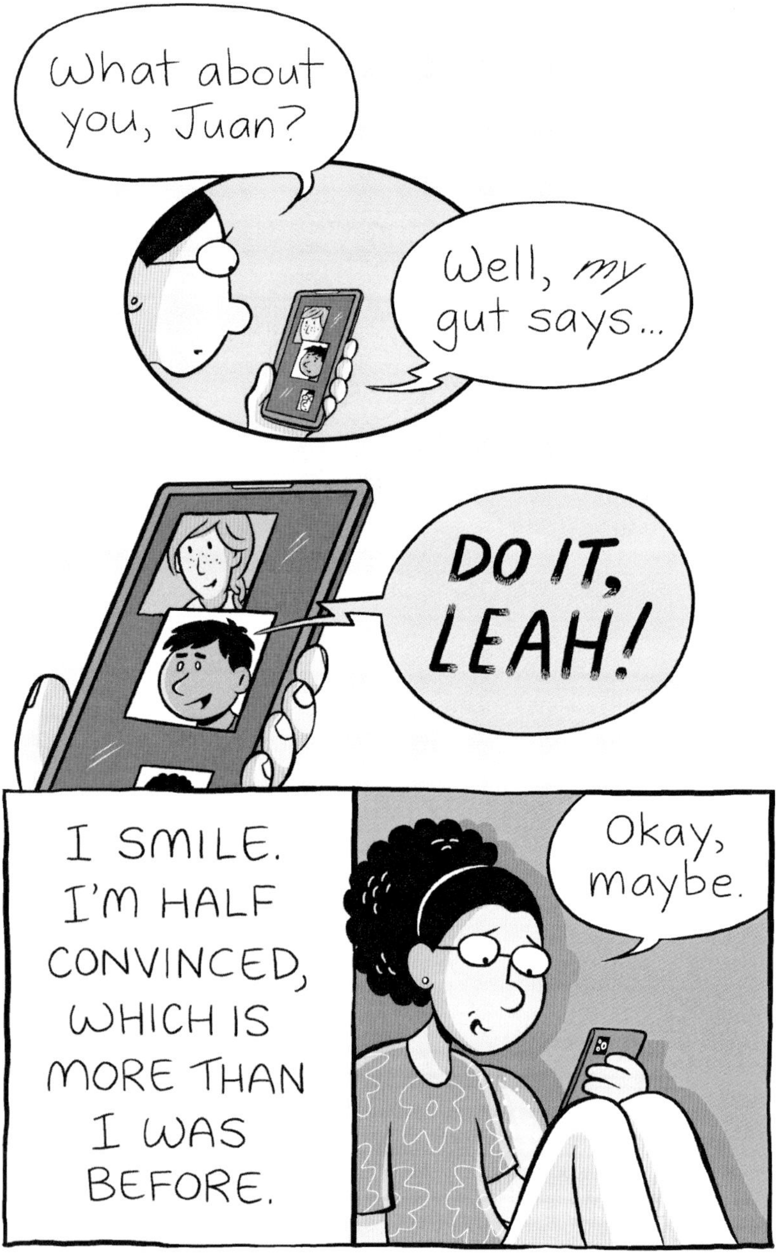

What about you, Juan?
Well, *my* gut says...
DO IT, LEAH!
I SMILE. I'M HALF CONVINCED, WHICH IS MORE THAN I WAS BEFORE.
Okay, maybe.

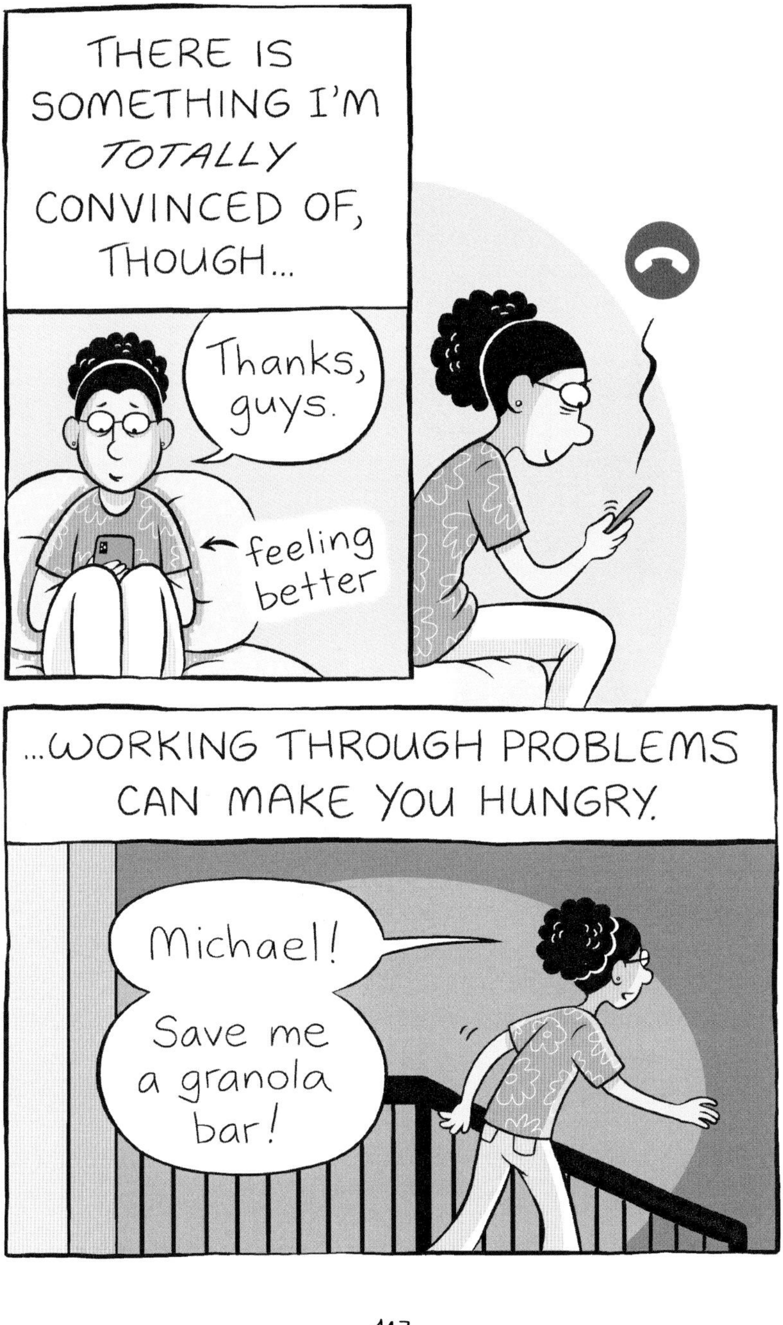
THERE IS SOMETHING I'M *TOTALLY* CONVINCED OF, THOUGH...
Thanks, guys.
feeling better
...WORKING THROUGH PROBLEMS CAN MAKE YOU HUNGRY.
Michael!
Save me a granola bar!

ANTHONY

Wednesday. I meet Leah for our next session.

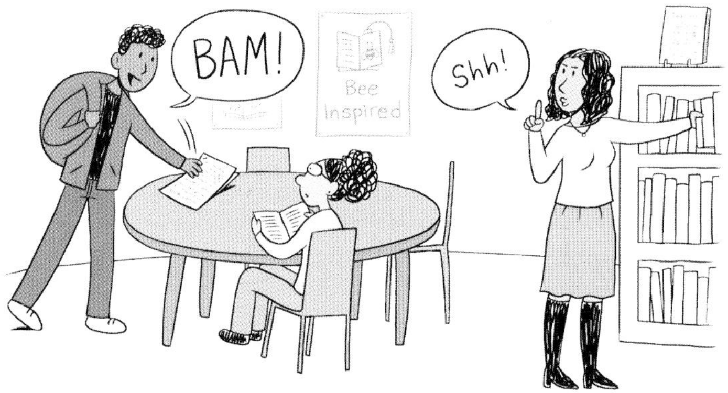
BAM!
Bee Inspired
Shh!

Leah, confused, picks up the paper. She scans it (with that superserious face of hers). Then she smiles.

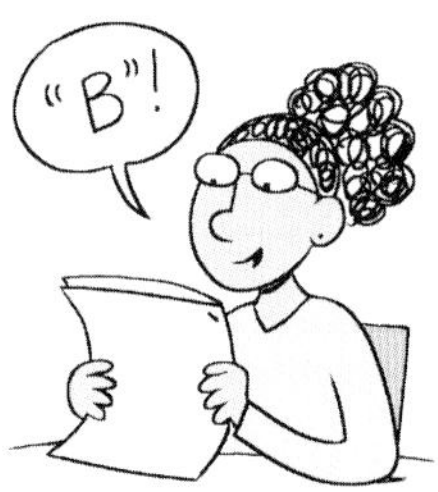
"B"!

Right? Marie Maynard Daly would be proud. Nope, she'd be "rhapsodic." See? I pay attention to the Winn Word of the Week.

Leah laughs. But it's not really a happy laugh. She must be thinking about what happened on Monday.

I make the mistake of asking:

You okay?

Yeah. No. I...

I was thinking about what happened on Monday and wondering...

She literally takes a deep breath.

Should We Say Something To Mrs. Langer?

principal

I don't even hesitate.

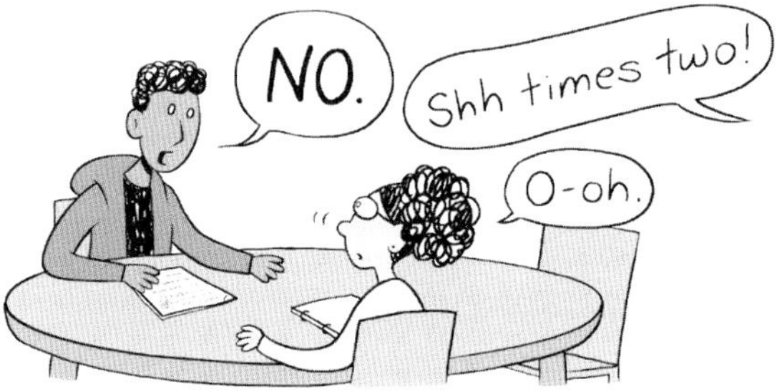
NO.
Shh times two!
O-oh.

Her face turns so red, it looks like a tomato.

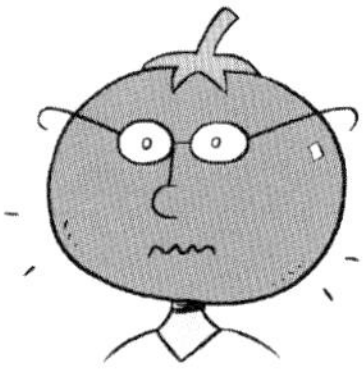

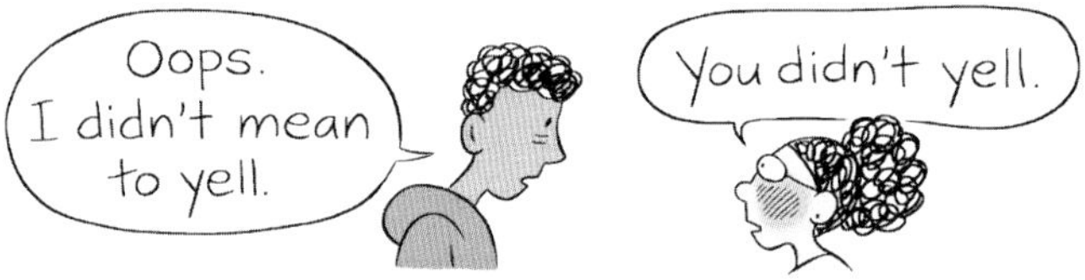
Oops.
I didn't mean to yell.
You didn't yell.

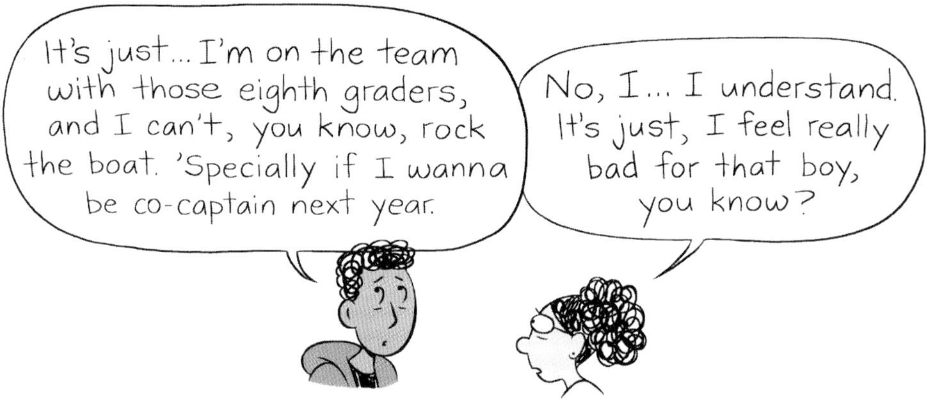
It's just... I'm on the team with those eighth graders, and I can't, you know, rock the boat. 'Specially if I wanna be co-captain next year.
No, I... I understand. It's just, I feel really bad for that boy, you know?

My mind instantly goes to a picked-on Leah in elementary school. I guess she can relate to this whole thing. The worst part is no one ever knew how nice she really is. I never knew. What I thought was butt-kissing was just her being smart and eager at school.

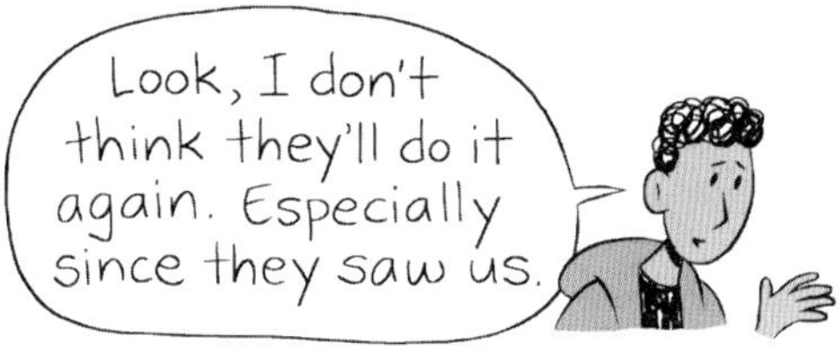
Look, I don't think they'll do it again. Especially since they saw us.

She looks kinda skeptical, but she doesn't say anything.

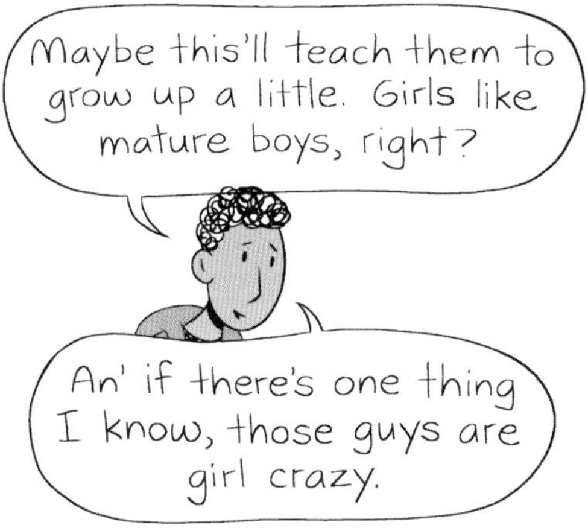
Maybe this'll teach them to grow up a little. Girls like mature boys, right?
An' if there's one thing I know, those guys are girl crazy.

Leah finally laughs for real.

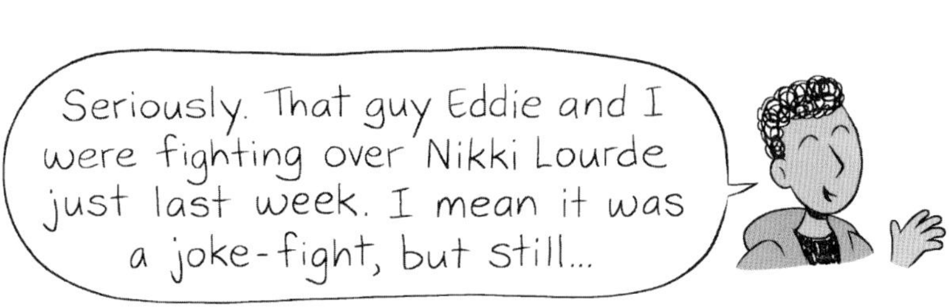
Seriously. That guy Eddie and I were fighting over Nikki Lourde just last week. I mean it was a joke-fight, but still...

My words trail off.

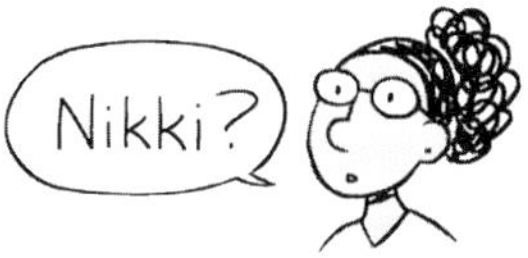
Nikki?

Oops.

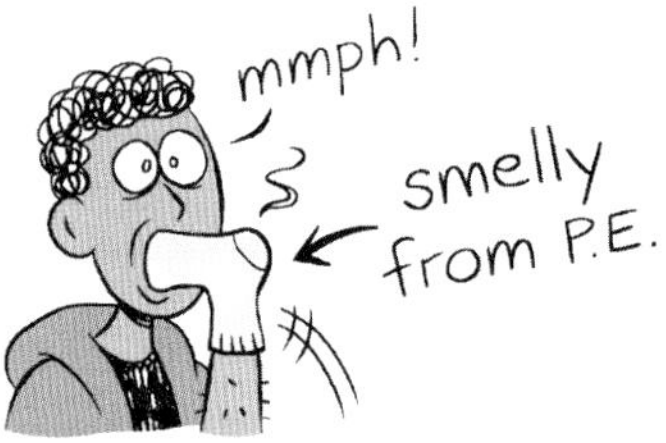
mmph!
smelly from P.E.

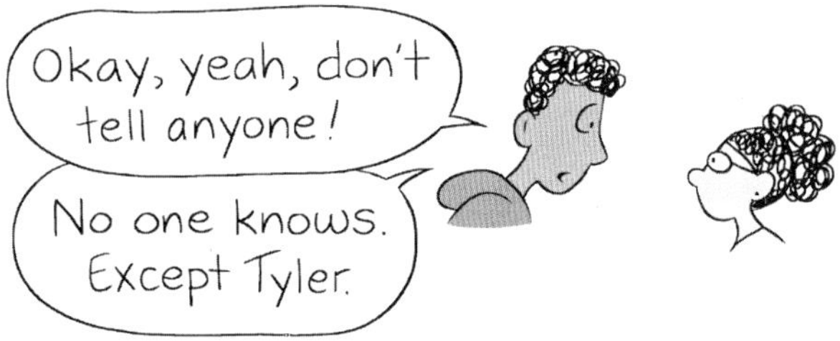
Okay, yeah, don't tell anyone!
No one knows. Except Tyler.

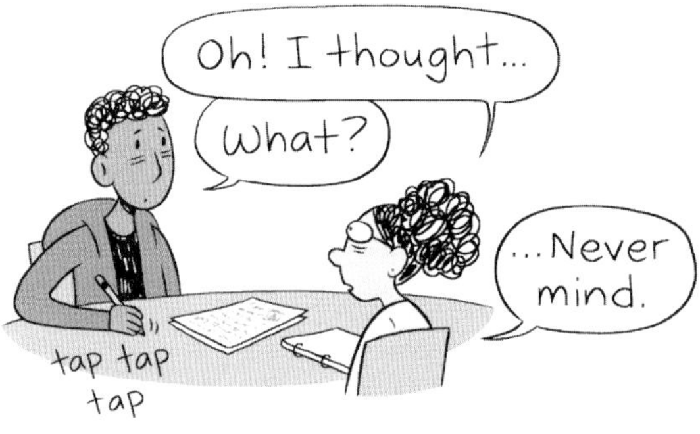
Oh! I thought...
What?
...Never mind.
tap tap tap

Me and my big mouth.

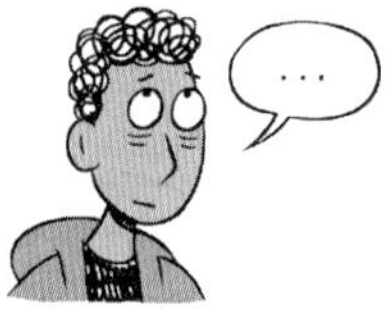
...

But maybe . . .

Maybe it's a good thing? It's a distraction from what happened on Monday. 'Cause I can't have Leah go telling on those guys, I can't. And, yeah, I do feel bad about standing there and doing nothing, but maybe I can make it up.

That's it. I'll be a friend. I'll . . . I'll share more. An' I'll work even harder to make her time with me worthwhile.

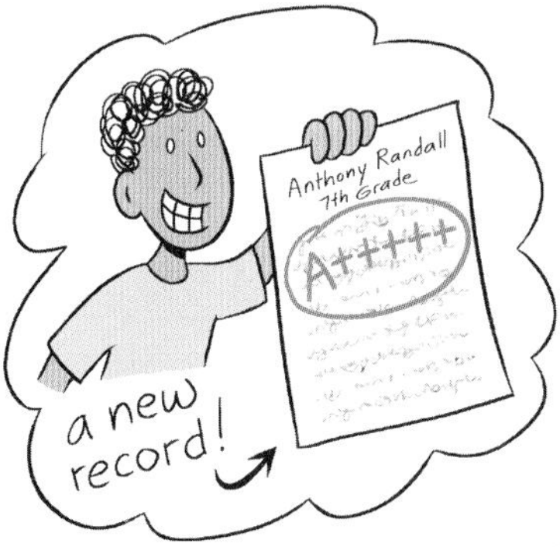
Anthony Randall
7th Grade
a new record!

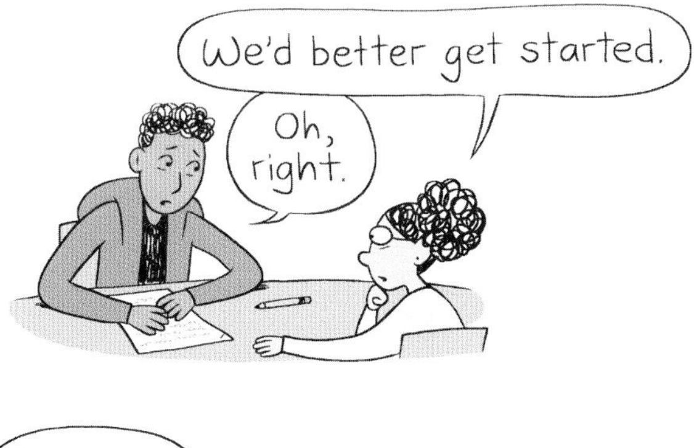
We'd better get started.
Oh, right.

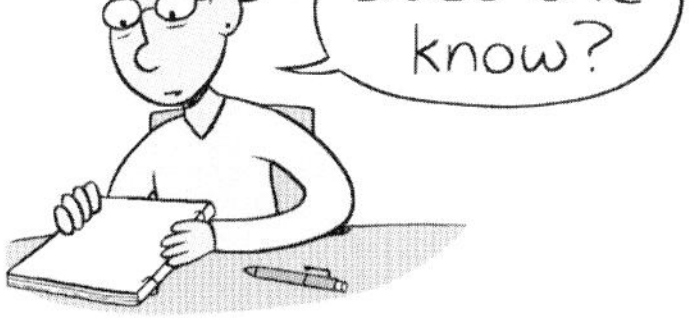
Does she know?

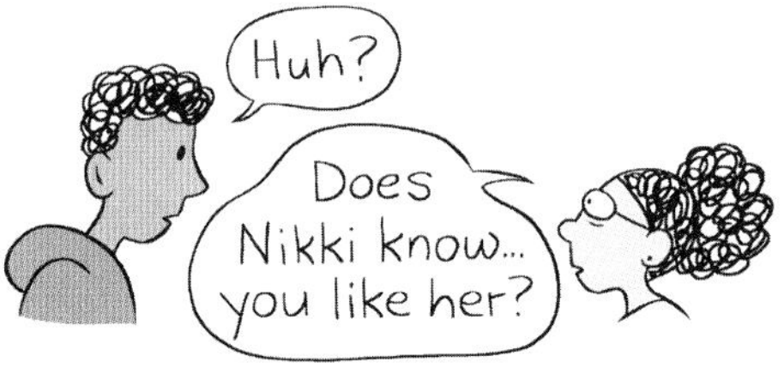
Huh?
Does Nikki know... you like her?

Oh wow. The (accidental) Distraction Plan is working. I'm still pretty embarrassed, though. I've worked really, really hard to make sure no one finds out about my crush. Tyler's the only one, but he knows how to keep a secret. I don't wanna get ridiculed by Joe or my teammates if I ask Nikki out and she shoots me down. Heck, I don't wanna get ridiculed by **her**.

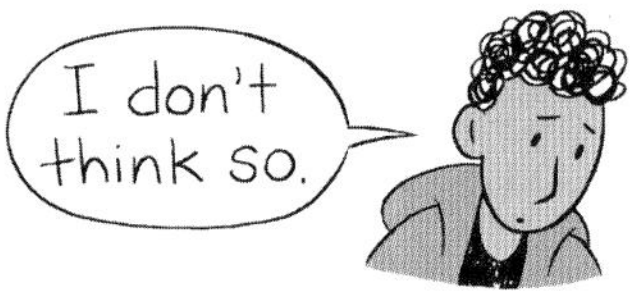
I don't think so.

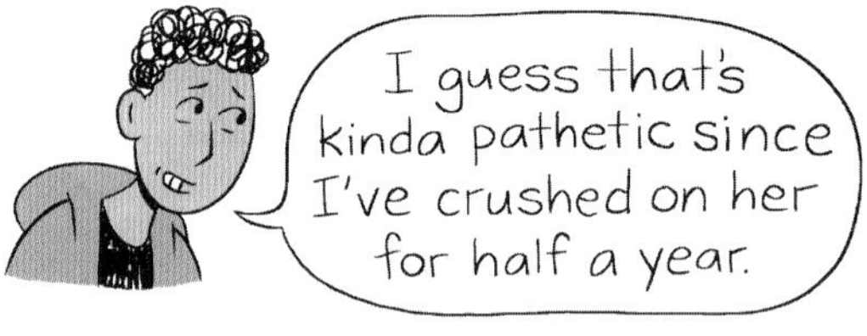
I guess that's kinda pathetic since I've crushed on her for half a year.

Holy cannoli,* I did it again.

Too much. Too much sharing. Now I wanna take it back.

*yum

I guess that's kinda pathetic sir I've crushed on for half a y
eraser

My face feels like it was shoved in a fire.

I have a crush too.

Wait, what?

You do?

She nods at a skinny kid in back.

Roddy Klein. He's in most of my classes. He's also my chemistry partner.

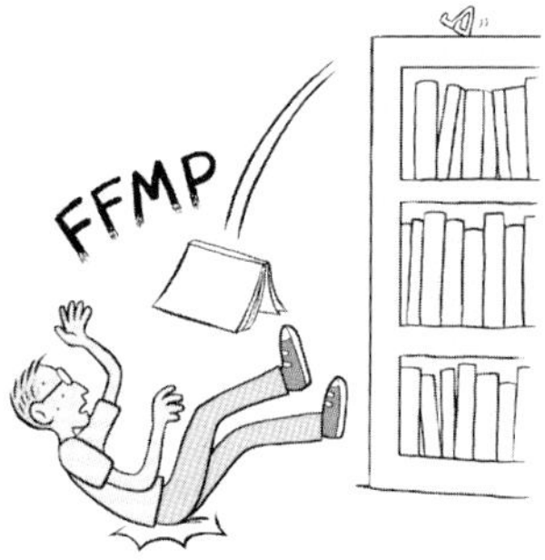
FFMP

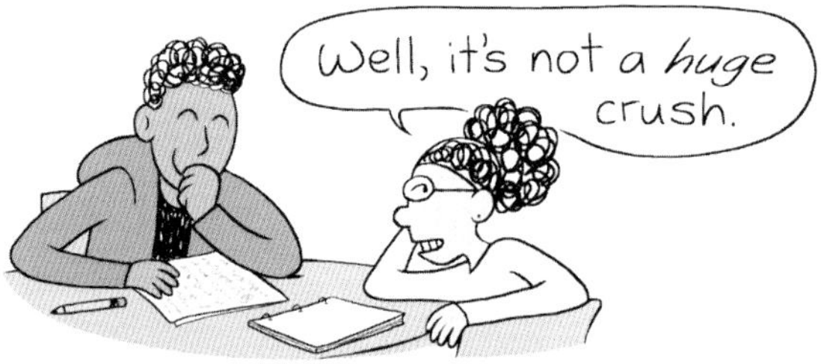
Well, it's not a *huge* crush.

I stifle a laugh.

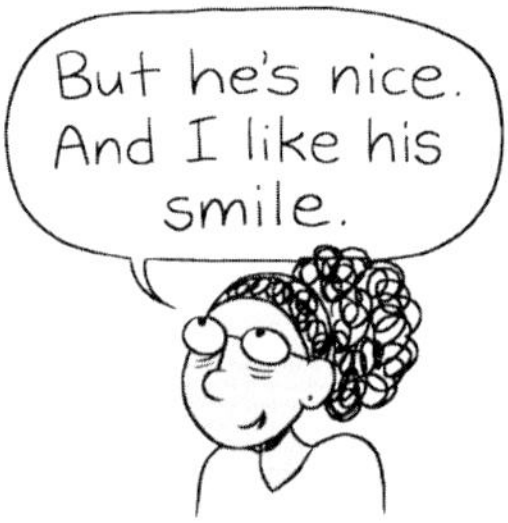
But he's nice. And I like his smile.

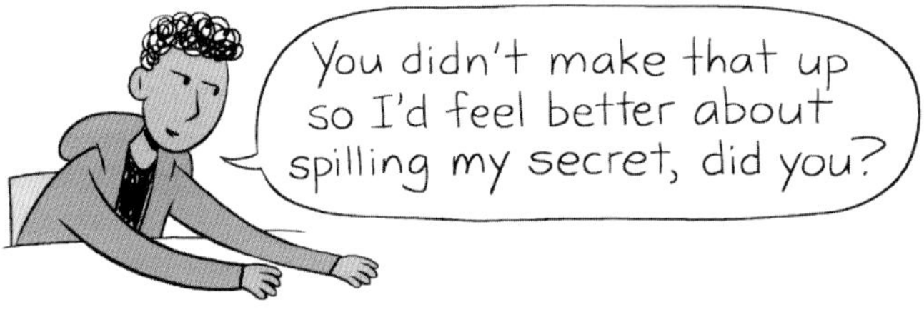
You didn't make that up so I'd feel better about spilling my secret, did you?

She quickly shakes her head.

No. I...
...I did it because you shared a secret with me. And I wanted to share one back.

I believe her.

And now I'm starting to think we **are** becoming friends. For real.

HOCOLATE
power bar

Make sure no one sees.

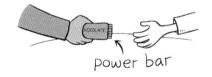

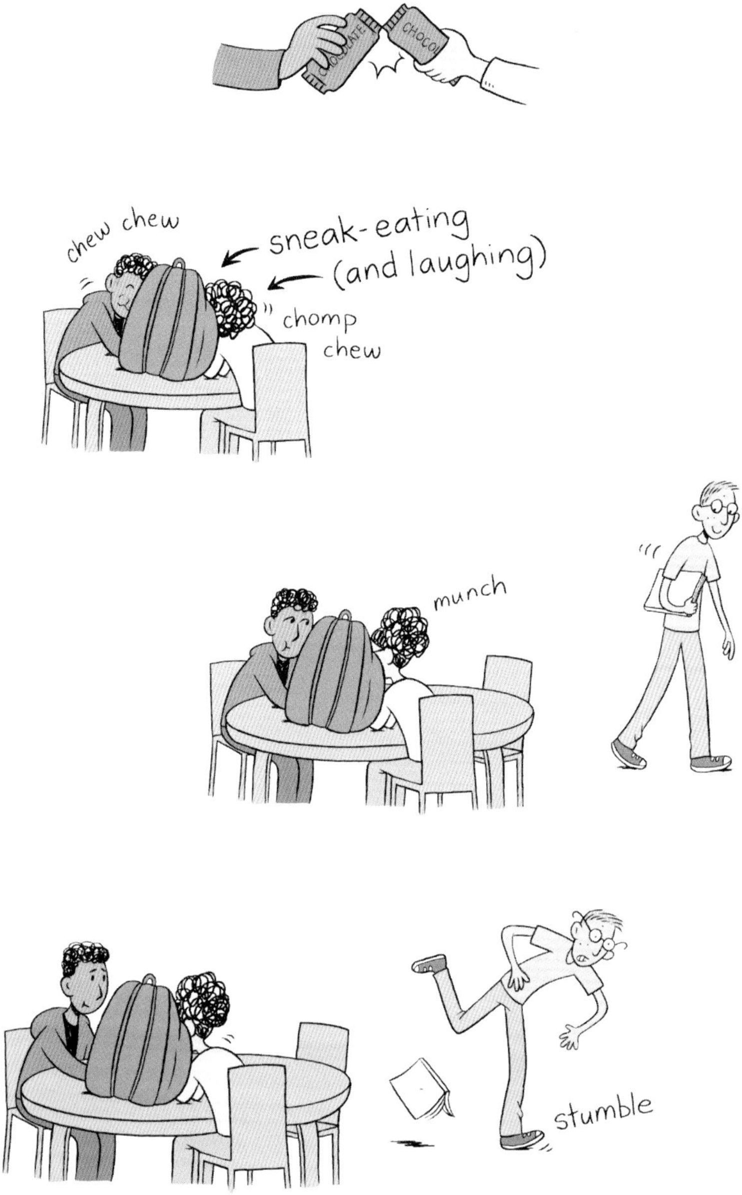
chew chew
sneak-eating
(and laughing)
chomp
chew
munch
stumble

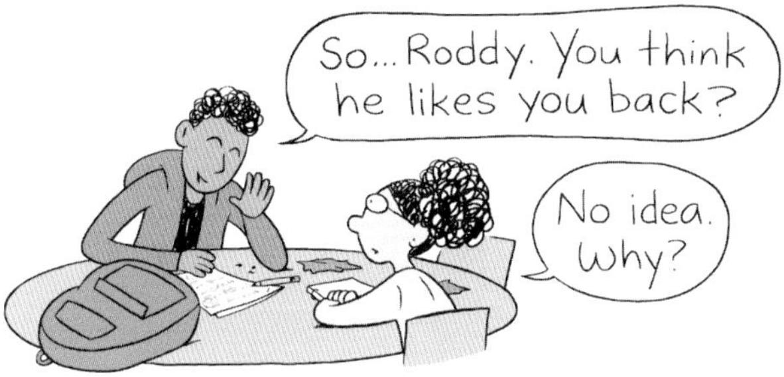
So... Roddy. You think he likes you back?
No idea. Why?

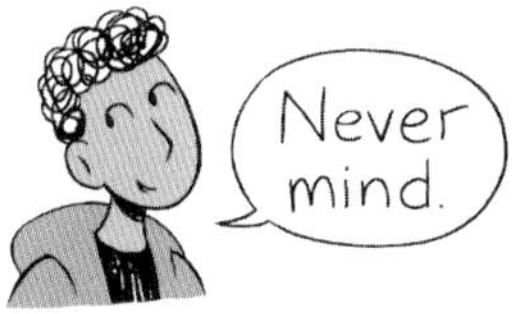
Never mind.

Leah

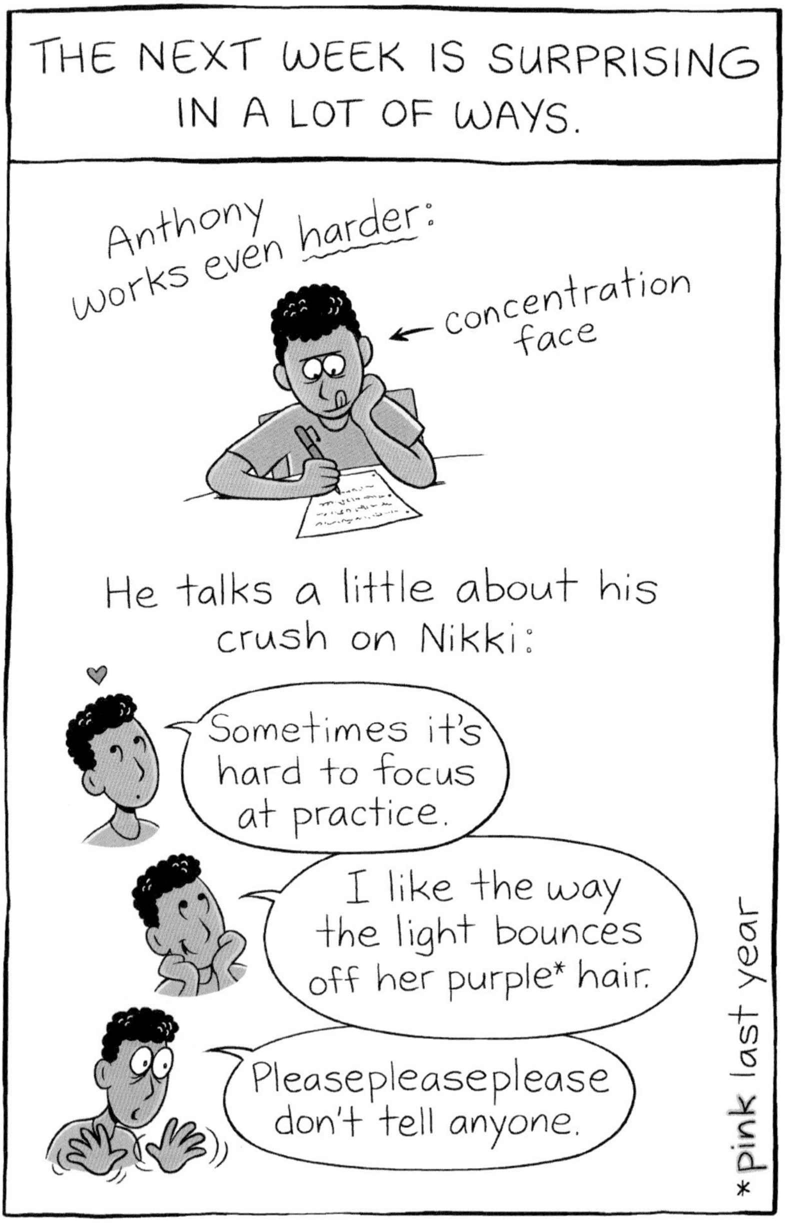
THE NEXT WEEK IS SURPRISING IN A LOT OF WAYS.
Anthony works even harder:
concentration face
He talks a little about his crush on Nikki:
Sometimes it's hard to focus at practice.
I like the way the light bounces off her purple* hair.
Pleasepleaseplease don't tell anyone.
*pink last year

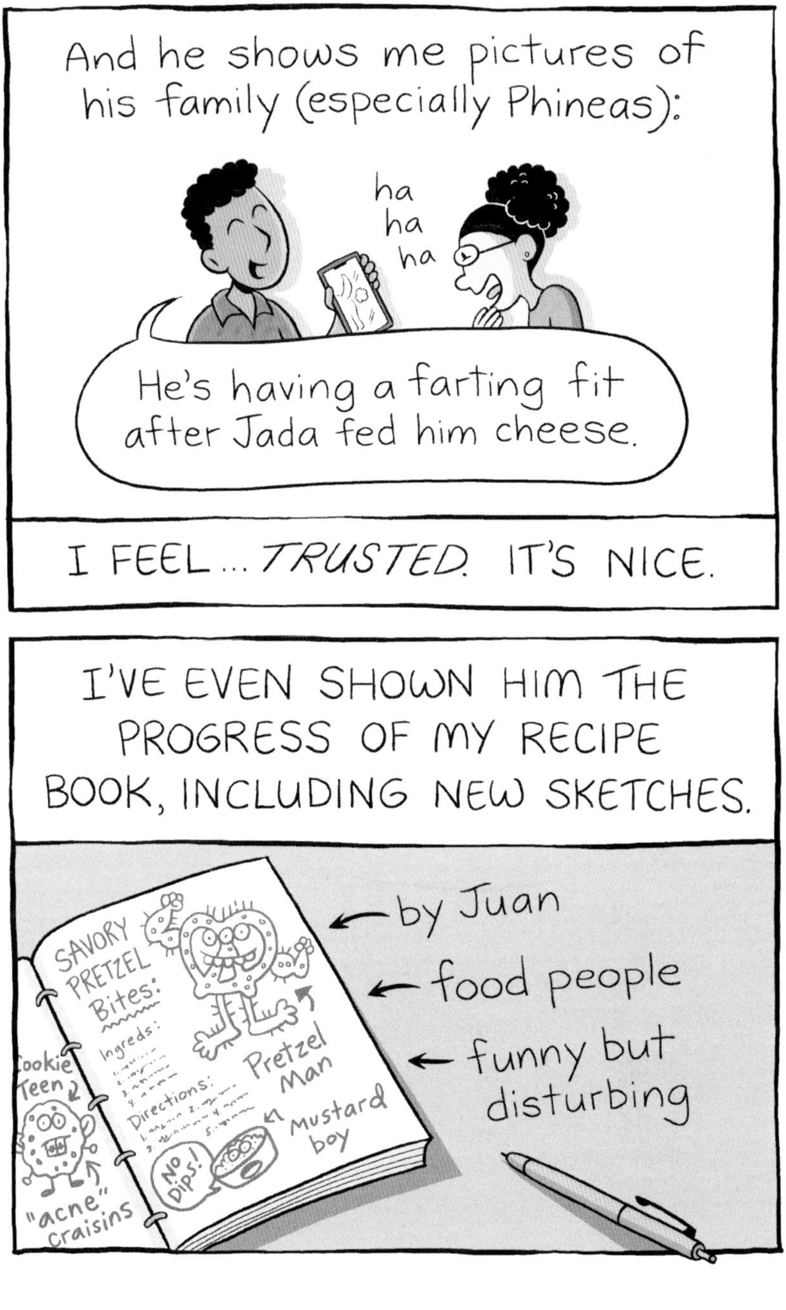
And he shows me pictures of his family (especially Phineas):
ha ha ha
He's having a farting fit after Jada fed him cheese.
I FEEL... *TRUSTED.* IT'S NICE.
I'VE EVEN SHOWN HIM THE PROGRESS OF MY RECIPE BOOK, INCLUDING NEW SKETCHES.
SAVORY PRETZEL Bites:
Ingreds:
Directions:
Pretzel Man
Mustard boy
No Dips!
Cookie Teen
"acne" craisins
by Juan
food people
funny but disturbing

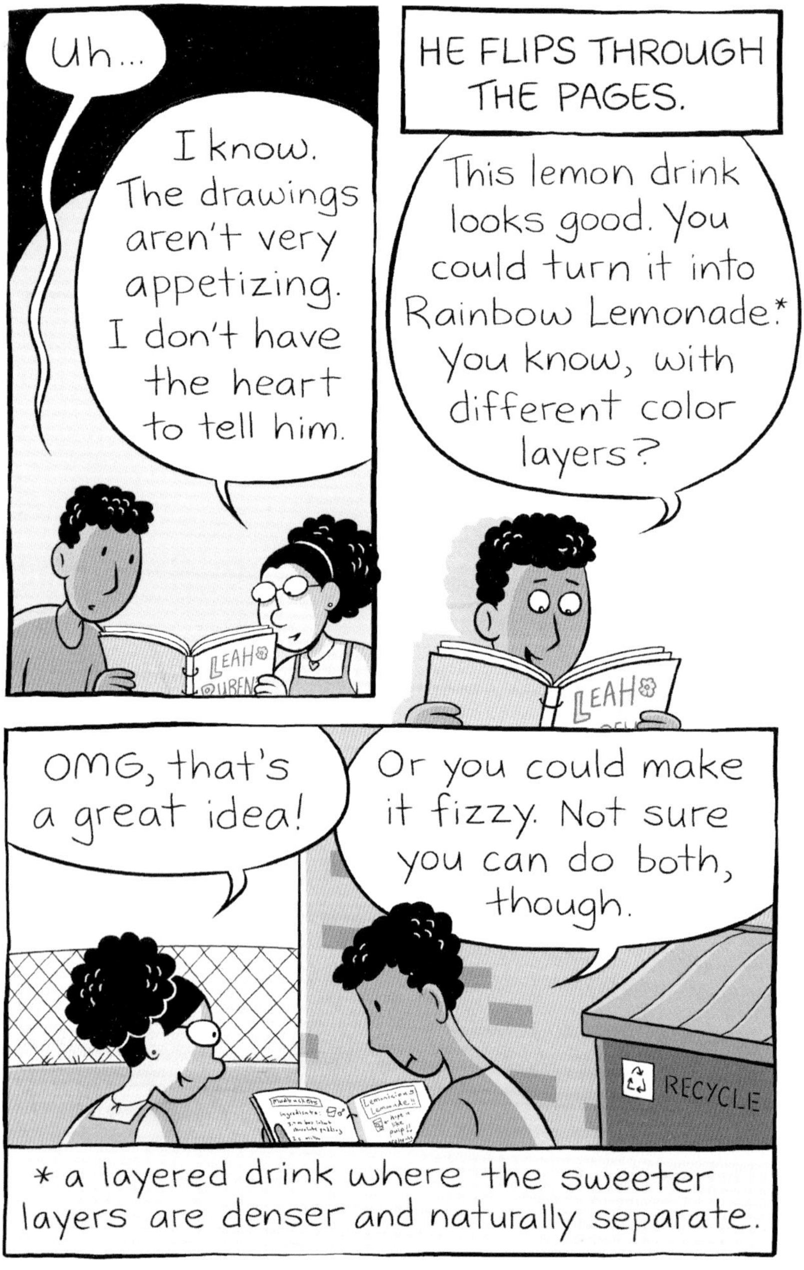
Uh...
I know. The drawings aren't very appetizing. I don't have the heart to tell him.
HE FLIPS THROUGH THE PAGES.
This lemon drink looks good. You could turn it into Rainbow Lemonade.* You know, with different color layers?
OMG, that's a great idea!
Or you could make it fizzy. Not sure you can do both, though.
RECYCLE
* a layered drink where the sweeter layers are denser and naturally separate.

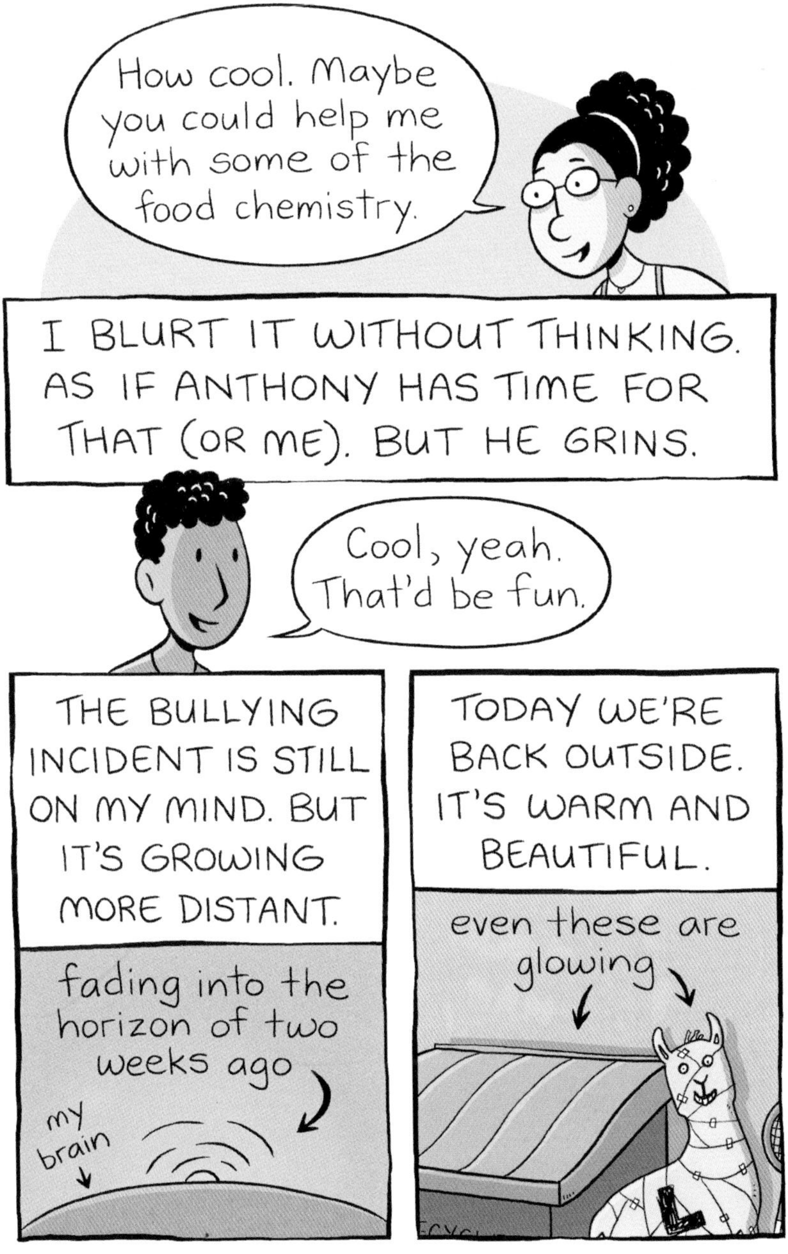
How cool. Maybe you could help me with some of the food chemistry.
I BLURT IT WITHOUT THINKING. AS IF ANTHONY HAS TIME FOR THAT (OR ME). BUT HE GRINS.
Cool, yeah. That'd be fun.
THE BULLYING INCIDENT IS STILL ON MY MIND. BUT IT'S GROWING MORE DISTANT.
fading into the horizon of two weeks ago
my brain
TODAY WE'RE BACK OUTSIDE. IT'S WARM AND BEAUTIFUL.
even these are glowing

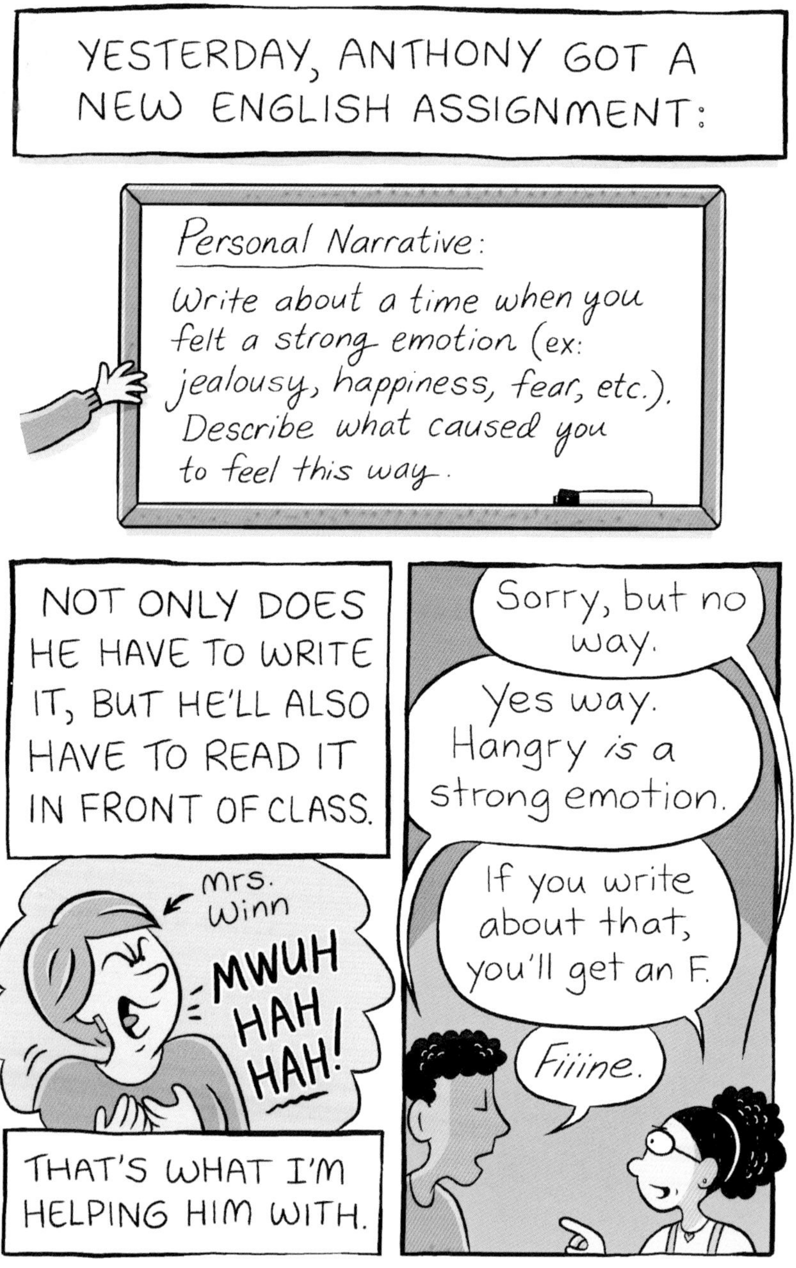
YESTERDAY, ANTHONY GOT A NEW ENGLISH ASSIGNMENT:
Personal Narrative:
Write about a time when you felt a strong emotion (ex: jealousy, happiness, fear, etc.). Describe what caused you to feel this way.
NOT ONLY DOES HE HAVE TO WRITE IT, BUT HE'LL ALSO HAVE TO READ IT IN FRONT OF CLASS.
Mrs. Winn
MWUH HAH HAH!
THAT'S WHAT I'M HELPING HIM WITH.
Sorry, but no way.
Yes way. Hangry *is* a strong emotion.
If you write about that, you'll get an F.
Fiiine.

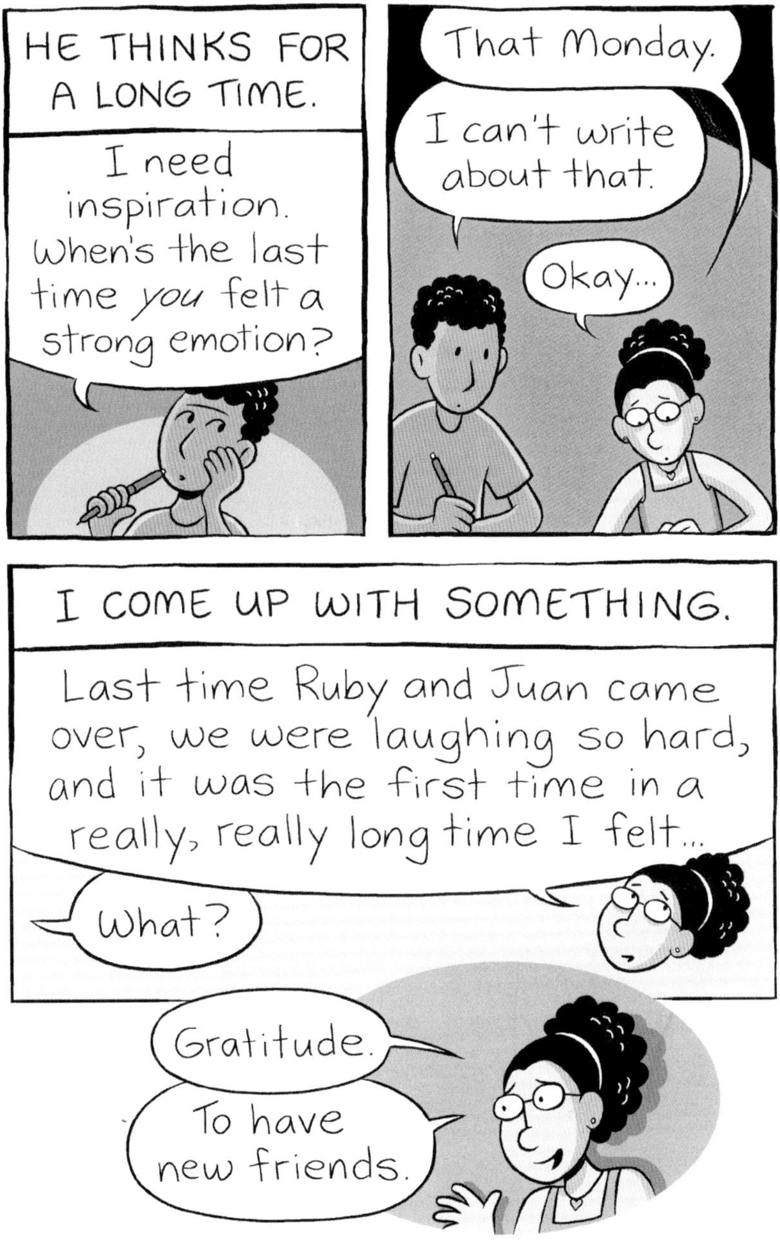

HE THINKS FOR A LONG TIME.
I need inspiration. When's the last time *you* felt a strong emotion?
That Monday.
I can't write about that.
Okay...
I COME UP WITH SOMETHING.
Last time Ruby and Juan came over, we were laughing so hard, and it was the first time in a really, really long time I felt...
What?
Gratitude.
To have new friends.

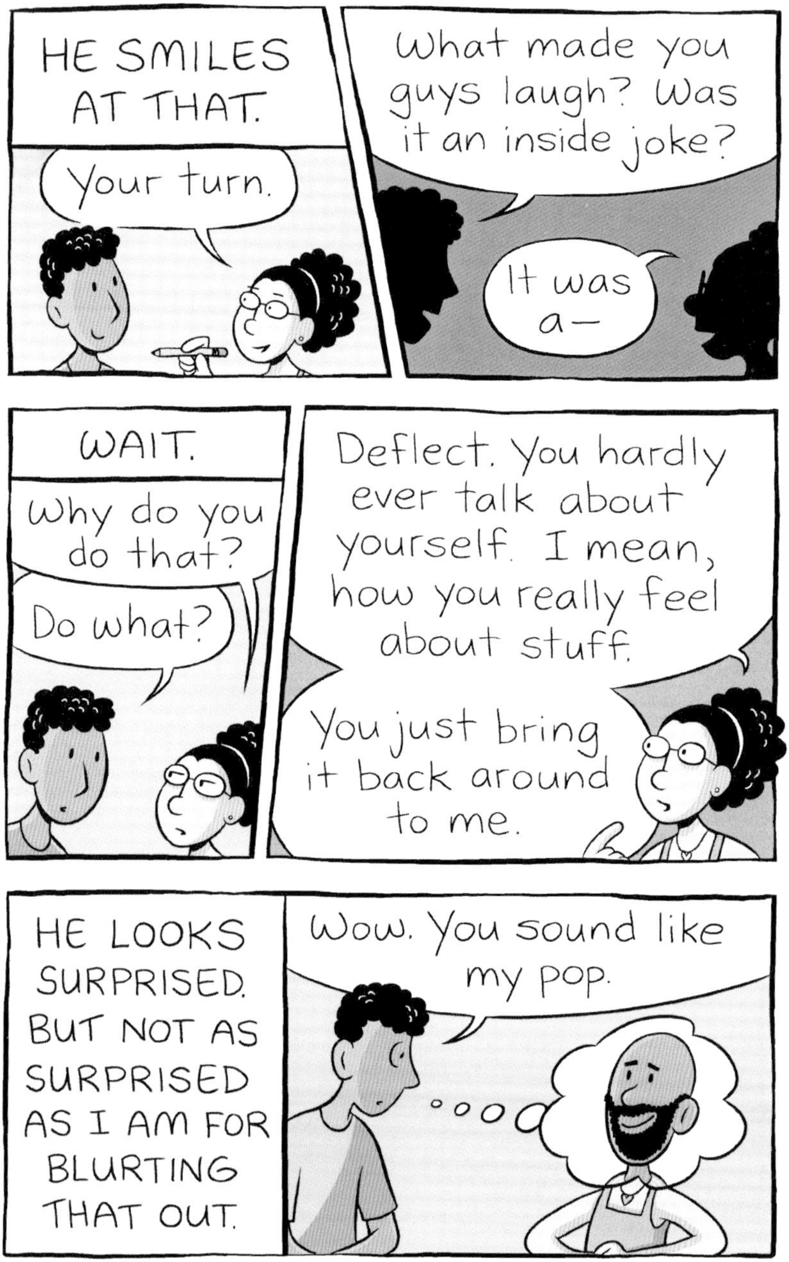
HE SMILES AT THAT.
Your turn.
What made you guys laugh? Was it an inside joke?
It was a—
WAIT.
Why do you do that?
Do what?
Deflect. You hardly ever talk about yourself. I mean, how you really feel about stuff.
You just bring it back around to me.
HE LOOKS SURPRISED. BUT NOT AS SURPRISED AS I AM FOR BLURTING THAT OUT.
Wow. You sound like my pop.

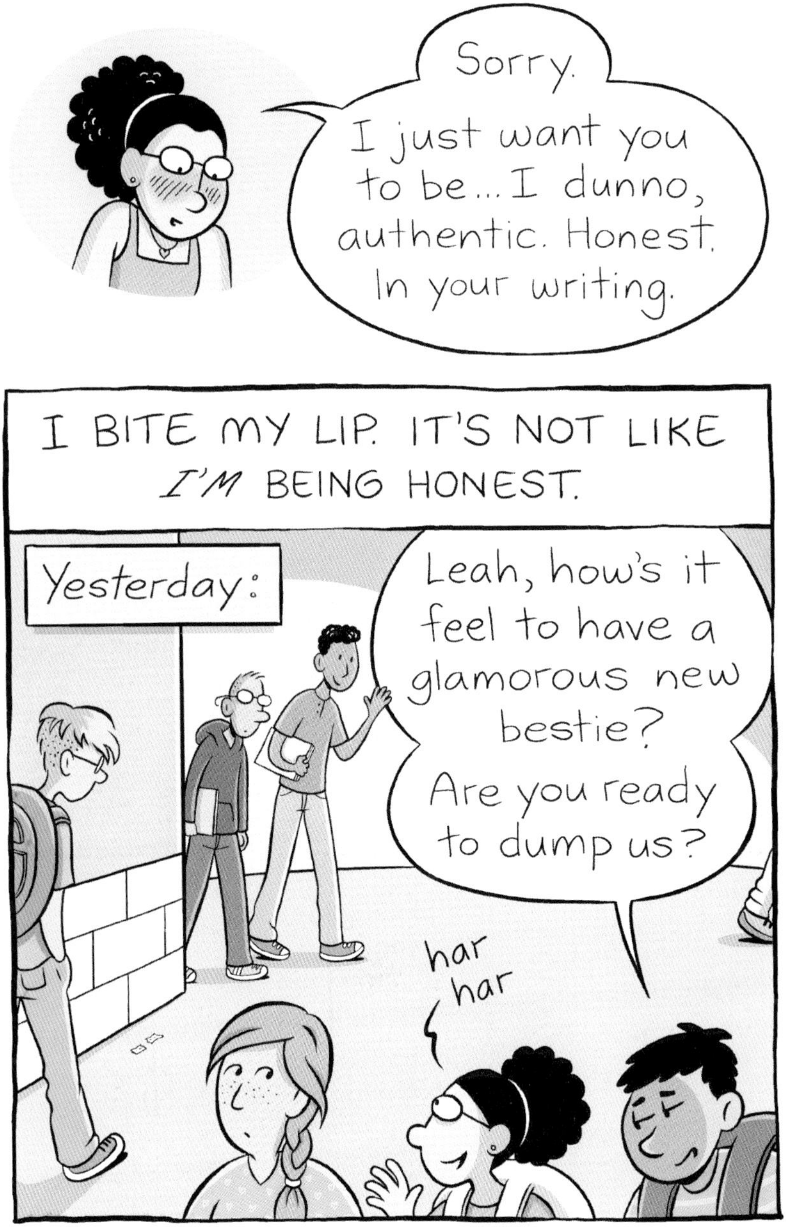

Sorry.
I just want you to be... I dunno, authentic. Honest. In your writing.
I BITE MY LIP. IT'S NOT LIKE *I'M* BEING HONEST.
Yesterday:
Leah, how's it feel to have a glamorous new bestie?
Are you ready to dump us?
har har

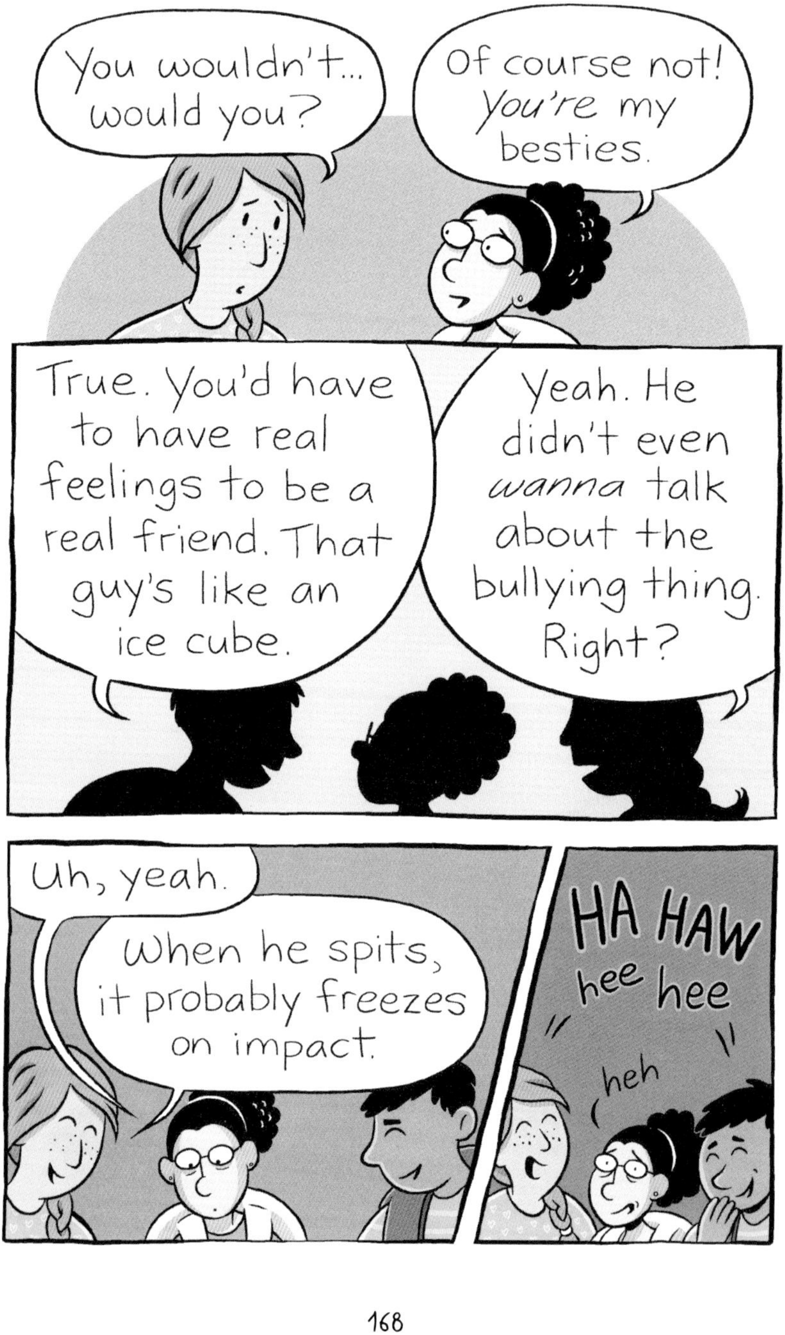
You wouldn't... would you?
Of course not! *You're* my besties.
True. You'd have to have real feelings to be a real friend. That guy's like an ice cube.
Yeah. He didn't even *wanna* talk about the bullying thing. Right?
Uh, yeah.
When he spits, it probably freezes on impact.
HA HAW
hee hee
heh

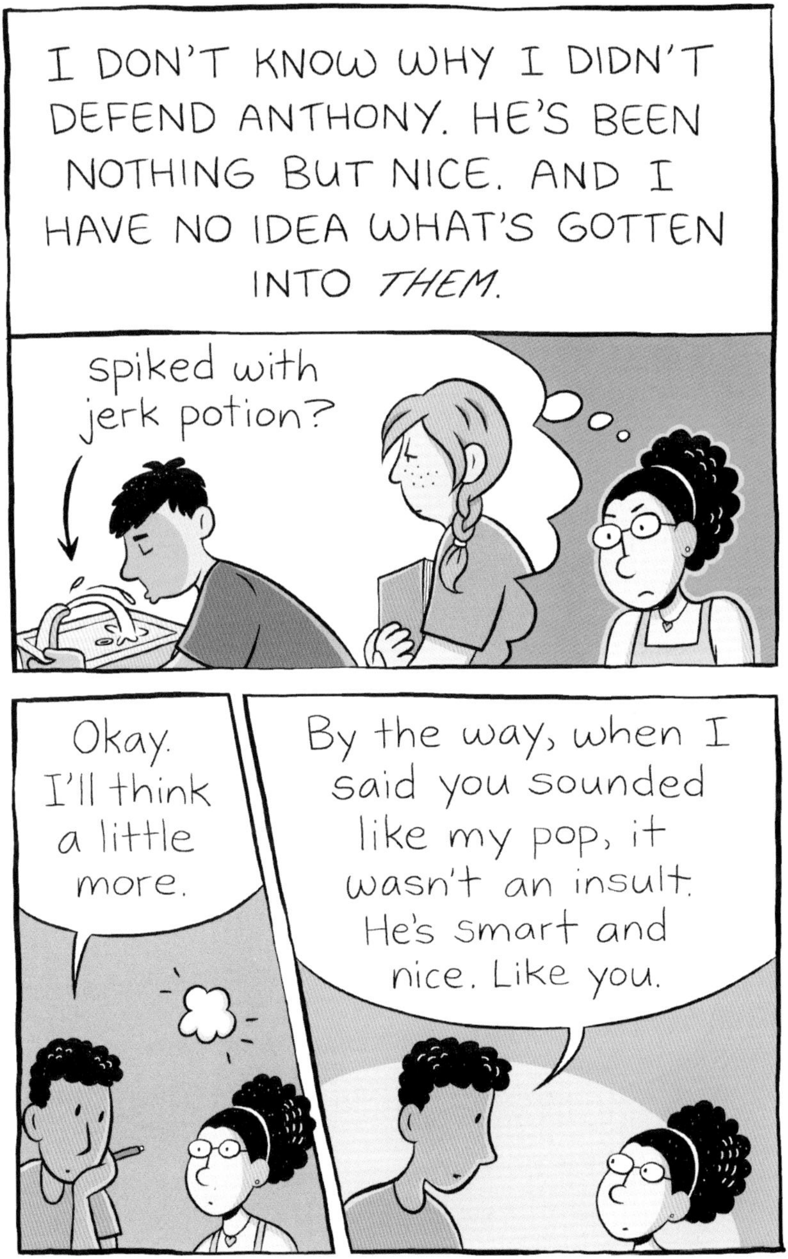
I DON'T KNOW WHY I DIDN'T DEFEND ANTHONY. HE'S BEEN NOTHING BUT NICE. AND I HAVE NO IDEA WHAT'S GOTTEN INTO *THEM*.
spiked with jerk potion?
Okay. I'll think a little more.
By the way, when I said you sounded like my pop, it wasn't an insult. He's smart and nice. Like you.

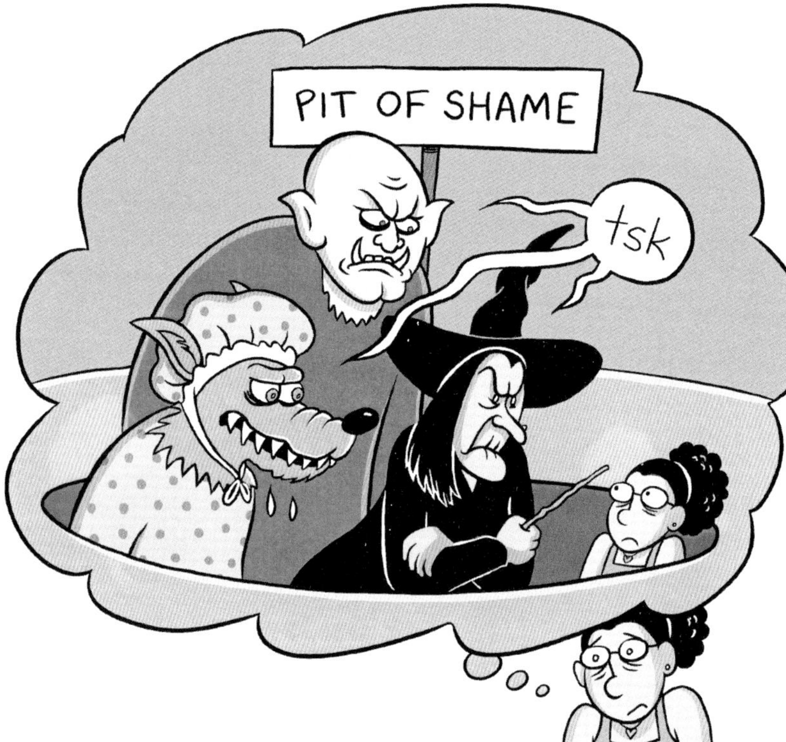
PIT OF SHAME
tsk

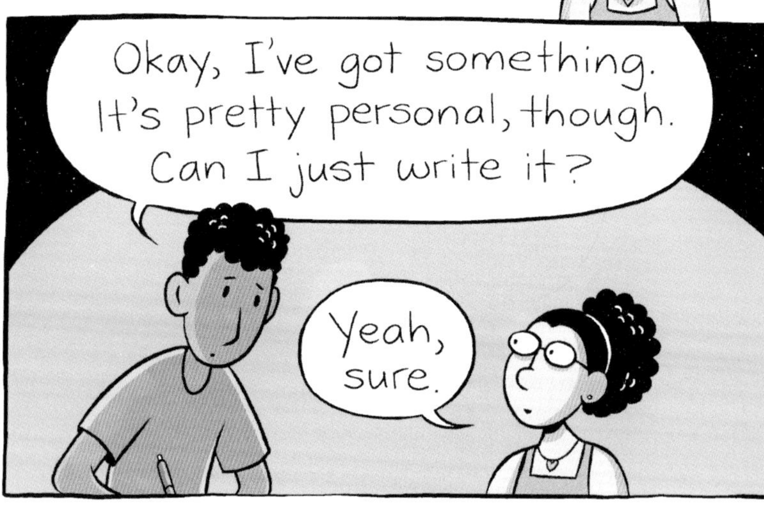
Okay, I've got something. It's pretty personal, though. Can I just write it?
Yeah, sure.

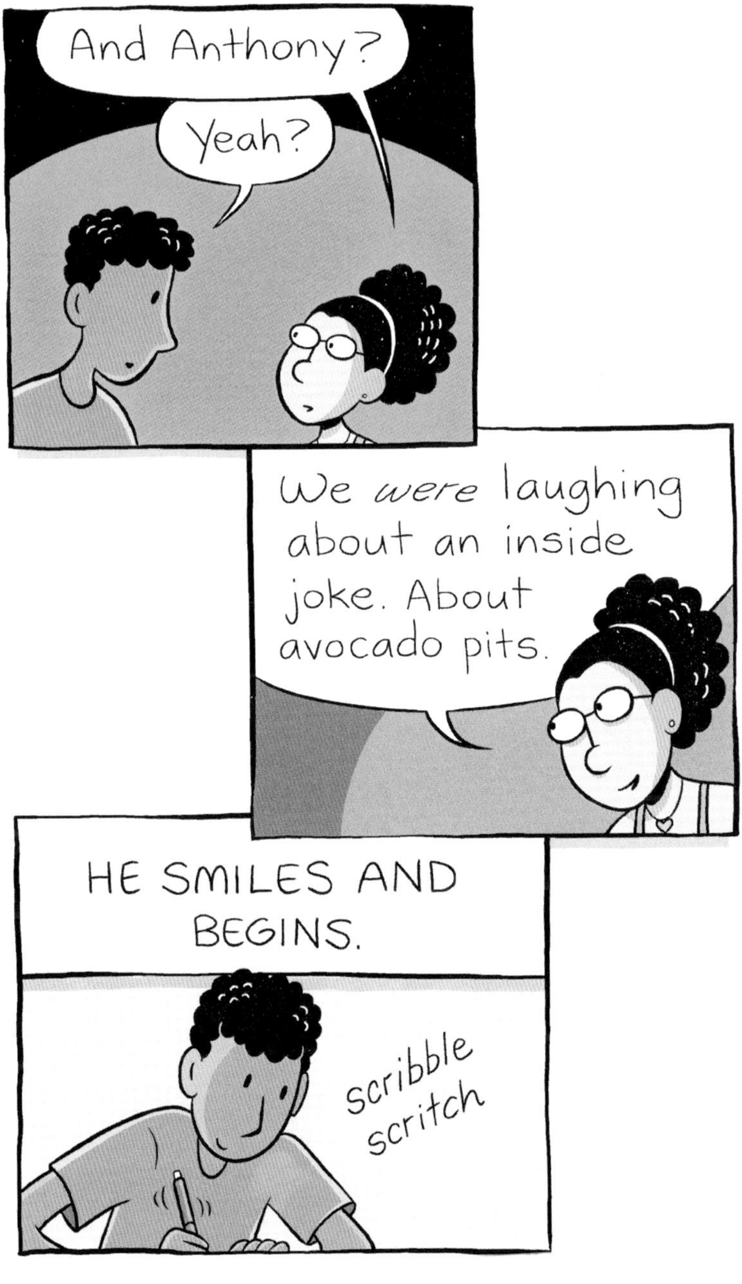
And Anthony?
Yeah?
We *were* laughing about an inside joke. About avocado pits.
HE SMILES AND BEGINS.
scribble
scritch

ANTHONY

I write and write.

I can't stop. It's like I opened the floodgates.

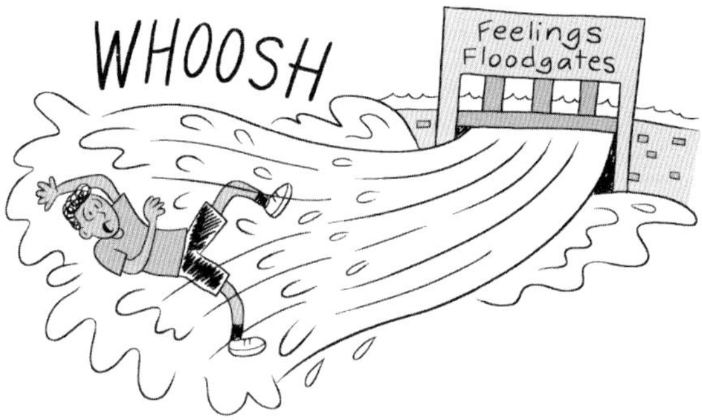
WHOOSH
Feelings Floodgates

My eyes even well up, but I fight it back. I hate crying. Not 'cause it makes me feel weak or anything—it just embarrasses me.

Leah works on her poetry. But I'm too engrossed to notice.

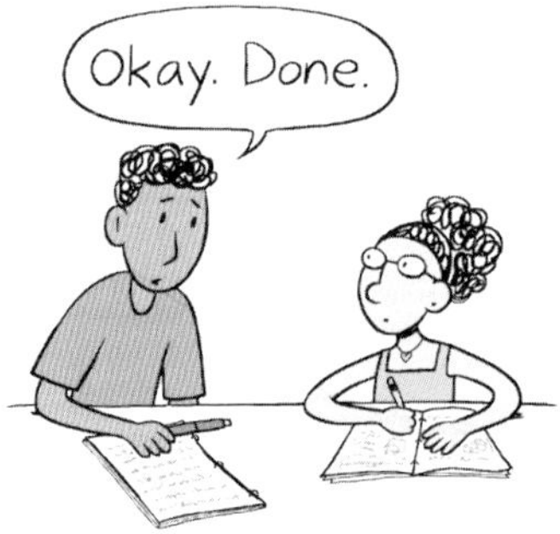
Okay. Done.

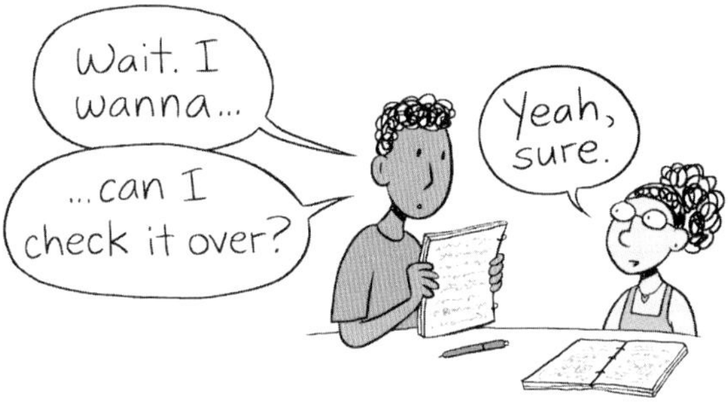
Wait. I wanna...
...can I check it over?
Yeah, sure.

I scan over my work, finding small mistakes along the way. I take my time to correct them and make other changes. Mrs. W would be elated.*

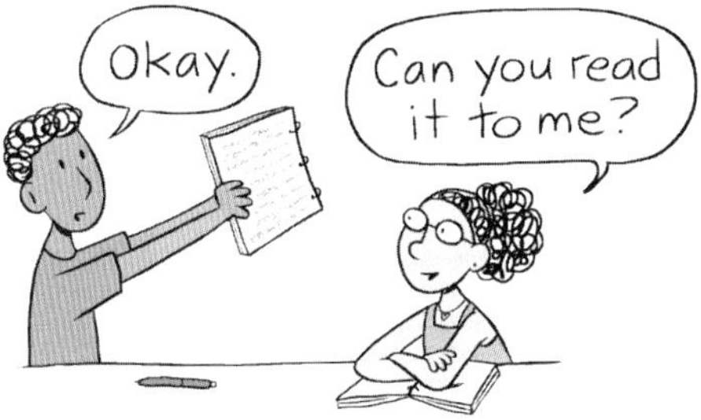
Okay.
Can you read it to me?

I start to protest. I mean, this stuff is personal. Too personal. And I'm not the greatest at public speaking. But then I remember we're **supposed** to read it out loud.

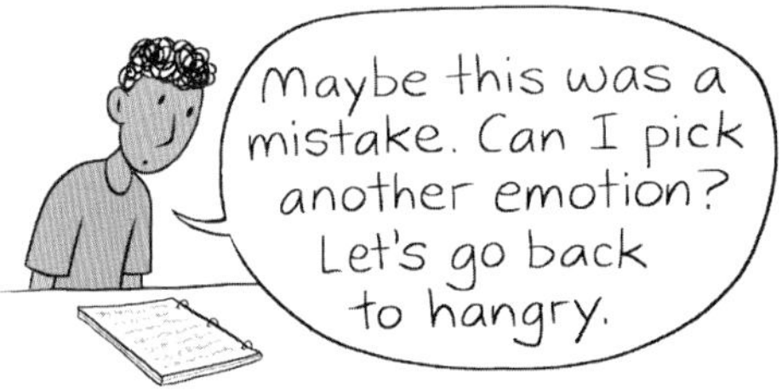
Maybe this was a mistake. Can I pick another emotion? Let's go back to hangry.

*last week's Winn Word

Leah shakes her head and gives me an encouraging smile.

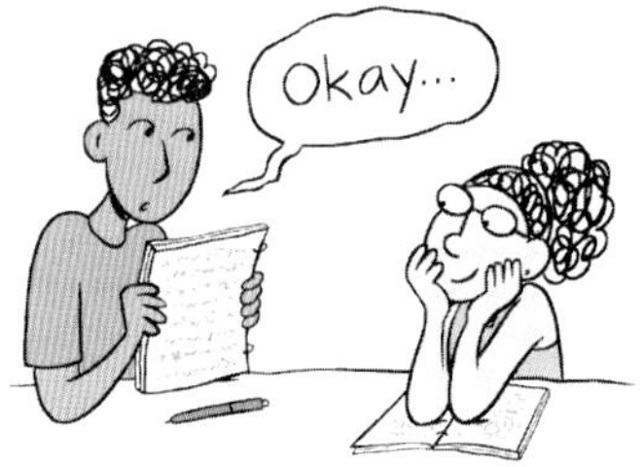
Okay...

I dive in. My voice is a little halting, but I keep going. When I finish, Leah is dead silent.

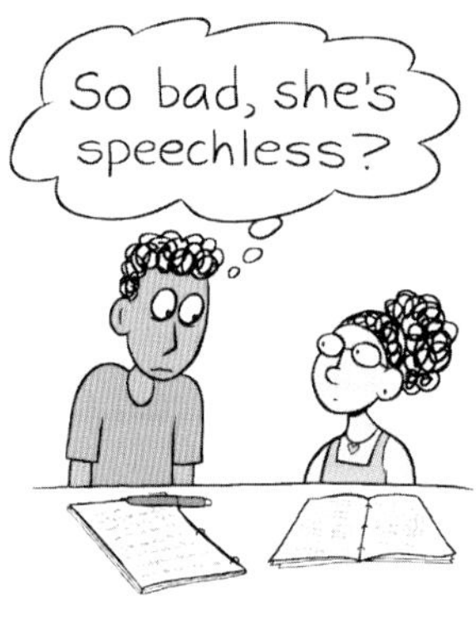
So bad, she's speechless?

She finally says:

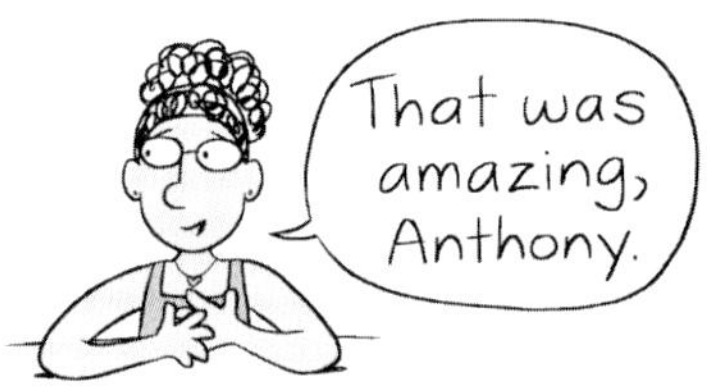
That was amazing, Anthony.

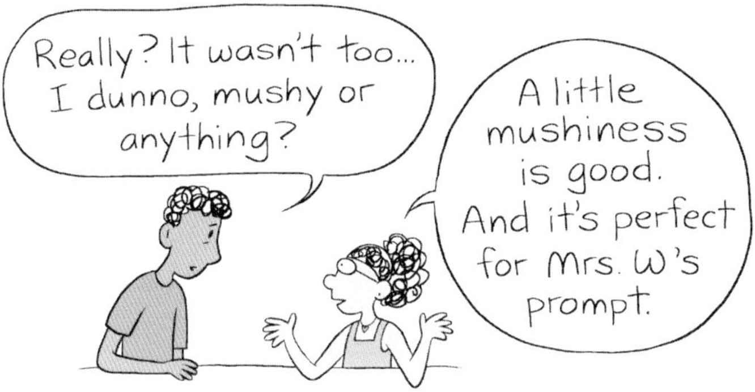
Really? It wasn't too... I dunno, mushy or anything?
A little mushiness is good. And it's perfect for Mrs. W's prompt.

I'm not convinced. But she throws me a look.

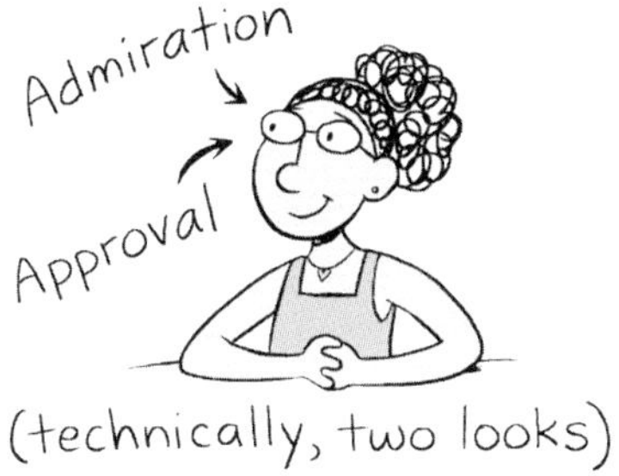
Admiration
Approval
(technically, two looks)

Whoa.

Suddenly, she's all serious again and gets down to business.

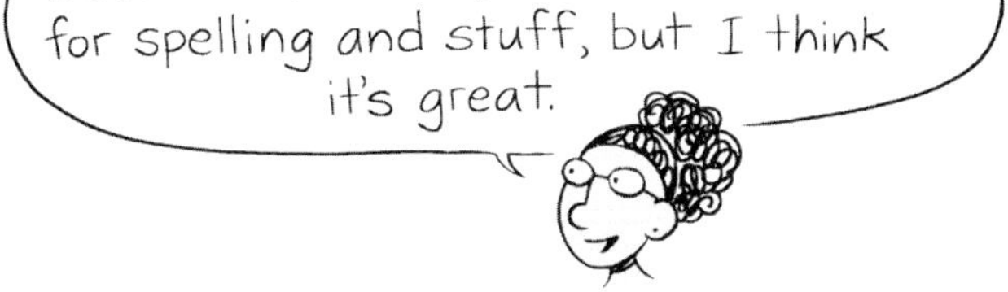
Before we leave, we'll check it over for spelling and stuff, but I think it's great.

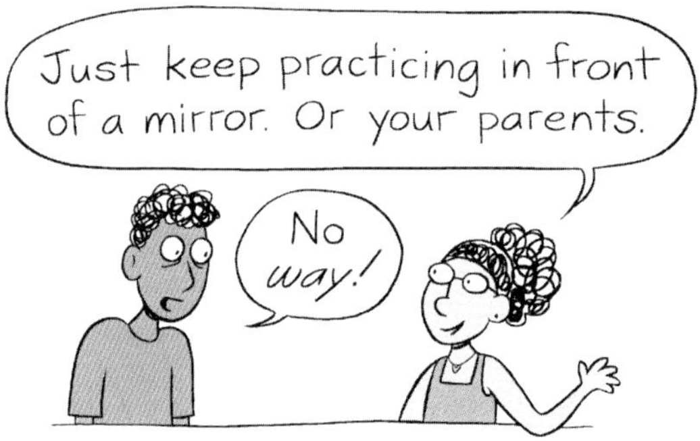
Just keep practicing in front of a mirror. Or your parents.
No *way!*

She laughs.

I feel more confident about my paper. That's when I realize: I trust her. Leah may be getting to know me better than anyone else at this point. Maybe even Ty and Jaime. I don't know if that's good or bad.

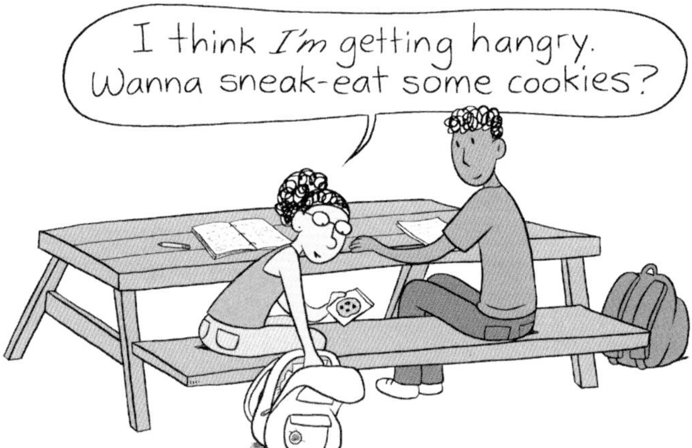
I think *I'm* getting hangry. Wanna sneak-eat some cookies?

I grin and hold out my hand.

All good.

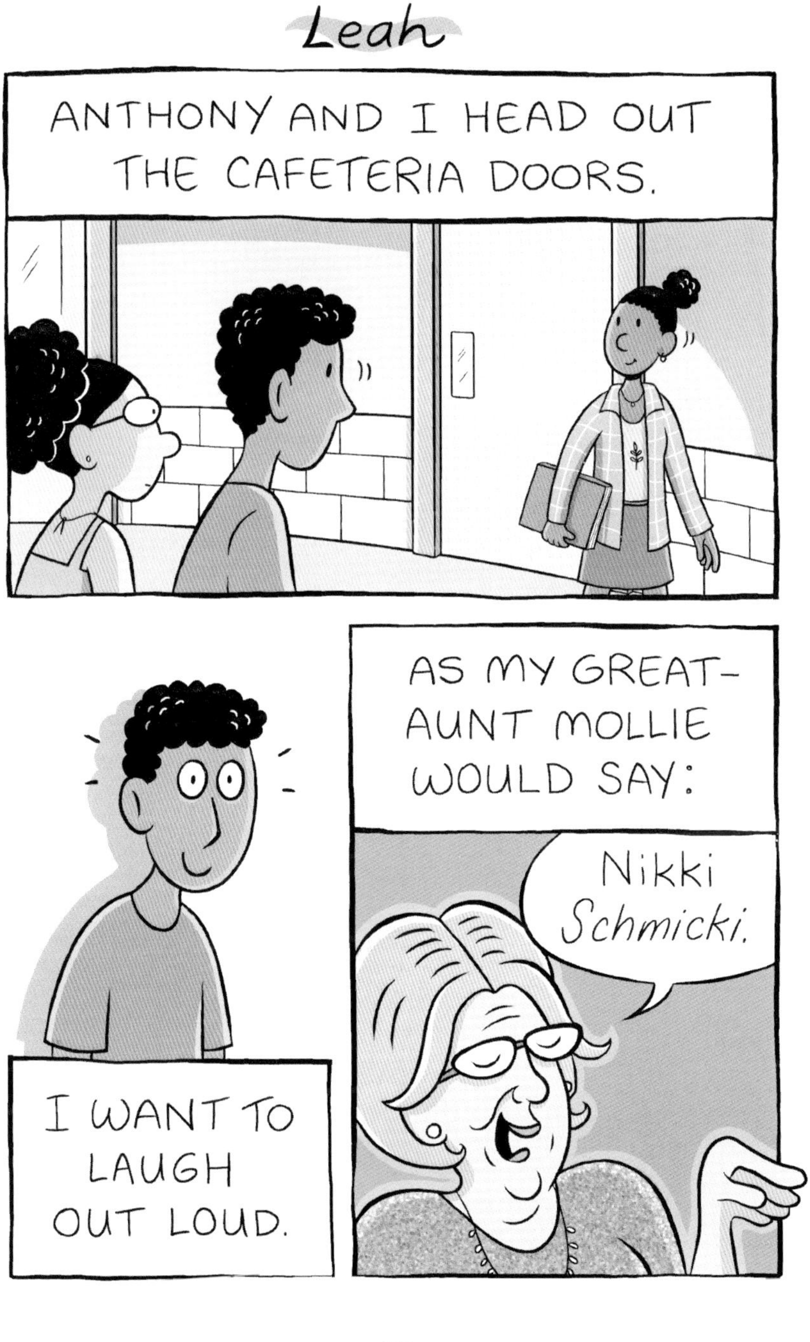
Leah
ANTHONY AND I HEAD OUT THE CAFETERIA DOORS.
I WANT TO LAUGH OUT LOUD.
AS MY GREAT-AUNT MOLLIE WOULD SAY:
Nikki *Schmicki.*

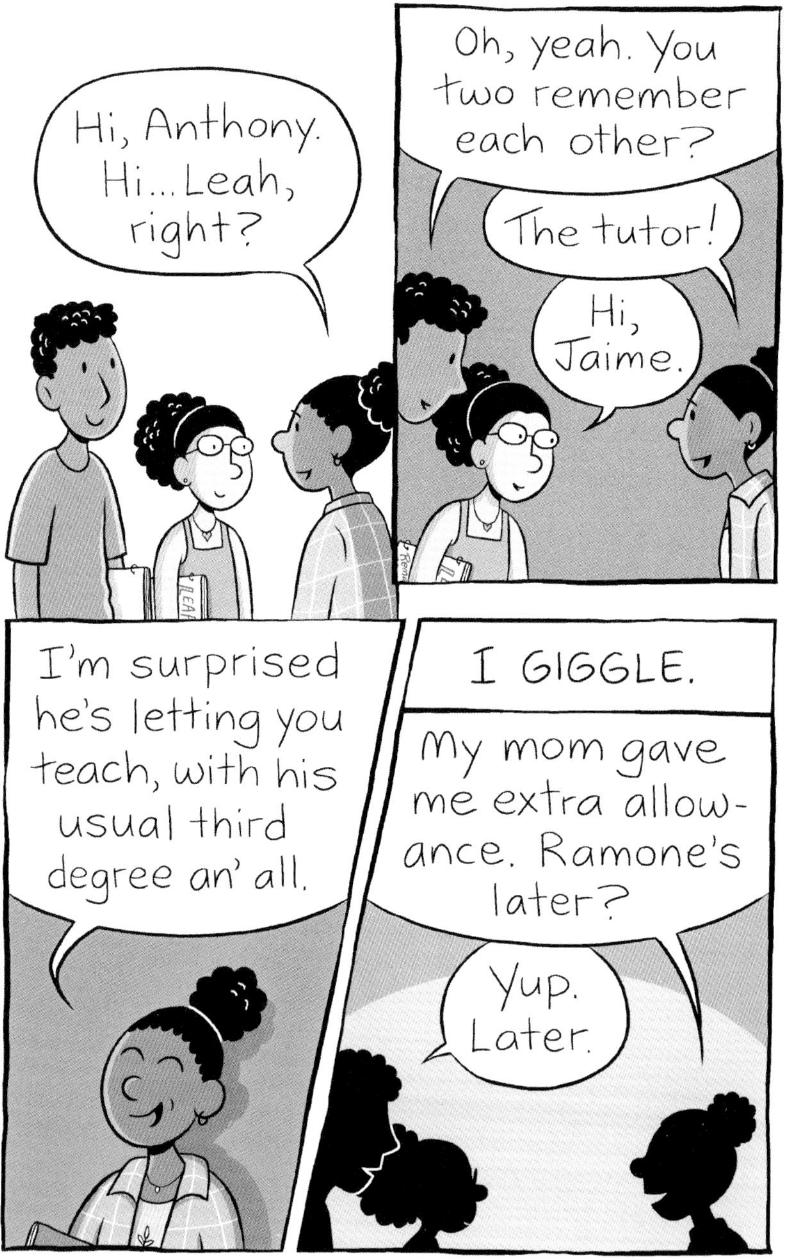
Hi, Anthony. Hi... Leah, right?
Oh, yeah. You two remember each other?
The tutor!
Hi, Jaime.
I'm surprised he's letting you teach, with his usual third degree an' all.
I GIGGLE.
My mom gave me extra allow-ance. Ramone's later?
Yup. Later.

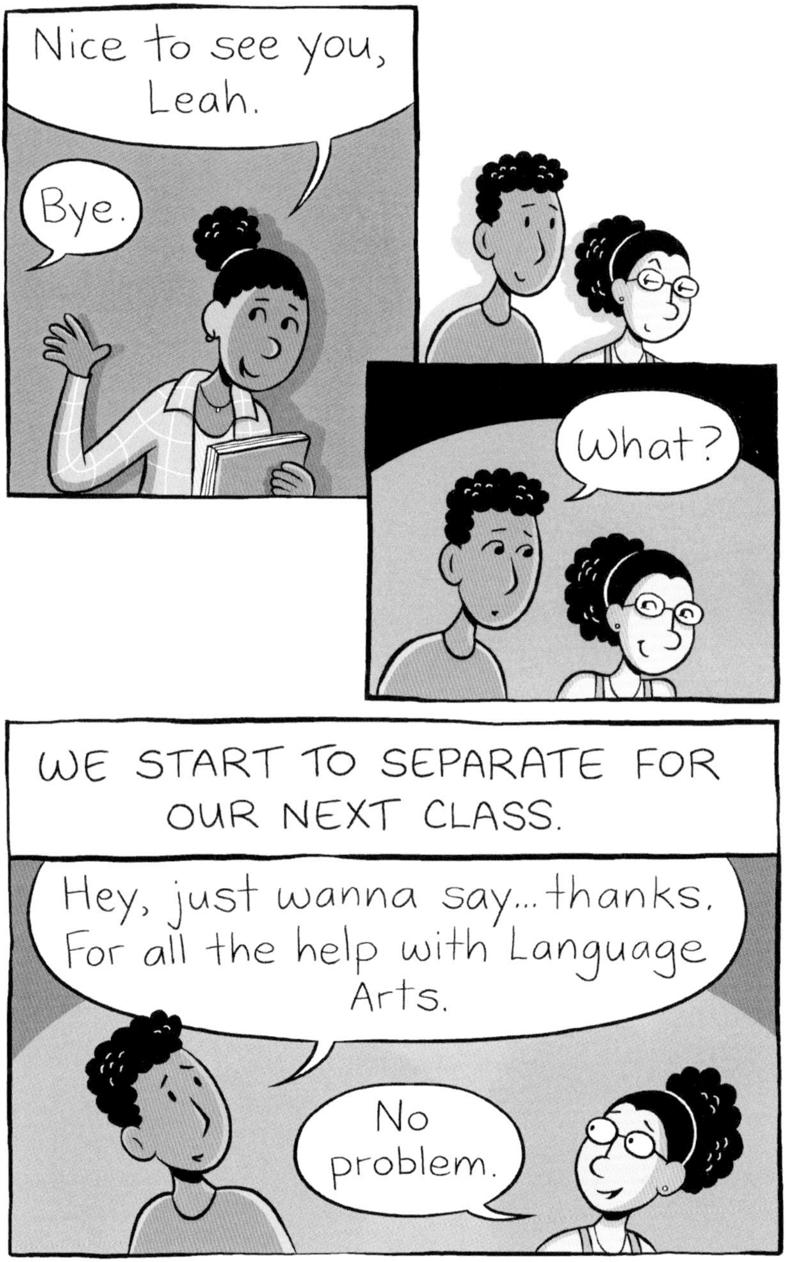
Nice to see you, Leah.
Bye.
What?
WE START TO SEPARATE FOR OUR NEXT CLASS.
Hey, just wanna say... thanks. For all the help with Language Arts.
No problem.

Good luck on the essay. Don't forget to practice.
Maybe...
I WAIT.
Maybe we can hang out after we're done tutoring.
WAIT, WHAT? MY CHEEKS FLAME UP.
No, no, I mean as friends. Like, work on that food chemistry stuff or go to Taystee's and actually *eat* food.
WOW. HE'S MAKING OUR FRIENDSHIP OFFICIAL.
Friendship Contract
signed,
Leah and
Mr. Kewel

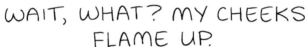

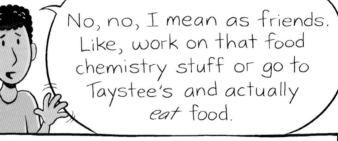

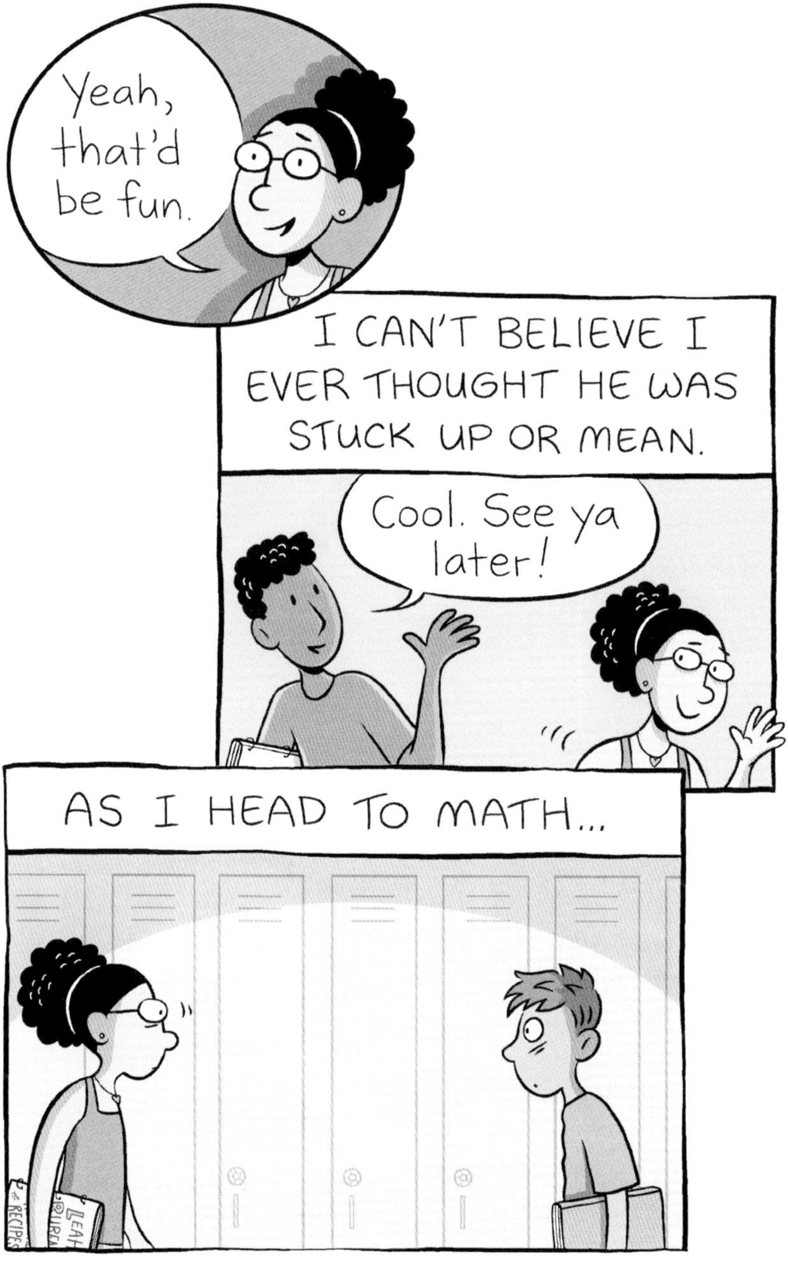
Yeah, that'd be fun.
I CAN'T BELIEVE I EVER THOUGHT HE WAS STUCK UP OR MEAN.
Cool. See ya later!
AS I HEAD TO MATH...

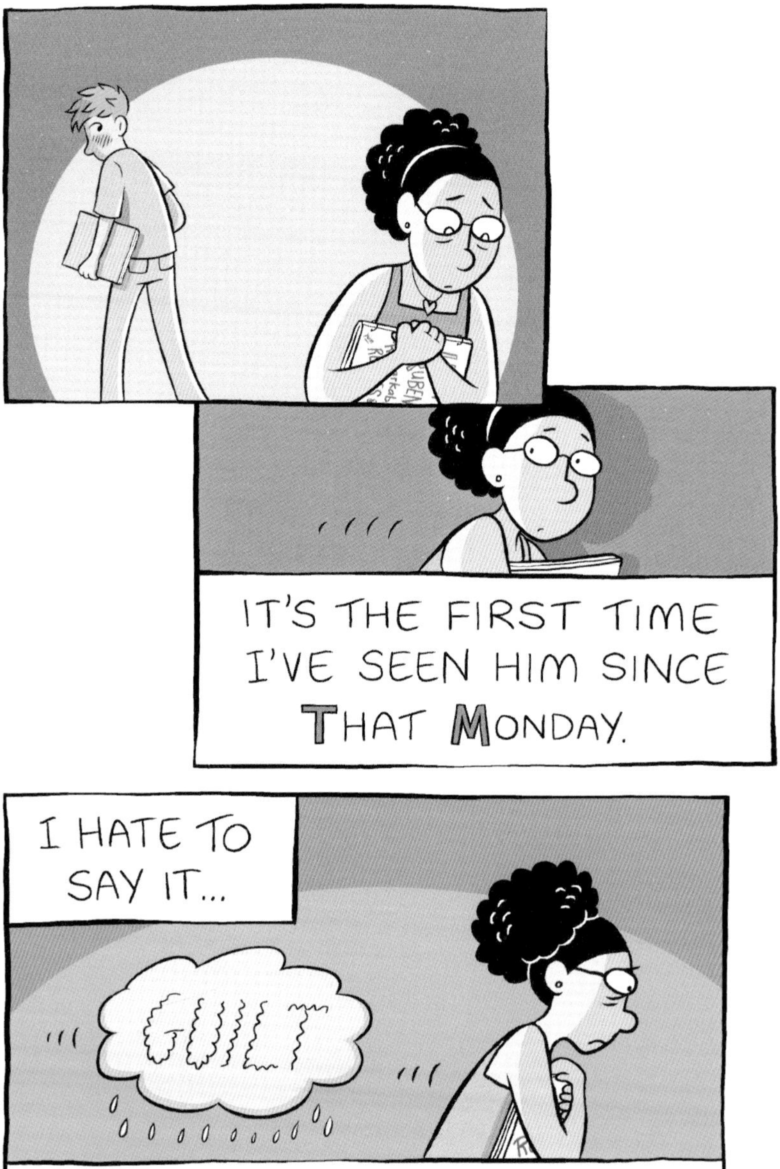
IT'S THE FIRST TIME I'VE SEEN HIM SINCE THAT MONDAY.
I HATE TO SAY IT...
GUILT
...I WISH IT WERE THE LAST.

ANTHONY

My hands are trembling. My palms are sweating. My cheeks are flaming. Basically, it's the way I feel whenever I see Nikki.

But this time it's not about her.

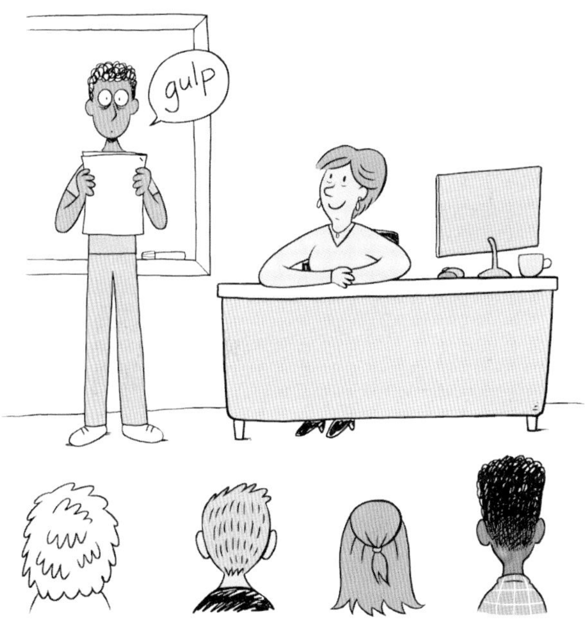
gulp

Well, unless you count the fact that she's here.

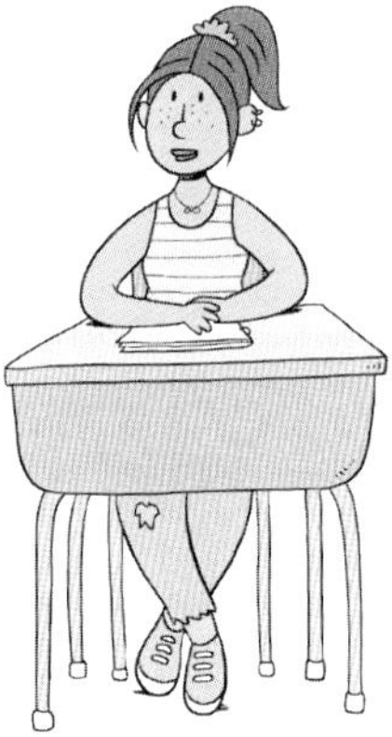

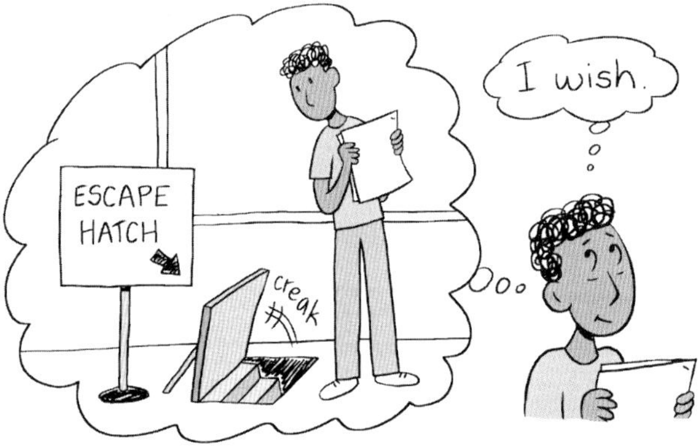
ESCAPE
HATCH
creak
I wish.

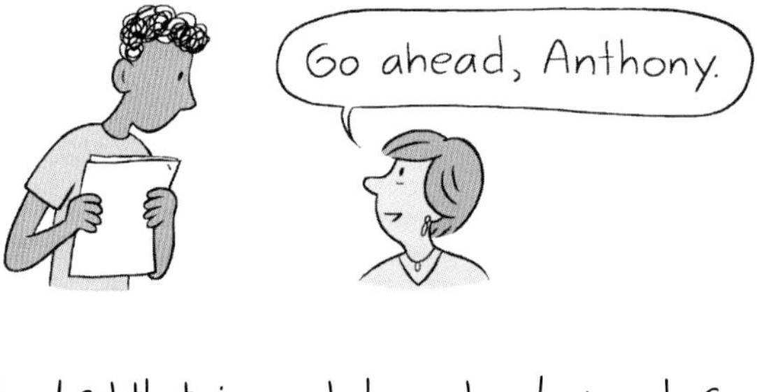
Go ahead, Anthony.

I'm thankful that six people have already gone before me.

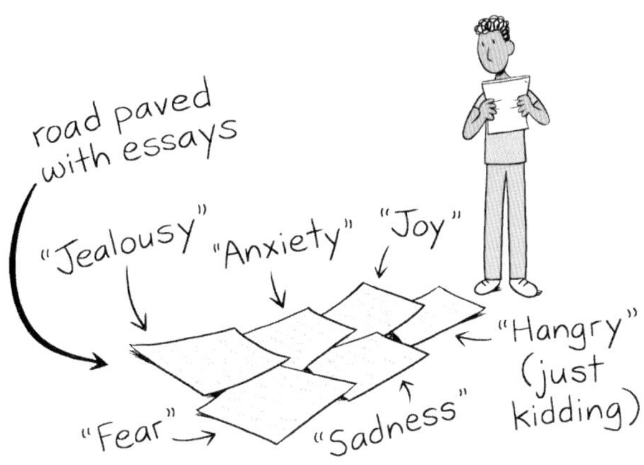
road paved with essays
"Jealousy"
"Anxiety"
"Joy"
"Hangry" (just kidding)
"Fear"
"Sadness"

Well, can't back out now.

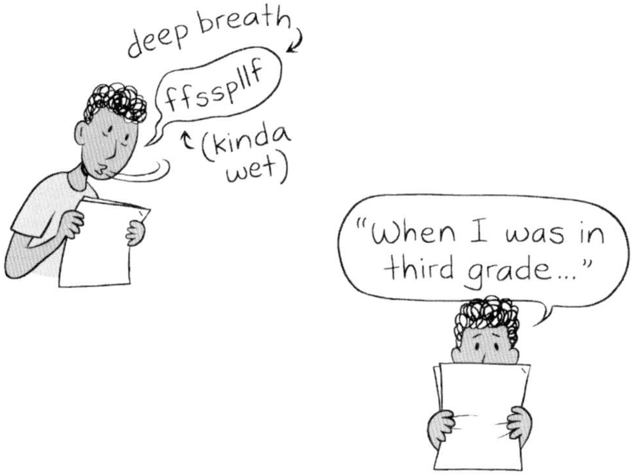
deep breath
ffsspllf
(kinda wet)
"When I was in third grade..."

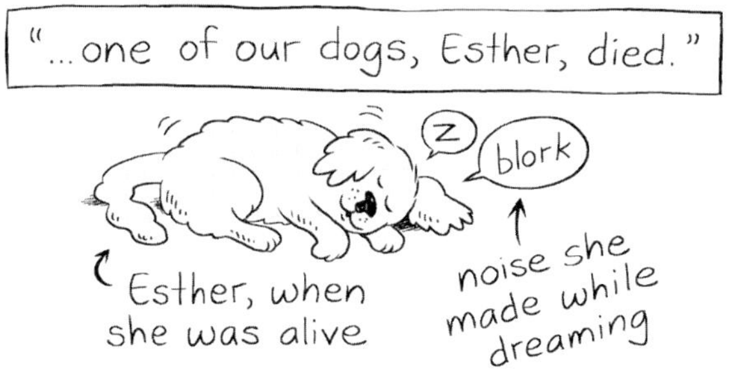
"...one of our dogs, Esther, died."
z
blork
Esther, when she was alive
noise she made while dreaming

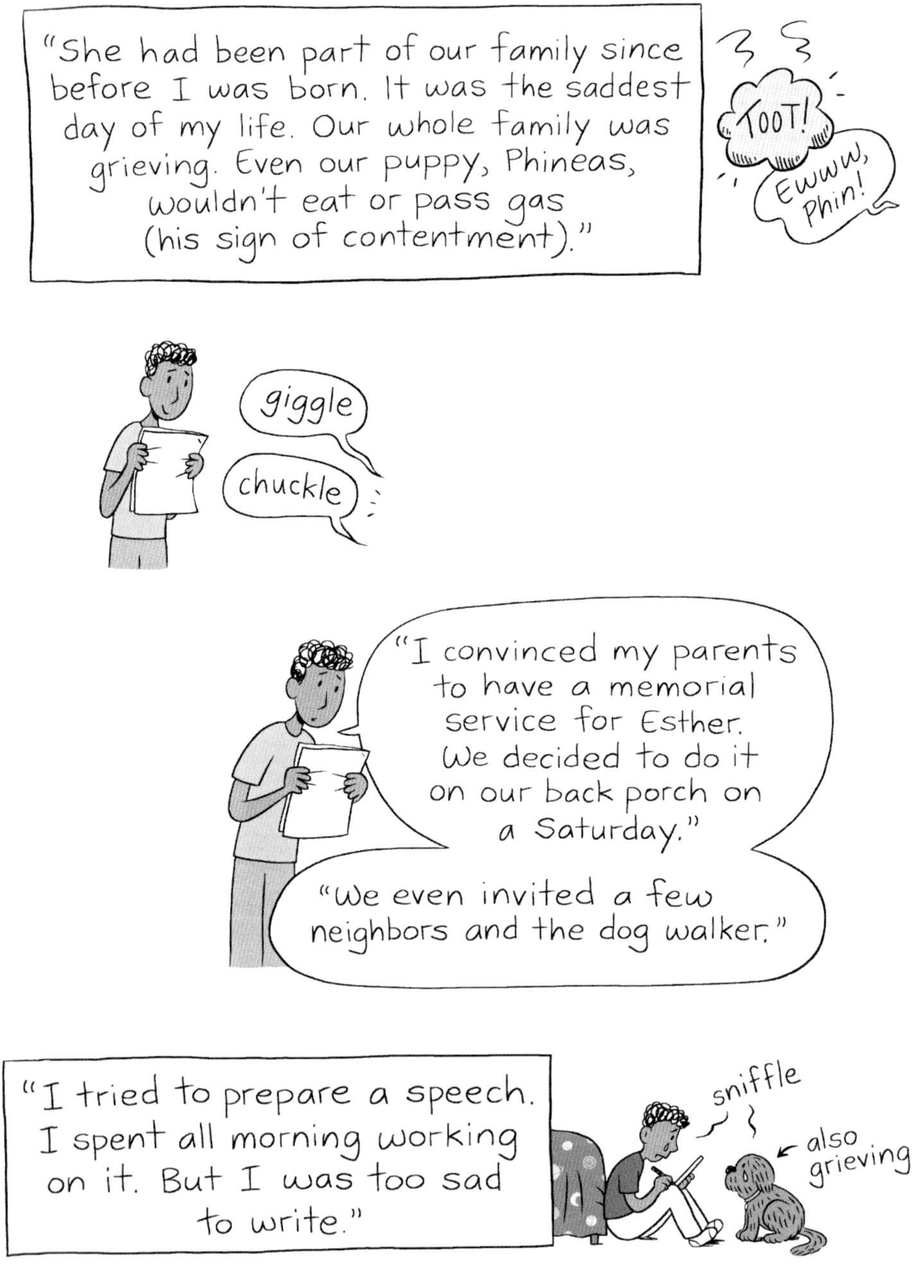
"She had been part of our family since before I was born. It was the saddest day of my life. Our whole family was grieving. Even our puppy, Phineas, wouldn't eat or pass gas (his sign of contentment)."
TOOT!
Ewww, Phin!
giggle
chuckle
"I convinced my parents to have a memorial service for Esther. We decided to do it on our back porch on a Saturday."
"We even invited a few neighbors and the dog walker."
"I tried to prepare a speech. I spent all morning working on it. But I was too sad to write."
sniffle
also grieving

"I just had a really hard time getting my words on paper. I must've torn up twenty pages out of frustration."

"In the end, I let my mom and pop make the speeches. Even my little twin sisters said a few words. I was the only one who didn't, and that was awful, considering I was closest to Esther."

"There was something else, though: I had been diagnosed with mild dyslexia the year before."

That's what that is?

educational psychologist ↪

2nd grade me ↑ (cool kicks) ↑

"I thought I had come a long way. But thinking about reading in front of everyone made me anxious, which always made the dyslexia worse."

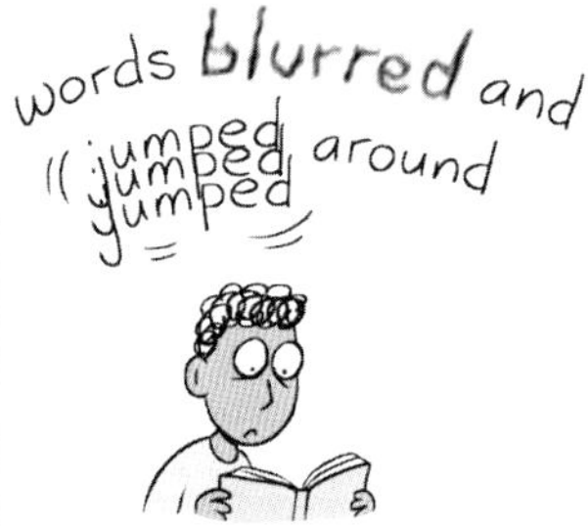
words blurred and
jumped
jumped
jumped around

"I had trouble reading from the start. Early on, my parents thought I didn't like it, even though I always *loved* it when they read to *me*."

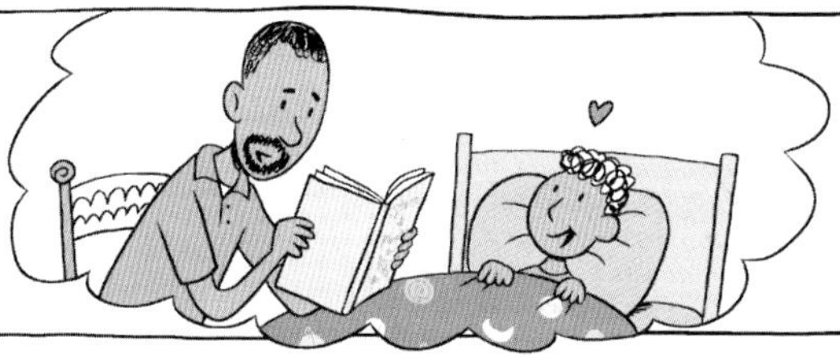

"Not only did I struggle, but I had a hard time concentrating or even putting certain sounds together. Luckily, my parents realized something was wrong and got me into a program. I started getting the help I needed."

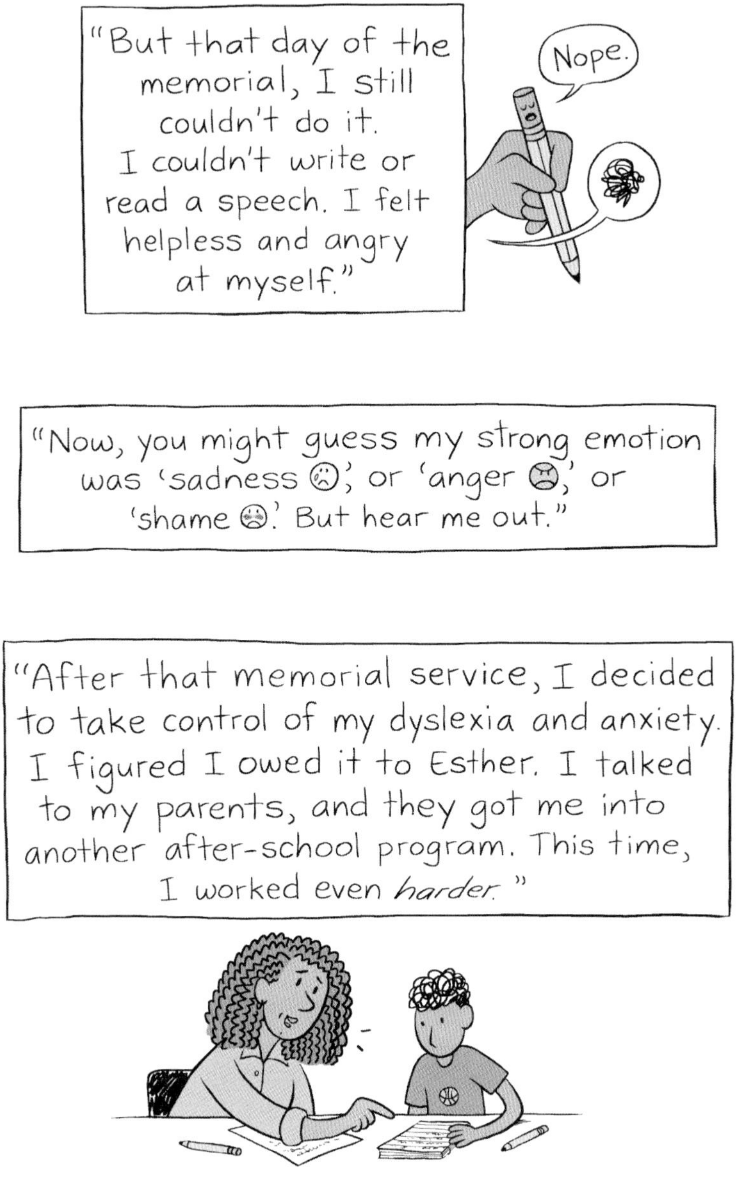
"But that day of the memorial, I still couldn't do it. I couldn't write or read a speech. I felt helpless and angry at myself."
Nope.
"Now, you might guess my strong emotion was 'sadness ☹,' or 'anger,' or 'shame.' But hear me out."
"After that memorial service, I decided to take control of my dyslexia and anxiety. I figured I owed it to Esther. I talked to my parents, and they got me into another after-school program. This time, I worked even *harder*."

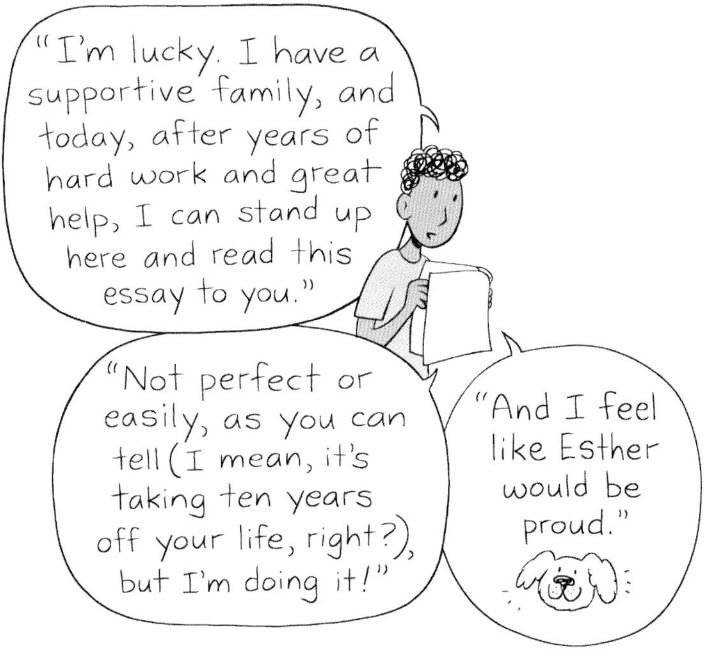
"I'm lucky. I have a supportive family, and today, after years of hard work and great help, I can stand up here and read this essay to you."
"Not perfect or easily, as you can tell (I mean, it's taking ten years off your life, right?), but I'm doing it!"
"And I feel like Esther would be proud."

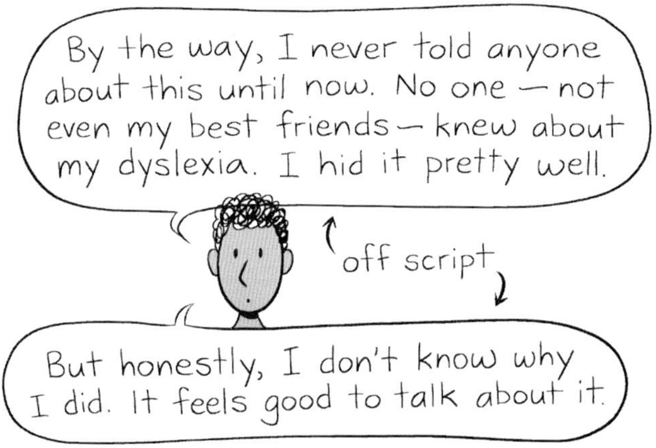
By the way, I never told anyone about this until now. No one — not even my best friends — knew about my dyslexia. I hid it pretty well.
off script
But honestly, I don't know why I did. It feels good to talk about it.

"I'm trying to express myself better and be a man of — not only action — but words."

Word **M**an
(can leap tall essays in a single structured paragraph!)

"And that is why today, despite my nervousness and stumbling, I am feeling this particularly strong emotion — the same one I felt after that memorial service for Esther:"

"Determination."

Silence.

I put my paper down, holding it against my stomach. My heart is beating out of my chest.

And then . . .

CLAP CLAP CLAP CLAP CLAP CLAP CLAP wipe WOO! CLAP CLAP

Whoa.

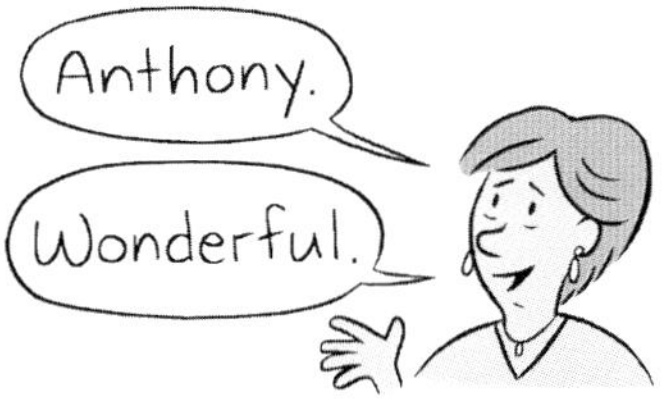
Anthony.
Wonderful.

Not really. I kept stumbling and stuttering. Still, compared to years ago, I was performing flawless Shakespeare.

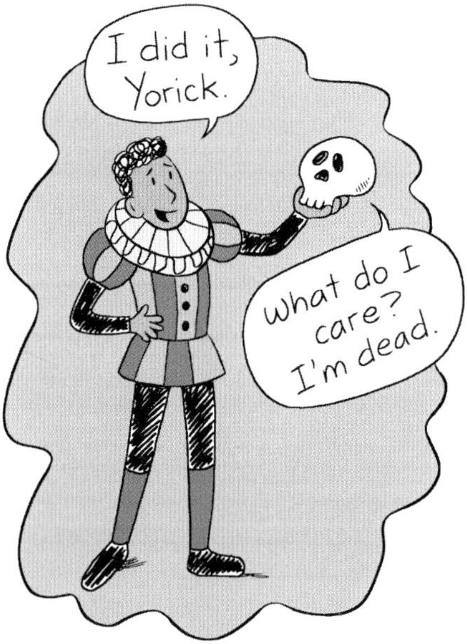
I did it, Yorick.
What do I care? I'm dead.

As I walk back to my desk, I'm feeling great (another strong emotion). Also, pooped. That took a lot out of me. But I think my parents would be proud.

I sit down in my assigned seat next to Tyler, who's looking at me like he doesn't know me.

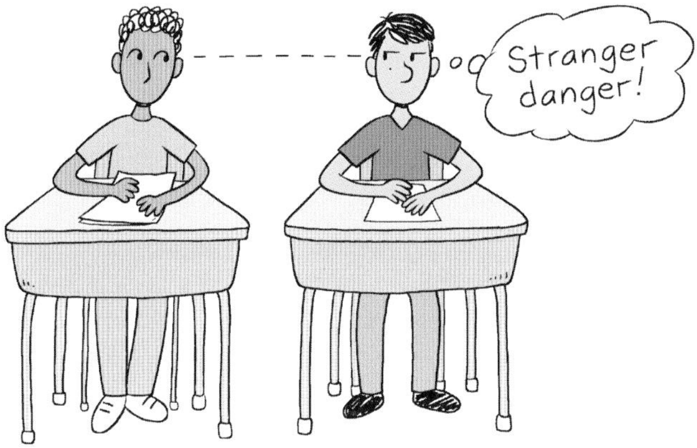
Stranger danger!

I guess I didn't think about how he'd react.

He knew I had struggles. But I never made a big deal out of my grades. Also, I didn't want anyone to feel sorry for me, including my best friend.

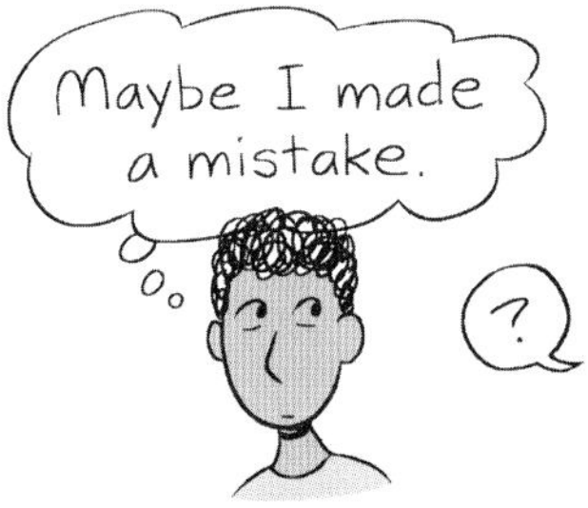
Maybe I made a mistake.
?

Two more students go up to read their papers.

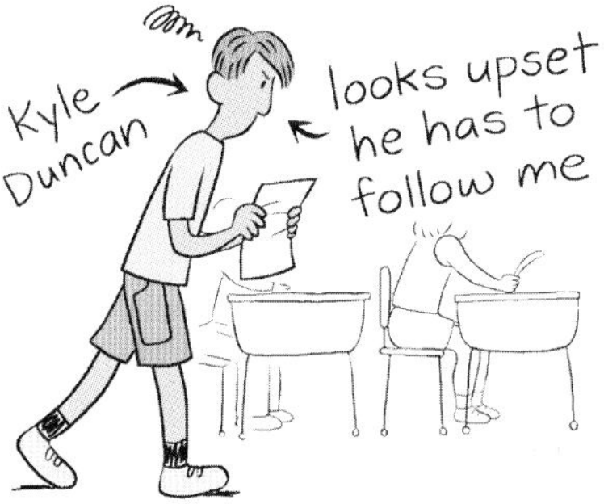
Kyle Duncan
looks upset he has to follow me

When the bell rings, Mrs. Winn calls me over. Ugh, not again. I just wanna get out of here.

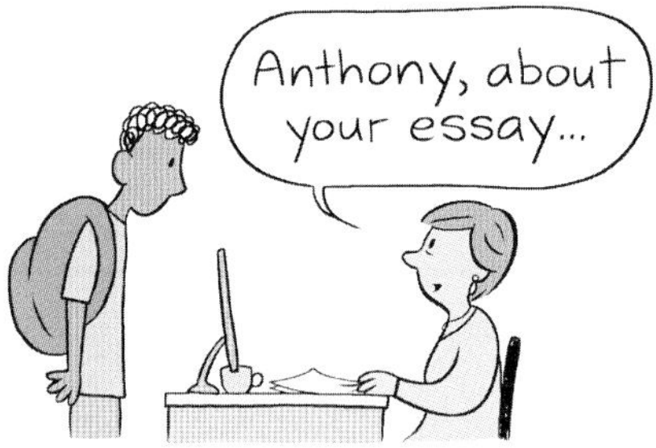
Anthony, about your essay...

Uh-oh. Did I screw up? She said she liked it, but—

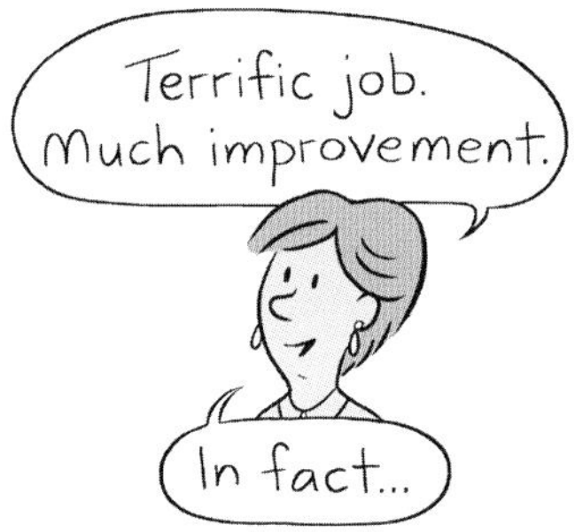
Terrific job. Much improvement.
In fact...

She waits until everyone leaves, and then she moves her monitor so that I can see my essay grade.

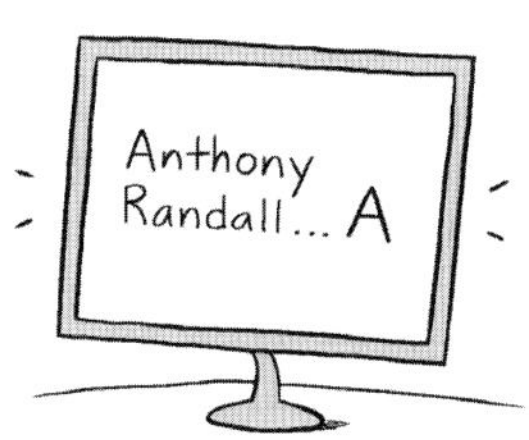
Anthony Randall... A

Wow!! Thanks, Mrs. W!
You earned it. Keep it up. And please...

...don't be afraid to ask for help if you're struggling.
I won't.

I head out. Sooo ready to go home and start the weekend. But when I step into the hallway, Tyler isn't there. I'm confused.

Hi, Anthony.

Uh-oh, I'm getting sweaty and trembly again. I adjust my backpack and hide my clammy hands in my pockets.

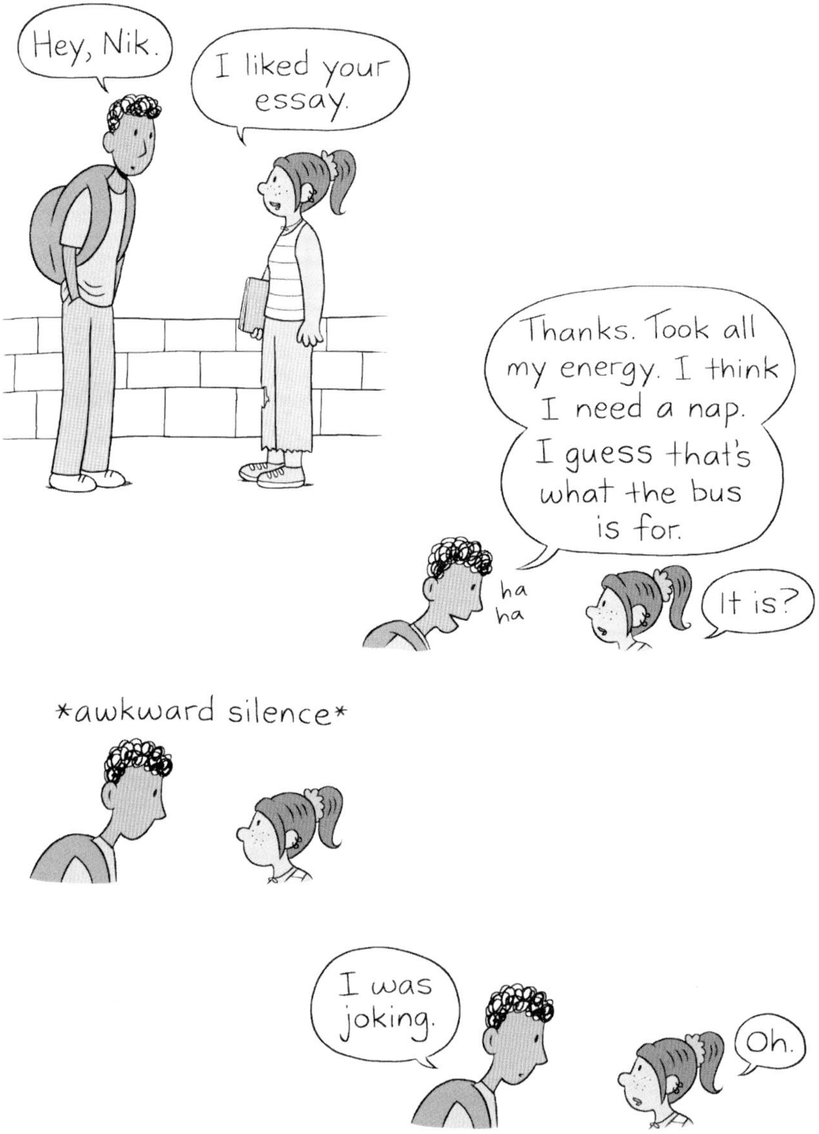
Hey, Nik.
I liked your essay.
Thanks. Took all my energy. I think I need a nap. I guess that's what the bus is for.
ha ha
It is?
awkward silence
I was joking.
Oh.

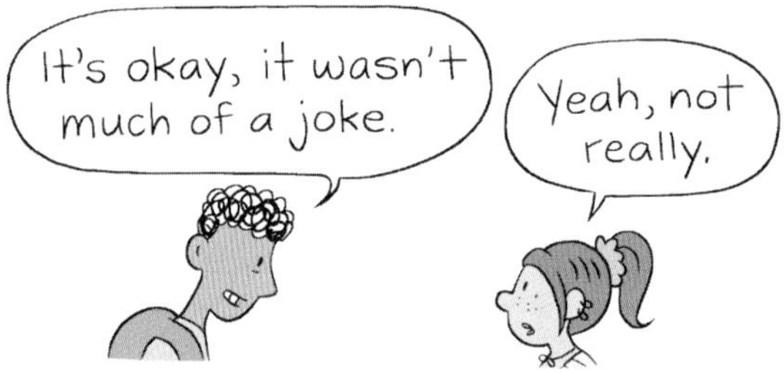
It's okay, it wasn't much of a joke.
Yeah, not really.

I laugh at that, but:

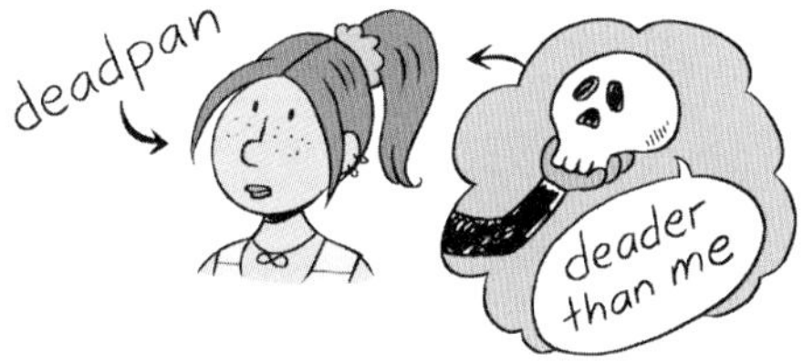
deadpan
deader than me

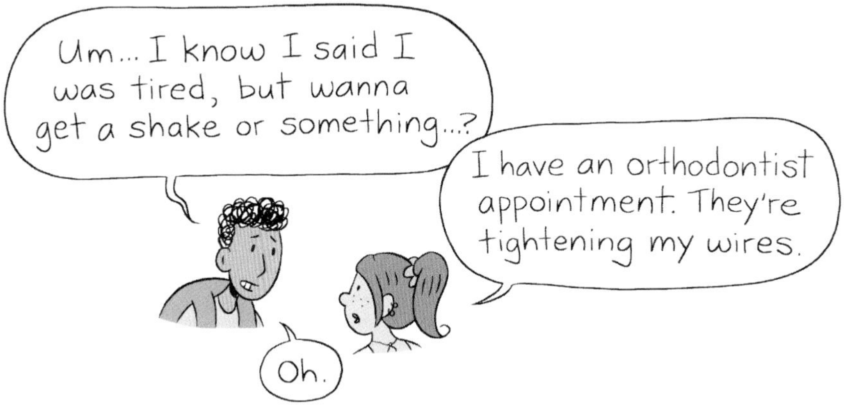
Um... I know I said I was tired, but wanna get a shake or something...?
I have an orthodontist appointment. They're tightening my wires.
Oh.

She doesn't offer up another day. Sweat is now pouring down my back.

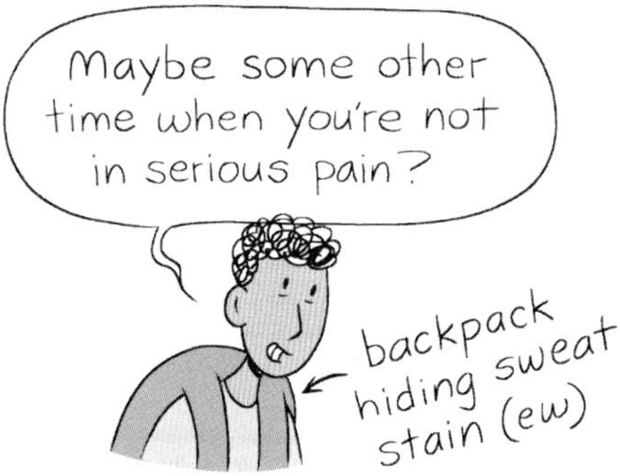
Maybe some other time when you're not in serious pain?
backpack hiding sweat stain (ew)

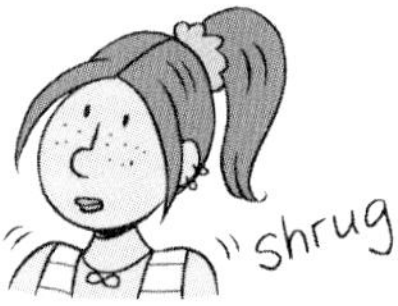
shrug

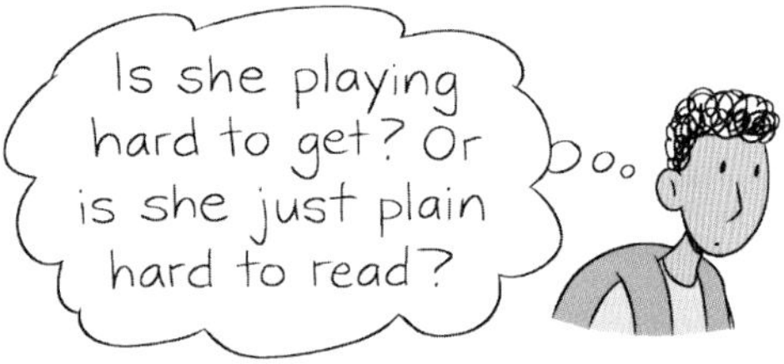
Is she playing hard to get? Or is she just plain hard to read?

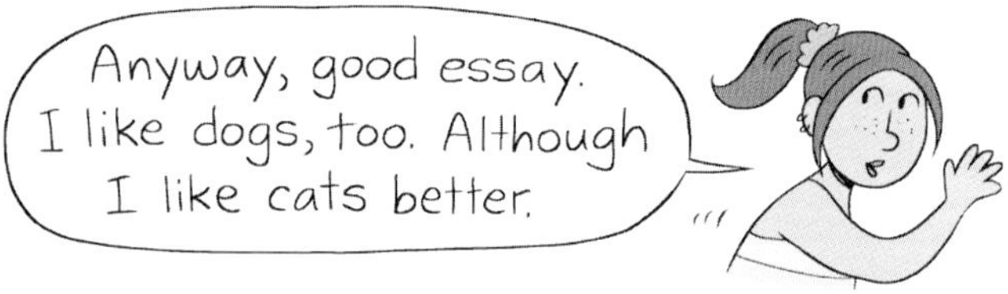
Anyway, good essay. I like dogs, too. Although I like cats better.

She walks away and joins her friends.

Cats? Seriously?

ACHOOFH!

sneezing at
the thought

I stand there, feeling awkward and kinda disappointed. Where was her sense of humor? I realize I've never seen her smile. I didn't even know she wore braces.

shaking
away
thoughts

Okay, I can't worry about Nikki now . . .

BRNNNNGGGG

. . . I have to find Tyler.

Leah

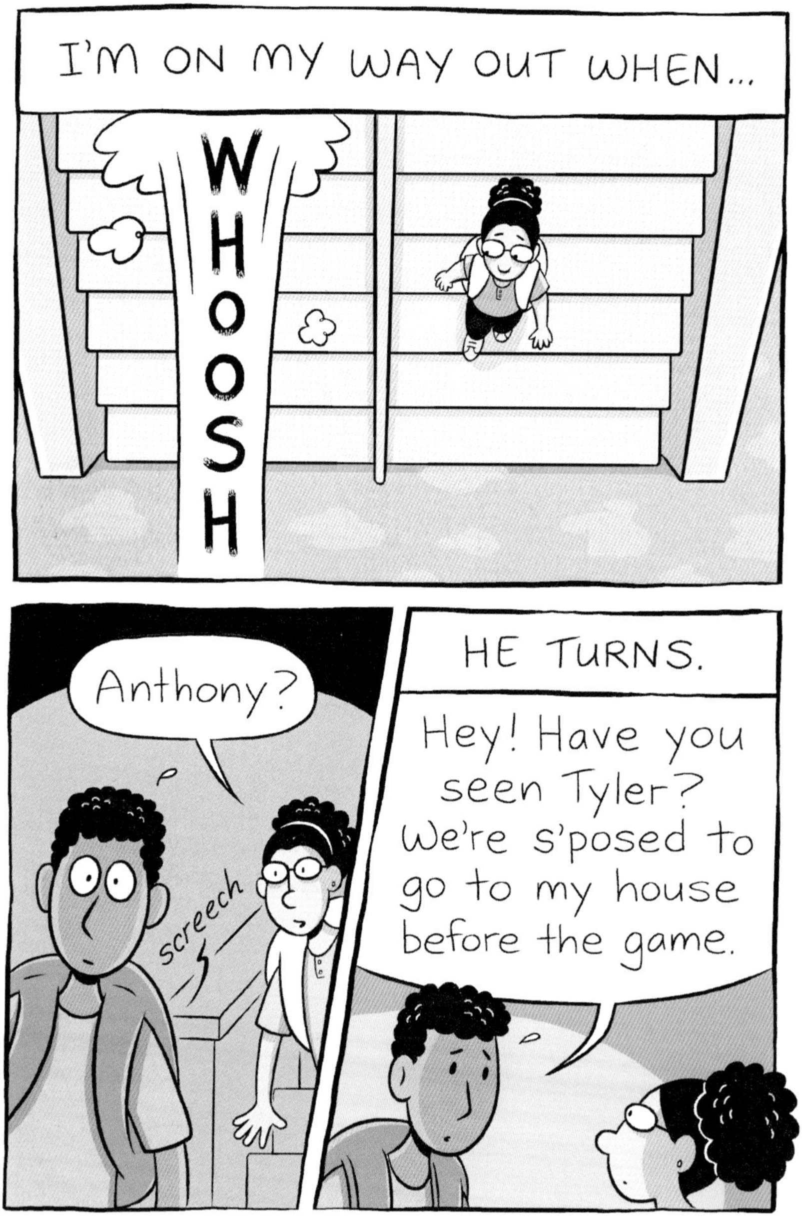

I'M ON MY WAY OUT WHEN...
WHOOSH
Anthony?
screech
HE TURNS.
Hey! Have you seen Tyler? We're s'posed to go to my house before the game.

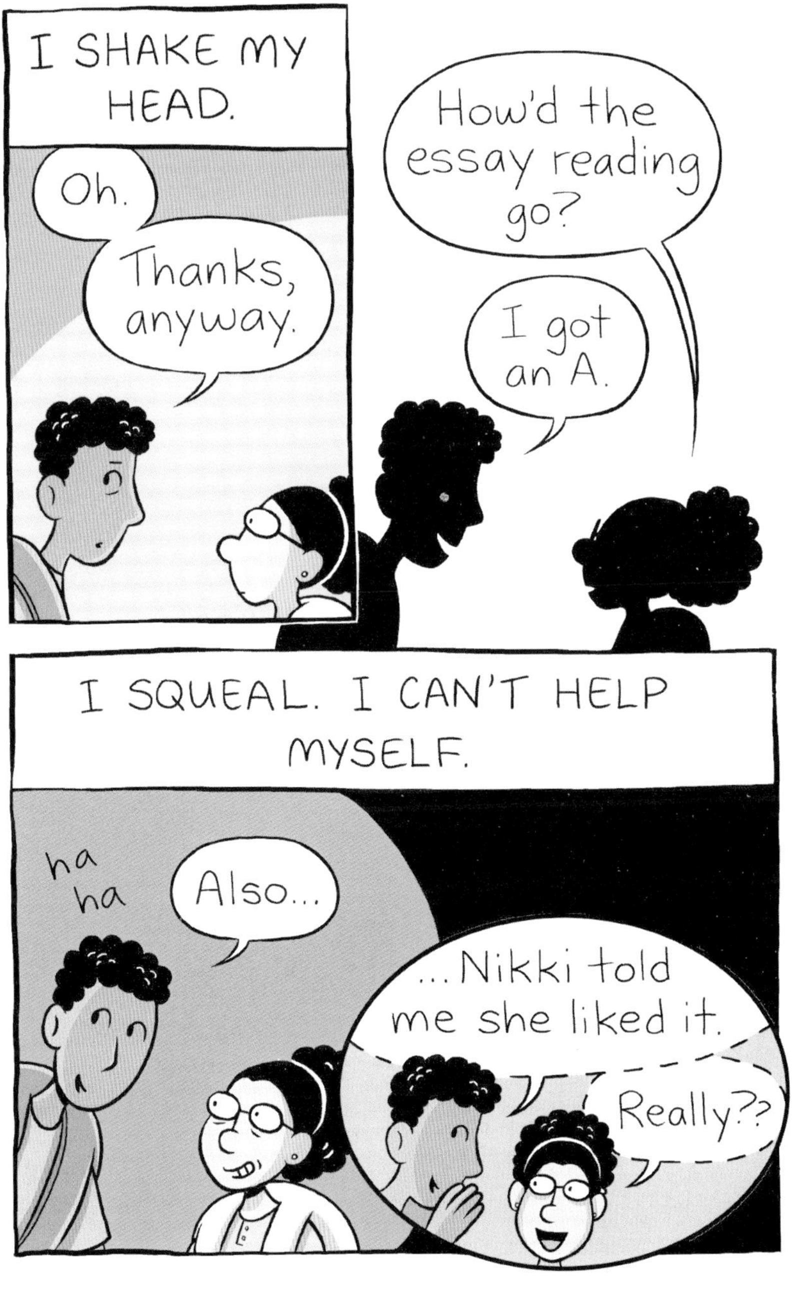
I SHAKE MY HEAD.
Oh.
Thanks, anyway.
How'd the essay reading go?
I got an A.
I SQUEAL. I CAN'T HELP MYSELF.
ha ha
Also...
...Nikki told me she liked it.
Really??

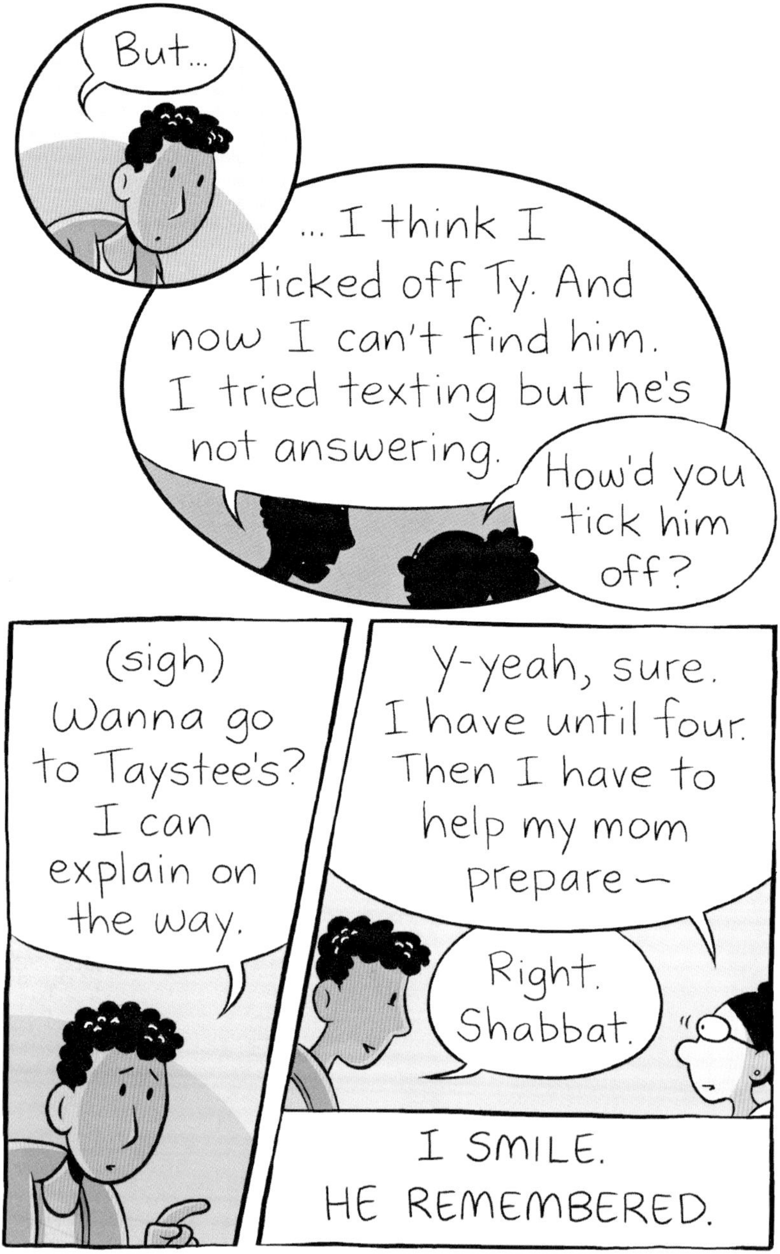
But...
... I think I ticked off Ty. And now I can't find him. I tried texting but he's not answering.
How'd you tick him off?
(sigh) Wanna go to Taystee's? I can explain on the way.
Y-yeah, sure. I have until four. Then I have to help my mom prepare—
Right. Shabbat.
I SMILE. HE REMEMBERED.

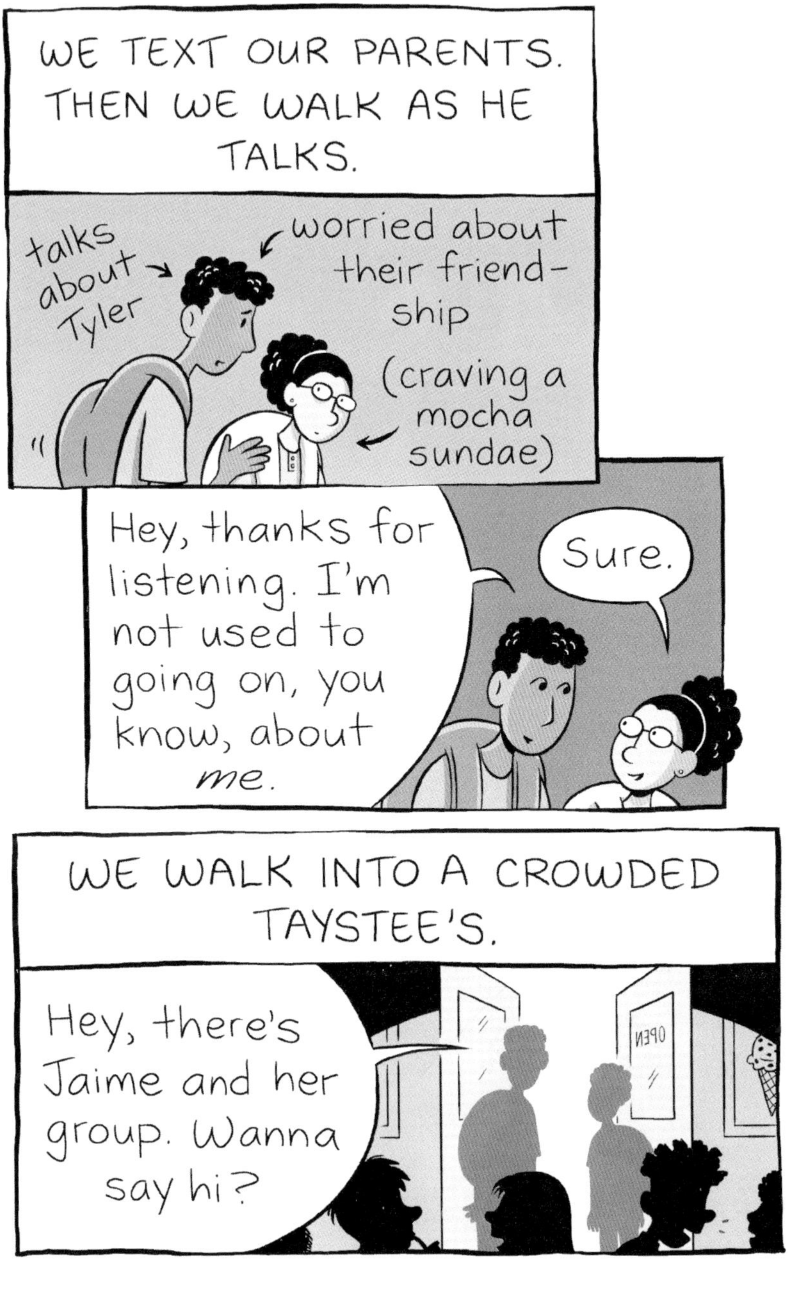
WE TEXT OUR PARENTS. THEN WE WALK AS HE TALKS.
talks about Tyler
worried about their friend-ship
(craving a mocha sundae)
Hey, thanks for listening. I'm not used to going on, you know, about *me*.
Sure.
WE WALK INTO A CROWDED TAYSTEE'S.
Hey, there's Jaime and her group. Wanna say hi?
OPEN

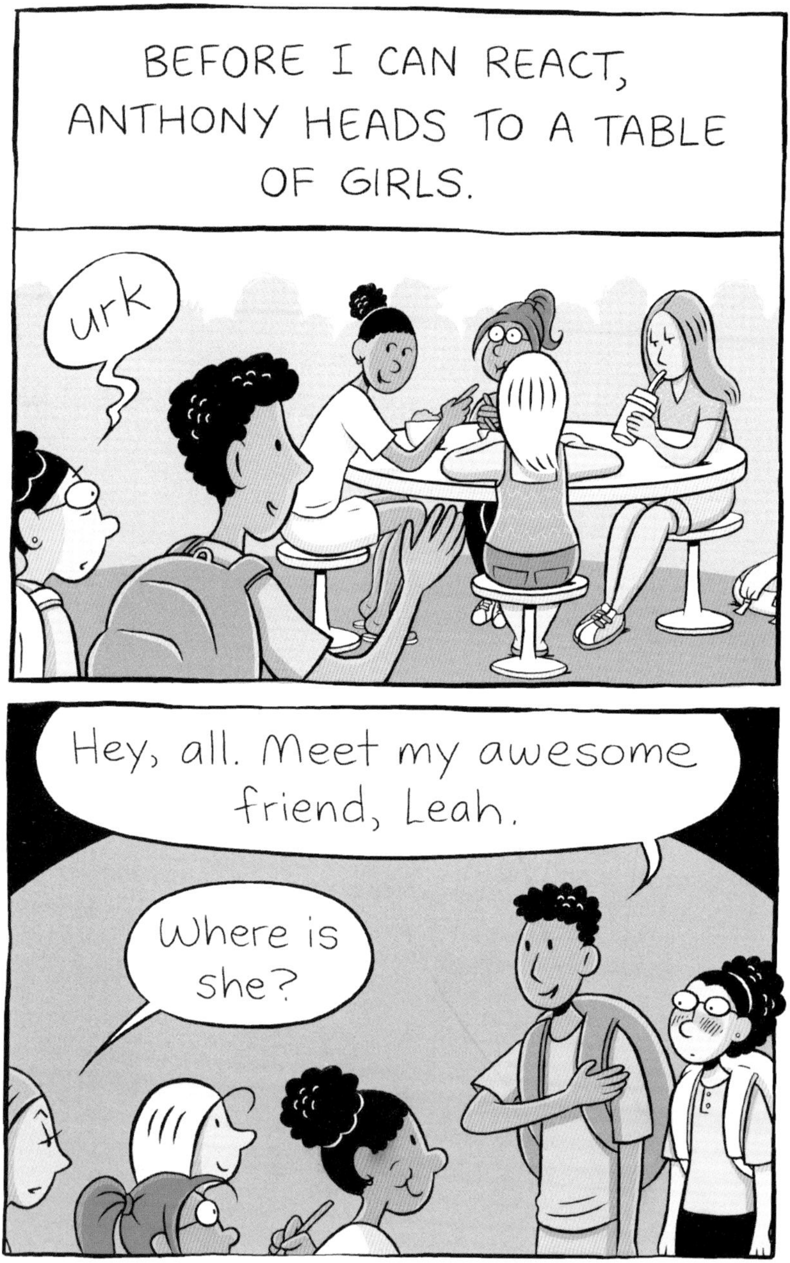
BEFORE I CAN REACT, ANTHONY HEADS TO A TABLE OF GIRLS.
urk
Hey, all. Meet my awesome friend, Leah.
Where is she?

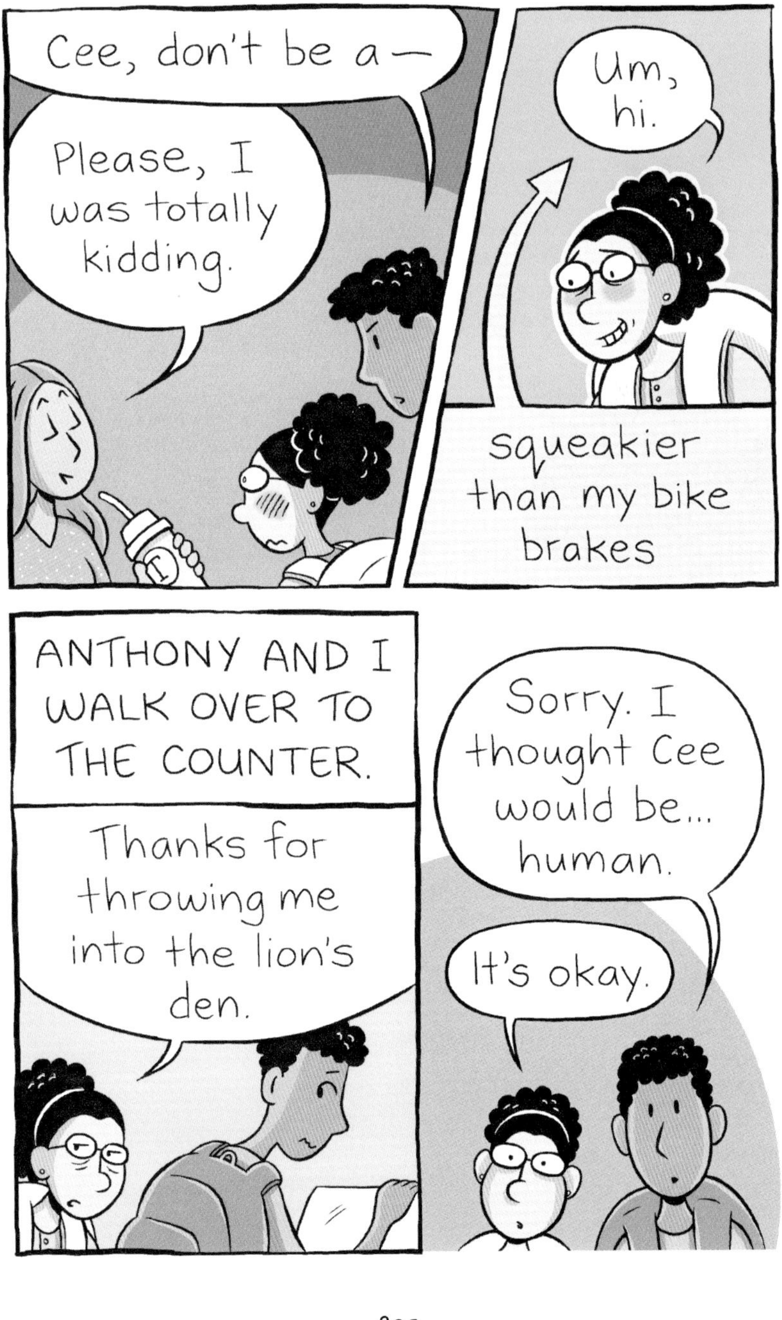
Cee, don't be a—
Please, I was totally kidding.
Um, hi.
squeakier than my bike brakes
ANTHONY AND I WALK OVER TO THE COUNTER.
Thanks for throwing me into the lion's den.
Sorry. I thought Cee would be... human.
It's okay.

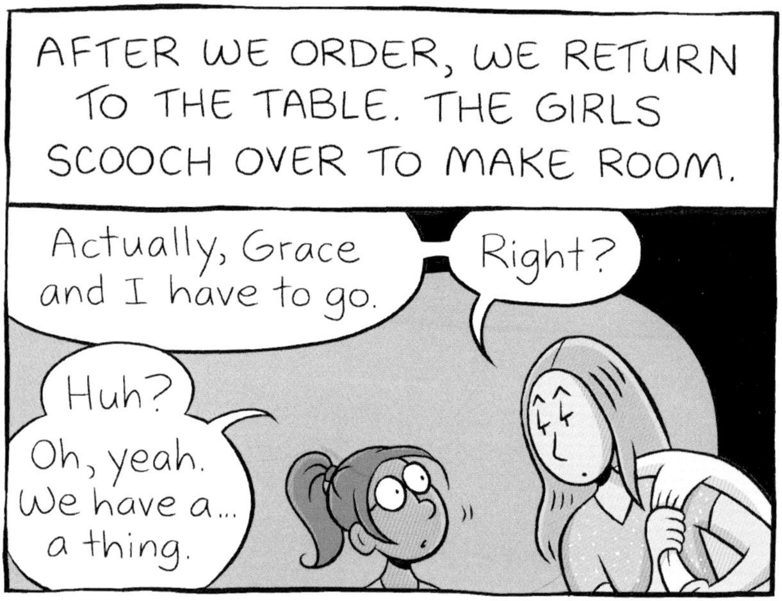
AFTER WE ORDER, WE RETURN TO THE TABLE. THE GIRLS SCOOCH OVER TO MAKE ROOM.
Actually, Grace and I have to go.
Right?
Huh?
Oh, yeah. We have a... a thing.

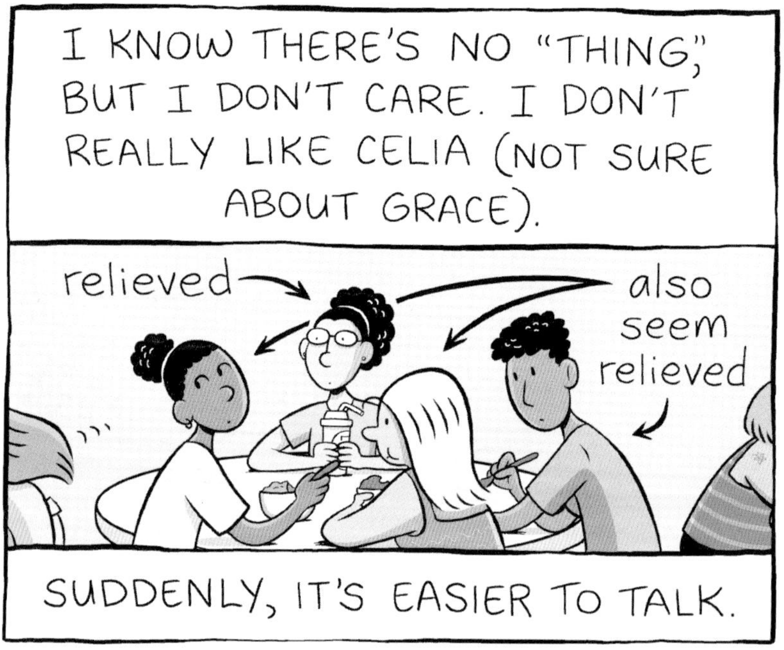
I KNOW THERE'S NO "THING," BUT I DON'T CARE. I DON'T REALLY LIKE CELIA (NOT SURE ABOUT GRACE).
relieved
also seem relieved
SUDDENLY, IT'S EASIER TO TALK.

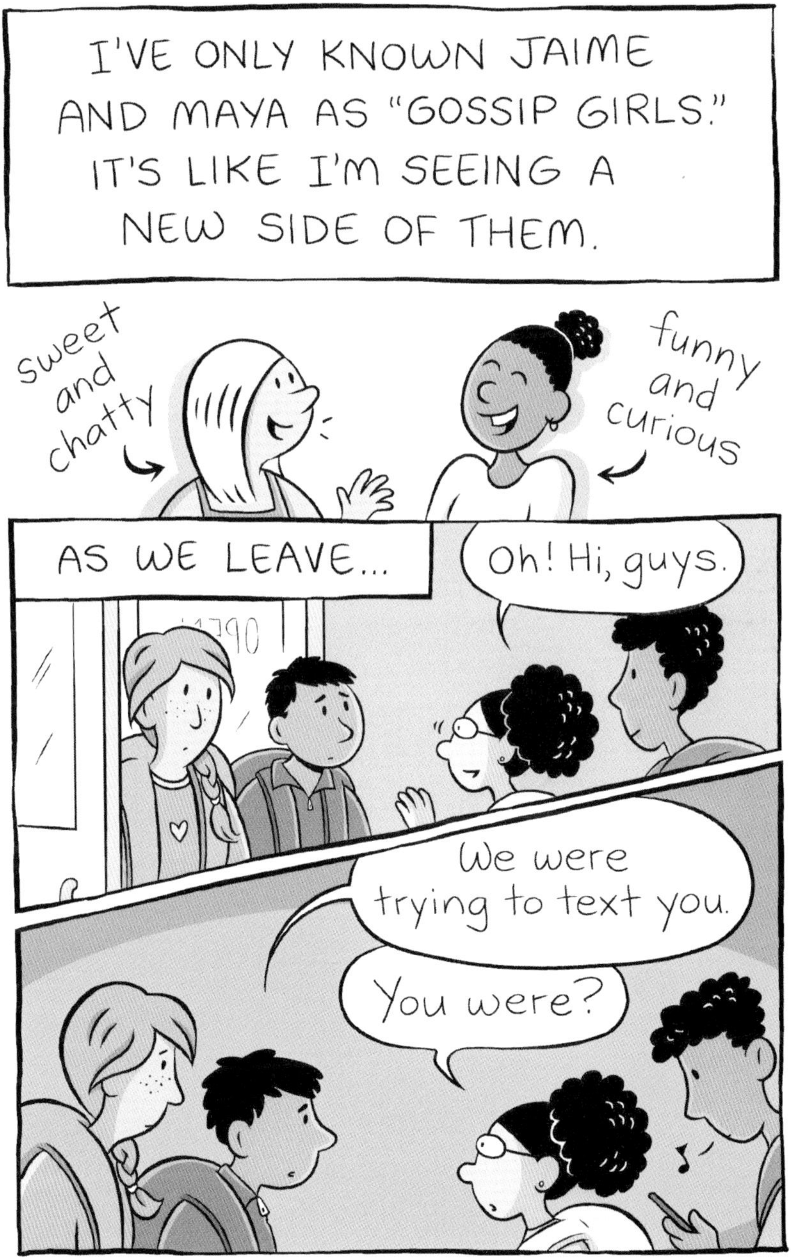
I'VE ONLY KNOWN JAIME AND MAYA AS "GOSSIP GIRLS." IT'S LIKE I'M SEEING A NEW SIDE OF THEM.
sweet and chatty
funny and curious
AS WE LEAVE...
Oh! Hi, guys.
We were trying to text you.
You were?

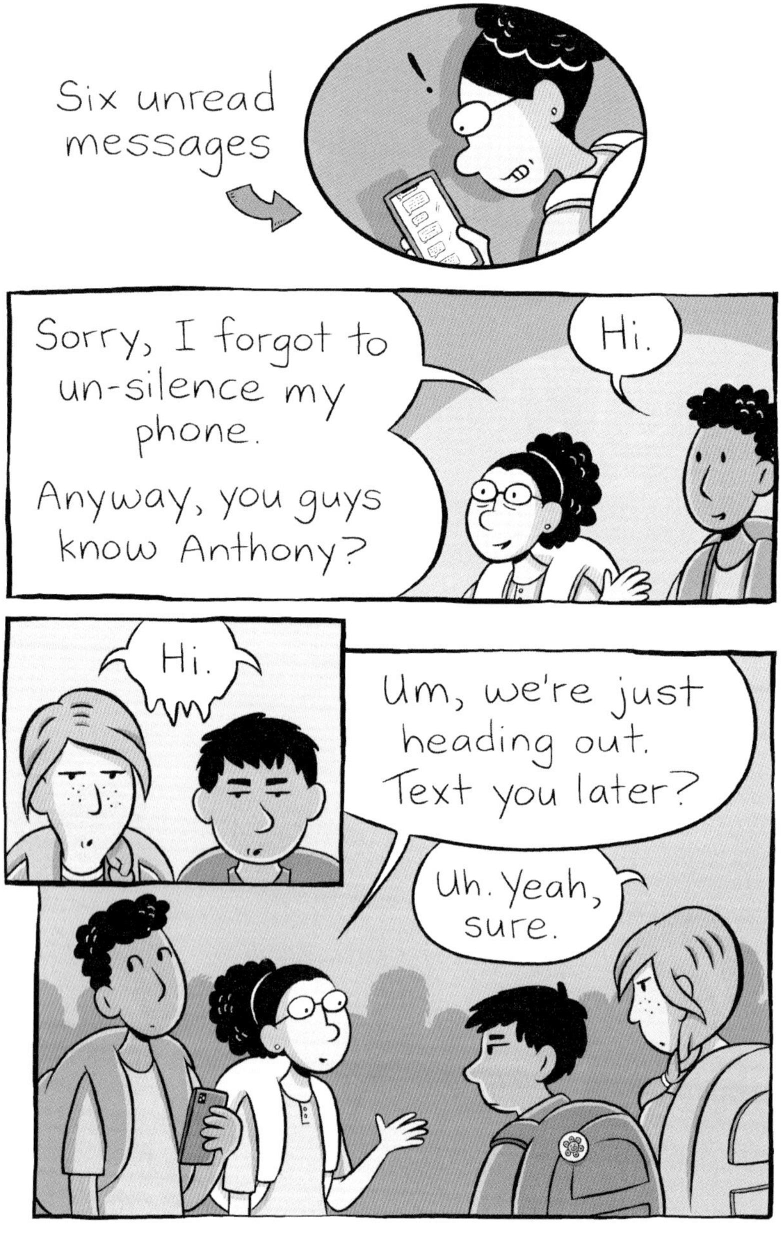
Six unread messages
Sorry, I forgot to un-silence my phone.
Anyway, you guys know Anthony?
Hi.
Hi.
Um, we're just heading out. Text you later?
Uh. Yeah, sure.

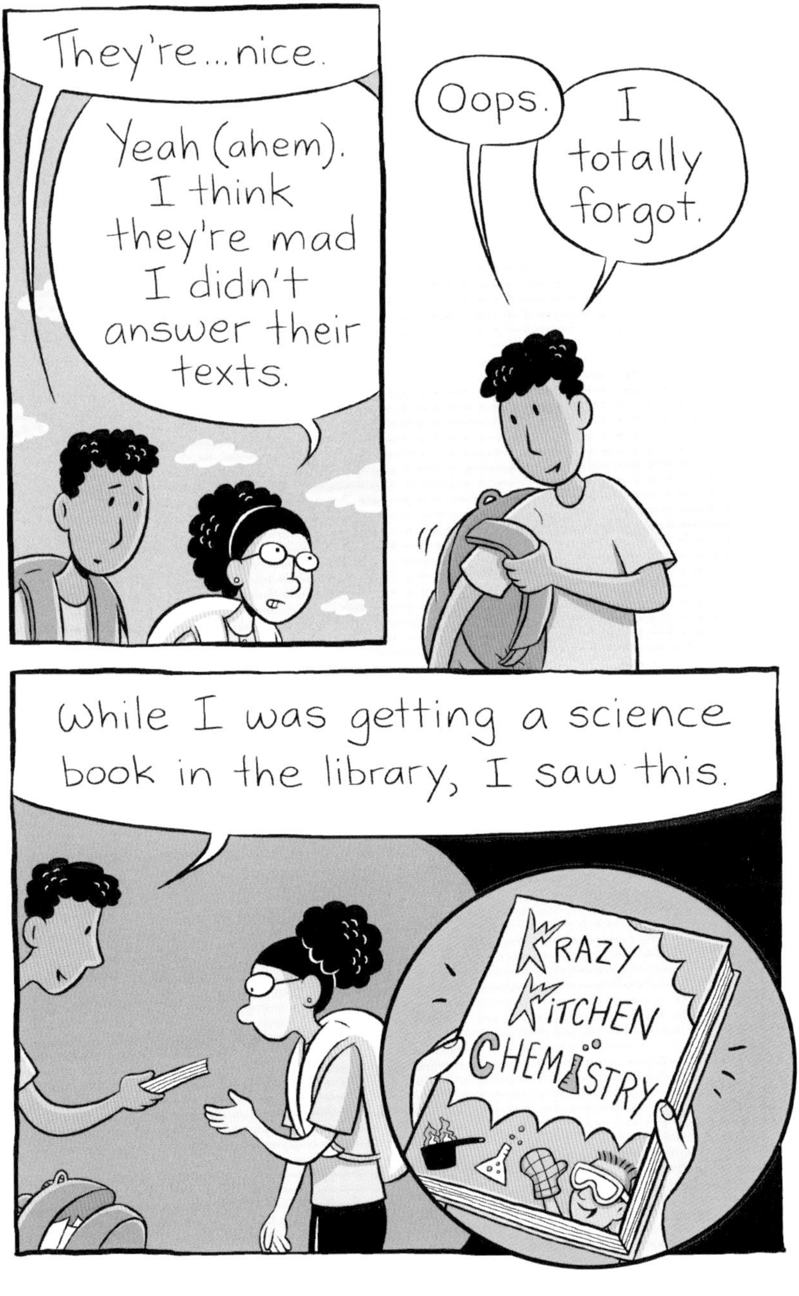
They're...nice.
Yeah (ahem). I think they're mad I didn't answer their texts.
Oops.
I totally forgot.
While I was getting a science book in the library, I saw this.
KRAZY KITCHEN CHEMISTRY

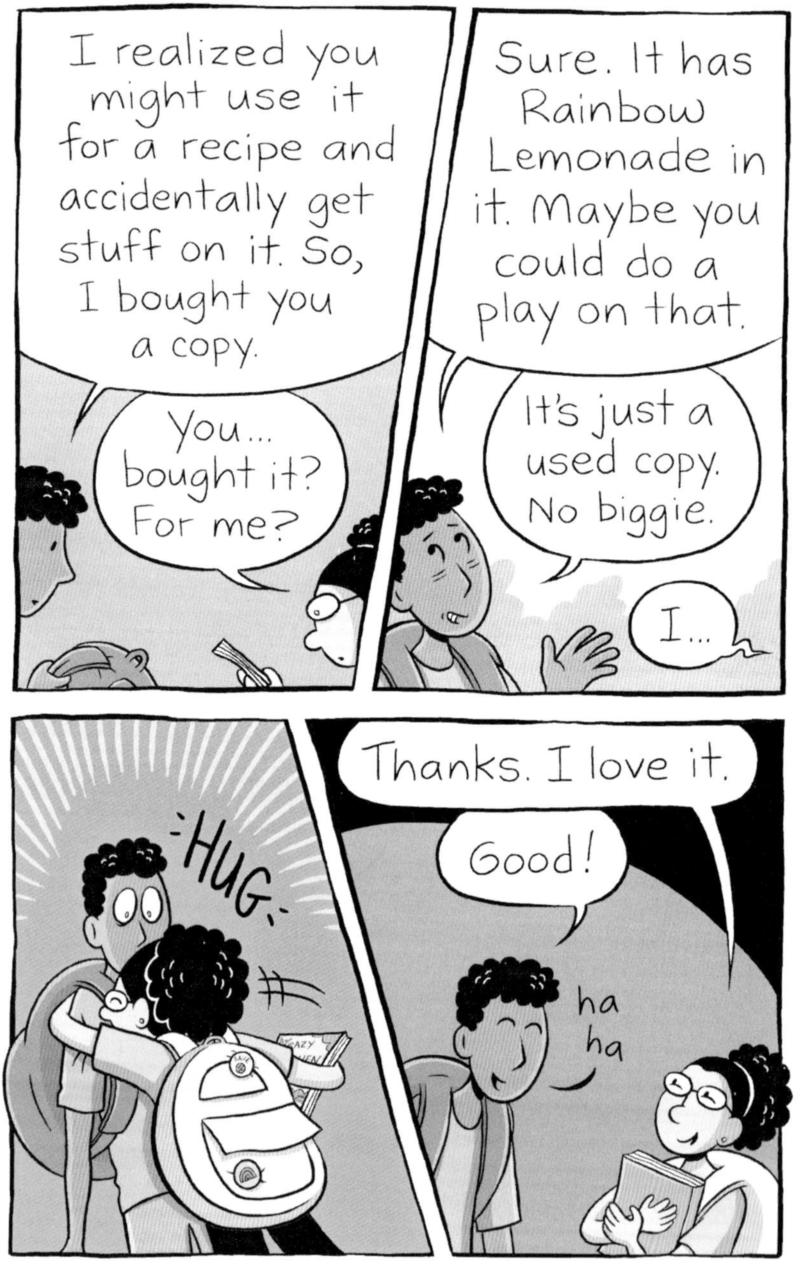
I realized you might use it for a recipe and accidentally get stuff on it. So, I bought you a copy.
You... bought it? For me?
Sure. It has Rainbow Lemonade in it. Maybe you could do a play on that.
It's just a used copy. No biggie.
I...
HUG
Thanks. I love it.
Good!
ha ha

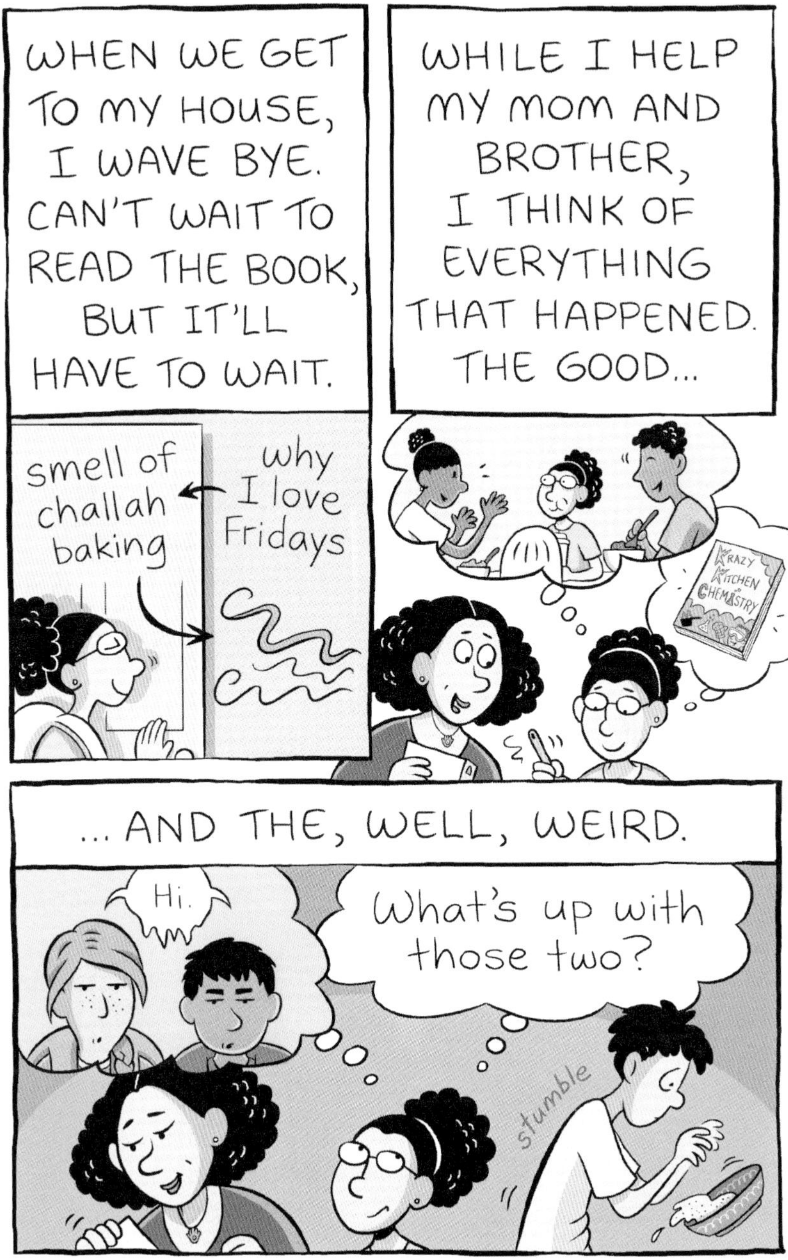
WHEN WE GET TO MY HOUSE, I WAVE BYE. CAN'T WAIT TO READ THE BOOK, BUT IT'LL HAVE TO WAIT.
WHILE I HELP MY MOM AND BROTHER, I THINK OF EVERYTHING THAT HAPPENED. THE GOOD...
smell of challah baking
why I love Fridays
KRAZY KITCHEN CHEMISTRY
...AND THE, WELL, WEIRD.
Hi.
What's up with those two?
stumble

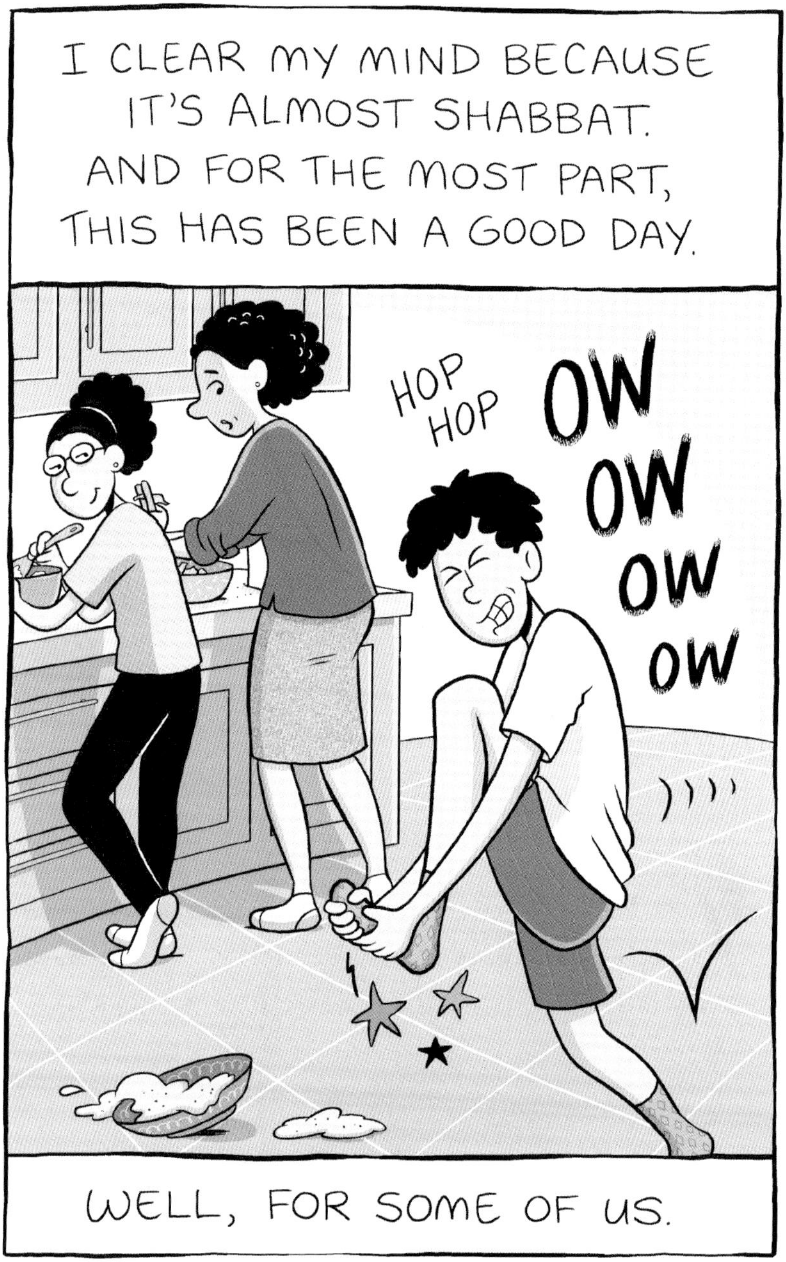
I CLEAR MY MIND BECAUSE IT'S ALMOST SHABBAT. AND FOR THE MOST PART, THIS HAS BEEN A GOOD DAY.
HOP HOP
OW OW OW OW
WELL, FOR SOME OF US.

ANTHONY

Music Room Monday.

    Despite the novelty of our room rotation, I'm having a hard time focusing. We're doing a poetry unit in class. My assignment is to identify poetic devices in a bunch of stanzas. This one is hard. I'm so bad at this stuff.

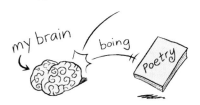

I'm also distracted 'cause of Tyler, who's mad at me. He never came over Friday afternoon, and he begged off when we all went to Ramone's after the game. But at least he was honest with me.

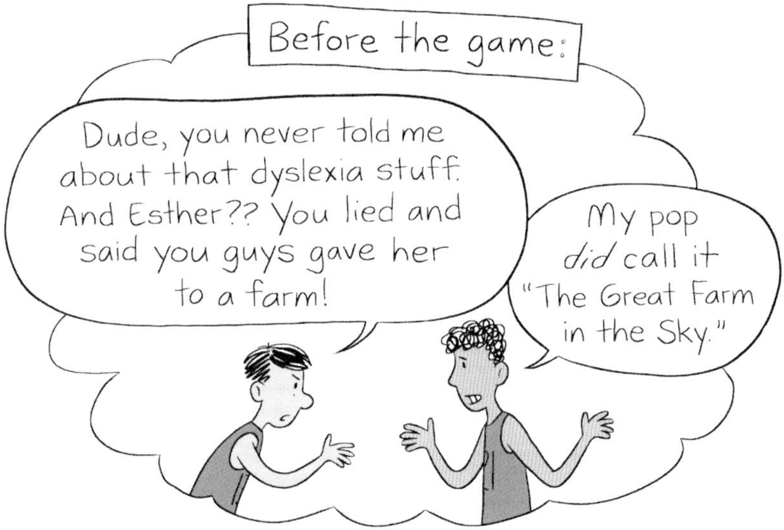
Before the game:
Dude, you never told me about that dyslexia stuff. And Esther?? You lied and said you guys gave her to a farm!
My pop *did* call it "The Great Farm in the Sky."

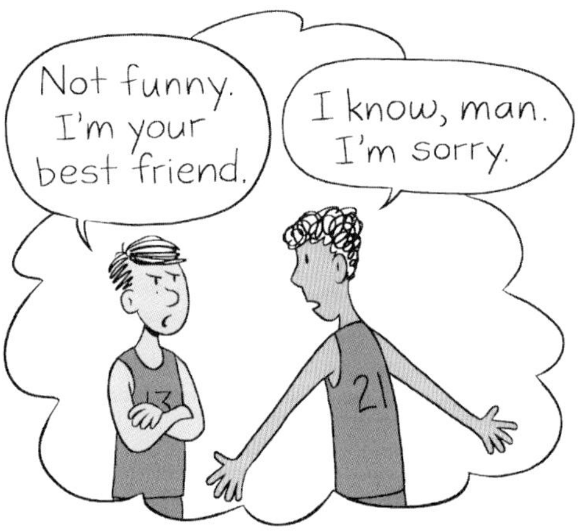
Not funny. I'm your best friend.
I know, man. I'm sorry.

He's still not talking to me, but I know him—pretty sure he just needs time to cool off. In the meantime, I try to stay on task. While I start a worksheet, Leah writes for the poetry club.

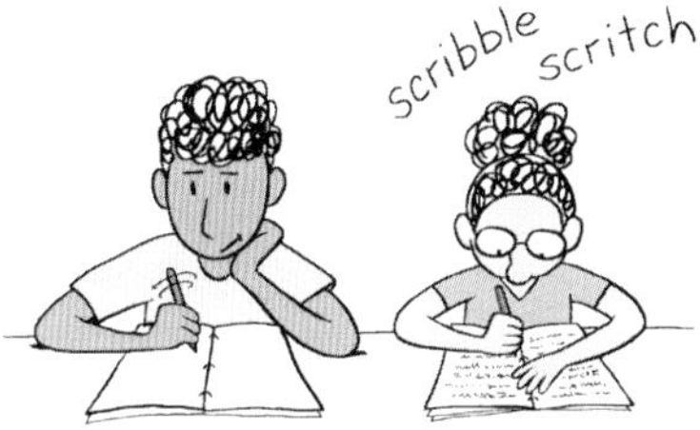
scribble
scritch

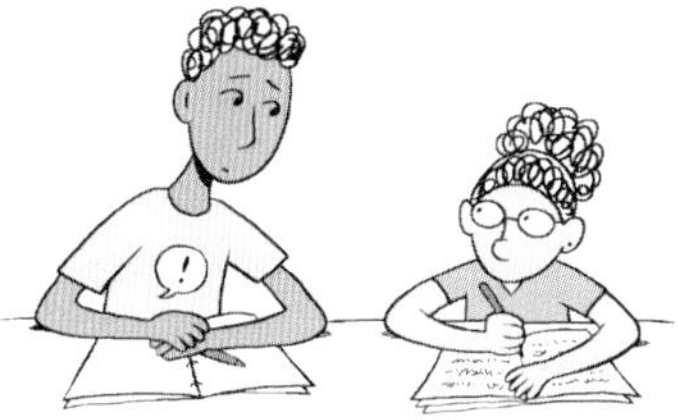

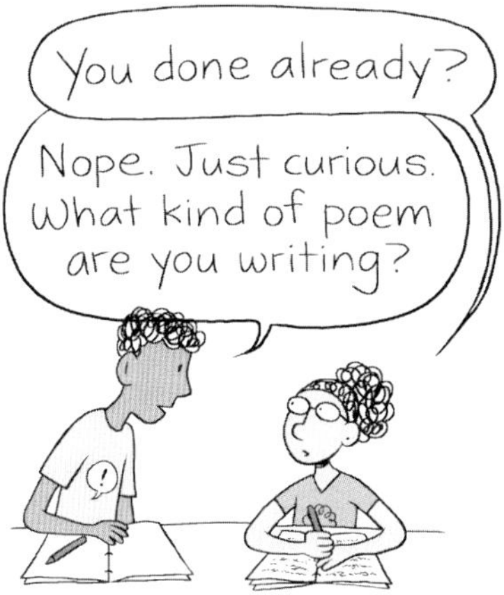
You done already?
Nope. Just curious. What kind of poem are you writing?

Leah shakes her head. She knows I'm stalling.

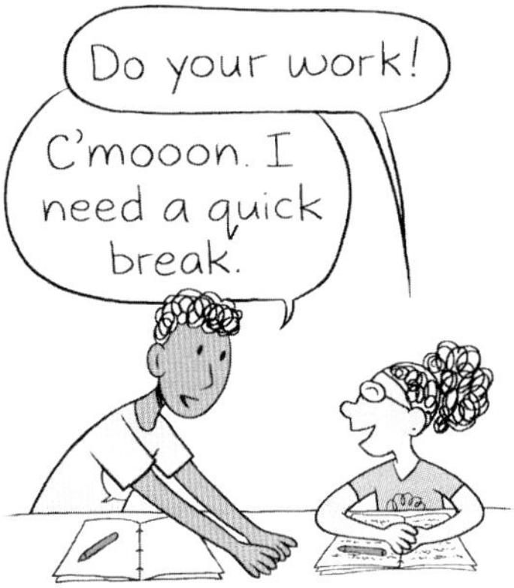
Do your work!
C'mooon. I need a quick break.

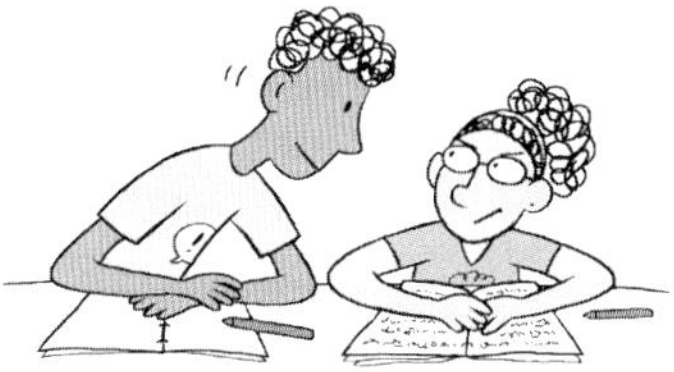

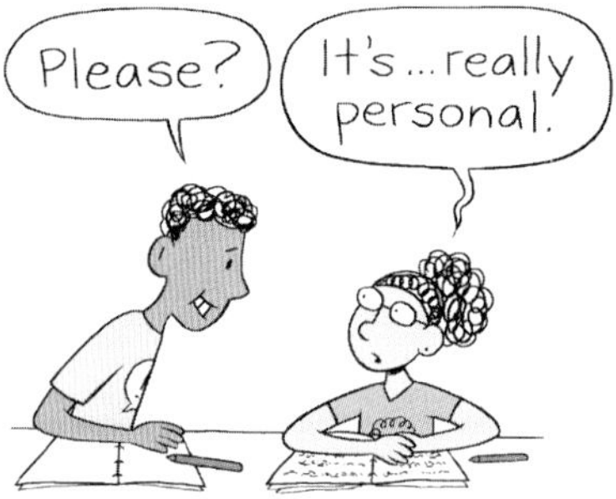
Please?
It's...really personal.

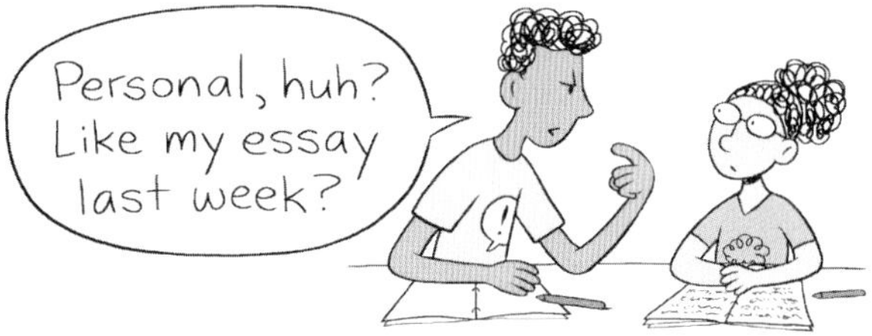
Personal, huh? Like my essay last week?

With that, she sighs and slowly removes her hands from the page.

Then she slides her notebook over to me.

I read it:

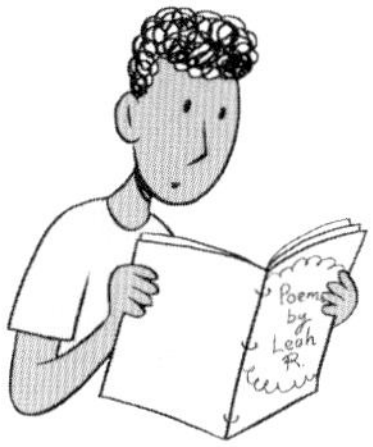
Poems by Leah R.

"My mother says
That when I was little
I bleated like a sheep
I brayed like a donkey
I whistled like the wind
In a hurricane

And then..."

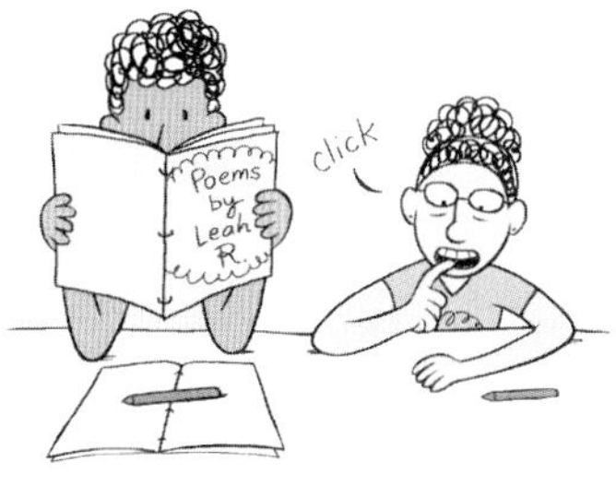
Poems by Leah R.
click

"And then came
The real storm
The one that took
My dad from our arms
And my breath away
Along with my voice

And then..."

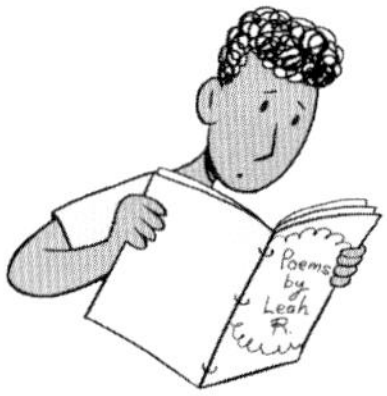
Poems by Leah R.

"And then came
The Silence.
The Shyness.
The voiceless animal
Who searched
For lost words
In the still air

Later..."

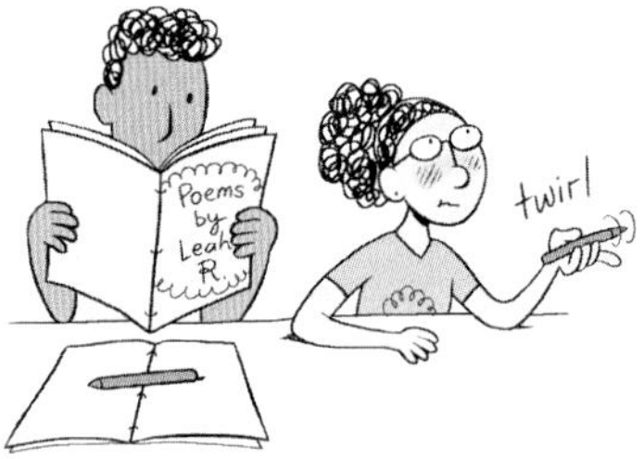
Poems by Leah R.
twirl

"I'd find it in books
In class
Inside me
The bullies tried to beat it down
The sadness tried to beat it down
But in the end

...a small chirp escaped."

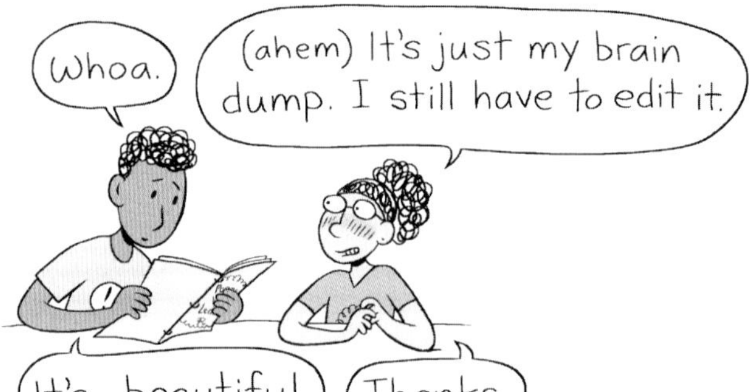
Whoa.
(ahem) It's just my brain dump. I still have to edit it.
It's...beautiful.
Thanks.

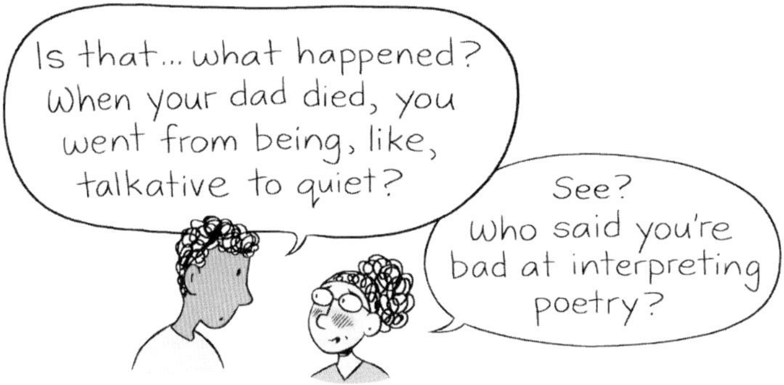
Is that... what happened? When your dad died, you went from being, like, talkative to quiet?
See? Who said you're bad at interpreting poetry?

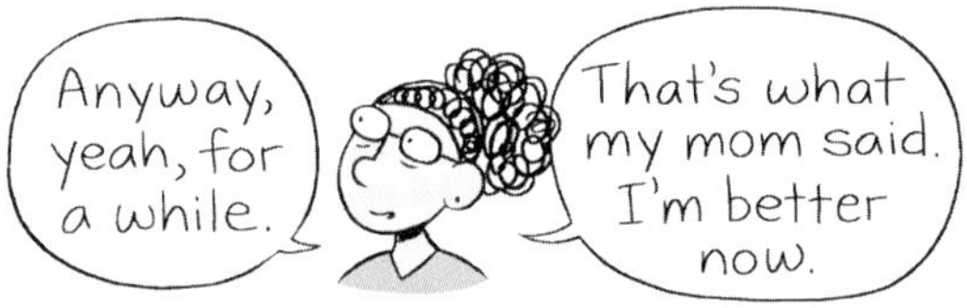
Anyway, yeah, for a while.
That's what my mom said. I'm better now.

We're quiet for a moment.

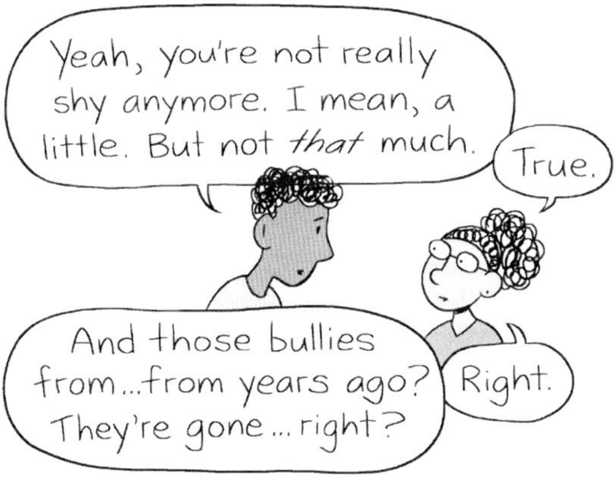
Yeah, you're not really shy anymore. I mean, a little. But not *that* much.
True.
And those bullies from...from years ago? They're gone... right?
Right.

I wanna say something else, but I don't.

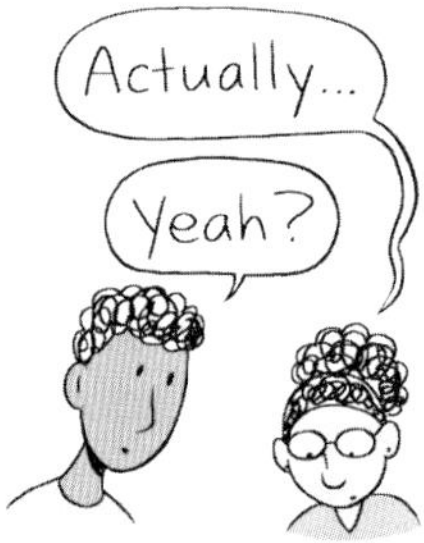
Actually...
Yeah?

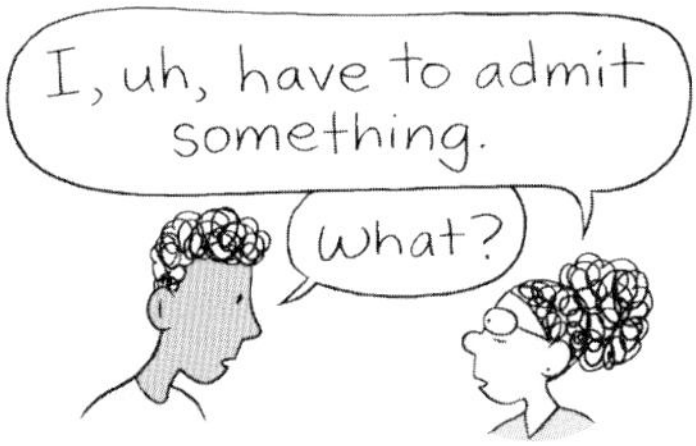
I, uh, have to admit something.
What?

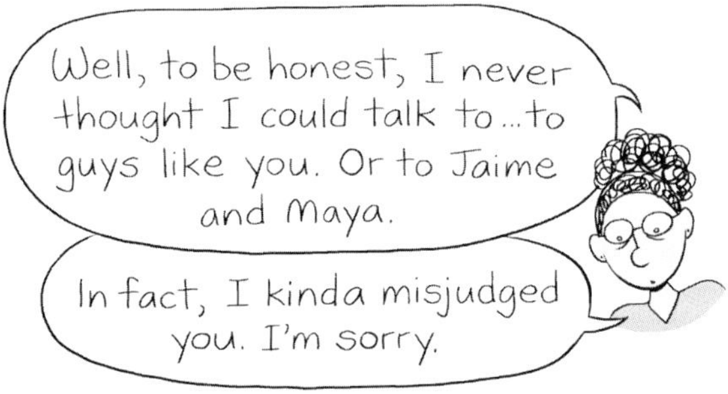
Well, to be honest, I never thought I could talk to...to guys like you. Or to Jaime and Maya.
In fact, I kinda misjudged you. I'm sorry.

I get it. She's talking about my friends and me, the "cool" kids. My face gets all warm but not in a bad way.

I don't say anything. I just smile a little and nod.

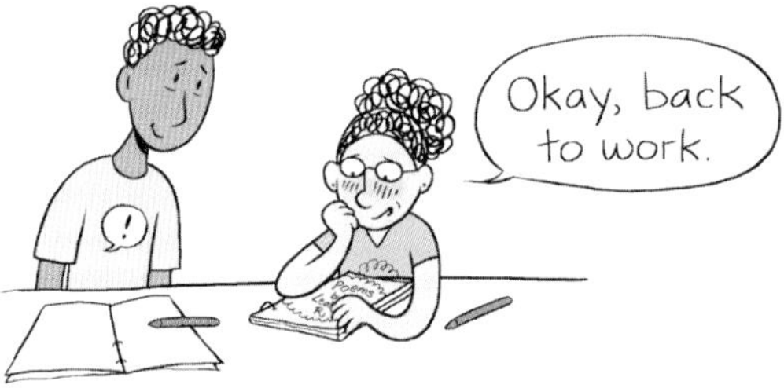
Okay, back to work.

Somehow, I manage to finish my assignment and check it over. Leah helps me with some answers and then has me do a few worksheets until the bell rings.

We walk out.

On our way to next period, we come to a cleared-out hall. It's kind of a shortcut where there aren't any lockers or classrooms. Leah turns to me.

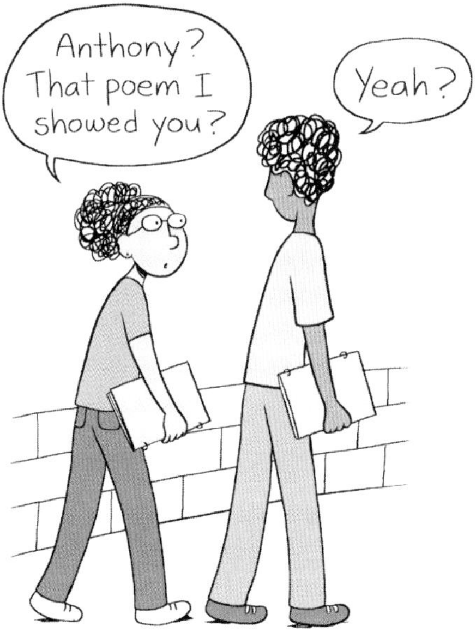
Anthony? That poem I showed you?
Yeah?

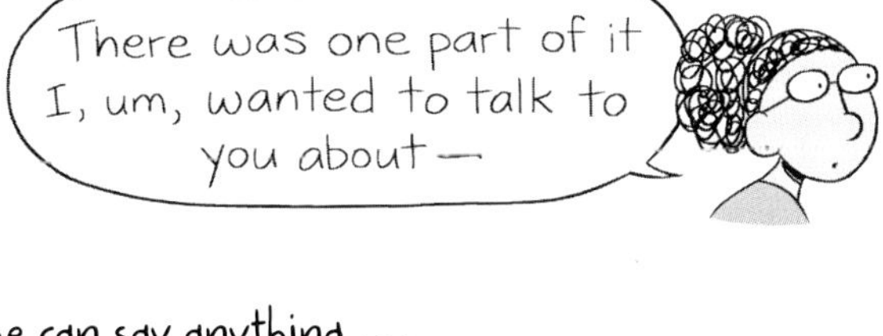
There was one part of it I, um, wanted to talk to you about—

But before she can say anything . . .

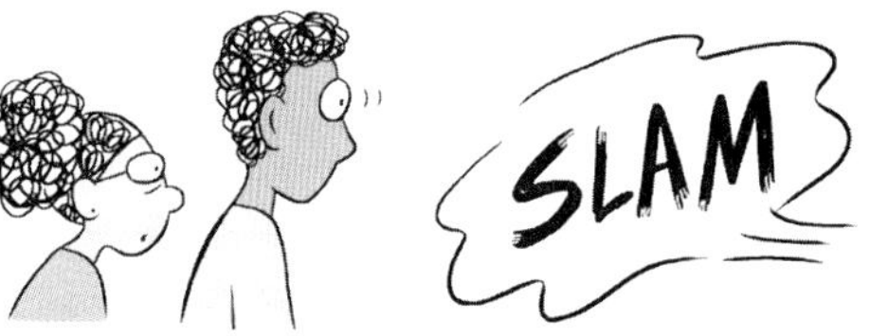
SLAM

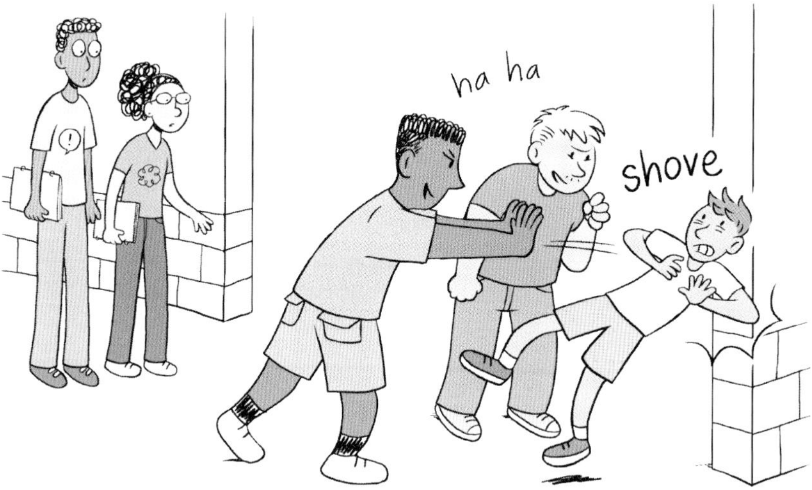
ha ha
shove

Then something unexpected happens.

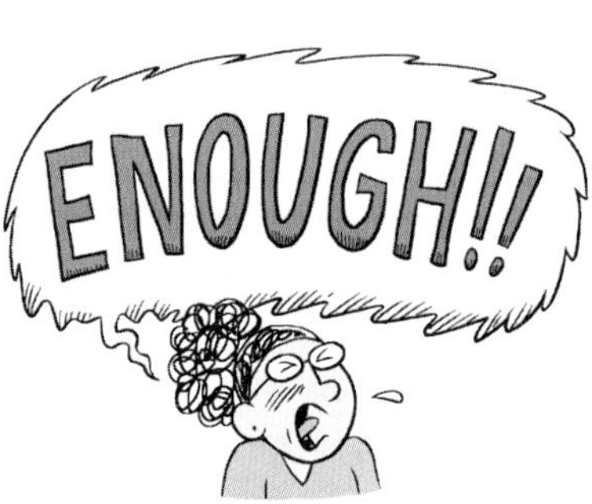
ENOUGH!!

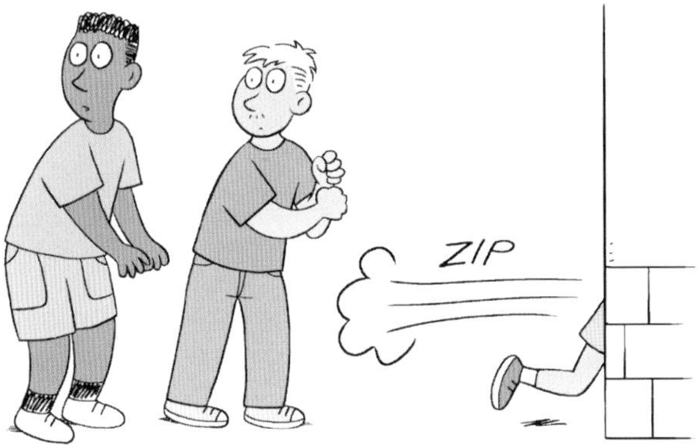
ZIP

I'm totally shocked, but the older boys laugh.

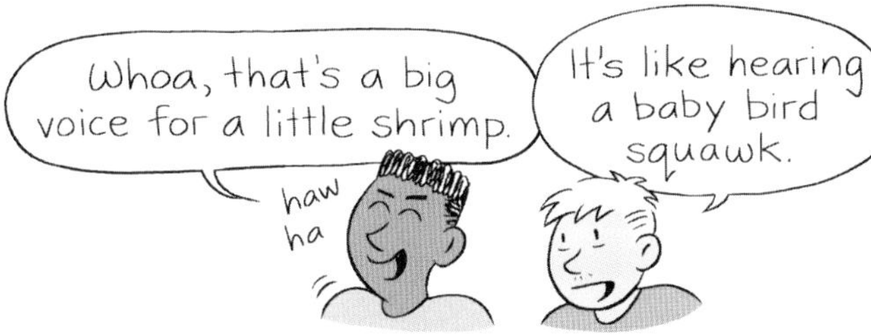
Whoa, that's a big voice for a little shrimp.
haw ha
It's like hearing a baby bird squawk.

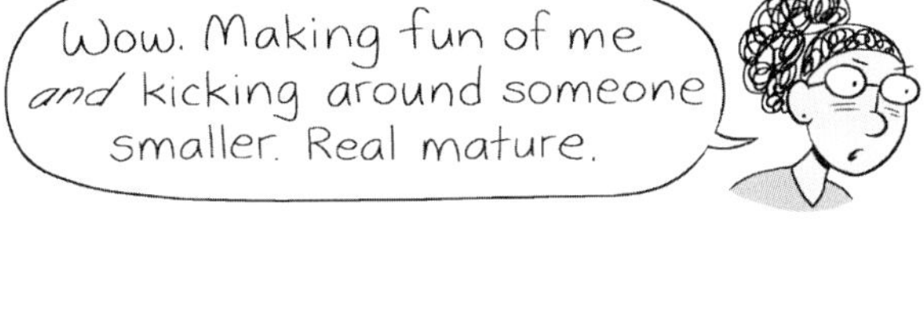
Wow. Making fun of me *and* kicking around someone smaller. Real mature.

That takes the wind out of their sails (as my pop says) but only for an instant.

Anthony, your little friend has a huge mouth.

Aren't you gonna tell her to shut up?

Truth is, I'm kinda frozen again. If I do the right thing, they'll make my life miserable. Heck, they'll make **Leah's** miserable.

Still, I've gotta say . . . something.

Hey, guys, you made a promise, right? You have amnesia or something?

I know *I* get hit in the head with the ball sometimes...

We never made a promise, bro. We just said "we hear you."

That little dude has a big mouth. He needed another lesson.

224

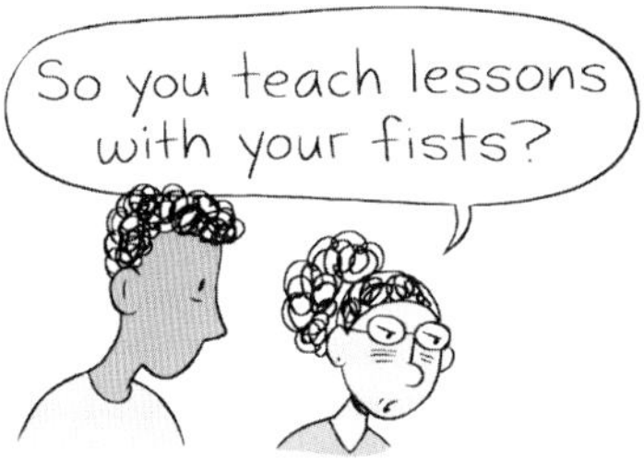
So you teach lessons with your fists?

Wow, she's not stopping. I wish she would; I'm trying to defuse the situation, not add more fire.

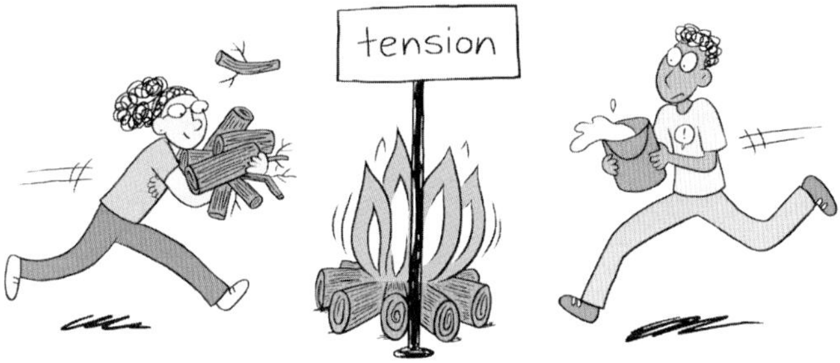
tension

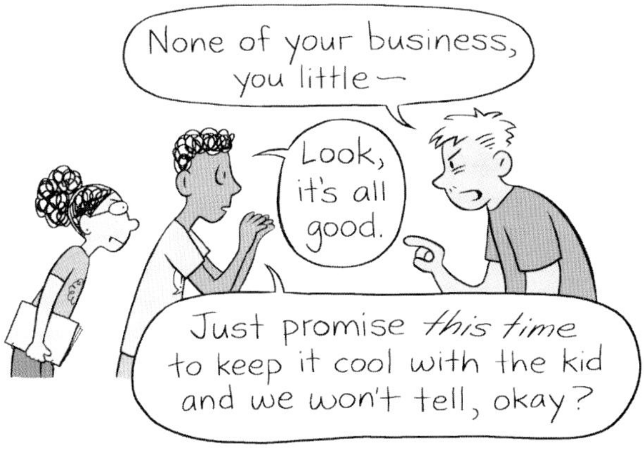
None of your business, you little—
Look, it's all good.
Just promise *this time* to keep it cool with the kid and we won't tell, okay?

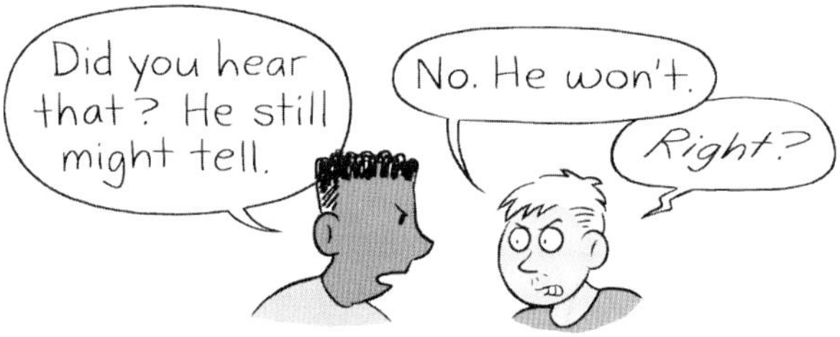
Did you hear that? He still might tell.
No. He won't.
Right?

Lucas and Eddie look directly at me. Not in a pleasant way. And I swear, in that moment, they look even bigger.

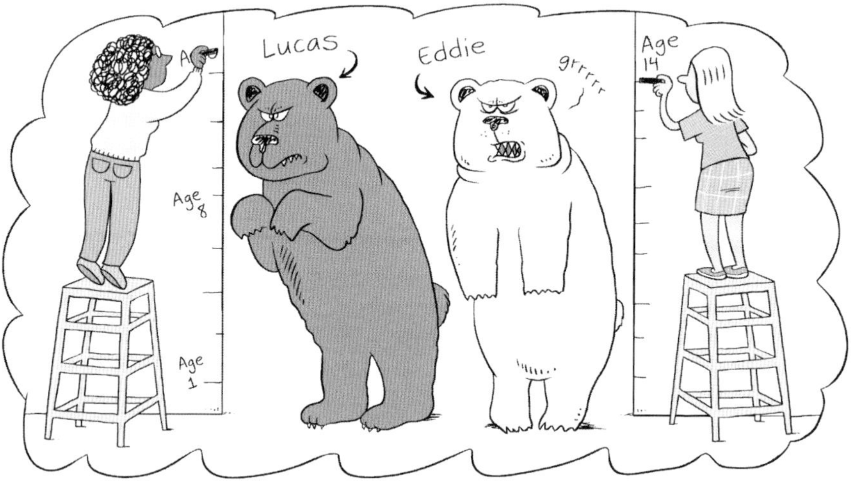
Lucas
Eddie
grrrrr
Age 8
Age 1
Age 14

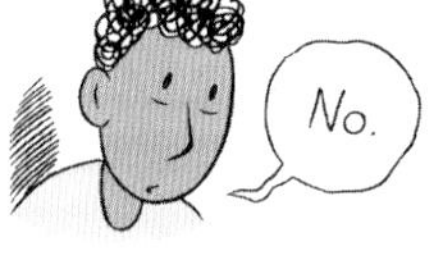
No.

Leah whips her head at me, her eyes practically bulging out of their sockets.

Then she turns and leaves. Not like she's frightened—like she's **mad**.

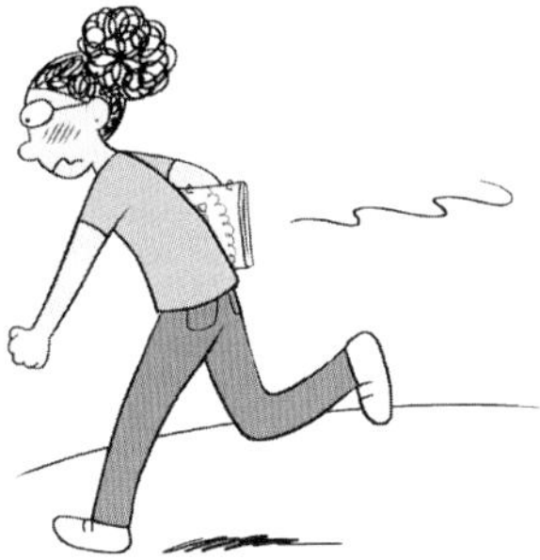

I stand there, not sure what to do.

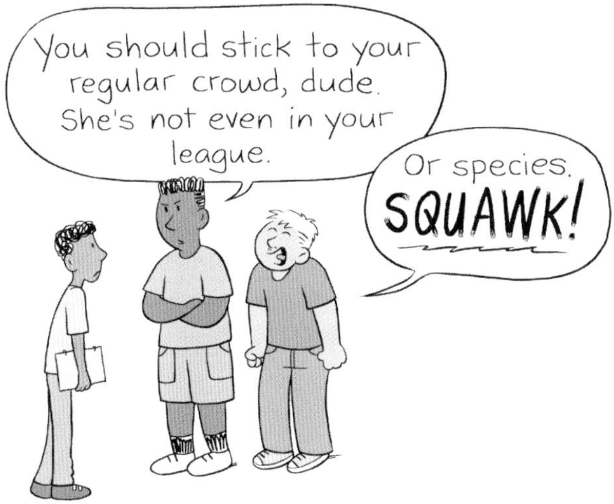
You should stick to your regular crowd, dude. She's not even in your league.
Or species.
SQUAWK!

I mumble that I have to get to class. Then I rush out of there. I can't think. Now I **really** feel like a robot.

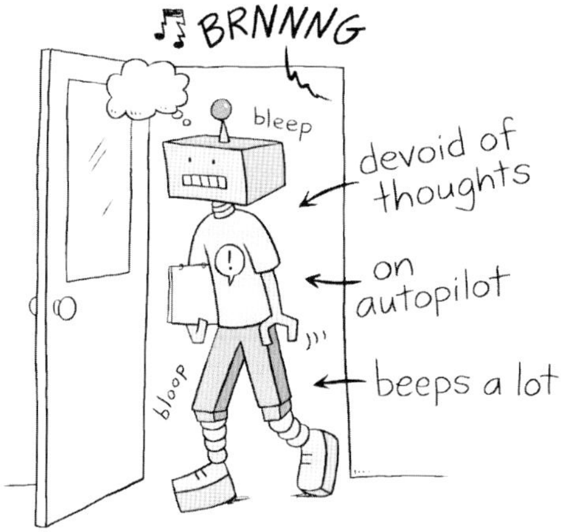
BRNNNG
bleep
devoid of thoughts
on autopilot
beeps a lot
bloop

After class, I wait for Leah. We need to talk.

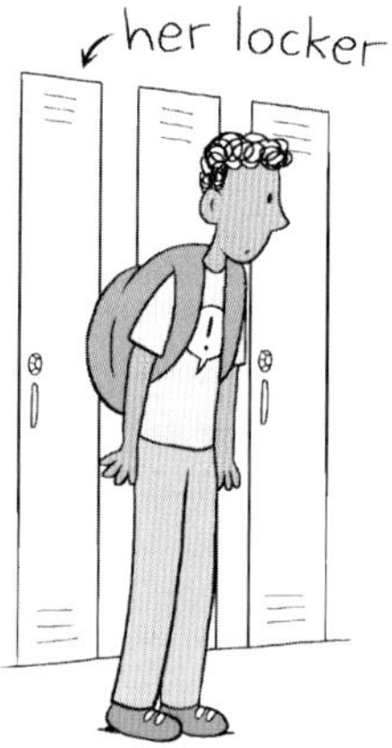
her locker

I can't find her.

But I've finally found something else.

common sense

I totally screwed up.

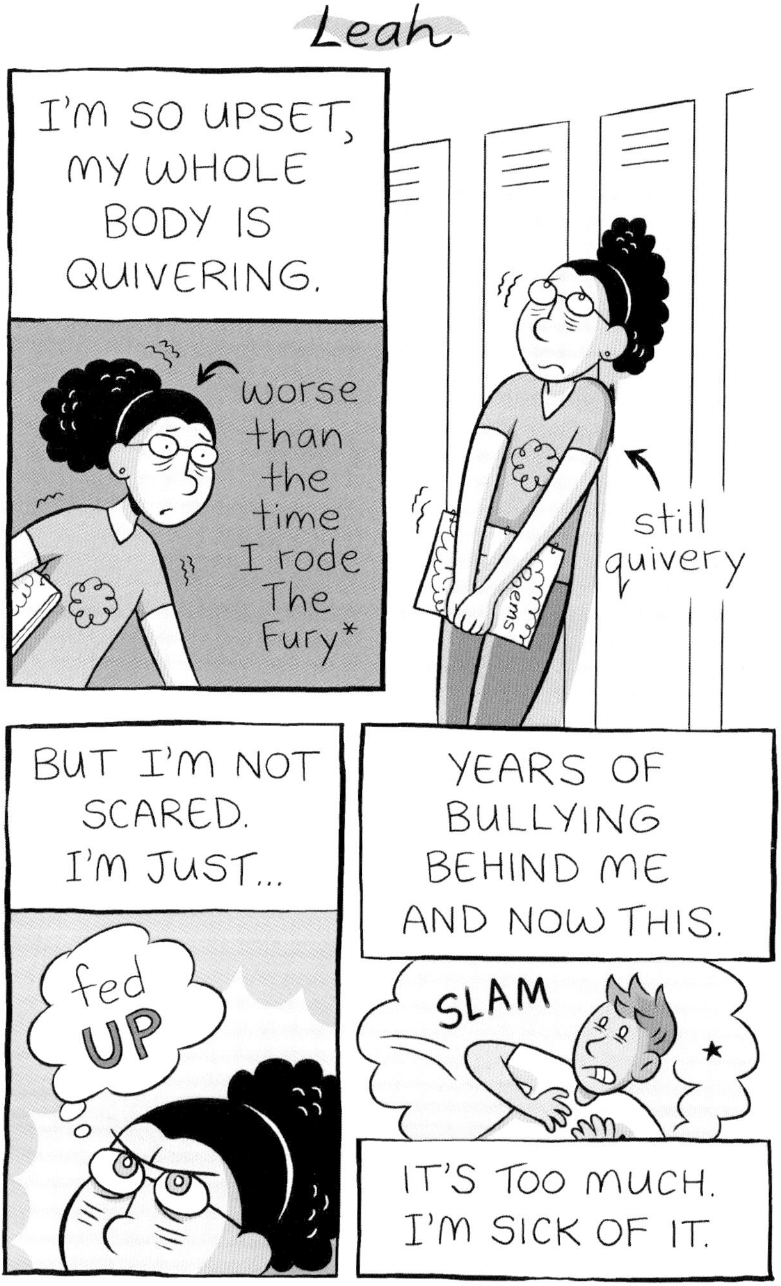
Leah
I'M SO UPSET, MY WHOLE BODY IS QUIVERING.
worse than the time I rode The Fury*
still quivery
poems
BUT I'M NOT SCARED. I'M JUST...
fed UP
YEARS OF BULLYING BEHIND ME AND NOW THIS.
SLAM
IT'S TOO MUCH. I'M SICK OF IT.

*huge roller coaster

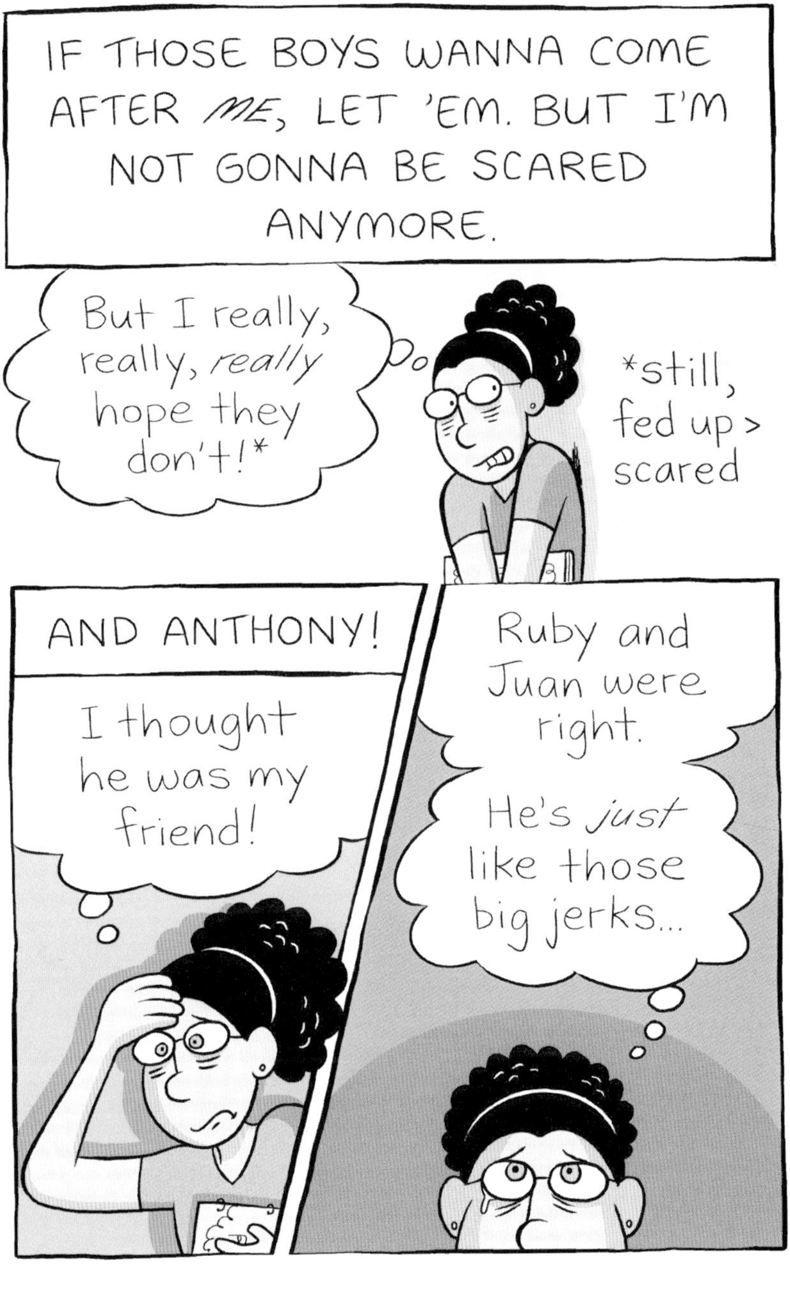
IF THOSE BOYS WANNA COME AFTER *ME*, LET 'EM. BUT I'M NOT GONNA BE SCARED ANYMORE.
But I really, really, *really* hope they don't!*
*still, fed up > scared
AND ANTHONY!
I thought he was my friend!
Ruby and Juan were right.
He's *just* like those big jerks...

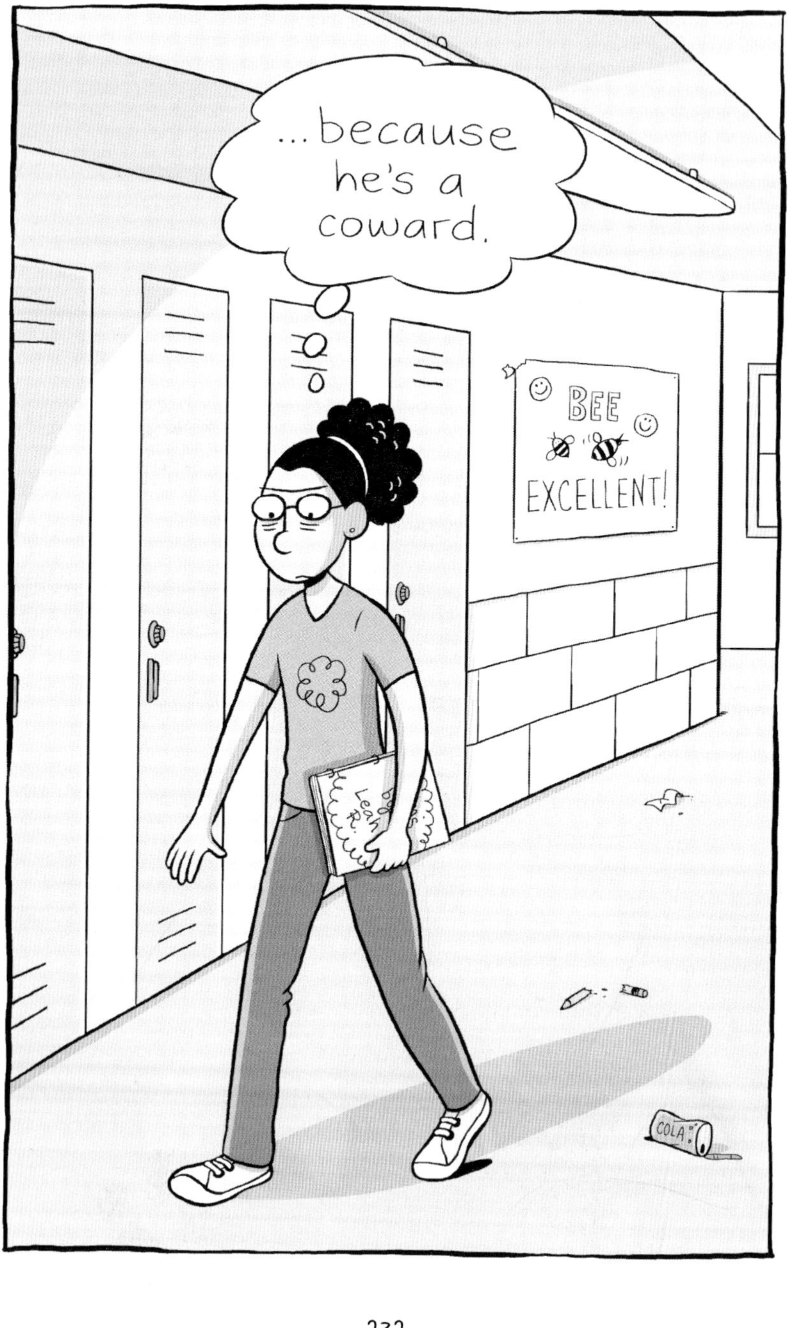
...because he's a coward.
BEE EXCELLENT!
COLA

ANTHONY

Oh man, I feel sick. I totally froze in front of Eddie and Lucas.

And Leah. I thought she was making things worse, but she was doing the right thing. Not me.

Screw-up meter:
royally
worse
I mean, wow
bad
can't go back
(I am hereish)

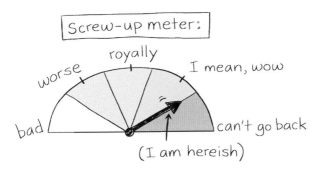

I've gotta fix this somehow.

I see Tyler and Joe heading out the door.

dim, but it's something

Maybe I can fix two wrongs at once.

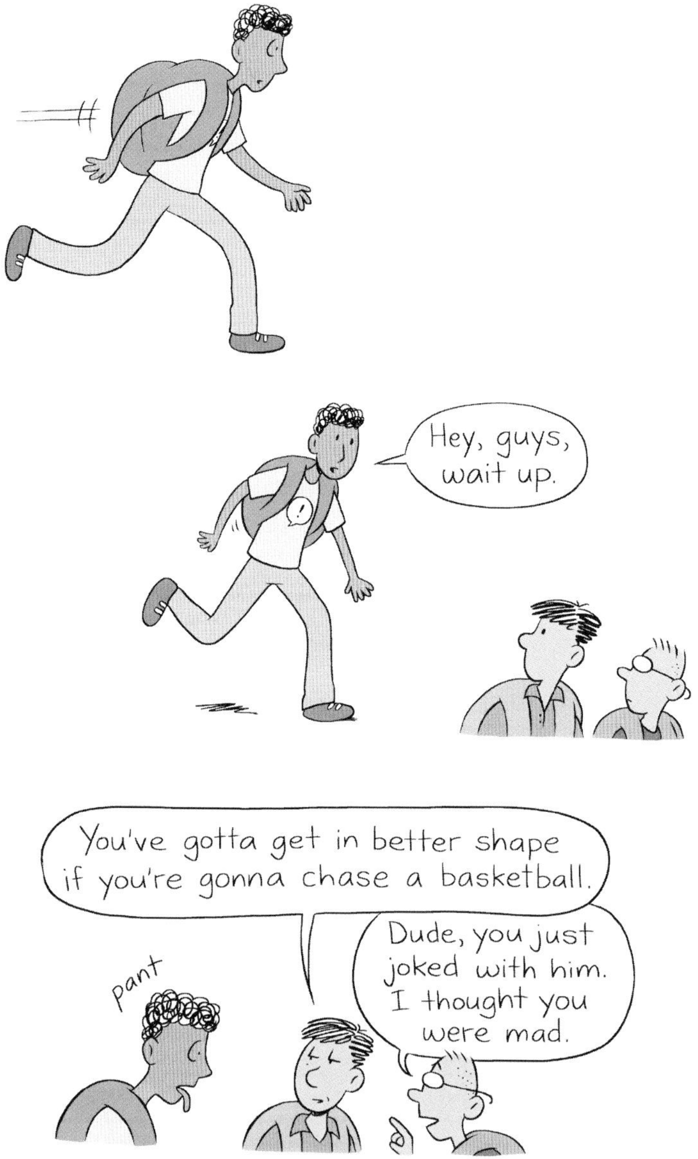
Hey, guys, wait up.
You've gotta get in better shape if you're gonna chase a basketball.
pant
Dude, you just joked with him. I thought you were mad.

That's right! Tyler looks like he just realizes that and scowls.

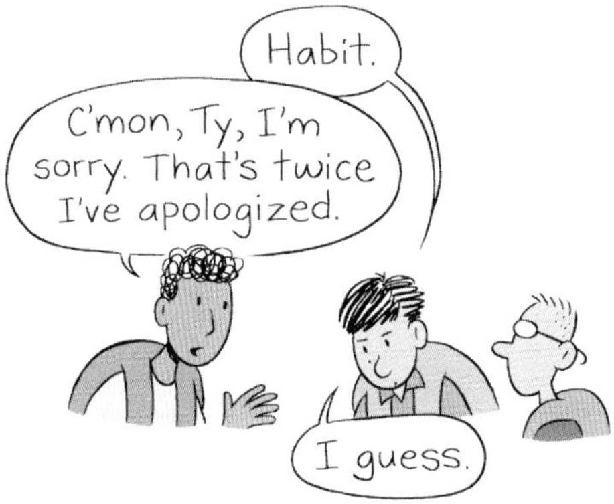
C'mon, Ty, I'm sorry. That's twice I've apologized.
Habit.
I guess.

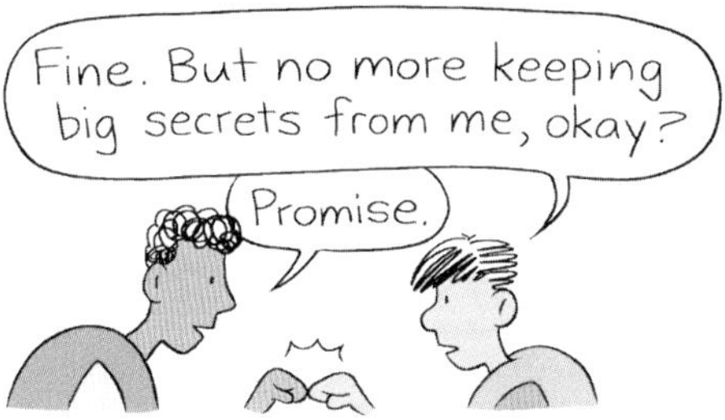
Fine. But no more keeping big secrets from me, okay?
Promise.

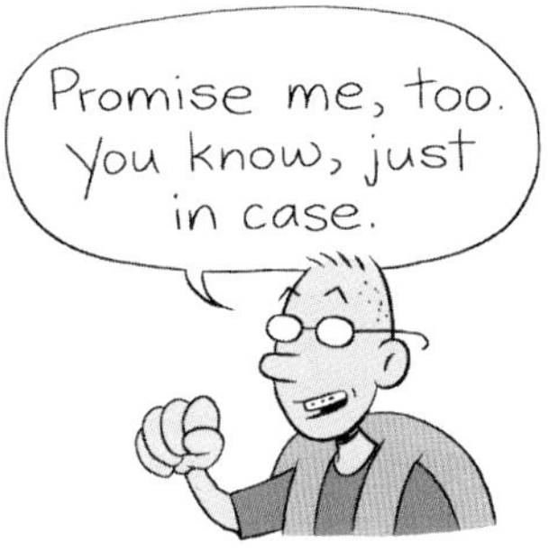
Promise me, too. You know, just in case.

I laugh and fist-bump Joe. Then I remember:

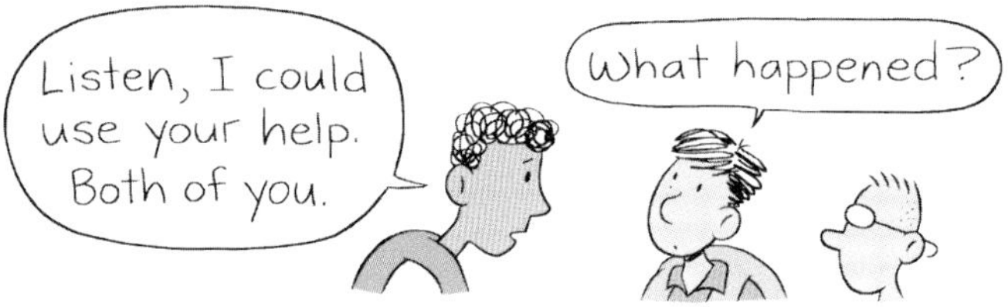
Listen, I could use your help. Both of you.
What happened?

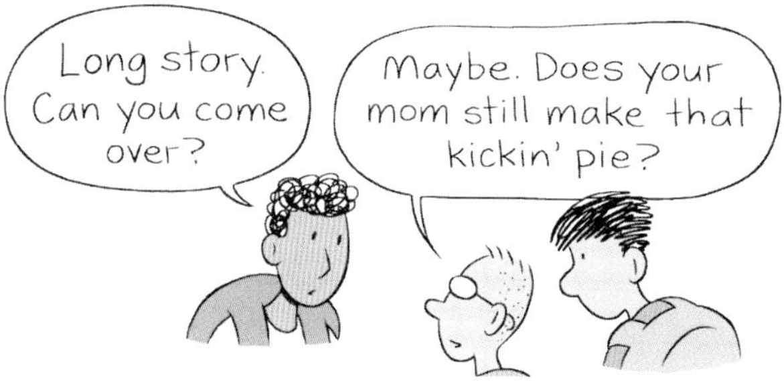
Long story. Can you come over?
Maybe. Does your mom still make that kickin' pie?

I nod.

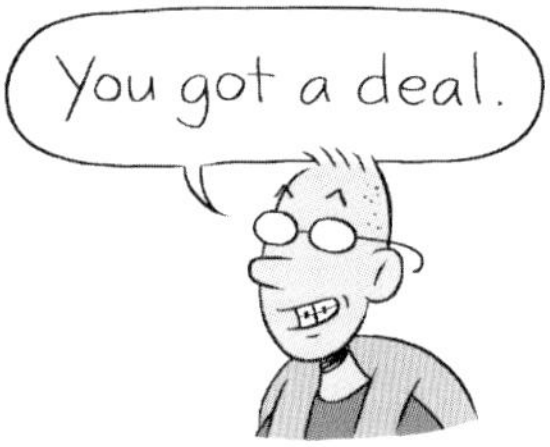
You got a deal.

Tyler stares at me and then strikes a "thinking" pose. He still looks a little mad.

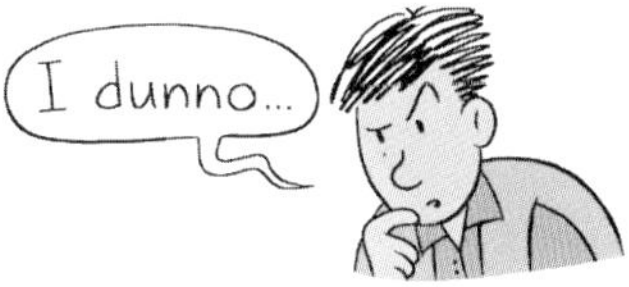
I dunno...

That's when I realize he's messing with me. I punch his shoulder.

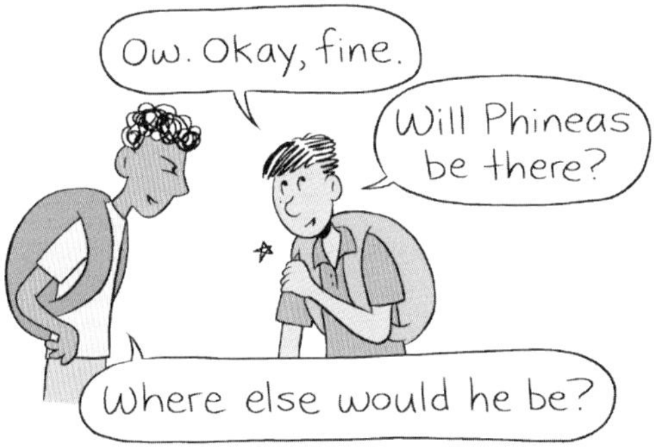
Ow. Okay, fine.
Will Phineas be there?
Where else would he be?

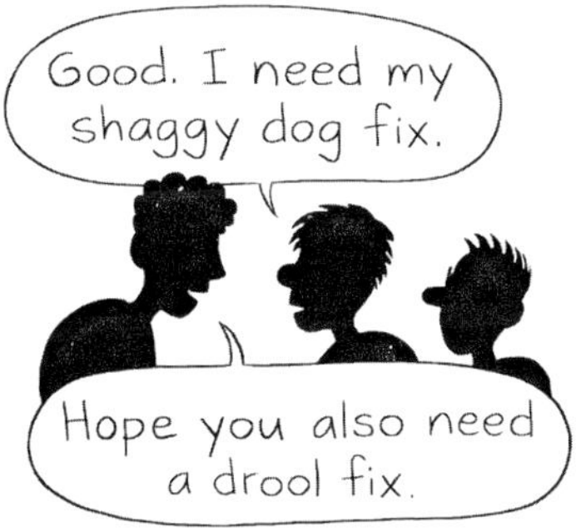
Good. I need my shaggy dog fix.
Hope you also need a drool fix.

We head down the block.

Leah

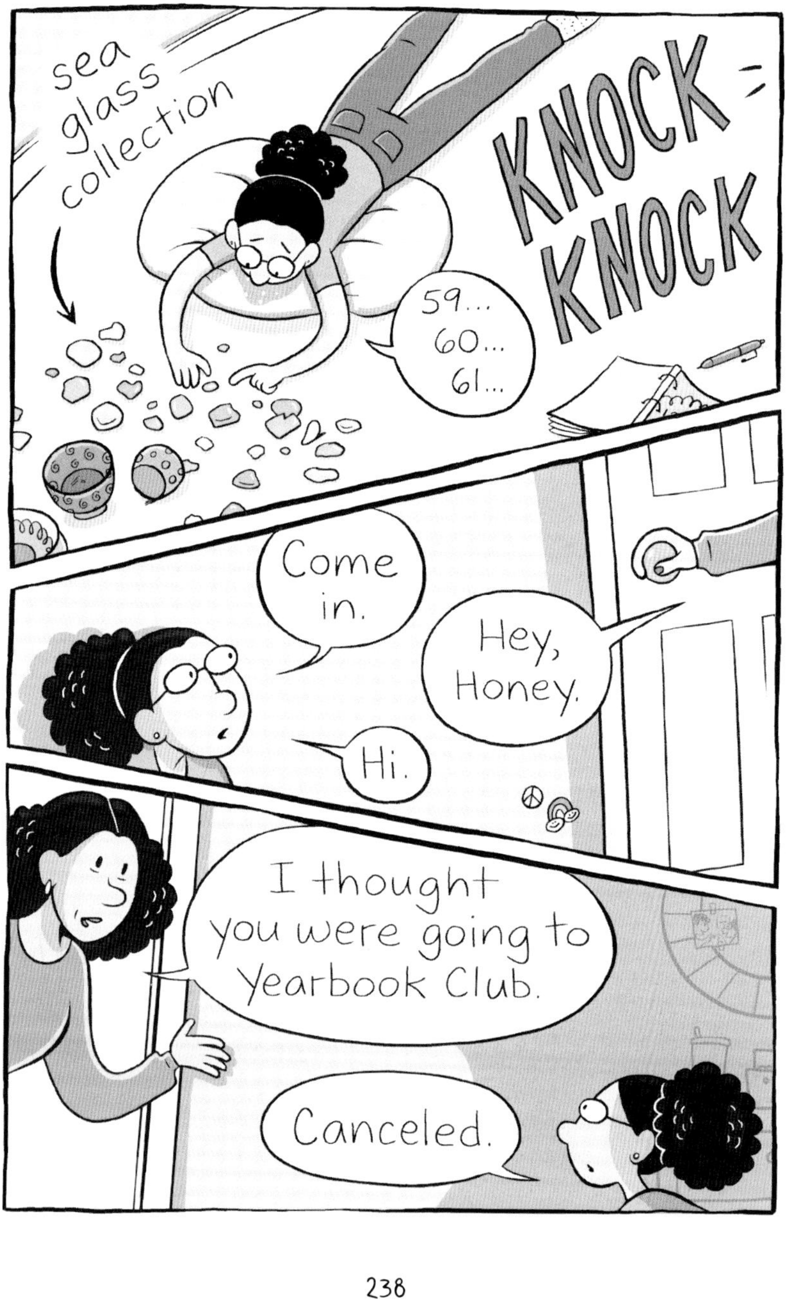
sea glass collection
KNOCK KNOCK
59... 60... 61...
Come in.
Hey, Honey.
Hi.
I thought you were going to Yearbook Club.
Canceled.

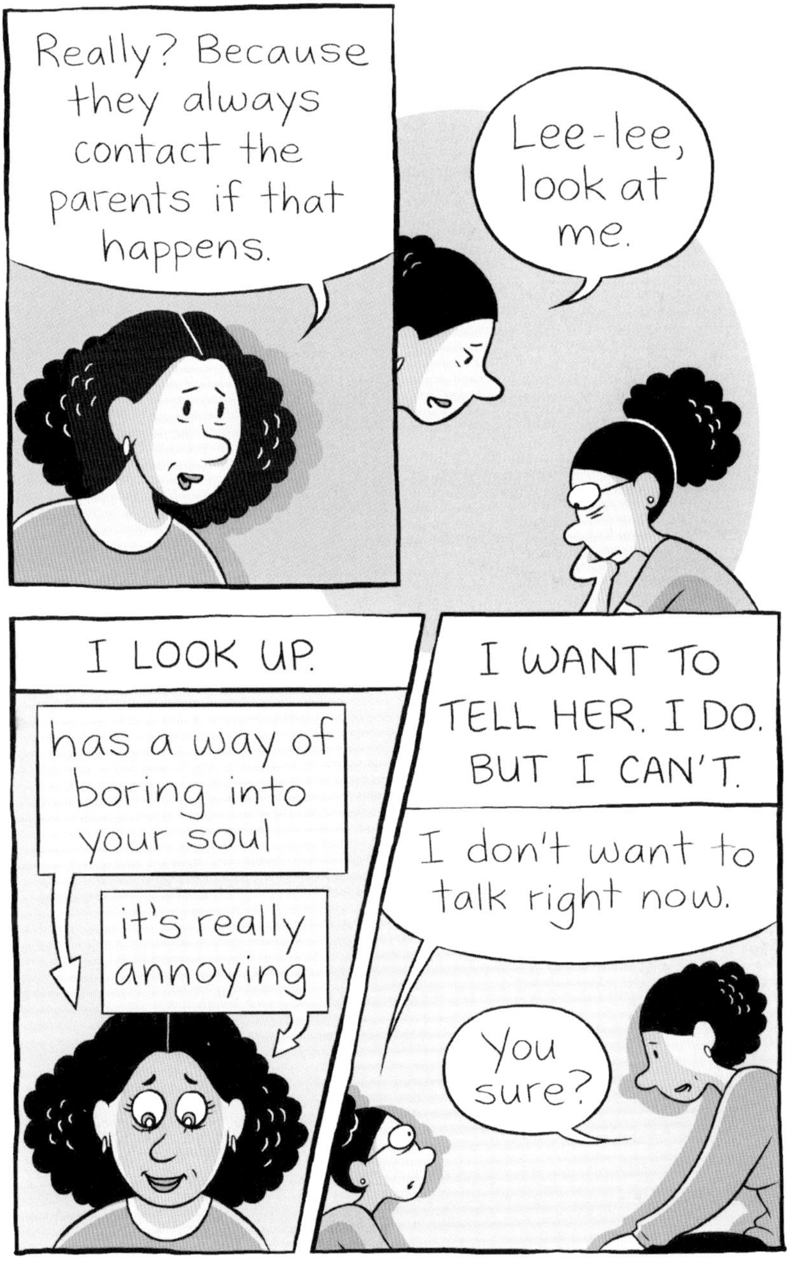
Really? Because they always contact the parents if that happens.
Lee-lee, look at me.
I LOOK UP.
has a way of boring into your soul
it's really annoying
I WANT TO TELL HER. I DO. BUT I CAN'T.
I don't want to talk right now.
You sure?

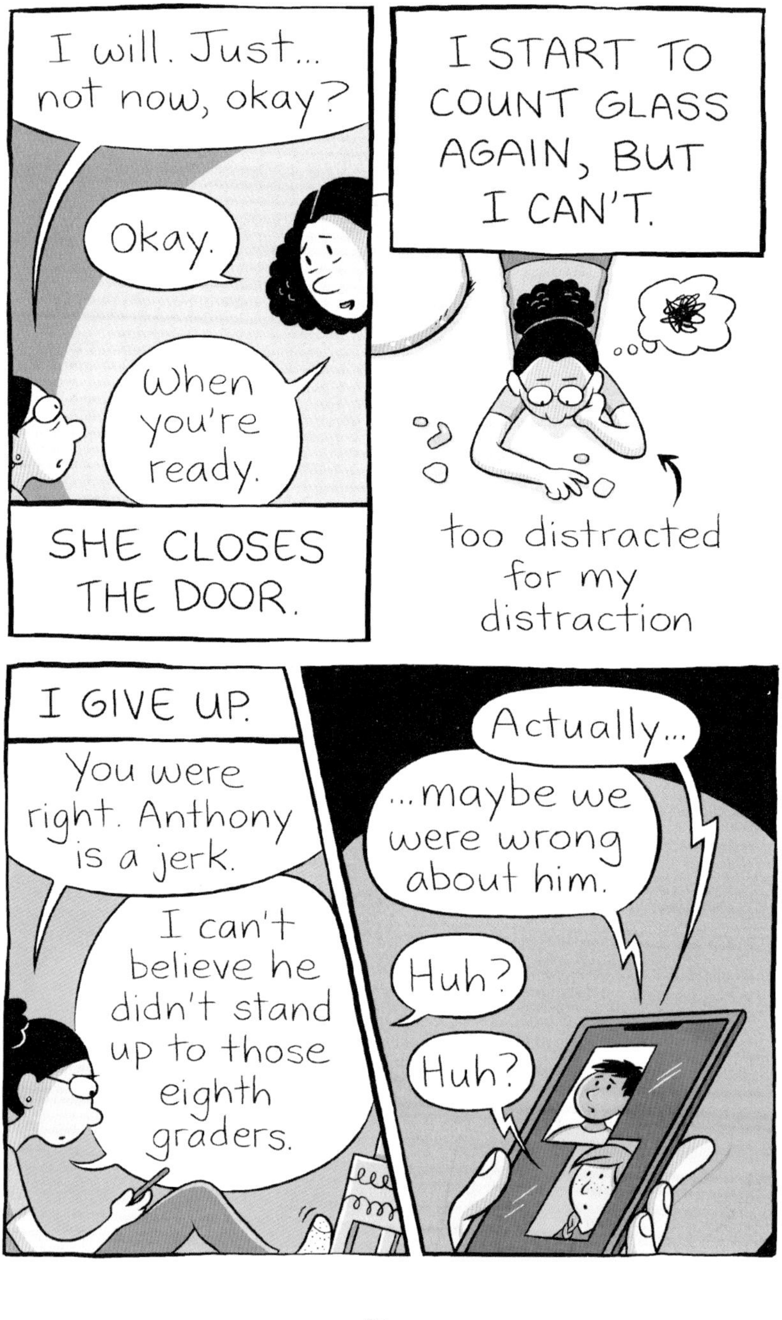
I will. Just...
not now, okay?
Okay.
When you're ready.
SHE CLOSES THE DOOR.
I START TO COUNT GLASS AGAIN, BUT I CAN'T.
too distracted for my distraction
I GIVE UP.
You were right. Anthony is a jerk.
I can't believe he didn't stand up to those eighth graders.
Actually...
...maybe we were wrong about him.
Huh?
Huh?

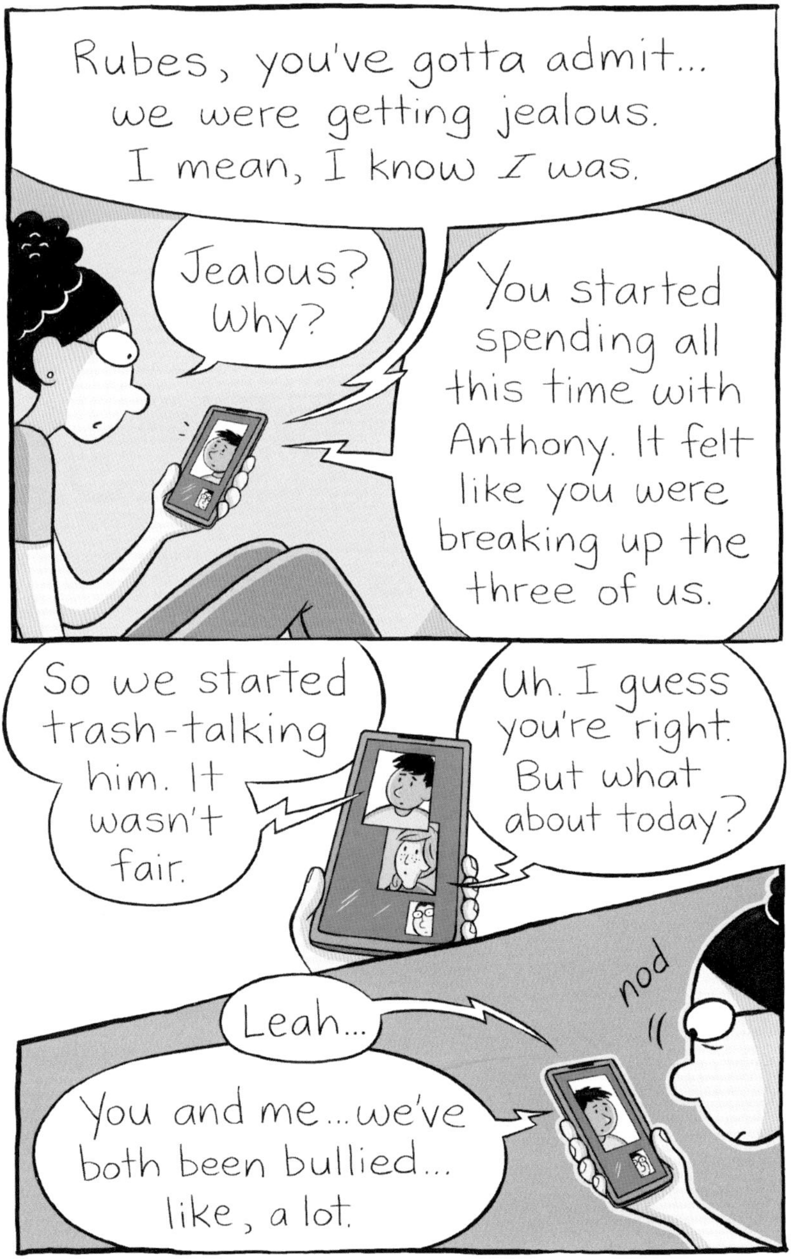
Rubes, you've gotta admit... we were getting jealous. I mean, I know *I* was.
Jealous? Why?
You started spending all this time with Anthony. It felt like you were breaking up the three of us.
So we started trash-talking him. It wasn't fair.
Uh. I guess you're right. But what about today?
nod
Leah...
You and me...we've both been bullied... like, a lot.

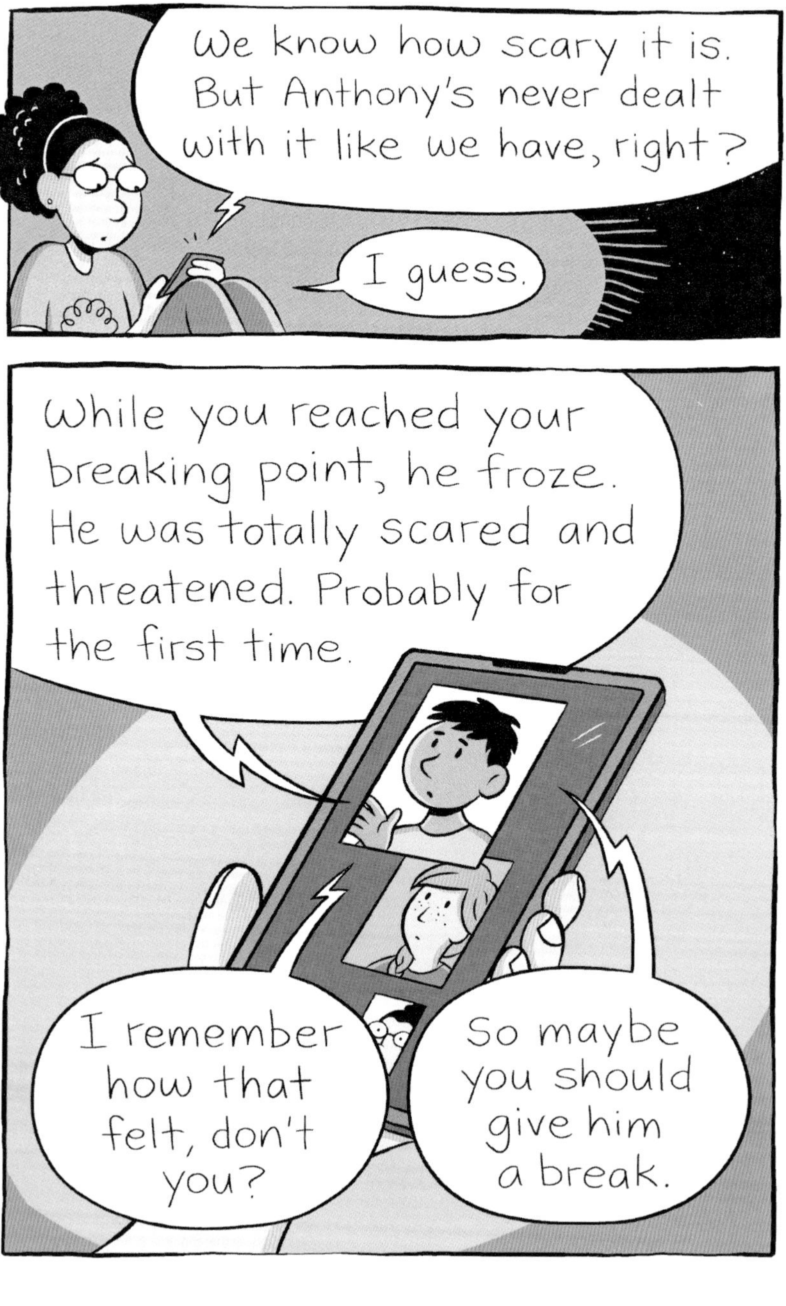
We know how scary it is. But Anthony's never dealt with it like we have, right?
I guess.
While you reached your breaking point, he froze. He was totally scared and threatened. Probably for the first time.
I remember how that felt, don't you?
So maybe you should give him a break.

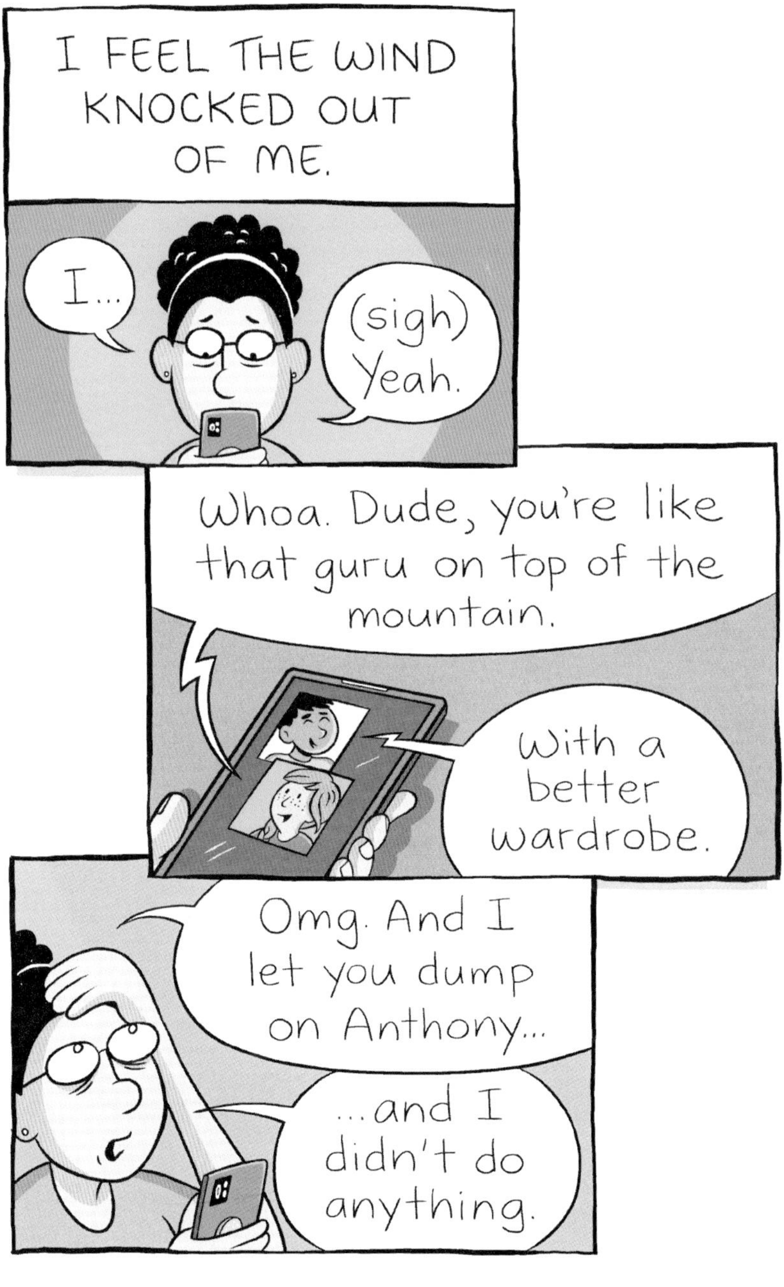
I FEEL THE WIND KNOCKED OUT OF ME.
I...
(sigh) Yeah.
Whoa. Dude, you're like that guru on top of the mountain.
With a better wardrobe.
Omg. And I let you dump on Anthony...
...and I didn't do anything.

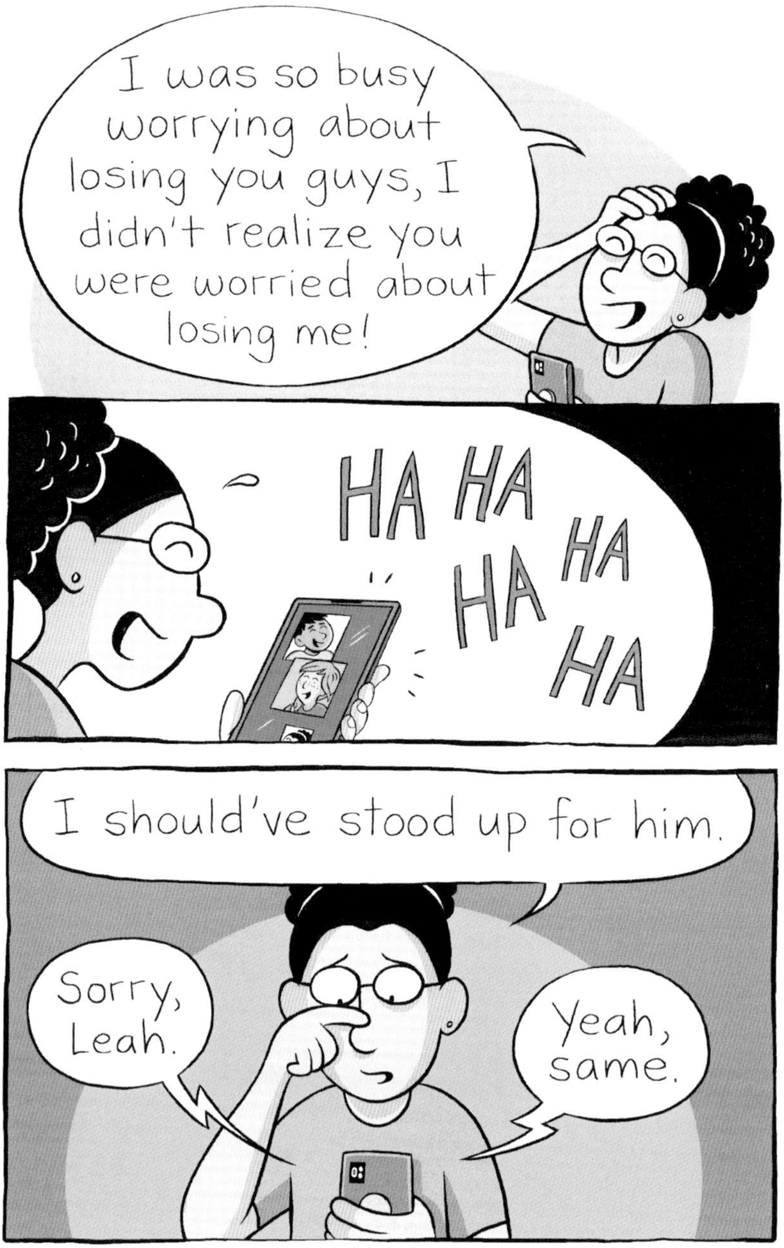
I was so busy worrying about losing you guys, I didn't realize you were worried about losing me!
HA HA HA HA HA
I should've stood up for him.
Sorry, Leah.
Yeah, same.

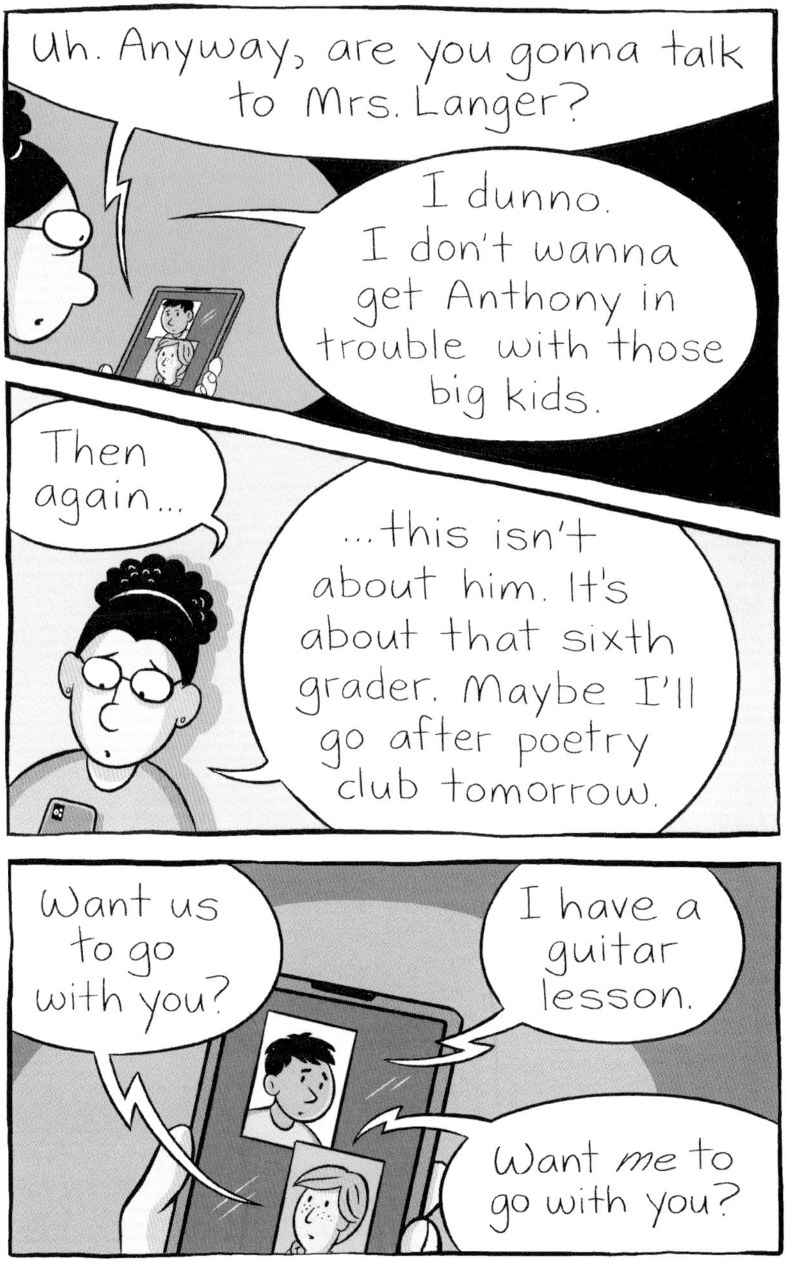

Uh. Anyway, are you gonna talk to Mrs. Langer?
I dunno. I don't wanna get Anthony in trouble with those big kids.
Then again...
...this isn't about him. It's about that sixth grader. Maybe I'll go after poetry club tomorrow.
Want us to go with you?
I have a guitar lesson.
Want *me* to go with you?

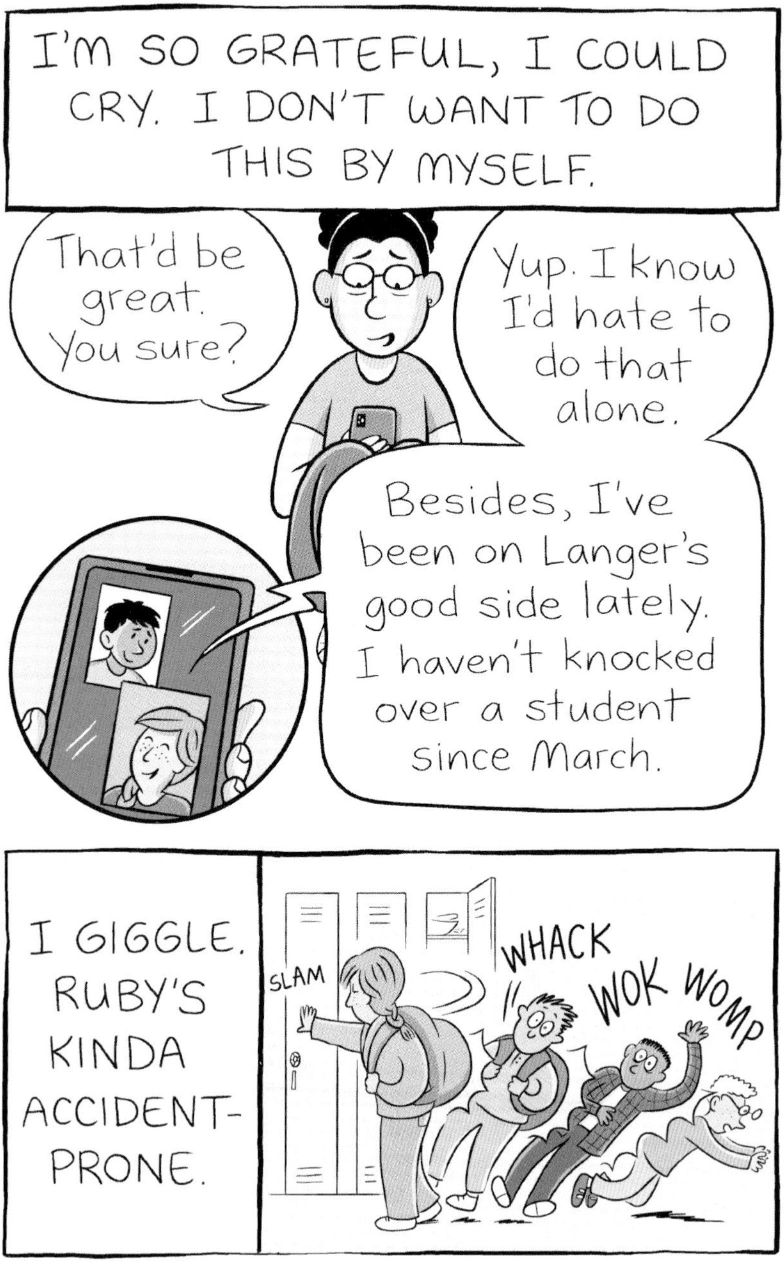
I'M SO GRATEFUL, I COULD CRY. I DON'T WANT TO DO THIS BY MYSELF.
That'd be great. You sure?
Yup. I know I'd hate to do that alone.
Besides, I've been on Langer's good side lately. I haven't knocked over a student since March.
I GIGGLE. RUBY'S KINDA ACCIDENT-PRONE.
SLAM
WHACK
WOK
WOMP

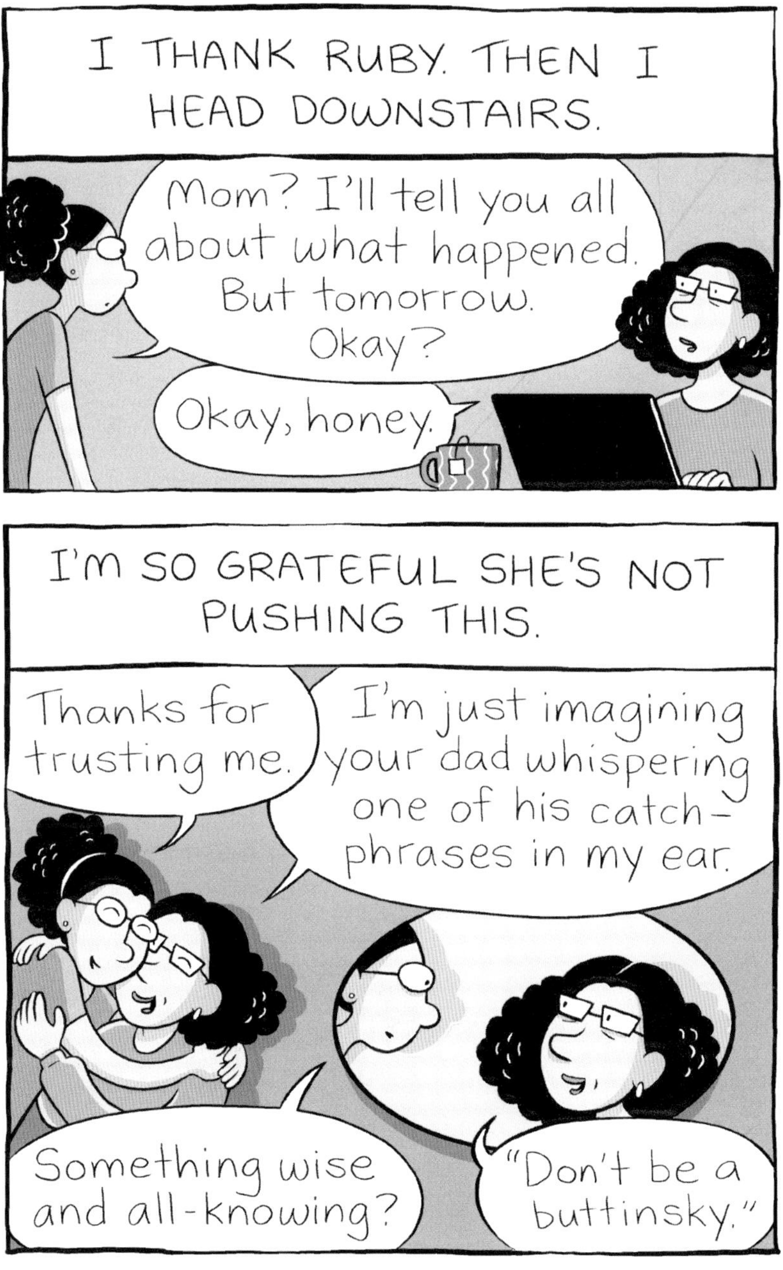
I THANK RUBY. THEN I HEAD DOWNSTAIRS.
Mom? I'll tell you all about what happened. But tomorrow. Okay?
Okay, honey.
I'M SO GRATEFUL SHE'S NOT PUSHING THIS.
Thanks for trusting me.
I'm just imagining your dad whispering one of his catch-phrases in my ear.
Something wise and all-knowing?
"Don't be a buttinsky."

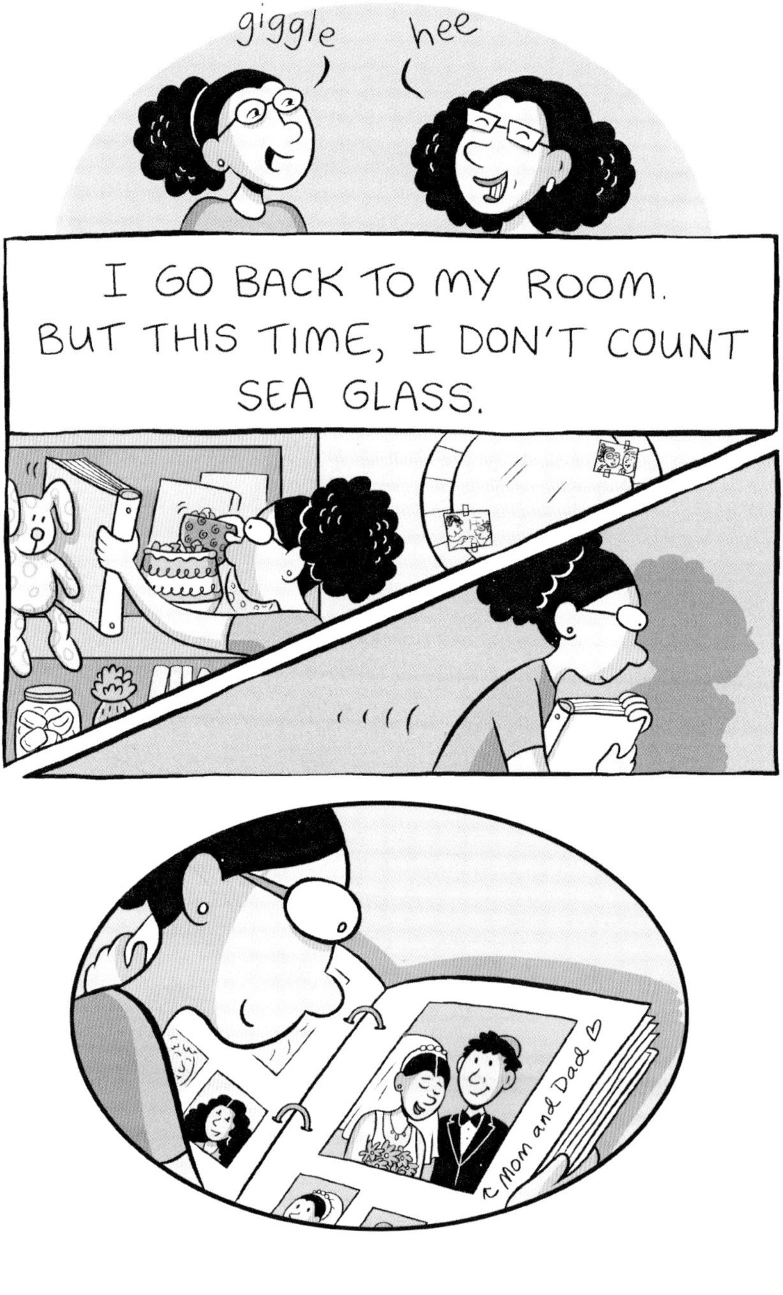
giggle
hee
I GO BACK TO MY ROOM. BUT THIS TIME, I DON'T COUNT SEA GLASS.
Mom and Dad

ANTHONY

Tuesday. We're in the locker room before practice. Me, Tyler, and most of the other seventh grade players. Oh, and Joe. He likes to hang out with us.

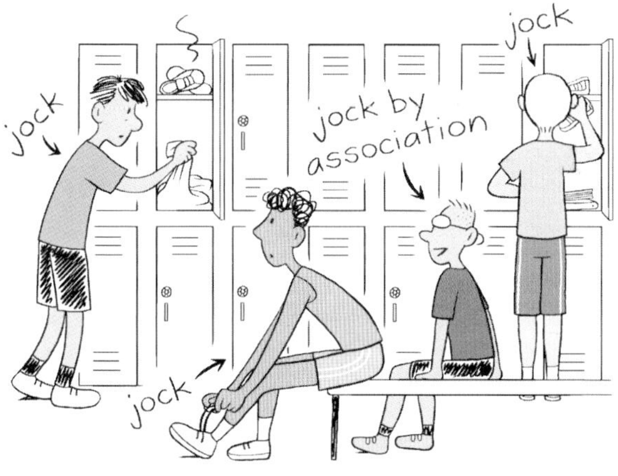
jock
jock
jock by association
jock

It always feels like the locker room is divided by age. I guess people in the same grade naturally drift together.

locker room map:
lockers
door to hall
7th graders
stray sock
bathroom*
(stinky)
bench
(no images necessary)
lockers
gum
6th graders
random cockroach
bench
showers
(no privacy)
extra wall (lucky!)
bench
8th graders
door to gym
lockers
* hasn't been cleaned since my pop went here

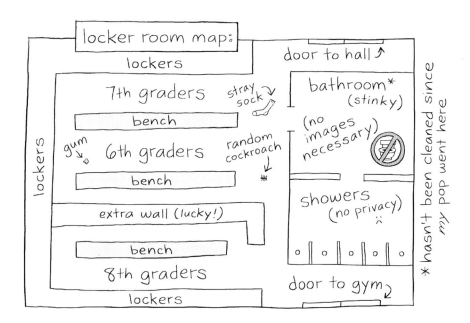

It's getting late. Coach Durdle absolutely hates tardiness. She's notorious for giving detention if you're even a second late. I've got a few minutes before she loses it and sends one of the sixth graders to get us.

tick
tick
tick
sixth grader in ready stance
(panicked)

I glance at Tyler, who nods. It's now or never.

I walk to the other side of the locker room where the eighth graders are. I never go here—feels like I need a passport. Lucas is tying his shoe and Eddie is tossing some stuff in a locker. There are a few other guys lingering, but they realize the time and head to the gym.

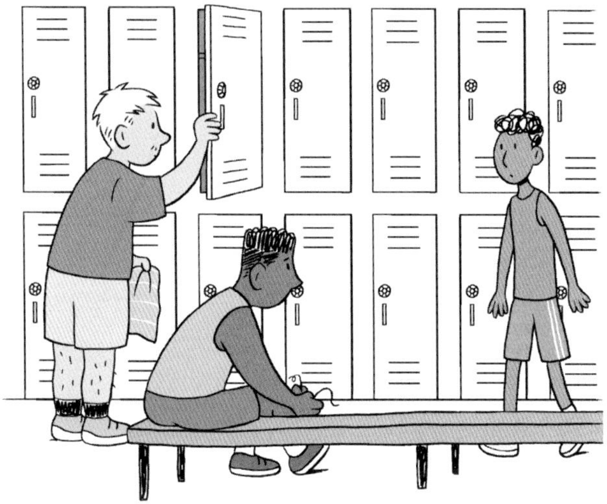

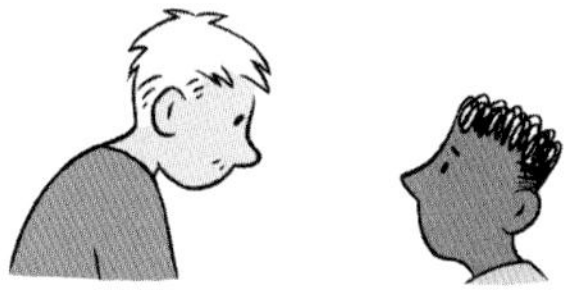

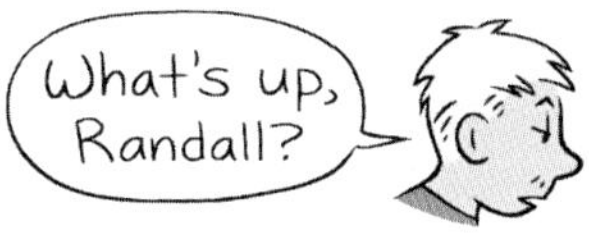
What's up, Randall?

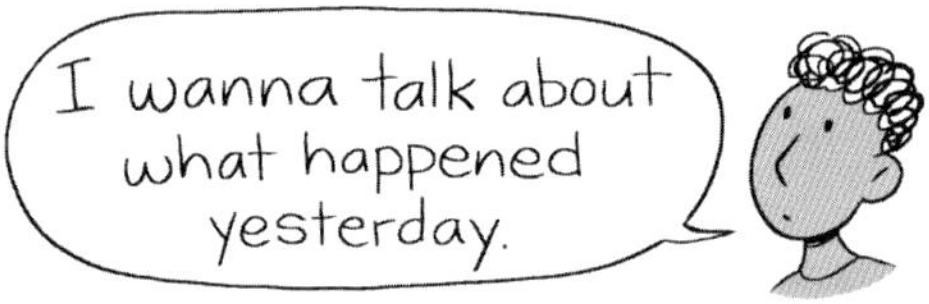
I wanna talk about what happened yesterday.

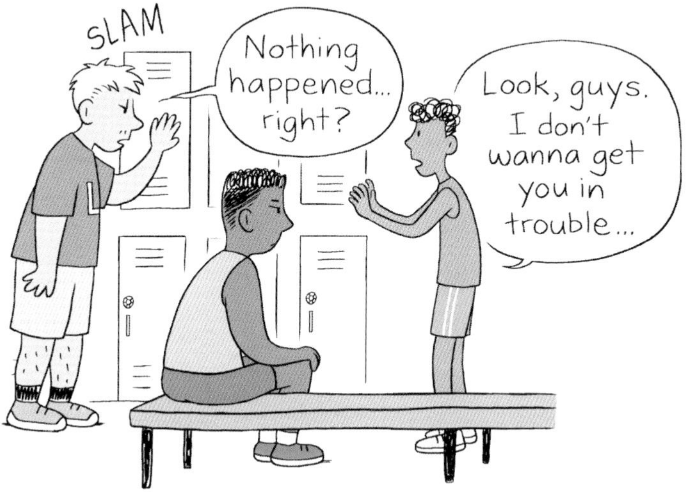
SLAM
Nothing happened... right?
Look, guys. I don't wanna get you in trouble...

Oh man, they're big.

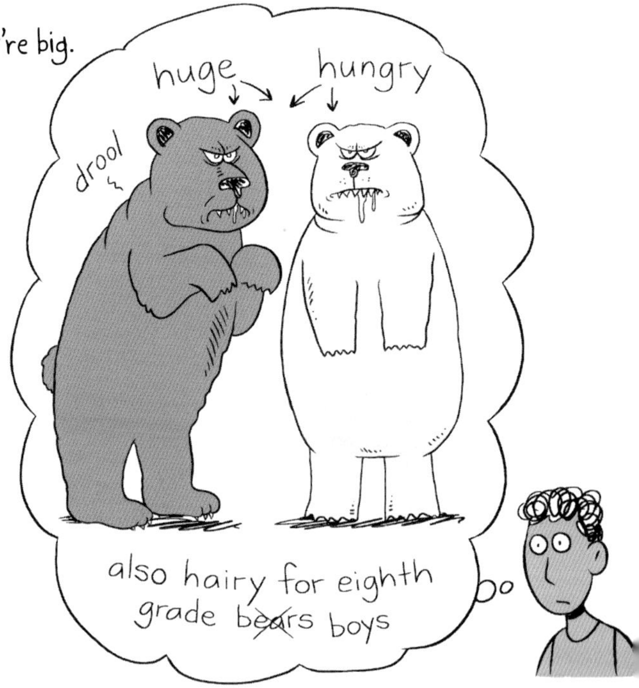
huge
hungry
drool
also hairy for eighth grade ~~bears~~ boys

...but you've gotta lay off that kid.

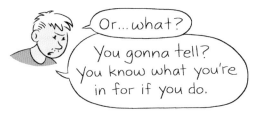

Or...what?

You gonna tell? You know what you're in for if you do.

Yep, I sure do.

That's okay. I'll deal.

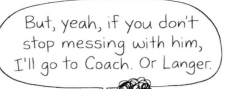

But, yeah, if you don't stop messing with him, I'll go to Coach. Or Langer.

HA HA HAW

Oh, Randall, we are gonna destroy you. Just wait.

Yeah, that's not gonna happen.

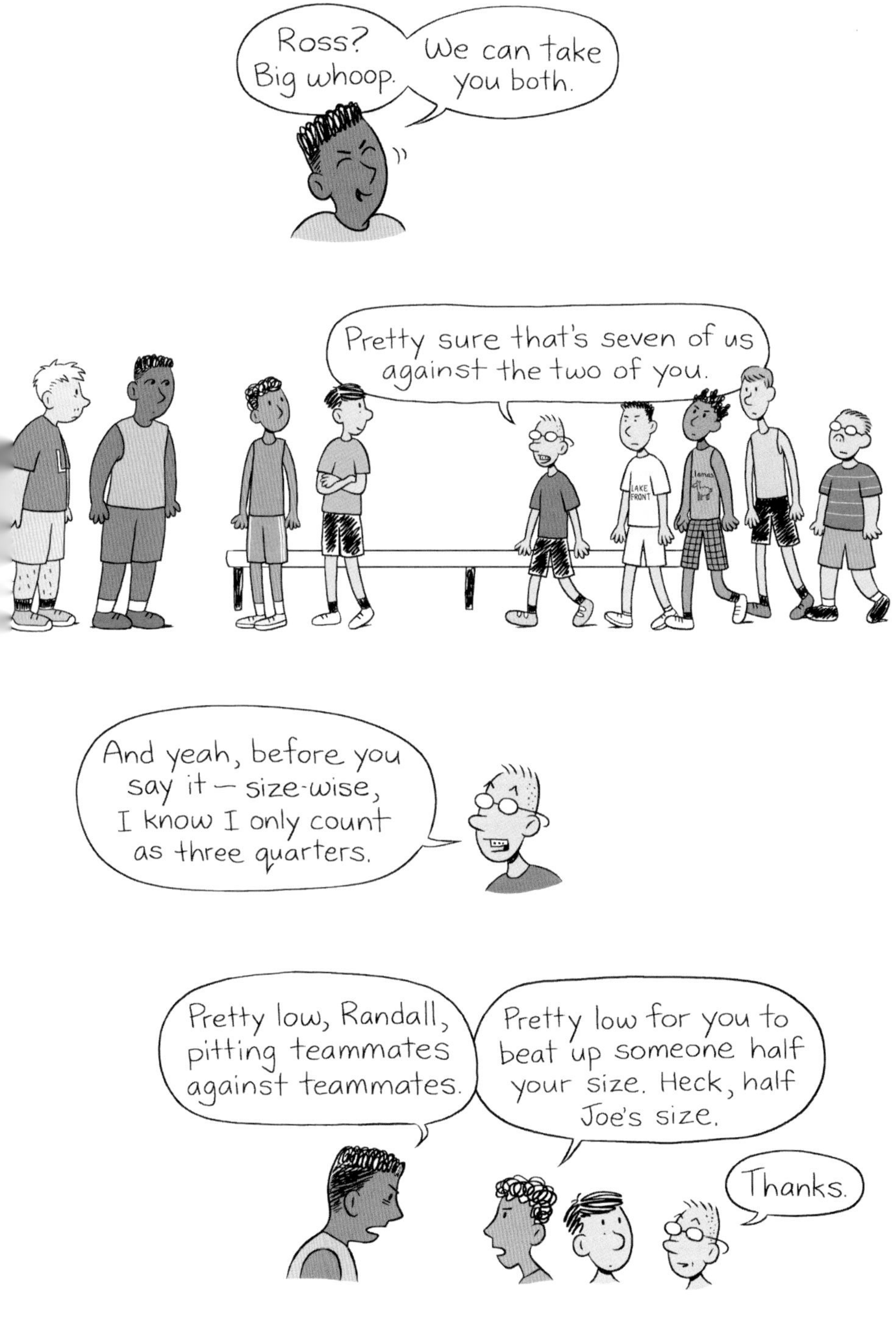
Ross? Big whoop.
We can take you both.
Pretty sure that's seven of us against the two of you.
And yeah, before you say it — size-wise, I know I only count as three quarters.
Pretty low, Randall, pitting teammates against teammates.
Pretty low for you to beat up someone half your size. Heck, half Joe's size.
Thanks.

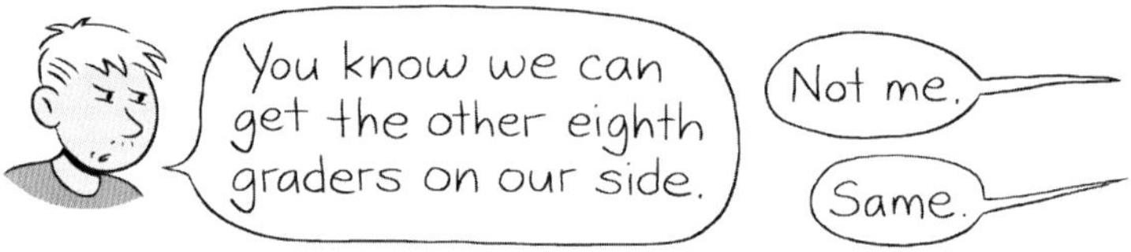
You know we can get the other eighth graders on our side.
Not me.
Same.

Two other (big) eighth graders, Nate Chen and Archie Katzenmeyer, step into view.

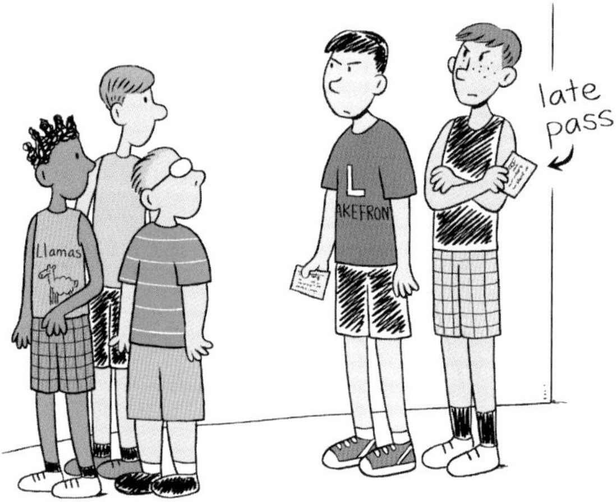
Llamas
L
AKEFRON
late pass

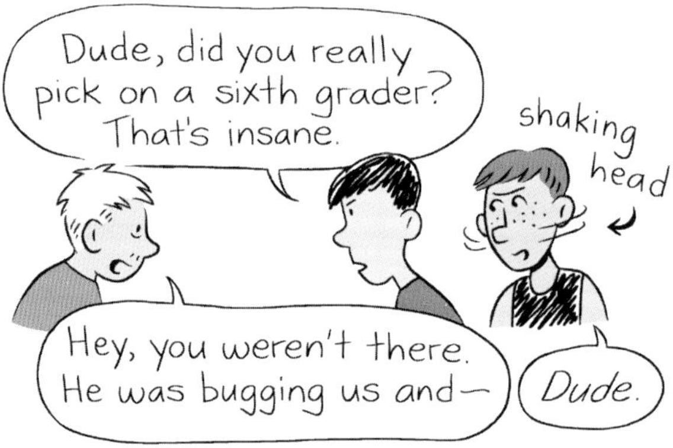
Dude, did you really pick on a sixth grader? That's insane.
shaking head
Hey, you weren't there. He was bugging us and—
Dude.

Eddie and Lucas glance at each other and then at the rest of us. They obviously realize they're done.

Fine. We'll lay off.

For real.

Yeah.

For the first time, I believe them.

The rest of us walk to the gym. When we're safely out the door, Ty and Joe high-five me.

That was freakin' brave, man. I thought they were gonna pummel you right there.

I would've said nice things at your funeral.

I take a deep breath and laugh nervously. What would I do without my friends and teammates? They really had my back.

gym

← death glare

tappa
tap
tap

Although, how we're gonna get out of **this** one, I have no idea.

Leah

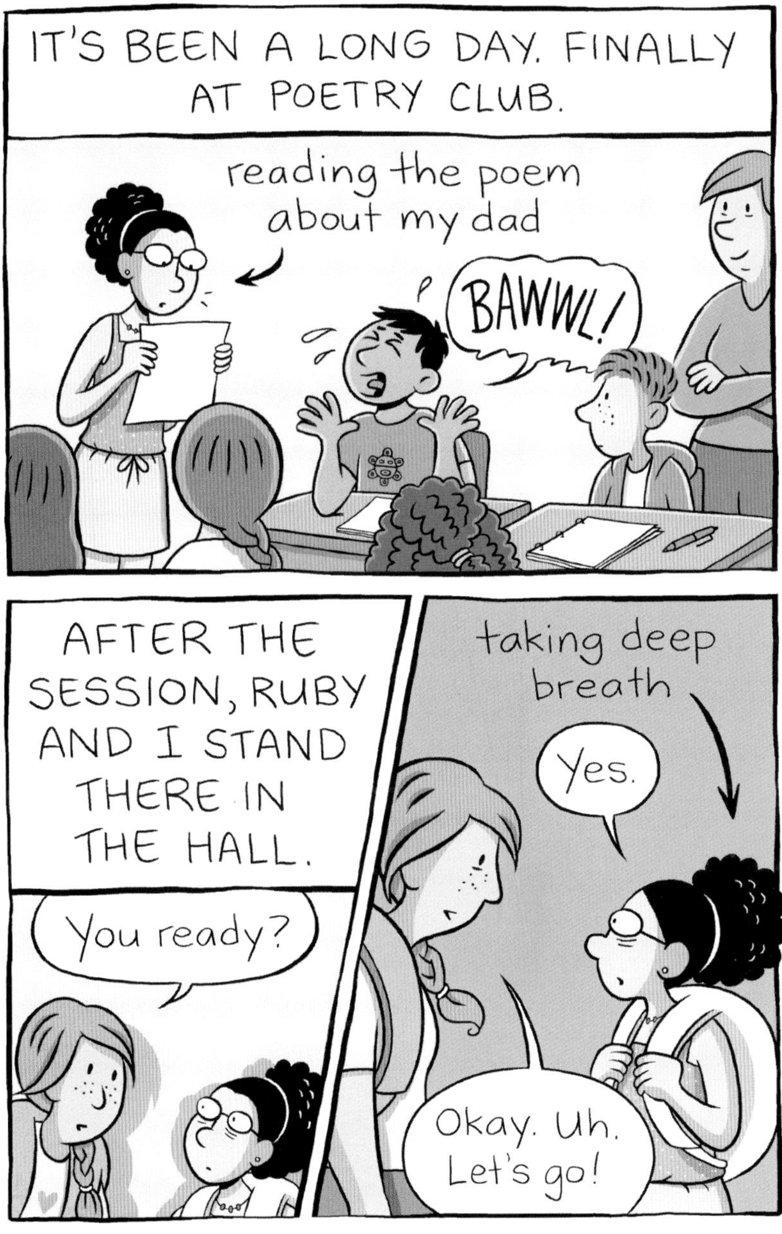

IT'S BEEN A LONG DAY. FINALLY AT POETRY CLUB.
reading the poem about my dad
BAWWL!
AFTER THE SESSION, RUBY AND I STAND THERE IN THE HALL.
You ready?
taking deep breath
Yes.
Okay. Uh. Let's go!

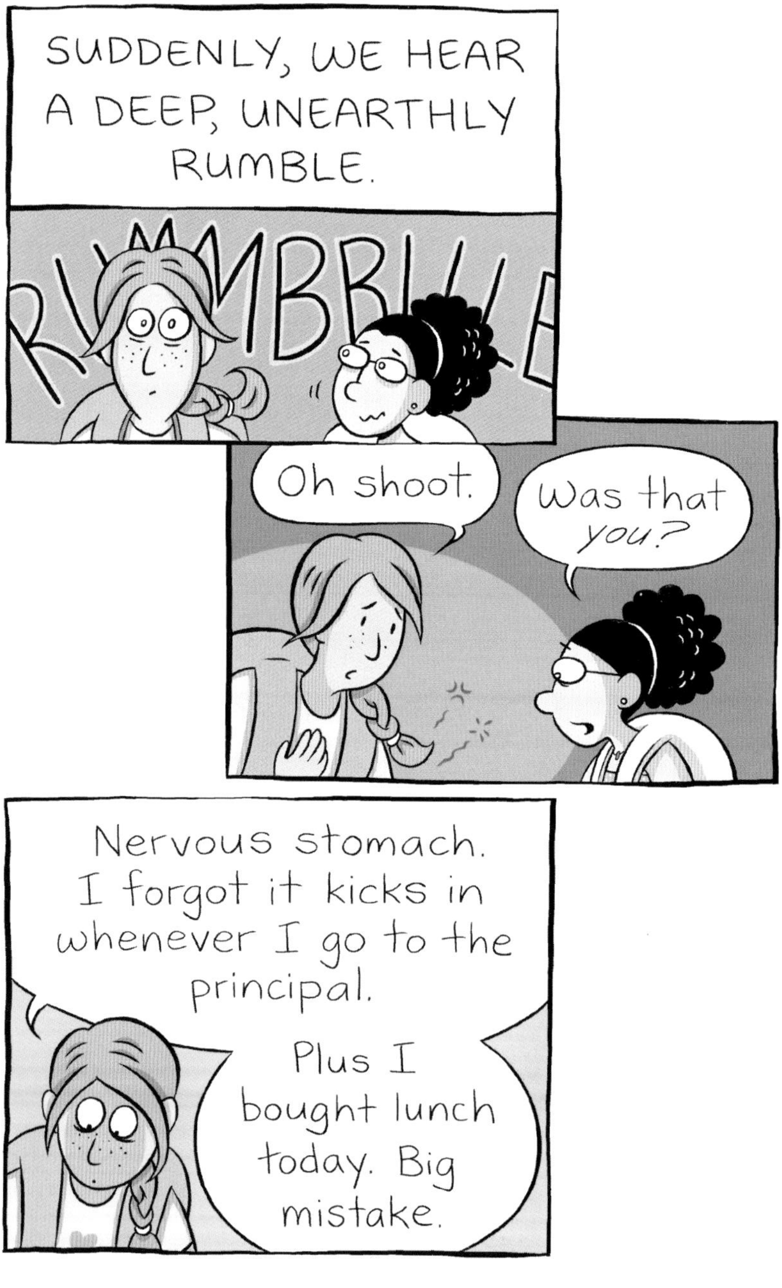
SUDDENLY, WE HEAR A DEEP, UNEARTHLY RUMBLE.
RUMMBRLLE
Oh shoot.
Was that you?
Nervous stomach. I forgot it kicks in whenever I go to the principal.
Plus I bought lunch today. Big mistake.

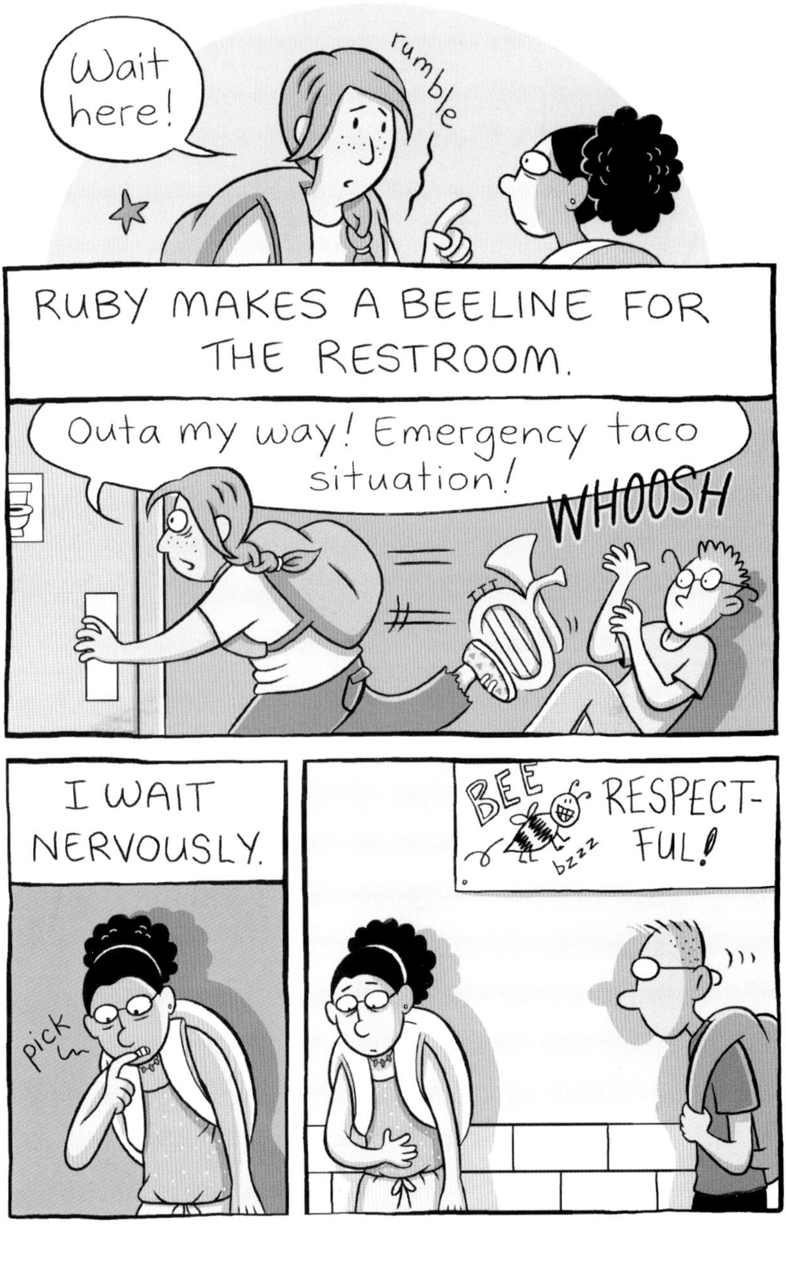
Wait here!
rumble
RUBY MAKES A BEELINE FOR THE RESTROOM.
Outa my way! Emergency taco situation!
WHOOSH
I WAIT NERVOUSLY.
pick
BEE RESPECT-FUL!
bzzz

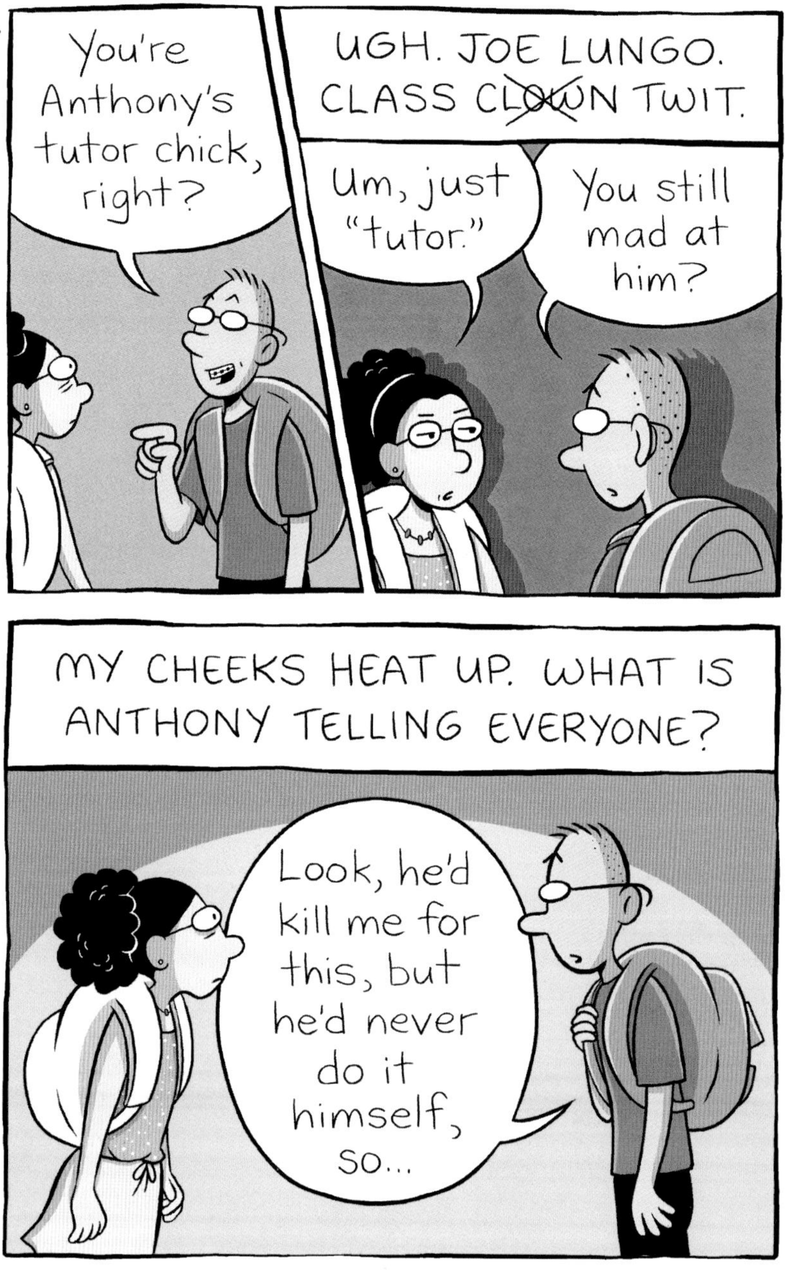
You're Anthony's tutor chick, right?
UGH. JOE LUNGO. CLASS CLOWN TWIT.
Um, just "tutor."
You still mad at him?
MY CHEEKS HEAT UP. WHAT IS ANTHONY TELLING EVERYONE?
Look, he'd kill me for this, but he'd never do it himself, so...

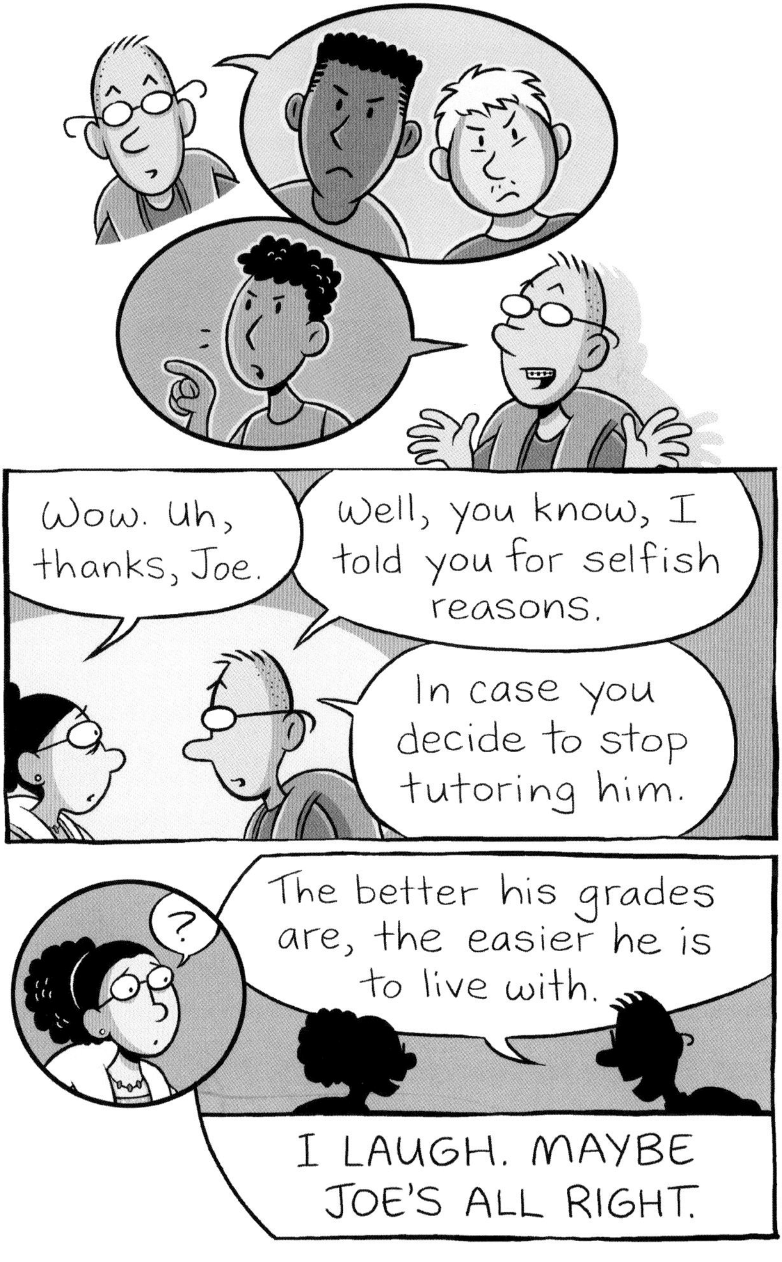
Wow. Uh, thanks, Joe.
Well, you know, I told you for selfish reasons.
In case you decide to stop tutoring him.
?
The better his grades are, the easier he is to live with.
I LAUGH. MAYBE JOE'S ALL RIGHT.

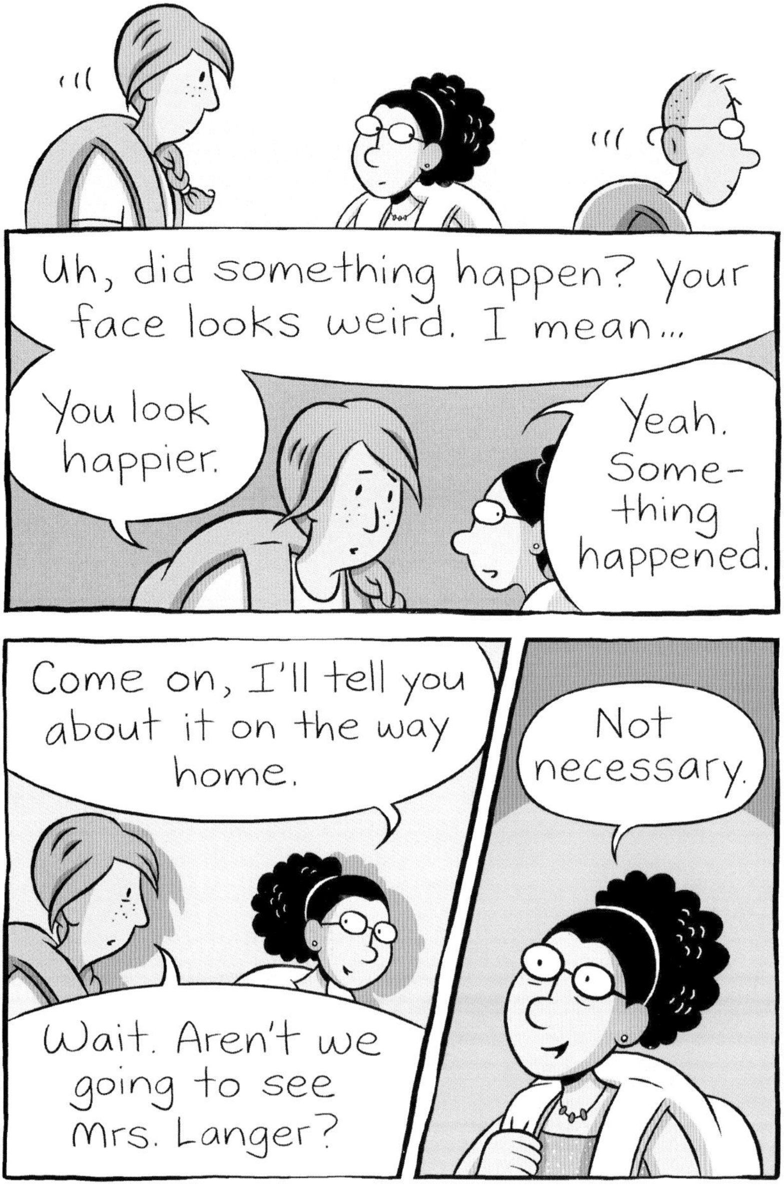
Uh, did something happen? Your face looks weird. I mean...
You look happier.
Yeah. Some-thing happened.
Come on, I'll tell you about it on the way home.
Wait. Aren't we going to see Mrs. Langer?
Not necessary.

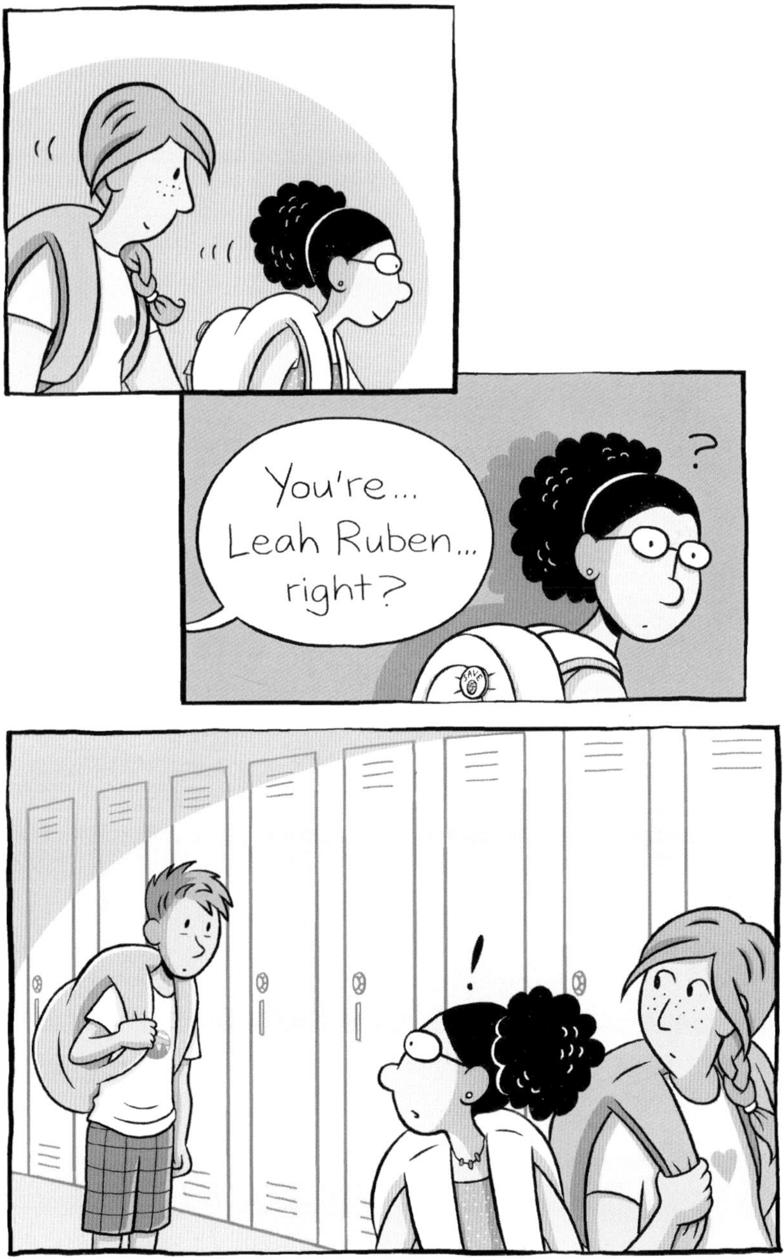
You're...
Leah Ruben...
right?

ANTHONY

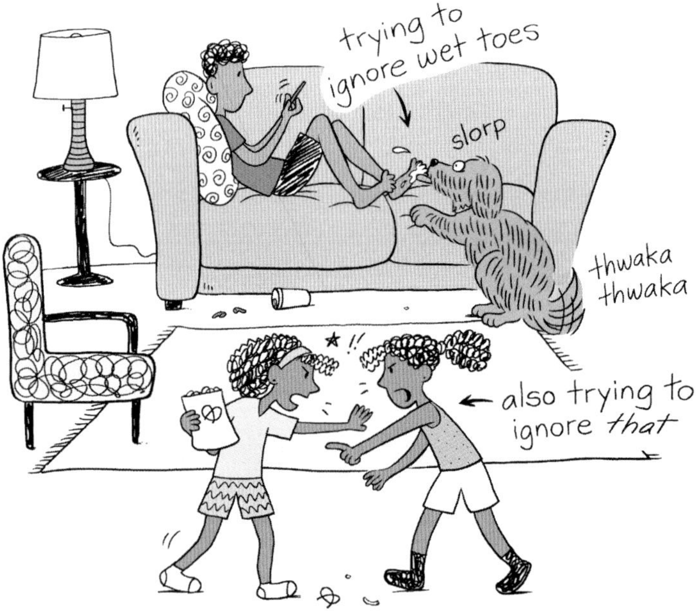
trying to ignore wet toes
slorp
thwaka thwaka
also trying to ignore *that*

I'm texting Leah.

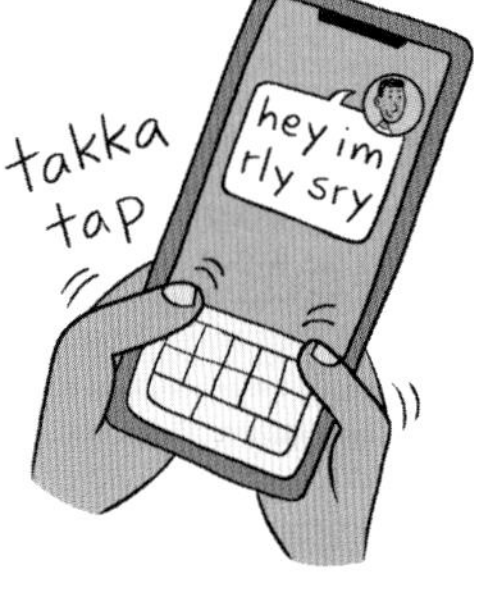
takka tap
hey im rly sry

Phineas tickles my feet, which makes me drop my phone.

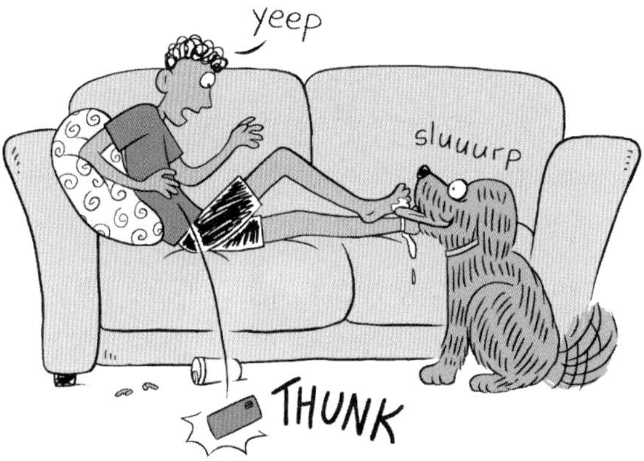
yeep
sluuurp
THUNK

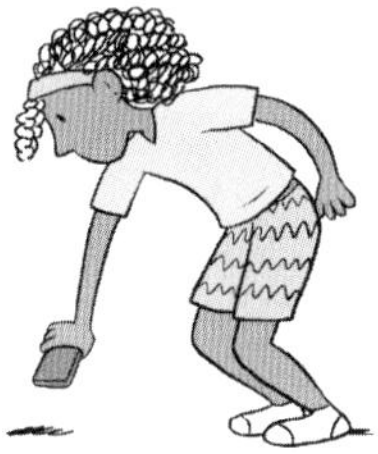

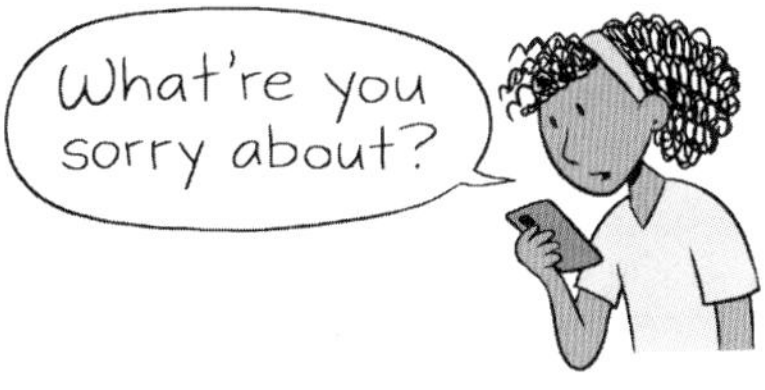
What're you sorry about?

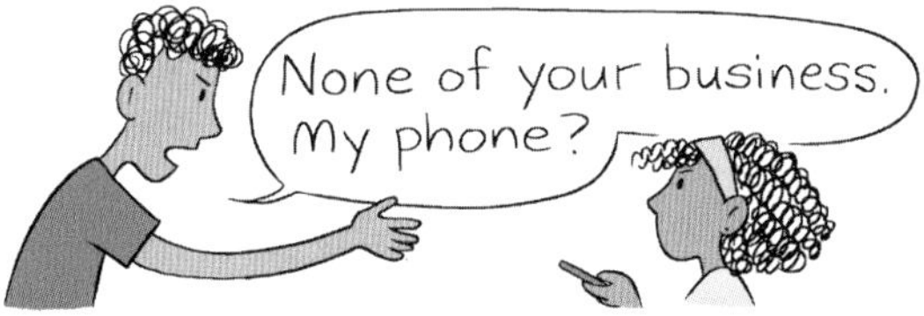
None of your business. My phone?

I hold out my hand and she slaps it into my palm.

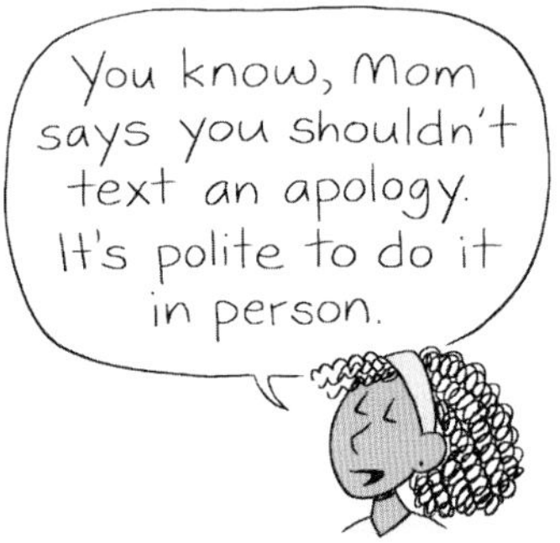
You know, Mom says you shouldn't text an apology. It's polite to do it in person.

I roll my eyes.

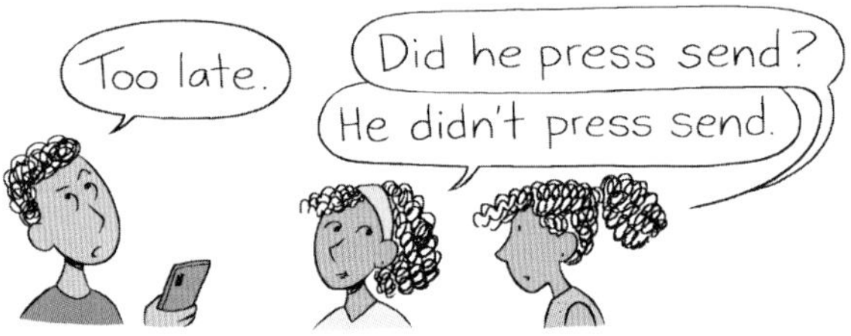
Too late.
Did he press send?
He didn't press send.

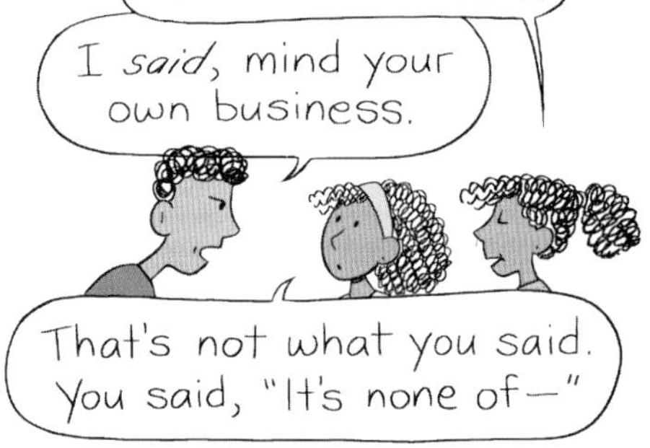
So it's not too late.
I *said*, mind your own business.
That's not what you said. You said, "It's none of—"

I tune her out and march upstairs to my room, closing the door.

As irritating as they are, the nosy twosome got in my head. They're right. I probably shouldn't apologize over a text. I delete it and type another one:

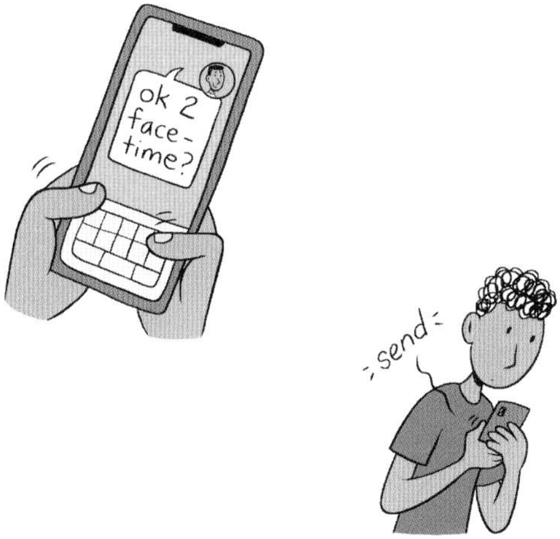
ok 2 face-time?
send

I know it's not in person, but I figure it's the next best thing. It'd be weird (and creepy, probably) for me to just show up at her house.

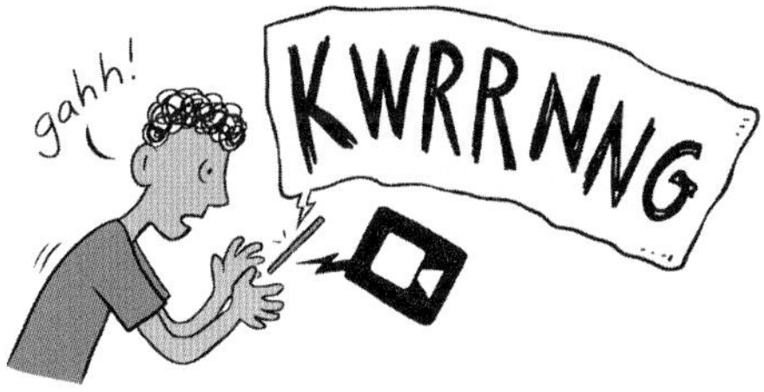
gahh!
KWRRNNG

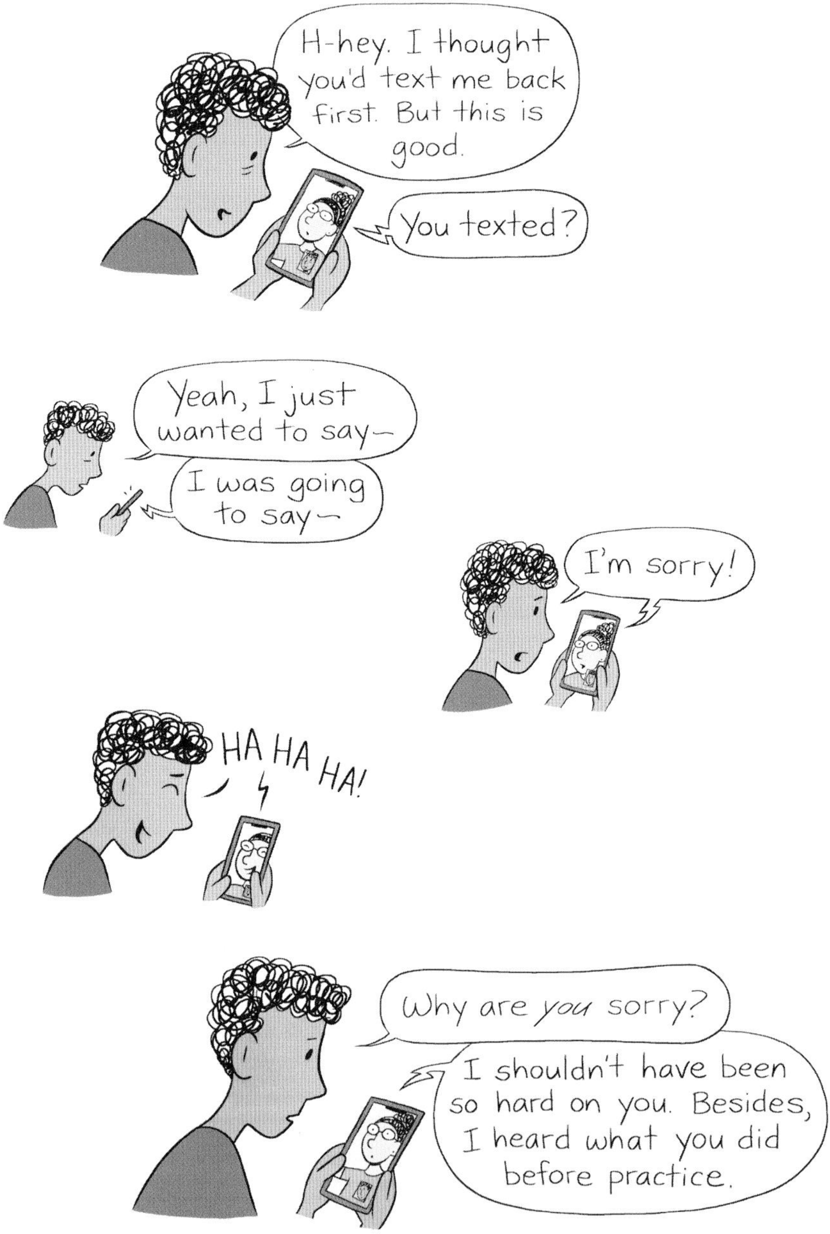
H-hey. I thought you'd text me back first. But this is good.
You texted?
Yeah, I just wanted to say–
I was going to say–
I'm sorry!
HA HA HA!
Why are *you* sorry?
I shouldn't have been so hard on you. Besides, I heard what you did before practice.

Wow. Word got around. (Why am I not surprised?)

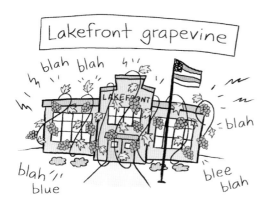

Lakefront grapevine

blah blah
blah
blah
blue
blee
blah

Well, I still feel bad...
...for being a chicken
and a jerk in front
of you.

Eddie and Lucas
were the real jerks.
But thanks.

There's an awkward silence. I hate those.

Um, I've got a question
for you.

Okay.

I pause.

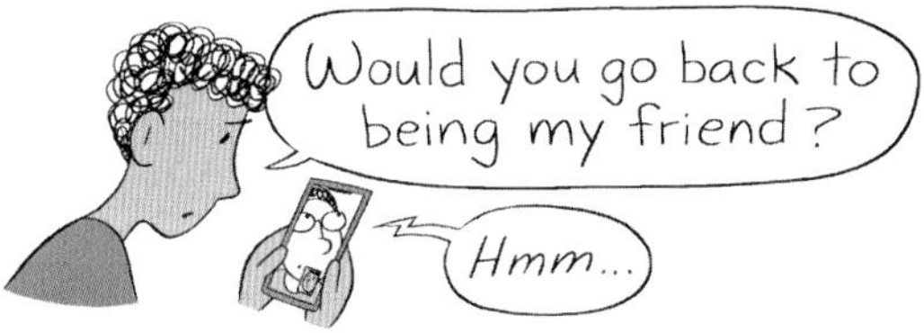
Would you go back to being my friend?
Hmm...

She takes a long time to answer. After panicking, I realize she's messing with me.

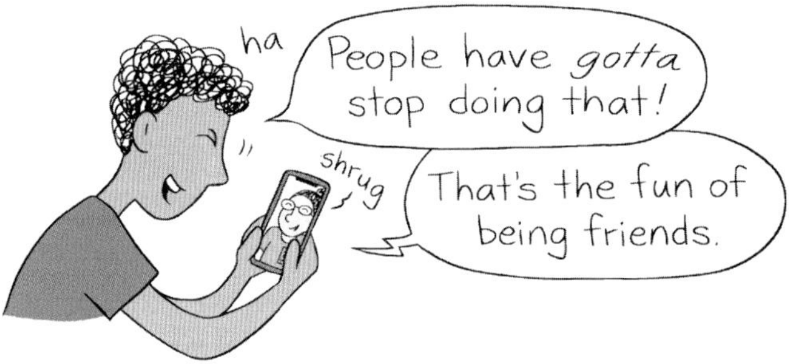
ha
People have *gotta* stop doing that!
shrug
That's the fun of being friends.

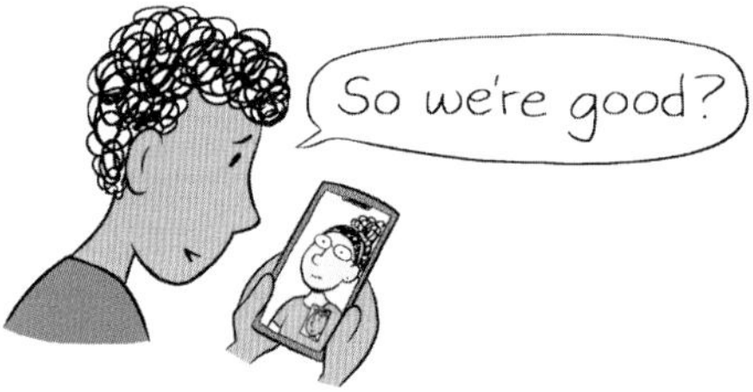
So we're good?

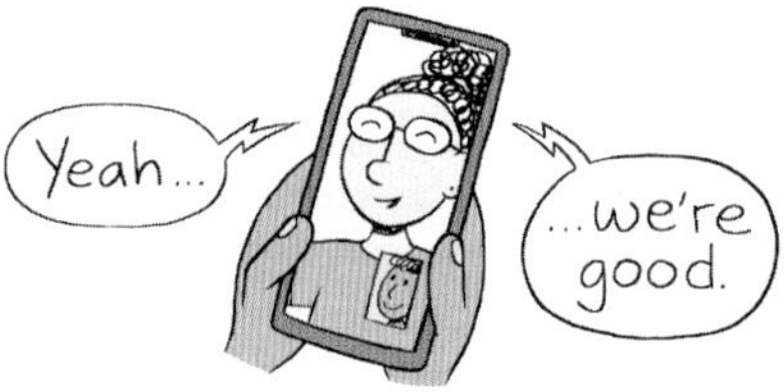
Yeah...
...we're good.

Leah

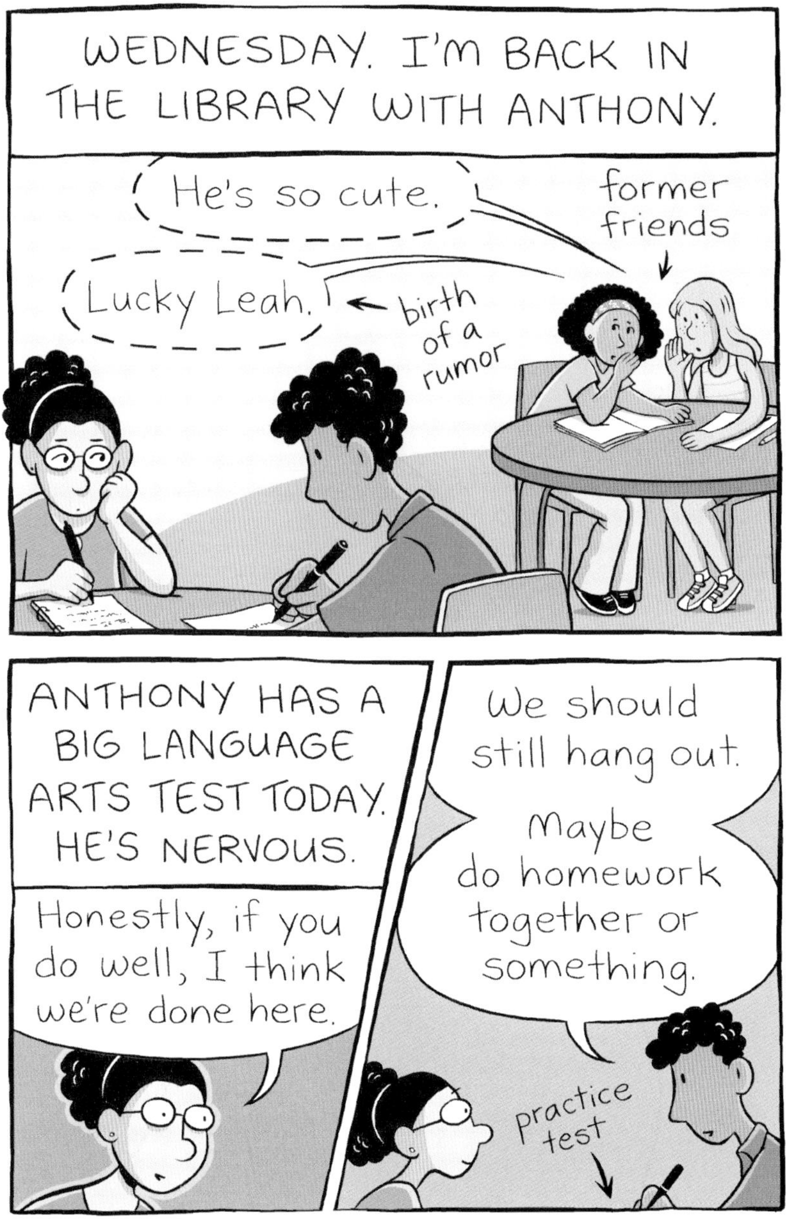

WEDNESDAY. I'M BACK IN THE LIBRARY WITH ANTHONY.
He's so cute.
former friends
Lucky Leah.
birth of a rumor
ANTHONY HAS A BIG LANGUAGE ARTS TEST TODAY. HE'S NERVOUS.
Honestly, if you do well, I think we're done here.
We should still hang out.
Maybe do homework together or something.
practice test

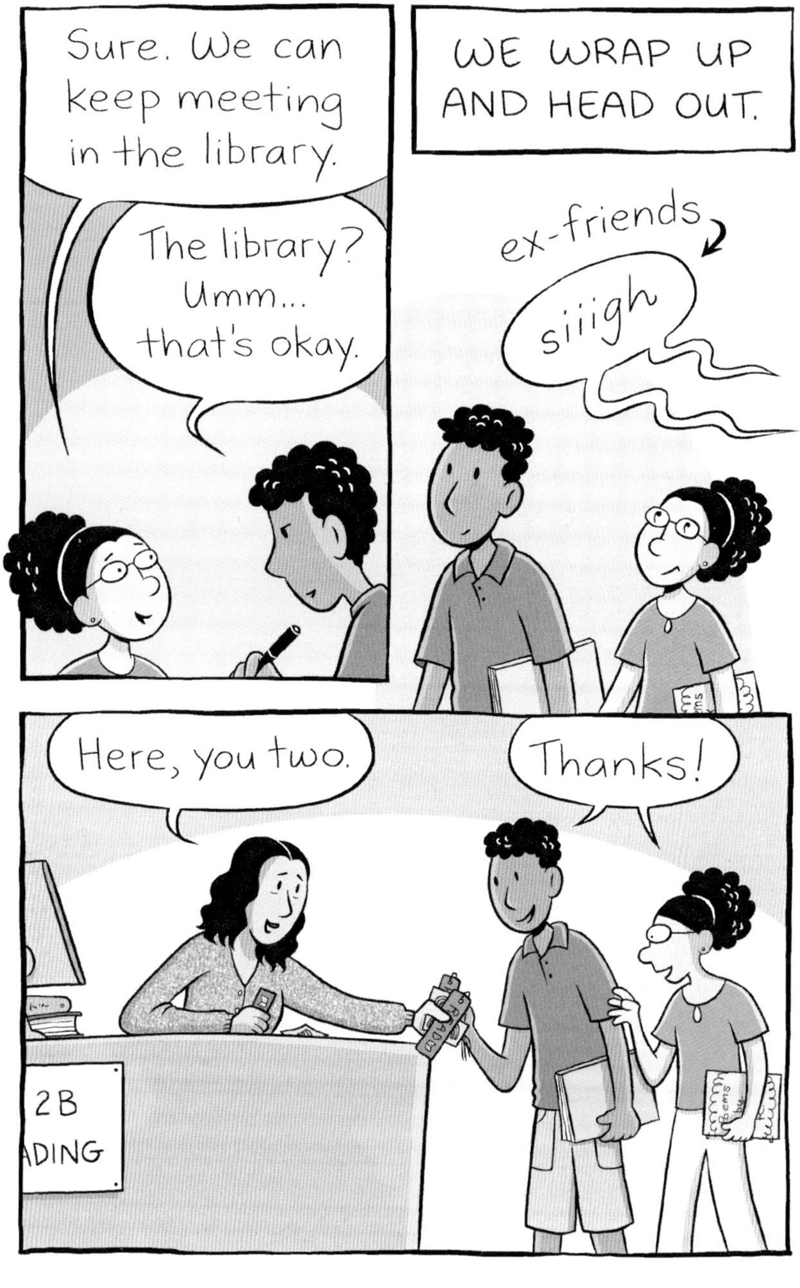
Sure. We can keep meeting in the library.
The library? Umm... that's okay.
WE WRAP UP AND HEAD OUT.
ex-friends
siiigh
Here, you two.
Thanks!
2B
ADING

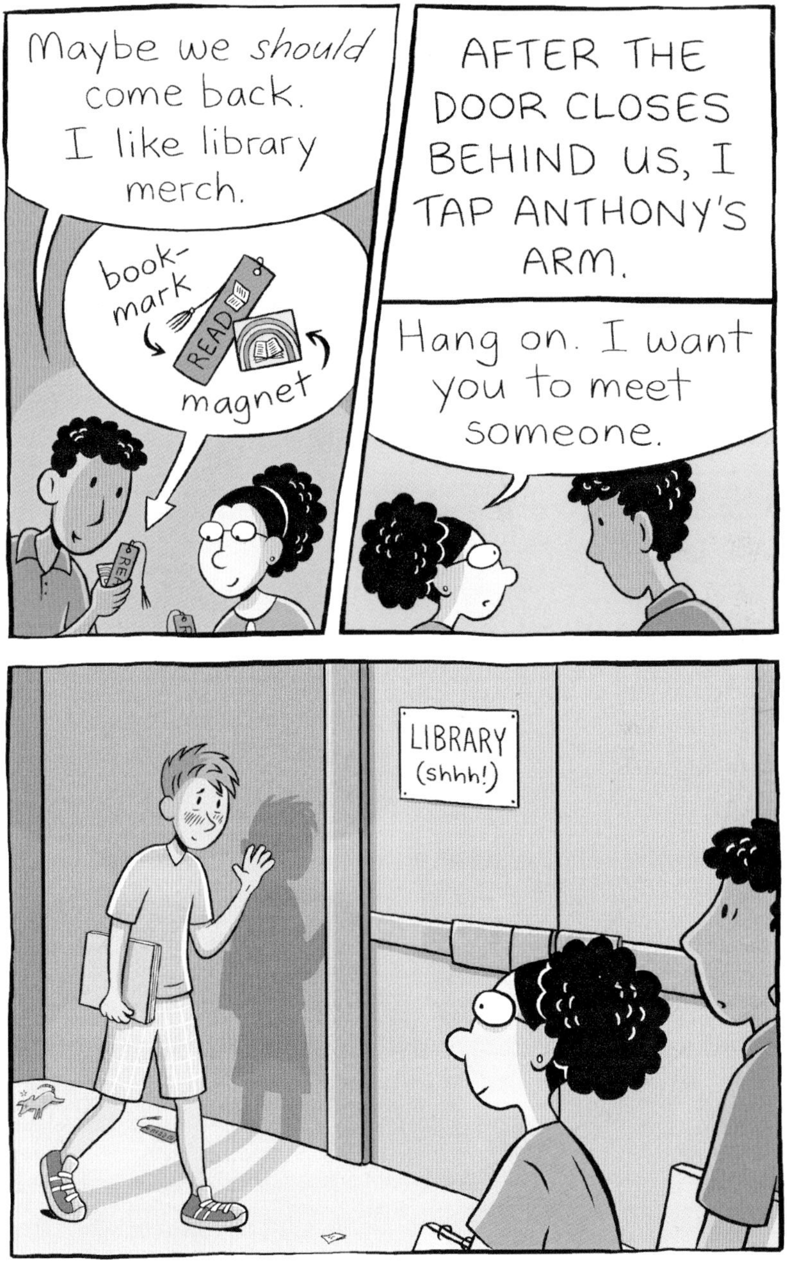
Maybe we *should* come back. I like library merch.
book-mark
READ
magnet
AFTER THE DOOR CLOSES BEHIND US, I TAP ANTHONY'S ARM.
Hang on. I want you to meet someone.
LIBRARY
(shhh!)

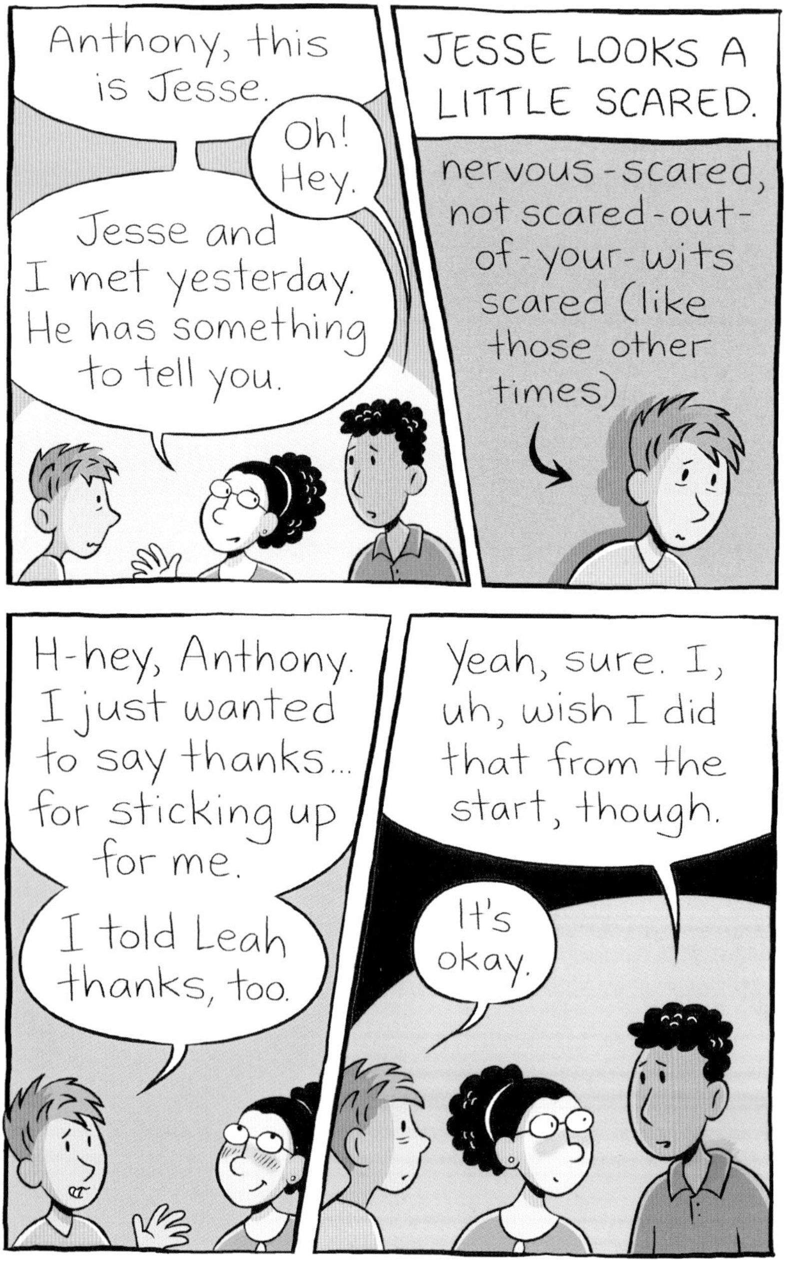
Anthony, this is Jesse.
Oh! Hey.
Jesse and I met yesterday. He has something to tell you.
JESSE LOOKS A LITTLE SCARED.
nervous-scared, not scared-out-of-your-wits scared (like those other times)
H-hey, Anthony. I just wanted to say thanks... for sticking up for me.
I told Leah thanks, too.
Yeah, sure. I, uh, wish I did that from the start, though.
It's okay.

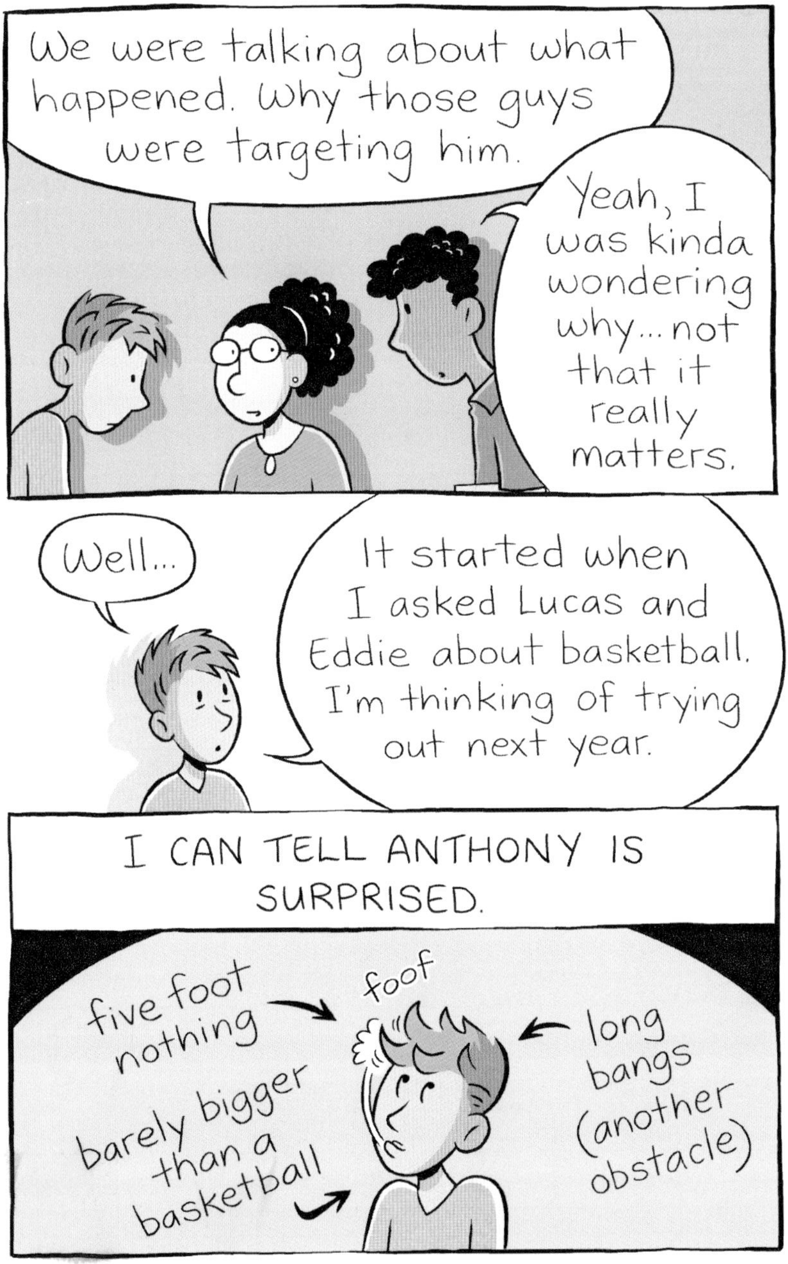
We were talking about what happened. Why those guys were targeting him.
Yeah, I was kinda wondering why... not that it really matters.
Well...
It started when I asked Lucas and Eddie about basketball. I'm thinking of trying out next year.
I CAN TELL ANTHONY IS SURPRISED.
five foot nothing
foof
long bangs (another obstacle)
barely bigger than a basketball

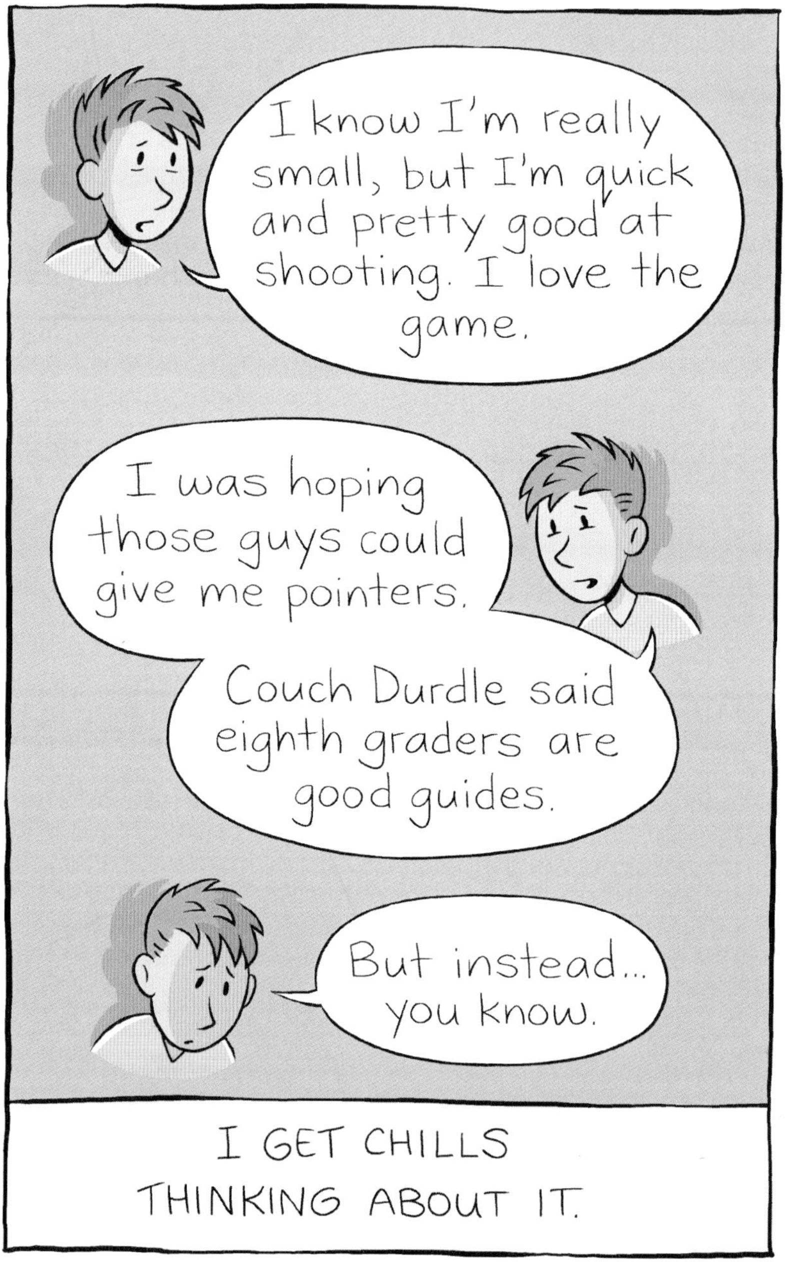
I know I'm really small, but I'm quick and pretty good at shooting. I love the game.
I was hoping those guys could give me pointers.
Couch Durdle said eighth graders are good guides.
But instead... you know.
I GET CHILLS THINKING ABOUT IT.

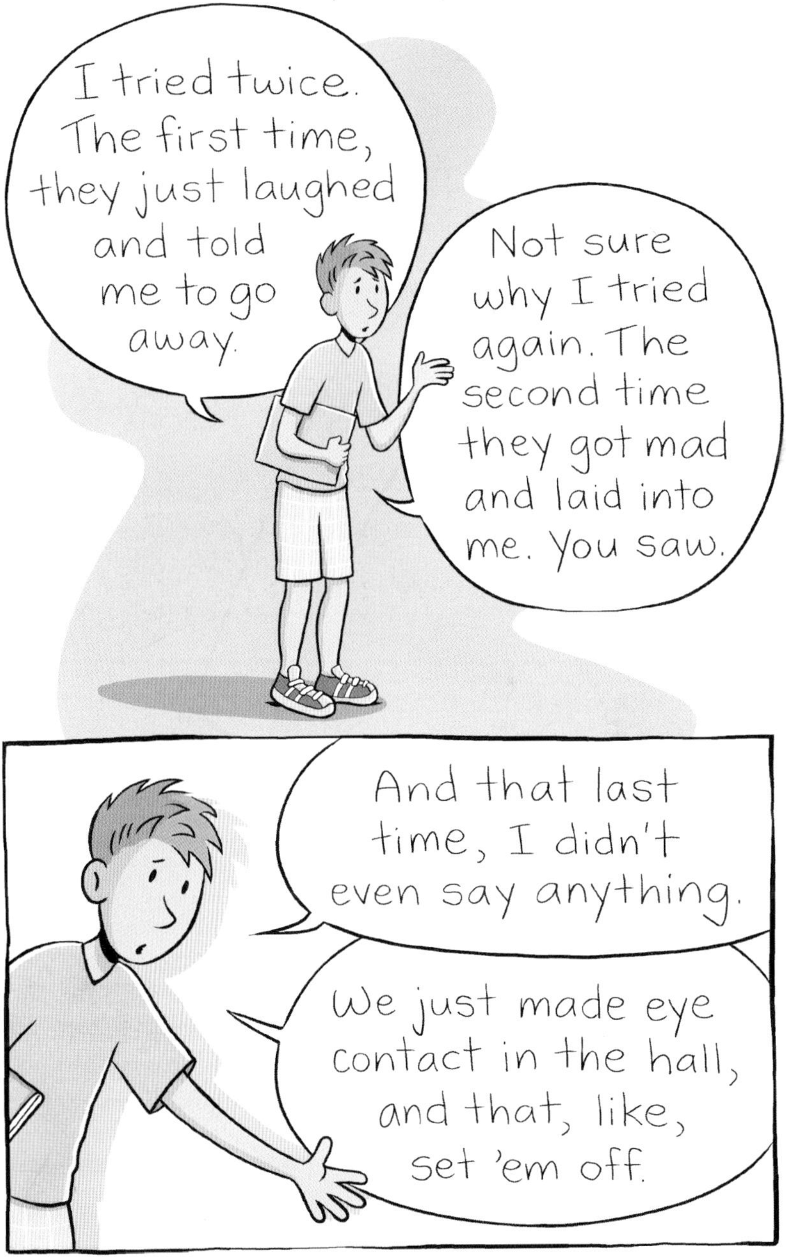
I tried twice. The first time, they just laughed and told me to go away.
Not sure why I tried again. The second time they got mad and laid into me. You saw.
And that last time, I didn't even say anything.
We just made eye contact in the hall, and that, like, set 'em off.

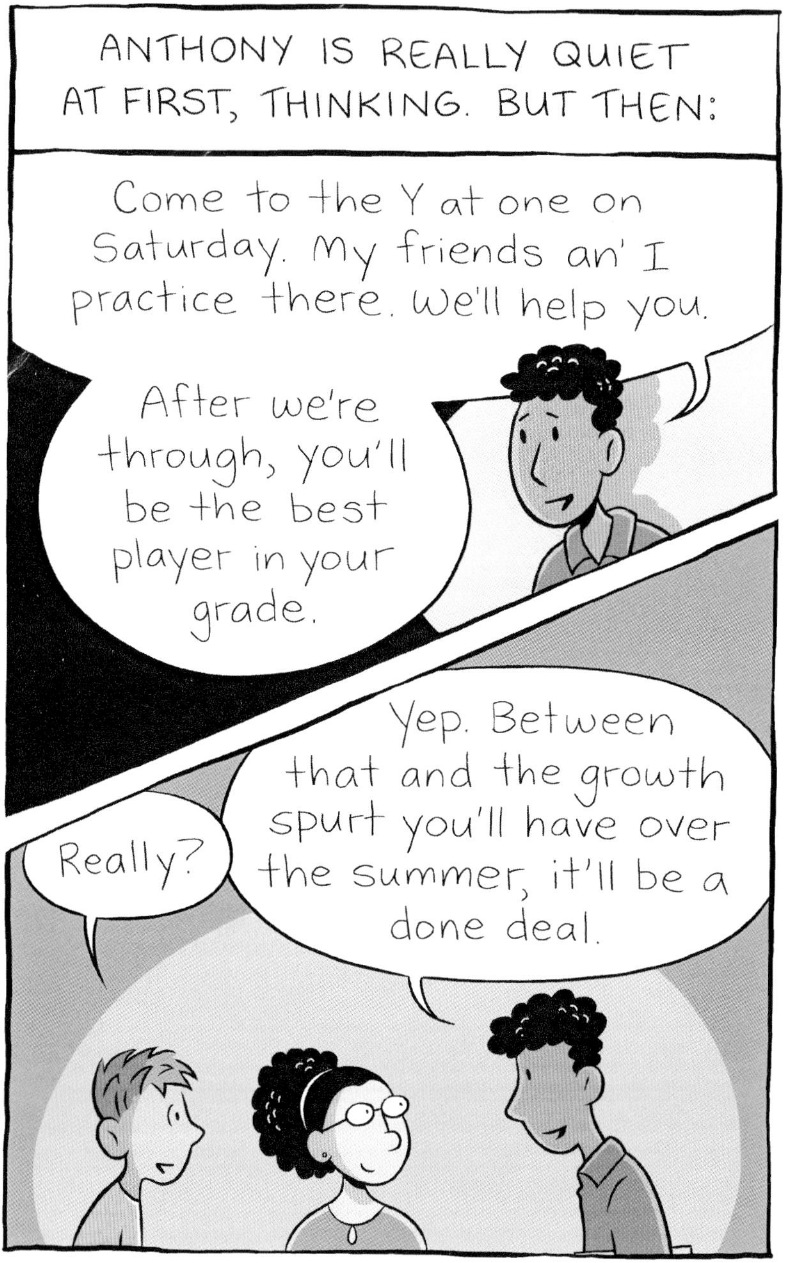
ANTHONY IS REALLY QUIET AT FIRST, THINKING. BUT THEN:
Come to the Y at one on Saturday. My friends an' I practice there. We'll help you.
After we're through, you'll be the best player in your grade.
Really?
Yep. Between that and the growth spurt you'll have over the summer, it'll be a done deal.

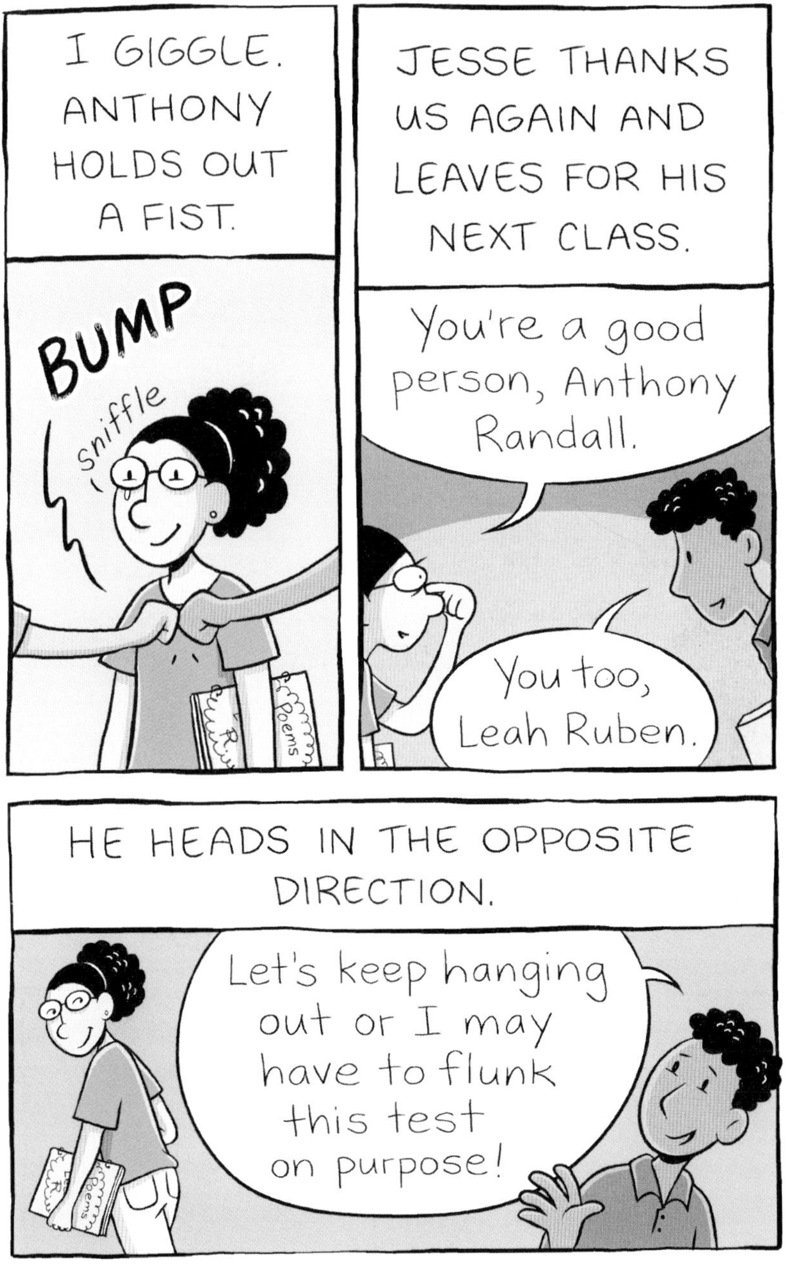
I GIGGLE. ANTHONY HOLDS OUT A FIST.
BUMP
sniffle
Poems
JESSE THANKS US AGAIN AND LEAVES FOR HIS NEXT CLASS.
You're a good person, Anthony Randall.
You too, Leah Ruben.
HE HEADS IN THE OPPOSITE DIRECTION.
Let's keep hanging out or I may have to flunk this test on purpose!

ANTHONY

Sunday afternoon. It's been a couple weeks and so much has happened.

First, I don't need Leah to tutor me anymore. My grades are finally stable at a solid B (one point shy of B+!). Feels like a miracle. I thanked her a **lot**, but she just looked at me and said:

You did it. You paid attention and worked your butt off.

That's no small feat. Especially with your history.

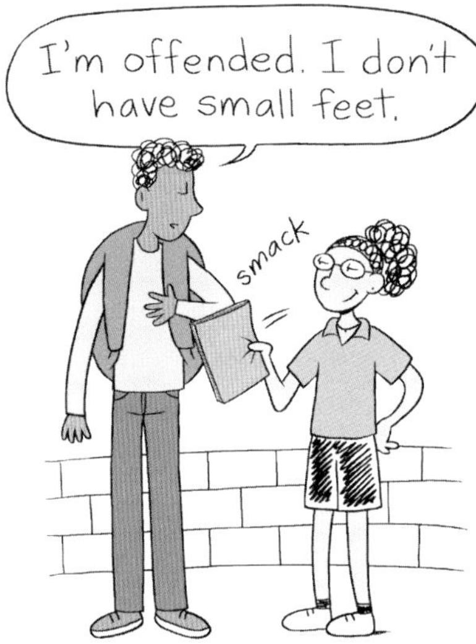
I'm offended. I don't have small feet.
smack

I haven't yet thanked her for something else.

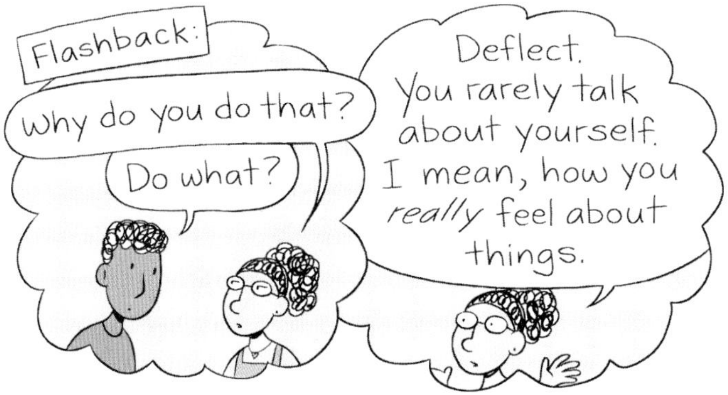
Flashback:
Why do you do that?
Do what?
Deflect. You rarely talk about yourself. I mean, how you *really* feel about things.

That led to writing about something really personal. And opening up about it in front of my class. And when the sky didn't part and lightning didn't strike me down, and people were actually

supportive . . . well, that blew my mind. I don't know why I held it in for so long.

Plus, now Ty and I talk more.

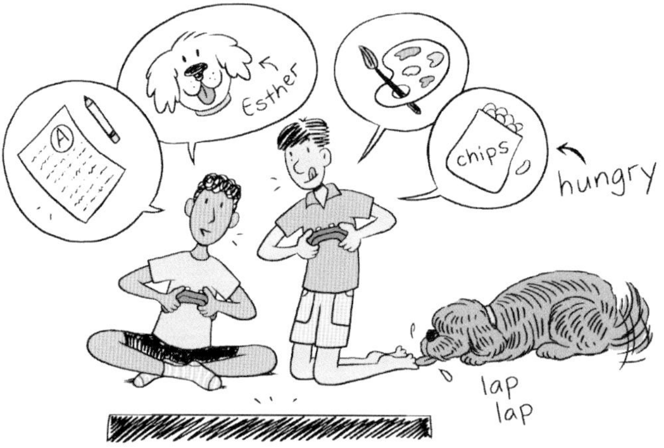

Esther
chips
hungry
lap
lap

If only we could break through to Joe, but there's still time.

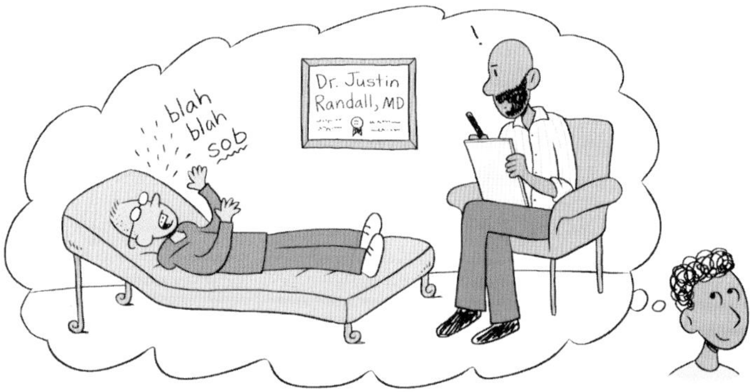

Dr. Justin
Randall, MD
blah
blah
sob
!

As for the sixth grader, Jesse: he came to the Y two Saturdays in a row. He's a fast learner and everyone likes him. Also, he didn't exaggerate: he's quick. No slouch at dribbling. And with the other guys' help, his shooting is already improving.

I even asked Ty's older brother, Zach, to come to the Y, which he did yesterday. Not only did he give Jesse pointers, but he also helped the rest of us with our crossovers and passes.

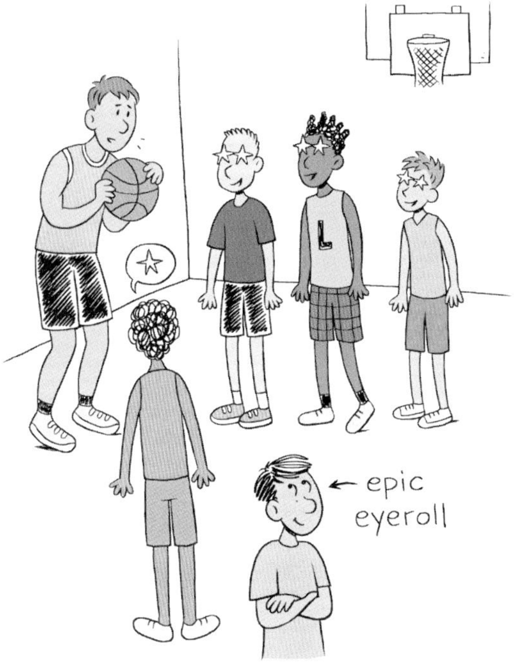
L
← epic eyeroll

As for my parents: they're really proud of me for raising my English grade. My mom even promised to take her badgering down a notch. My pop forgot himself and laughed when she said that. Which led to some bickering. Which led to my sisters and me sneaking away to take Phineas for a walk. Which led to me treating them to ice cream. Which led to my sisters telling me:

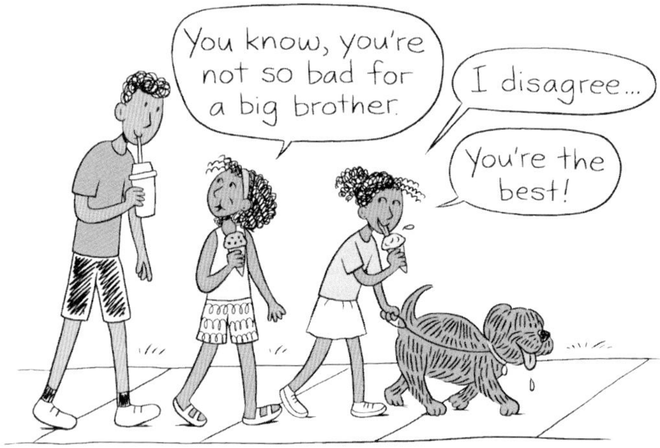
You know, you're not so bad for a big brother.
I disagree...
You're the best!

Okay, so I know that was coming from their stomachs more than their hearts. But still. Makes me realize how much I love those two twerps . . .

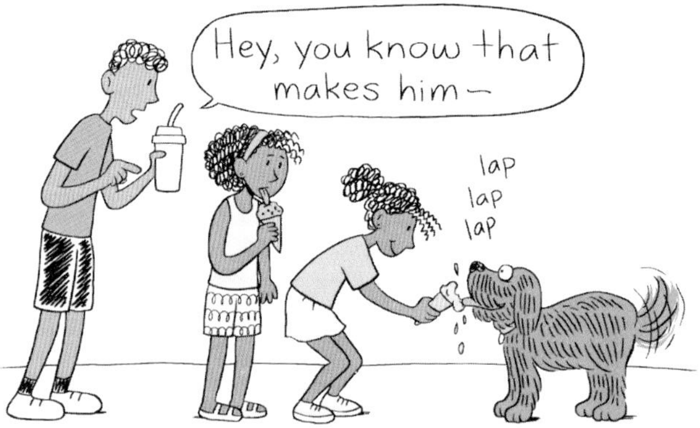
Hey, you know that makes him—
lap
lap
lap

HA HA
HA HA
TOOT!

. . . most of the time.

Anyway, all that's good. Great, even. But there's something that's still bugging me . . . a lot. I tried shoving it in the back of my mind, blocking it out, telling myself it doesn't matter anymore, all that. But I dunno . . . maybe it's 'cause I'm opening up more or something. I just can't let it go.

hey, meet at ramones? i need a slice
tap click tak
hey meet at ramones? i need a slice
. . .
hey meet at ramones? i need a slice
sure see u in 10

I tell my mom I'm meeting a friend at Ramone's. She's busy FaceTiming Aunt Lily.

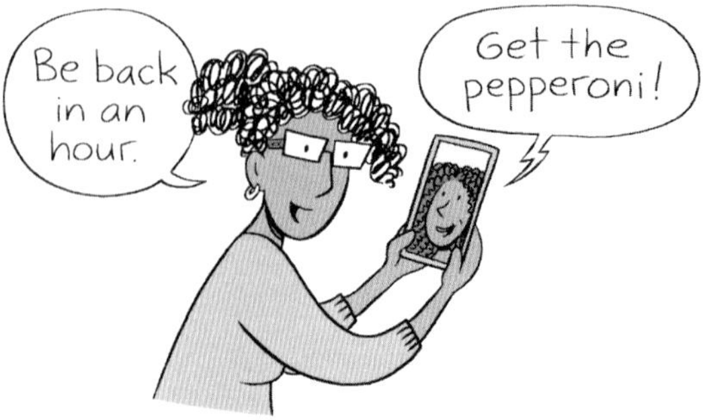
Be back in an hour.
Get the pepperoni!

The restaurant is only a couple blocks away, so I grab my bike and go. They have a weekend deal for kids thirteen and under: two slices for three dollars. So, it's not unusual to see a lot of Lakefront students there.

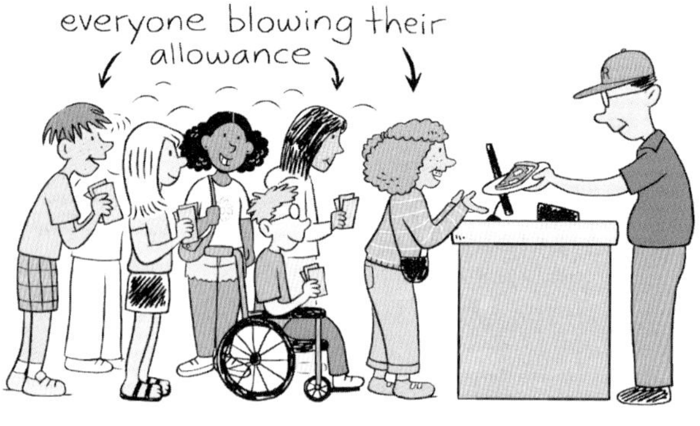
everyone blowing their allowance

Today is cloudy and a little rainy, so not many people are out. It's pretty dead inside the restaurant. I get there first and grab a booth in back.

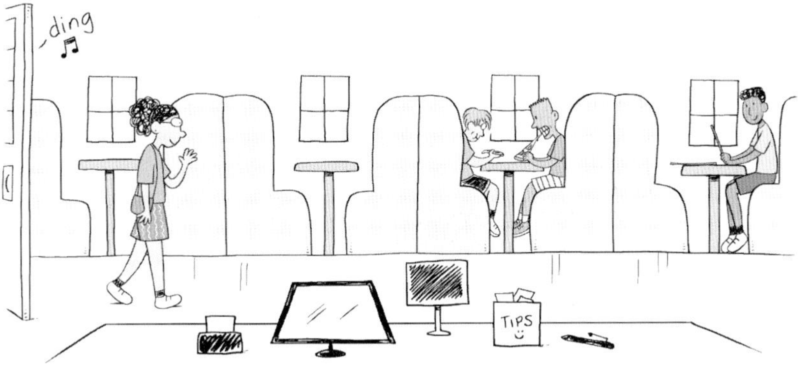
ding
TIPS

Leah and I have started hanging out more. This is the second time we're meeting at Ramone's.

We order a couple of slices.

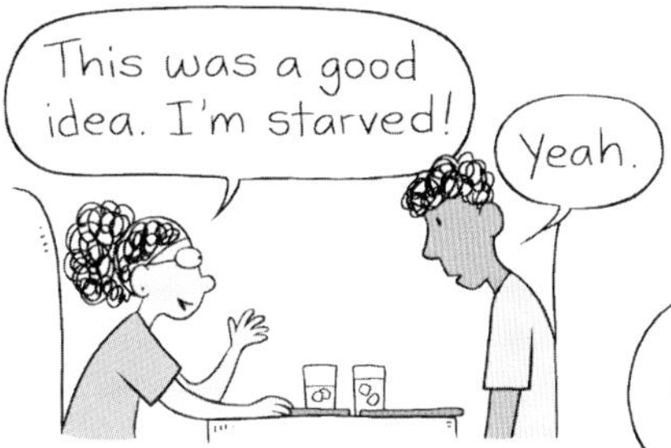
This was a good idea. I'm starved!
Yeah.

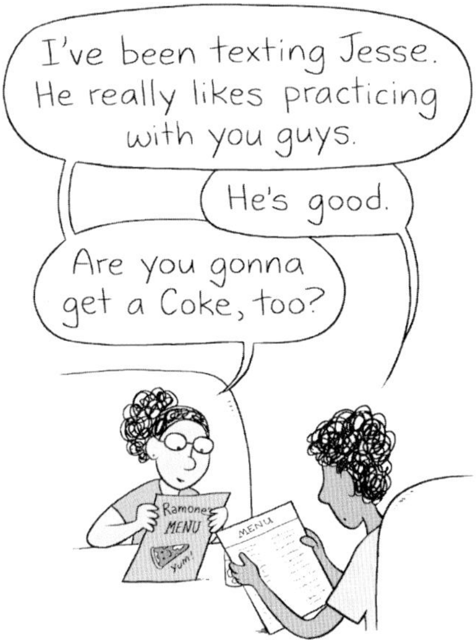
I've been texting Jesse. He really likes practicing with you guys.
He's good.
Are you gonna get a Coke, too?
Ramone's
MENU
yum!
MENU

I shrug. Leah studies me.

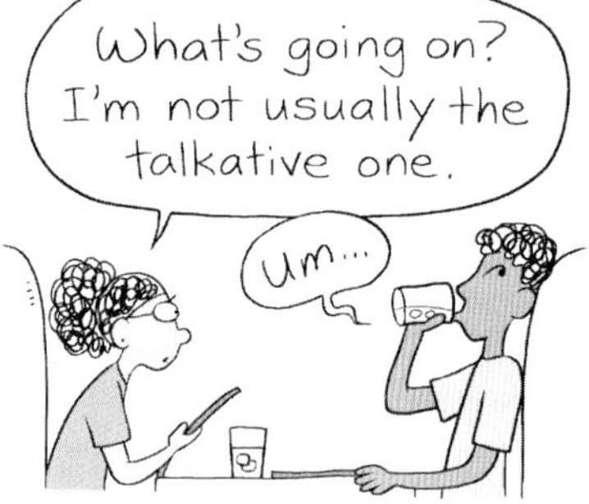
What's going on? I'm not usually the talkative one.
Um...

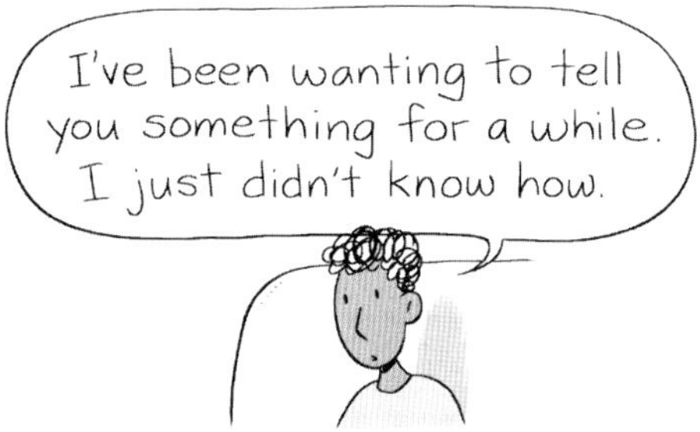
I've been wanting to tell you something for a while. I just didn't know how.

She waits.

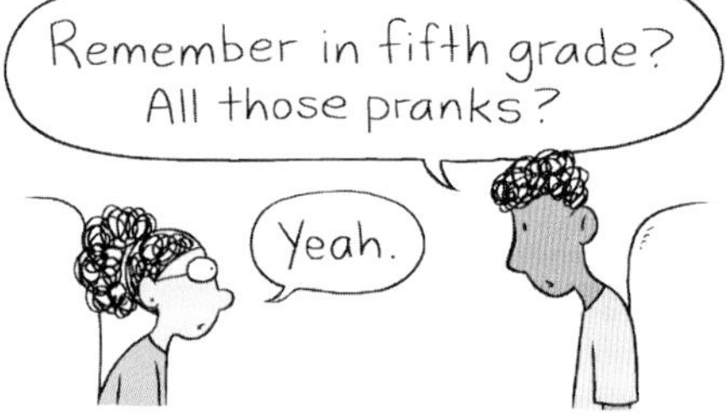
Remember in fifth grade? All those pranks?
Yeah.

I take a deep breath.

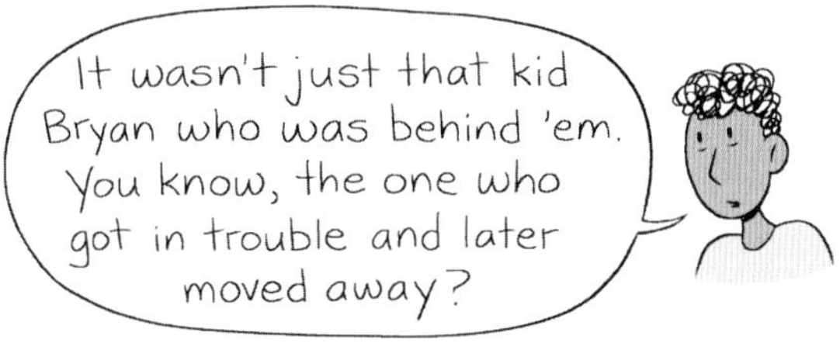
It wasn't just that kid Bryan who was behind 'em. You know, the one who got in trouble and later moved away?

Leah looks confused at first.

And then it dawns on her.

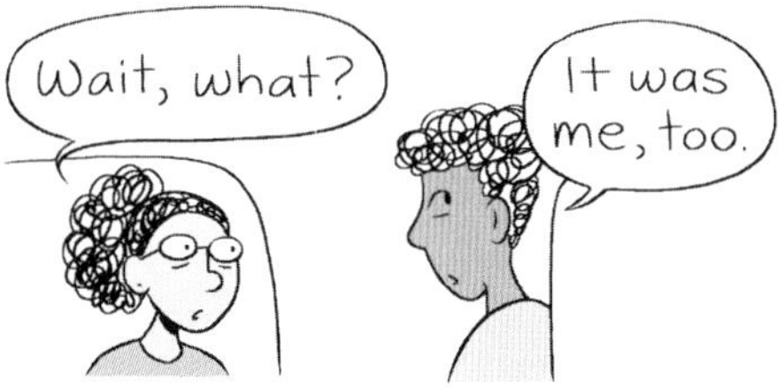
Wait, what?
It was me, too.

She shakes her head.

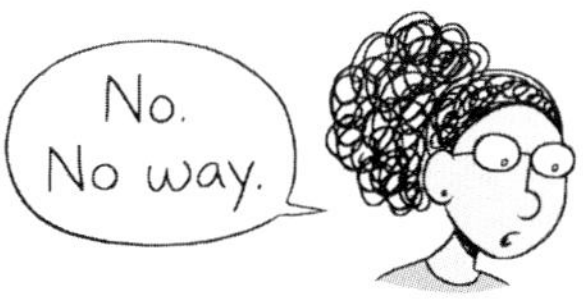
No. No way.

I nod. She stares at me.

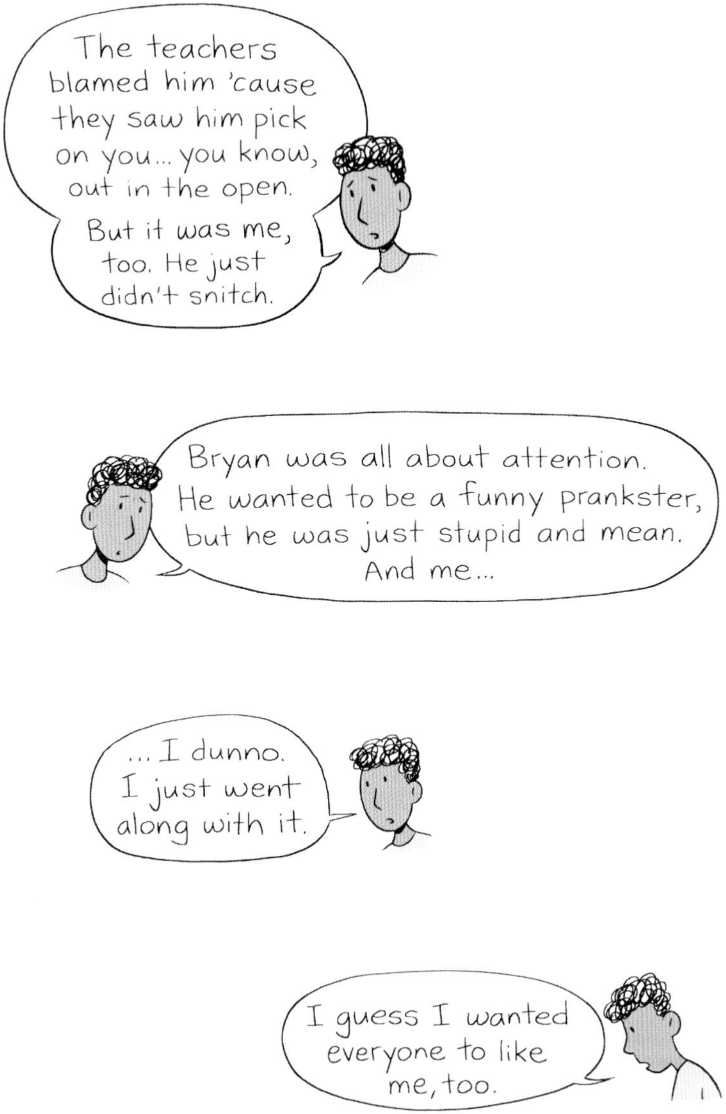
The teachers blamed him 'cause they saw him pick on you... you know, out in the open.
But it was me, too. He just didn't snitch.
Bryan was all about attention. He wanted to be a funny prankster, but he was just stupid and mean. And me...
...I dunno. I just went along with it.
I guess I wanted everyone to like me, too.

She's still staring.

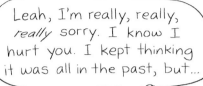

Leah, I'm really, really, *really* sorry. I know I hurt you. I kept thinking it was all in the past, but...

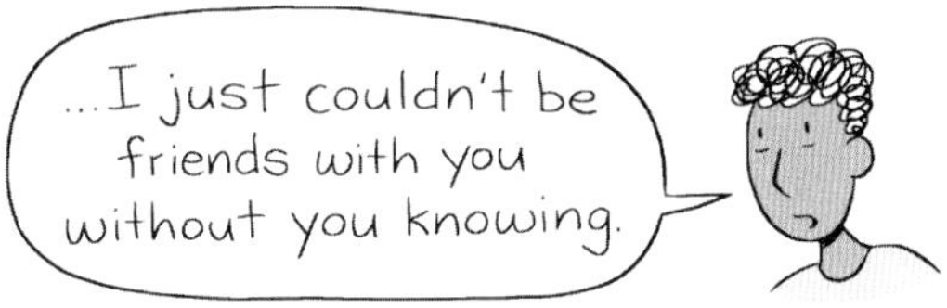

...I just couldn't be friends with you without you knowing.

Staring.

worried she's developed some kind of eyeball disorder

Um?

Say something?

She doesn't.
She gets up and walks out.

Wow. Hope you have an appetite.
Not anymore.

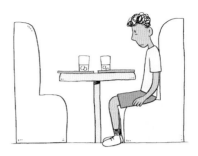

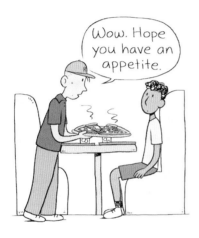

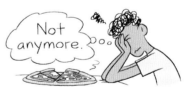

Leah

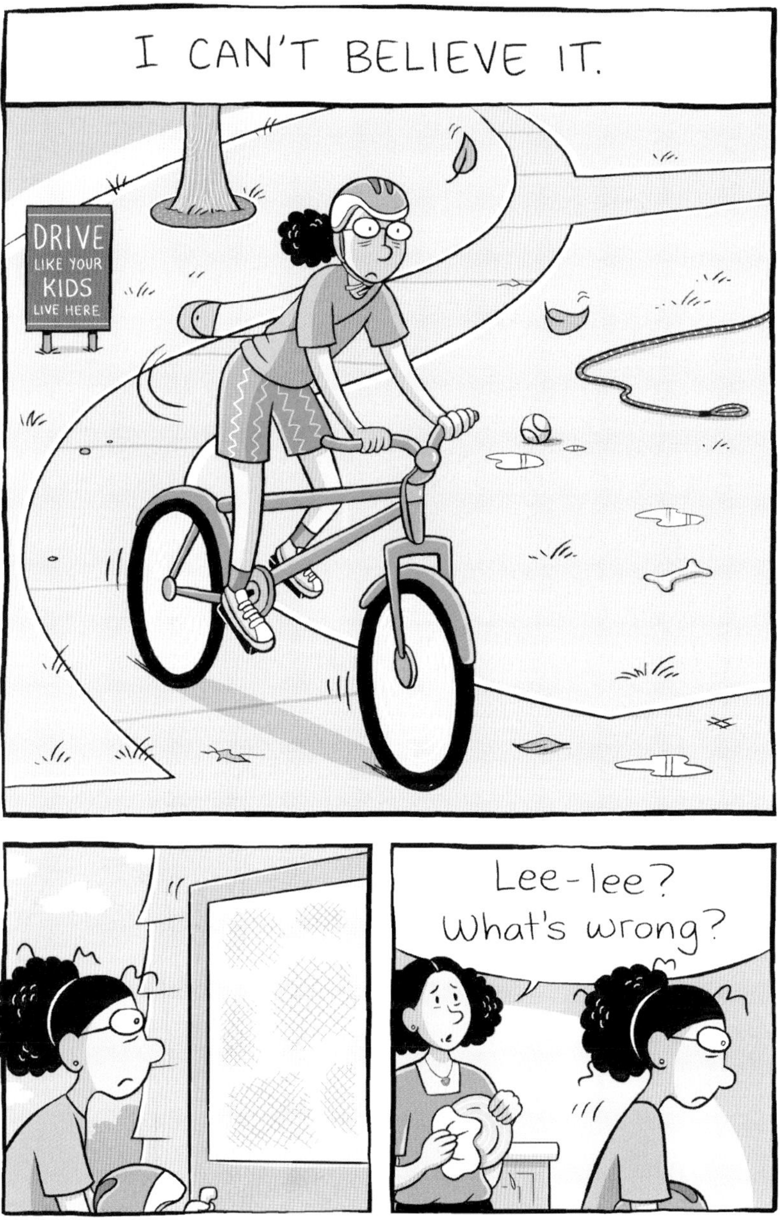
I CAN'T BELIEVE IT.
DRIVE LIKE YOUR KIDS LIVE HERE
Lee-lee? What's wrong?

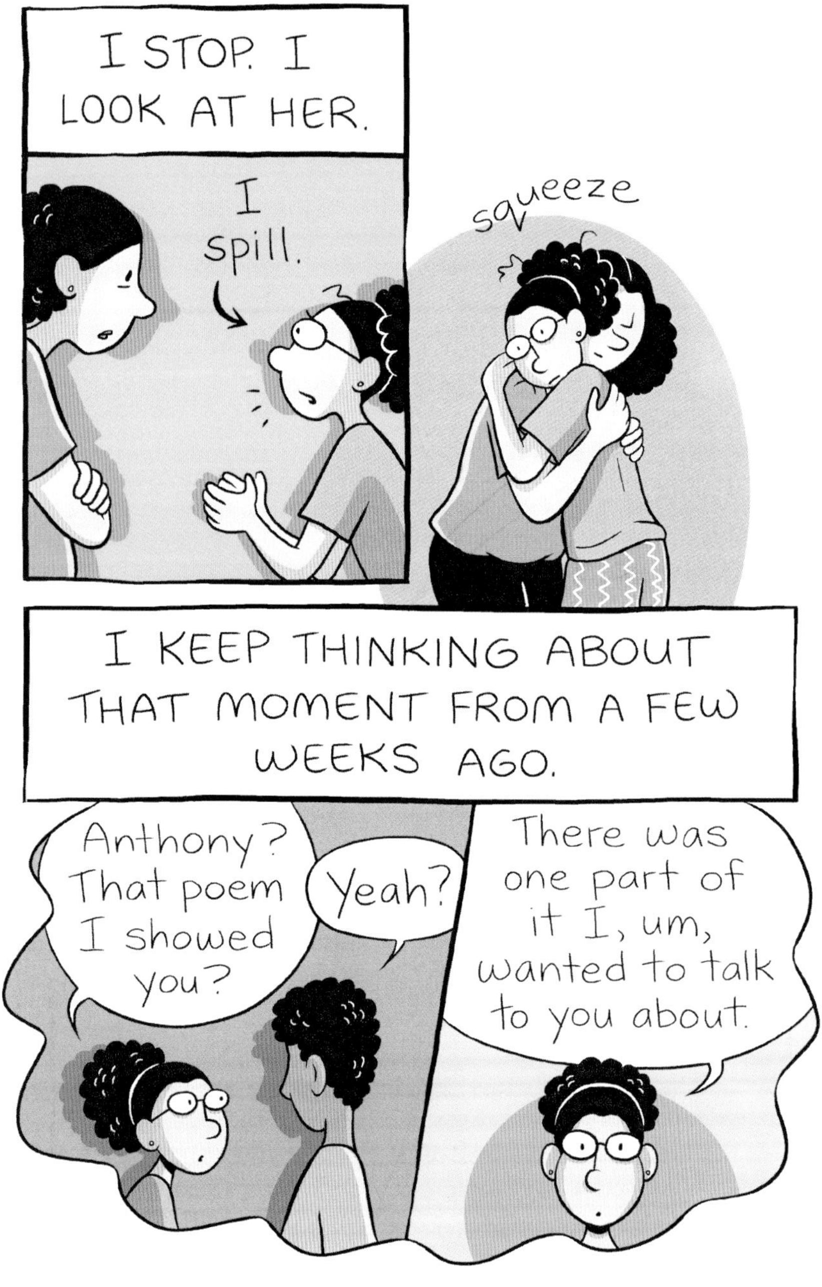
I STOP. I LOOK AT HER.
I spill.
squeeze
I KEEP THINKING ABOUT THAT MOMENT FROM A FEW WEEKS AGO.
Anthony? That poem I showed you?
Yeah?
There was one part of it I, um, wanted to talk to you about.

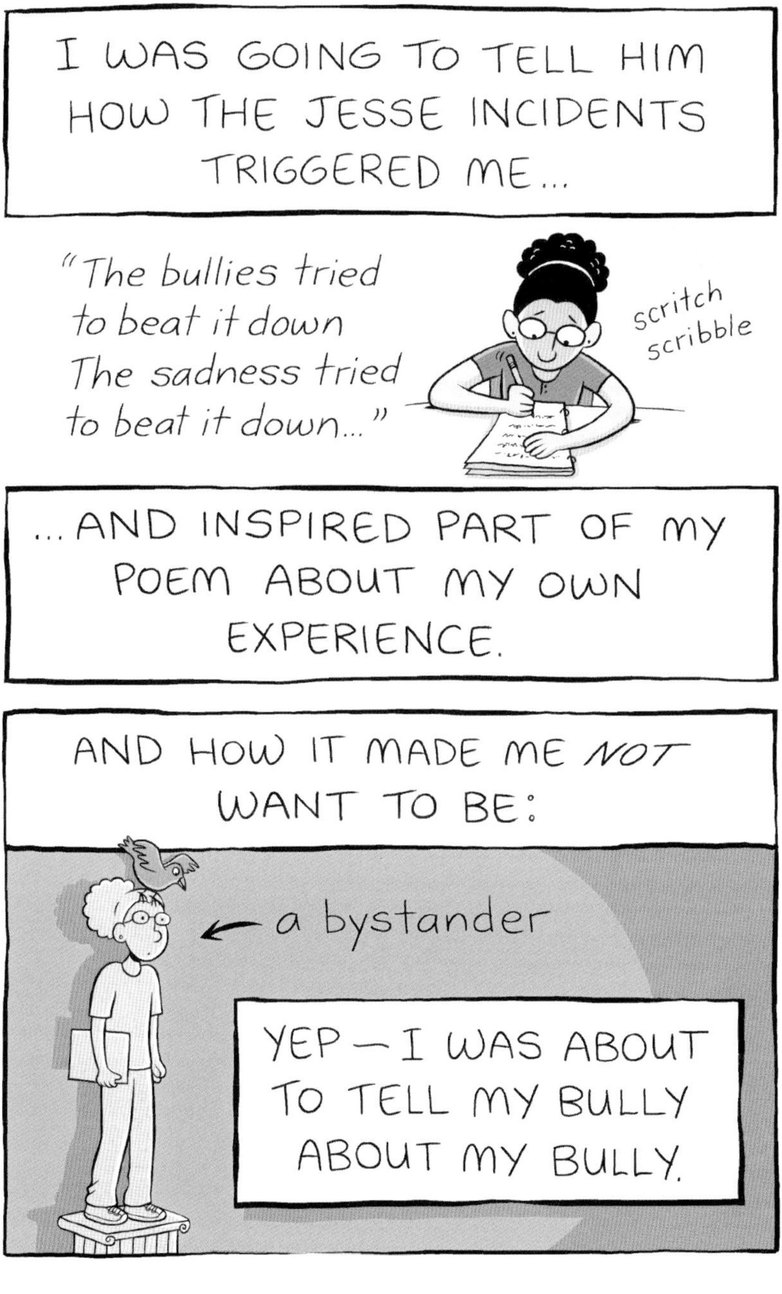
I WAS GOING TO TELL HIM HOW THE JESSE INCIDENTS TRIGGERED ME...
"The bullies tried to beat it down
The sadness tried to beat it down..."
scritch scribble
...AND INSPIRED PART OF MY POEM ABOUT MY OWN EXPERIENCE.
AND HOW IT MADE ME *NOT* WANT TO BE:
a bystander
YEP — I WAS ABOUT TO TELL MY BULLY ABOUT MY BULLY.

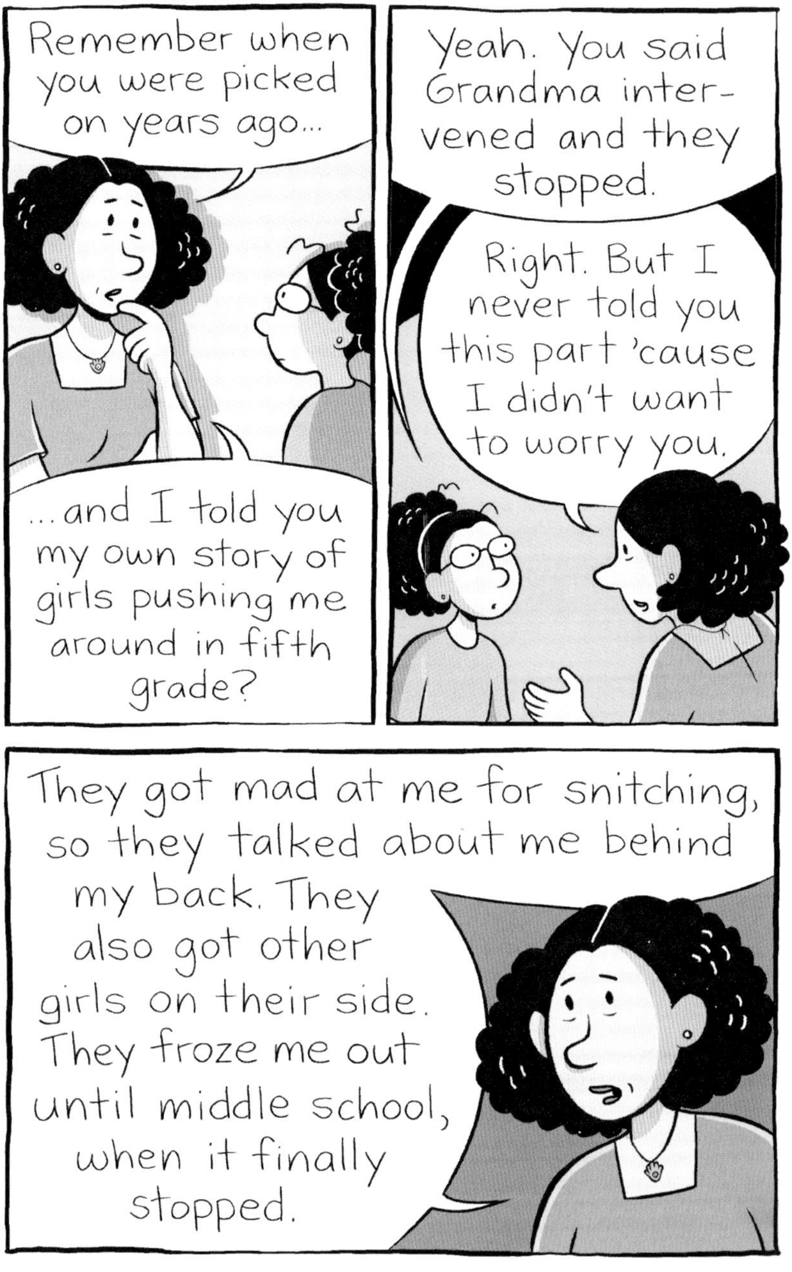
Remember when you were picked on years ago...
...and I told you my own story of girls pushing me around in fifth grade?
Yeah. You said Grandma inter-vened and they stopped.
Right. But I never told you this part 'cause I didn't want to worry you.
They got mad at me for snitching, so they talked about me behind my back. They also got other girls on their side. They froze me out until middle school, when it finally stopped.

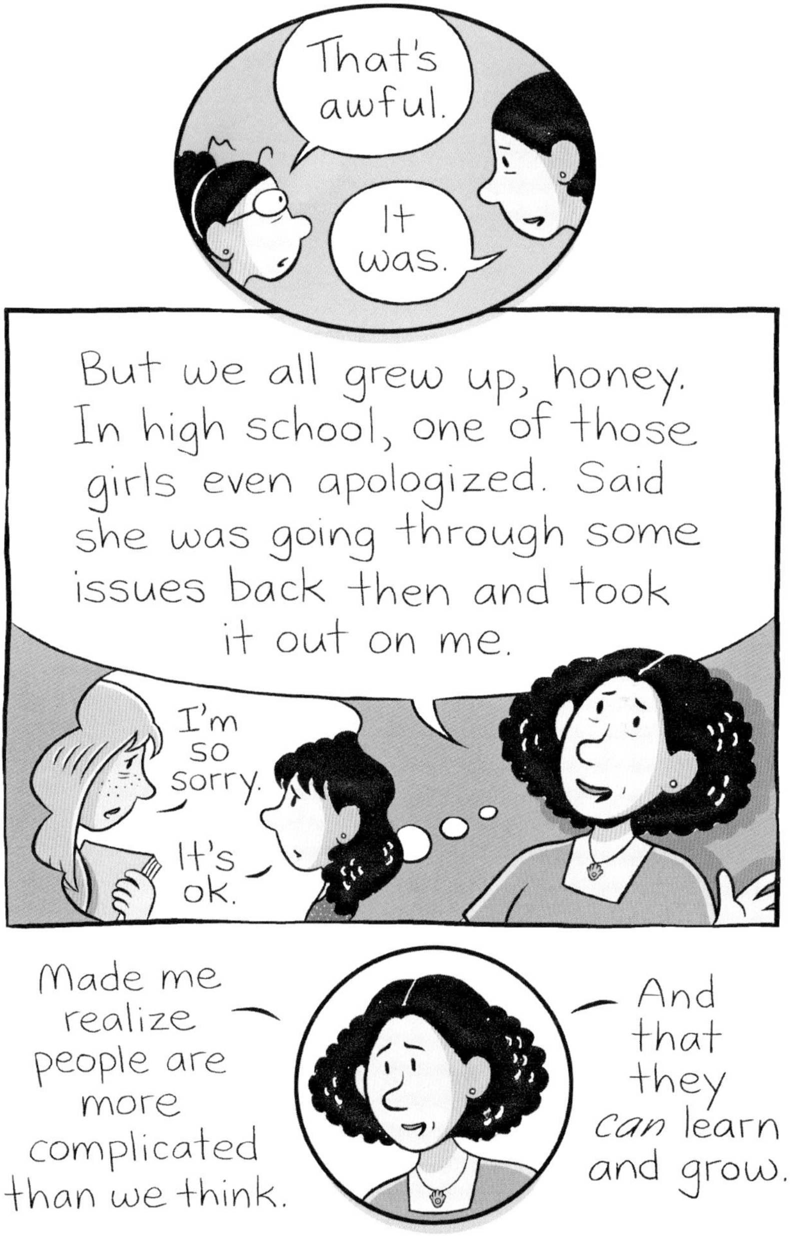
That's awful.
It was.
But we all grew up, honey. In high school, one of those girls even apologized. Said she was going through some issues back then and took it out on me.
I'm so sorry.
It's ok.
Made me realize people are more complicated than we think.
And that they *can* learn and grow.

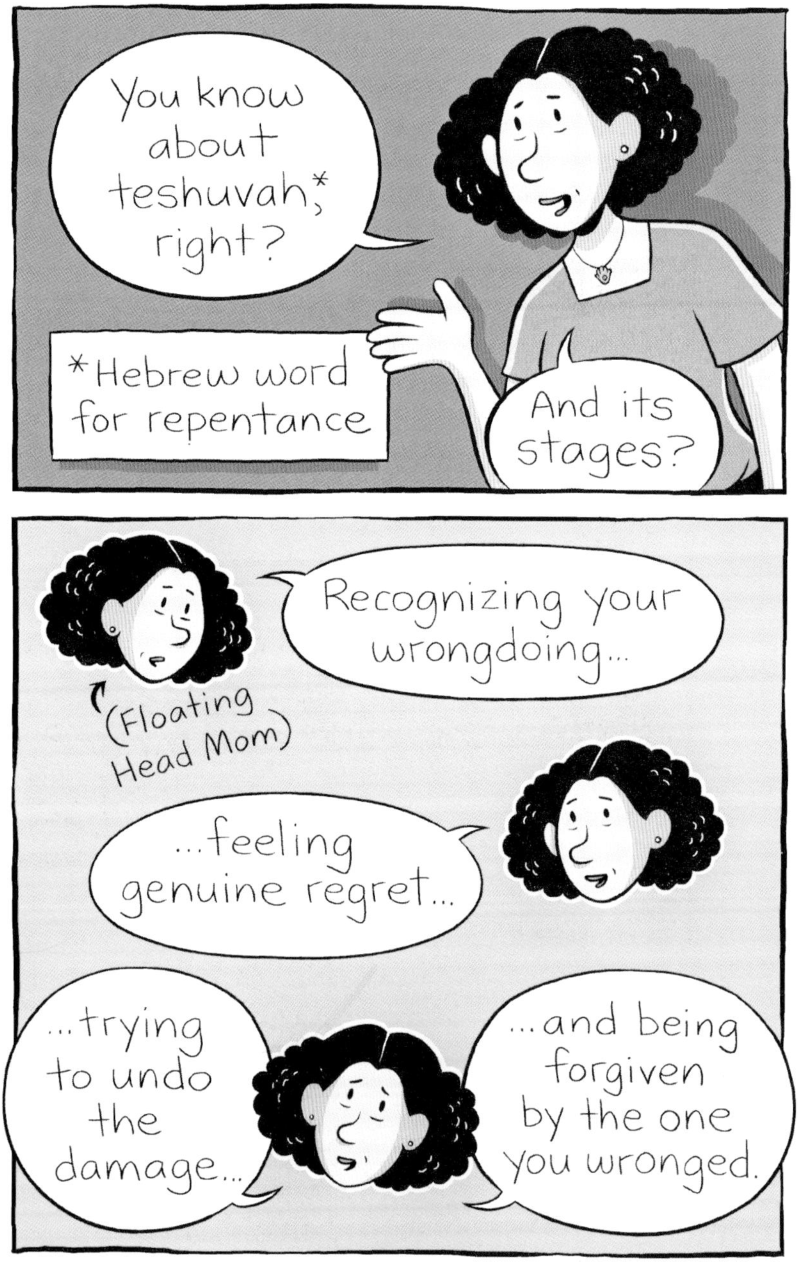
You know about teshuvah,* right?
*Hebrew word for repentance
And its stages?
Recognizing your wrongdoing...
(Floating Head Mom)
...feeling genuine regret...
...trying to undo the damage...
...and being forgiven by the one you wronged.

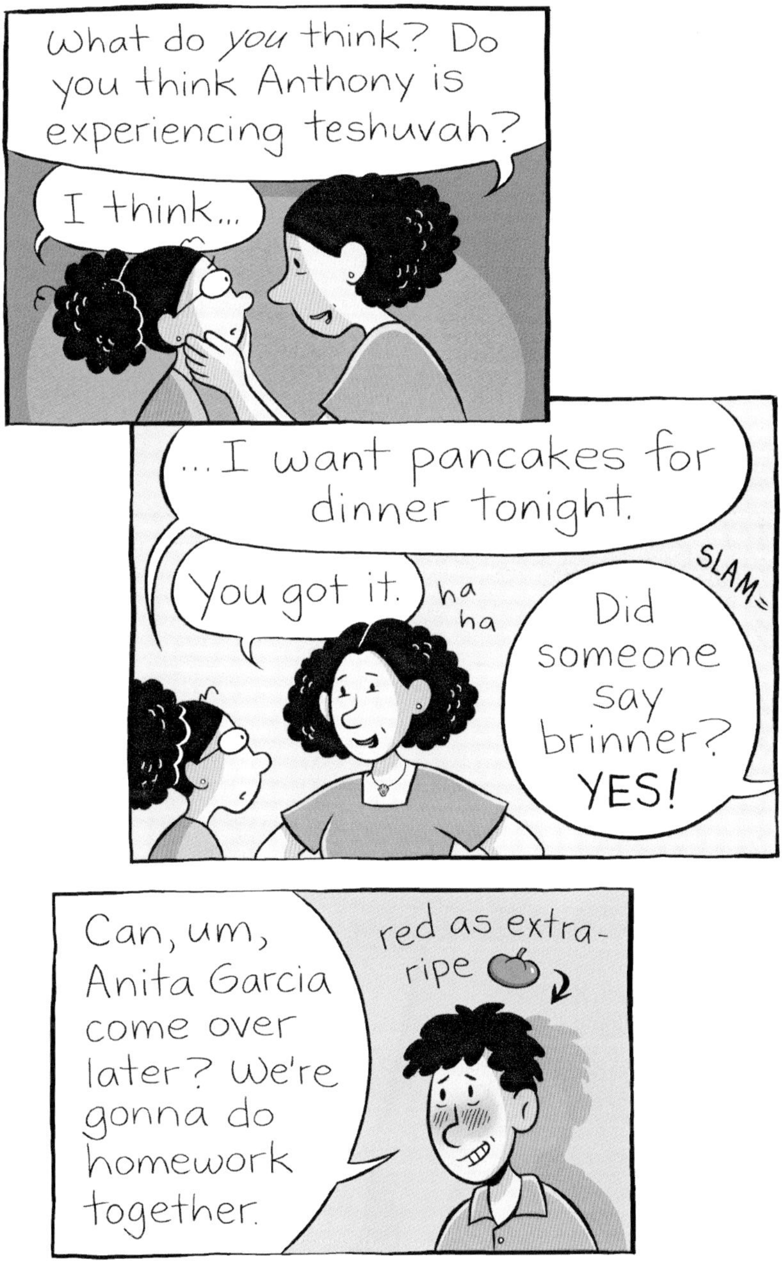
What do *you* think? Do you think Anthony is experiencing teshuvah?
I think...
...I want pancakes for dinner tonight.
You got it.
ha ha
SLAM
Did someone say brinner? YES!
Can, um, Anita Garcia come over later? We're gonna do homework together.
red as extra-ripe

WOW. MAYBE THE GOSSIP GIRLS ARE PSYCHIC.

Sure. But stay in the living room.

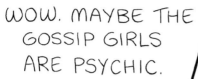

pancake batter →

GUESS I HAVE A LOT TO THINK ABOUT. BUT I DO FEEL BETTER.

Mom? What about the other girl? Did she apologize, too?

No, but in high school, she got dumped by her then-boyfriend... who eventually married me.

Not sure what the Hebrew word is for "divine payback."

HA HA HA HA HA

302

ANTHONY

Monday afternoon. The final bell rings.

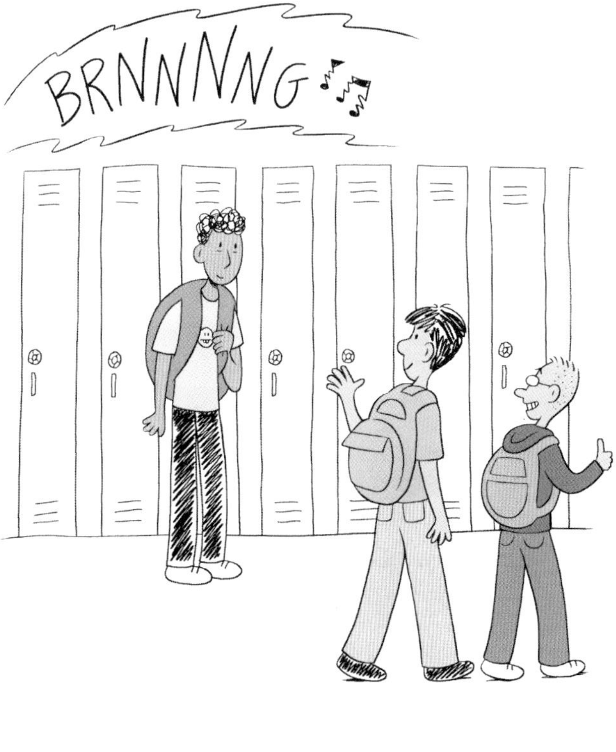
BRNNNNG

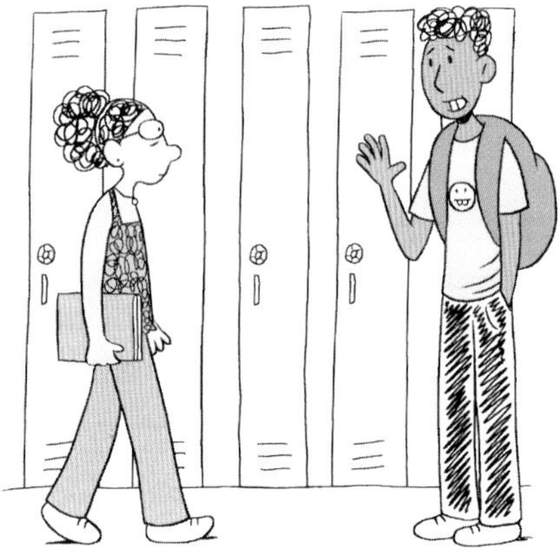

If I were smart, I'd just leave Leah alone. Forget about being friends with her. I've already hurt her enough.

So why don't I?

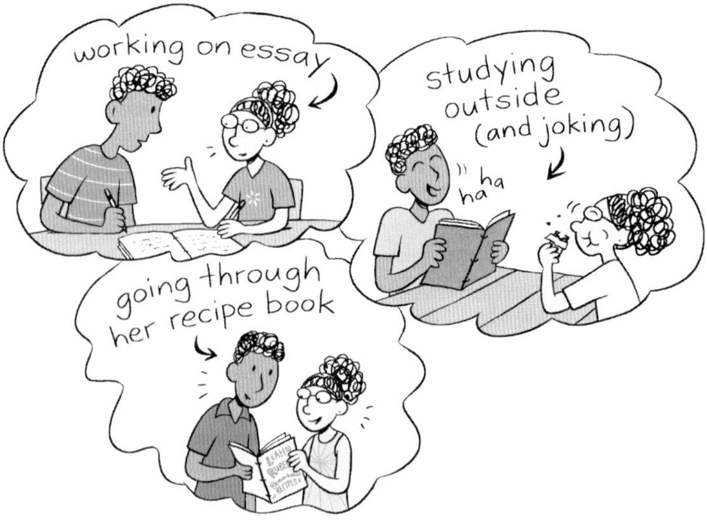
working on essay
studying outside (and joking)
ha ha ha
going through her recipe book

I guess it's hard to let go of people who get you.

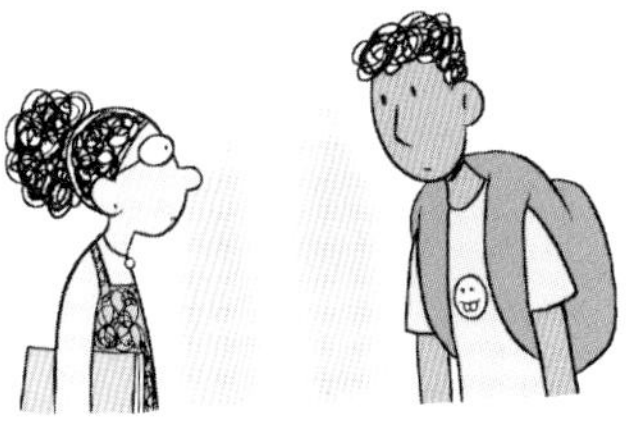

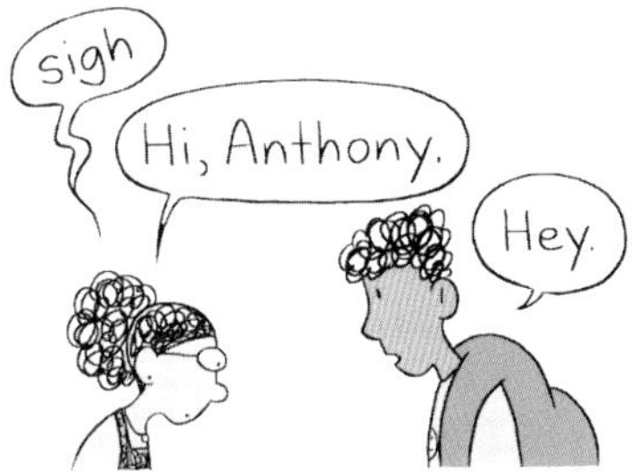
sigh
Hi, Anthony.
Hey.

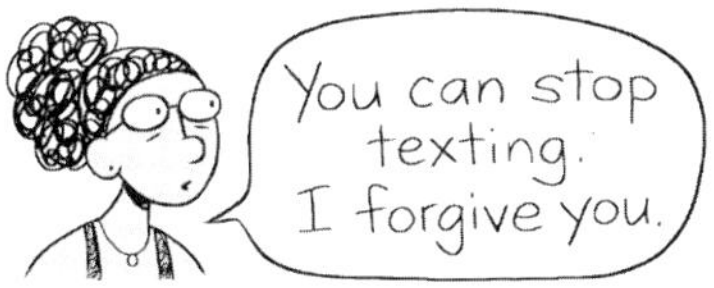
You can stop texting. I forgive you.

I exhale.

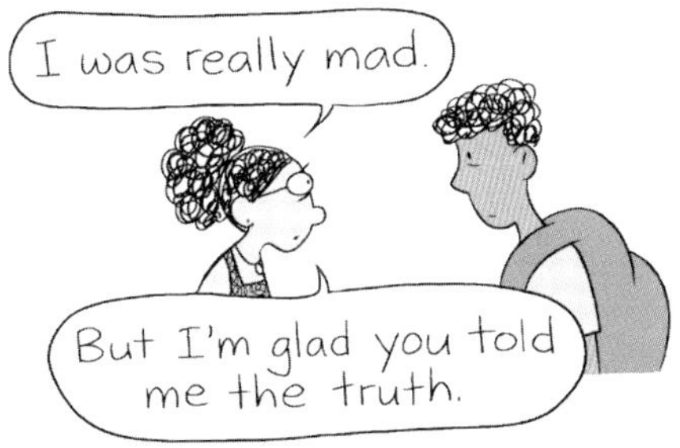
I was really mad.
But I'm glad you told me the truth.

Can we...walk home together? I don't have practice.
Okay.

We step into the afternoon sun. It's so nice out, warm and bright.

One question, though.

Was Tyler in on it, too?

I shake my head.

Even back then, I knew what I was doing was wrong 'cause I was too ashamed to tell him.

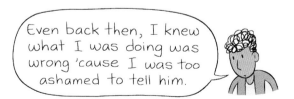

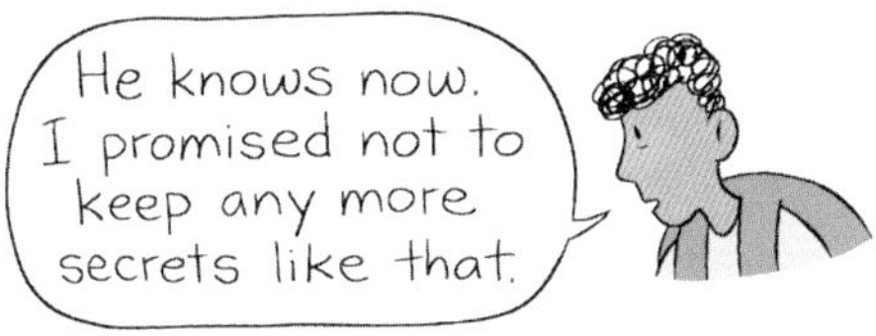
He knows now. I promised not to keep any more secrets like that.

She smiles. We hear some chatter from behind.

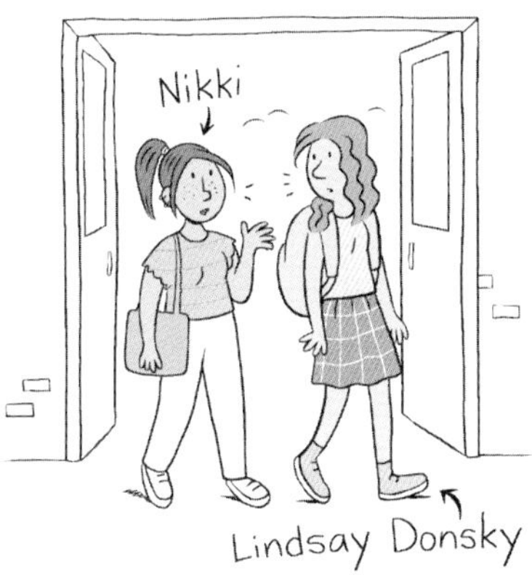
Nikki
Lindsay Donsky

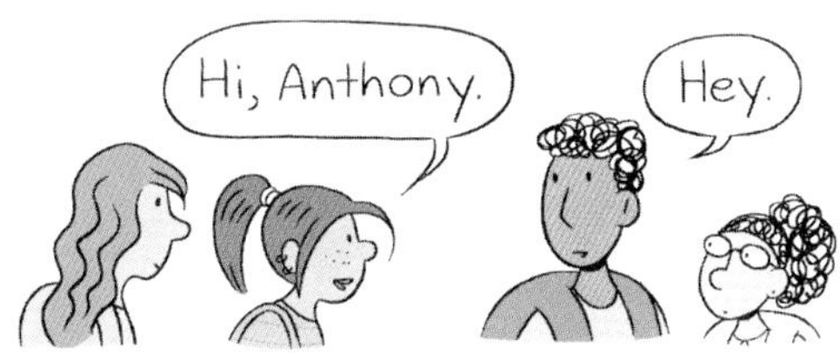
Hi, Anthony.
Hey.

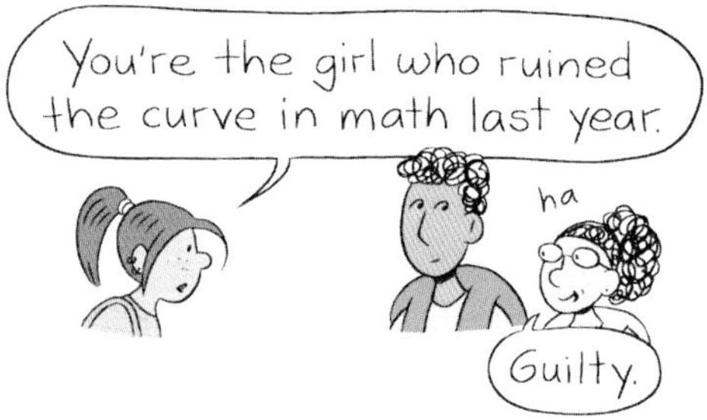
You're the girl who ruined the curve in math last year.
ha
Guilty.

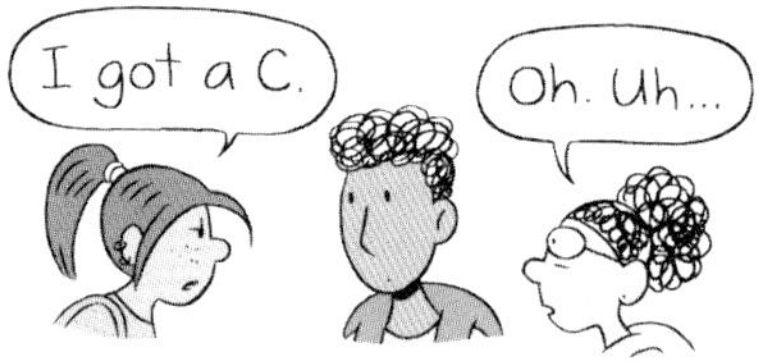
I got a C.
Oh. Uh...

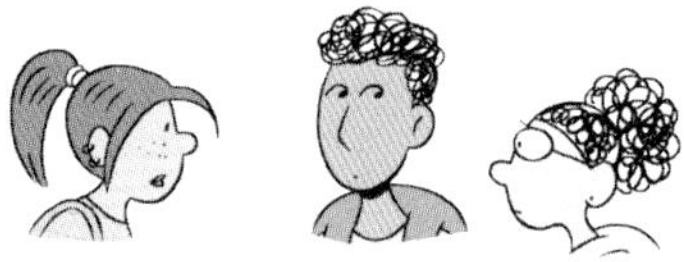

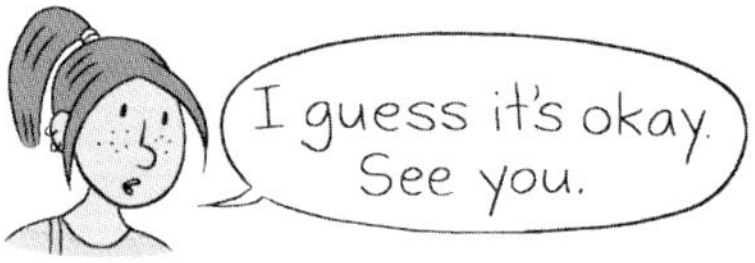
I guess it's okay. See you.

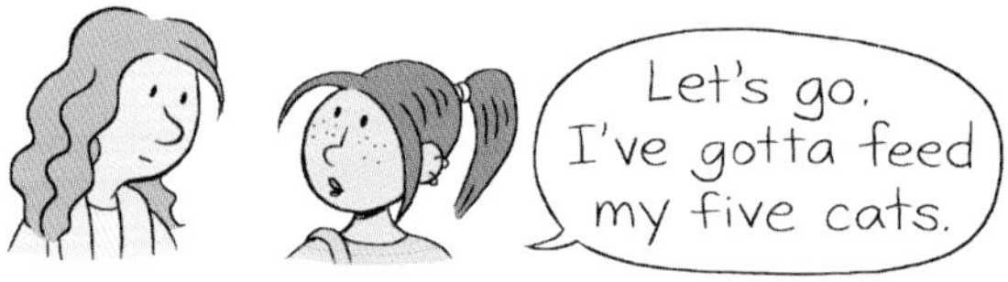
Let's go. I've gotta feed my five cats.

I shudder. Leah throws me a questioning look.

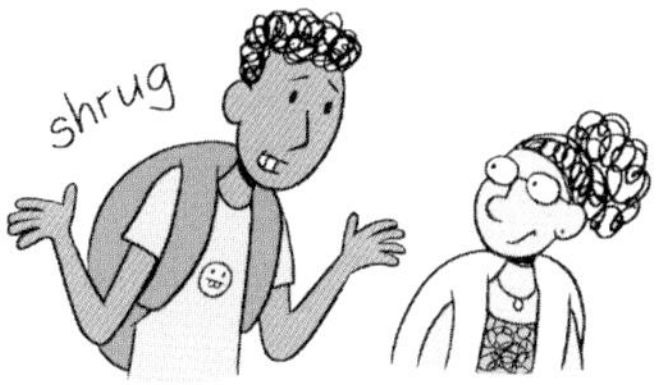
shrug

I'm starting to question things myself. Like now: I'm wondering why I've been crushing on someone I barely know.

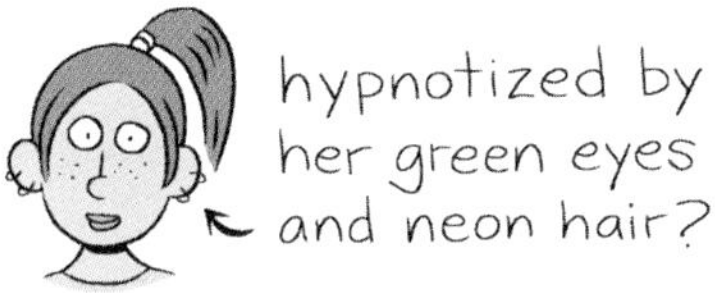
hypnotized by
her green eyes
and neon hair?

Oh well. Not something I have to figure out this minute.

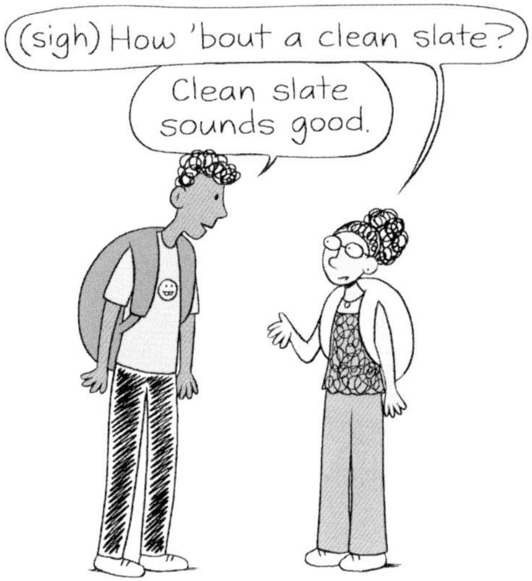
(sigh) How 'bout a clean slate?
Clean slate sounds good.

We fist-bump.

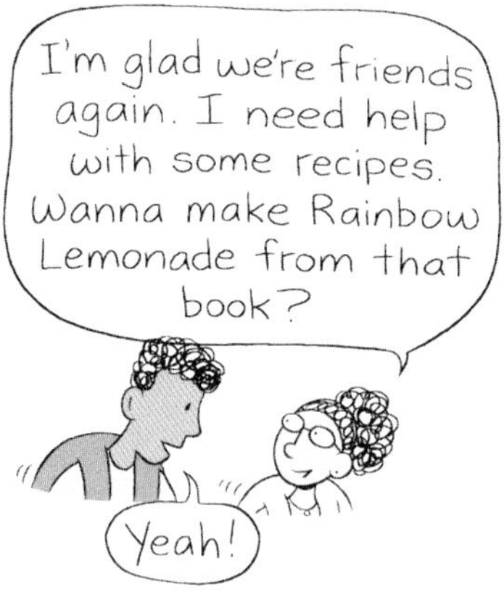
I'm glad we're friends again. I need help with some recipes. Wanna make Rainbow Lemonade from that book?
Yeah!

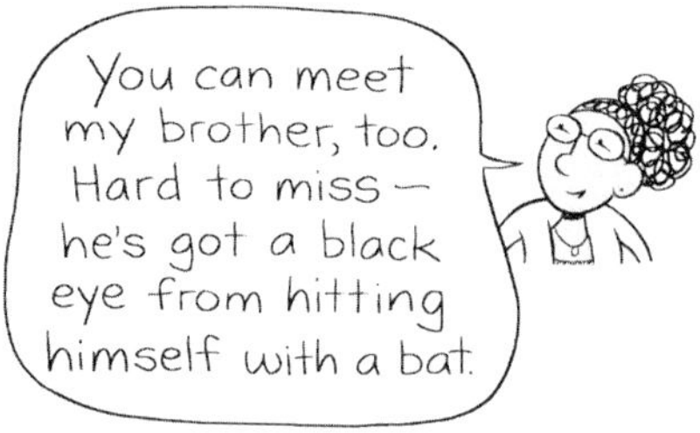
You can meet my brother, too. Hard to miss— he's got a black eye from hitting himself with a bat.

We walk to her house and the tension breaks. We talk about chemistry-related combos for her notebook. I suggest using methyl cellulose, a jellifying agent. (My parents are Food Network nerds and I like the molecular gastronomy stuff.) She agrees to try and we get excited, coming up with other ideas like using foams and emulsifiers and . . . I forget what else.

It's nice to have a clean slate. It's also nice to talk about stuff like this with someone who's just as into it. In fact, at this moment, I suddenly feel a strong emotion . . .

gratitude

. . . for having a new friend.

EPILOGUE
ANTHONY

Back in the library.

Not for tutoring. I think we just got so used to doing school-work together, we kept it going. We meet during study hall once or twice a week. Not every day, 'cause Leah just started tutoring someone else.

guess it's not just for Halloween

Today, I notice Roddy Klein.

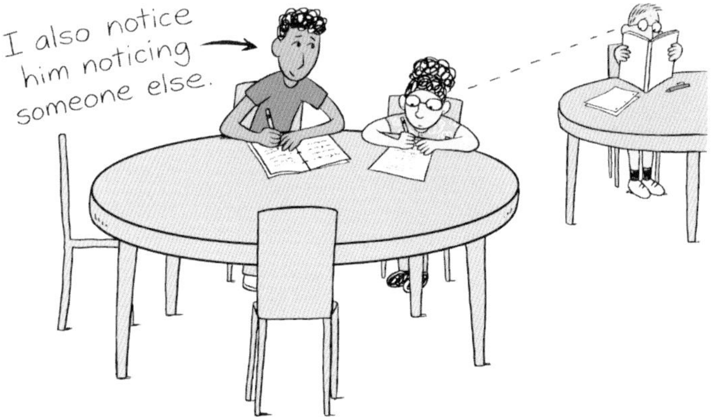
I also notice him noticing someone else.

Speaking of this stuff . . .

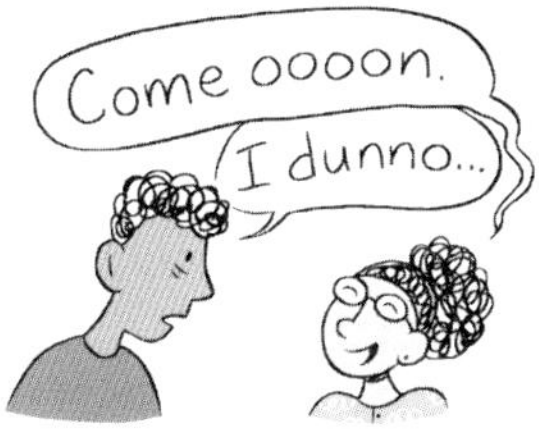
Come oooon.
I dunno...

Leah's been coaxing me to ask out my own "crush." But I've already been burned once. I think?

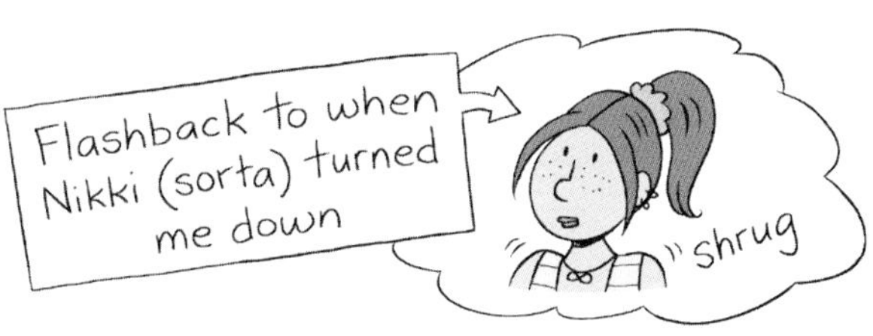
Flashback to when Nikki (sorta) turned me down
shrug

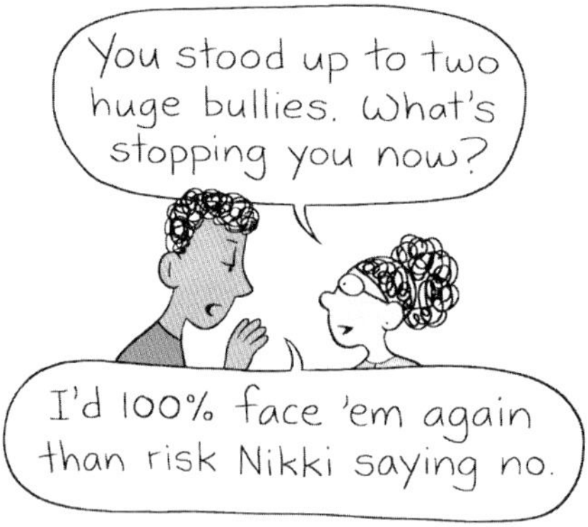
You stood up to two huge bullies. What's stopping you now?
I'd 100% face 'em again than risk Nikki saying no.

Also . . . I'm not even sure I'm crushing as hard. But I don't say so. I don't know what I feel, really.

Leah just shakes her head.

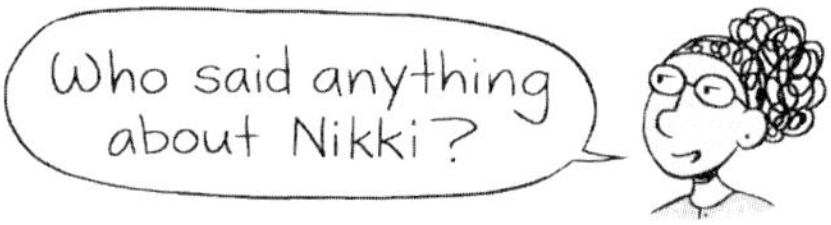
Who said anything about Nikki?

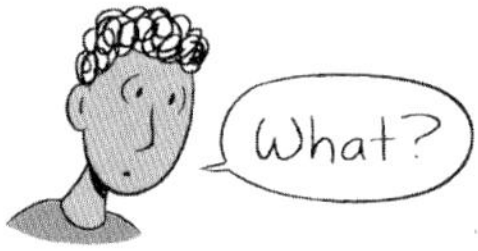
What?

I'm totally confused. I mean, I'd gone on and on about her. Before I can say anything, the bell rings.

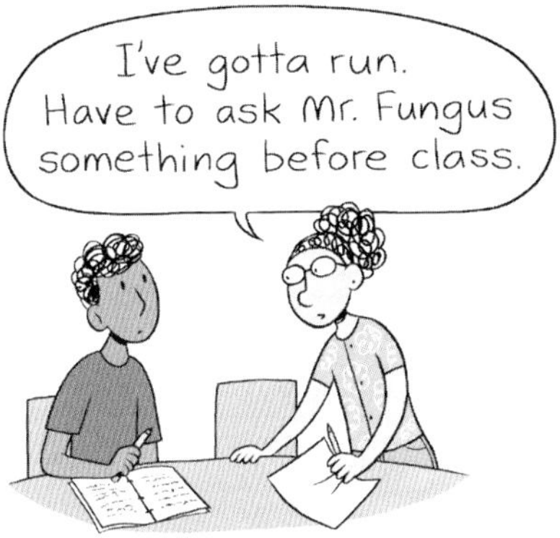
I've gotta run. Have to ask Mr. Fungus something before class.

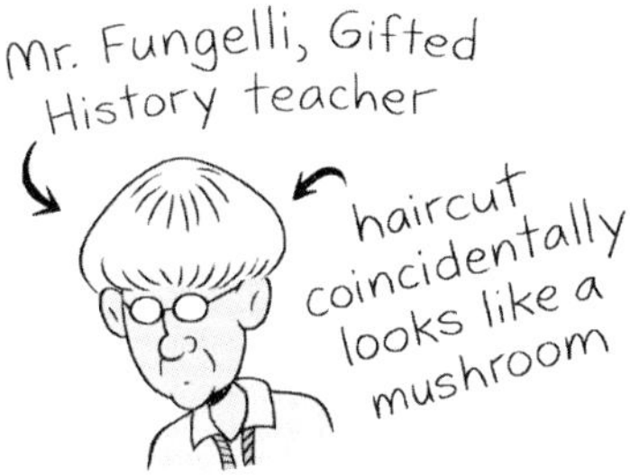
Mr. Fungelli, Gifted History teacher
haircut coincidentally looks like a mushroom

As Leah gathers her stuff, Jaime and Maya walk in.

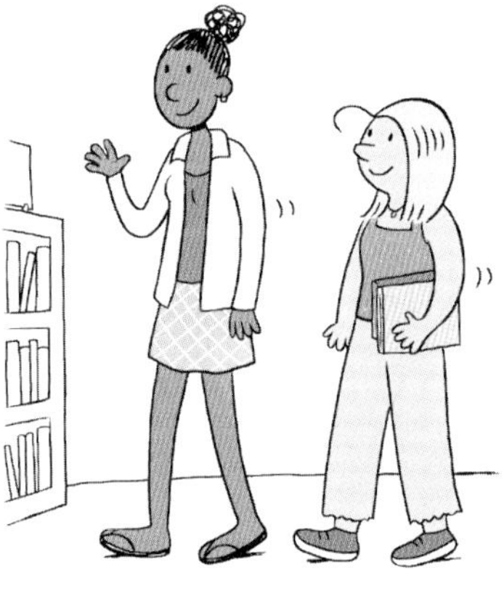

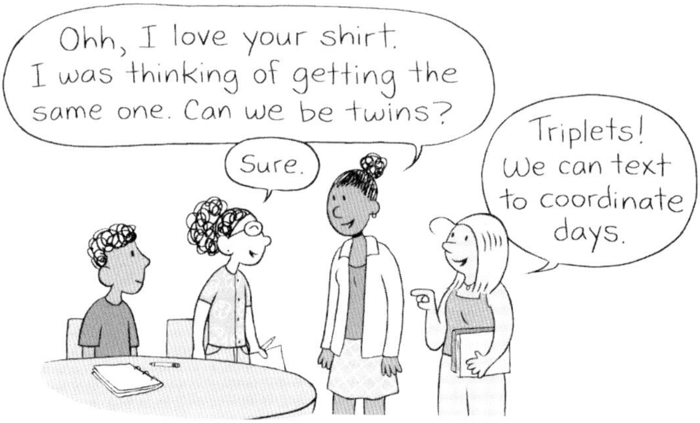
Ohh, I love your shirt. I was thinking of getting the same one. Can we be twins?
Sure.
Triplets! We can text to coordinate days.

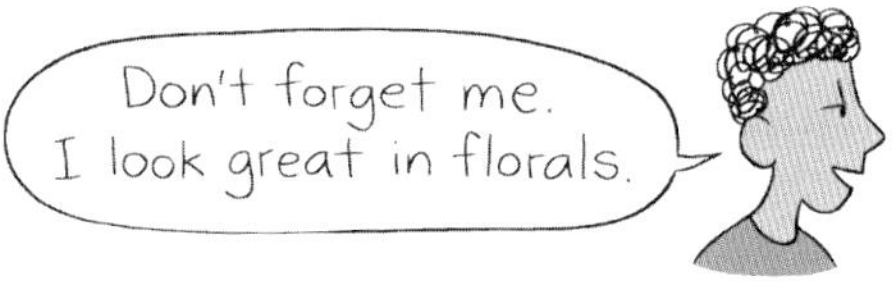
Don't forget me. I look great in florals.

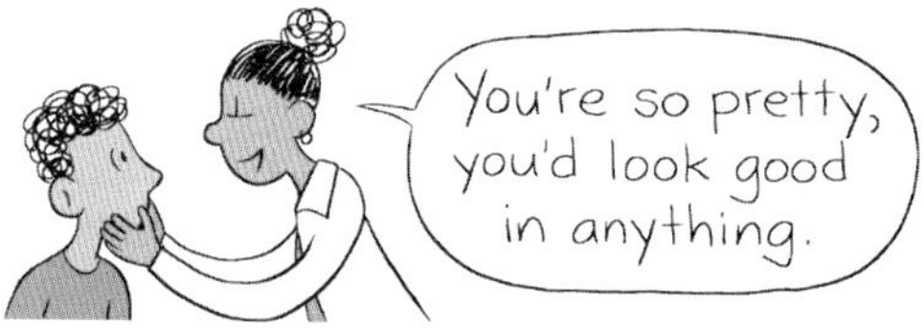
You're so pretty, you'd look good in anything.

I know she's teasing, but whoa. My insides do a flip. That freaks me out. Jaime? My festie?

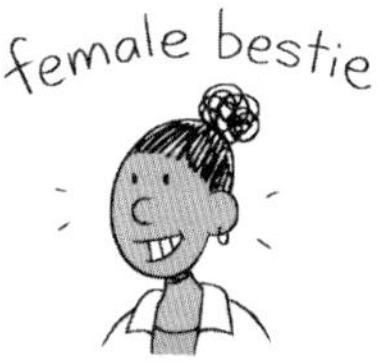
female bestie

Leah grins slyly at us as she heads out. What is that?

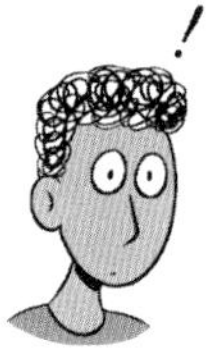

OMG. She's even smarter than I thought.

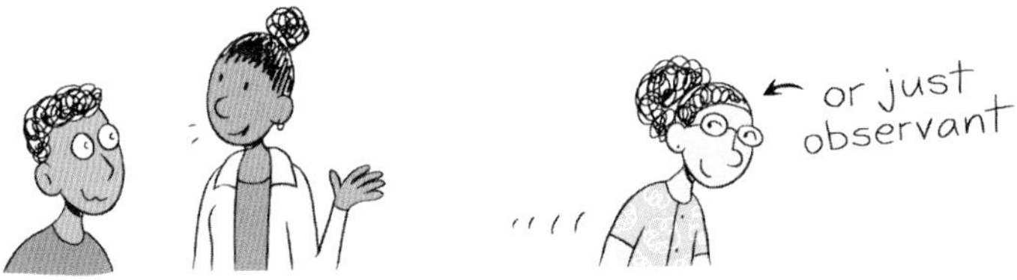
or just observant

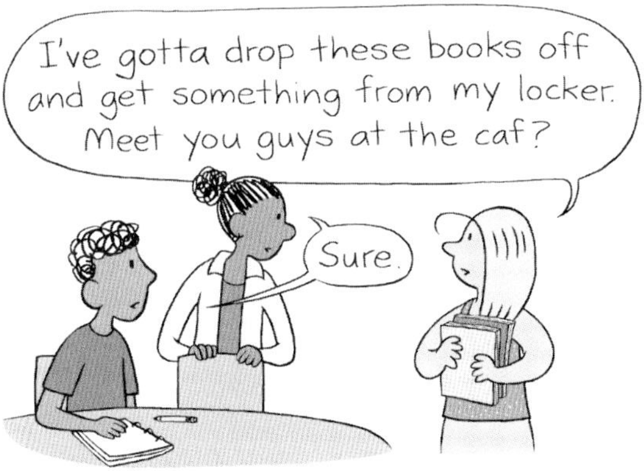
I've gotta drop these books off and get something from my locker. Meet you guys at the caf?
Sure.

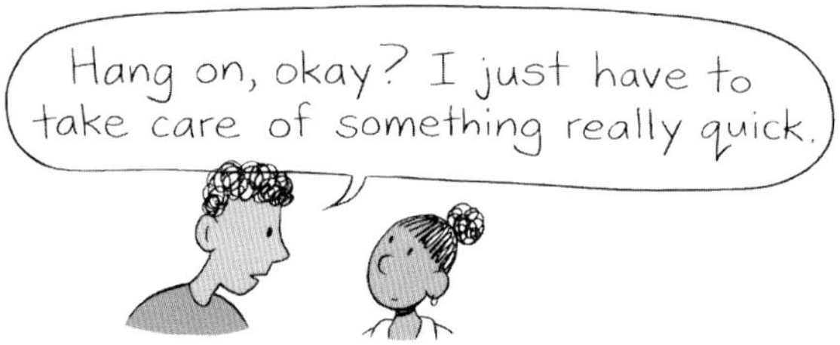
Hang on, okay? I just have to take care of something really quick.

I disappear for a minute. When I return, Jaime and I head out.

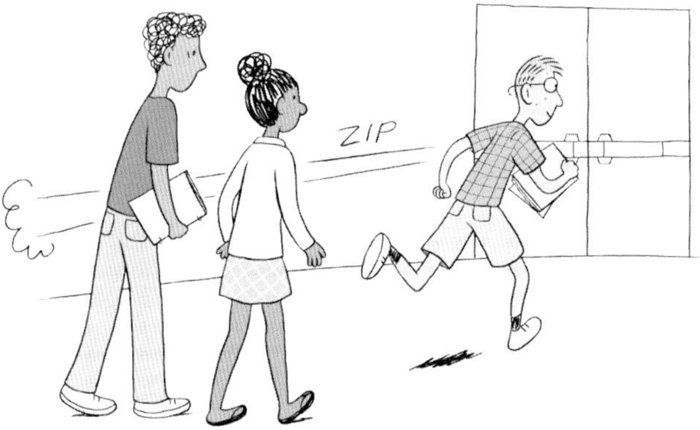
ZIP

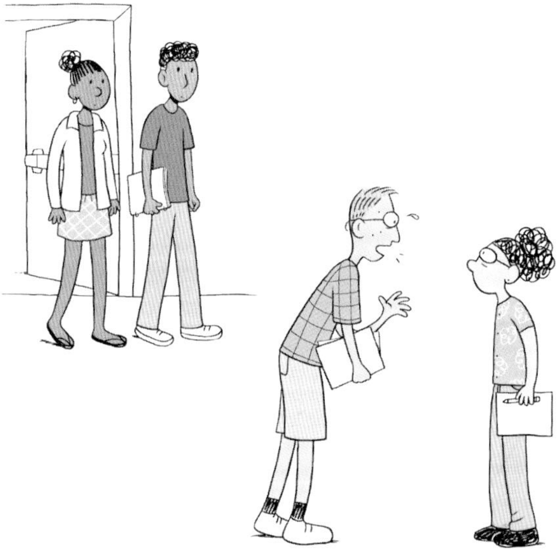

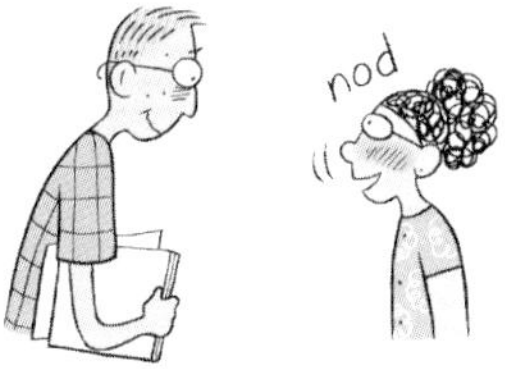
nod

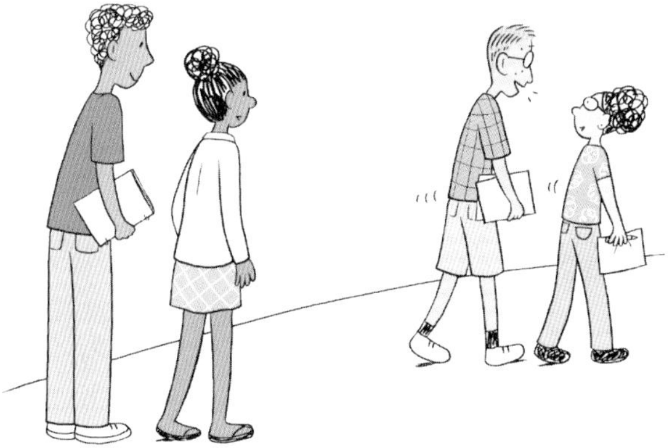

Jaime squints at me.

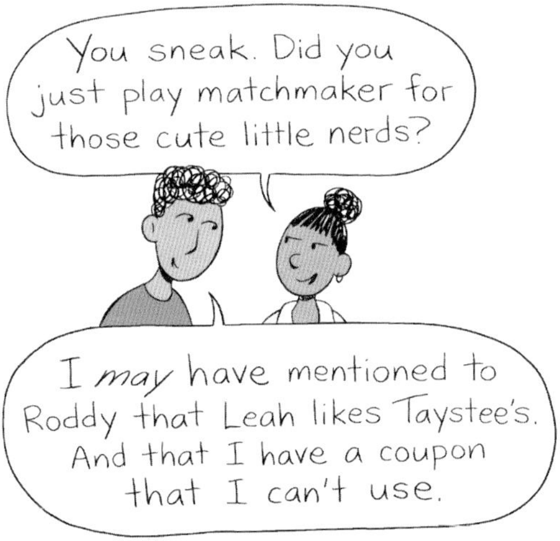
You sneak. Did you just play matchmaker for those cute little nerds?
I *may* have mentioned to Roddy that Leah likes Taystee's. And that I have a coupon that I can't use.

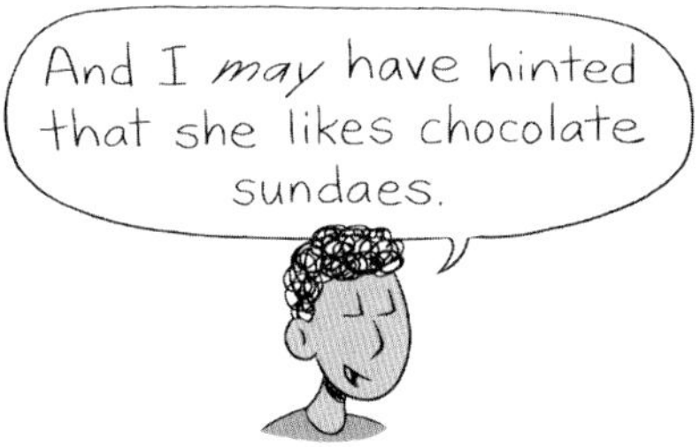
And I *may* have hinted that she likes chocolate sundaes.

Jaime laughs and I soak it in.

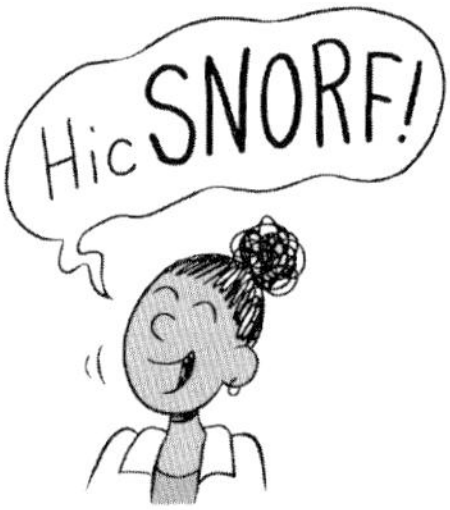
Hic SNORF!

We head out, walking and talking about our upcoming games. I even admit how nervous I am (especially about my layups). I've **never** admitted that. Especially to girls.

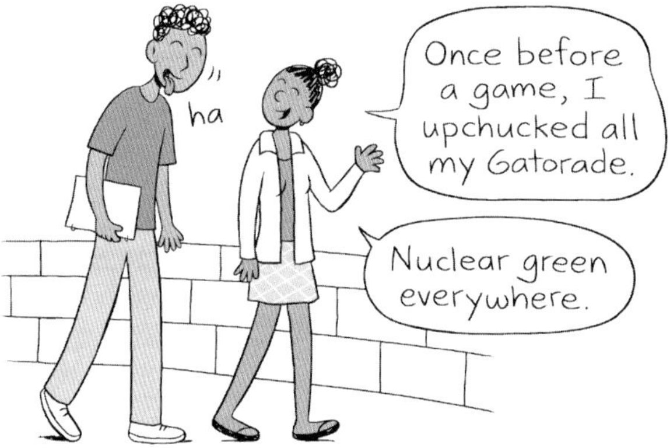
ha
Once before a game, I upchucked all my Gatorade.
Nuclear green everywhere.

But maybe "cool and laid-back" don't define me anymore.

And maybe . . .

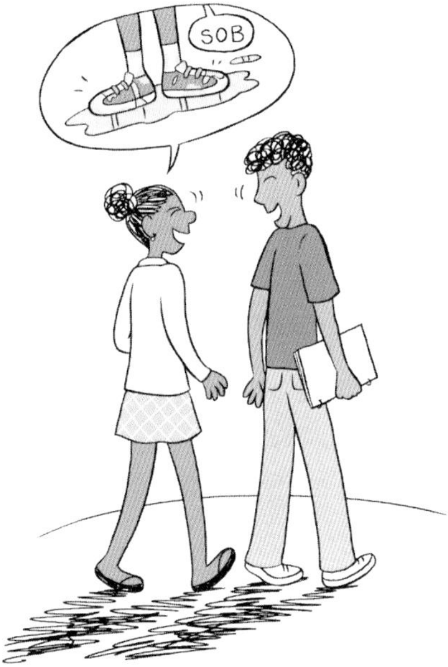
SOB

. . . I'm okay with that.

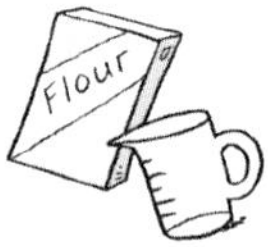
Flour

From the RECIPE BOOK of Leah Ruben:

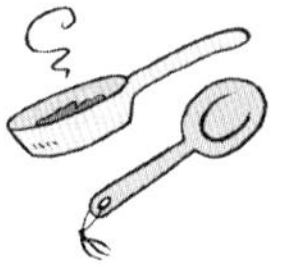

Mudbuckets:

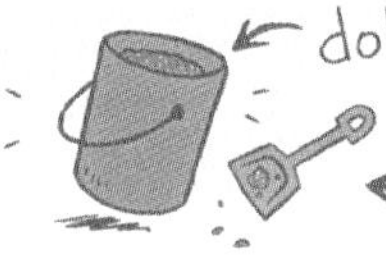
dollar store mini bucket
mini shovel (spoon)

Ingredients:

- 3.4 oz. box instant chocolate pudding
- 2 cups cold milk
- 8 oz. Cool Whip
- 8 oz. Oreos cookies, crushed
- optional toppings: extra crushed Oreos, gummy worms, chopped nuts

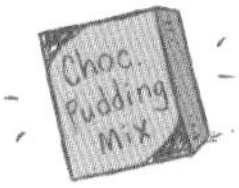
Choc. Pudding Mix

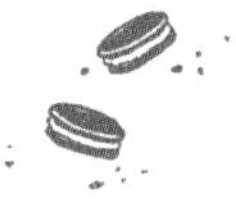

Instructions:

1. Whisk pudding mix and milk 1-2 min. until well-combined.
2. Let stand for five minutes.

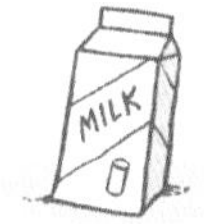
MILK

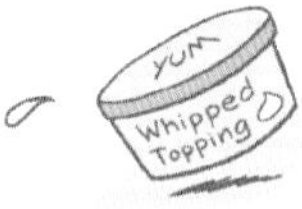
YUM
Whipped Topping

3. Stir in Cool Whip and crushed Oreos.
4. Pour into bowls or mini buckets. Refrigerate for 1 hour.
5. Add toppings and shovel into face!

Serves 4-8, depending on portion size. (Watch out, it's *RICH*.)

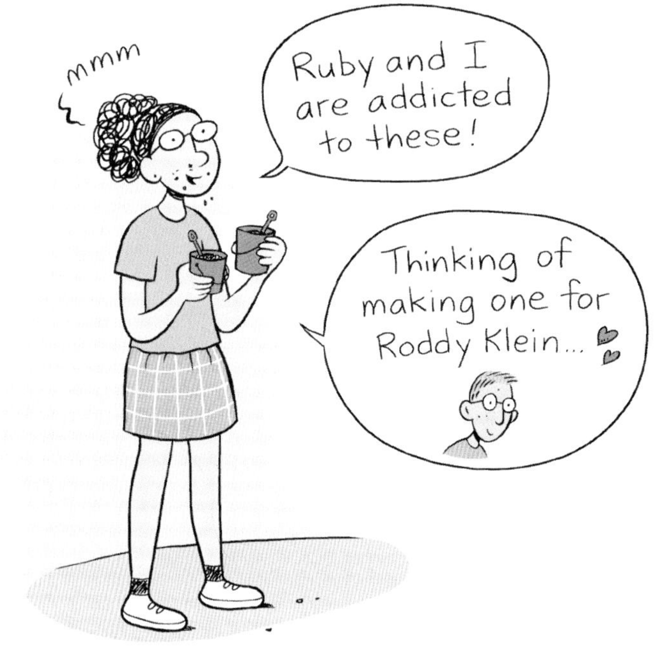
mmm
Ruby and I are addicted to these!
Thinking of making one for Roddy Klein...

Rainbow Lemonade*

*or Fibonacci Lemonade, after the inventor

Ingredients:

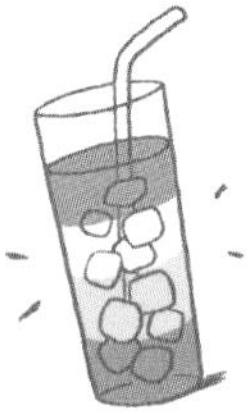

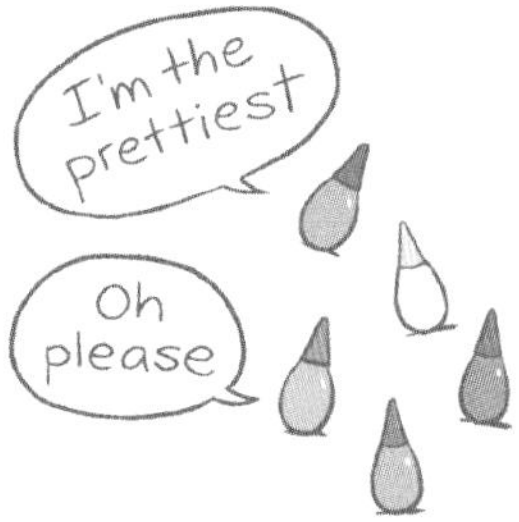

I'm the prettiest
Oh please

- lemon juice
- simple syrup
- water
- food coloring
- five cups + one tall glass filled with ice cubes

Instructions:

Make your five mixtures.

1. First cup: add 3 tsp. lemon juice, 5 tsp. simple syrup, 1/2 cup water, and a few drops of RED food coloring.
2. Second cup: add 2 tsp. lemon juice, 3 tsp. simple syrup, 1/2 cup water, and a few drops of YELLOW food coloring.

3. Third cup: add 1 tsp. lemon juice, 2 tsp. simple syrup, ½ cup water, and a few drops of GREEN food coloring.

4. Fourth cup: add 1 tsp. lemon juice, 1 tsp. simple syrup, ½ cup water, and a few drops of BLUE food coloring.

5. Fifth cup: add 1 tsp. simple syrup, ½ cup water, and a few drops of PURPLE food coloring.

Slowly pour your first mixture into the glass, directly over an ice cube. Repeat with the remaining mixture.

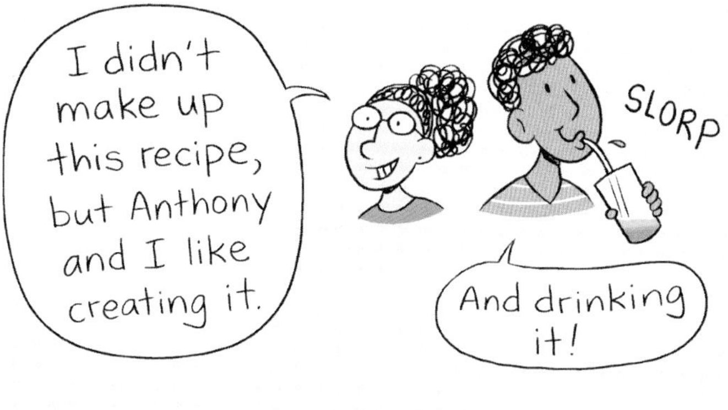
I didn't make up this recipe, but Anthony and I like creating it.
SLORP
And drinking it!

Yogurt Rigatoni*

*or any shape noodle
you like

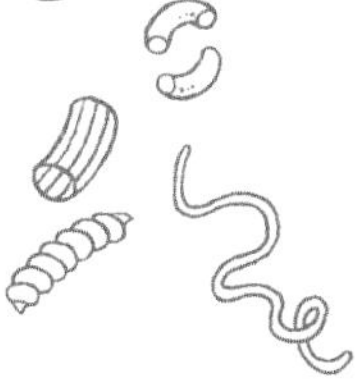

Ingredients:

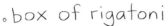

- box of rigatoni
- plain yogurt (Greek yogurt works)
- grated Parmesan cheese
- 1/4 - 1/2 tsp. minced garlic
- salt and pepper

Instructions:

This is simple. Cook the rigatoni. Dump any amount of yogurt on your pasta (don't heat up the yogurt!). Mix in Parmesan, garlic, and salt & pepper to taste.

Yum!

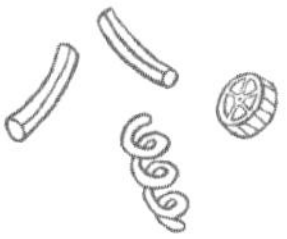

garlic
(stinky but delic!)

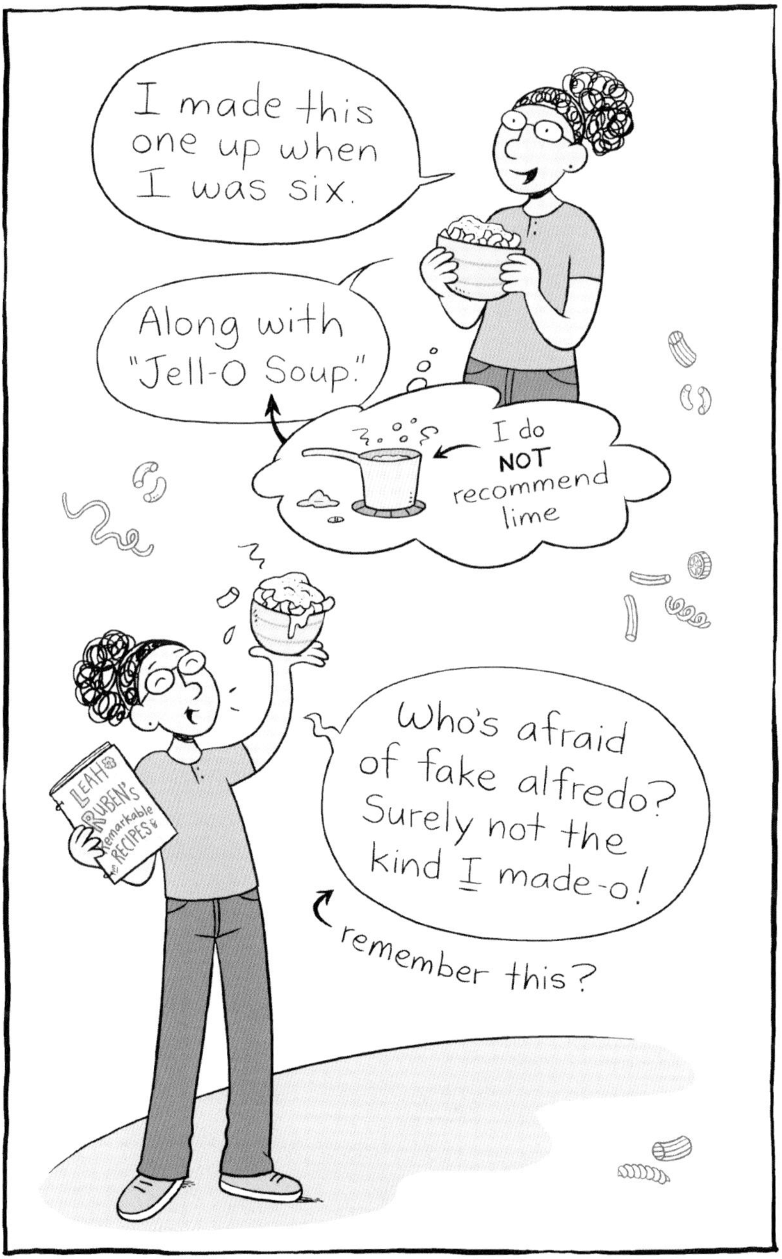
I made this one up when I was six.
Along with "Jell-O Soup."
I do NOT recommend lime
LEAH RUBEN'S Remarkable RECIPES
Who's afraid of fake alfredo? Surely not the kind I made-o!
remember this?

ACKNOWLEDGMENTS

How I love unexpected friendships. I've had a few myself, and they've made my life richer. They challenge preconceived notions about people and relationships, and they are endlessly surprising. The same goes for fictional characters, which is why I enjoyed writing about Anthony and Leah's blossoming—and unlikely—friendship.

I couldn't have done it without the following people:

My amazing editor, Donna Bray, who helps enrich my stories and characters so that each book is the best it can be.

My wise and thoughtful agent, Dan Lazar, whose support knows no bounds.

Laura Mock, Amy Ryan, Taylan Salvati, Sabrina Abballe, Jon Howard, Gwen Morton, Patty Rosati, Puige Pagan, and the rest of the continuously hardworking, talented team at HarperCollins.

Mike, Mollie, Nikki, and Rosie, who continue to spoil me with love, encouragement, and—in the case of Rosie—dopamine from belly rubs (hers, not mine).

All my family and friends, who continue to have my back and are so supportive. Lucky me!

And, of course, all my readers. Thank you for sending me your main character suggestions (I'm filing 'em away!) as well as beautiful letters and emails that never fail to make me smile. You're the best!

Rosie waiting for her belly rub